The Moonlit Cage

Also by Linda Holeman

The Linnet Bird

The Moonlit Cage

LINDA HOLEMAN

First published in Great Britain in 2005
by HEADLINE REVIEW

An imprint of HEADLINE BOOK PUBLISHING

3

Cataloguing in Publication Data is available from the British Library

ISBN 0 7553 2293 2 (hardback)
ISBN 0 7553 2461 7 (trade paperback)

Typeset in Bembo by Avon DataSet Ltd,
Bidford-on-Avon, Warwickshire

Printed and bound in Great Britain by
Mackays of Chatham plc, Chatham, Kent

Headline's policy is to use papers that are natural, renewable and
recyclable products and made from wood grown in sustainable forests.
The logging and manufacturing processes are expected to conform to the
environmental regulations of the country of origin.

HEADLINE BOOK PUBLISHING
A division of Hodder Headline
338 Euston Road
London NW1 3BH

www.headline.co.uk
www.hodderheadline.com

To the strong women in my life –
my mother Donna, my sister Shannon,
and my daughters Zalie and Brenna.

With thanks for all your stories.

India and Afghanistan, 1845

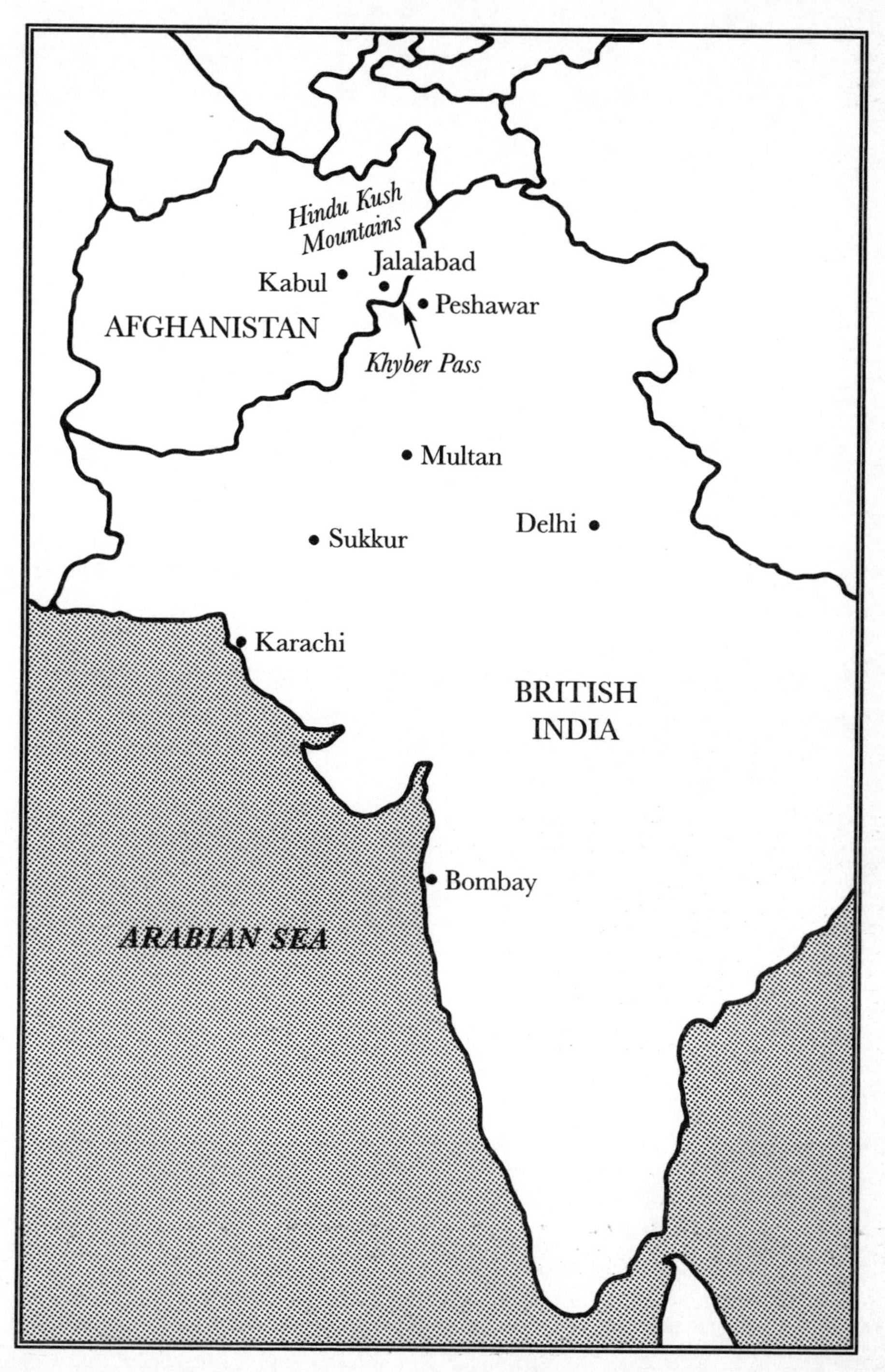

CONTENTS

Some Kiss We Want

There is some kiss we want
with our whole lives, the touch of
spirit on the body . . .

At night, I open the window and
ask the moon to come
and press its face
against mine.
Breathe into me.

Jelaluddin Rumi, thirteenth century

PROLOGUE

Atlantic Ocean, 1856

I HAVE ALWAYS BEEN told I was wicked.

This is my story, then: full of my wickedness and my attempts at goodness, of power found, lost, and found again. Of beliefs destroyed and rebuilt, of faith in oneself and in others. The strength carried in poetry and fables, in dreams and desires. It is a story of love and of hatred, all the contrasts you know, and have already experienced; all the pieces that make up the whole, make up a life – intricate as the veins in a leaf, the patterns of the stars, the seeds in a pomegranate.

The pomegranate is difficult to find here, in this land I sail from, this damp land with its layers of greys and greens, the land not my birthplace. I have been brought one of the crimson, hard fruits today, as a special gift, for a special reason. In time you will learn of it.

I've cut open the pomegranate, and the seeds are in a white bowl in my lap; I reach into the cool, smooth porcelain and bring one seed to my mouth. It is plump and sweet against my lips, then its taste floods over my tongue, filling me with memories of my own country. My *watan*.

Now my thoughts of that place and my life there run through me, but unlike the seed on my tongue, this taste is bittersweet. There are so many twisted threads that were woven together, slowly and steadily, to create the crooked tapestry that became my life. In my mind I can see the hands that held those threads – those of my grandmother with her past, hidden life in the *zenana*, of my Tajik father and mother, of the dirty Kafir whore, and of my Pushtun husband. And sometimes, although such thoughts are blasphemous, I even see the hands of Allah, with silken filaments looping between His most holy of fingers.

It is still difficult to speak these thoughts aloud, for in my *watan* women are punished for far less than daring to think that Allah would care about the life of one obstinate and ill-mannered Tajik girl.

And although I am safe now, my mind opening like the captured moth released from the palm, old habits die hard, and I still hold many of my reflections and desires close.

Please read my story and, as you do, ponder this question: Am I truly wicked? And when it is over, you can be the judge.

PART ONE

In the Shadow of the Hindu Kush, Afghanistan, 1845

CHAPTER ONE

MY GRANDMOTHER WAS called Mahdokht – Daughter of the Moon.

There was nobody like my grandmother in our village; she was looked upon as an outsider even though she had been brought to Susmâr Khord as a bride by my father's father. She was not a Tajik; she was not even of this land. She was, she said, a Circassian, born in a country of mountains – the Caucasus Mountains, which rose between the Black and Caspian Seas. She had been beautiful, with fair skin and thick, lustrous hair of brown streaked with a colour like gleaming honey.

My grandmother told me the stories of her life in other places, stories in great detail that seemed clear and true, even though she could no longer remember what time of year it was, what she had last eaten, or the names of many of the people in our village. When she told me her old stories her face grew calm, and she had a look of being at the same time awake and yet dreaming.

She told me that because of her great beauty, she, like many of the other girls from her mountains, with their pale skin and large eyes and wild manes of hair, were sold by their parents. They were much sought after by the sultans of the land called the Sweet Waters of Asia, where the water bore the name Bosporus. She was taken there when only eight years old, on a long and wearying journey. She had been born a non-believer with another name, but when she arrived at the *zenana* of the sultan she was renamed and trained in the ways of Islam. She could not remember the name she had been given by her parents, as no one had spoken it to her in over seventy summers.

Because she was so young, much younger than the other mountain girls on that first journey, she was given to the sultan's daughter. The princess treated her as a living plaything; she bathed her and braided her hair and dressed her in fine clothing. 'A child doll, I was,' my grandmother said, treated with gentleness when the princess was happy, slapped and pinched when a foul mood overtook her.

After some time, when the child Mahdokht grew more mature, the princess became weary of her pretty plaything. She sent her to live cloistered with all the other girls and women, where she became a slave concubine. I didn't know the word concubine; my grandmother simply shook her head when I asked its meaning.

She told me that because of the teachings of Islam, she accepted that her personal fate was set before she was born – written on her forehead, she said, tapping her lined brow with her fingertips. Trapped within the walls of the *zenana*, she spent her time in an idle life. In the days she bathed and perfumed her skin and learned to sing and dance and recite poetry, and she ate wonderful food prepared by slaves beneath her. She spent her nights smoking a pipe filled with *keyf*, which gave her magical dreams, and listening to the poetry and stories of the other captive women, stories which told of their own lands, or stories born from loneliness and boredom.

'Tragedy and love, Daryâ,' she said. 'Suffering and joy. These are the four corners of a life.'

She taught me these songs and poems in Persian, the language so like the common Dari spoken by all in our Tajik village, but even more beautiful with its slight variations.

'It was very wonderful?' I asked, trying to imagine a life where one did not work, where there was only eating and sleeping and telling stories. How could it not be wonderful?

But my grandmother's face closed. 'Sometimes. But we were closely guarded by the beardless men – those who have been cut so they are men but not men – and there was danger, always danger, within the walls of the *zenana*.'

'Danger?'

'The *zenana* was also a treacherous place,' she said. 'There was idle gossip, and the lies of rivals, and often girls disappeared – poisoned, their bodies flung to the bottom of the Sweet Waters. That is why I escaped; I knew my time would come also, for I had seen I was a threat.'

'But why were you a threat? How did you escape?' I had asked, but at this point my grandmother would tell me little of her life after the *zenana*.

She didn't speak of these things when my mother or father were nearby; the secrecy was obvious, and I didn't question this, even though I was a girl who questioned many things. I loved these stories; the idea that she – and therefore I – was part of another tribe filled me with a wild, sweet longing for something I couldn't name, but which slid over and through me, slippery and enticing. I looked at her and tried to see the beautiful girl from the faraway mountains. But to me she looked like the other old women of our village, just another grandmother – a *mâdar kalân* – with thinning white hair and a whiskery chin and dim eyes sunken in a nest of wrinkles. I saw nothing of myself in her. My hair had no streaks of honey; it was such a dark brown as to be almost black. And while my eyes were not grey like hers (mine were green), Mâdar Kalân told me that when she looked into my eyes she saw her own in shape and in the framing of thick dark eyelashes she had once had.

One of the things she wouldn't speak of was how she came to Afghanistan; I sensed it was not her choosing to live out her life in this small farming village of Susmâr Khord. She had seen too much, knew too much, to be content here. She sometimes spoke of another man, not my grandfather, who had died before I was born – one she called her true husband, her only beloved. She talked of her other children by him, born long before my uncle and my father, who, she always said, had been a gift from God: my father, born to her in a time of life when women are no longer fertile, was a son to bring a daughter-in-law to care for her in her old age. She sometimes cried, telling me of those other children – those alive and yet lost, and those already in paradise, like her first child, born dead in the *zenana*, and my father's older brother who had died at the hands of men wearing red coats in the battle in Kabul.

'These men of the British Empire,' my grandmother said, 'they wish to take this country. Their own country, Inglestân – England – is not enough for them. They believe there is none finer than their blood, pale, thin, and it should be spread throughout all the world.'

She sang then, in a cracked and rusty voice, the foreign song I had long ago memorised. She told me what the words to this song meant: the people of England ruled everything, even the water of the oceans, and that they would always be rulers, and never be slaves. *Rule, Britannia, Britannia, rule the waves*. I liked the twisting foreign words on my tongue, and often sang the song under my breath.

'There was a painting, a painting I remember now,' she said, looking at me after we had once sung the song together. 'I think it is your face in the painting.'

I knew then, by her fading voice, by the distant look in her eyes, that she was going away from me, from our village, and back to another time and place. I waited, patiently, for I knew this pattern, knew she would return.

'The painting, Mâdar Kalân?' I gently reminded her, finally.

She blinked and looked back at me. 'The painting hung in the home of the man who held my heart in his hand. He came from that faraway place, from England, all the way to Ankara, in Turkey, where he found me after I escaped from the *zenana.* And he desired me, for it was my time of greatest beauty. He bought me from the master who then owned me, but he treated me with more kindness than any other man I had known. He gave me a son and a daughter. Beautiful. Beautiful,' she said. 'With skin like milk. My babies.' She fell silent, and then tears came from the corners of her eyes. I had heard of these lost children many times, but she had never before mentioned a painting. I leaned towards her and softly wiped her face with the edge of her headscarf.

'It's all right, Mâdar Kalân,' I said, speaking in Persian, as she did. 'Don't cry. What was the painting of?' I prompted.

'There was fighting, as always,' she said, still in that other time. 'He ran, one child under each arm. He turned to call to me. But it was too late. He disappeared, and I . . .' She wept. 'My little ones, my little ones. What happened to them? What happened to my beloved?'

I took her hand between mine and stroked it. 'The painting, Mâdar Kalân? What of the painting?'

She shook her head, as if trying to clear her thoughts. 'It was of a woman. She wore a helmet, and carried a shield and a weapon with three teeth; she wore the fighting armour of a man.'

'Who was she?'

'She was the British Empire,' my grandmother said, and again sang the song.

I waited until she was done. 'What do you mean?'

'The British Empire is like a powerful woman.'

'A powerful woman? What woman has power?' I knew, as I asked, that my grandmother must be confused again. Women were not powerful in Susmâr Khord.

But she didn't answer; she was dozing with her head drooping forward on her thin, loose-skinned neck. I studied her as she slept, wishing I could go inside her head and see all she had seen, know what she knew.

In spite of the marvellous stories Mâdar Kalân spun into the air for me, she now had to be watched like a child. She wandered about the house in the middle of the night, grew anxious about which sleeping quilts were hers, and sometimes forgot to go to the screened corner of the courtyard, soiling herself and then striking her chest in shame.

My mother was busy with the cooking and cleaning of the house, and my father, of course, would not be expected to care for a woman. I was the only child, and so it fell to me to tend and watch over my grandmother. But it was not a duty; it gave me a quiet happiness to help her, such was the fierce, somehow protective love I felt for her. She was the only person who brought something large to my own small and cloistered life, who made it seem possible that there were other lives and other worlds beyond the walls of our village, that there was more beyond the horizons bounded by the fields and mountains.

And no matter how many times she repeated herself, telling me again and again about the places she had seen, the rivers and cities, deserts and too many wonders of the world for me to keep count, the same stories and poems and songs, over and over, tales of the *zenana* with its love and betrayal, joy and death – I didn't mind. Sometimes she would ask me questions about her stories, ask me to repeat them to her, and I wondered whether she wanted to listen to me to see if I had remembered what she had said, or whether this was because the familiar tales were beginning to fade, like her memory of the day, and she wanted me to make them clear to her again.

On fine evenings I would help Mâdar Kalân up the rough ladder to the flat roof, pushing her from behind, and then I would clamber around her and pull on her twisted hands, pulling and tugging her off the ladder and on to the roof. I supported her while she caught her breath from the climb, and she would lean heavily on me as she settled herself on the small faded rugs there. Our house was on the outskirts of the village, so from our roof we could see the fields spreading out around us, the purple shadows of the mountains in the distance.

We would sit together as the sun went down, waiting for the night sky with its moon and stars. She knew the meaning of the pathways of the stars, and had stories about the shapes they created. Mâdar Kalân told me that here, in my *watan*, the sickle moon was a male, and it was believed that women should revere and sit at the foot of the moon in the same way that we should sit at the feet of men. But, she also told me, in other, faraway places, the moon is a woman.

'Is it a different moon, then, in these different places?' I asked.

She shook her head. 'It is like the belief in Allah. Not all believe in him, but have their own gods.'

'Isn't Allah all-powerful?' I asked, aghast at this declaration, the first time she spoke of Allah the Merciful in this way.

'Only to those who worship Him,' she said. 'There are many people who pray to different gods, just as there are people who believe what they will about the moon. Some say the moon is a woman, full and round in times of plenty, thin and pale in times of hardship. I don't know about Allah, child. I just don't know. But this' – here she pointed skyward – 'I know. That there is only one moon, one sun, but more stars than there are people on the earth.'

Looking at my grandmother as she spoke, her face pouched and uneven in the moon's glow, I was reminded of that round, pale moon with its shadows and markings. I thought I understood why someone in a faraway place, so long ago, had decided on her name. And I decided to believe that the moon was, indeed, a woman. Of my grandmother's strange talk about Allah and other gods I wasn't so sure; perhaps it was only her confusion.

But I would never speak to anyone about either.

'Do you think I'll ever see any of the places you have known?' I asked her.

'Yes,' she said. 'You will. I know this, for you are like me. People who are content often remain in one place,' she said. In the darkness I saw the whites of her eyes. 'Those who are not move about, looking for the contentment that eludes them.' She looked back at the sky. 'Your power will not allow you to find contentment easily.'

I made a sound of annoyance, but Mâdar Kalân continued to speak as if she had not heard me. 'This village – this country – is not the only world,' she said. 'This you will come to see in time. You have the power, Daryâ. You will not be content here. You must go.'

'Where will I go?' I asked, an unexpected thump of dread filling my stomach.

She continued to look at the sky, slowly shaking her head as if arguing with an unheard voice. 'It is there that you will find what you seek.'

'What I seek? But I don't know—'

'No, you don't know yet. But one day you will take out your power, and use it to live the life you desire,' she said. 'A life such as I once knew, for too brief a time. A life where you are truly alive.' And then she said no more.

Even though I was young, I understood her hopes for me – that I not live out my life as my mother did, and as she herself had in her later years. But how was this to happen? I knew only my village of Susmâr Khord, set in a low valley in the shadow of the Hindu Kush. Its houses were made of mud mixed with crushed limestone and straw, low mud walls enclosing the compound of each house. Within our compound was a storage shed, a small corral for the animals, the summer cooking area of raised, tamped earth where we could also wash dishes and clothes, and the secluded area for our private business. The spread of carpets in the shade of our lime and mulberry trees was for my mother's visitors, so they could sit in seclusion and talk with their faces uncovered.

My father was a farmer. The fields were fertile; water was diverted from the streams that ran from tributaries of the far-off rivers on to the carefully levelled plots of thin soil in the winding valleys south of the Hindu Kush. When the cooler days of autumn arrived, and the last of the winnowing of the grain was completed, my father, like a number of the other men, also had a winter trade. During the cold unproductive months in Susmâr Khord, he would pack his tools and ride to Kabul, where he could earn money working as a carpenter, repairing the homes of the wealthy city dwellers.

My father worked hard, and was good with his hands. He kept our home well-maintained. We rarely went hungry. But he was often angry, disappointed, and this arose from the fact that a man who had only one daughter was to be pitied. He longed for a son to help him with the work and bring him self-esteem. I know that my father felt that he was less of a man than his fellow villagers because of his lack of family. With his father and brother dead, there was no elder to sit on the roof with him, talking at the end of a long hot day in the field. His mother was no longer able to reprimand and support her daughter-in-law in the running of the house.

There was no noise and bustle; no brood of children to scold or boast about. There was only me.

More and more he took this frustration out by striking me – for not bringing his tea quickly enough, for not noticing the water jug was almost empty, for not lowering my eyes when he reprimanded me. For nothing more than the fact that I was a girl.

And because of this my own anger towards him burned within me.

My feelings for my mother were more complex. I didn't love her with the clear and bright light I had for my grandmother. And I felt none of the venom that burned in my chest towards my father. My mother was quiet and simple. She did what was expected, passive and accepting. I saw her as I saw so many of the other women of the village, finding pleasure in the home and in quiet companionship with other women, with raising their children. And I saw that she expected me, once I was no longer a child, to find happiness in the preparation of our meals, in sweeping the raised wooden floors and arranging the rugs and quilts in our simple one-roomed house with its curtained sleeping area for her and my father. She shook her head, her lips tight, at my disinterest in cleaning and sewing, at the number of cups and dishes I broke, clumsy in my haste to finishing washing and drying them.

I could not be content with these simple household chores, or with the long, gossipy visits of our neighbours in the warm courtyard. I was always restless, always needing to move. I didn't feel I belonged with the other girls and young women in Susmâr Khord; I was unlike them – different, even, to my best friend Gawhar. And maybe this was another bond I shared with my grandmother. Although she was accepted and treated with respect in Susmâr Khord – for her husband had carried some power in the village – she had always been looked upon as an outsider, even now, when so old. And didn't I feel this way as well? Although born in Susmâr Khord, somehow I thought of myself as an outsider, dissatisfied with the constraints of my simple and yet good life, although I couldn't name the reasons for this discontent. I was regularly in trouble with my mother, and even more so with my father. I could not be obedient.

⋆ ⋆ ⋆

That summer, in the hot August of my eleventh year, I grew more and more tense, more edgy. I wanted more than daily trips to the bread oven or well in the town square, more than sitting on the roof at night and looking at the stars. Mâdar Kalân slept much of the time now, some days not rising from her quilts even after I had helped her wash and eat.

I wanted to know what the mullah instructed the boys in the mosque; I wanted to hear him speak of the Koran, to hear the holy words which came from his mouth. His lips, buried within his thin white beard, were thick, and glistened with a purple hue.

The mosque was mud-coloured, like the rest of the buildings in my town, although on one inner wall was a glorious design of the Tree of Life created from tiles – tiles of blue to frighten the evil *jinn*. The tiles were indigo and cobalt, azure and turquoise, and I longed to run my hands over their cool, glazed, smooth surface. Behind the mosque was a dusty, deserted courtyard with only a few ancient and gnarled mulberry trees. But it was here, in this place where nobody seemed to visit, that I crept one afternoon, hearing the drone of voices from inside the mosque. I dared not look in the window, knowing the mullah might spot me, but crept along the wall. And then I saw it: a crack in the wall, between two high, narrow windows. The crack was low down; I had to bend my knees to peer through it. But it gave me a clear picture of the mosque. There were the backs of the boys; they sat on worn cotton prayer rugs. The mullah, standing before them with a Koran in his hands, led them in his low, monotone voice as he read from the book. The boys swayed back and forth rhythmically as their voices repeated the mullah's words. I felt as if thin, invisible threads, fine as those of the spider, attached their words to the mullah's, and his words were attached to those on the page. Everything in me yearned to know this connection, to feel this learning.

We had a Koran on a shelf above our door; my father had told me never to touch it, for it would be wicked for my hands to pollute it.

And yet the day I made the discovery of the hole in the wall of the mosque, I went home and waited until there was no one there but my grandmother, who watched me without speaking. I took my father's Koran into my hands and gently caressed its creased and torn pages, wondering at the black, twisted forms on paper so thin it was almost transparent. This was blasphemy in itself, but my need to know its secrets was greater than my obedience.

The next day I hid the holy book under my long dress, tucked into the waist of my loose trousers. And then I sat in the dusty courtyard behind the mosque with the book in my hands, following the mullah's words, mimicking the boys swaying on their mats. I whispered almost soundlessly while around me chickens scratched in the dirt and the earth smelled sour and the leaves of the twisted mulberry trees rustled in the summer breeze. Day after day I returned to my place behind the mosque while my mother assumed I waited for our bread at the oven in the centre of the village. I didn't think I would be seen.

And even if I was caught, what of it? I was often punished for my disobedience.

How was I to foresee that this time would be different?

CHAPTER TWO

IT WAS VERY hot the day the world changed. Everything was still, and there was only an occasional whisper of air sluggishly churning the sultry air. I was at my spot in the courtyard of the mosque, kneeling, the book resting on my thighs. I didn't touch it, for my palms were wet with sweat. The mullah's droning voice took on the tone of a large, buzzing insect, matching the sound of the flies that lit on my damp forehead. I brushed them away with quick, annoyed slaps, shaking my head and trying to focus my thoughts. The sun had moved so that the leaves of the mulberry no longer protected me. I thought I might leave, but at that moment a shadow fell over me. I looked up, my legs tensed to run, but it was only Basaam. He was a few years older than I, a dull-witted, mainly harmless boy who spent much of his time following the younger boys – for the boys his age shunned him – and doing what they asked of him: usually silly acts of humiliation that made them laugh. He would beam as he made a fool of himself, pleased for the attention and what he must have thought was friendship. But on occasions I had also seen an unexpectedly sharp expression in his usually vacant eyes, as if for brief moments he was aware that he had not been blessed, that he did not have the same respect as the other boys. At these times his shuffling, grinning and amiable character would change, inexplicably, as if a sharp finger had poked him once, hard, on the back of the head, and awoken a cruel side. I had seen him push down a little girl and step on her fingers. Another time, when he couldn't keep up with the boys running ahead, he had grabbed a small dog who innocently trotted by, twisting its neck as the animal snarled and snapped in pain and confusion. He had dropped it only when its teeth sank into his thumb.

But on this day Basaam smiled at me in his usual wet, open-mouthed grin, and I put my finger to my lips. He did the same, nodding vigorously and smiling even more broadly so that I saw his discoloured back teeth, strung with saliva. Then he wandered away, kicking at pebbles. The mullah did not allow him into the mosque to study with the other boys, I knew, because he couldn't concentrate and made loud noises which distracted the others.

I turned my attention back to the mullah. But a short time later a shadow fell over me again, and this time I looked up in annoyance, opening my mouth to tell Basaam to go away. But it was my mother, appearing at my side with no warning sound of footsteps. She grabbed my arm as I glimpsed Basaam's shirt-tail disappearing round the corner of the mosque.

My mother glared at me, her fingers gripping my upper arm so tightly that it ached. 'Daryâ, you evil girl,' she whispered, her words clipped and hard even though spoken so quietly. She took the Koran from me, glancing at the crack in the wall. Then she crouched beside me, moving her head so that she could see what I saw. 'Here near the boys, watching such things. It is not allowed. Lower your eyes, now.'

But I wouldn't lower my eyes. All I ever heard was that I wasn't allowed to touch, to hear or to watch because I was a girl. I shook my arm to free it of my mother's grip. 'Stop it. You're hurting. And why am I so evil because I want to know of our holy book?' I demanded, knowing, as I did so, that there was no answer she could give. Some things just are.

She made a hissing noise and I fell silent, but I still scowled at her. She tightened her grip, dragging me up. I pried her fingers from my arm and walked in front of her, staring straight ahead. I would not have anyone see her treat me so. We passed other women; some shook their heads as they saw me striding ahead of my mother, my chin up, my steps long and ungraceful. I had known for some time that they pitied my mother for having such a bold, wayward daughter, and I thought, as they passed me, that more than one sent a grateful prayer to Allah for their own modest, obedient daughters.

Once inside our house my mother grabbed my arm again, throwing me on to the rug nearest the wall before reverently returning the Koran to its shelf. She didn't allow me food or water for the rest of the day. My grandmother, from her dark corner, cast glances at me, and I longed to run to her and bury my head in her lap, as I had often done when my mother scolded me or my father slapped me. At one point, when my mother's back was turned, I made a motion to rise and go to my grandmother, saying, pleadingly, 'Mâdar Kalân', but she shook her head, patting the air with her knobby, twisted fingers, and I knew this time was different. This was not like spilling the clay urn of water because I tried to run with it, or burning the rice because instead of watching it I watched the clouds. It was not like hiding in the fields when I should have been doing chores, or taking another woman's loaf of bread from the oven when I tired of waiting for ours to bake. It was not like making a face at the cranky old man who always sat on the steps of the *chây-khâna* with a cup of *chây* – tea – in his hand.

Perhaps, I began to realise, what I had done was not one of my silly, childish acts of defiance. Turning from my grandmother's worried face, I lay down with my back to the room, wrapping my arms around my empty belly.

My head throbbed with the heat, and my dry throat ached. After some time my father's heavy footsteps approached our house, but before he entered my mother went outside. I sat up and faced the door, heard the rapid, distressed murmur of her voice, and then my father's louder one. When he stormed into the house his face was dark, his lips a straight line.

He came towards me and I jumped up. 'You will be punished for your inappropriate conduct,' he shouted, staring at the wall over my head as if I were too disgusting to look at. 'No daughter will embarrass me in this way.'

I knew it was wrong to listen to the mullah, but I couldn't understand the depth of his anger. I also knew better than to question him, but continued to study his face, trying to make sense of his rage.

'Lower your eyes,' he roared, as his gaze came back to me. 'And cover your insolent face.' He reached out and yanked my headscarf so that it fell over my face. I did not yet need to wear the veil; my woman's time had not come. 'I stopped for a glass of tea at the *chây-khâna*, but left in shame when others laughed about your behaviour. Women can't stop their wagging tongues. Already everyone knows of your rude and disrespectful actions.'

He loomed angrier than I had ever witnessed: a large, watery shadow through the thin fabric of my headscarf. 'Have you learned nothing yet? Do you dare to show me no respect, to stare into my eyes as if you are my equal?' he shouted, and I dropped my chin. But he was enraged, and now I understood. It was not only because of what I had done, but because of how he had felt in front of his friends. He raised his hand and struck me, on both sides of my face, and my headscarf fell to my shoulders. He had slapped me before, often, but never with such force. The strength of his second blow knocked me down, and I fell on to my hip and elbow. And then his hard, work-roughened hands rained blows on to my shoulders and back. I heard my grandmother cry out, and I curled into a tight circle, trying to protect myself. But now he pulled me up. 'I shall show you how a disrespectful daughter is treated,' he said, and dragged me through the room, my feet tripping on the rugs. I was shocked, unable to breathe properly. I stumbled behind him into the fading sunlight. At first I thought he would take me to our courtyard to beat me further, but he led me away from our house and towards the village square.

The streets of our village fanned out from the square like spokes in a wheel, and there were no connecting lanes. I was glad that most people would be in their courtyards behind their homes at this time of day, walled within their own privacy, and hoped that few would witness me being pulled through the streets.

We came into the centre of the square, a large area of hard earth, shaded from the sun by the leafy canopy of walnut and pomegranate trees around the border. I saw the mosque directly across the square from the *chây-khâna* and beside the teahouse the well and bread ovens.

I thought then that my father would take me to the well, would dash water on me in an attempt to cleanse me of my evil ways.

'This girl has disrespected the ways of Allah,' he shouted, his voice so loud and unexpected that I flinched. The two women at the ovens looked at us, their hands still, and men appeared at the door of the mosque and the *chây-khâna*. 'She has behaved in a manner shameful to the village. She must be taught a lesson.' That he would shout out about my disobedience, draw attention to me, so that all might look, was unbelievable.

As he pulled me through the square and past the well with such purpose it occurred to me, with a sickening thud of disbelief, what he was about to do. To one side of the mosque was an old chenar with a rope secured around one high, thick limb. It was used for disciplining boys, but in my life I had only seen two incidents of a boy hanging there by their hands, and they had been tied there by the mullah, not by their own fathers. Their planned crimes had been violent and malicious, unacceptable by all accounts, and all the men of the village – including their fathers – had agreed that they must be punished. What I had done was nothing in comparison with them.

But now my father slapped my palms together and wound the thick, fraying rope around my wrists.'You want to act like a boy?' he muttered. 'Well, then you will be treated like a disobedient boy. Perhaps this will teach you a valuable lesson – that girls do not behave as you have, and more importantly, that they do not have wicked, impure thoughts.'

He made the rope tight, so tight that my fingers immediately tingled. He yanked on the other end of the rope that was looped over the limb, and my arms were pulled up over my head. Then he tugged even harder, and my toes rose from the ground. He secured the rope to a sturdy peg which had been implanted into the bark for this purpose. He tossed my headscarf at my feet. 'Let everyone see your shame,' he said, and then walked away, his feet throwing up small clouds of thick dust.

But I would not be shamed. I stared out at the empty square, hoping someone would come so that I could show them my pride. Let them look at me. It was my father who should feel shame. This was not how girls were disciplined; they were disciplined at home, out of sight. But I knew then that the people of our village would be embarrassed by what my father had done, and would not venture out from their closed doors. It would be appalling to see a girl hanging in the rope meant for wild and unruly boys, only the tips of her toes touching the dust. But then again I was not like the other girls; would any of them take pity on me? I doubted it.

After some time I grew disoriented from lack of food and water, from the stinging welts on my cheeks and back, from the pain in my hands and wrists and the burning in my shoulder blades. I let my head hang forward; my hair had loosened from its long braid and hung at the sides of my face. Staring at my bare feet, I saw the dust beneath them swirl and eddy into odd patterns. The evening wind, still hot from the day, was rising; I began to sway in its strength. The edges of the headscarf at my feet teased and curled, and then gracefully floated along the ground. As I swung, gently, from side to side, the limb over my head creaked in rhythm. The rope bit into my wrists. My arms were numb but my shoulders felt as if they were tearing from my body. I closed my eyes. After what felt like a long while I drifted into a strange, dreamy state where I could not feel any part of my body. I thought of Allah, then. Was this his wish – that I be treated so for only wanting to know His word?

'Daryâ.' I thought, for one confusing instant, that Allah had called me, and would speak to me. But then it came again and I realised it was my grandmother's voice, low and soft. 'Daryâ,' she murmured, and I opened my eyes and lifted my head. 'Daryâ *jan*.'

The wind had stopped, and the dry air was still now. The sun had not yet set, but the sky had taken on a bruised, shadowy look. A cicada screamed, once, its high tone vibrating in the silent square. It was as if the village had died while I swung in creaking circles. Mâdar Kalân held out a crimson slice of melon. She reached up, her arm and hand shaking with the effort of placing the melon to my lips. One stout stick lay on the ground at her feet. Her other gnarled hand gripped another. I understood what effort it had taken for her to come here; she had not left the house in months, her feet and ankles swollen and discoloured with her great age.

'Mâdar Kalân,' I whispered, stretching my neck towards the melon, opening my lips.

And then she dropped as if her legs had been cut from beneath her, and I saw blood run from her temple on to the ground. She lay on her side under my feet, the melon beside her like a second curve of blood on the dust.

'Mâdar Kalân!' I cried, shocked out of my stupor. 'Mâdar Kalân!' I looked about the empty square for help, strange sounds coming from my throat. I saw only Basaam. He stood with his back against the wall of a house, and in his hand he held a slingshot.

'The old woman,' he said, his voice loud and carrying to where I now twisted, like an insect on a hook. 'She didn't know her place. Like you. She is disobedient.' And then he smiled, the same smile I had seen when he discovered me hiding behind the mosque earlier in the day, and I realised then that it was not an empty, mindless smile, but one of hidden cunning.

I looked down and saw that my grandmother's eyes stared at her own hand, curled loosely beside her. She blinked, slowly. And then a dog barked, a man shouted. A woman's voice cried out in alarm.

Within minutes my father came and cut me down. He first attempted to untie his own tight knots, but his hands shook, and he pulled out his knife and sawed through the rope. I fell to the ground, my arms dead and useless as stones. Unable to get to my feet, I made my way to my grandmother on my knees. Other women had already crowded around her; I recognised my mother's thin wail. I pushed through them with my hips and shoulders. My hands, still tied at the wrists, would not do my bidding, would not lift to touch her, so I lowered my face to hers and rested it against her cooling skin, her leathery cheek sticky with her own blood. She smelled of the almonds she loved to chew. 'Mâdar Kalân,' I whispered. 'I'm sorry.'

Her eyes closed then, and my father stooped and picked her up as if she were no more than a child. As he strode through the gathering crowd it parted. My mother followed, wailing loudly now, and finally I was able to get to my feet. I pulled the rope from my wrists with my teeth and trailed after my mother, my hands and arms burning with pain as they awakened. They were dead slugs at the ends of my arms, and I shook and shook them as I followed, crying silently.

In our house I lay on the quilts beside my grandmother, my hand holding hers while my mother washed away the blood and pressed a damp cloth to the swollen temple. I stayed there while Yalda, the midwife, came and studied my grandmother's eyes and face and hands, and gave instructions to my mother as she handed her a small gourd. I stayed while my mother mixed the potion into cooled tea and held it to my grandmother's lips, and, as the house grew dark, still I stayed, stroking her face. I thought she had fallen asleep, but suddenly I heard her speaking, little more than a mumbling of foreign words.

'What did you say, Mâdar Kalân? I can't understand,' I said, leaning on one elbow.

Her head turned and she looked at me. 'You have come at last, little sister,' she whispered in Persian. 'I waited so long.' Then she spoke in the foreign tongue again.

'No, I am not your sister. Look. Look, it is me. It is Daryâ.'

'Do not weep for me, sister,' she murmured, again in Persian. 'I am happy to go to paradise.'

'No,' I said. 'No, you will not go yet. Please, Mâdar Kalân. Please stay.'

Her eyes grew clearer; this I saw even in the shadows. 'My Daryâ *jan*,' she said, and her lips formed a faint smile. 'When I appear before my beloved in paradise I will, like the crescent moon, become young and beautiful again. My beloved with his pale skin, the man who loved me more than any other, will already be there, waiting for me. And he will forever be thirty and one years. He is my beloved, and I his. I go to him as he waits at the gates of paradise. Be happy for me.'

I tried to nod, and I couldn't stop my sobs.

'Will you remember what I told you, Daryâ *jan*? Will you choose to sit at the foot of the moon, or will you leave here and go to where you can be free?'

'How will I know what to do, where to go, without you to guide me, Mâdar Kalân?' I whispered, weeping. 'What do you mean, be free?'

'You will know. It will be clear to you.' Her voice faded, and she spoke Dari once more. 'Now it is my time. I will go to paradise. And you will go where you must. Remember your power, Daryâ *jan*, remember your power, always.'

I said, 'Yes, yes, Mâdar Kalân. I will remember,' and she closed her eyes and a sigh, as light as the whisper of one leaf twirling on its stem, escaped from her mouth.

I slept, but woke with a start, sitting up in the grey light of early morning. I saw that Mâdar Kalân's eyes stared at the smoke-darkened ceiling, and her body had grown still and cold, and I wept anew, even though she had asked me not to, had asked me to be happy for her. My mother came and looked upon us, then fetched my father. And still I lay beside my grandmother, my head on her flat breast, until my father pulled me away so that the women of the village could prepare her for burial. My mother whispered that Basaam had taken my place in the rope. She looked at me anxiously, apologetically, as if she hoped this unimportant information would lessen my pain.

I watched as Mâdar Kalân was washed and wrapped in a white shroud. Carried by my father and his friends, her body was taken to the village's burial place that evening. She was placed into a freshly dug, stone-lined rectangular opening, her body returned directly to the earth. When we came back to the silent house my mother had me help her with the preparations for the special bread made of farina, cinnamon and nuts which, she told me, would represent my grandmother's body.

For the next forty days the villagers came by to visit and mourn, to drink tea and eat the sweet concoction.

After the fortieth day, verses from the Koran were chanted and my mother and all the women of the village covered their faces and prayed. I prayed with them. We finally sent the spirit of my grandmother to rest.

I knew then, with certainty, that she had indeed left the earth and had taken her place in paradise. And I knew that there was no one who would ever again love me as she had, or who would speak to me about power.

But I would not forget what she had told me, what she had said I must do. I knew she watched me from paradise, and I would not disappoint her.

CHAPTER THREE

Mâdar Kalân was always in my thoughts. Following her burial the days and weeks and months in the village moved forward with the steady, practised pace of a faithful donkey. While alone, beating rugs in the courtyard, walking to the well or oven, gathering droppings for fuel in the pasture, or sitting on the roof, I still recited Mâdar Kalân's Persian poetry and sang the songs she had taught me. I thought about the far-off places she had described, but when I tried to imagine them – or even the cities of my country my father spoke of – Kabul, Jalalabad, Herat, or Kandahar – they did not appear real. It was as if images were held in front of my face, and I gazed on them, but without my grandmother's presence they were lifeless and flat, threatening to grow too faint to be seen. I learned that in the dark they were clearer, brighter, than when washed thin and pale by daylight, and so I held them tightly in my head, only letting them out when I lay in the darkness, waiting for sleep.

It was summer again; I had passed my twelfth birthday. My mother told me that surely my woman's time would soon come, and even though my body was changing as I grew taller and my dresses and trousers fit in a different way, it did not happen. The hot wind moaned and whined with unusual persistence, and flies swarmed with even more abundance than usual. Because of the wind and flies, we kept the wooden shutters closed, making the house airless in the oppressive heat. My mother cried endlessly, rocking back and forth on the floor. I begged her to stop, to rise and wash herself, to eat. I held her hands, so cool and papery in spite of the humid room. Her belly was swollen again. The last three times – the times I was old enough to remember – the baby had been born dead. Each had been a boy. She said she had had a vision; it would occur again, the baby would be a dead boy, and also, this time, she would die.

She would not be comforted.

Over and over my mother wept that if only I had been born a boy, if only she had not had the great misfortune to have her only living child a useless girl, life would not have taken this path for her. Had I been a boy, her husband could hold his head high, and she would know she would be supported into her old age by her strong son, and revered and treated with respect by her daughter-in-law.

Every time she said this a stab of something that I thought was sadness made an ache in my head, behind my left eye. After some time I realised it was not sadness, but anger, and, in the same moment, recognised that I hated my mother for speaking these words. The final time she uttered them I shouted at her, raising my hand and knocking her cup of tea from her hand. 'Yes, I am a girl!' I yelled. 'A girl. What would you have me do?' I hit my chest with my palm. 'Cut off my breasts?'

My mother drew back as if I had struck her. 'Daryâ,' she breathed, looking at the overturned cup, the tea pooled on the carpet where we sat facing each other. 'That you would speak so? That you would treat your own mother with such disrespect?' she said. 'How dare you act this way with me? I shall tell your father when he arrives.'

'Tell him,' I said, my voice low and hard. I stood and stamped on the cup. It shattered, and I ground the fragments into the carpet with the ball of my bare foot. I felt the shards of thin clay cut into my flesh, but didn't flinch, for the pain brought a strange pleasure. 'And he will simply beat me again.' I lowered my voice and bent towards her, staring into her face. 'He always says that my behaviour is your fault, that you haven't taught me properly. And each time you tell him of my disobedience you only show him that he is right. So tell him. Weep, and look for pity, and tell him how Allah has cursed you with such a wicked daughter.'

Her face had grown pale; now it looked as if it were carved from wood. She turned from me, picking up the broken clay and mopping the rug. She didn't cry for the rest of that day, glancing at me when she thought I wouldn't notice. Although I told myself I truly had been wicked to shout at my mother, to knock the cup from her hand and stamp on it, like a small, nasty boy, I felt, in that moment, a strange awareness of something new. It was disturbing, and yet, at the same time, I liked it. It was large and warm, sitting just under the skin of my chest. When I breathed deeply it grew in size, like the cavity that held my ribs.

I knew then that grandmother had been right. What I felt growing within me – as my body grew on the outside – was simply the power she had always spoken of. When I saw the fear in my mother's eyes – fear, and also a grudging respect – I knew then that I was stronger than she, as strong as the son she wished me to be.

I was not yet thirteen, and I knew that day that I possessed power. And once I allowed it to flow through me, it was as impossible to rein in as the swollen river which overruns its banks.

I was betrothed to my mother's cousin's son Ishrat. I would marry him a year after my first unclean time. I had never seen him; he lived in the village my mother had come from – Kamê Bara, two days' hard ride to the west. We had been betrothed when I was born and Ishrat was ten years old. I tried not to think too much about this, and usually I didn't, for it failed to seem like a real thing in my head. But then Gawhar's marriage approached.

Gawhar and I had been best friends for our whole lives. She was sweet, with a slow smile. She talked too much about unimportant things, and never argued about anything, even when I purposely tried to make her disagree with me. I easily grew impatient with her confused look when I raged about something: my mother making me collect an extra basket of droppings from the field behind our house, my father forbidding me to ride our mare as a punishment for my outspokenness, a comment I had overheard at the well. I fumed and seethed about many small things then – before I had anything larger to occupy my thoughts. Sometimes Gawhar cried quietly when I was full of anger.

'Why do *you* cry, Gawhar?' I asked, shaking her shoulders, annoyed with her easy tears. 'This is my life.'

Gawhar didn't have an answer that made sense. She'd look at me, shaking her head. 'You mustn't be so . . . so unsettled, Daryâ. It does you no good.'

Unsettled. She used the word regularly. I would bite my bottom lip with impatience at this gentle word. Unsettled. Surely I was more than that. But Gawhar, I came to realise, was very settled. She accepted what she was told, and did not question the choices made for her. As her wedding day approached, we whispered about what would happen. We both knew of the act that happened in the darkness when parents thought their children slept. Neither of us had seen our parents in this act which we knew created children, but for the last few years had realised what it was the dogs, the stallions and mares, the rams and ewes, the roosters and hens were doing. I had taken a new interest in watching the mating of the animals – stealthily, for I instinctively knew I would be punished if seen watching. But this past spring, as I had seen a ram clambering on to a surprised-looking ewe, and watched his haunches jerk, something low in my belly thumped, once.

But for humans, we had no name for this act, and just called it 'It'. Gawhar worried greatly about It, sometimes covering her face with her hands and saying, as I wondered aloud at the strangeness surrounding what must be done to produce a baby, 'Don't talk about it any further, Daryâ. It's wrong to speak of such things. Our husbands will know what must be done, and we will learn about It from them, as it should be.'

And now, when I looked at my mother's swollen belly, and thought of what my father had done to made this swelling, I shuddered with revulsion. But when I thought about the unknown man who waited for me in Kamê Bara, It wasn't as revolting. Perhaps because I made him tall and very handsome, with fine, unlined skin and clean clothing that smelled of the valley's breeze and sweet wormwood. And he would never make me cry as my father did my mother, and he would smile tenderly at me when I uncovered my face after our wedding and he rested his eyes on me for the first time.

Thoughts of my imaginary husband, with his smile and his long, slender hands on my body, filled my head more and more.

Eventually the heat lessened, and the fields were cleared. My father spent many days and evenings in silence on the roof, gazing at the far-off mountains. He made no move to prepare his tools, and made no mention of when or if he would journey to Kabul. And then one day after breakfast, without a word to my mother, he got on his horse and rode off.

When he didn't return at the end of the day I looked at my mother. 'Where has he gone? To Kabul?'

She shook her head. 'He took nothing. Perhaps just for a long ride.'

He did not return for two days. When he did come back, he boldly swept into the house, smiled at my mother for the first time in weeks, and even touched my head as he passed.

Later she whispered, 'A little solitude in the hills is good medicine for a man.' And she smiled at me.

I was sure things would be better now: both my parents smiling on the same day.

But within a few days my father was once again surly and pensive. Off he went, and returned a few days later, grinning and presenting my mother with a huge solid round of goat cheese.

I smiled, too, watching for my mother's pleased reaction at this gift. But instead I saw something that looked like a prickling of fear. She carefully set the cheese on to a plate and continued with her sewing, glancing at it every now and then as if she were waiting for it to come alive and leap at her.

'Mâdar?' I whispered, when my father had gone behind the curtain, lowering himself to the pallet with a quiet groan of pleasure, 'What is it? Why does Pâdar's gift not make you happy?'

My mother looked at the curtain. She held up her fingers in a signal that meant I should wait. I noticed her fingers were no longer thin, but puffy and waxen. I waited, stitching quietly, until we both heard low, steady snores.

'The cheese is made by the Kafirs,' my mother said then.

'In Kafiristan?' I had heard of this evil place, knew its border lay to the east, perhaps five hours' ride, high into the distant jagged mountains.

'Land of the Infidels,' my mother said, the words strangely harsh. 'Non-believers. They pray to wooden idols. It is said that the women wear no veil even in the presence of strange men. They have no morals, these women.' She looked at the cheese again, and her lips pulled into a hard, tight knot, then she threw down her sewing, pulled herself to a standing position, her hand on the small of her back, and went out into the autumn air.

I thought about what she had said that evening as I ate a wedge of the creamy, delicious cheese. Non-believers or not, the Kafirs knew about cheese.

Two days after he had brought my mother the cheese, my father washed and dressed with care, winding a fresh white turban round his head. It was early; he had just finished his prayers as the sun rose. My mother and I sat on cushions at the low table, drinking our morning tea.

'Where do you go?' my mother asked, watching him comb his beard. She held her cup halfway between the table and her mouth.

'I have business,' he replied, his voice clipped.

Mâdar put down the cup and fidgeted with the edge of her dress. 'Is your business with the Kafirs?'

Pâdar turned to her. 'Yes,' he said. 'What of it?'

Now Mâdar stood and came to him. Looking at the floor, she said, 'But Kosha, those people . . . the stories . . .' Suddenly she lifted her head, although her gaze did not go beyond my father's chest. 'Take Daryâ with you,' she said, and my mouth fell open.

Pâdar glanced at me. 'Why would I take the girl?'

'I cannot deal with her. She argues, she is lazy, she upsets me. I would like to be free of her, if only for a short while. And I'm not well. Things do not feel right with this new child.' She put her hand on her belly.

I was not lazy, and opened my mouth to say so, but then I thought of riding away from the village and so I closed my mouth. If I started an argument I would only make my father angry. And yet I already knew he would never agree to take me with him.

'Impossible,' he said, as if reading my thoughts. 'There is no reason for her to accompany me.' He turned and went out, and I heard the low murmur of his voice as he spoke to his horse.

Mâdar gripped my arm. 'Go with him, Daryâ. You must.'

'Why? He said no, that I couldn't—'

My mother's lips trembled. 'Daryâ, I fear he . . . this business he speaks of . . .'

'*What?*' I said, shaking off her hand. 'Say it quickly.' Her expression was unlike any I had seen before. 'Tell me why I must go.'

Now my mother's eyes filled. She closed them, and her jaw clenched. 'I think he sees a woman.'

'A woman?' I felt my face twist. 'A woman?' I repeated. '*Pâdar?*' The thought was inconceivable. 'No. He wouldn't.'

'If you go with him, he will be shamed. He will not . . .' Her eyes flew open, and we looked at each other. 'Come. Quickly,' she said, and again took my arm. In spite of my disbelief at what she had just told me, I was surprised at her insistence, at the firmness in her fingers. We went into the courtyard, where my father readied the tall gelding.

Mâdar stared into his face, again surprising me. She rarely looked directly at my father. 'Do I ask you for anything, Kosha?' she asked, her voice uncharacteristically bold and, when she was met by silence, added, 'Do you hide something from me?'

Now it was my father who surprised me: he dropped his own eyes. There was something large and dark in the courtyard with us; its presence was clear. We both waited for my father's reply.

'If you hide nothing, then take Daryâ,' my mother said then, in that same loud and confident voice.

My father put one foot into the stirrup, making a clicking sound with his tongue. 'All right. She can come,' he said, and my heart leapt to my throat. As I went towards the corral, he added, loudly, as if I had already disobeyed, 'But when I conduct my business you say nothing, and do only as I say.'

I ignored him, leading out the mare. As I looked at my mother she nodded, and then raised her chin. Her face shone with a new and determined strength, and suddenly I saw what she might have looked like when she was my age, young and hopeful.

I was flooded with a strange admiration for her.

CHAPTER FOUR

WE HAD THE two horses, a spirited grey gelding and a sturdy brown mare. I loved the mare, Mehry, who was, as her name indicated, kindly and gentle, and I thought of her as mine, because neither my father nor mother ever rode her. It was I who fed and watered her every day, and slowly rode her in the field behind the village to give her exercise. I often brushed her gleaming chestnut coat, and fed her pieces of spoiled fruit, and she thanked me by nuzzling my neck with a nose soft as the finest silk. Now I rode behind my father, away from Susmâr Khord. I frequently turned back to look at my village in the soft glow of early morning, feeling the wonder of seeing it from a distance for the first time. I was surprised at how small it looked as we started a slow, uphill climb. I had thought its streets long and twisting, its mosque and teahouse grand. Now it appeared small and insignificant, fading into the brightening valley, the mud-coloured houses with wisps of smoke rising from their chimneys becoming part of the earth. Beyond the houses stretched the freshly ploughed fields, and over them hung a low mist. The wide, rushing stream that ran down from the foothills to irrigate the fields was now nothing more than a narrow, glittering thread. I thought of my grandmother's premonition, that I would see so much more of the world than our village, and knew that this was at least the beginning.

After a number of hours riding we entered a high, narrow gorge, and then we were into a heavily wooded area, always climbing. The rough path led through tall, dark pines. At times the path was so steep and rugged that we had to dismount and lead the horses by their embroidered bridles. I wiped my sweat-covered face with my sleeve, swatting at the teeming gnats and flies that gathered in clouds about my eyes in the warm autumn air. On the horses again, then off. On and off; it was a tiring ascent. I knew we had ridden at least four hours, and

I was thirsty and my stomach grumbled, but my father appeared full of energy and paid me no attention. As we mounted the horses where the forest was thinner and the path more well-defined, he grew even more intent, urging the horse on. I wondered at his anxiety to arrive.

Finally my father reined in so suddenly that Mehry banged into the rear flank of the gelding. I looked beyond my father and saw a confusing jumble of buildings on the mountainside. It was an intricate and complicated fashion of homes, strung together layer after layer, some seemingly on top of each other. They were made of wood from the trees around us. Pâdar prompted his horse forward again, and I followed; at the first house, we dismounted. Even though it was not necessary, I pulled my headscarf across the bottom of my face, securing it behind my shoulder so that only my eyes were visible.

A group of young women passed us; they wore nothing on their heads, and were carrying huge triangular woven baskets on their backs. Stacked high with firewood, the baskets were held in place by torn strips of cloth tied across their chests. As the ragged group toiled by, one of the women stumbled and fell to her knees under the weight of her burden. I stepped forward to extend my hand to help her up, but my father gripped my arm fiercely, holding me beside him until the girl had regained her footing. Bent over almost in half, she adjusted her load with scarred fingers, her arms trembling with the effort, then continued on her way.

'*Bari*,' Pâdar muttered, his first word to me since we had left the village. 'Here the people are either *bari* – slaves – or noblemen. You mustn't come in contact with the *bari*.'

I nodded, then followed him to a doorway over which hung a spectacular pair of horns. 'What are they?' I asked as we tethered the horses and he took a black horsehair bag embroidered with golden threads from his saddlebag.

'Ibex. They are a sign of the owner's prestige among his people,' he told me. 'He is an important man here – in this village of Wamed. We have arrived. Say nothing.'

We had to stoop to pass through the low doorway, and once inside, I blinked rapidly in the smoky dimness. It was difficult to make out anything; the air was thick and, as I rubbed my burning eyes, I saw that the walls of the room were blackened. I realised there must not be a hole in the roof to let out the smoke from the cooking fire.

A man rose from a pile of cushions in one corner. He was short and older than my father, his face fanned with wrinkles. As he smiled, I saw that his front teeth were stained green from *naswar*, a mixture of finely ground tobacco and spices. When his smile broadened, there was only a discoloured band where his lower teeth should have been. I knew that he must have kept the *naswar* under his tongue constantly, and it was this that had caused his gums to rot. There was one old man in our village with the same mouth; my father said that those who could not control their desire for *naswar* were of weak character.

'Greetings, my friend,' the man said in halting Dari, hugging my father and kissing his cheeks just a little too hard. 'You are well?'

'Yes. You are well?'

'Yes,' the man said. 'We are happy you have returned to us.' He ignored me.

'I am honoured to be a guest in your home once again, Namoor,' Pâdar replied. 'I have brought a few small trinkets to show my appreciation of your kindness.'

As he opened the embroidered bag, women and children appeared out of the smoky shadows. Like the *bari* I had seen, none of the women wore any head or face covering. Pushing each other for a better look, the small crowd clustered around my father, and I was forced to step back. From the bag he pulled tiny amulets, simple jewellery, and a small woven rug. I gasped at the unexpected sight of the gifts; he must have spent money from the crop to buy presents for these people.

It had been a long time since my mother – apart from the unwelcome cheese – had received a gift of any sort.

With a pompous air of ceremony my father put the gifts into the grasping, outstretched hands. The women and children faded back into the shadows. Once this was done, Namoor, grinning broadly, motioned my father to sit, then loudly clapped his hands. I stayed where I was, uncertainly, by the door.

A girl appeared from behind a strip of cloth hung over a doorway within the house. She carried a tray loaded with plates of bread and honey covered with clarified butter, bowls of black walnuts, and steaming glasses of tea. Saliva rushed to my mouth, and, without meaning to, a tiny sound came from between my lips.

Namoor looked in my direction and raised his chin. I kept my scarf over my nose and mouth, but stared at him.

My father simply said, 'My daughter.'

Namoor nodded as if unconcerned, and then motioned for the girl to set the tray between him and my father.

I moved slightly so that my back was supported by the sooty wall, and watched, hoping my father would allow me something to eat or drink. But he ignored me.

The girl who had brought the tray did not leave. She was a few years older than me, and pretty, although there was something cunning in her face. Her body was large and soft, and, when she passed my father a cup of tea, her long, dark eyes flashed boldly at him. And then I saw that her hand lingered on the cup, and I also saw that my father's fingers brushed hers. I looked away, angry at both of them. I remembered my mother's words about the Kafirs and their shameless behaviour, and her worry over my father's interest in another woman. But surely he wouldn't be attracted to a girl such as this one, bold and sly?

'My daughter Sulima has missed you these last days,' Namoor said, and my father laughed loudly, as if the man had told a very funny story, and looked at the girl.

A sick emptiness that had nothing to do with hunger ground in my belly. I had never seen him look at my mother – or anyone – like this. He looked like a child who has had his favourite food placed before him.

'Namoor,' my father said, 'your daughters are all beautiful, and your sons strong. Your three wives are fertile. You are a lucky man. I could only wish for a tiny piece of such good fortune.'

Now my face grew hot, anger buzzing in me at my father's shameful behaviour.

'She', here my father tossed his head in my direction, 'is all I have to show. One sickly wife is not enough to produce a large family.'

I stood straighter, so hot I thought that if I opened my mouth flames would emerge. And how I longed to speak or rather to shout at my father for embarrassing me in this way, to speak of me – and my mother – to this stranger in such a disrespectful way. And at the same time I had to watch him and the girl steal glances at each other. I saw that Namoor also watched the disgusting display, his eyes narrowed slightly as if thinking deeply, or calculating.

The girl brought me a cup of tea, but even though I longed to take it, I refused with an angry shake of my head. She shrugged lazily and returned to sit on a cushion between her father and my father. After many cups of tea my father rose, and I, too, stepped forward with a jerky, indignant step, assuming we would now leave. But he shook his head at me, and with his elbow pushed me back as he passed, and I realised he was simply going outside to relieve himself.

With him gone, Namoor and Sulima spoke in hurried, whispered tones. Even if I could have heard them I would not have understood, for they spoke their own language. It was as if I were not there. Sulima's voice grew louder, petulant, and she flung her long hair about as she openly argued with her father. She waved her plump arms, the many bracelets on her wrists clanking and rattling. Her father slapped her face; she spat back into his. There were no sounds from the others, the women and children, who still lined the walls of the room. A small boy rushed forward when his father's back was turned, grabbed a handful of walnuts and then scurried away.

I could not look away from this shocking exhibition between the father and his daughter. As the door opened their voices stopped as abruptly as they had started, and Sulima smiled sweetly at my father, while Namoor lovingly patted his daughter's hand.

'Are you ready to discuss business?' Namoor asked my father, and in turn my father glanced at me.

'Let us go to the *chây-khâna*,' Namoor said then, taking out a small container. He opened it and held it to my father, who shook his head. Namoor dipped his tongue into the *naswar* and deftly rolled it under his tongue. And then they left me, alone, in this dark, smoky hut full of women and children who neither spoke my language nor believed in Allah.

I didn't have time to worry about my fate. The minute the door closed behind my father and Namoor the children lunged at the food that was left on the plates, shoving it into their mouths with dirty hands, pushing each other with their elbows and shoulders and arguing in high voices. Many had sores around their mouths, and their hair was matted. Within the next instant they came at me, babbling as they pulled at my clothing, yanking my headscarf so that my face was uncovered. I swatted at their hands. 'Go away,' I said, fighting them off while trying not to hurt a small one who tottered around my knees.

Sulima stood in front of me then, plump hands on rounded hips. She barked out a sentence, and the children stepped back. At another sentence they returned to the shadows in disappointed silence.

'I learn Dari from my father,' she told me. I simply stared at her, my eyes narrowed. She looked me up and down. 'You skinny, like . . .' she put her two fingers up at the sides of her head, and made a little up-and-down movement with her shoulders, and I knew she meant rabbit. *And you're fat as an old ewe*, I thought, but refused to speak to her. Then she pulled my headscarf off my shoulders. 'I keep,' she said, starting to wind it around her neck. 'Mine,' she added, smiling that slow crafty smile I had seen her give my father

'No,' I said, 'it's mine. Give it back.' I grabbed it but she slapped my hand, holding tight to the scarf. We each held an end, pulling, and then one of the women – perhaps her mother – came and pounded on Sulima's back with closed fists, and as both our grips lessened she grabbed the thin scarf and wrapped it around her own shoulders, tying it in a firm knot over her chest. Sulima wailed loudly, hitting the woman's shoulder, but the woman ignored her, picking up the smallest child and walking through the curtain into the other room.

The food was gone and, seeing I had nothing more to offer, the women, including Sulima, disappeared – some behind the curtain and some outside. Only a boy of perhaps six remained, and before leaving, he urinated loudly into the fire, causing the flames to retreat and hiss, sending up a new wave of smoke. And then he, too, left. Alone, I took my father's cup and drained the last few drops of cold, sweet tea. Acting like one of the dirty children, I took up the plate that had held the bread, and licked it clean, savouring the smears of honey left there.

And then I sat near the door in that smoky, wretched room for what felt like for ever, hearing the noise of the women behind the curtain, the wailing of an infant, the peevish voices of arguing children, the clatter of pots and dishes. I felt naked without my scarf to cover my face. I waited for my father to return and take me from this place where I felt little but misery.

What had drawn my father to this place? What prophet could have called his name, pulled him on an invisible cord to a place of infidels? It couldn't have been a prophet, I argued with myself. It would have been a *jinn* – an evil spirit such as the one which lived within the girl

Sulima. I saw that she had bewitched my father, and knew her to be evil. The *jinn* take many shapes, and, surely, they had taken hers.

I was exhausted when we finally arrived home, just as the sun was setting. It had been such a confusing journey. As well as having all the silent hours on the ride home to think, over and over, about my father's shameful behaviour towards Sulima, he had done something else puzzling and disturbing. We had been walking beside the horses and, without warning, when the setting sun reflected off the line of poplar trees at the edge of the village, he threw back his head and gave a loud, happy snort that turned into a full arc of laughter. And then he shouted, 'Allah be praised!' His words echoed in the still countryside, golden in the fading rays of evening light. I couldn't remember when I'd last heard him so openly joyful.

'What brings you pleasure, Pâdar?' I asked, speaking to him for the first time since we'd left the Kafir village. There was obvious sarcasm in my voice, but my father ignored it, simply shaking his head, still smiling broadly. He strode on, his steps so long and elastic that I had to almost run to keep up, tugging Mehry's bridle as I hurried. She was as tired as I after the five hours each way. As we drew close to our home, Pâdar's footsteps slowed, his mood changing. He grew visibly anxious, pulling at his beard and muttering to himself as if arguing with an unseen person. I knew what caused this; soon he would face my mother.

She met us in the courtyard, carrying a large basket of chopped hay for the horses. She set it down and straightened slowly, smiling at us. 'Was your journey pleasant? Food is prepared; I made your favourite mulberry bread, Kosha.'

I was disappointed to see her back to her usual meek self. I wanted that angry light in her face again.

Pâdar ignored her, striding into the house without a word. I led the horses to buckets of water and let them drink. Mâdar stayed where she was, holding a handful of hay. She brushed her palm with the prickly ends, over and over. I waited for her to ask me what had happened, and knew she was as nervous as I. My back to her, I brushed Mehry's side with a soft rag.

Still my mother neither spoke nor moved. When I moved to Mehry's other side, I glanced at her over the animal's back. She studied the hay in her hand as if it held the answers she looked for. Finally she said, so softly that at first I wondered if it was only the wind in the mulberry tree, 'Daryâ?'

I brushed harder.

'Where is your head covering?'

I shrugged. 'Bad-mannered children took it,' I said, not wanting to tell her the truth.

'What did you do? Whom did you see? What of the Kafirs? Whom did your father do business with?'

I stopped the rag then. 'Just an unpleasant old man named Namoor. Pâdar ate and drank tea with him, and then they went to the *châykhâna*. He left me there, in Namoor's house, alone with the women and children. They were all dirty and rude, and showed me no hospitality. I didn't like them,' I finished, my voice petulant, and weak with weariness and the anxiety of avoiding the truth.

I bent my head and brushed again, this time harder. The mare's skin rippled with pleasure at the pressure. Mâdar came to me then, and touched my arm.

'Did you see anything . . . strange? Is it as I feared, or have I been foolish, and sent you on this unpleasant journey out of a tired wife's mere suspicions?'

Staring at her hand on my sleeve, I saw, in my head, my father's fingers brush Sulima's. And in that moment I knew I wouldn't – couldn't – fool my mother, couldn't tell her what she wanted to hear: that there was nothing to worry about. I wouldn't speak of what I had seen, but as I raised my head and looked into her face, I knew my expression told of my dismay. We simply looked at each other, and in that long moment I felt a kinship with her such as I had never known. All my feelings of annoyance with her fled, replaced by something that felt like pity, but was not. It was a shared anger.

And I knew then that I must no longer play the role of the sullen daughter. Even though I still waited for my unclean time, when I would truly be a woman, I knew that this day – as had happened on the day I caused my grandmother's death – I had grown ever older in my soul.

CHAPTER FIVE

THE NEXT FEW days passed in strained silence. My father spent most of his time on the roof, watching the sun rise and then sink below the distant mountains that were home to the Kafirs. My mother and I worked side by side; now I was careful not to upset her. She moved slowly with her great bulk, her face lined and grey.

Three nights after our journey to the Kafirs I was awakened by my parents' voices, by unexpected light in the darkness, and the sound of their movements. I rose to find my father awkwardly standing in the middle of the room as my mother lit some wild rue. The strong bitter scent reminded me of my mother's other deliveries. But those times the herb had not protected the baby from the evil eye.

'Fetch Yalda,' Mâdar said, supporting her belly and leaning heavily against the wall. But before I left, she and I prayed together that this baby would be alive, and be a boy.

I ran through the dark streets to the midwife's, my way lit only by the light of the full moon. I knocked on Yalda's door, panting out that she was needed. She nodded sleepily, rubbing her eyes and taking her large cloth bag from a hook near the door.

I ran home again, unable to wait for her. She was old, swaying awkwardly as she walked, and I knew it would take her some time to reach our house.

My father brushed past me as I hurried through the door. 'Fetch me from the roof when it is over,' he said brusquely, and I knew that he, too, was anxious about the outcome of this birth.

Yalda finally arrived, breathing heavily, and went behind the curtain that separated my parents' sleeping area from the rest of the room. I waited outside the curtain.

'I want Daryâ here,' I heard Mâdar whisper, and I grew warm at her words. Unmarried girls were not allowed to be present at birth. The other times my grandmother had been here to help. But my mother had no other female relative in our town.

Yalda pulled aside the curtain, looking closely into my face. She was kind, and had been a friend of my grandmother's. One side of her face and one of her hands were badly scarred from having been burned in an accident when she was young. The fingers of the burned hand were curved inward, but for all their stiffness it appeared they were still able to move as she wished. I stared back into her face, seeing the mottled, puckered flesh, the eye in its pulled socket, the lip exposing part of the gums. I grew uncomfortable under her scrutiny, and then she suddenly nodded. 'Yes,' she said. 'This girl should help.'

I don't know what she saw in my face, but I felt a rush of gratitude.

'Fetch some water so that we may wash our hands, and bring another bowl of warmed water as well.'

I did as I was told and, after washing my hands, tucked my hair behind my ears. It had come unbraided when I had run to get Yalda, and now swung about my waist. Almost choking on the acrid odour of the rue that burned in the corners of the house, I squinted in the dim light of the lamps, lit with a twist of cotton dipped in oil. Beside her on the floor, Yalda arranged a pile of clean rags, the bowl of water I had brought her, a dish of salt, another of ashes, a small axe, a sharp cooking knife, and a length of braided thread.

Now my mother groaned, pushing herself from the pallet and squatting over a square cloth Yalda had spread on the floor. Her feet were planted on two large flat stones covered with the cloth. Around her ankles were strung the amulets blessed by the mullah that I remembered her wearing at the end of her last pregnancy.

'Bring the clarified butter, Daryâ,' my mother said through clenched teeth. 'It is prepared near the fire.'

Again, I did as I was told, and gave it to Yalda, who held out her hand for it and motioned for me to support my mother from behind. Pressing myself against my mother's back, I put my arms around her and let her weight slump against me. Even with the baby inside her, she still felt light in my arms.

Yalda tied up my mother's sleeping dress, then dipped her undamaged fingers into the clarified butter and massaged Mâdar's belly, pushing in circles. Mâdar stiffened suddenly, then called out quietly. The sound eventually rose to a thin, quivering cry. When it died to a whimper, I heard my mother's teeth chattering, and saw that her thighs were trembling violently. Yalda massaged harder, this time pushing in a downward direction, and at my mother's next gasping cry, Yalda went to her knees, slowly and painfully, and peered between my mother's thighs.

'It is time, Anahita,' she said, and my mother growled, deep in her chest, and it seemed as though she stopped breathing. I felt her body tighten as she crouched lower. But she made no other sound. I watched over her shoulder.

Yalda reached between my mother's legs, and called the names of the prophets. I watched as she guided a tiny head down, and in a rush, a body followed the head and shoulders in a gush of fluid. 'Hold her, Daryâ, hold your mother,' Yalda said quietly as my mother began to slide to the floor.

I did my best to keep her from collapsing on to the stones and now dirtied cloth beneath her. Yalda, still on her knees, blew into the baby's mouth, ears and nose. Still it lay unmoving in her hands. She held it upside down by the ankles and massaged its back firmly, finally giving it a quick, hard tap. I couldn't see whether the baby was a boy or a girl. A suddenly angry cry filled the room, and Yalda smiled at my mother, and at me, and then lay the squalling baby on the pile of clean rags beside her. She pushed on my mother's abdomen, pulling on a thick cord that I saw still attached the baby to the inside of my mother.

'The protector of the child is no longer of use,' Yalda said, and then muttered, 'Love of life, in the name of Allah.' When the odd, bloody thing she waited for slid from my mother's body, she reached toward her tools. She took up the kitchen knife, and at that my mother wailed in disappointment. 'Not the axe, Yalda?' she cried, and then I knew that the choice of the kitchen knife must mean the baby was a girl. Yalda quickly cut the cord with the knife and tied it close to the baby with the braided thread.

I helped my mother on to the pallet, not looking at her. The baby was alive. At least one of our prayers had been answered.

Yalda ignored my mother, who was weeping quietly. She sprinkled ashes from a bowl on the floor on to the baby's stomach, then folded the bit of protruding cord over and bound it in place with a clean cloth. Next she took a small packet from the folds of her dress and poured the contents into the basin of water. I saw the water grow red-brown.

'Henna?' I said to Yalda. 'You will decorate my mother?'

Yalda shook her head, taking the wailing baby into her arms. Holding it over the basin with one arm, she scooped handful after handful of the warm bathwater over the tiny body. 'To protect the baby from the evils of the first forty days.'

The baby's cries lessened, and then stopped. It squinted into Yalda's face as she continued to calm it with the water. When the little thing was clean, Yalda rubbed it dry with a soft rag. 'Hand me the salt,' she instructed, and as I did so, Yalda sprinkled it over the baby's body. 'To toughen the skin,' she murmured, and I was grateful she did not appear to mind telling me why she did these things. I had expected her to ignore me, but I saw now that she was instructing me in the ways of birth.

Dipping into a small pouch tied around her waist, she neatly lined the baby's eyelids with a blue powder, then tightly bound her in a large piece of white cloth embroidered with powerful eye-beads – also blue, for everyone knows the *jinn* are afraid of blue – made from brilliant porcelain. I had seen my mother take this cloth from the storage chest the week before.

Finally, Yalda handed the sleepy baby to my mother, who wordlessly took her. I knelt beside my mother and my new sister while Yalda gathered her belongings. Before she left, she touched my shoulder.

'You performed well this first time,' she said, and I lowered my eyes, suddenly shy from the unfamiliar praise. Then she took my hand in her own undamaged one, turning it over and studying it. I saw her good eye momentarily flash – whether with gladness or shock I do not know – and she let go of my hand abruptly. I waited for her to speak of what she saw, to tell me of her thoughts, and stood in front of her, expectantly.

She opened her mouth, and I leaned forward. 'Go and tell your father he has another daughter,' was all she said, and disappointment sat heavily within me.

Three days after the birth, the mullah was called in for the naming ceremony. Mâdar suggested the baby be called Nasreen, the name of a close childhood friend of hers. Pâdar shrugged indifferently; it was apparent another daughter's name was of little importance to him.

The old mullah, in his white clothing and turban, held Nasreen and whispered into her ear, 'God is Great! God is Great! I am a witness that there is no God but one God, and that Mohammed is his prophet! God is great! God is great!'

Mâdar smiled slowly, her face wan. Pâdar smiled as well, but his manner was distracted. He held his new daughter and looked down at her as if puzzled, or unsure about his feelings. It was obvious he was disappointed, but he patted Mâdar's head and gave her a thin bracelet of pounded silver. I saw it was similar to the bracelets he had given to Namoor's women, and I had to turn away, a bitter taste in my throat as my mother beamed proudly and slipped the bracelet on her wrist.

On the seventh day a small celebration was held, and friends brought gifts. The women stayed inside with Mâdar and me, talking and singing. The men sat outside with Pâdar. It was a good day. Nasreen was passed from woman to woman, and they all sighed, saying 'poor thing', because even though she was perfect, it was of course a bad omen to say good things about a child's health for fear of calling in the evil eye.

Everyone laughed as Nasreen squalled suddenly, as if annoyed with all the handling.

'Will this one be headstrong, like her older sister?' Masa, Gawhar's mother, asked, grinning at me. 'Always looking for a fight?'

'Don't suggest such a thing,' Mâdar laughed, and the women joined in. I smiled, too, but my face was tight.

Masa understood my false smile, and put her arm around me. 'Come, Daryâ, we only joke. What would your mother do without you, alone in this house with no other woman?'

'This is true,' my mother said, smiling fondly at me. 'She has helped so much since Nasreen came.'

At this my smile was genuine; with the safe birth, I wanted to believe that now our lives would be happier, that Pâdar would forget about the Kafirs. And Sulima. And perhaps, if Nasreen had been a boy . . . but we would never know.

Finally, ten days after Nasreen's birth, Yalda came to the house and helped my mother with her ritual purification bath. I watched all that Yalda did, memorising her words, the herbs she used, the way her large, rough hands touched Mâdar and Nasreen with gentleness. I admired her.

That evening I went to my pallet in the corner of the room, leaving Pâdar sharpening a scythe and Mâdar sitting with Nasreen who was dozing fitfully against her shoulder. Mâdar looked calm, stroking the baby's back and breathing comforting sounds each time little Nasreen snorted or squirmed. I knew my mother was relieved to have her time over, and pleased – she had given birth to a girl, true – because at least the child was healthy. Although there were still thirty days left when the *jinn* could swoop in and take Nasreen's life, Mâdar did not appear to worry. In the lamplight, I saw her kiss the baby's head.

I dreamed of horses and a howling wind. And then I was sitting straight up in bed, realising it was not the wind but my mother's scream which penetrated my dream. I had no idea how long I'd been sleeping; it was dark in the house except for the one lamp, still lit, on the low table in the centre of the room, and it was beside the table that Mâdar stood, screaming.

I jumped up and stumbled towards her. Mâdar was screaming as if attacked. Now Nasreen's high, thin wail joined Mâdar's. *At least she isn't dead*, I remember thinking. Nasreen isn't dead. What else could cause Mâdar to scream in this horrible manner? She stood, arms at her sides, mouth open in a black hole full of dreadful sound. Nasreen lay on the cushions at her feet, still swaddled, as if my mother had simply dropped her there. I was sure our neighbours would soon come running to see what had happened. My father stood to one side, staring at the rug where a large bulging sack lay.

'What's happened? What is it?' I shouted, grabbing my mother's arm and shaking it. I picked up Nasreen and held her against me, cradling her head, and her wails softened. 'Pâdar? What's happened?' Neither of my parents answered. I took my hand from Nasreen's head and shook Mâdar again, and she looked at me, and then covered her mouth with her hands, stifling her own screams. The silence was a relief. Tears streamed down her face. She took one hand from her mouth and pointed, with a shaky finger, at my father.

'What? What is it?' I asked him.

But he grabbed the bag and left, through the curtain and then the door, out into the black night. I heard the whinny of the gelding, and then the sound of galloping hooves. I looked back to Mâdar. She wrenched Nasreen from my arms, causing the baby to cry out again.

'Go. Go after him. You know where he goes,' Mâdar said, her face drained of colour.

'I – what do you mean? Where is he—'

But she cut me off. 'Go. There is no time.' She walked in small circles, patting Nasreen's back briskly. 'He told me of his plans. He said I could no longer manage on my own, that you were not enough help. I told him' – she stopped, squeezing her eyes together, her mouth turning down – 'I told him in a few months my body will heal, I can still bear another child, and the next one could be a living boy. But he –' she broke down again, dropping to her knees and rocking Nasreen back and forth. 'Stop him, Daryâ. Take Mehry and go after him. Please. Make him see I cannot live with –' she swallowed, then drew a deep breath. 'But another Tajik woman – a second wife – I could live with this, if it was done properly. With planning, arrangements. With consideration. But not, no, I cannot . . .' She was unable to speak the words.

I stood as if stuck to the floor.

'A dirty Kafir, Daryâ,' she finally said. 'He chooses a dirty Kafir, a non-believer, lazy, surely unable to even boil rice or make nan.' She shook her head. 'I will kill myself, Daryâ. I won't live with the disgrace of him bringing a woman like that to our village. Into our home. Stop him.' She sobbed again. 'Go after him, Daryâ. Maybe you can . . . you can . . .'

'Mâdar,' I whispered. 'I have no influence over him. You know this.'

'But I cannot let this happen without doing something, Daryâ. If I were not in this state – if I didn't have the baby – I would go myself. But I can't, Daryâ. Please. Please,' she begged, weeping, and I could not say no to her. Even without Nasreen, even if her body was healed and healthy, she would never have ridden after my father. She knew this as well. But she also knew I could, and would. I leaned down and put my arm around her shoulder, briefly pressing my cheek to hers.

'I will go, Mâdar,' I said.

She gripped my hand, her own hand trembling, and when she let it go I ran outside.

But the mare was gone as well, and this filled me with an even deeper horror. I looked back at the house, but couldn't bear to face Mâdar again, to tell her that Pâdar had taken both horses. Of course he had taken Mehry to bring Sulima back to our home. I hurried into our neighbour's courtyard. At my footsteps, the old grandfather called down from where he slept on the roof, 'Who is there?'

'It is I, Daryâ. I must borrow one of your horses, *bâbâ*.'

'But there won't be light for another hour, child. Where do you ride?'

I didn't answer, throwing a blanket over the back of one of the smaller mares and climbing on. I rode out of the courtyard, heading in the direction of Kafiristan.

CHAPTER SIX

AT FIRST I was guided by the light from a bone-coloured moon hanging low in the sky. I could not see my father, although surely he could not be too far ahead of me. I frequently stopped the little horse and listened, and occasionally, far in the distance, could hear the sound of hooves on rocky ground. The night air was cool; I shivered in its thin bite and wished I had grabbed a thicker shawl as I ran from the house. As the sun rose I lowered my head and said my prayers, knowing Allah would forgive me for not taking the time to dismount.

I did not catch up with my father for the whole distance. Instead of the air warming as the moon went down, the further I went into the mountains the colder it became. Overhead the dark pines whispered as their branches brushed against each other, but otherwise it was eerily silent. I was afraid, imagining I saw the faces of *jinn* leering from between the crowded trees. I prayed aloud as I rode, but my voice was weak to my ears. When an unseen crow suddenly cried loudly and unexpectedly I jumped, my heels digging into the horse's sides, and she started and lurched into an uneven trot on the wet, root-filled path. The trees swayed now as the wind grew in intensity, and flurries of snow swirled around me. The sky grew darker, even though it was only mid-morning as I finally rode into Wamed.

In a sheltered area at the side of the house with the ibex horns I put the borrowed mare beside Mehry and the gelding. An old, sway-backed donkey was also tethered there. The donkey brayed crankily at me, showing square yellow teeth and trying to nip me as I passed him on my way to Namoor's house.

I didn't care about courtesy now; without knocking I opened the door and almost drew back at the blast of hot, fetid air. The fire in the middle of the room roared, and brought out the underlying smell of stale food and urine and unwashed bodies. Through the smoky haze I made out my father and Namoor. They sat on the pile of dirty cushions; Namoor reclined, but my father sat straight in the place of honour – furthest from the door. The horsehair bag lay open between them, and I saw all manner of gifts, obviously brought by my father. This time there was no one else in the room.

My teeth were chattering, my fingers numb. I closed the door and rubbed my hands together.

My father stared, his mouth open, then rose and strode toward me. 'What are you doing here?' he demanded. 'You followed me? Leave at once,' he said loudly. And then quietly, so that only I could hear, he said, 'You have shamed me.' His voice grew bold again. 'You will be punished. Severely punished. Leave!'

'Mâdar sent me,' I answered, staring into his face. There was no point in reticence; my father had already told me I would be punished. 'Pâdar, don't—'

'Silence!' he roared, and lifted his hand. I flung up my arm to protect my face, and Namoor chuckled and slapped his knees with his palms. 'Your first wife sends a messenger, does she?' he said, now laughing aloud. 'But it doesn't appear to be well wishes.' His laughter rose, and then he stood. 'It warms my heart that you are, like me, a man who does not stand for insolence.'

At this, my father lowered his hand and glanced back at Namoor, then looked at me. In that one moment, I saw something in Pâdar's face, something that made me think my presence here, in this vile, dirty hut, might change fate, that perhaps –

'Daughter!' Namoor called then, loudly, as if sensing the importance of timing. Sulima appeared from behind the curtain immediately, obviously waiting. 'Good news, daughter! The honourable Tajik, Kosha, has come for you in marriage. Is this not a joyful day?'

Pâdar turned from me to her as if he were a kite, bounced on an updraft of wind. With a small smile, Sulima flickered her eyes once at my father, then lowered them demurely. I saw the side of my father's face flush, and with that I knew he was lost. My mother's hopes were futile against the spell this girl had wrapped around my father. And I? I was as little use as one of the flies that swarmed about the crusted dish near my foot.

'Well, then, my friend,' Namoor said to my father, 'as soon as the marriage is completed will you leave for your home immediately?'

'But what of the wedding feast? Surely it must be here, where the bride's family and friends can partake in the ceremony. I will send my daughter home, and remain here until the feast is prepared.' Pâdar smiled warmly.

A slight sheen of perspiration on Namoor's upper lip glinted in the flames of the fire. 'Ah. The ceremony. We do not hold with much ceremony here. Who among us feels it worthwhile to spend time and money on such a common occurrence as a marriage? For births and deaths we have certain rituals. But weddings, bah!' He threw up his hands in feigned disgust, shaking his head.

My father's smile faded.

Now Namoor winked boldly at Pâdar. 'And we must not let her' – here he tossed his head in Sulima's direction – 'think she is too important. Marrying a Tajik and moving to a faraway home will be exciting enough for her. Isn't that right, my girl?'

Sulima still didn't raise her head, nodding as if shy. Her transparent act made me want to slap her face.

'And also,' Namoor continued, 'you haven't much time. The snows have begun early; within a few days they may cover the pass, and I'm sure you want to take your new wife and get back to your home. A wedding would take days to organise. No, I think we should just be about it as quickly and simply as possible. It can be done this afternoon, and after tonight,' another wink and green-toothed grin, 'you can get away early tomorrow morning.'

Something about his wink, and what I knew this one implied, made bitter bile rise to my mouth. I swallowed, imagining my father and Sulima in a contorted position, and my throat burned. I looked at her bold, deceitful face, her bare head and naked arms, her full body. I could not picture her in our warm, clean house, sitting at our table, going behind the curtain with my father. I had to swallow the sourness again. And what of my mother? Did he think so little of her? She had served him with obedience and silence, had borne him five children – two living and three dead – had cared for his own mother with tenderness and consideration, had never given him reason for a moment's shame in the village. Any shame he had experienced was due to me. But now it would be he who would bring shame. Shame would be upon my mother's head. I didn't care what the others thought of him – or me – but I cared what they thought of my mother. I didn't want her to have to hide away in the house, afraid to go out to the well knowing others gossiped about her.

Yes, there were a number of second wives in Susmâr Khord, even a third one, but they had been carefully chosen from other Tajik villages, the marriages arranged with thoughtful attention to the first wife. The second wife could be a source of help within the home, of sharing chores and child-rearing, and I knew that even deep friendships between the women could be established. Gawhar's mother Masa was a second wife, and she and the first wife treated each other as sisters; to Gawhar the first wife was a favoured aunt, another source of love and support.

A respectful husband would never behave as my own father did now.

With a sudden sinking feeling, I wondered if I were more like my father than I had ever considered. Had I not, in the past, often acted without thinking, or with thoughts of only myself and what I wanted? I shook my head at my internal argument. Although I was no longer a child, I was not yet fully a woman. My father was a man. His behaviour could not be excused.

Now Pâdar nodded at Namoor. 'Fine. We will leave tomorrow.'

'Good. I will speak to the girl's mother,' the older man said. 'She will see that the girl has all she needs. And of course there is the matter of her dowry. You will not be displeased. Sit, my friend. Eat and drink while you wait.'

Namoor and Sulima disappeared into a back room, and a few moments later a scrawny child in a short ragged dress, the flesh of her bare feet and legs purplish with cold, appeared carrying a chipped wooden tray. On the tray was a bowl heaped with boiled corn, round bread, a bowl of melted cheese, and green tea in a small glass. As the girl stepped around the cushions slowly and carefully, I saw that one of her eyes was filled with a gluey substance. She set the tray on the floor in front of my father and stepped back.

Still, my father did not look at me. It was a repeat of my first visit here, him eating, ignoring me, while I stood by the door, hungry, anxious. I watched him dip a chunk of nan into the greasy cheese and ram it into his mouth, but he appeared to have trouble swallowing. Finally he did turn, but didn't meet my eyes.

'Your mother acted unwisely in sending you.' He cleared his throat, as if the food had lodged there, and looked down at the edge of the cushion he sat on, running his fingers over its tattered fringe. 'A father's business is none of a daughter's concern.'

'It is a concern if it affects our family,' I answered, aware my father did not expect me to answer, knowing I would only anger him further. Knowing that if I were a son my father might listen to my reasoning.

'I am allowed up to four wives, if I can afford it. I do nothing wrong,' he said, now looking at my face, defending himself as if indeed he were in conversation with another man. 'If one wife does not suffice, take four. So says the Koran. We do not argue with the Holy Book.' His voice was loud.

'I know this.' My own voice was as loud as his. 'But I also know such delicate matters of new wives are handled openly, with discussion. And in this case the new wife is not even . . .' I stopped. 'The one you have chosen is not one of us,' I finished. I had stopped myself from calling him Pâdar as we spoke, as I didn't want him to think of me as a child any more, but a woman. 'Do you not think what it will do to Mâdar? Do you think so little of her? For her to lose part of her power as a wife to this . . . this Kafir? How will she hold up her head in the village?' *And did you think, for even one moment, how much deeper a wedge this will drive between you and me? Do I mean so little to you, Pâdar? Do I?*

'You have no right to give your opinion,' he argued. 'And now you have spoiled this day for me,' he said. 'This is a joyful occasion.'

I waited a heartbeat. 'And are you joyful, then?' My voice was low, hard. 'I do not see joy on your face. I see only misery. Misery you have brought upon yourself, and upon your family.'

But I had misread him. It was not misery that I saw, but carefully controlled anger. He stood suddenly, and his foot knocked into the tray. The tea and liquid cheese spilled.

'*Bas!* Enough. I want you to leave,' he said, his voice harder than mine. The muscle in his jaw clenched. 'Return to your mother, and tell her to prepare room for my new wife. That is all. Do you understand?'

What power did I hold here? I thought of my grandmother's words, and of the strange look on Yalda's face when she had studied my palm. But it appeared they were wrong; I was no more than my father saw me, a useless female who could only be tolerated, and punished for her ill behaviour. I reached for the rope that served as a handle of the door. But when I pulled on it and the door swung open, a rush of freezing snow blew in. I looked back at my father. 'You expect me to travel home in this storm?' I asked him. I didn't know whether I wanted him to say yes or no. While I wanted him to force me to leave, not wanting to witness anything further here, at the same time there was still a tiny whisper of hope that if I remained, perhaps the day would not go as everyone here expected. I saw then that maybe I had been wrong in expecting power to rise up and make itself known. Perhaps this was the shape and form of power; it was useless on its own, and needed direction.

My father looked out into the snow. Nothing was visible except the hulking shape of the house directly across from Namoor's.

'What is all this about?' Namoor called cheerfully, coming back into the room. 'Shut the door, girl. Kosha, you won't send your daughter out in such weather? Let her stay! She will enjoy the wedding. We are to be connected now, tied through this marriage.'

I grimaced at his words, not caring how rude I appeared. To be connected to this foul man, to this horrible family . . .

Namoor didn't notice my expression, or didn't care. 'Come, girl, sit by the fire. I will go and command food for you.'

My father was silent as I stepped in front of him and went to my knees near the blaze. Finally he sat on his cushion again. 'What Namoor says is true. The pass through the mountains will be difficult to find in this snow.' He picked up a piece of nan again, studying it. 'You will ride home with us tomorrow.'

I didn't answer, and suddenly he looked at me. 'And, Daryâ . . .' I was surprised at his hesitation, 'you will not question this decision any further. You may never question any of my decisions. You are no longer a child. You must become more like your mother. And just as you cannot question my decisions, in time you cannot question those of your own husband. If you continue as you do, you will not find contentment within your life. Only loneliness and misery.'

I didn't know how to respond. My father had never spoken to me in this manner, his voice soft, as if pleading. I should have remained quiet, should have allowed him to try to be kind to me, to try to make me understand. But whatever it was that made me me, Daryâ, wouldn't allow it.

'Contentment? As you make my mother content this day? Has her obedient behaviour not brought her loneliness and misery?' I replied, so quietly it was almost a whisper. Then my voice rose again. 'No. It's not her behaviour that's brought these things upon her. It's you. It's you who are the cause of her misery.'

And of course it came then, as I had expected. He slapped me, not so hard that I fell, but hard enough to feel my tooth bite into my cheek, and I knew he thought of me as he always had, a forward and wicked daughter, and knew that I would continue to disappoint him for all the days I lived under his roof.

Within an hour, word of the wedding had spread through Wamed. Through blowing snow I walked with my father to the *chây-khâna* where it appeared most of the village had assembled to watch the proceedings. The wind was losing its edge, and, as my father and I waited on the wide wooden steps, it died completely, and the sky grew lighter. Soon just a light snow fell softly on to the onlookers.

My father indicated I was to move to one side and sit on the cold, damp wood. I crouched where he indicated, my shawl held across my face with my teeth, and I studied the villagers. The men were dressed in drab, heavy wool shirts and woollen leggings under their knee-length pantaloons. Some had the adornment of a dagger in their belts. The sheathes that held the daggers were beautiful; even from my position I could see the symbols of undulating fish etched into the beaten silver. The handles were distinctive, a crescent shape with the head and tail of a fish curving down towards the case.

The men were barefoot in spite of the cold, and I saw how badly their feet were scarred, many missing toes. Their scalps were shaved but for one long lock hanging from the back of their heads, and some wore flat-topped brimmed hats. In contrast, my father looked prosperous. He had brought his finest clothing for the occasion; although he still wore his riding trousers, a loose, very white cotton shirt hung to his knees. Over the shirt my mother had kept so bright and spotless was a vest she had, only last year, painstakingly embroidered with designs of many coloured threads. I felt a strange ache at the thought of her working over my father's clothing, taking pride in him looking so well-cared for.

He had unwound his white *longi* from his head and instead of the usual turban now wore his new and beautifully decorated *kolah*. The hat was cylindrical in shape, and had been made in the bazaars of far-off Kandahar. It was intricately woven with silver and gold threads. I had only seen him wear it once – less than a week earlier, at the gathering to celebrate Nasreen's birth. That he had worn it on that day, such a happy day for my mother, and wore it now, changed the ache into something that burned more deeply and painfully than the anger I had carried earlier. Now I worried not about what my father was about to do, but what would happen when we returned to our home.

I tried to push away thoughts of my mother as I looked at the women in the crowd. They wore long, brightly coloured dresses. It was easy to distinguish the more illustrious from the *bari* by the rows of cowrie shells that decorated these dresses. The shells must have been used for barter, or had great significance, for the women whose dresses had the most shells stood in the front of the crowd, while those with fewer or none were relegated to the back. They wore nothing on their heads and, like the men, their feet were bare. The women talked loudly, laughing and jostling in the crowd, and it appeared they had no shame in front of their men. They stared at my father – and at me – pointing and talking amongst themselves. I longed to understand their language. I sensed they admired my father's fine clothing. As for what they thought of me, I will never know, but it was apparent that some found something about me comical.

Finally the bride arrived, flanked by three older women. Her short-sleeved dress was bright red; in the cold, her fleshy arms were mottled. Peeking out from under the calf-length dress was another skirt, this one white – although rather dirty and grey – and trimmed with a layer of matching red. Under the skirts was a pair of red trousers. She wore many heavy brass bracelets on her plump arms and, like everyone else, her feet were bare. On her thick dark hair perched a beige cap covered with cowrie shells.

As she came up the steps towards my father I noticed a small commotion in the crowd. A young man, missing his eye-teeth, spoke loudly. He suddenly called out Sulima's name, and she turned. Men near the younger man spoke sharply to him, one slapping his head so that his hat flew off. I saw Sulima look at him, and him at her, and in that moment I knew there was a connection between them. But then Sulima gave that sly smile that I was already growing to know too well, and turned her back on the crowd and the young man. Whether my father, too, sensed what I did, I don't know; I believe he was too taken with this strange, bold young woman, and his future with her, to consider – or, perhaps, care – what she had done in her past.

As Sulima stood beside my father, a very bow-legged man tottered out from the gathered crowd. His age was undefinable, although his eyes appeared ancient. Namoor helped him up the slippery steps, and he shakily joined the hands of Sulima and my father, then, continuing to hold them together, he bowed low over them.

He raised his head and said one word. His voice was waspish, high-pitched. Sulima nodded. Then he muttered a few sentences. When he stopped, Sulima gave a one-word answer.

The ageless creature then turned to my father, said the same one word as when he'd started his speech to Sulima, then stopped. He leaned forward, peering up into my father's face, then turned to Namoor and seemed to be questioning him.

Namoor replied, and at his words, the old man laughed, although it came out unpleasantly, more like a gargling deep within his throat. He rushed through the few mumbled sentences. When he finished, there was silence. Sulima nudged my father with her elbow and said a word. My father repeated it, and the old man nodded and dropped their hands.

He turned and, with a stifled belch, extended his own hand to Namoor. Tightening his lips, Namoor dropped a few coins into his palm.

There was a moment of uncomfortable silence, during which my father shuffled his feet on the step, and the crowd realised there would be no invitation for even a cup of tea, and dispersed. I saw the young man sullenly staring at Sulima, and she, aware of his long looks, tossed her head in a haughty manner, the cowrie shells dancing and tinkling. Namoor slapped my father on the back and kissed both his cheeks with wet smacks, while the women from Sulima's family chattered and laughed.

'Come, son-in-law,' Namoor said. 'We will have tea here. Your new wife will fetch her belongings and say goodbye to her mother and the others, and then she will join you.'

At this my father started. 'Here, in the *chây-khâna*? You allow women?'

Namoor shrugged. 'For this special occasion, of course. You will spend your night here. In this way you will not be disturbed.' He pushed at my father's shoulder with his open palm, grinning.

I put my head down, studying my fingertips, red from the cold. As any daughter would be, I was deeply ashamed at having to share these things with my father.

My father could not look at me, although I watched him. I had arranged my shawl so that there was only a slit for my eyes. He and Namoor and I went inside the teahouse as my father waited for his bride. The *chây-khâna* was dirty and cold, although there was a small fire in the brazier in the room's centre. Two tiny, high, open windows allowed in the only light, and as I looked into the dark corners, I saw, with horror, that a large wooden head, the size of a small man, stood in one. The face crudely carved into the wood seemed to stare at me, and I quickly turned so that my back was to the blasphemous idol.

A boy carried in tea, and at a word from Namoor he brought the tray to me. I drank the first cup of hot, sweet liquid quickly, and when the boy passed again, I held out my empty cup and nodded. He made a sound of annoyance, but brought me another. The relief of the quiet and the warming effects of the tea made me sleepy. I had managed to eat a few bites of dry nan from the tray in Namoor's house, but it was difficult to chew and swallow with my thoughts in such turmoil. Now I leaned back against the cushions, overcome with exhaustion from both the long ride and the events of the terrible day. I had not done what my mother had so desperately hoped I could accomplish. I would have to look upon her face when we arrived home, and see the devastation there. I closed my eyes and welcomed sleep, wanting even a brief escape from my thoughts.

Something awakened me. I opened my eyes, shivering in the chilled darkness and frightened at being alone in this strange place with the horrid idol. I saw two light squares on the walls, and realised they were the windows. But then the sound came again, and I knew I wasn't alone, and I also knew that it was this very sound that had pulled me from sleep.

It was Sulima. She was giggling, a low, furtive giggle. The sound came from the far side of the room. There was the rustling of clothing; I heard a moan from my father. I covered my ears, squeezing my eyes shut. But after a minute I slowly took my hands away. Now Sulima was whispering, her voice quick and demanding, and although I couldn't make out what she said, the confident insistence with which she spoke to my father made me think that what she did with him was not entirely unfamiliar to her.

Did my father not think the same thing? But before I could contemplate this idea any further, my father made a sound that could have been a laugh or a sob, and Sulima giggled again, and then there was a steady rhythm, and I knew I no longer wanted to listen. I turned to the wall, pulling a cushion over my head, and hummed tunelessly under my breath so that I did not have to hear the event taking place on the other side of the room.

CHAPTER SEVEN

When we prepared to ride home to Susmâr Khord the next day, things grew even worse, although I could not imagine that anything could make me feel more terrible than I did this grey, miserable morning.

As I climbed on to our neighbour's mare, I saw my father helping Sulima on to the gelding, which struck me as odd; the gelding was tall and lively. Would it not make more sense for Sulima to ride Mehry? But then Pâdar swung up behind her, and I looked at him, and back to Mehry, then slid off the borrowed mare. My anger at my father loomed even larger as I imagined he rode this way simply to be close to Sulima. But as I reached to undo Mehry's tether, he called to me.

'What are you doing?'

'I'll ride Mehry and lead the little mare,' I answered.

'No. Leave Mehry where she is.' And without saying anything else he urged the gelding out of the narrow gate, and then I understood. Along with the gifts in the horsehair bag he had given Mehry to Namoor as the bride price. '*No!*' I shouted at Pâdar's back, and stayed where I was, my hand on Mehry's chestnut flank. 'You cannot give away Mehry. Please, Pâdar!' My father didn't turn around. 'Pâdar,' I screamed, putting my arms around Mehry's neck. She shied at my voice in her ear, and Namoor came from his house.

This time his expression and voice were not friendly as they had been the day before. 'Get away from her,' he said. 'She belongs to me now. Go on your way. You have no further business in Wamed.' He came towards me. For the first time I realised we were the same height.

'I will go', I said to him, 'when I have said goodbye to my horse. *My* horse,' I emphasised, hoping the anger in my voice would prevent him from seeing the tears in my eyes.

I turned from him and buried my face in her soft mane. Would

Mehry have enough to eat, and a warm blanket placed on her back during the coldest weather? Would anyone brush her, or bring her the soft apricots she loved? I knew the answers, knew by the state of the children, of the donkey, and I was filled with such an overwhelming sadness that I wept against her, no longer caring if the miserable Namoor saw my sadness. I whispered, my lips against Mehry's silk neck, that I always had and always would love her. That I was sorry for what had happened, and, if I could, would spirit her from this place. I sensed, by her absolute stillness, her lowered head, her ears stiff and forward, that she understood my sorrow, and somehow this comforted me. I finished weeping, and with an aching throat kissed her velvet muzzle and mounted the borrowed mare.

Without looking back, I rode away from Wamed, hoping I would never see it again.

Although it was cold, there had been no more snow, and it was a brilliant day. Depending on the angle of the path, the sun came through the trees in blinding shafts which gave the impression of moving from light to dark and back to light in an uneven pattern that made me blink and occasionally rub my eyes. I rode far behind my father and Sulima, not wanting to be near enough to hear if they spoke to each other, to see the way their bodies touched.

As we descended from the forest and into the valley, there was no snow at all, and the air was noticeably warmer. But I could not feel any warmth; I was frozen, outside and inside. I could not bear to think about Mehry, left behind, for I felt that somehow I had failed her. And I also couldn't bear to visualise my mother's face as the three of us arrived home. I had been her only hope, and it was as if I had failed her as well.

When the familiar shape of Susmâr Khord rose from the valley floor in the distance, my father stopped his horse, and eventually I pulled up beside them. He had dismounted and helped Sulima down, and his hands lingered on her waist. It was very warm here, the air still, and Sulima impatiently shrugged off the blanket she had wrapped around her as we came down through the snowy pass. She still wore her red bridal dress, which clung tightly to her curves. My own dress was like that of all the women of our village: long and shapeless, hanging to my ankles. The sleeves covered my arms to the wrist. Sulima's hair was not only uncovered, but wasn't even braided or pulled back. It was loose and tangled, pieces of it stuck on to her perspiring cheeks and forehead. Away from her own people, Sulima now looked almost naked. I was ashamed for her, and wondered if my father felt the same way. Surely he must.

Sulima and my father drank water from the flask he took from the side of his horse. He began to retie it, then glanced at me and raised his chin, questioning if I wished to drink.

I was thirsty, but shook my head. Sulima's lips had been on the flask.

We slowed the horses as we approached our house. The sight of it started to thaw some of the ice inside me. I saw my father point to it and say something to Sulima. She looked over her shoulder at him, frowning, her voice questioning. Her almond-shaped eyes were deeply ringed with kohl. When my father nodded, she tossed her head as if annoyed.

My mother, obviously alerted by the sound of the horses, appeared at the doorway, holding Nasreen. There was a look on her face I had not expected. All this time I had prepared myself for her horror, her disappointment that I had not been able to stop my father. I expected her to shriek, or weep loudly. But this was not what happened. Her face was stiff, hard, her eyes dry, and I knew what I read there was deep anger, and a dark gladness filled me. She simply glanced at my father, studied Sulima with an open look, and then turned her back and went into the house.

I returned the mare to our neighbour's corral, glad that I had this reason not to enter the house with my father and Sulima.

When I had wiped down the horse and given it water, Hasti, the woman of the house, came out. She did not question my taking the horse and staying away with it for two days and a night. By her silence, and the way she and I did not look at each other, I knew my mother had told her of the shameful situation. There had never, to my knowledge, ever been a Kafir in our village. And now one would live next door to her.

I could stay away from my own home no longer. I heard Nasreen's loud cries before I got to the doorway. My mother stood by my pallet. Nasreen lay on it, wailing desolately. I glanced at my mother, again expecting to see despair. But again she surprised me. She appeared calm, her shoulders straight, her face composed. I didn't understand.

Where was the weak, wailing woman I knew? Sulima was walking around the room, idly inspecting the simple furnishings with an insolent look on her face. My father looked from Sulima to my mother, obviously unsure of how to handle this situation. My appearance seemed to relieve him in some way; he came towards me.

'Daryâ, you must help Sulima get accustomed to our way of life. She is closer in age to you. Your mother needs all her energy to care for the new baby, and so it is fitting that you show Sulima. . .' His voice had been loud so as to be heard over Nasreen's cries. Now it trailed off, as if he wasn't sure what it was, exactly, that Sulima needed showing. And I knew that for all his bluster, he could not help but feel, in his own, familiar surroundings, the enormity of what he had done. That it was apparent in a way it hadn't been in the strange, foreign place of the Kafirs. I wondered if even the night he had shared with Sulima was momentarily forgotten.

'Why does that child cry?' he shouted, suddenly. 'Anahita! Can you not stop this noise?'

My mother stooped, gracefully, I suddenly thought, watching how her dress moved with her, and picked up Nasreen. My sister's cries slowed to long, quivering hiccups.

'Tea,' my father said. 'We will now have tea. We have ridden many miles.'

It appeared Mâdar didn't hear him. She looked at me, then carried Nasreen across the room, past my father, past Sulima. 'Come, Daryâ. We will go and visit Yalda.'

My father stepped in front of her, stopping her. 'It grows late. I asked for tea. And there is no meal prepared. It is not fitting that –'

My mother slowly walked around Pâdar as if he were a bush, a rock. 'Have your new wife prepare your tea and food. Come, Daryâ.' Now she looked back at me, that unfamiliar look still carved on her face.

I started to follow, but stopped at my father's roar. 'Daryâ! You will not go with your mother. Prepare our meal.'

I looked from my mother to my father, caught between them.

Then my mother held out her hand. 'Come,' she repeated, softly. 'Your father has a woman to look after him. We do not need to worry ourselves.'

I drew in my breath, then walked towards my mother and took her hand. It was warm and dry. Holding my mother's hand as I had not held it in many years, I felt younger – and yet older – than I had ever felt. My shoulders tensed, waiting for the sound of my father's feet as he crossed the room to pull me back, to strike me. But there was no sound, and as we went through the doorway, I couldn't help myself.

I turned my head just the slightest, for I had to see my father's reaction. He stood with his mouth open, his face unreadable. And beside him stood Sulima, arms crossed over her chest sulkily. Then I left with my mother, filled, suddenly, with the fiercest love for her I had ever known. Love, and something else. Pride.

And for that moment I wondered if perhaps I carried within myself something of my mother after all, a strength I never knew she possessed. Perhaps a strength she had never known she possessed.

When we were only a few steps from the house, my mother stopped, wordlessly putting Nasreen into my arms. She pulled her shawl over her face and walked ahead of me, purposefully, but I knew, by the shaking of her shoulders, that she cried. Though she had managed to hold on to her dignity in front of my father and Sulima, I saw now what effort it had taken.

We went to the home of Yalda, and there my mother cried out the shameful story. Yalda sat beside her, rubbing her back in slow circles as my mother did to Nasreen to comfort her. She wiped my mother's face with her large, good hand, and my mother melted against her as if Yalda were her own mother.

'A house with many women is like a ship in a storm,' Yalda said. 'But the storm will calm, Anahita. It will calm in time.'

Yalda's son, older than my father, came to the door, and my mother and I immediately covered our faces. 'Go to the *chây-khâna*,' Yalda ordered, and he backed out, obviously not wanting to be a part of the women's business in his home.

Nasreen fussed in my arms, turning her face towards me, her tiny mouth opening and closing on the fabric of my dress. I brought her to Mâdar, and at this Yalda slowly got to her feet. 'Your child needs feeding,' she said. 'As do we.' She looked at me, and I went to her side, and helped her prepare tea and heat the pot of pilau over the fire. The smell of the rice, with its chunks of goat meat and dried apricots and mulberries and walnuts, made saliva rush to my mouth; I had not had anything to eat or drink except for a few bites of nan and the sweet tea in the *chây-khâna* in Kafiristan the day before. I realised now that my legs were curiously weak, and my head drummed with dull pain as I stirred the pilau with the wooden spoon.

Mâdar stopped crying as Yalda and I worked, and now looked down at Nasreen as the baby fed. When the pilau and tea were ready we all ate and drank. I tried to eat slowly, but my hand shook as I scooped up the pilau, spilling much of it on to my lap. When we were done, Yalda rubbed her hands together, as if wiping dust from them.

'And now, Anahita, return to your home, and hold your head high. Never forget you are the first wife. You have the weight. But be wary. Do not let the Kafir cast the evil eye in your direction. Remember always that the power of Allah is stronger than the *jinn*.'

My mother nodded, and I felt myself nodding with her.

Everything in the house was now changed. Mâdar slept with me, Nasreen tucked beside her, while my father and Sulima shared the pallet behind the curtain. I wondered how Mâdar stood it, hearing Sulima's low laughter, the hushed whispers. Sometimes Mâdar cried at night, and when she did, I put my arms around her, and she leaned into me as she had to Yalda, and I felt myself grow larger at those times, my arms, strong and sure, around my mother. One morning, as my mother and I stood shoulder-to-shoulder spreading washed clothing on the bushes in our courtyard, I saw that I was taller than she. It pleased me.

Sulima and my mother didn't speak; I spoke to both of them, passing on messages from one to the other. At times I felt like the middle bead on a string, pushed back and forth from either side. I hated Sulima for what she had done to our family. And it was clear she hated me. She sometimes pinched me or tried to trip me for no reason that I could see, except that she had a miserable nature, and had grown up with cruelty. Or maybe she hated me because she saw I was my mother's ally, and that without me present she would wield more power.

Sulima hid this nasty side from my father for at least the first while, smiling prettily when he looked at her, laughing coyly at almost everything he said, and openly touching him, stroking his arm or picking up his hand and laying her cheek against it. And at this behaviour, which to me was tasteless, my father would strut about the house as if he were a rooster in his house of clucking hens.

It was hard for me not to hate him as much as I hated Sulima as I watched their silliness and my father's obvious pleasure in the life he had created for himself. It was the first winter of my memory that he did not go to Kabul to work; instead, each morning after breakfast he went to the *chây-khâna*, preferring to spend the long cool days sitting and drinking tea and talking with the other men who also spent the winter in the village. When he returned for the evening meal he sat like a king on the cushions, surrounded by his women – his two wives and two daughters. There were a few unpleasant moments when I was reminded of Namoor.

Sulima always went to bed early, pulling on my father's hands, glancing at my mother from beneath half-lowered lids as if taunting her. The only small good grace my father had was to wait until Mâdar and Nasreen and I were settled in bed before he blew out the lamp and joined her.

As for Sulima's role as second wife to help my mother, she made it perfectly clear that she had no intention of working. After the first few tries I hadn't bothered to show her how we made our nan and pilau, or our methods for cleaning the house, or the routine of washing our clothing and bedding. These were her opportunities to bully me physically; as well as not wanting bruises I didn't want to be near her, as she smelled unwashed, her skin and hair oily. I wondered how my father did not care about this, but it was too personal a matter to bring up with my mother. Sulima had absolutely no interest in Nasreen, and never once picked her up or even looked at her.

It was very clear that Sulima simply wasn't interested in anything except eating and taking long naps every afternoon and what she did with my father behind the curtain. She spent a lot of time putting on her kohl and lip colour, and trying on her many pieces of jewellery which she had brought as her dowry, gazing at herself in the small mirror she had also brought. Of course she didn't join us in the mosque, for she was a non-believer, and didn't want to be in the company of the other village women. When women came to visit Mâdar – and many did, those first few weeks, to catch a glimpse of this strange new wife of Kosha's – she would pretend she couldn't understand them, sitting blankly during the conversation.

But she was smart. I knew she listened to my mother and I as we spoke, and her stilted Dari was improving rapidly. Sometimes I heard her speaking it to my father at night, and was surprised at how easily she had learned it. That she hid her obvious cleverness from my father – along with her unpleasant nature – was troubling. I would have preferred it if she really was as vacant as her stares at the other women seemed, and if she really was as useless as her feigned incompetence at anything that resembled work.

Pâdar did insist, when she left our house, that she wear a headscarf and pull it over the bottom of her face. The first time he instructed her, she argued with him, refusing. He slapped her face. Without the slightest hesitation she slapped him back, and Mâdar and I both gasped in horror. Pâdar caught her wrist in his hand and narrowed his eyes at her, and a strange smile came to his mouth, as if he had somehow enjoyed her terrible disobedience. And she smiled back, her usual sly smile, gently pulling her arm away.

Then Pâdar said, without looking at Mâdar, 'Take Daryâ and Nasreen and fetch fresh water from the well.'

'But there is a full—' I started, but Mâdar yanked on my arm, and when I turned to her in confusion, I saw her face closed and hard. She grabbed Nasreen and tilted her head at me, and we left.

'Does Pâdar not want us watching as he beats Sulima the first time?' I asked, although there had been something about my father and Sulima's behaviour that was odd. And Sulima had shown no fear. Instead, it was as if she was in control.

'Your father has a new side to his face,' she said, her spine rigid as she marched with long strides. I had to hurry to match her steps, and Nasreen bounced against her shoulder. 'Perhaps I should learn from Sulima, and then your father would call me to his bed again.'

I was uncomfortable at my mother's talk of bed with my father, but in the next instant understood. My father enjoyed Sulima's boldness, and wished to be with her because of it. I hated Sulima even more deeply at that moment. 'Sulima has nothing to teach anyone,' I said. 'She is nothing but a lazy Kafir whore.'

My mother stopped and turned to me. 'Daryâ! Such language. It is not fitting . . .' her voice trailed off, and she and I studied each other.

'The name fits the wearer,' I said, and my mother said no more, but as she walked again her steps slowed, and my arm touched hers as we went into the square together.

CHAPTER EIGHT

ONE MORNING SULIMA rose long after Pâdar had gone to the *chây-khâna*. Her hair uncombed and her eyes smeared with the previous day's kohl, she shuffled into the main room where Mâdar stirred yogurt and I played with Nasreen, shaking a small amulet on a string in front of her, eliciting excited squeaks. She was growing sweetly, had just begun to laugh, and one tiny pearly tooth showed through her bottom gums when she was barely three months old.

'Where is the *qaimak-chây*?' Sulima asked, yawning and stretching. The special tea, with lumps of salty boiled curds floating in it, was her breakfast favourite.

'Pâdar finished it before he left,' I told her. 'Make some green tea instead. I would have a cup, and –' I looked at Mâdar. She nodded. 'And make enough for Mâdar as well.'

Sulima scowled at me. 'Don't tell me what to do. I'll just have the yogurt.' She dipped two fingers into the bowl Mâdar was holding.

I saw Mâdar's mouth tighten as her hand gripped the bowl. Sulima tried to take it from her, but Mâdar wouldn't relinquish it. As they both pulled, the yogurt spilled on to the rug. Sulima let out a cry of anger, then stomped her foot and went back behind the curtain, and we heard the clinking of her jewellery, and low muttering.

While my mother cleaned up the yogurt I made green tea. Nasreen had fallen asleep. In the silence, as Mâdar and I sat and drank, my back comfortably against the wall, I studied my hands, wrapped around my cup. My fingers were long, thin, and I thought how ugly they looked, the nails broken from work, the skin around them red and ragged. I put down my cup and tore at the tiny pieces of skin with my front teeth, thinking of Sulima's soft hands, her long, carefully shaped nails, stained meticulously with betel juice.

There was a sudden shriek from behind the curtain. 'Who took my kohl?' Sulima shouted in fluent Dari, rushing back into the room. 'I need it. It was you, wasn't it, you little witch?' She ran at me, and I jumped up. Nasreen woke, howling. 'You sneaky thief,' Sulima yelled, and grabbed my shoulders. 'If you don't tell me where you've hidden it I'll slap you until your teeth rattle. Tell me, you horrible girl.'

My head shook back and forth so violently that I felt as if my neck would snap. I heard my mother's voice, loud, demanding Sulima to stop, and saw her face over Sulima's shoulder. I put my own hands on Sulima's arms, gripping as strongly as I could. 'Stop it!' I cried. 'I never touched your kohl. Why would I—' But at that moment a particularly violent shake slammed the back of my head into the wall. It was as if my head cracked open from the inside, and I felt myself sliding down the wall. From far away I heard Nasreen's cries, my mother's voice calling, and the whine of Sulima's voice, but it all blended into one roar, and I couldn't understand anything that was being said.

When I woke, I was lying on the rug. Mâdar was bathing my face with cool water, and my father was also there, with Hasti from next door peering anxiously beside him. The house was silent. And then my father lifted me and laid me on my pallet. I wondered, as if in a strange dream, why he was here, and why he carried me; why he didn't tell me to get up and help my mother instead of lying on my bed in the daylight.

But I was too tired, my head strangely heavy, and I slept.

When I next opened my eyes, Sulima was sullenly grinding chickpeas, which was odd – Sulima working. Beside her, my mother busily patted nan into shape. And she was humming as if content, or pleased with something. By the light in the room, I knew it was early morning and, bit by bit, I remembered what had happened the day before. I knew I had slept through the rest of that day and the whole night, and yet remembered nothing of the sleep. My head throbbed in a terrible way, and even when I moved my eyes it caused more pain.

My mother never told me what my father had said to Sulima, but for the next while she was more quiet than usual, and her face carefully blank. She even did a few chores occasionally, although often her work had to be redone, as what she did she performed carelessly. And then, a few weeks later, Sulima announced that she was with child.

I heard my mother's intake of breath at Sulima's proud statement.

I'm sure my mother knew, as well as I did, that the child would be the boy my father had so desired.

As Sulima's time drew nearer, she became increasingly rude and irritable. She was even more petulant with Pâdar. One night when he reached in front of her for a plate of mutton she swiped at his hand. At the attempted slap my father stopped chewing, his face growing red and seeming to increase in size. I noticed his face did not hold the pleasure it had earlier in their marriage when Sulima had shown her disrespect and slapped him. This time he slowly rose, stood glaring down at the girl for a long time, then brusquely turned and strode out the door, muttering to himself.

I tore my nan into small pieces, looking from Sulima to my mother. My mother continued to eat as if nothing had happened, but Sulima hoisted herself up from the cushions arranged around the bowls of food on the floor and walked into the bedroom as quickly as her cumbersome body would allow, swishing the curtain closed with an angry twitch.

Mâdar reached over and gently smoothed my hair back from my forehead, an uncommon gesture of tenderness from her. I thought she looked pleased.

The next morning, after Pâdar had gone to the *chây-khâna*, Mâdar rearranged the sleeping pallets and quilts so that there were now two sleeping areas in the main room. I watched her as I swept the carpets covering the raised wooden floor with a twig broom. When she was done she stood back and put her hands on her hips, smiling.

'Sulima is restless at night with her increased size, your father tells me. It is better for her to have space to herself to sleep. So now there is room for her here, and your own bed there,' she told me, and I knew that she would spend her nights with Pâdar again, and I so wanted to see Sulima's face at that moment. But Sulima stayed behind the curtain the rest of the day, and I was glad, even though I knew my gladness was a meanness of spirit.

A month later, I was outside stacking sticks and twigs when I heard Sulima give a tiny, sharp scream. Out of curiosity I went inside and saw Sulima bent over, clutching her huge abdomen, her feet spread wide. Between them was a pool of clear liquid. My mother stood at her side, looking down at the liquid.

'Anahita,' Sulima wailed, saying my mother's name for the first time since she had arrived at our house less than a year ago.

'Yes, yes, it is time,' my mother said calmly. 'Daryâ, mop up the waters. Sulima, stand there,' she instructed, bustling about the room. She spread a large sheepskin on Sulima's bed, and helped her lie upon it. 'You should wear these,' she said then, bending over Sulima's ankles to tie on the birthing amulets.

'No,' Sulima panted, kicking her foot so that the amulets flew from Mâdar's hand. 'I will not wear those Muslim trinkets.'

My mother made a sound with her lips, picking up the amulets. 'Daryâ, go and fetch Yalda while I tend to Sulima. And take Nasreen; I can't watch her with this one needing me.'

I nodded, going to Nasreen who was sitting in the corner banging wooden spoons on the floor. She had learned to walk, but was still slow and unsteady. I squatted, and she obediently climbed on to my back, her little arms and legs clinging tightly around me. She squealed with joy; she loved to go for walks with me like this.

By the time I reached Yalda's door, I was breathless from hurrying through the village with Nasreen's weight on my back. It was hot, the late summer air humid. I told Yalda the news and then rested, giving Nasreen a drink of water from Yalda's clay urn and taking some myself while the midwife prepared her birthing bag. I walked back with Yalda through the village. She hobbled so slowly that I was able to hold Nasreen's hand as she toddled beside us for part of the way. I felt none of the urgency I had a year earlier as I ran through the night to bring Yalda back to help my mother. I was not interested in helping Sulima with the birth.

I needn't have worried. When we entered the house, my mother was already on her knees in front of Sulima, who sprawled on the floor with her back against the pallet, screaming and pulling at her own hair. Her knees were bent; her dress pushed up. My mother cupped her hands, ready to catch the baby. There had obviously been no time to even have her stand upon the stones. I turned and left, carrying Nasreen, and within a very short time, immediately following a horrendous scream that seemed to last for ever, I heard a newborn wail.

I waited a few more moments, then entered the house. Yalda and my mother talked, quietly. I heard Yalda say, 'And so quickly. Definitely not her first; you saw yourself that –' She stopped when she saw me, and busied herself with cleaning the small axe.

When she was done she nodded at me. 'You can find your father and tell him he at last has his son,' she said, and I realised then that I had not even gone to the *chây-khâna* to look for Pâdar to tell him it was Sulima's time.

I crossed the room. Sulima had her eyes closed, and the baby lay loosely in the crook of her arm. I looked down at him. He had very dark hair, and his skin, too, bore a darker stain. He looked unlike Nasreen and unlike me, and for this I was glad.

Yusuf, Sulima's son, grew quickly. He was healthy and robust, and although I did not think I would love him as I did Nasreen I found it difficult to resist his dimpled smiles. Pâdar had him blessed by the mullah, saying that Islam had passed through him to the child, and thus Yusuf was born a Muslim. Sulima said nothing about any of the proceedings.

The only thing she took a brief interest in was dressing him in the fine outfit Mâdar had made for him. As she had worked on it Mâdar had told me that even though Yusuf was not hers, he was a child of the house, and it would be an embarrassment for him to appear uncared for. So Sulima put him in the beautifully decorated outfit, and with obvious vanity carried him to the well in the centre of the village to have the other women look at him and declare him handsome. I knew it was basic conceit for her to enjoy attention as she showed off her baby. The women usually ignored Sulima as she did them, and all of them – apart from Yalda, who studied her openly – were awkward in her presence. Even those who had come to our home to see her shortly after she arrived had lost interest, and it was clear that some were fearful, turning from her and pulling their scarves across their faces when she came into view.

I sometimes wondered what my father thought of her now. He beamed with pride when he picked up his son, but other than that he treated Sulima rather carelessly. And she didn't seem to care. Shortly after Yusuf's birth she began to take long afternoon walks into the fields beyond the village. She would leave Yusuf sleeping on her pallet, and splash cool water on her face, comb through her hair, and then wander out, returning a few hours later. I wondered at this, and asked Mâdar her thoughts on this behaviour, but my mother just shook her head.

'Let her go. She is more work than help anyway. It is easier without her here.'

Something had changed in Mâdar. Even though Sulima's arrival had been devastating, in some strange way I was starting to realise it had brought my father a new understanding of my mother, and he treated her with more consideration than he had in the past. Mâdar's pleasure at this was unmistakable.

'And maybe she has finally learned to find some happiness in the sunshine, instead of lying in the dark house most of the day,' Mâdar finished.

It did appear that Sulima was happier these days, especially when she returned from her walks. Her cheeks carried an unusual colour, and her dark eyes were bright within their ring of kohl.

Two months after Yusuf was born we celebrated Ramazân. I was excited, as always, at this time of year. It was a joyful time, for we knew that the gates of paradise were open, the gates of hell were shut, and the devil was in chains. We had nothing to fear.

Or so I believed.

Every morning for twenty-nine days, my father and mother and I rose in the dark and hastily consumed handfuls of dates and raisins, followed by as much rice and meat pilau, nan and tea as we could hold. As soon as I had finished eating I stood in the open doorway, holding a white and a black thread in the air. When we could distinguish the white thread from the black thread, dawn had officially arrived, and nothing more could pass our lips until the sky was once again dark.

Sulima, of course, continued to eat as always. Because Nasreen and Yusuf still took their mothers' milk, they did not have to conform to the doctrine.

At the end of this twenty-nine days of showing our devout obedience, three days of celebration, known as Id-al-Fetr, or Little Id, began. It was a time of great rejoicing, as the physical hardship of the fast was over for another year. In our village Little Id meant new clothing and much visiting between friends for two days. On the final day, the men retired to the mosque for a day of unbroken joyful prayer, while the women prepared a huge communal feast. For this one day each year they were allowed to use the *chây-khâna*.

For the two days of visiting, Sulima stayed at home, as usual, with Yusuf while Mâdar, Nasreen and I went on social calls. On the third day, as my father left for the mosque, I stepped outside and gazed at the autumn countryside. During the relentless days of summer, a dust fine as powder misted the landscape and everything grew colourless in the scorching sun. But now, with the sun losing much of its strength, the far-off mountains and our valley became a patchwork of brilliant colour.

I saw the beauty surrounding me as I had never seen it before, and something in my chest turned over slowly as I looked out at the valley that lay in the shadow of the great Hindu Kush. I had seen this familiar sight all of my life, but I don't believe I ever saw it as I did that day, with the orchards in their final lushness, and the fertile, terraced fields.

I thought of my grandmother's words again – that I would leave this place. But when? How? For so long that thought had been a solace, something to dream about. And yet now, pleased with the developing closeness between my mother and myself, and happy in my new clothes, the pleasant visits with friends, the anticipation of the up-coming feast, and caught up in the beauty around me, I wondered if the world outside this village could actually be a better place.

Later that morning, Sulima was still in bed when I roused her, telling her Mâdar and Nasreen and I were almost ready to leave for the day of food preparations at the *chây-khâna* with the other women. 'Will you come? Pâdar asked that you attend.'

Sulima shook her head. 'No. I felt sick all night and I'm staying in bed today. Take Yusuf with you so he doesn't bother me while I'm trying to sleep.'

I looked at the baby, lying apart from Sulima. His eyes squeezed shut, he was ferociously sucking on a damp rag. 'But what of his feedings? You know Mâdar has no extra milk, what with the fasting.' My mother had occasionally fed Yusuf her own milk when he cried piteously and Sulima was nowhere to be found, out on one of her walks. But in the last few weeks she worried that might not even have enough for Nasreen.

'She can do it today,' Sulima said.

'But you're always overflowing,' I argued, seeing the soaked front of Sulima's dress.

She crossly drew the quilt up over her. 'Then take a sack of goat milk and his rag,' she answered, with obvious annoyance. 'Just keep soaking his rag in the milk and let him suck on it. He doesn't care how he gets it.'

I studied Yusuf's perfect fingernails and miniature sculpted ears. Now almost three months old, he looked so forlorn, lying alone and almost hidden in the bedding with his sour rag. I knew how much more content he was snuggled against his mother's breast, his eyes either studying Sulima's face with his dark eyes, long and narrow like hers, or closed blissfully, his small clenched hand batting at the round fullness that was his main source of comfort.

Now I gathered him up, feeling that the cloth he lay on was soaking wet and cold. Obviously he had been lying on the same cloth since Sulima had taken him to bed with her the night before, and now he smelled strongly of urine, and his bottom was an angry red.

I carried him to my sleeping quilts, which I had not yet rolled and stacked against the wall. Despite the chill morning air outside, the house was warm. When the cold nights began, my father built a small contained fire at one end of the front room, under the raised floor, before going to bed. The heat tunnelled along, rising up through the floor. He would get up every few hours to check on the fire and add more rounds of dung to the flames.

Leaving Yusuf wrapped in my quilt, I stepped outside into the courtyard. On the kitchen platform Mâdar was boiling a large pot of rice and chopping up two stringy chickens to contribute to the feast. Nasreen slept in a sling across her back, her cheek pressed against Mâdar's shoulder.

'Is there warm water? Sulima insists we take Yusuf, and he needs bathing,' I said.

Mâdar gingerly handed me a small pot from the side of the fire, and I carried it back to the house.

Spreading one soft cloth under the little boy, I began to wash him with another. Yusuf stared up at me with his mother's eyes, solemnly watching my mouth as I sang quietly. I realised I was singing the old foreign song about the Britons ruling the waves, and knew it was because I had earlier thought of my grandmother's words. I rubbed

Yusuf's downy head with the washing rag, and a few drops of warm water ran into his eyes. He blinked quickly, then broke into a large gummy grin, followed by a low chuckle. I felt an unexpected happy flush, and wondered why tears suddenly stung my eyes. Why would hearing Yusuf's first laugh make me feel both happy and sad like this? I wrapped him warmly and hugged him close.

In that instant, I longed to hold my own baby. I had never before had this feeling, even with Nasreen. I thought of my marriage, coming ever closer, even though my unclean time was so slow in appearing.

For those few moments, thinking of my earlier time in the morning sun, and now this affection I felt for Yusuf, I believed that perhaps I could, after all, find happiness as a wife and mother. That perhaps I was more like the other village girls than I had thought, and would somehow find the strength for obedience and acceptance. That perhaps my grandmother's visions of a different life for me were simply the confused dreams of an old woman.

I know now that often, when what we see as truth seems the most intensely powerful, things are on the verge of change.

CHAPTER NINE

WHILE THE MEN had begun their prayers at sun-up, we left our home a few hours later, meeting friends on the way to the *chây-khâna*. We sauntered, talking and laughing, enjoying the relaxed freedom. The light-hearted mood was festive, as all the men would be secluded in the mosque until sundown, and there was no need for us to stifle our talk or laughter, and the women pushed their headscarves well out of the way.

With Yusuf in the sling across my chest, I held Nasreen's hand. Gawhar joined me, holding her own little brother's hand, and we walked behind Mâdar, who carried food in two large cooking pots.

I was always happy to have a chance to spend time with Gawhar; as we grew older our time together was curtailed as we were called upon more and more to carry out women's chores in our homes. Now we only ran into each other at the well or bread oven, or while we gathered goat and sheep droppings for fuel on the hills outside Susmâr Khord. Seeing her now, I thought, again, about my betrothal.

'What of your marriage, Gawhar?' I asked. 'Has the date been set?'

Gawhar's round, sallow face took on a deeper colour. 'Yes. In the first month of spring.'

I felt a rush of sadness. 'And then you will leave.'

'But not so far, Daryâ. My new husband's village is only a day's walk.'

I thought of the young brides who had come to our village from the countryside and from other villages. Most looked frightened and bewildered; I knew that many did not immediately or easily fit into their new husband's homes.

'I hope that I will be able to return to visit my mother when my husband's mother allows it,' Gawhar chattered on. 'It is a good marriage arrangement. And perhaps, when you are also a wife, we will both be allowed to return for special celebrations, and be able to see each other.'

'Perhaps. Although my mother's village – Kamê Bara, where my betrothed lives – is far to the west.' I couldn't imagine it – leaving Susmâr Khord and moving into another village, another house, with a mother-in-law to obey and care for. To leave my mother, and Nasreen and even little Yusuf, and all that was familiar . . .

'But did you not tell me Kamê Bara is much larger than our village, Daryâ, with its own bazaar?'

I nodded. 'So my mother says.' It struck me then that my mother had never returned to Kamê Bara during my lifetime. For the first time, I thought of her as one of the young brides arriving in Susmâr Khord. And I realised she never spoke of her own parents, of any brothers and sisters she might have had. Why hadn't I asked her? Completely opposite to my grandmother, who had lived in the past, my mother spoke only of her life in terms of what was today, and what would be tomorrow. Is this what happened to women? That eventually your own family was lost to you for ever, and you didn't speak of them again? Must it be this way?

'But surely the laws will be stricter in Kamê Bara, Daryâ? You may have to wear the *châdari*. Did your mother wear one?'

'She didn't say.'

'Think how it will be to shop for anything you need, without having to wait for the peddlers to bring their wares. You are lucky about that, Daryâ, although not about the *châdari*. I can't see you not being able to look at the world as you wish. A *châdari* would be especially difficult for one like you.'

My happiness was trickling away. To be able to only view the world outside one's own courtyard through a small square of lace would indeed be a prison. Well, I thought, with a toss of my head, I would not do it.

'So although the village I go to is even smaller than Susmâr Khord,' Gawhar went on, unmindful of the worm of dread she had placed in my head, 'and I will not know a bazaar, I will still have the freedom of wearing only the veil. I am especially lucky to be a first wife, given that I am so young. Now all I hope for is a gentle mother-in-law, and, may it please Allah, my sons will arrive quickly.'

I wished Gawhar would stop her bothersome prattle. As she went on, seemingly unaware that I didn't comment, I tried to picture the face of my new husband beside me on the quilts, his hands lifting my wedding dress. And I tried to picture standing on the birthing stones, feeling the pain a woman should expect.

But for some reason I couldn't imagine any of it.

Mâdar hurried from the *chây-khâna*, just as we arrived a few minutes after her, holding out her arms.

'Quickly, Daryâ, give me the children. I've forgotten my jar of sesame oil at home. Run back and fetch it for me. It's beside the large grain bin.'

I slipped the sling over my head, and passed Yusuf to Madâr. I hurried through the square, hearing the murmured chants of the male voices in the mosque grow fainter and finally fade completely. Then I walked with long, easy strides. I was wearing a new dress of rich orange and trousers of dark green. On my feet were wooden clogs, carved, by my father, with traditional designs. The clogs, which I only wore in the coldest weather, or in the spring when the mud was deepest, or, like today, for special occasions, had high, awkward heels. I stopped and took them off. Carrying them in one hand, I picked up the edge of my dress with the other, and then ran. The rooftops were empty, and I knew there were no men or boys to see me, and nobody to remind me I was almost a woman now, and should not be running through the village, my headscarf blowing back and my mouth open to swallow the cool air. I felt the urge to yell, to jump, as I travelled through the deserted streets with long springy bounds, the earth hard beneath my bare feet.

I arrived at our house and entered quietly, mindful that Sulima was probably sleeping. But I saw that she was not on her pallet, and knew then that she had lied, that she had used her illness to avoid coming to the *chây-khâna* and most likely roamed the fields and hills behind the house.

But as my hand closed around the neck of the bottle of oil, I heard a familiar low laugh from behind the curtain. The laugh I had not heard in many, many months. Gawhar had whispered to me certain facts her older married sister had told her: that a man was not allowed to approach his wife in the last few months of her pregnancy, and then again for forty days after the birth, due to the impure state of the mother. Bad luck might befall her or the baby at this time should she share her quilts with her husband. But even though more than two times forty days had passed since Yusuf's birth, still, Sulima slept alone on her pallet, and my father with my mother behind the curtain.

I knew I should leave, run back to the *chây-khâna*. But then the laugh came again, this time stopped in the middle, and then other familiar and disturbing sounds began. I knew what was happening, that Sulima performed the act. I thought that my father still desired her after all, and felt a small hard knot of disappointment.

But in the next instant I realised I had seen my father leave this morning, and if he had returned to the house he would have passed me as I made my way to the *chây-khâna*. How could what I heard be true? My curiosity was huge, although with it was a dark sense of foreboding.

Walking across the rugs on my bare toes, I put my face against the side of the wall and pulled the curtain open a few inches. The room was shuttered, but a candle burned on a low table near the pallet. I stared at it – the wide pallet Pâdar once again shared with Mâdar – and it was a long moment before I could make out the moving tangle of arms and legs. Then I saw Sulima's head, thrown back in what appeared to be unrestrained joy. Her eyes were closed and her mouth open in a loose, unconscious smile. There was a naked rounded back, moving in rhythm on top of her. Her hands stroked the back with a gentle urgency. I saw this, and a man's head.

But it was not my father's head. This one was shaven, with only the tail of hair of the Kafir men.

And in that instant, as I understood that I was seeing Sulima and a man not her husband performing this act of marriage, and that this could cause her to be stoned to death, Sulima opened her eyes. The unexpectedness of it made me draw in my breath. At the sound, Sulima's eyes darted to where I stood, only my face showing at the side of the curtain.

Her mouth clamped shut and she pushed the man away from her and scrambled off the edge of the pallet. He opened his own mouth and made a questioning sound, and before I stepped back I saw his profile and missing eyetooth, and knew it was the young man from Wamed who had cried out to Sulima on her wedding day to my father.

Now Sulima yanked back the curtain and came towards me, her

sleeping dress undone and flying away from her body. I lowered my eyes in shame at her nakedness, but not before I saw her belly, sagging loosely, the extra skin from her pregnancy shaking with her quick movements. A series of purplish marks stretched across her abdomen and down the front of her heavy thighs. Her breasts were unpleasantly swollen with milk now, the large brown nipples cracked.

I turned, in panic, but Sulima's hand shot out and closed over my shoulder like the talons of the eagle as it snatches the rabbit. She spun me around, her clutch so tight I heard the ripping of the stitches in my dress.

'If you tell anyone what you saw here, I'll curse you, you evil girl,' she hoarsely whispered, spraying my face with a thick shower of garlic-smelling saliva. She gripped both my arms with her hands, turned claws. 'Look at you, creeping about to spy on me' – here she gestured with her chin at my shoes in my hand – 'so that you can bring trouble on my head. But you won't get away with it. You won't get away with it,' she repeated.

I shook my head, my mouth open.

'You stand there with your wide eyes, acting as if you don't understand. Of course you understand; are you not more clever than your mother, than your father? You think I don't see what you try to hide from me?'

My power. Did she see my power?

'But all your wits are useless against the most potent Kafir spirits, girl. Useless. If I call on these spirits they will come to me, they will come into me like teeth grow in the mouth, like hair on the head. They will live in me, and with their aid I can bring down a curse unlike anything you have ever known or imagined. It is I who carries the power in this house, Daryâ, and you know it, don't you?'

I just stared at her, my mouth still open. I gasped; I couldn't breathe, and I was growing dizzy.

'Terrible things will happen to you. Perhaps I'll curse you with a pox, and your face will be a desert of craters. Everyone will recoil from you in disgust.' She leaned even closer, the whisper turning to a snarl. 'Or I may think of something far worse. Under your dress you may grow the tail of a serpent; your feet will be cloven. I can think of many things. Do you wish me to curse you? Shall I call down the spirits right now?'

I shook my head, still unable to speak, hardly able to pull breath inside me. I pressed the bottle of oil against my chest with one hand, trying to pull away, but Sulima held me close to her, as if we were lovers. She had grown huge; she filled the room, so that all I could see was her face. Her words rang with a horrible truth, and I knew, at that moment, that she could do what she said. And more. I thought of Yalda's words about belief in Allah being stronger than the evil eye. I tried to pray, but nothing came to my lips, to my mind. Sulima had overpowered me. Yalda didn't know. She didn't see what I saw this day. Prayers could do no good against this force. I was sunken in fear as I had never known it.

'Will you tell what you've seen?' Her voice was a booming echo, coming from somewhere beyond the house, from the distant mountains.

I shook my head again and again. I kept shaking it, my lips trying to speak, but they only trembled. Sulima's face swam before me, frozen into the terrifying mask of a *jinn*, her mouth a grimace, breathing garlicky fire, her features swirling, rearranging themselves into monstrous proportions. I heard whimpering, the sounds Yusuf made when awakening, hungry, and realised it was my own voice.

And then Sulima's mouth relaxed into a slow smile, and she changed from a *jinn* back to a girl. She had seen inside me, and recognised my terror and belief in her potency.

She knew that her secret was safe.

The rest of the day passed as if I walked through sleep. I don't remember going back to the *chây-khâna*, nor finding my mother, but then she was taking the oil from me, touching my forehead.

'What is it? Your face is white, and so hot. You are ill?'

I simply stared at her, unable to speak.

'Is it your unclean time?' she whispered now, studying me. 'It is past due. I was a year younger than you. Could it be this? Do you have any sign?'

I shook my head again, still incapable of making a sound. The thought of my first unclean time had always filled me with an unknown dread. Now, in comparison to what was making me ill, it would be a simple and welcome occasion.

'Why do you not answer?' my mother asked, looking more closely into my face.

It was as if Sulima had sucked my voice into herself with her own mouth as she spoke. I knew the *jinn* could do that.

'Now you annoy me, with your piteous look. How can I help if you won't tell me what it is? Go and sit with Gawhar and the children in the shade on the other side of the *chây-khâna*. When you feel better come back and help.'

Gawhar also questioned me as to why I was so pale and quiet, but when I didn't answer she shrugged and chattered on about her up-coming wedding plans, and slowly I felt my spirit return to my body as Gawhar put Yusuf in my arms, and Nasreen clambered over me.

But the afternoon stretched endlessly. I alternated between looking after the little ones and setting crockery on long wooden trays, cutting open muskmelons and watermelons, filling bowls with curds, breaking eggs and beating them, and cutting chunks of meat and threading them on wooden skewers. The older women cooked the mountains of rice and hills of nan.

Finally the smallest children were fed, and shortly after, the men arrived from the mosque, hungry after their day of prayer. I saw my father, but turned away, unable to look at him in case he read what I could not stop seeing and feared appeared on my face – Sulima and the man from Wamed, writhing together in the quilts he shared with my mother.

There was much joking and laughter from the men as we served them, and then we sat outside while they ate. Small boys were allowed to run in and out of the *chây-khâna* snatching bits of food from the bowls and showing off on this special occasion. Much later, the men returned to the square for more conversation under the sheltering trees, and we ate our meal. I had waited all year for this elaborate feast: *torshi*, the mixture of pickled aubergines, beans and chillies; a variety of pilau, with chunks of mutton or chicken or tomato buried in the centre; mutton meatballs mixed with onion, tomato and boiled eggs. And yet now I could eat nothing; I knew if I put anything in my mouth it would make me sick.

My mother frowned when I shook my head as she passed the special treat at the end of the meal. The *faludah* was a thick paste, prepared by mixing milk and wheat flour in a porous container and boiled for a whole day. I remembered that the year before I ate so much of it that my mother worried I would be sick. This day, just looking at it made my stomach roll.

All the women congratulated each other on the food, so different from our usual meals of pilau and nan. At last we gathered the cooking pots and utensils, and the families returned to their homes in the lengthening shadows of dusk.

My arms were full of dishes of leftover food as I followed a few steps behind my mother, who had Yusuf in the sling. My father walked in front, carrying Nasreen.

'Why did Sulima not appear today?' he turned and asked Mâdar. My heartbeat quickened and my arms grew curiously weak; I was afraid I might drop what I carried.

'She claimed she was ill,' Mâdar said.

Pâdar only snorted.

My nervousness increased as we approached the house. When we traipsed in, my eyes darted from one corner to the other. But everything appeared to be in place; the curtain was pulled to one side, and I saw the pallet was made with fresh quilts. Sulima also wore a clean dress, her hair braided neatly and her face expressionless.

'Did all go well at the feast?' she asked my father.

When he didn't reply, Mâdar said, 'Yes, but my legs ache with standing all day. Help Daryâ clean the dishes and pots.' She looked more closely at Sulima. 'It appears you are rested and no longer ill,' she said, with obvious sarcasm.

'Yes, thank you,' Sulima answered, her own voice light and pleasant. 'Now, come to the courtyard, Daryâ, and we will wash the pots.'

I shrank back as she approached.

'Give me those spoons. They aren't dirty. I'll put them away for you,' she said, loudly, her back to my father and mother. As she took the spoons from me with one hand, the other snapped around my wrist like a trap, and twisted until tears sprang to my eyes. Sulima glared at me, then dropped my wrist and busied herself putting away the spoons.

The night was torture. I tossed and turned, falling into a fitful sleep, dreaming and waking over and over. I dreamed of Sulima and my father running through bushes, their faces torn by brambles. As I stared at Pâdar's ripped and bleeding face, it turned into my own. I screamed.

Suddenly my mother was there, kneeling beside me, and the room was no longer black; she held a lit lamp. She set it on the floor by my quilts, and stroked my hair. 'Just a dream, daughter.'

I opened my lips. They were so dry I felt a tear at the corner of my mouth. My chest rose and fell, my nightdress trembling with the pounding of my heart.

'What is it that distresses you so?' my mother asked, but I had no words. 'I will fetch the *stamboul*,' she said, and reached to a shelf over my bed. She took down a small earthenware pot, tightly covered with dried goatskin and tied with thread. As she undid the thread and lifted off the cover, the scent of hundreds of tiny dried fruits rose into the air, blocking out the oily smell of the lamp. She held the pot under my nostrils, waving it back and forth slowly.

'This will soothe you back to sleep,' she said, and I closed my eyes, trying to breathe in the pleasant odour.

After a few moments Mâdar returned the *stamboul* to the shelf and turned to leave.

'Will you leave the lamp? Please?' I begged.

She looked at me again, and nodded. When she had gone behind the curtain, I glanced at Sulima's pallet, but the wavering shadows of the flickering lamp created a large, humped beast crouching under the covers. I pulled my quilt over my head and prayed to the prophets for protection from the evil within my own home.

CHAPTER TEN

A WEEK AFTER THIS, the autumn winds turned colder, and my father cleaned and repaired his carpentry tools, preparing for his work in Kabul. I knew he would have to labour many long months; I had heard my mother's harsh whispers to him about her money worries. Sulima's bride price, last winter's lost season of work, and the feeding and clothing a second wife and two new children required caused a strain upon the household.

He rode away with a handful of other village men then, and we knew we would not see him until spring.

The terror Sulima had put upon me never left, and it was more than a month before I could be near her without my body – first my hands, and then my legs, and then my whole body – trembling, ever so slightly. I hid this from my mother; it was not difficult, as she was always busy with both Nasreen and Yusuf. Sulima paid her son less and less attention.

By her new sulkiness, and her sudden onsets of weeping as she ventured to the roof, I knew it was unlikely that Sulima saw the boy from Wamed again. The weather had grown too cold for her to roam the fields; I thought now that surely she had been meeting him there in those first months after Yusuf's birth – and maybe even before – and that during the winter it would be impossible for him to ride down through the snow-filled passes. One day I looked at Yusuf – who looked so like his mother – with new eyes, and wondered if he actually was part Tajik, or all Kafir.

When my mother wasn't near, Sulima would look at me – long, menacing stares – and at these frightening episodes I turned my head, eyes downcast, praying silently. No one had ever made me so afraid; even when my father lifted his hand over me for the obstinacy that still rose, hard and defiant, within me, I felt only anger. The bruises he inflicted faded, and I easily forgot the pain.

Sulima's threat was of a completely different nature. It was a pain – although it hadn't touched my body – that went inside me, far beneath my skin. I could not forget what she had said she would do to me; her words never left my thoughts for more than a few hours, and I spoke with exaggerated caution when she was present. I avoided being alone with her, following my mother in and out of the house as if I were the age of Nasreen. This meant I lived in a constant nervous state of wary watchfulness which made it difficult for me to enjoy my food, or to sleep deeply. Mâdar commented on my thinness, the more deeply bitten skin around my fingernails, and the darkening patches under my eyes.

When my unclean period finally arrived, she nodded, saying that she had known this was what had troubled me. 'When it is slow, it plays within the body as the hold of a *jinn*. And', she went on, briskly, 'now you will regain your former good health.'

While I knew that she was happy with the beginning of this woman's time because she believed what she said about the *jinn*, I knew that she also rejoiced because I could now marry. There had been no other girl in our village who had remained unmarried so long past her thirteenth birthday and well into her fourteenth year, as I had, and this was a source of embarrassment for both her and my father. Gawhar, whose wedding approached, was only thirteen, but her unclean time had already visited her for two years.

But within a few months it became apparent to her that this did not help restore my health, and then my mother began to wonder aloud if I carried within me some sickness.

I knew she was right, for I carried the sickness of fear.

Somehow that long, difficult winter passed. Sulima had become more and more withdrawn, even – like me – seeming to lose her interest in food. She slept a good deal of the time, and now there came hours when I could almost forget about her threats, although as soon as she sat up on her pallet and looked across the room at me I felt the old trembling return.

It was unpleasant to be outside for too long, and our routine was dull. Without my father our days were much more simple, and often Mâdar and I would bundle up the babies and spend the afternoon visiting friends. We never considered leaving Yusuf with his mother; the little boy was much happier in the midst of activity, and it seemed unnecessary and almost unkind to leave him behind. The only time she held him was when she fed him, and even then it was with an irritated expression.

In the evenings, because there was no need to worry about preparing the meal my father must be fed, Mâdar and I would sometimes just eat nan and jam, drinking cups of hot black tea. We'd settle ourselves around the *sandali*, our feet stretched towards the warmth of a brazier we kept lit under the low table covered with a thick quilt. When the babies were asleep we worked, in comfortable silence, sewing and embroidering. Outside the cold wind from the mountains moaned, and some mornings I scraped a thin layer of snow off the flat roof.

I often thought of my grandmother on those long silent nights around the glowing lamp on the low table, its heat trapped underneath by the quilt, our feet and legs warm. I had rarely spoken of her aloud since her death, but now, in this long winter, with the menace of Sulima always near, I wanted to comfort myself. I thought that if I shared some of her stories with my mother it would help. It might help me remember the power she had spoken about, my power, suppressed now by Sulima. I wanted to dream again about a different life, one where I was not afraid within my own home. But the first time I began one of her stories my mother shook her head.

'Your grandmother's life, before her marriage to Kosha's father, was a shameful one. It was not wise for her to speak of such things to the child you were, and now it is best if you forget an old woman's addled and most likely untrue tales.'

Out of respect for my mother I did as she asked, and never again mentioned my grandmother's stories. But that didn't mean I forgot them.

The weather turned warmer; I attended Gawhar's wedding and although I didn't cry with the other women as she rode to her new husband's home on a decorated pony, I waved until she was out of sight. My mother talked with the other women of my wedding, which would take place immediately following the heat of summer. In this way I would be a bride at least by my fifteenth birthday.

'Any longer and her betrothed would give up waiting. And then Daryâ would have to be passed off as a third or fourth wife, as a favour to an old man,' an aunt of Gawhar's said unkindly, cracking a nut with her broken front tooth.

My mother stiffened. 'My cousin is an honourable man. He waits patiently,' she told the woman.

I asked my mother for news of her cousin, of his looks, his family, what his mother was like, but she would say little. She had not seen my betrothed since she left Kamê Bara, and he had only been a child. 'I remember a lively, mischievous boy with bright eyes,' she said, but that could describe any boy in our village. 'And your father checked, and confirmed that he will be a good provider. You have nothing to fear. Your future mother-in-law is an ordinary, decent woman.'

I wondered if this was really all she knew, or if she said so little on the matter because she didn't want to frighten me. Perhaps my cousin had a hump on his back, or his mother was a cruel woman who would use me as a slave.

Gawhar came home for a visit after her third month of marriage. Her plain face had a new glow; it was alive in a way I hadn't noticed when she had been an unmarried. I asked her details: how did her mother-in-law treat her? Did she have to work much harder than at home? And, more importantly, how did it feel when her husband came to her under the quilt? Did it hurt? But Gawhar's face only grew more and more flushed at my questions, and she shook her head.

'You will know soon enough, Daryâ,' she said.

'I don't want to leave Susmâr Khord when autumn comes,' I said quietly to my mother as we worked beside each other in the courtyard. She had told me my wedding would be in the first month after the long heat, as this was the most successful month for marriage. It was a sunny afternoon when the wind blew sweetly and the scent of spring was everywhere. Mâdar had decided, with my father due to arrive home from Kabul at any time, to clean all the bedding and floor coverings. She shook small rugs briskly and threw them over bushes to air, and now, with short, thick branches, we beat larger carpets hanging over thick ropes tied between the trees in the courtyard.

'You know you must, Daryâ,' Mâdar said. 'The betrothal has been sealed for all these years; it would be unthinkable to make any change to the plans. The family of the groom would be deeply shamed. Besides, there is no choice. There are no unmarried men in our village who are old enough to be established in a way fit to take on a first wife. And none of the older men would be rude enough to take on a second, younger wife from our own village women.'

'I know,' I said. But I had grown fearful in an inexplicable way since Sulima's threatened curses. While I wanted to be away from her presence, the thought of leaving my home and all that was familiar had taken on a dark, unpleasant tone. I still gazed at the stars at night, still thought of their paths through the sky, and the paths on the earth my grandmother told me I would follow, but the fear I carried now threatened to smother any sense of power I had once known.

I climbed the ladder to the roof, and Mâdar handed me up some of the quilts to spread there to freshen in the sun and wind. As I finished I saw Sulima standing in the furrowed fields behind our house, shading her eyes and staring east.

'What do you look at?' Mâdar called to me.

I came down the ladder. 'Sulima. She gazes towards her home.'

My mother shrugged. 'There is nothing for her here, and she knows this. You understand that if your father had spoken to me, asked me if he might bring in a younger wife to take away some of my burden, I might have accepted another woman with relief, and treated her as a sister, as it should be. He could have gone to any of the neighbouring towns, or . . .' she stopped. 'But that is an old story. I have told it in my head so many times that it has lost its potency. And now Sulima has also lost her influence over your father. Her own son cries when she picks him up. She has no friends in the village, and has never once requested to go back to visit her family. And nobody from her own village has ever come to ask about her.'

You are wrong, Mâdar. The rounded back and shaved head of the Kafir stood in front of my eyes.

'I'm sure Sulima imagined a Tajik life as very grand, and that Kosha would continue to shower her with attention and gifts. She is not so much older than you, Daryâ.' Mâdar laid her hand on my arm. 'I see how you shun her. It saddens me that you will not be with me for much longer, but unfortunately Sulima will always be here.' She sighed. 'Allah's plans are not always easily understood.'

I stared at my mother. She didn't know I was not shunning Sulima, but protecting myself from her evilness. Like Gawhar, Mâdar believed in the simple rules of life: stand silently by your husband, raise your daughters to be quiet and obedient, keep a clean home, and, perhaps as importantly, do not hold anger in your heart. Forgive. She had forgiven my father for his poor choice; I saw now that in her own way she had even forgiven Sulima for being born an infidel. She had no idea of Sulima's power, had never seen her as I had, transformed into a *jinn* who could steal life away.

And I knew I was not good like my mother, or like Gawhar. I carried within me something black and uncontrollable, and I wondered how I would live the rest of my life with it.

Later that day Mâdar told me that I was to dust and sweep out the sleeping room behind the curtain. She was going into the square to see what a passing peddler had brought. I wanted to go with her, and not stay home with Sulima, but this time my mother did not allow it. 'Your father may arrive home any day. Surely the roads from Kabul are clear now,' she said.

As soon as she was gone Sulima looked up from her jewellery. She had dumped it on her pallet and was sorting through it. 'So. Your mother has left you alone, has she?' She gave a slow, menacing smile.

I turned away. 'I have much work to do,' I said, then looked over my shoulder. 'Would you like me to air your bedding?'

'What are you saying? That I'm dirty?'

I shook my head. 'No. No, Sulima.'

'Then don't tell me what to do.'

'But I didn't –'

'*Be quiet!*' she said loudly, and at that Yusuf, sitting on the floor at my feet, whined. 'And shut him up as well. You know how his crying bothers me.'

I reached down and picked up the little boy, instinctively backing away from Sulima, watching her as she piled her jewellery back into its bag and put it on the low shelf over her pallet. She whirled unexpectedly, and I jumped back, catching my breath, and Yusuf's mouth curved downward as he clutched my shoulder. 'I see you watching my jewellery,' she said, and I shook my head. 'Are you thinking of stealing something from me?'

'No. No, Sulima,' I said, shaking my head. 'I wouldn't.'

'That's right,' she said, coming nearer. 'You wouldn't. Because if you did, or you said anything you shouldn't, you know what would happen, don't you?'

I nodded, breathing rapidly. She came close, and again I pulled away, but before I could stop her she reached out and gave one of Yusuf's tufts of baby hair a hard yank. He screamed, burying his face in my neck, and I put my hand on the back of his head to protect him as Nasreen ran to me and clung to my skirt.

But Sulima didn't hurt her son any further. 'I'm going for a walk,' she said. 'And I'll know if you've so much as touched my jewellery bag. You remember, don't you? How I can see everything you do, even if you don't know I'm watching?'

I lowered my gaze, holding Yusuf closer. How could I forget?

Once she had gone I took a deep breath and prepared a piece of nan sweetened with a smear of honey for each of the children. When they had eaten and were again calm I took them behind the curtain with me, and gave them wooden blocks to play with. I threw open the shutters and let a warm draught fill the room, then I took a cloth and dusted the walls. My mother had already put the fresh quilts back on the pallet, although the rugs remained rolled in a corner. I got on my hands and knees and swept out under the low pallet with a rough bundle of switches lashed together. Large balls of webby dust rolled out; we had not cleaned under the pallets since before Ramazân. I heard my mother come in, humming, and as I pushed the broom as far as I could, it hit something far against the wall. I lay on my stomach and forced the heavy object out with the end of the broom.

It was a dagger, thickly covered with dust, its blade sheathed in a silver case I recognised too well. The knife of the Kafir who had been in this bed with Sulima.

My mother called in an excited voice. 'Daryâ! Children! Come. It's your father, home already.'

As Nasreen ran into the other room, Yusuf crawling behind her, I held the knife by my side, hidden in the folds of my dress, and pulled aside the curtain as my father came into the house. Mâdar was smiling.

'You're early, Kosha! I really didn't expect you home for four or five days.'

'The weather turned so quickly that we all decided we would get an early start on the planting. There was much work to be done in Kabul this year because of the earthquake tremors last autumn, but there were many extra men. We had the best season in a long time.'

He set the heavy saddlebag down and stiffly lowered himself to the cushions. 'It is good to be home. Come, little ones,' he said, spreading his arms to Nasreen and Yusuf. Nasreen went to him, but Yusuf stayed back, sucking his fist.

'His memory is still young,' Mâdar said. 'He will remember you in a few moments. Now, I will prepare food,' Mâdar said, still so pleased-looking. 'Daryâ, come and help.'

'Wait, wait for a moment,' my father said, one arm around Nasreen, who stood at his side. 'Come and sit, both of you. I have brought presents.' He glanced around the room. 'Where is Sulima?'

'She went for a walk,' I said. My fingers clutched the dagger. It was too late for me to try and hide it.

'Well, we won't wait for her.' As my mother sat beside him, holding Yusuf on her lap, my father dug in the saddlebag and, with a flourish, held up a large bolt of soft, beautifully woven burgundy and navy silk. 'For you, Anahita, for a festival dress. Bought from a Turkoman. They make the finest silk. I also have some glass beads to sew on it . . . here. Here they are.' He handed her the fabric and a small cloth bag. My mother took them, her smile filling her face.

'And look,' he said, bringing out small carved toys. 'For you, Nasreen,' he said, handing her a camel with jointed legs, and a long snake made in many painted segments. She took them, smiling shyly, holding them against her. 'And for my son,' he said, and dangled a wooden knife in front of Yusuf. But Yusuf turned his head away, still sucking his fist, looking petulant. Pâdar set it on the floor.

'Daryâ,' he said, studying me. 'You have grown even taller since I left. Now come. I have brought something for you as well.'

I stood as if my feet were planted into the rug.

'Well? Do you not wish to see what I have?' my father asked.

Still I stood, not moving. 'Daryâ,' Mâdar said. 'Do not be disrespectful. Go to your father.'

I went across the room slowly, my right hand clutching the knife, keeping it deep in the folds of my dress.

'For my oldest daughter,' my father said, 'her first piece of jewellery. She will wear it as a bride.' He slowly pulled his hand out of the saddlebag, displaying a long silver chain with a small lapis lazuli hanging from the end.

'It's beautiful,' I said, but my voice sounded odd in my ears.

He held it towards me. 'Take it.'

I reached for it, awkwardly, with my left hand, as I moved my right hand behind my back. My father cocked his head, smiling, and I felt sweat over my lip.

'Daryâ!' Mâdar scolded. 'Thank your father. What have you behind your back?'

Before I realised what she was doing, she stood and pulled my arm away from my body. Both my parents stared at the dagger. Then my father stretched out his hand, palm up, towards me. I placed the dagger there.

He sat down on the cushions again, and turned it over and over in his thick, scarred fingers. 'Why do you hold this?'

I wiped the sweat from my top lip. 'I – I don't know.' It was as if my mind was as frozen as my body. I couldn't think of one sentence, one explanation. Usually I had an argument for every question. The fingers of my left hand now closed around the pale stone of the necklace. It was smooth and cool.

'You don't know? Where did it come from? Anahita? Do you know?'

'No,' my mother said. 'Daryâ? We wait for an answer.'

I knew I had to speak. And I couldn't think of a lie. 'I found it under the pallet,' I whispered.

'Under *our* pallet?' my mother asked. 'But whose is it? I have never seen a dagger in this shape, or decorated so.'

'It is a dagger of the Kafirs,' my father said then, his voice low.

'Oh, well then, it's Sulima's,' Mâdar said.

But my father shook his head, slowly and heavily. 'Women do not have these daggers. Only the men.'

'But then how –' Mâdar stopped, and her expression changed from puzzlement to fear.

My father stood so suddenly that he trod heavily on my foot. I tried to move away from him, but his foot pinned my own. I looked into his face, and saw that it had grown scarlet.

'Anahita,' he said now. 'Go and find Sulima. Say nothing to her. Just bring her back to me.'

I had never heard this tone, even when he had been so angry with me over the years, even as he beat me. But this was different, and I was filled with a horrible sense of knowing what was to come.

CHAPTER ELEVEN

TEN MINUTES LATER, Sulima trailed into the house after Mâdar. My father and I had sat in silence while we waited. I was trembling uncontrollably. Nasreen happily played in front of us with her camel and snake, and beside her Yusuf sucked the dull end of his wooden knife.

'Kosha,' Sulima said. My father stretched out his open hand, and she looked at the knife there.

'Daryâ has shown this to me,' he said, and I closed my eyes. Why? Why did he say it in this way? Why did he say my name?

Sulima turned to me, and without thinking, I clapped my hands over my eyes so that I might protect myself from what I feared I would see in her face – that ghastly, monstrous face of the *jinn*.

'Sulima?' My father barked her name with such fierceness that I took my hands away and looked from him to her. 'Your guile is great indeed.'

At these simple words, Sulima's eyes rolled up into her head so that only the whites showed. My father could not see this, as she still faced me.

'Will you explain how a dagger from one of your men came to be –'

But before my father could finish the sentence, Sulima dropped to the floor as if struck by an unseen hand. On her back, her hands balled into fists, she beat the wooden floor with dull thuds. Suddenly her heels joined in the rhythmic pounding. Then she struck the back of her head on the floor as well, over and over. She hit it so hard that it bounced up with each jolt. Tiny gasping screams puffed out of her pursed lips.

My father bent over her. 'What is it?' he shouted down into her face, then, as the girl's shrieks grew louder, he looked at my mother helplessly. 'Anahita!' he yelled. 'Stop her!'

Mâdar rushed towards Sulima, who had begun clawing her own face and ripping at her hair. Her long nails tore open her skin, and blood oozed out from the deep scratches on her cheeks and neck before Mâdar could grab her hands. Nasreen ran to me and clutched my legs, burying her face in my skirt, while Yusuf sat, howling in fear. Instinctively I swooped him up; his terrified screams echoed in my ear.

I knew what I was seeing; I had heard stories of women possessed by *jinn*, but had never imagined it to be so horrible.

'Help me hold her, Kosha,' Anahita called over the unbearable din as Nasreen now wailed as well. While my father held Sulima's kicking feet, Mâdar pinned Sulima's hands down and chanted.

'In the name of Allah, Most Gracious, Most Merciful,' she repeated, over and over, hoping the holy phrase would frighten away the spirits. My father joined in loudly, and I realised I was saying the phrase over and over, although in my head. *In the name of Allah, in the name of Allah.*

Time stretched on indefinitely. And then Sulima's frenzied activity slowed. Her head still flailed from side to side, and her lips had a bluish tinge, but her screams subsided. And with her cries dying the children's quieted to whimpers. Eventually the room grew still; the heavy breathing of the adults and the shorter quavering gasps of the babies were the only sounds. It appeared that Sulima had fallen into an exhausted form of sleep, although her eyes were half open.

My parents looked at each other over the inert body, and then cautiously loosened their grip. When Sulima remained still, they sat back on their heels. My mother rubbed her sweating face with the hem of her dress. 'Lay her on our bed,' she told my father. 'I will see to her scratches. Daryâ, calm the children – sing to them, tell them a story, anything.'

Yusuf had buried his face against my neck, and now only moaned. I took Nasreen, hiccuping, to my pallet, and put them both there. I gave them each a drink of water, and then put their new toys in their laps, but they showed no interest. I drank water, too, and tried to sing, but only croaks emerged. My throat was tight, my mouth dry, no matter how much water I swallowed.

Through this, my father sat on the cushions, unmoving, holding the dagger again, and staring at the curtain.

* * *

Half an hour later Mâdar emerged from the sleeping room with a rag and bowl of water. I saw it was pink with blood. She hooked the curtain up over a nail on the wall. A small lamp burned by the bed.

'She sleeps now, but we must watch for another attack. Her scratches are deep, but hopefully will not scar.' She glanced at my pallet, where I sat with Nasreen and Yusuf, an arm around each one. By the slump of their little bodies, I knew they both slept. I lowered them to the quilt and covered them with another.

Mâdar lit a thick candle. 'Why should she be possessed, Kosha?' she asked as the candle flared. 'I have only seen a few other possessions, and they were unstable, weak young women unable to cope with the death of a child or husband, or the constant viciousness of a mother-in-law's tongue. What caused the *jinn* to come to Sulima? She does not even believe in them.' She folded and unfolded the rag as she studied my father's face, then continued. 'Should we attempt a cure? Tomorrow we could bind her to one of the large trees near the mosque. She is not a Muslim, but perhaps if we pay the mullah handsomely he will pray for her, and the *jinn* will flee. Kosha? Do you think it is wise to do so? I have seen it work before. Although of course the women were believers . . .' Her voice trailed off as she waited for my father to reply.

He finally looked up. 'It was not the *jinn*. Sulima herself called this fit to come upon her so that she would not have to deal with the truth uncovered today.' He held up the knife, and the silver glinted in the wavering light of the candle, making the body of the fish appear to undulate. 'She is an adulterous wife. She has made a fool of me with a man of her village. This is the proof.'

My mother shook her head. 'No. When, Kosha? How could she bring a man to our home? All winter, either Daryâ or I were at home; Sulima was not alone for any period of time except for an hour or so when we visited.' She looked at me. 'Is this not true, Daryâ?'

I nodded.

'Sulima is of a devious nature. We shall not know how she accomplished what she did, nor with whom, nor how often. But her infidelity is obvious.'

There was no possible reply. We all sat in silence for a long while. Then, slowly and quietly, my father rose from the cushions and walked into the sleeping room. Through the open doorway we saw him looking down at the still form on the bed.

With a sudden growl that made us both leap, my father grabbed Sulima around the neck. Sulima sat straight up with a strangled cry, clawing at my father's hands. By the light of the lamp I saw that her eyes bulged, and her tongue protruded from between her open lips. Mâdar ran to pull at my father.

'Stop, Kosha, stop,' she cried. 'Don't kill her. She is the mother of your son. No more!' She sobbed now. 'Think of the punishment for killing her, Kosha. It is up to the mullah to decide how she will be disciplined.'

Kosha squeezed Sulima's throat for only another second, then abruptly loosened his grip and threw her back against the quilts. She gave one huge gasp. My father turned and strode from her, and then out the door. Sulima lay with her head hanging over the edge of the pallet, choking and retching.

My mother also left her, coming to sit beside me. After a long silence, I quietly asked, 'What will happen now, Mâdar?'

She put her arms on her knees and laid her head upon them. 'Tonight your father will probably sleep at the *chây-khâna.* As for tomorrow . . .' she lifted her head, and I saw the fine lines radiating from the corners of her eyes, the deep creases beside her mouth. 'As for tomorrow,' she repeated, 'only Allah knows the fate of us all.'

I opened my eyes to the first light teasing at the windows; the room was freezing. Mâdar and I had fallen asleep without closing the shutters, and cold air had filled the room. We all slept on my narrow pallet – Mâdar and Nasreen and Yusuf and I.

But it was not my uncomfortable sleep that had awakened me. It was something else, something unfamiliar. I raised myself on one elbow, listening, but now there was only silence, an uncanny stagnancy within the walls of our home. I glanced at Nasreen and Yusuf; they still slept, curled against each other like exhausted puppies between my mother and I. Mâdar was asleep on her back, her mouth open. I eased out from under the quilt, tucking it back around the children. The tip of my nose and my fingers were cold. I would start a fire.

Straightening my shoulders and then stretching my arms above my head, I glanced towards the curtain, still held open by the nail. The pallet was a jumble of quilts and pillows, and there were clothes thrown about the room. But Sulima was not there.

'Is your father back?' Mâdar whispered as she sat up, rubbing her eyes. Her skin had a yellow cast.

'No. And Sulima is not here either.'

My mother shook her head, falling back on the pallet. 'Daryâ, I am too weary to think, or to move. Please, look outside – in the courtyard, on the roof. See if you can find Sulima. Go to the *chây-khâna* and rouse your father. Tell him to come home; we must speak of what is to be done.'

Not taking the time to start a fire, I ran into the courtyard and climbed to the roof. I gazed into the fields, thinking perhaps Sulima was there, but the countryside was empty, pale vapour hovering low over the ground. In that moment pink streaks broke over the mountains, and I heard the call of the mullah. His voice echoed eerily over the rooftops of the village, and I knew the most devout were starting their first prayers of the day. I climbed down again, and went towards the centre of town to fetch my father.

As I reached the village square, I was surprised to see a small crowd gathered there. Some women held water jugs. They stood in the open where the new growth on the trees formed a fresh, leafy bower. But they were silent, and, inexplicably, this filled me with dread. There was no reason I could think of for anyone, men or women or children, to stand so quietly in the square, ever – and certainly not so early in the morning.

I approached, and for some reason, the crowd parted, letting me through. This in itself was puzzling. And then I saw her. Sulima, her dress torn at the front so that part of her breasts were shamefully exposed, her hair a coarse mess of tangles, her cheeks covered with long, freshly scabbed rakes, faced them. On her throat were dark bruises. A few feet away from her lay her decorated bag. Gold and silver bracelets, rings, anklets and earrings – not just hers, but also things I recognised as belonging to my mother – spilled out on to the dusty street. My father stood beside Sulima, clutching her arm.

And then I knew Sulima had tried to leave, but my father had been waiting for her outside our home. He must have dragged her to the square to declare her adultery, to have the mullah announce her punishment. Surely she would be stoned.

But Sulima threw off his hand. It was clear she no longer feared him as she had the night before; there was no terror or shame in her face at all. Tension thickened the air. Sulima looked into the circle of faces surrounding her. And then her eyes fell on me. Such hatred filled her face that I involuntarily gasped and put my hands over my mouth. She stepped forward, and, as one, the crowd behind me stepped back.

She muttered under her breath, staring at me. Now words rushed from her mouth, an incomprehensible combination of Tajik oaths and indistinguishable Kafir words and grunts. Spittle trickled from the corners of her mouth as her eyes glazed over. I saw that Sulima was putting herself into a trance again, although a different one to that I had witnessed the night before, different, even to when she had turned into a *jinn* before my eyes. My father pulled at her arm again, but she whirled on him, attempting to claw his face with her fingernails, and he involuntarily ducked, moving away from her.

Immediately the villagers spread out, whispering prayers for protection. 'She is a *jinn* in disguise,' a man murmured, and the rest of the crowd murmured in assent. 'First she tricked Kosha, and now she is in our midst, spreading her evil,' the man continued.

'Do not look at her!' a woman behind me cried out. I turned to see her pull her veil completely over her face, and other women do the same. 'She is a pagan,' the woman continued, her voice shrill. 'She has no benevolent god to beg favours of or give thanks to. Instead, she calls upon wicked spirits to help her achieve her goals. Cover your eyes, good people!' the woman screamed now, backing further away, and I looked back at Sulima. It was a mistake. She stared into my face, and somehow I was held with her eyes. I couldn't move. Why didn't my father come to help me? Was he, too, frozen into stone as I was?

A child whimpered, and then absolute silence fell. Sulima slowly walked towards me, still babbling, her chin shining with drool. When her face was only six inches from mine, she stopped. Her eyes focussed, and I saw the pupils – tiny, hard, black points. A heinous smile appeared, and the incomprehensible words stopped. Now she spoke loudly and clearly, in perfectly understandable Dari.

'I curse you, Daryâ, evil woman who has brought this trouble on my head. I warned you, but you ignored my warning.'

I wanted to open my mouth to protest, to tell Sulima that I had not told her secret, that it had all been a mistake, an accident of timing, but my jaw didn't work.

'And because you caused this, you must be cursed. I won't curse you with simple pains of the head or sores of the skin. I will curse you with a lifetime of misery.'

A heavy sigh ran through the crowd. Sulima continued, her voice a loud screech. 'You will be barren. Only a hard, coiled knot – like the twisted body of a black snake – will form where a child should grow. Barrenness. You'll be a dried-up empty hag, shunned by all men, despised by everyone. You shall become withered and old, with no sons to honour you or daughters-in-law to care for you. You will be worthless, less than the dust beneath the feet of the camel. You will die alone.' Her voice rose to a wail, and she threw back her head, her arms reaching to the blue of the morning sky.

She then turned and walked away, stooping to pick up her bag, shoving her own and my mother's jewellery back into it. She did all these things slowly and precisely, without glancing around her or showing any apprehension. She walked away from the square, and I watched her as if a flame danced before my eyes, its heat making her image a wavering, distorted shape. The heat became greater, burning my eyes from my head, and it was white in its intensity, surrounding me with silence.

I remember nothing more of that day.

CHAPTER TWELVE

In our quiet village, a year had passed since Sulima left, but this year was my undoing, for I was ruined.

Although our family never again mentioned Sulima, I knew with certainty that she would have returned home. Her father would beat her severely, but, after all, he had our mare, and Sulima had taken her dowry back with her. I could imagine her now, laughing at us all in the arms of the man with no eyeteeth, or perhaps in the arms of other men. Her life would return to what it had been, while mine was destroyed for ever. Word of the curse had raced from village to village with the speed of a flock of small, swift birds.

At first there had been a strange release for me: I no longer had to live in fear, for the fear had been realised, and that brought its own twisted freedom. I was made ill by the curse for the week after Sulima's departure, sleeping deep, feverish dreams. But when I finally arose from my pallet, clear-headed, I understood the enormity of what had happened to me.

Although my father hurried to Kamê Bara, to try and reason with my mother's family, my betrothal was broken, my mother's cousin's son freed from the pact. According to my father, all of the Tajiks in the villages from ours to Kabul had heard of the death of my future. That death floated above my head continually, like ash in the wind. There was no hope for me to be married; I was, as Sulima had decreed, now worth less than the dust beneath the feet of the camel.

The men of Susmâr Khord – the older men who had known me since my birth, as well as those near my own age – all feared me now. Such was their belief in a curse by an infidel that even to be near me might be detrimental. When I passed them, my scarf covering my nose and mouth, my eyes lowered, they also averted their eyes, touching their amulets. From under my lowered lids I detected the movement of their hands to chests, and knew they placed their fingers on the small pouches there, often blackened by years of wear. The pouches contained a few words from the Koran, blessed by the mullah. I knew the men beseeched protection from me should I suddenly look in their direction. I asked my father if prayers from the mullah could lift the curse. But his dark look, as he turned from me with a quick shake of his head, gave me the answer. I knew then that the blessed amulets might offer protection but all the prayers and blue beads in the village could not reverse Sulima's curse.

Even the other women were nervous in my presence. Sulima's curse had not only placed barrenness upon me, but also made me an outcast in my own village, and at first my mother and I were no longer visited, and no friendly invitations came to us.

I told my mother then that she was to make it clear that I chose not to see anyone. In this way, although the women would no longer come to our house, she could still be invited to theirs. The only person who still spoke to me, smiled at me, and was unafraid to be seen with me was Yalda. She called me to her house to drink tea and to help her prepare her remedies. One day as I ground roots, putting all my anger into the satisfying crush of the stone against stone, she put her hand on my arm, and I stopped.

'Sometimes, Daryâ, a curse may be a blessing,' she said.

I snorted. 'A blessing? A curse brings only misery, Yalda. I can assure you there is no blessing in my life.'

'We cannot know the shape of the curse. Perhaps it will not work in the direction it was intended. I have seen this. It depends not only on the giver, but on the receiver. Your own power also plays a part in determining the strength of the curse.'

I ground again, creating a rasping rhythm, angered further by her use of the word power. My grandmother had spoken of this, and yet it was clear I held none. 'There will be no blessings for me in Susmâr Khord,' I said, annoyed with her.

'Perhaps not. But perhaps when you are elsewhere –'

'Elsewhere? Where would I go?' I said too loudly, looking into her good eye, wondering what she, and my grandmother before her, thought they knew. They were both wrong; my destiny was now to forever be a scorned woman in my own small village.

And then I apologised for my rudeness, for I was grateful to Yalda.

My time with her helped pass the slow daylight hours when other women my age drank tea and gossiped, or laughed together at the well, or cooked for their husbands, or tended their babies. And the wisdom she imparted gave me things to think about as I lay on my quilts at night, listening to the soft, even breathing of Nasreen and Yusuf.

The nights were the most difficult. Knowing I would never share my quilt with a man, would never stand upon the birthing stones, or feel the small arms of a son or daughter around my neck, and would have no one to care for me in my old age, could bring on a grief so deep I could not contain it. At these times, no matter how cold the night, I climbed to the roof. The sky was my only consolation.

I may as well have had the face of a goat and the hump of a camel. I thought of my own vanity; before Sulima's curse I had sometimes studied myself in the small, clouded mirror my father had brought back from Kabul many years earlier. I had been pleased with my image. I remember admiring the sweep of my hair, which, when unbraided, hung to my waist in a shining black curtain. I found my face, wider at the forehead and narrowing to a firm chin, to be a pleasing shape. And I had especially liked my own wide green eyes, surrounded by thick lashes. Yes, how vain I had been, how young and foolish.

Now I could no longer see anything pleasing in my face or body. I had grown too tall, taller than most of the other women. Indeed, perhaps I was camel-like after all, with long, ungainly legs and arms. My face, as well, had become too thin to be pleasant. In such a narrow face my eyes looked overly large and startled. No, I decided one day, my face was not that of a village goat; more of an ibex, sister of the goat, the horned creature who bounded through the forests. A man in our village had brought an injured one home a few years earlier as a pet for his children. It had died, but for its few weeks in captivity I remember the look in its eyes as I stroked the bony, trembling head, and I had sorrowed for the wild creature.

I was past sixteen. Now I kept my hair tightly braided at all times, finding its length and weight a burden, and avoided the mirror. I learned to walk with my eyes fixed on the ground, using shadows and my own intrinsic knowledge of the familiar routes through my village. I was destined to live under my father's roof for the rest of his days. And my hope was that his death would come after Yusuf had become a man and taken a wife. Perhaps Yusuf would allow me, out of pity, to live with him and his family.

Nasreen and Yusuf were both growing up, and I worried for my little sister. She was only four, but if she wept in hunger or frustration my father shouted at her. She kept her head down when he was present. And yet when Yusuf howled for the same reasons, my father laughed, praising him for his loud voice and demands to be attended to. I saw that Nasreen was like my mother, and unlike me. In one way I was glad, for it meant she would have less physical pain in her life. In another way I sorrowed, for it only meant that she would have a different sort of pain. The pain I knew only too well, the one which grew in a deep, dark place under the bones that shielded my heart.

As I have said, I was always an embarrassment to my father. But now, with the curse, his embarrassment was one hundredfold more. And so he found me a husband. I had not realised the lengths he would go to in order to be rid of me.

The ochre hills turned pale green with spring growth as I sat on the roof. My mother stood in the courtyard, scouring pots with sand. My father came from the mosque and spoke to her; neither were aware of my presence as I watched them from above.

My father's voice was quiet, and Mâdar's hands grew still. Then she set down the pot and shook her head. My father spoke again, and this time my mother's voice rose, and I could hear her words.

'But we'll never get to see her again.'

'I have no choice, woman!' My father's voice was louder than my mother's. 'Her fate is sealed if she remains with us.'

I silently moved further back on the roof.

'Perhaps we could find someone very old, someone who would take her on as a youngest wife, the fourth. He could take her knowing she could give him no children – and surely he would already have many – but he and the other wives could use a young and strong woman with many years of hard work in her.'

'But we couldn't expect a bride price, then,' my father argued. 'This is the only solution. They know nothing of her or the curse, and will only deduce that she is barren after a few years, long after it's too late to return her. No one will be blamed.'

'Except her,' my mother said. 'Perhaps if we wait another year or two, Kosha, people will forget –'

I heard the clang of pots being pushed, or kicked. 'Don't talk foolishness! You know that in a few years the situation will be even worse. By then any man who didn't know of the curse would wonder why she has not married earlier, and suspect a problem.'

Now my mother wept.

'If only my brother had sons before he was killed,' my father went on, his voice tight with anger. 'One of them would have to take her off our hands, and we would even get something in trade. No. I can't wait. I need a bride price after last summer's crop failure.'

'And your losses with the birds?' my mother said, and there was the smack of flesh on flesh, and I knew my father had struck her face. He had taken a chance on a game of *Qwak* the past winter in Kabul, Mâdar had told me, certain he would win back enough money to cover the losses he had incurred with Sulima: first her bride price, then her taking my mother's jewellery. The partridge he wagered on was predicted to win over all the other birds, but it had been injured just before the end of the game, and instead of earning a wealth of extra afghanis, my father lost all he had made for his winter's work.

'So it will be done,' my father said now. 'I will ride to their camp tomorrow. They are moving on to their summer pastures in a few days. The timing is perfect.'

My body went cold. *Their camp*?

Mâdar surprised me by speaking further, even after being hit by my father. 'Please, Kosha. Reconsider. They are such a warring tribe, the Ghilzai, always feuding with the Durrani.'

The Ghilzai? They were Pushtuns. Worse, they were nomads. Surely my father could not –

'*Bas!* Stop your snivelling. You know there is no other way. Some young man from the Ghilzai camp will be happy to take on a robust young wife, no questions asked. They don't allow their women to marry outside the Pushtuns, but the men love to bring Tajik and Baluch women in with their own. Our women are well-respected and can work like mules. And even better, the nomads don't care about dowries. Should they agree to take her, she need bring nothing to her new husband, and hopefully he will be willing to trade at least two horses for her. They have superb Kabulis.'

'You think of the figure you would cut on a powerful steed? You would trade our daughter for the prize of owning enviable horses?'

'Stop. You talk in circles. I will go to them tomorrow. Tell our daughter what to expect.' There was a moment of silence, and then my father's voice came, more quietly. 'At least she will still live in the valleys and mountains where she has grown up. She is strong, and brave.' He stopped, and when he continued his voice was even softer, and I leaned forward to hear. 'It is because of my actions that her life has been ruined. I have prayed to Allah for forgiveness,' he said, and I closed my eyes.

My father's voice was gentle, as it was when he spoke to Yusuf, showing him how to eat pilau with his fingers, or teaching him how to climb the ladder to the roof. If only he could have shown this gentleness to me even once. I would have tried so much harder to please him, had I but known that he saw me in a way I did not believe anyone saw me. And still he continued.

'She demands respect, even though everyone is afraid of her. I think, truly, that perhaps Daryâ will find a life with the nomads – once she is used to their ways – that will not bring her any greater sadness than marrying an elder of the Tajiks and being a lowly fourth wife. You know she is unlike the other girls. And because of this, she will survive, Anahita. In your own heart you know Daryâ will survive.'

The pleasure of hearing my father speak so glowingly of me was lost in the reason for his words. *Daryâ will survive*. His words echoed in my head long after he left the courtyard, and my mother slowly gathered her pots and went into the house. Survive? Is this all I could expect of my life?

Much later, when I knew I could trust myself not to cry, I went inside. Mâdar sat on the cushions, limply holding an empty cup. She looked up at me, quickly, and then away. I sat across from her.

'Mâdar. I was on the roof when Pâdar spoke to you of the nomads. I heard him.'

My mother shook her head, placing her hand over her mouth for a moment, then removing it. 'You know I tried, Daryâ. I do not want to lose you for ever. But your father must do what he feels is best, and we must obey.' She reached across the space between us and took my hand in hers. 'The greatest sorrow for a woman is to think of her daughter growing old alone. Every woman must have a husband, Daryâ.' She closed her eyes for a moment. 'I have dreamed since you were born of your marriage to my cousin's son. She and I lived together as children, and I loved her as a sister. It pained me to speak of her, as I thought I would never see her again when I left Kamê Bara. It is better not to speak – even to think – of painful things. The best way is to let them retreat, to try and forget. This my own mother taught me before she died. But knowing our families would be tied, through our children, brought me great pleasure, and I thought that Allah had smiled on me, and that my cousin and I might once again be united, and . . .' her voice trailed off.

'You never said this.' Why was everything kept secret from me? I did not believe what my mother said: that pain retreated when left alone and not spoken of. I knew my own pain only grew larger and uglier in my head, day by day.

'What good would it do? If I had talked overly of it, if I spoke too longingly of my desire, perhaps I would have unwittingly called a curse down myself. And look what has happened. Do you see?' She pressed my hand more tightly between her own, and I saw her eyes, so like mine, turn a darker green, as mine did just before tears came to them.

'I am sorry,' she said. 'But I must be cruel for you to understand. You are undesirable now, Daryâ, worthless in every way. No Tajik will ever want you. If you have any chance for a life where you must not hide away, it may be with the nomads.'

I nodded. Her words did not hurt me. She told me nothing I didn't already know.

I didn't sleep that night, trying to imagine life with the Ghilzai. I didn't speak Pashto, and wouldn't understand what was said to me. I knew the people of Susmâr Khord were wary of the Pushtuns, even though they didn't come to our village, for it was too small for them to venture in to trade. But my father had known many Ghilzai from his time in Kabul; he had told us stories of their fierceness. There were numerous tribes, each with its own chief, and intertribal disputes over small matters sprang up quickly. Many ended in bloodshed and even death. They lived with violence, he had once said, and now I thought of myself in the midst of violence.

I would live in a tent in the winter, a yurt in the summer. My life would be one of movement, of impermanence. I would never have my own home, nor any possessions save what was necessary to survive. Survive. That word again.

And then I wept, my quilt tightly over my face so that my parents would not hear me and think me weak. I brought forth the image of my grandmother, and hoped that this was part of the plan she saw for me among the stars. Eventually I silently crept up on the roof to stare at them, willing my journey to be a safe one.

The next afternoon my father rode towards the hills. For the last few weeks I had seen tendrils of smoke spiralling upwards from the distance, and in the still evening air I occasionally heard far-off, muffled bleating. I did not question this; it was common in the spring.

Through the day I fretted endlessly, unable to complete a task, dropping things, forgetting why I crossed the courtyard, letting a pot boil dry.

It was dark when my father finally returned, Mâdar and the little ones already asleep. After I served him supper he went behind the curtain, and I, too, went to my pallet. I heard my mother's questioning murmur, and my father's lower reply. I strained to hear what was said between them, but their voices remained whispers.

I did sleep, even though I thought I wouldn't, and Mâdar woke me before it was light.

'Come, daughter. You must prepare yourself.'

I sat up, holding the quilt to my chest. 'What will happen?'

With a tilt of her chin, Mâdar beckoned for me to come away from Nasreen and Yusuf. Still in my nightdress, the quilt wrapped around me, I followed her to the far side of the room.

'Sit,' she said. 'Would you like some morning tea?'

I nodded, my mouth suddenly dry. My mother had never served me, except for the few times I was ill. But instead of preparing tea, she sat across from me. She played with the fringe of the carpet, watching her own fingers as she spoke.

'When Kosha went to the Ghilzai yesterday,' she said, 'he found the chief to be a sensible man. He has a son, this chief, whose wife recently . . . left, to return to her family, Zadran Pushtuns in the south. Apparently the arrangement was not satisfactory, and now the son looks for another wife before they go to their summer camp.'

I swallowed with difficulty. 'Did Pâdar see the son?'

Now she met my stare. 'No, but he said the chief is quiet-spoken and a distinguished figure; Kosha was impressed by him. It is often the case that the son resembles the father in character, is it not?' Her voice was falsely cheerful on this sentence.

'So.' I took a deep breath. 'Pâdar drew up a contract?'

'Yes. The Ghilzai chief will give him three fine Kabulis. As long as the conditions are met . . .'

'Conditions?'

By her hesitation, and the way she let her gaze fall back to the carpet, I knew this was not something she wanted to tell me. Her eyelids were puffy. When she finally looked back at me, her eyes were streaked with red, and I knew that like me, she had wept much of the night. 'The main condition,' she said, 'being that you are pure.'

I sat up straighter. 'But Pâdar must have told him of my virtue,' I said, hearing indignation in my voice. 'All the girls of Susmâr Khord are virtuous at the time of their marriage.'

'Yes. But daughter,' here her eyes bored into mine, 'we are used to marriage between families, or lifelong friends. Our word is sufficient. But to the Pushtuns, Kosha is a stranger. The chief was willing to take his oath of your innocence, but the son was not so accepting. You must understand his thinking. The tribe will not lose three of its best horses on a marriage arrangement in which every detail is not perfect. The Pushtuns are men of great pride and honour. Especially when – well, the confirmation of an unknown woman's purity is necessary.'

'But if they do not accept Pâdar's word, how –'

'It may be difficult for you, Daryâ.' Now Mâdar became brisk. She stood and moved to start a small fire, busying herself with preparing the tea, her back to me. I knew it was an act, an attempt to appear as if this conversation were normal, that there was nothing to fear. 'Two respected women from the Ghilzai will come later today, and they will see for themselves that you are pure. They will know what they look for. They will lay their hands upon you.' She still hadn't turned around.

'They will . . . touch me? No! I will not allow it,' I said, horrified, standing. 'No. Mâdar, you cannot let them –'

Unexpectedly my mother turned and took me in her arms. 'I'm sorry,' she whispered. 'You know I would never wish this upon you.' She held me tightly, in a gesture of comfort she hadn't used since I was very small. 'They will not hurt you, if you do as they say.'

CHAPTER THIRTEEN

BEFORE THE GHILZAI arrived, my father called me to join him on the roof. He had never done this before, and I knew it was not to be a pleasurable talk.

We sat side by side, stiffly, in the gathering strength of the afternoon sunshine. I looked out over the flat roofs of the nearby houses with their walled gardens. In the shade of poplar and lime trees in the courtyard next door, I could see the first shoots of green rising from the small patch of tilled ground, and there was a drone of hornets hovering over the rotting blossoms of a peach tree. I looked the other way, at the terraced fields against a backdrop of indigo mountains. I waited for my father to speak.

'Your mother has told you what will occur soon,' he said. It was obvious that his discomfort matched my own.

I nodded, focussing on the mountains.

'You understand the seriousness of the situation, Daryâ. This will be your only chance for a woman's life. It is abnormal for a woman not to marry. You know this.'

I nodded again.

'Therefore it is vital that you make a good impression today, and, more importantly, that no word of the curse be breathed while the Pushtuns are around Susmâr Khord. This morning I spoke to the mullah, and explained the hope of the marriage arrangements. He is calling a village meeting as we sit here, and will instruct every man to avoid speaking of your . . . unfortunate circumstances.'

He stopped, but there was nothing for me to reply. I felt him turn to look at my profile.

'If all goes as it should, you will marry a chief's son. Most village girls would be pleased and grateful to marry into such a prestigious role.'

At this I could hold my tongue no longer. 'But you know nothing of the man you are proposing to be my husband.' My voice was low, but the anger was audible. 'Nor of his family. You only met his father. The son may be crippled, or an idiot, for all you know. Did you even ask to meet him, to see if he is suitable?'

My father stood. 'You ungrateful girl. Considering your problem, do you not realise the wonderful arrangement I have found for you?'

I looked up at him. The sun behind his head made a ring of light, and turned his features black. I forced myself to be calm. 'Oh, yes, Pâdar. I realise.'

My toneless quality angered my father further, as I knew it would. 'Do you believe yourself to be a princess? You are only a skinny, worthless Tajik girl. Do you believe you could do better than to be daughter-in-law to a Pushtun chief?'

I continued to stare at him, not lowering my eyes, my voice, even. He wanted me to give him cause to strike me, to take out his own regret on me. But I would not do this. 'No, Pâdar. I could not do better. I understand what a burden I am. Surely today I am the luckiest woman in this village.' There was sarcasm in my voice, but not enough to make my father raise his hand.

After a moment he sat again, and I could see his face once more. 'I think we know each other well, my girl. Perhaps, inside, you truly are the son I hungered for. From which ancestor did you inherit this unfeminine superiority, this urge to make sense of the world, instead of simply accepting it for what it is?'

'From your own mother,' I said, without a moment's hesitation. 'Am I not like her?'

He sighed, then nodded. 'This I have always known. And she died before her time because both you and she refused to act in the proper ways.'

We sat in silence. I thought of Mâdar Kalân, as I know he did.

'The Pushtuns will not tolerate a woman who is too clever, Daryâ.' He stood, crossing his arms over his chest. 'And now this conversation has taken a direction that is not proper between father and daughter.' He turned to leave, but stopped at the edge of the roof and looked back at me. 'This marriage must work, Daryâ,' he said. 'You understand that, don't you? You can return to visit, but you will never be welcome to live in Susmâr Khord again. This is your one chance. Remember this, and make the best of your new life.'

And then he left me alone on the roof, and I thought of all the things he had said. I wondered how to hide the cleverness he spoke of, when I lacked the ability to predict what I said would be viewed as clever. And that I could never again live under his roof.

An hour later voices were heard outside the house. I sat very still, dressed in my latest Ramazân dress, my hair down and brushed until it shone. I wore my headdress, and kept the veil across my nose and mouth.

Mâdar took Nasreen's and Yusuf's hands. 'I will be outside with the children,' she said. She went to the doorway, then turned back to me. 'It is an older man who has brought the women. He speaks Dari with Kosha.' She started to leave, then looked back at me as if she wanted to say something. But instead she only gave the shadow of an apologetic smile.

After what felt like a long while, two women entered our home. They were unveiled. I jumped up and stood with my eyes lowered. At a strange word from one of them, I looked up. The older woman motioned, with an impatient wave, for me to remove my veil. Then they studied me, and while they did so, I took in their appearance as well.

Each wore a long loose dress which reached to within six inches of their ankles. The women were obviously wealthy, and wearing their finest clothing for this betrothal meeting. The dress of one was green velvet, the dress of the other, burgundy, and both were heavily embroidered with gold. Dozens of coins were sewn to the material, creating a soft jingling when they moved. Under their dresses the women wore flowing blue pantaloons; on their feet were soft, open-heeled leather shoes. Simple black headscarves covered their hair.

Both had dark complexions, and their eyes were heavily ringed with black kohl. But what was most astonishing were the tattoos on their faces. A series of small, dark circles – some no more than dots – covered their foreheads and extended down the sides of their cheeks. One of the women had the dots all over her lips. With a touch of panic, I wondered if I would have to be tattooed.

Having looked me over, just as I had them, the shorter, younger one spoke to me in a questioning tone, and I shook my head. The other woman, taller and heavier, then spoke in Dari. Her words were slow, chiding.

'If you are to marry into the Ghilzai, you must learn Pashto. Only a small number of our tribe speak Dari, and only when necessary. It will not be tolerated for you to expect to speak your own language among us.'

I nodded.

'I am Hanouf,' the older woman went on, 'and this is Bibi.' The younger woman smiled at me, and I felt a tiny relief at Bibi's friendly, curious look. She was not much older than me.

Now Bibi glanced at Hanouf, who was surveying the room. The men's voices could be heard clearly through the open doorway. At a burst of laughter, Hanouf said, 'We will go behind the curtain.'

My heart gave one painful thump, and then kept up a steady race. My face grew hot. I awkward twisted the ends of my veil in my hands.

'Come,' Hanouf demanded, striding across the room and pulling aside the curtain. 'Go down,' she said, with a toss of her head.

Trying to control my breathing, I lay on the pallet. Bibi stood to one side, but Hanouf knelt at my feet, and, with one quick and unexpected movement, shoved up my skirt and pulled down my trousers, bending my knees. As she forced my legs apart I covered my eyes with my arm and turned my face to the wall. No one had ever seen my body except for my mother, and even she had not seen it for at least five years.

I gasped, and instinctively my knees tried to close as Hanouf's long fingers came towards my most secret of places, but the woman firmly pushed my legs apart again. Her hands were strong and hard, her movements so sure that I knew I dare not fight against her.

'Be still,' she said, and then worked two of her fingers into the place I thought would never be touched by anyone but my husband.

Tiny, involuntary breaths that sounded like hisses came out of my clenched lips as she dug and probed somewhere within me. My mother had said it wouldn't hurt, but it did; it felt as though she were tearing my flesh, and I held my teeth together tightly. My legs trembled. She withdrew her fingers with the same brusqueness, and a long, shaky cry escaped my lips.

Hanouf pulled my skirt down with another quick jerk, and then she and Bibi left the room. I pulled up my trousers and turned on my side, hugging my knees. When I heard my mother's voice, I crept from the pallet and peeked behind the edge of the curtain. Mâdar had told me I must not be in the room while the negotiations were being made.

She offered the women a smooth wooden tray holding a foot-high conical sugar loaf she had made for the occasion. Hanouf reached out her hands for the tray, and Bibi pulled an embroidered kerchief from the front of her dress and handed it to Mâdar.

As my mother accepted it, I knew the marriage was imminent. With the traditional exchange of the two items which would be used in the wedding ceremony, the betrothal was sealed.

After the women and their escort had ridden off, I sat on the pallet once more. Mâdar came in and sat beside me. She picked up my hand and squeezed it, and I put my head on her shoulder. We sat in silence.

The next day the women returned, and once more sat with my mother. This time I was allowed to be present. Once again, the man who had brought them stayed outside with my father, and I didn't see him.

Hanouf returned the wooden tray which had held the sugar loaf. On it was a Pushtun outfit I knew I would wear on the day I rode to the camp, and a silver necklace with a fish pendant. I did not look at my mother; I knew the fish to be a sign of fertility, and felt the weight of our sham at that moment.

'Take the necklace, Daryâ,' Mâdar instructed, as if reading my thoughts. 'It is a ritual gift for a bride.'

I picked it up and held the smooth, slender fish tightly in my hand.

'We leave for Badakhshan in five days' time,' Hanouf said. 'All arrangements must be complete by then.'

'Of course,' my mother said. 'My husband has spoken to the mullah. He will perform the ceremony in three days. This will give us time to prepare the village wedding feast. My daughter will come to your camp on the fourth day.'

The other woman nodded. 'It is agreeable.'

'The wedding will be scheduled for late afternoon, in the mosque,' Mâdar continued. 'The feast will take place afterwards. Members of your tribe who so wish are, of course, invited.'

'Just the men of the groom's family will attend the wedding,' Hanouf told her. 'They will return to the camp afterwards, and the next day, when the bride comes to us, we will have our own celebration.'

The women stood to leave. As they walked towards the door, the coins on their dresses clinking, Mâdar called after them. 'May we know the name of my daughter's intended?'

Hanouf turned back and looked at me, her face expressionless. After a second's hesitation, she answered. 'He is called Shaliq, and is the second son of our chief. Bibi and I are the second and third wives of the eldest son, Hafeez.' Her eyes were locked on mine.

'We will now be sisters,' she said, and then she and Bibi disappeared.

The morning of the wedding my head was heavy, my throat scratchy and sore. I hadn't been able to sleep properly for so many nights, and now I couldn't believe that what my parents had talked about only a week ago was a reality. I had already packed a small bag with my belongings – my three dresses and one pair of wooden clogs. My jewellery consisted of the lapis lazuli necklace my father had given me that horrible time and the fish pendant sent by my husband-to-be.

The night before Yalda had come to our house, and she and my mother had decorated my hands and feet with henna. The designs were intricate and lacy, and I admired them in the early morning light before I rose from my pallet. As I folded my quilts, knowing that tonight would be my last night to sleep alone, Mâdar came to me.

'I have a small gift for this great day,' she said, her voice a little too loud, as if convincing herself that the day was, indeed, great. She held out a finely scrolled gold *halhal*. 'It was given to me on my own wedding day by my uncle. He told me that some day I would pass it on to my oldest daughter.'

I took the delicate ankle bracelet and turned it over in my hands.

'Thankfully the Kafir did not manage to find all of my jewellery,' Mâdar said, reaching out to run her finger along the scrolling on the hoop. I flinched at the memory of Sulima, and Mâdar put her hand on my shoulder. 'I am sorry. Now you must try and drive the thought of Sulima's curse from your mind, daughter. Even if her words did not carry the power she hoped for, if you dwell on them for ever, it is possible that the *jinn* will see into your mind and ensure that the words are a reality. Now, I have put the wedding dress out on my pallet. Come and see.'

I followed her, and she held up the thickly pleated ankle-length white dress of fine muslin, which she had spent hours yesterday pressing with flat hot rocks, wrapped in cotton. The yoke was intricately embroidered with hundreds of tiny red and blue flowers with twining green leaves.

'You will be so beautiful in this, Daryâ. I wore it at my own wedding, as did my mother before me. I am only sorry that you must leave it behind for Nasreen. You know that only the youngest daughter can carry it with her to her husband's home.'

'I am honoured to wear it.' I touched the delicate flowers. 'Mâdar?'

My mother looked up from the pile of veils she was folding for the wedding ceremony.

'The wedding night. I'm afraid I will not know what to –'

Mâdar's hands grew even busier with the veils. 'It is a shame you have no older sister to talk to you of this. But there is nothing for you to do. Your husband will know all there is to know. Do not question anything; accept whatever happens, and it will go easier. After the first few weeks of marriage your body will adjust to your husband's needs. This nightly release is not necessary for us, but most important for a man.'

I wished she would look at me. 'Why is it more important for them than for us?'

'Daryâ. You and your questions.' She finally stopped folding, and sat heavily on the pallet. 'Because good women are comforted by other things. Like the satisfaction of preparing a well-received meal, of having a clean home, and bearing children. Women who do not enjoy the pleasures of the home and look for gratification elsewhere are punished by Allah for their wanton desires.'

I thought of Sulima. She had taken what she wanted, and gone where she wished. She had left her burdens with us – her son with my mother to raise, her curse with me to shoulder. It did not appear to me she had been punished – but then again, it was not Allah she worshipped.

'But could it not be possible, Mâdar, for a woman to enjoy both things – the home as well as the . . . other, the way men can?'

'Such talk, Daryâ. Where do these ideas come from? Of course not. Men are created to enjoy; women to give enjoyment to them. This is important to remember; we must not expect rewards here on earth.' She stood again, her mouth a straight line. 'We have talked enough. You ask improper questions for a woman. Perhaps you have had too much time to dwell on your own desires. But you will have no time to think of these things from now on. You will have to work without complaining, and be careful of how you act and of what you speak. You will no longer be in your family home where inappropriate ways are forgiven. You will be among strangers, judged at all times. Even though you will be a Pushtun wife, you are still a Tajik. You must not forget that, and take pride in your family and your people, and behave in such a way to make us proud. The Ghilzai will be demanding, but I know you can be obedient if you only set your mind to it, and keep your mouth closed.'

It was similar to what my father had told me, on the roof. 'Keep my mouth closed?'

'Your voice must be silenced when you are married. This is the way it is. Life will be easier for you if you do only what is expected. Now, put on the marriage dress.'

As she had spoken, I had watched my mother's face grow more and more disturbed. I knew such a long speech about delicate matters had been difficult for her. And I knew she had no more answers, for the facts she had told me were all she knew in her own married life.

And yet I could not believe that my mother's grim words about the joining of a man with a woman under the quilts could be totally true. For the last year my own body had often seemed a stranger. Now I sometimes awoke in the night with puzzling dreams of the animals, of a heat I didn't understand, and, knowing I was being evil, put my hands under my nightdress and touched my own body. It had brought me a strange comfort, yet at the same time a huge sadness of knowing no man's hands would ever touch me and marvel at the softness of my skin.

Surely my mother, wanting me to be a chaste wife, was keeping some secret from me. The muffled laughter I had heard from Sulima when she shared the pallet with my father, and the look of delight on her face when the boy from Wamed had moved over her – surely it meant that an act which was meant purely for the release of the man and the creating of a child could not be entirely repugnant for a woman.

Although, of course, Sulima was a non-believer. Maybe only non-believers were allowed this pleasure, and good Muslim women were not.

The shadows outside lengthened as I slipped the *halhal* on to my ankle. Within a few hours I would be a married woman, and within another day I would know the truth.

CHAPTER FOURTEEN

I ENTERED THE MOSQUE with my father. I had rarely been inside except for special ceremonies such as weddings, instead worshipping at home as was proper for women.

I tried to keep my eyes lowered as I entered the cool, dark building, breathing in the scent of the sweet grass scattered on the mud floor, but it was impossible. At least my father didn't reprimand me for looking around. Light came from the tall narrow windows facing east. Perhaps it was the altering of my vision through the sheer white headdress, or the soft light from those windows, but a sense of calm I hadn't felt for so long washed over me in the stillness of the quiet, empty mosque.

A curtain had been suspended from the ceiling, splitting the long room in two so that the women would be separate from the men. While the men would hold their celebration here after the wedding, the women would spend the evening in the *chây-khâna*. I would not see the groom during the ceremony, nor directly afterwards. I would only come face to face with my new husband, with Shaliq – the name tasted strange on my tongue – the day after the wedding. Then the men of Susmâr Khord would accompany me partway to the Pushtun camp, my father had told me. The men of the Ghilzai would ride out to meet me and bring me to Shaliq.

My father sat on a thick carpet, richly woven with bird motifs, at the front of the room. I knelt, as he had earlier instructed me, behind him. I clenched my hands together under the voluminous white folds of the ancestral wedding gown, glad for the excess of material, for my hands were damp, and trembled.

Within moments there was a shuffling sound I recognised as the walk of the mullah. My father and I stood.

The elderly man, his full beard dyed a bright red to indicate that he had made *hajj* to Mecca, lifted my veil and smiled at me. His religious duty exempted him from the usual taboos of viewing a woman's face.

'The bride is indeed radiant, Kosha,' he said, and lowered my veil.

'Yes. It is a happy day for her.'

'Are you ready, child, for the vows?' the mullah asked me.

I nodded.

'Good. When the groom appears and the mosque holds all of its children, the ceremony will take place. Sit and praise Allah while you wait.'

He and my father went to the other side of the curtain. I heard the rustling of their clothing as they knelt and lowered their upper bodies until their foreheads touched the floor, then the murmurs of their prayers. I sat, facing ahead, until I heard stifled laughter, whispers and coughs as the room behind me filled.

Finally there was absolute silence, and then heavy footsteps on the men's side of the curtain, and I knew that the groom and his family had arrived. My hands would not be still, no matter how tightly I clutched them.

The mullah appeared on the women's side and beckoned. I came forward, and, at a tiny wave of his fingers, knelt down again, close to the curtain. From his position, I knew he could see both of us – myself and the groom.

'There is no God but Allah, and Mohammed is his prophet,' the mullah announced, and the ceremony began. In unison, the crowd repeated his words. He then opened the Koran and began reciting. I stopped listening after some time, and was aware of the ache in my knees. I was shocked that I would think of such a simple complaint at such an auspicious occasion.

Finally he closed the book and once again beckoned with both hands, palms raised. I stood, and the curtain swayed with my movement and a similar one on the other side.

The mullah directed his eyes to the men's side. 'Do you, Shaliq, son of Kaled, take this woman, Daryâ, for your wife?'

The voice was almost too low for me to hear the murmured assent.

'You will provide for her in all ways?'

Again, the low murmur.

The red beard now quivered in my direction. The mullah's expression was solemn and his eyes suddenly stern. 'Do you, Daryâ, daughter of Kosha, take this man, Shaliq, for your husband?'

As I had been told to do, I hesitated. The mullah asked me the second time, and still I waited according to custom. On the third time, when he asked if I would take Shaliq as my husband, I was allowed to answer with a clear 'Yes.'

Now my father, carrying the sugar loaf my mother had presented to the Pushtun women on their betrothal visit, came to our side of the curtain with three of his friends. He held the tall loaf high over my head while another man rapped it sharply with a tiny axe. The cake shattered into many pieces, raining down over my thinly veiled head.

'Good fortune will fall on her,' the three friends said, nodding at my father. My mother came and gave my father a handful of veils. My father and his friends carefully lowered six of them over my head, praying for happiness, prosperity and security. Before gently dropping the seventh and last veil, my father knotted it with a green turban cloth, then tied the connected length around my waist.

'I release you from my authority into the authority of your husband, in a pure state,' he said, enunciating the ritual words so that all present in the mosque could hear. 'For the sake of the family of Kosha, carry honour with you always.'

With the final phrase, dignified clapping echoed through the mosque, and my mother removed the heavy veils from my head, leaving on the original white translucent one. Then she walked with me down the length of the mosque so that all the women could see me in my newly married state. I kept my eyes on the floor, and never knew what expressions the women's faces wore at the deception the whole village had carried out that day.

Mâdar and I led the way to the *chây-khâna* where the prepared feast awaited; immediately women hurried back to the mosque with steaming pots and bowls for the men. I sat on a raised cushion, but kept my white veil completely over my face. In this way, although I could see the women and they me through the gauzy cover, I knew they felt safer. I was relieved when it was time to go home; my head had not ceased pounding, and I was unable to eat any of the food Mâdar brought to me. The *chây-khâna* had not held the usual joyful sounds of a wedding feast. The women ate, and then, with a few words to Mâdar, left.

No one lingered to laugh and tell their own wedding stories or tease the new bride.

* * *

That night I managed a few restless hours of sleep, but was awake before the first chirping and twittering of the birds in the courtyard. While my family still slept I bathed myself and dressed in the new Pushtun dress and pantaloons Hanouf and Bibi had brought.

The wedding ritual called for women of the village to come at daybreak and prepare me to meet my new husband. But when my mother and father rose, and had had their tea and nan and fed the children, only Yalda and our neighbour Hasti waited outside.

My father took Yusuf, who, at almost three, was no longer considered a baby, and went to the square. Nasreen, looking pallid and anxious, with eyes like full moons, watched as Yalda and Mâdar brushed perfumed oil into my hair, then braided it, weaving in a good luck cloth that was the seven colours of the rainbow. Hasti kept up a quiet beat on the *dayrah* she had brought with her. The gentle tapping of her fingers on the oiled goatskin stretched tightly over a rounded willow frame reminded me of Gawhar's wedding. I thought of the many village women crowding into Gawhar's home as they worked over her, and the loud laughter and songs about men which had made Gawhar blush furiously. There had been many *dayrahs* played that day.

I felt a curious detachment, neither joy nor sorrow. I was sad to be leaving my home, but underneath the sadness there beat, in rhythm with Hasti's fingers, a tiny excited pulse. I did not believe I would never again see my mother and father, Nasreen and Yusuf. The route of the Ghilzai must bring them through this valley regularly, and surely my husband would allow me to visit Susmâr Khord at those times.

The ceremonial procession to the nomads took place in late morning.

Hasti had bid me a happy life and quietly left; Yalda remained for a few minutes. She simply held both my hands in hers; I was aware of the toughened, uneven surface of her burned hand. She gripped tighter, looking into my eyes, then just nodded.

'It will be well,' she said, and with those simple words, a weight lifted from me. She carried some strange foresight, I knew instinctively, and saw that she believed in me, and in my future, and this meant more to me than any other assurances from my mother.

It was more difficult than I had ever imagined to leave Mâdar. After Yalda limped away, leaving us alone except for Nasreen, Mâdar held me tightly and we wept together, her voice a low wail and mine a quiet sobbing. 'Allah's will,' she wept. 'This is Allah's will.'

Is it? Or is it my father's will?

Watching us, Nasreen also cried, burying her head in my skirt. I dried my face and picked her up and told her I would come back and see her, and that she must be a good girl and help Mâdar, and that she should also hold her head up and look at the world around her. I told her she should look at the night sky and think of me. I tried to remember, in those last few moments with my little sister, something important that my grandmother had told me, tried to pass on something she might need, but nothing came to me. Nasreen nodded solemnly at me, although she was too young to truly understand, and I held her warm body close, breathing in the smell of her neck.

My father, holding Yusuf, waited for me outside, and I went with them. As we neared the end of the street where we must turn, I looked back at my home, and saw Mâdar in the doorway, holding Nasreen's hand. She raised her other hand to me, and I returned the wave, and then she was gone from my view. I pulled down the thick veil to cover my face now, as we approached the square and the friends of my father's who waited there. They were not to see my face, and I was glad.

In the square I mounted a horse and rode slowly out of town beside my father, who held Yusuf in front of him in the saddle. The men of the village rode behind us, singing. 'We bring the bride, we bring the bride,' they chanted.

Half a mile from the village there was movement on the top of a rise. The men of the Ghilzai were waiting.

We stopped, and I heard faint music. As the parade of nomads drew closer in a swirling cloud of dust, the music grew louder. It was more solemn than any music I had heard, and rang with an ancient quality. The Ghilzai men sang, their voices savage to my ears. They were accompanied by the beating of different-toned drums, and despite the coarseness of their voices, I found the strange melody compelling.

One man rode ahead of the others, his black horse high-stepping with measured precision, almost as if his inner animal ear kept time with the rhythm of the crowd behind him. The rider held the reins of three beautiful buff Kabulis, and even from a slight distance I could see the traits – the small heads, thick necks, tight bellies and delicate hooves – which made them so desirable to my father. As they neared I saw the watchful intelligence in their eyes. Not far behind another man led a beautifully decorated camel, its face raised in a haughty, disdainful manner, as if the noise and confusion surrounding it was distasteful.

Many young men danced and twirled in the sienna dust that rose around them. To me they appeared wild. They did not wear the tightly wrapped *longi* of the Tajiks, allowing their long black hair, which was past their shoulders, to sway and bounce as they danced to the hypnotic music. Some of the older men, walking at the end of the procession, did wear black *longi*, but with one end dangling over a shoulder, not tucked in neatly as the men of my village did.

Now I could make out the man riding in front, leading the Kabulis. My heart leapt. His carriage was straight, and his face was thin but strongly boned, his forehead high and noble. Was this my husband? In the next instant I realised it could not be. He was too old, his black hair streaked with grey, and obviously too powerful and self-possessed to be a man without many wives, one who had to choose a wife from a Tajik village. I also remembered that I had been told I would be brought to my husband, who awaited me in the camp.

The man reined in his horse in front of my father, and held up his hand. Immediately all noise and activity stopped, and there was no sound but the pawing and snorting of the horses.

'May Allah be with you. May you never be hungry,' he said.

'May you never be poor,' my father answered respectfully. I watched the way his eyes lingered on the three horses. 'I have brought your son's wife.'

This was my father-in-law, then. With such a handsome, virile face, surely Shaliq would also be dignified and attractive, I told myself. Perhaps my father had, after all, made the right decision.

The man looked at me, and I lowered my head, although I knew my face was only a shadow.

'Welcome to the Ghilzai,' the man said. 'We have prepared the bridal camel for you.'

My father jumped off his horse and held my veil firmly, in case it slipped as I climbed down from my own horse. None of the Ghilzai men must see my face before my husband.

One of the young, bare-headed man led the camel forward. Its rubbery lips and slack jaw were held together by gaily braided strips of orange, yellow and black cloth that went over the muzzle and then back behind its sloping head. Large orange and black tassels swung below each ear, and a huge green plume bobbed between the animal's small, crafty eyes. Over the tooled leather saddle a canopy had been fashioned: a light wooden structure, covered with large, colourful shawls which created a tiny tent on the camel's back. At a hard whack to its thick rump it groaned loudly, but lowered its front legs, hissing crankily the whole time, until it was kneeling.

My father helped me place my foot into the hanging stirrup, and I climbed into the saddle. I had to grasp the rough hair on the camel's heavy, serpentine neck as the beast rose jerkily at another word from its master. I had never before been on a camel; it felt as high as sitting on our roof at home, and I held on tightly.

My new father-in-law rode closer, reaching up to pull the shawl, which was folded back on the frame of the structure, down over my face. Before he did so, I saw him stare through the veil for an instant, and in his eyes I saw a look I did not understand. As the shawl dropped I was in darkness, and could see nothing. There was a quiet exchange of words between my father and father-in-law, but I could not make them out. And then, suddenly and unexpectedly, Yusuf's high, clear voice called out.

'Daryâ! Me go too!'

At the little voice, my lips and chin trembled. I had managed to retain my dignity since I had turned the corner on my home and mother and sister. Secluded now, I threw back my veil, breathing in great gulps, and put my hand tightly over my mouth. I heard my father reprimand Yusuf, and thought of how I had combed his tousled hair only yesterday. I assumed my father might come to the shawl and say goodbye, but with no warning, the camel swayed forward. I fell to one side with the awkward gait, and righted myself, pulling my veil over my face again. The pounding music and singing began again.

I was blind inside my tiny, shadowy prison, deaf with the loud music and shouting voices. Surrounded by strangers and yet alone, I left the only life I knew.

CHAPTER FIFTEEN

I ROLLED AND PITCHED on the camel's back. Finally it stopped, and the drums and voices grew fainter. When the noise was only the whisper of a rhythm, the shawl in front of me was thrown back. I squinted, for even my veil could not keep out the glare of the noon sun.

In the blaze of light someone ordered the camel to kneel once more, and as I shaded my veiled face with my hand, saw that it was my father-in-law. He beckoned me to climb down. A large black tent sat directly in front of me; my father-in-law pulled back a door flap, and, still without speaking, motioned for me to enter. I did so hesitantly, expecting that I might come face to face with my new husband. But in the sunlight flooding through the doorway I saw only sleeping quilts, cooking utensils, and Hanouf.

'Greetings, Kaled,' she said.

He nodded, setting my bag on the ground, then disappeared.

'Come. Sit,' Hanouf said to me.

I lowered myself to the quilt opposite her.

'Your husband enjoys a small men's party. By late afternoon there will be a number of Ghilzai from other camps who will come to wish the new couple well. Once Shaliq meets you he will take you out to introduce you to our people, but before he does, I will speak with you. It is the job of Shaliq's mother to do this, but it is not possible.'

I frowned. 'She is dead? I have no mother-in-law?' I had not expected this situation.

'No. She lives. But . . .' Hanouf was hesitant. 'Your father-in-law has chosen me to speak for her. Remove your veil.'

I did as I was told.

'These things you should know,' Hanouf said. Then she added, 'Take water if you wish.' She motioned to a sweating pot beside me, and I gratefully filled the small gourd that floated on the surface of the water, and drank. Then I waited, watching Hanouf. Her tattoos seemed to have grown darker since I saw her last, or perhaps I had forgotten how many there were.

'Allah has smiled upon Shaliq,' she said, nodding at me, and my face grew warm at the compliment. Nobody here knew me. They did not see the shadowy outline of a *jinn*'s curse when they looked upon me.

'Your mother-in-law is called Utmarkhail. She is Uzbek. Although she lives among us, she has chosen a life of solitude. She has not shared her husband's or son's tent for many years.' She smiled. Her teeth were red from betel. 'But you should consider yourself lucky. Do you know the saying that wicked daughters-in-law whisper? A mother-in-law is the scorpion hiding under the floor mat.'

I tried to smile back, but my face was stiff, uncooperative. I wanted her to know I was grateful to her for trying to put me at my ease.

'Shaliq is not an easy man,' Hanouf said, her own smile fading, and her words, as well as her face, made me uncomfortable. 'Last year he sent his wife back to her parents, forcing them to refund her bride price. He did this because she had been two years in the marriage without producing a child. He has grown very discontented in all ways this past year.'

I swallowed, my throat dry even though I had just drunk. 'Perhaps if Allah the Omnipotent grants a child to our union immediately, my husband will feel a lightening in his soul,' I said while asking, silently, for forgiveness. Where would I go if Shaliq rejected me as well? My father had made it clear I could never return home.

'We all pray for this,' Hanouf went on, and I brought my mind back to the present, 'although for reasons we cannot question Allah did not see fit to allow a child to be planted in either of Shaliq's wives.'

I blinked. 'Either wife?' I repeated.

A line appeared between Hanouf's thick eyebrows. 'There was another wife before the last. She was twelve when he married her, frail and childlike, completely unfit to carry the prestigious burden of first wife. Kaled did not approve of this marriage, but Shaliq insisted, seeing the girl in another camp and desiring her. But she fell ill before long, and died on the caravan route to our winter pasture in the second year of their marriage.'

She looked at my hands, and I realised I was twisting the veil in my lap.

'So. After two fruitless marriages, it is important that this one work. You must allow for Shaliq's . . . impatience. He is the second born of three sons, and the only from Kaled's second wife. There were daughters, as well, but they have all married into other camps. Shaliq's is a difficult role, carrying neither the honour of first-born – my husband, Hafeez – nor the cherished, pampered position of last. Although the youngest brother, Razak, was taken by fever five years ago, before even marrying, Shaliq is still bitter over what he sees as the unfair circumstance of his birth order. He will never be chief of this tribe. That falls to Hafeez.' She stopped as shouts and laughter rang out, then she rose.

'Your husband approaches, so I will leave you.'

I made a grab for my veil, but Hanouf shook her head. 'There is no need to cover yourself from your husband. And even in camp, when there are no strangers present, you may remain uncovered. The men of our tribe may look upon our faces, and we are treated with respect by them. In a small camp it is as if we are all related.'

But this time I wanted to cover my face. I didn't think I would be able to look at my new husband for the first time without a veil between us.

Hanouf left, and the clamour outside the tent suddenly dispersed. I heard Kaled's voice and the voice of another man, this one lower and rougher. They spoke in Pashto, and I couldn't understand their words. The conversation ended as the flap was pushed aside. I jumped up, ignoring Hanouf's words and throwing my veil over my head so that it covered my face.

The man who entered turned and secured the flap, then faced me.

Immediately I was flooded with disappointment. This man had none of the towering dignity of his father. From his Uzbek mother he had inherited the squat body and bowed legs common to that tribe. His long black hair was coarse, hanging limply around his flat face. His nose was broad, his lips full and indulgent. I concentrated on his eyes, for they were fine and the only feature that I saw of his father – they were almost black, and had a pleasing almond shape and thick, dark lashes. I knew I had no right to feel this quick flash of disappointment. A person's looks, I knew well, did not convey what was in their heads and their hearts.

He stared through the veil; I saw that our eyes were at the same level due to my ungainly height.

'You have cost our tribe dearly,' he finally said, his Dari heavily accented with the more guttural Pashto nuances. 'My father spent a great deal of time and money acquiring those Kabulis last year.'

I could think of no reply.

'Remove your covering so that I can see if you are worth it,' he demanded now.

I did so, and a slow smile spread over Shaliq's face. Somehow the smile did not make me feel as I thought it would when I dreamed of this moment as a girl. 'You will do,' he said. He sat on the quilt and patted the spot beside him.

I did so, facing straight ahead. I felt my husband studying my profile, and raised my chin. Without warning he reached out and lightly ran his hand over my breast as if needing to assure himself of something. I gasped involuntarily, but closed my mouth and remained motionless. In the next instant he stood, pulling me up by the arm. He smiled, a natural smile, and I let out my breath slowly, for this natural smile made him more attractive.

'Come. Many Ghilzai are travelling to our camp for the celebration.' With the reckless enthusiasm of one much younger than his years, he almost dragged me outside, and I put the back of my hand in front of my eyes, shielding them from the sun after the dimness of the tent. I started to pull my headscarf so as to cover myself, but Shaliq stopped me.

'I will allow everyone to see my new wife.'

At least he is not disappointed in me, as I am in him, I thought, then shook my head to drive away the thought. *I must no longer think like a young girl. I am a wife, and before tomorrow's sun rises, I will truly be a married woman. Tonight in my prayers I must ask Allah for his forgiveness for my uncharitable nature.*

I had no time to think further on this as Shaliq pulled me between the huge black goat-hair tents, shaped, I thought, like misshapen butterflies. Men and women worked side by side, laughing and talking, while barefoot children scampered freely. The girls played as well as the boys, screaming and laughing with each other. Their shrieks of excitement were accompanied by the almost continuous barking of dogs and mournful bleating of goats and sheep. Occasionally the querulous roar of a camel could be heard above the din. The babble of voices speaking and shouting in Pashto, so much choppier than my own soothing Dari, was discordant to my ears.

I had never imagined such a bold world as this existed. Even the infidel village of Wamed did not carry this freedom. An old man brushed by me, his arms piled with sheepskins, and I automatically lowered my eyes, staring at the ground. The old man stopped and spoke to Shaliq. In a moment I heard my own name, and looked up.

'Welcome, Daryâ, wife of Shaliq,' the old man said, his toothless gums working over the words, his hooded eyes still able to sparkle.

I could only nod, embarrassed by the attention.

As we passed another tent I heard whispers, and saw two girls, younger than me, but approaching marriageable age, staring from the open doorway. Their dresses were similar to my own, but much shorter. Both girls wore dozens of silver bangles on their wrists, and chains of silver coins about their necks. Neither had tattoos on their faces; I wondered if these came with marriage. They had bright red cloths covering their hair, which hung beside their cheeks in long braids. I was suddenly conscious of the new style my mother and Yalda had given me this morning: the cluster of many braids at the back of my head, which befitted my new marital status – at least among the Tajiks of Susmâr Khord.

I smiled at them, unsure of their reaction, but was immediately rewarded by their friendly grins, and then they whispered again, one coming to touch my headscarf, which was so thin and fine compared to their own thick head cloths.

Shaliq pulled me away, and a sea of strange faces swarmed in and out of my line of vision, most speaking Pashto, but a few welcoming me in my own language. My mind whirled, trying to remember names. My face ached from smiling. Finally we stopped, and Shaliq sat in a large clearing in the middle of the tents. Many fires burned and the smell and sizzle of cooking meat filled the air.

I stood beside him, filled with uncertainty, my face hot as so many eyes – both men's and women's – viewed my open face. I fought to keep my hands at my sides, and not bring them up to cover it. A woman with a plain, but serene and gentle face, came to me and put her hand on my shoulder.

'You may sit. We will enjoy food in your honour.'

I smiled gratefully at her, moving to sit behind my husband, but she motioned for me to sit beside him, and then she sat beside me. Kaled was opposite me, and beside him sat a tall, slim man with the same noble forehead. Seeing the small children around his legs, Bibi beside him, holding a baby on her hip, and Hanouf there as well, wiping the face of one of the children, I knew this to be the eldest son, Hafeez.

'I am Myassa,' the woman beside me said, 'first wife to Hafeez. I know you have already met my sister-wives. As the family of the groom we will eat first, and then the rest of the tribe will feast. Later there will be games.'

The back of my neck was tight and strained, and although I hadn't eaten anything since just after dawn, my stomach rolled at the rich, greasy smell of the food being ladled into large earthenware bowls. Before the bowls were set down, long white cloths were spread on the ground in front of the honoured family. The cloths were clean, although yellowed with age and many washings, patched and carrying the stains of numerous feasts.

My new husband dived into the food with enthusiasm. There were vast pyramids of yellow rice, which I knew to be flavoured with saffron. I recognised saddles of roast lamb, skewered sheep's liver, and golden mounds of chicken. The food was accompanied by small rounds of nan floating in oil and onion. I nibbled on some nan, all that I dared to put into my stomach, and watched as Kaled dipped three fingers into the hot rice, kneaded it, rolled it, and slipped the ball into the mouth of a little girl – no older than Yusuf – who nestled confidently against his chest, and I knew her to be his grandchild. Beside me, Shaliq chewed and slurped his hot black tea noisily. I tried not to watch, but out of the corner of my eye I could see his lips working furiously as he cracked a chicken bone and quickly sucked out the marrow.

Finally everyone seemed to have satisfied their hunger. With a loud belch, Shaliq rose, and the rest of the family did so as well. Myassa walked beside me as Shaliq hurried ahead to the gaming field behind the tents.

'Which are your children?' I asked, stepping aside as the brood rushed past, their voices shrill and their faces still greasy from the meal.

'Mine are the two tallest boys, that girl in the orange dress, and the smaller girl Kaled carries. The girl and boy who chase each other are Hanouf's. And Bibi, married to Hafeez only two years ago, carries her son in her arms, and another child within her.'

'Hafeez must be very proud.'

'Yes. He chose his wives carefully, and there is no discord. Although

Hanouf and I have both buried children, we are still blessed with these living, another favour of Allah the Merciful. And now it will be your turn.' She smiled, and her features softened, making her less plain.

It caused me deep discomfort to have come to these warm, friendly people on the wind of a lie. 'If Allah the True One deems it fitting,' I answered, hoping my voice did not betray my thoughts.

We approached a level area between sloping plains, and Myassa pointed to a spot shaded by a large myrtle tree. 'Come. We will sit there with the children, out of the late sun.'

I looked to the west, where the sun was beginning its descent. I did not want to think about darkness falling, and the return to the black tent with Shaliq.

Hanouf and Bibi joined Myassa and me, and the children tussled and wrestled with each other. Again, I could not help but notice how the girls acted no differently to the boys. Bibi kept smiling at me, and I was sorry we could not yet speak to each other.

'How do you say "well done" in Pashto?' I asked Myassa. When she told me, I pointed to Bibi's abdomen and hesitantly repeated the word. '*Shâbas*, Bibi.'

Bibi laughed delightedly, and patted her belly, nodding and replying.

'She thanks you,' Myassa said. 'You will learn our language quickly. Your tongue twists with ease.'

We all looked to the clearing as voices rose. 'What are they doing?' I asked, watching two pairs of men standing in a circle that had been created by dragging a stick through the soft earth. Each man was bound to his partner by a piece of felt secured with strips of hide around the inner leg.

'They will play Rope and Circle,' Myassa said. 'The games of our tribe are only strength and sport. The games of other tribes usually involve animals fighting to the death, but Kaled does not allow it. He has a soft heart, and does not wish for blood activities.'

'Too soft, in this case,' Hanouf said, her brow stern. 'Sometimes I fear our sons will not grow to be proper warriors if they are not allowed to see fighting to the death.'

'Stop grumbling, Hanouf,' Myassa said. 'You know all our men are strong and fearless fighters, and our sons will be, too.'

How odd, I thought, to speak of fighting and death so casually, but then the game began. One pair of men used a rope to whip the legs of the other pair. As the whip lashed towards them, the men of the second pair leapt as one into the air to avoid the stinging blows, trying to stay within the boundary of the circle. Without weapons, they attempted to touch their opponents with their feet, shod in leather. After a short but exhausting time of lashing and leaping, one slight man succeeded in hitting his target with his toe, and a loud cheer arose. The four men slapped each other on the backs and shoulders, and each took a long drink from a goatskin bag. The whip was exchanged, and the defeated pair now had their turn to avoid the whip.

As the game went on with different pairs entering the circle, I noticed more bonfires blazing on the hills surrounding the encampment, and saw, by the brightness of the flames, that dusk fell. There were continuous greetings as visitors rode into camp, and I watched as friends greeted each other in joyful embraces, the older men often grasping each other's beards and bestowing passionate kisses on both cheeks. Soon drumbeats came from the far end, opposite the game field.

Rope and Circle was replaced by wrestling. Men placed their chins on their opponent's shoulder and wrapped their arms around each other's waists, taking a firm hold on the back of their trousers. Then they attempted to lift, trip, drop, or somehow get their opponent on the ground, and be declared the winner.

Myassa stood and picked up the little girl who had fallen asleep in her lap. 'I will put this one to bed,' she said to me. 'The games, and more food for the men will go on late into the night. Hanouf, will you bring the children when you come?'

As Hanouf nodded, Shaliq appeared in front of me. My mouth went dry. 'We will go now,' he said.

I couldn't look at Myassa or Hanouf or Bibi. My head down, I followed my husband to the tents. On the way, Shaliq plucked a thick, smouldering stick of wood from one of the bonfires. He led the way through the tents, not glancing back. I stumbled in the near-darkness, my legs unwieldy and awkward. I was light-headed from exhaustion and my inability to eat. Now I struggled to swallow as my throat was tight with nerves.

The noise throughout the camp had grown louder with the influx of visitors. I caught glimpses of men dancing in the firelight between the tents, and the dogs, distressed by the onslaught of strangers in the camp, never stopped baying.

All I wanted was quiet. And sleep. Was this the way a bride should feel on her wedding night? Without warning I saw Sulima's face, joyful and free as the boy from Wamed moved over her.

We reached Shaliq's tent, and he threw the flaming torch into a nearby fire, and pulled back the flap. Stooping, I followed, seeing Shaliq by the faint light that reflected through the doorway. He immediately lowered himself on to the quilts spread over large sheepskins on the packed earth, hooking his hands behind his head and staring at me.

I looked away, my pulse beating so loudly in my ears that I grew dizzy.

'Shut the flap,' he said, touching the quilt beside him, and ducking his chin at it.

I did as I was told, and the tent was completely dark. In the blind warmth of it, I moved slowly towards where I knew my husband lay, my hands held in front of me, afraid of tripping over something in the unfamiliar darkness. My foot touched the edge of a sheepskin, and I crouched, feeling for the quilt, then knelt and crawled forward. I could hear Shaliq's heavy breathing as I lay on my own back beside him. I was still in my ceremonial clothing. Would I sleep in it? I couldn't undress and put on my sleeping dress with this stranger beside me.

In the next moment there was a stealthy rustle, and with one swift motion Shaliq had positioned himself over me, his legs straddling mine. I smelled onion on his breath, and caught my own, lying rigidly with my arms at my sides. He pulled up the long hem of my dress and yanked at the waist of my Pushtun pantaloons. As I felt the thin material give a warning rip, I quickly reached up and untied the drawstring, my hands tangling with his as I tried to wriggle them down over my hips. He moved off to kneel beside me and, with both hands, pulled the pantaloons to my ankles, then off. I felt my *halhal* dig into my flesh, and my leather shoes came off with the pantaloons.

Shaliq nudged between my legs with one of his knees. Even though I knew what I must do, my legs were strangely uncooperative, the muscles in my thighs tight and unwilling to relax and open. Now Shaliq took hold of my knees, forcing my legs apart, and then moved between them. I turned my head away, my eyes staring into the blackness, and balled my hand into a fist, bringing it up to my mouth. My other arm stayed at my hip, clutching the edge of my dress. Shaliq grunted, and I felt something hot as a burning torch pressing into me where Hanouf's fingers had probed days earlier.

This is my husband. This is his right. I opened my mouth and jammed the back of my hand into it, biting down as the pain mounted with each of Shaliq's insistent stabs. It seemed there was a closed door which Shaliq could not penetrate no matter how hard he battered. And then, with one particularly forceful shove, there was a new pain, this one dry and sharp and raw, a pain with such unexpected intensity that I couldn't stop the cry that burst from my lips around my hand. I squeezed my eyes shut and felt my face contort, as if I were a small girl waiting for danger to pass, and now sucked on my hand, trying not to make a sound. My instinct was to strike Shaliq's back with the fist in my mouth, pound him as he was pounding into me, but I knew I mustn't, couldn't.

Shaliq emitted a gruff cry and moved rapidly, his hands on either side of my shoulders as he rocked back and forth. I do not believe I breathed, my hand and mouth now still, although my stomach heaved with repugnance and something close to disgrace. Humiliation, perhaps. I was humiliated by this assault, even though I knew it was proper. I waited for the end.

It was over quickly. After one long hoarse sigh, Shaliq moved out of me with a brusqueness that made me gasp a second time. There came a quieter sigh, and I heard the movements of his own clothing, and then he lay beside me again, his back to me. He pulled a quilt up over us both, and within only moments, his deep snores filled the tent.

I lay in the darkness, my legs apart, my dress around my waist. Tears ran from the sides of my eyes into my ears. Finally I took my fist from my mouth, and realised my hand hurt, that I must have bitten through the skin. I thought of my own clean pallet, and the crowded warmth of Nasreen's and Yusuf's little bodies against mine. I thought of the stillness of our village at night, only the wind murmuring through the leaves of the mulberry trees and whispering at the wooden shutters. I thought of the roof, and lying there, looking at the map of the stars.

I listened instead to my husband's snores, the dogs' howling, and the wild, unbridled music accompanied by the shouting laughter of strange men. I moved my legs together, pulling down my dress and turning to my side so that my back was to my husband's, and felt pain that was both inside my body and within my heart. I wept, soundlessly, into the blackness of the goatskin Pushtun tent.

I wanted to go home. I wanted my mother.

I wanted to be a Tajik girl again.

CHAPTER SIXTEEN

AFTER THAT FIRST night I had little time to weep over my own confusion or desires. I was awakened early the next morning by my husband taking me again. It hurt even more this time; my flesh was still torn, but, as I would quickly learn, Shaliq's regular intrusions on my body were always brief. For this small mercy I was grateful.

He left the tent immediately afterwards. I lay there, hearing the coughing bray of a donkey, the bold crow of a cock. Myassa came through the flap, gracefully balancing a covered bowl and an armful of clothing. She left the flap open, and as the early light came through, I hurriedly pulled down my dress under the quilt as I sat up, embarrassed to see my pantaloons in a heap at the foot of the bed. Myassa appeared not to notice my discomfort. 'I waited for Shaliq to leave,' she said.

I looked at her kind face, and then, unbidden, pictures of what had happened the night before, and, even worse, only moments earlier, came to me, and I was filled with revulsion and shame, and lowered my head.

'Come. I have brought you warm water,' she said, her voice so matter-of-fact that I was able to look at her. 'And here is camp clothing – the *kamis* we wear for every day. The ceremonial dresses are too long for ease in work.' She held up long-sleeved shirts which I knew would fall to my thighs, as hers did.

As I splashed water on to my face Myassa smiled. 'I did not think you would like to go to the stream with joking well-wishers this first morning.'

I said nothing, and at this Myassa raised her eyebrows. 'Perhaps you would prefer if I were not here, either.'

'No. I'm sorry,' I told her. 'I –' To my horror, I felt my lips tremble. I would not cry in front of her. I pressed them together tightly, aware that I was frowning.

Myassa set down the bowl and kneeled in front of me. 'You have pain?'

I couldn't look at her. 'A little.'

'I will bring you some sheep fat,' she told me. 'Use it before your husband comes to you. This helps.'

I raised my head to look at her. Sheep fat?

She understood my confusion, and now her smile was comforting. 'Perhaps it is different among the Tajik women. Perhaps you do not discuss such matters.'

I didn't understand what matters she was talking about.

'You put it where he joins with you,' she said. 'Just a little. The men never know. And until your body has loosened, it can help. After your first birth you should have no more difficulties.'

Then I understood, my cheeks flaming. I covered my face with my hands.

Myassa's hands came on to mine, pulling them away, and I was forced to look at her. She gazed down at the purplish circle of teeth marks on the back of my hand, briefly covering it with her own. 'It will be better, Daryâ,' she said, and at her sympathy I had to shut my eyes to hold back the tears.

Then her voice became practical again. 'There is no place for great modesty in camp, Daryâ. We live too closely. Soon you will grow comfortable with our ways.' She glanced towards the open flap. 'There is much work to be done,' she said. 'We start our journey to Badakhshan today.'

'Badakhshan? Where is this place?'

'It's high through the mountains. The lambs have been born, and the shearing done before we stopped outside your village. Now we will go ever higher for the flock to graze on the long, tender grass they will find there.'

I thought of their fat-tailed sheep – Karakul – with curly thick wool.

'On the way,' Myassa continued, 'we will stop at more villages to trade the wool and some of the sheep for our supplies.' There was a shout from outside. 'But before I leave you, Daryâ, I must quickly tell you Shaliq's story. In this way perhaps you will understand him – and maybe find some forgiveness for his ways.'

Could she know what had happened in the tent, how he had shown me no respect or tenderness, but took me roughly, wordlessly, as if I were of no importance? 'Yesterday Hanouf told me of his former wives, and of his insecurity as second-born.'

Myassa nodded, settling more comfortably on the quilts. 'But there is more. Because Kaled does not have a wife but for Utmarkhail, who cannot be counted as such, I have taken on the role of the head woman for his family. The stories have been given to me. It is my duty to see that as a family, there is close alliance. Without it, our life, with so little privacy and stability, begins to fall apart. Anything that I tell you about our family – the family of Kaled – is for this family only. The words we speak remain within the walls of our own tents, and are not spoken of in other tents. It must be so; gossiping is not looked upon kindly. Do you understand? Can I trust you?'

I nodded.

'Shaliq is indeed a difficult man, but in the years I have been married to Hafeez I see that his unhappiness stems from how unsure of himself he feels. And while Kaled is a kind and fair man, he does not look at Shaliq with the same love and respect as he does Hafeez, or as he did his younger son, Razak.

'Three daughters were born to Kaled's first wife, Husna. And then came Hafeez. The year after his birth, Kaled had gone north, farther than he had ever ventured before, to buy horses. The Turkomen of the Uzbeks breed the finest horses. Kaled hoped to buy some and then sell them for a higher price in Kabul, but he miscalculated. He was stranded by heavy winter snows among the Uzbeks, unable to come back through the mountains.

'He was young and hot-blooded, and without a woman for four dark months. During this time he met Utmarkhail, and she bewitched him.'

I nodded, thinking of my own father and Sulima.

'Kaled brought her back from the steppes as a second wife, and she quickly gave him Shaliq. But within a short time she showed signs of an unstable mind, and made life most terrible for Husna, the first wife.'

I found the mirroring of these lives with mine strange. Unsettling, and yet in some unknown way it brought me an understanding. Perhaps it was so with many husbands and wives and children. Perhaps what had happened in my own home was not as shocking as I had always believed it to be.

'While Husna carried the child that was to be Razak, Kaled left camp again for many months,' Myassa went on, 'trading and selling horses. Utmarkhail and Husna fought bitterly that winter; even though he was a small child, Hafeez remembers the unhappiness of the tent. Shortly after Razak was born in early spring, while Kaled was still away, Husna died suddenly and mysteriously. Utmarkhail said that it was a tainting of the blood from the childbirth, but everyone suspected she had poisoned Husna. By the time Kaled returned, Husna was buried. Nothing was ever proven, but within a few months Kaled took his daughters and Hafeez and moved into his cousin's tent. The wife of his cousin had taken Razak to her breast along with her own child after Husna's death, and they all lived together for many years. Kaled wanted to take Shaliq as well, as he worried for the boy under Utmarkhail's care, but the woman refused.

'And so Utmarkhail and Shaliq lived alone, although of course Kaled continued to provide for them, and forbade anyone to treat them with disrespect. But gradually, as Utmarkhail exhibited more and more signs that the *jinn* had destroyed her thinking, everyone stayed clear of her. And of course Shaliq suffered, as a child, with such a mother. When he was older, and no longer under her influence, he simply moved to the tent of his father. But the years with her scarred him, and he has never felt that he rightly belonged. And so he blusters and swaggers, trying to prove to everyone that he is just as worthy as Hafeez is, and as Razak had been.'

'What of her now? My mother-in-law?'

'She no longer speaks, nor comes from her tent. She remains inside, in the dark, eating for much of the time. Even when food is scarce, she sneaks out and steals from others to feed her appetite, which is much larger than any man I have known.'

My face must have shown some sign of fear, for Myassa reached over and patted my hand. 'She will not bother you, child. She cares for nothing and no one. As long as her belly is full she is of no consequence to anyone. You will always prepare extra food; Shaliq will take it to her. This has been my job when Shaliq was without a wife. Now it will be yours.' She rose. 'Use the water while there is still some warmth to it, and dress. I will send Bibi to help you take down the tent.'

And so I would begin the trek to the province of Badakhshan, and the rest of my life.

* * *

I watched in amazement, half an hour later, as Bibi untied a few knots and gave hard tugs on the winter tent made of *palas* – black goat-hair cloth woven into panels – and it gracefully collapsed in a whooshing rush of air. I had already packed up all of our belongings. And in less than an hour, the entire camp – which I found later to have over one hundred and fifty men, women, and children – was dismantled. Everyone, down to the smallest walking child, had a job to do.

Shaliq appeared only once, briefly, while I worked with Bibi. He silently took his saddle and a goatskin water bag I had set outside the tent, and left, heading towards the corralled horses.

I watched as the strong, humped camels were brought forward, and, although nasty, seemed impervious to the weight that was heaped upon them. The ugly beasts were incongruously decorated with bridles of bright red, blue, and white beads. Some were further ornamented with additional feathers, ribbons, and bells, and I wondered if the Ghilzai hoped that improving their appearance would do the same for the animal's dispositions. Each family had a camel to transport their belongings, and huge, tottering piles of tents, bedding, pots and pans and wooden cages of squawking chickens were secured on to the animals' backs. Young boys with loud voices and stout, knotted branches milled around the camels, keeping the hissing, spitting creatures in an orderly line.

Other camels were outfitted with roughly constructed wooden carriers, like small crates, which sat on either side of the camels' humps. Into these small children were set, comfortably padded with sheepskins and blankets, and a mother climbed into the opposite crate, to balance the load, to watch that none of the more curious little ones attempted to climb out, and to keep the great swaying neck of the camel in line with long wands of willow branches.

Some camels also carried the elderly, and I wondered which of the shawl-covered women was my mother-in-law.

The horses were lashed together in groups of three or four, and one man on a horse held the lead to each small group of the long-legged, graceful animals. Many of the men mounted horses, and would ride alongside the caravan of animals. Older children and younger, childless women walked in the soft dust beside the camels. A few carried the newest lambs in blankets tied on their backs.

Finally, the huge flock of sheep was brought to the end of the caravan. Surrounding them were the camp dogs, who ran, endlessly barking, around the bleating sheep. Little boys chased after the occasional lamb who ran out of the group in wild-eyed confusion, panicked at being unable to find its mother. A few dozen bearded goats mixed with the sheep.

I joined Bibi, her baby in a sling, and Hanouf in the noisy, chattering crowd of women, and the caravan began its journey. I saw that Myassa rode on a camel which carried Hanouf's children and her own daughter.

We walked all day, stopping only briefly to give the animals water and eat the bread and cheese we carried with us. At first I had stared around me as we walked, feeling a small nudging of pleasure at the freedom of walking through the countryside as I had never done before. Of course I thought of my grandmother, putting back my head and searching the bright sky. Was she watching this journey, nodding?

But by late afternoon my legs ached painfully, my feet felt swollen within my soft shoes, and I was hot and dusty. I would not complain, or ask when we would stop, as I saw how the other women and children walked with no apparent discomfort. But I was relieved when a man on horseback trotted down the long winding line of camels and horses and sheep and bodies, calling out in Pashto, and I knew, from the nods and murmurs of the others, that we would soon stop.

But in spite of my aching body, I could have walked through the night to avoid spending it with Shaliq.

For the next two days the caravan travelled slowly but steadily through the fertile upland country. Just before evening of the second day a village came into sight. I knew it was Tajik, and stared at the outlines of the buildings sitting proudly in the green valley, the late sun casting long shadows on the smooth walls. The familiar odour of dung burning on a hearth wafted towards me on the warm evening breeze, and I longed to run towards that place that was so like my home.

'What is this village?' I called to Hanouf.

'Pani Mar,' she answered, and a dull thump of dread came into my chest. A cousin of my father's lived in Pani Mar. It was suddenly difficult for me to breathe.

'Will we stop here?'

'Yes. Some of the men will go to the teahouse this evening, and find out if the Tajiks would like to trade – although this town does not usually want sheep.'

I followed her in silence, hoping a Tajik bride was not important enough to be discussed by men in a teahouse. I found it difficult to eat before Shaliq left for the village, and spent the evening alone in my tent, too worried to sit with the other women.

I lay under a quilt, waiting, imagining what would happen should my secret be disclosed. My heart jumped wildly when I heard the return of the men, and I sat up, staring at the flap, both hands clutching the quilt at my chest.

But Shaliq entered the tent silently and said nothing, and when he extinguished the candle and came under the quilt, the usual pattern of our nights took place, and I knew I was still safe.

Ten days later I came into my unclean period. Although I knew I would, knew that no seed of Shaliq's would ever be planted within me, I still felt a surprising sense of disappointment. But there was also a small relief, relief that I would have at least five nights of peace without Shaliq's nightly attentions. He would sleep in another tent, I knew from the other women, according to the Pushtun custom for women's unholy times.

I didn't know how to tell him the embarrassing fact of my time; we rarely spoke of anything except for his requests or demands and my replies. So that evening I simply held out a stained cloth when he came into the tent after he had eaten his meal.

His lips tightened as he stared at it.

'I'm sorry,' I said. 'But it is only the first month.'

He nodded.

'A man such as you . . . surely we will have many fine sons,' I said, hoping a compliment would soften his mood.

He nodded again.

'What would you wish to name your first son?' I asked, feeling that Shaliq and I – for the first time – shared something. Even if it was disappointment.

'I have always dreamed of a son named Baksh,' he said, and something in his voice and his eyes actually brought out pity in me. For that moment I could understand how frustrating his childlessness made him, and could almost forgive him for his rough treatment of me.

'Oh, yes,' I agreed. 'A good name. And our son will, as his name predicts, be a gift to you.' I handed him the quilt I knew he preferred, and he took it.

'May Allah bring you peace in your sleep,' I said, softly, and he turned and left, and for the next five days I only caught glimpses of him, astride his horse in the slowly moving caravan which continued to thread its way upward into the hills.

I wondered how many more months he would accept the unclean cloths I knew would always appear, and for how long he could be appeased with soothing words.

After almost thirty long days of travel, of setting up the tents at evening and taking them down at sun-up, we reached Badakhshan. I breathed deeply with pleasure when Hafeez rode back, one early afternoon, to tell us to make camp at the edge of a great meadow of springy green grass that would be our home for the summer months.

'Now we will set up our yurts,' Myassa told me. 'They are cooler and more roomy than the tents. Much more practical for warm weather.'

She helped me put up the structure supported with long sticks which were placed securely into the ground and bound together at the top to form a cone. The poles were then sided with reed matting; the rounded roof was a covering of black felt, left open where the sticks met at the top to allow more air to enter the yurt. As it had been when we stopped and set up our tents every night of the voyage, each family positioned their yurt so that no door faced its neighbour. When my yurt was up I helped Bibi with hers. Then I prepared food and left it over the fire for Shaliq and his mother, slipping away to explore what would be my home for the next months.

Winding through the grassy banks of the vast valley, surrounded by the craggy snow-capped mountains, was a wide, peaceful river, the Panjshir. I had heard of the Panjshir, and knew that in places it was dangerous and fast-moving, with thundering rushing torrents. And yet here, in this secluded valley, it ran quietly. Backwaters formed narrow peninsulas of land and tiny islands in its broad surface. I shielded my eyes with my hand in the bright sunlight, following the winding course of the water further, and could see the formation of a small lake at the end of the valley. The mountains, casting deep purple shadows, sent down waves of cool breeze which gently lifted and rippled the skin of the water. Arranged with almost balanced perfection at various spots along the river's banks were huge rocks, covered with orange and green lichen.

Golden summer flowers – I would later learn their names to be potentilla and ranuncula from Bibi, who was patient in teaching me Pashto – attracted the valley's insects. Hosts of tiny cream-coloured butterflies with dark grey markings fluttered and dived above the small blossoms with frantic movements, in contrast to the sleepily buzzing bees clambering amongst the flowers.

The long grass was many different hues of green, and the swaying heads of hollyhocks, which I recognised, were shades of ivory, brilliant pink, and deep purple. I sat in the deep grass, staring at the water, feeling, for the first time in my month as a wife, a small sense of peace. I realised I had not prayed as regularly as I had in Susmâr Khord; Allah's name did not cross the lips of the Ghilzai as often as it had with the people of my village. I lowered my head. Now I would pray, and thank Allah for bringing me to this place of beauty. It would feel good to say a prayer that came from my heart.

But as I closed my eyes, heavy tramping nearby disturbed me. I turned to see who came, ashamed at having been caught resting when I should have been working. But the intruder did not appear to notice me. She was a huge, veiled woman, jiggling with layers of fat under her stained and stretched kamis. Lowering herself heavily to her knees, she grunted as she hit the ground with a dull thud. I knew it was Utmarkhail; this was the only Pushtun woman I had never seen before. Hanouf had pointed out her figure, slouched on a camel at the end of the caravan, her face always covered. Once Shaliq set up her tent each evening she would disappear into it, still heavily veiled, but I occasionally caught a glimpse of the woman's bare, monstrous ankles and shabby, split shoes as she laboriously lurched through her tent door. I was reminded of a giant insect scuttling for safety. Now she threw back her veil and began working through a patch of wild strawberries. Red juice trickled down her chin, and by the way her slack lips smacked I knew she no longer possessed teeth. Her jowls trembled as she stuffed handfuls of the ripe fruit into her mouth.

I was wary of coming face-to-face with this strange woman who was my mother-in-law. And as if reading my thoughts, Utmarkhail's head darted up, her mouth, hanging open, full of mashed fruit. Her lumpy nose rose in the air like a wary fox.

She stared at me, and even at that distance, my flesh crawled at the lunacy I saw in the small, bright eyes. I stayed perfectly still. After a few seconds the woman slapped at the air in front of her face and then continued with her busy picking and eating. Her jaws working furiously, she moved among the plants a few more minutes. Then she pushed herself to her feet, lowered her veil, and shuffled off in the opposite direction to me.

Sighing with relief, I lay back in the grass and looked at the sky. I thought about my life. I found I could not think clearly when always surrounded by the women and children of the camp; no longer did I have any time alone, any privacy. I missed it, and realised that my thoughts – which could roam when I lived in Susmâr Khord and sat on the roof by myself – had grown smaller, honed in. Strange, that in a tiny village my thoughts were expansive, while in the width and breadth of the countryside we travelled through they had diminished.

While we walked in the caravan I was always surrounded by talking women, by the laughter or tears or demands of the children, by the sounds of the animals. I had little time to think uninterrupted; instead, I listened to the other women, trying to follow their Pashto, sometimes joining in. The talk was women's talk: of children and food and clothing, of childbirth and illness and death, of weather and cycles. Talk that I had heard between the women of my own village. It was the same, different only because of the different life.

I didn't mind it, this talk: it kept me distracted, kept me from thinking of my own village, of my husband's nightly needs and wondering how long he would put up with a wife who did not give him a child. Of my fate when he would no longer accept me. But I longed for something more, for talk of stars, of distant journeys. Surely some among the Ghilzai had ventured far in their roamings. Surely there were wondrous stories of foreign places such as my grandmother had seen.

Perhaps now that we would be in one place for a number of months, I would find that the talk in camp turned to these things. That my own head could again grow full with the stories I remembered, and that my grandmother would come to me in my dreams, and remind me of my power.

I had forgotten about my intended prayer.

CHAPTER SEVENTEEN

FIVE MONTHS HAD passed since I came to the Ghilzai camp, and now the summer – our time in the valley – was nearing its end. I had worked from daybreak until sundown with the other women, making the sheared summer wool into felt, milking the goats, and preparing food. At times I felt we were like donkeys, working silently, endlessly carrying loads, stopping only to eat and drink, sleeping deeply at the end of each long day.

There was no talk of the moon or the stars. We were usually asleep, exhausted, before they made their appearance. I was able to speak Pashto well enough to be understood. I didn't like the way the words felt – sometimes lodging harshly in my throat, and I longed to speak the gentle, melodic tones of my own language. But once I had demonstrated my knowledge of Pashto, nobody bothered to speak Dari to me.

Shaliq did little. Kaled and Hafeez and others spent most of their time working with the horses in the rough corrals. There were beautiful Arabians that they broke in order to sell in Jalalabad in the winter. In contrast, Shaliq sometimes fished in the stream running off the Panjshir, or idly sat in the warm summer sun, drinking tea and talking to other men who joined him.

My husband wanted my face marked with ornamentation. I said I didn't want the marks, but he growled that the choice was not mine, and sent me to Hanouf.

'They're not only for beauty, but for enhanced fertility and protection from disease,' she told me, as she prepared a powder made from the bark of the acacia tree and husks of a strange, dark seed. She added cold tea to the mixture and stirred it.

She cleaned my face, and with a sliver of bone which she first placed in boiling water over the fire, she pricked the skin of my forehead and chin. 'Shaliq prefers a simple design,' she said, her tongue touching her top lip as she worked. I sat perfectly still; she worked quickly and with a steady hand and it hurt only a little. With a clean cloth she continually wiped away the small drops of blood that welled up under the sharp tip of the bone. Then she'd wipe the bone and dip it into the dark paste and smear it over the tiny circular punctures.

Finally she sat back on her heels and nodded. 'In a few days the scabs will fall off, and your *harquus* will shine on your face.'

I reached up to touch one, but she stopped me. 'Don't wash your face until the scabs are gone. And don't worry. The cleansing fire of the examining angels will burn them off before you enter paradise.'

I had no mirror, and could only see my face as a wavy, murky reflection in the river, or the strange, tiny image in the pupils of those I spoke to. I felt I had grown taller still in the last few months, and I sensed my body leaner, the bones beneath my flesh more evident. My hands, too, had become stronger through the labour, and darkened by the sun. The women were mostly kind to me, although often lost in their work, dealing with their own responsibilities. In spite of the busyness of the camp, inside I was lonely.

At first I often attempted to speak to Shaliq after he had rolled off me in the dark, when I knew he was calm and satisfied. I asked specific questions about what he had done that day, or some small event that had taken place within the tribe. He answered in brief sentences, although he was sometimes pleased to tell me of his prowess at a game he had won. I thought it might bring us closer if I could arouse in him even the slightest interest in my own former life, so different to this one, and tried to tell him of my Tajik village. But if I spoke too long he would turn over, and soon his muffled snores began. After a while I stopped trying for a conversation between us.

Once, in those early days, again thinking of Sulima and the obvious pleasure she knew with her man, I tried to slow his rapid nightly routine by stroking his shoulders as he climbed on to me. 'Shaliq,' I whispered. 'Wait. Please. Let me get comfortable so I –'

He surprised me by stopping. But then I didn't know what to do, and my body gave me no clues. I lifted my head, pressing my cheek against his, feeling his stubbled skin, but still, I knew of nothing further to attempt, felt nothing that Sulima's face had shown. 'Come to me, husband,' I finally said, and although he was not quite as hurried that night, I felt an even deeper loneliness and frustration when he was done.

My main pleasure through those first months with the Ghilzai was the beauty that surrounded me. I felt a wave of peace come over me when I had a chance to look at the mountains, to smell the earthy river and the sweetness of the waving grass. My favourite times were those when I stood in the water of the Panjshir to wash clothes. Then, as I pounded and thumped the wet clothing against the smooth river rocks, I sang my old Tajik songs. Every so often I even sang the strange foreign one about Britannia. I recited the Persian poetry my grandmother had taught me. The singing and poetry brought me joy, yet also sadness.

I was losing the part of me that was the Tajik Daryâ. I no longer knew, with complete certainty, who I was, with a new language tumbling from my lips, my hands rough as a man's, and my face marked with *harquus*.

Shaliq beat me the first time when my unclean time came that fifth month. I should have been prepared; the fourth month he had stared down at the bloodied rag and I saw the fury in his face. He had grabbed his sleeping quilt and stomped through the doorway of the yurt. But as he did so, he snatched up an empty cooking pot from the ground beside the fire and hurled it through the yurt opening. It happened so quickly and unexpectedly that I had only a second to dodge it, and the heavy pot glanced off my shoulder, immediately raising a tender welt that turned into a dark, ugly bruise.

This fifth month I sensed my time was late by the thinning of the moon. I carried my small, hopeful secret for three days. The nights had grown cooler and the sun was slower to rise in the mornings; the dawn crisp. Now we were kept busy making stacks of the flat travel nan, fat worked into the dough to create a hard, tasty bread that would keep for over a month. There was a feeling of restlessness within the camp as all prepared for the descent back through the mountain passes and high plateaus and down past the Laghman province and my home. I wondered if I would be allowed to visit my family. The plans were that we would arrive at our winter camp outside of Jalalabad before Ramazân. We had huge quantities of felt to sell, as well as a great many extra containers of clarified butter and dried whey. With the lambs now close to maturity, and the prancing Arabians broken, the tribe was hoping to turn a good profit, both in traded goods and coins.

As the light in the sky faded I hummed, walking back from the river, a huge basket cradled in my arms. There was a sultry heaviness in the air. I had washed all our clothing and bedding in readiness for the many weeks of travel. It would be difficult to find the time and energy to scrub clothes and let them dry when we travelled, so I was content in knowing we would have enough fresh items to last most of the trip.

As I passed the horses in the corral they whinnied and shied, bunching together and then breaking apart and trotting restlessly in their enclosure. There was a faint, distant rumble from over the mountains, and I understood their behaviour. Thunder. It didn't surprise me, after the weight of the air all day.

I hoped the thunderstorm wouldn't ruin the evening. There would be a small celebration to mark the end of summer camp, with a *landay* performance, as well as the men of the camp dancing their ceremonial *atan*. I looked forward to it; we had done nothing but work, and it brought me pleasure to think of the planned festivities.

The basket was cumbersome, and as I shifted it to my hip, I felt a sudden heavy cramp in my abdomen, and the hope I had held close to my heart immediately evaporated. I had let myself believe that it had happened, that Allah the Just had listened to my prayers and seen fit to grant me the only wish I asked for. In the last few days I had let dreams, filmy as summer clouds, form. I imagined that should there be a baby, I would be allowed to stop at Susmâr Khord as we passed it on one of our future journeys, and show my parents their first grandchild. I would prove that Sulima's curse had been weaker than my belief in Allah and His merciful ways.

But now, as the familiar cramp intensified, all those dreams were blown away like the shimmering heads of the flowers gone to seed in the meadow.

My walk slowed, and I stared into my laundry basket as I reached the outlying yurts, hoping no one would speak to me; my mood was soured. As I slipped between two of the yurts, avoiding the open doorways, I heard men's raised voices. Unconsciously listening, I realised that one of the voices was Shaliq's, the other Qul, husband of Faiza, a young woman my age.

Qul's voice was languid, teasing, while Shaliq's responses were heated and barely concealed his anger. I knew the men of the camp were forbidden to fight with each other; their hostility must be kept for other tribes. Their fists could not be used upon each other; instead, any animosity was taken out in gaming, or with *turbruganay* – a word game which stopped just short of open insults.

I had seen how some of the men were adroit at twisting words in such a manner that their true meaning was disguised under light banter. Only later, when the recipient of the words dozed, or relaxed over a cup of tea, would the smack of the verbal sparring strike.

And I had also seen that Shaliq, lacking conversational skills, was often a hapless victim when it came to this word game. His response to the jests he was subjected to was usually angry muttering and a string of oaths.

I heard my name, and stopped. No one could see me, between the yurts.

'After all, my friend,' Qul said, 'she certainly has a body that moves as if it was meant for a riot of pleasure.'

My face burned at such familiarity. Because I was not a Pushtun, not tribal born, I knew some felt they could take more liberties with my dignity. It happened to my face with a few of the women, but I hadn't realised the men also spoke of me with a lack of respect.

'And how fortunate that your father was willing to spare no expense in finding you a wife,' Qul went on. 'Especially since there are unmarried girls still within our own camp. But of course they are spoiled and ungrateful, to refuse the offers of a man such as you.'

I listened with growing distress. I had occasionally wondered why Shaliq had not married any of the Ghilzai; why his father had chosen a village girl for him. Now that I knew how much less rigid the rules were for the nomads, I realised that the Ghilzai girls themselves had chosen not to accept Shaliq. It made him less appealing than he already was.

I could not hear Shaliq's reply.

'Yes, Shaliq. This is true. But as the son of our chief, it is even more important for you to have many sons. Perhaps the weakness of your first wife and the unpleasant personality of the second frightened your seed. But there can be no excuse with a woman such as the one you have now.' He laughed heartily, as if Shaliq enjoyed the biting words with him. 'Perhaps you had better rest even more in the daylight hours so that you are not so tired when you pull up the quilt.'

More muffled words followed, then Qul's voice, clear, came again. 'Come, my friend. Sit down. The tea is still hot.'

Shaliq's heavy footsteps pounded out of the yurt and towards the river. I hurried home and quickly spread the clean clothes and bedding over the rope strung between a pole of the yurt and another firmly planted pole close by. The cramping continued; when I checked it was as I feared.

I stoked the fire and heated up a large pot of Shaliq's favourite food which I'd prepared earlier – rice with *dhye* – sour curds poured into a well in the centre. The flies were thicker than usual, and I waved a small leafy branch over the cooling nan, trying to keep them from lighting on it. More distant grumbling came from far away, and now I was sure there would be rain. A hot breeze appeared from nowhere, bringing dust, thick and bitter and old-smelling. It tugged at the reed yurts and teased my head covering into fluttering wings around my face. When I finally saw Shaliq approaching, a scowl on his flat face, I poured melted butter over the rice mixture.

'Your meal waits, Shaliq,' I said, as he looked into the steaming pot. 'I have also made the cake you love, of pounded almonds and the last of the raisins.'

Shaliq squatted, not waiting for me to dish it into a bowl, but scooping the greasy rice into his mouth with his fingers so quickly that I wondered that he didn't choke, hardly chewing before swallowing. He wiped his hands and face on the cloth I offered him, then took the chunk of cake and crammed it into his mouth.

As I dished out my own meal and sat down to eat, Shaliq suddenly grabbed me by my braids. Shocked, I put my hands up over Shaliq's, trying to ease the strain on my scalp. Without a word, he dragged me into the tent as easily as if I were one of the lambs.

'Stop, Shaliq! What is it?' I asked, although I knew, knew that he would take out his anger towards Qul on me. My scalp burned; Shaliq kept his grip tight on my waist-length braids.

'You make a fool of me,' he growled. 'All the newest brides in this tribe expect a child. All but you.' His hand pulled tighter.

'But we have not been married as long as the others; I have not been a wife for as many months as—'

'*Chuptiyâ!*' he roared. I fell silent as he demanded, and he let go of my hair and pushed me to the quilt. I looked up at him, truly fearful for the first time. I had never seen him so enraged. Before I could protest, he hooked his hand in the top of my pantaloons and ripped them down. As he did so, his face, flushed, grew rigid, his jaw clenched. I struggled to pull my *kamis* down to cover the tell-tale absorbent fleece, although he had already seen it and knew.

Now his chest heaved, and his eyes were mere slits. I crawled backwards, away from him, my eyes fixed on his face, but in two steps he was in front of me, and snatched me up by the front of my *kamis*. He slapped my face once, twice, three times, so hard that my ears rang and I lost my balance.

As I fell, I turned over and crouched, as I had done as a girl with my father, covering my head with my arms. Shaliq pounded my back and shoulders with his iron fists. I was eventually beaten down to my stomach, and I felt the sharp toe of Shaliq's leather riding boot forcefully ram into my ribs. I screamed with the shock of it, and suddenly the yurt was silent except for Shaliq's raspy, laboured breathing.

The silence swooped around me as if all the sound and movement of the camp had stopped with that one, high, panicked scream.

I lay motionless, afraid to move in case I brought on another attack. Finally Shaliq left the yurt. I slowly drew my knees up under my chest and then sat back on my heels. One of my ears had such a loud humming in it that I wondered if I were deaf; I shook my head to clear it but the gesture brought new agony.

Nobody came to the yurt. Had anyone actually heard my scream, or was the silent camp simply inside my head? Or had they heard, but would not interfere? That was more likely. Shaliq was my husband; he had every right to treat me however he chose.

Men were all-powerful in every matter, after all. Although Shaliq's seed, no matter how strong, was obviously not potent enough to combat a Kafir curse. *But how many more months, or years, will this continue? Now that he has beaten me once, will it occur every month? If the curse holds, surely Shaliq will eventually kill me.*

My own thoughts terrified me. I would not let this happen; I would not let my husband end my life. I tried to find a comfortable position, lying on my side with my knees drawn up, and sought to comfort myself with pictures in my head. Pictures of the *zenana* with all its women, or of a foreign room with a painting of the woman with the helmet whom my grandmother said could be me. Of children with skin like milk. But I could see nothing; Shaliq's blows had knocked them from my inner sight.

I could only think of my curse. But perhaps there was some way, some way known to these nomad women, to be rid of it. Or to make Shaliq's seed contain even more power. As I thought of this, another small voice inside my head asked what I had never wondered before: *why is it that neither of his other wives conceived, either?* Surely they were not cursed as well. There could be no such coincidence.

The pain of my bruises and cuts came over me in waves. I closed my eyes. The noise of the celebration began, but I would not be attending.

The rain started after the final music and laughter died away. It poured down all night; thunder crashed, and occasional flashes of lightning brightened the inside of the yurt. When I came out the next morning the rain had stopped, although the sky was a smudged mass of roiling clouds. We all worked hastily, taking down our yurts and packing up the camp. The trotting, bleating sheep and goats were driven ahead, followed by the women and children. The wretched camels slumped along behind us, and lastly came the men and horses.

I turned for one last look at the camp. The flattened, yellowing grass showed the imprints of the yurts. Water dripped miserably from the ragged leaves of the stands of walnut, almond, myrtle and oak trees that grew in profusion nearby. Branches, torn down in the wild night wind, lay scattered about the soggy ground. The leaves, which only a few weeks earlier had been a rich green, now wore their autumn colours, but without the hint of reflecting autumn sunlight that had given them such splendour only yesterday. No proud gleam of bronze or copper, no rich reds, no radiant canary yellow or tangerine fluttered in the stillness; the downcast, trembling leaves all appeared the same humble dun shade.

How sad, I thought, to leave this once-glorious place in such a state. It was as if the camp had aged overnight, perhaps like an artfully painted woman of the *zenana*. Although mysterious and beautiful in the shadows, in the harsh reality of daylight she was revealed to be a faded hag, bearing only a faint resemblance to the former vision.

As well as sadness, I was also full of bitterness that morning, remembering how I had come to this once-beautiful place with hope.

* * *

We trekked to our winter camp. We set up the black tents. The months passed, and Shaliq's treatment of me became more brutal. He didn't care that the others saw my puffy, discoloured eyes, my limping walk. He openly spoke of his disgust with me.

'You are truly a worthless wife,' he said, over and over. 'My father wasted his horses on you. How much longer do you believe I will allow you to eat my food, to shelter in my tent? Any slave could do the work you do. You are worthless,' he repeated.

Worthless. The word continually rang in my head. *You will be worthless as the dust beneath the feet of the camel*, Sulima had said. And it had come true.

Yalda had told me, on my wedding day, that it would be well. She was wrong. Where was my bright future, the one my grandmother had predicted? Was I not trapped here, with the Ghilzai, trapped as surely as I had been in Susmâr Khord after Sulima's curse?

One early afternoon, as I was inside the tent sewing, Kaled came to sit by the fire with Shaliq. I paid no attention to their words until I realised that Shaliq was complaining about me.

'But she does not carry a child. How much longer can I go without a son?' Shaliq's sulky voice carried inside. I bent my head over the tiny tight stitches of the new shirt I was making for him, bringing the lamp closer.

'It has not been so very long,' Kaled answered. 'You must wait.'

'I'm tired of waiting. I have always been waiting. This one is useless. Could you not have found someone more receptive?' Shaliq's voice rose. 'Look at Hafeez's wives. All three are productive. It seems you pick unsuitable wives for me on purpose.'

I held my breath, the needle poised in mid-air, wondering how Kaled would respond to this disgraceful outburst. A heavy cloak of fear settled over me as the long silence continued. Finally Kaled spoke.

'An ungrateful son is a wart on a father's face – to leave it is a blemish, to cut it a pain.'

More silence followed the comment, and then Kaled continued. 'A child is conceived more readily in hope and consideration than in cruel greed, my son. You know that Hafeez will succeed me as chief. But as our camp grows, there is always the chance that you, as my second son, may start your own following. Do you think of this?'

I waited, surprised at Kaled's words. Shaliq, as chief of another Ghilzai tribe? It seemed an impossible image. Shaliq could not hold the respect of others; who would obey his commands but me?

'But the honour of being a chief does not pass on without responsibility,' Kaled went on. 'The Ghilzai want the strongest man as leader – not only strong in the sacks of grain he can lift, the ewes he can carry. They want to see strength within his face in his dealings with the chiefs of warring tribes as well as with the old women and the smallest children. Think. Think, Shaliq, before you speak and act, as I have said since you were a child.'

I set down my sewing, listening to Kaled. Again I thought what a kind, wise man he was. How had a son such as Shaliq come from him?

'Even now the tribe sees how you treat your wife. Everyone hears, and sees the marks upon her face, and they know how she suffers at your hand. It's an embarrassment, Shaliq, and a similar pattern to that with your other wives. You beat them, and it does nothing. A woman won't conceive any faster because she's tortured.'

There was a low sentence from Shaliq, interrupted by Kaled. 'Yes, it is your right to beat your wife. But beatings are for disobedience, or for wanton acts. It's not seemly for a man who may one day be chief to earn the disrespect of his people through an impatient and uncharitable nature.'

Although I heard no reply, I knew that Shaliq's face would be knotted with anger, his lips tight with unspoken words. I sent a small plea to Kaled.

Please be especially wise at this moment. Talk no more tonight. The resentment burning in Shaliq over your words will later erupt, and I will feel the sting of his wrath.

As if he had heard my thoughts, Kaled suddenly said, 'Come. Let us leave our ugly talk behind us. Ride with me now, while there is still light. We will journey far up into the next pasture, where last week I saw a herd of strong young horses. We will sleep in the grass, and in the first light of dawn, perhaps we will surprise them and be able to catch one or two.'

'But you always take Hafeez.' Shaliq sounded like a child accusing his parent of favouritism.

'You never express a desire to help with the chase, although you, too, have a quick hand with horses.'

'Hafeez will join us?'

'No. Just the two of us.'

I heard the hiss of satisfaction, and then Shaliq swaggered into the tent, his face alight with smug pleasure. 'Pack a bag with food. I will go with my father, north, beyond the pass.'

While Shaliq gathered up his riding whip, a skin waterbag, and rolled a quilt into a narrow length to fit behind his saddle, I filled a saddlebag with enough bread, hard cheese, cooked mutton, wild rhubarb compote, and tea leaves to last both men for two full days. I added a small cooking pot and two cups, then followed Shaliq out of the tent. As I handed him the heavy bag, I glanced at Kaled.

'Good luck in your quest,' I said softly. 'May Allah be with you.'

Shaliq was already disappearing between the tents on his way to the corral.

'And may your dreams be peaceful,' Kaled answered.

I smiled, and Kaled nodded, then turned to follow his son. As I watched his strong back and straight shoulders, I thought, as I had so many times, how far the second son had fallen from the tree of his father. I could only pray that Shaliq would think of what his father had said to him the next time I showed him the soiled fleece.

CHAPTER EIGHTEEN

SHORTLY AFTER WE returned to our summer camp in Badakhshan, Faiza, Qul's wife, was the first to approach me with a possible solution to my inability to conceive. She came to me carrying a small leather drawstring bag.

'It is *bui-moderan*, Daryâ. Green tea, mixed with special herbs which make it extremely hot and sharp to the tongue. At your next woman's time boil it in water and drink it for three days. It's important to only try this at your unclean time, for then the womb is open and will accept the stimulants. I had been married three months with no sign of life in my belly, but tried this tea and . . . well, you know my little Jabbar was the result.'

I thanked her, trying to smile as I looked at the sleeping baby cradled against her chest. I found it difficult to think of this; Faiza was a year younger than I, with one small child in her arms and already another growing within.

And so I drank the boiled tea, almost gagging on its bitter taste, but it did not work for me as it had for Faiza.

Dulfiya, the tribe's *dai*, brought me other dried herbs. 'First try boiling them in goat's milk, and drink it,' she instructed me. The midwife's close-set eyes and bulbous, crooked nose made me think of a large bird, but her gentle spirit shone in her wide, square-toothed smile. 'If it doesn't work, the next month try adding more of the herbs to hot clarified butter, then mash the mixture into cooked grain and eat it. Too much must not be introduced into the body at one time, as these herbs contain strong medicine that cleanses the womb, but can also cause severe aches in the stomach.

'Also, Daryâ, remember, only hot foods while you try to induce a pregnancy. Cold foods drive the heat away, and heat is a stimulant for the man's seed. Avoid cold water, buttermilk, yogurt – anything that does not keep your insides warm at all times.'

Looking into Dulfiya's eyes, I was reminded of Yalda, and wanted to lean against her, to tell her about the curse. But I must tell no one. Thinking of Yalda, sadness coursed through me. I needed to see my mother, to feel her arms around me. Shaliq had not allowed me to go to Susmâr Khord as we had passed within a few hours of it on our way down to our winter camp, and then back up in the warm weather. I tried to imagine Nasreen and Yusuf another year older. I could see Nasreen learning to cook and clean, her own slow, sweet smile so like our mother's. And Yusuf – had he ridden on a small pony yet? Did my father take him to the *chây-khâna*, and sit on the roof with him?

Would Shaliq ever allow me to visit my family?

I followed all of Dulfiya's directions explicitly so as not to arouse suspicions.

I believed these ancient remedies would be rendered useless under Sulima's power. And of course Dulfiya's medicines proved fruitless. Then Myassa came to me.

'Now it is time to try *post-poshidan*,' she told me.

I translated to myself. 'The wearing of . . . skins?' I asked, puzzled.

'Yes. For the first time, we will try the less forceful path. We will kill a chicken. Then, for one day, we bind its skin to your abdomen, which will have been prepared with a mixture of cloves and turmeric. The heat of the spices will draw the hot quality of the skin into your body. The same day you will eat the chicken's flesh, cooked with ginger.'

I wrinkled my nose. 'A chicken skin? For a whole day?'

Myassa tutted. 'It is not painful, my girl, and will be worth it if you conceive the next month, don't you agree? If you do not, then we will go a step further.'

'And the next step? What is it?' I asked, knowing Myassa waited for me to enquire, although I didn't really want to know.

'The larger the skin, the stronger the power. We will try the hide of a freshly slaughtered ewe. It will be wrapped around your body, wool side out, for two days and two nights. You must not move during this time.'

I made a face of revulsion, but Myassa continued, unperturbed.

'Of course, for the forty days after the application, you are not allowed any cold foods, as this would lessen the benefits of the *post-poshidan*.'

I nodded. And so it would continue.

I underwent the chicken skin, and in due time, the sheep skin. The second procedure was uncomfortable and humiliating. As I lay on a sleeping quilt the second day, covered with the layer of bloody, stiffening flesh and fur, trying to ignore the flies that settled about my face in the putrefying stench, I distracted myself from the discomfort by sending out strong thoughts to a faceless, lost child who might be waiting at Allah's side for a mother.

For one brief moment, falling into a restless state of sleep that was almost trance-like, I saw myself, as if from a far distance, dressed in strange clothes, cradling a tiny baby, a child whose feature I could not see. Joy filled me, although there was something else, something I could not name. Try as I might, I could not see the face of the child. And then the image faded, growing further and further away, and I cried out, pleading for it to return. There was cool water on my temples, and I looked into Myassa's serene face as she wiped my face with a wet cloth.

'You had a vision, Daryâ?'

I nodded, weakly, and Myassa smiled. 'It is normal. Were these pictures good or bad?'

'Good. I think. Although . . .' I hesitated, unable to put into words the feeling of quiet distress that had accompanied the image.

'Was there a child?'

Again, I nodded.

Myassa nodded. 'It is a sign, Daryâ. I think this time we will have success.'

I felt a tiny tentacle of hope reach out within me, but the unknown and disturbing feeling did not assure me.

Four weeks later my blood flowed dark and heavy. Myassa summoned the *dai*.

'Can we not try anything else?' she asked Dulfiya. 'It has been over a year, and still nothing. What of the use of a *degcha*?'

The small pot? I looked from Myassa to Dulfiya. The older woman studied me. 'There is but one physical route left, Daryâ. It may be that your womb is not positioned properly within your abdomen, and discourages entry of the seed. I will try to move it to the appropriate site. Let me see.' She pulled at the front of my *kamis*.

My heart sank. I knew the difficulty was not with my womb.

'Come. Come, girl. Show me. This is not the time for modesty.'

Staring at the woven wall of the yurt, I waited while Dulfiya's strong, wrinkled fingers probed and massaged my stomach.

'Hmmm,' she said, not looking at me as she worked. 'It feels as if the womb is aligned just so. There is no obvious displacement. But it could be that it is tipped inside. Myassa is right.' She let my *kamis* fall into place and looked into my face. 'On the chance that this is the case, I must use the *degcha*. Do not be afraid,' she said.

'I am not.'

She nodded. 'The method is far more simple than the wearing of skins, although if not used with knowledge, it can cause damage. I have done this many times over my years as a *dai*. It will straighten you, inside, and once this is done, the womb should be positioned with its mouth ready to grasp the seed. Come to me on the last day of your time. This is when you will be most receptive.'

Four days later I went to Dulfiya's yurt, carrying a small, delicately stitched cotton bag with a drawstring of thinly braided goat hair. Myassa had told me I must take the *dai* a token payment for her services.

Now Dulfiya wasted no time on conversation. 'Lie down and uncover your abdomen.'

When I had done so, she greased my skin with clarified butter. Taking a flat round of raw dough, she spread this over the butter. She left the tent, briefly, returning with a small clay pot. The *degcha*. It was wrapped in a thick cloth, and I could see smoke rising from the circular opening at the top.

'Within is a burning rag, secured to the bottom of the pot. I will place the mouth of the pot on the dough. The dough will take the heat, and the fire will not burn you. But do not move.'

'What will it do?' I asked, eyeing the hot container.

'As the air in the pot is exhausted by the flame, it will create a sucking sensation on the damp dough, and this, in turn, will pull hard on your skin. Hopefully, the pull will be great enough to also pull your womb into place.' She began the procedure.

As I was subjected to the warm, drawing, almost tearing, sensation on my skin, I felt a rush of despondency. All of these administrations. And to what end? It was clear that the curse was too strong to be overcome by medicines. Dulfiya was wasting her time, as had Myassa and Faiza. No one could help me; Allah did not see fit to rescue me from my predicament.

A sickening jolt in the pit of my stomach, not caused by the *degcha*, followed this last thought. Did Allah not think me worth his attention, then? Had I truly been such an ungrateful daughter, a disobedient, wilful and wicked female that he felt it right I should suffer with childlessness and my husband's wrath? Had I not attempted to be a better person, to go to the Ghilzai with lowered eyes, to be a nomad wife, working endlessly, obeying my husband and suffering his assaults? Shaliq never went hungry or dirty or without relief of his nightly need. I complained to no one when he beat me, and did I not try to follow the expectations of Islam?

Perhaps my grandmother had been wrong about me, and my father right, when he said that I saw myself as more than an ordinary woman, and looked – expected – more than others. I seemed unable, inwardly, to accept my fate with grace, so often questioning Allah's ways . . . and perhaps this was why the curse had not lifted. In an unusual rush of self-pity, tears filled my eyes.

'It hurts?' Dulfiya asked, surprised.

Ashamed, I shook my head. 'No. No, the tent is smoky from the *degcha*. My eyes burn, that's all.'

When the fire in the pot burned itself out, and the container cooled to Dulfiya's touch, she removed it and pulled the blackened dough from my skin. 'We will hope for the best, Daryâ. If this last step is not successful, well, as I told you, there is little else to be done. Except . . .'

I was wiping my skin clean of the grease and tiny remnants of sticky dough with the cloth Dulfiya handed me. Now I stopped. 'Except what?'

'Well, we know that if external methods do not work, the decision is in Allah's hands. You might ask Kaled if you could visit a *zyârat*, and pray there. Praying at the site of the tomb of a saint carries more power, and Allah's ears may be more open to your words. There is such a *zyârat* close to our winter camp, on the other side of Jalalabad. It is said to have much potency, and many have undertaken cures there.'

'Thank you, Dulfiya,' I told her, 'for your help today, and for your words that give hope.' I handed her the token gift, and she bestowed one of her infrequent, yet remarkable smiles upon me.

As I hurried back to my tent, I touched my abdomen lightly with my fingertips. Nothing felt different, but then there had never been anything wrong with my womb. The affliction brooded within my spirit.

A few months later, in our winter camp – my second winter with the Ghilzai – I thought of Dulfiya's advice about the shrine, and made the decision to approach Kaled. Since my marriage to Shaliq, I looked forward to my father-in-law's infrequent visits to our tent or yurt. He spent most of the time he was in camp with Hafeez and his family. But Kaled's voice was soft when he spoke to me, and a number of times I caught a pensive look on his face as I served him. The look made me think he carried guilt for the man his son had become.

I no longer even considered attempting to coax anything resembling kindness from Shaliq. I knew there was nothing there, no shred of compassion. I took his beatings with a studied acceptance, eventually learning his pattern for abuse, how to best protect myself, and how to prepare solutions which would ease the pains of the cuts and bruises.

Now I waited until Shaliq was busy with the herd, then carried a large fresh cake of dried apricots and almonds to Hafeez's tent, for the children. I knew Kaled was there, preparing for a trip to Jalalabad. There were great mounds of felt to sell.

He was sitting outside the huge tent – the largest in camp. It housed Kaled, Hafeez, his three wives and their increasing brood of children. Although Myassa believed she would bear no more children, as her body had been badly torn after the last birth, Hanouf had given birth to her third child, a second son, the winter before. Bibi's second child, a daughter, was past one and already Bibi carried another. So Hafeez's wives had given birth to nine living children. A sign of Allah's extraordinary approval.

Now the two babies, Hanouf's son and Bibi's daughter, climbed all over their grandfather, pulling at his long hair, sucking at his shiny earring, and poking inquisitive fingers into his ears and mouth. Kaled laughed, and I felt a surge of new respect as I watched him tickle his granddaughter's neck and then blow on her fat little stomach. I had never seen my father play with Nasreen in such a way; I knew he thought it might make her feel she were as important as Yusuf. But Kaled did not seem to fear such a reaction.

He looked up as I stood in front of him. 'Greetings, daughter. All goes well?'

'Greetings to you, Father. Yes, as Allah is my witness. I bring a cake for the children. I'll take it inside.'

As Kaled moved to let me pass, I stopped. 'And I wish to speak to you, if I may.'

He nodded.

I ducked inside and exchanged a few words with Hanouf, who was tending to Bibi. The woman's first stage of her pregnancy was making her ill. I quickly left the tent, and taking Hanouf's son from Kaled, put him on my lap. I buried my face in his thick, soft baby hair and smelled deeply. His scent reminded me so strongly of Yusuf that I closed my eyes in pleasure. When I opened them, I was embarrassed to see Kaled watching.

'He is so like my little brother,' I explained, my cheeks hot at my open display. 'I think of him every day, imagining the tall, strong boy he is becoming.'

'I know that Shaliq again denied you the privilege of visiting your home as we came down from the mountains,' Kaled said.

I played with the small curls at the baby's nape.

'You miss your family a great deal?' my father-in-law asked.

I could only nod, lowering my head to kiss the little boy's ear.

'Perhaps Shaliq will have a change of heart over the winter,' Kaled said. 'Susmâr Khord is less than a day's journey when we move upwards again in the spring . . .' he let the sentence hang, then continued, 'but of course it must be his choice, as your husband. Not mine.'

'Yes. I know.' The baby suddenly sucked vigorously on his dimpled fist, then looked around. 'He's hungry,' I said, watching as he squirmed off my lap and crawled into the tent. I heard Hanouf's murmurs, then silence.

'He's a clever boy,' I said. 'Not yet a year, and already he doesn't wait for what he wants, but goes in search of it.' I smiled at the little girl still sitting with Kaled; the child lay back against him, sleepy and relaxed.

'What did you wish to speak of, daughter?'

It was difficult to bring up so personal a matter, but Kaled's concerned voice helped. 'The *dai* and other women have tried fertility methods on me, and all have failed,' I said in a quiet voice, my eyes lowered, embarrassed. I pulled my head covering in front of my mouth and nose; it gave me more confidence to have my face half covered as I spoke of such an indelicate subject. I had considered asking Myassa to speak for me, but sensed that Kaled would respect me more for approaching him directly.

Now he sat in silence.

'There is only one option left. The *dai* spoke to me of a *zyârat* on the other side of Jalalabad. She says it is one with much power, of the Muslim martyr Murtaza, and Allah is often most merciful to those who perform their prayers there.' It was hard to continue. 'Could you allow me, at some time over the winter, to visit this tomb? I do not ask my husband, as any mention of my . . .' I stopped and took a breath. It must be said. 'My inability to conceive incites great anger. If he knows the truth of why I wish to visit Jalalabad, he will grow even more disturbed. But you travel into the city many times while we camp here, and you often take some of the women. I know it would be a large imposition to—'

'When do you wish to go?' he interrupted.

I looked at Kaled for the first time since I had sat opposite him. My mouth opened. I had not expected this reaction; in fact, I had prepared myself for accepting that he would not allow me to do something without my husband's knowledge.

'So? When do you wish to make this trip? I plan to go into Jalalabad in two days, the second market day. I will speak to Shaliq. Hanouf is also going; she'll be selling the extra vats of dried whey. This could be your purpose as well.'

I was so surprised, so grateful, that I reached out and took Kaled's hands in mine, and pressed them to my forehead. 'Thank you, my father,' I said, my voice loud and sure. I looked into his face. 'Thank you,' I repeated.

CHAPTER NINETEEN

In the dark I put on clean clothing and stepped outside, leaving Shaliq snoring heavily. I breathed deeply; the air was crisp and cool, and the grass covered with a thin rime that crunched underfoot. It would be gone as soon as the sun rose, for even in the coldest months, this low warm district in the river basin – almost entirely surrounded by hills – rarely had temperatures that allowed snow to stay.

I looked to the eastern sky, where the morning glow sent streaks of the palest shell-pink into the faint shadow of night stars. I closed my eyes and said my first prayer. I had always been secretly glad that women were not required to follow the same procedures as men: washing their eyes with water – or, if none was available, with dust – removing their shoes, covering their heads, and prostrating themselves as they prayed to Allah at dawn, noon, mid-afternoon, sunset, and after nightfall. And it was even more informal in camp. I saw that the other women simply closed their eyes for a moment, praying as they fed children, scrubbed clothes in icy streams, and sweated over hot cooking fires. And so I did the same. I knew that Allah heard our words, too, even though not uttered as loudly as the men's. He was a Just God, after all.

I could still hear Shaliq's snoring through the tent walls. He had grudgingly given his consent when his father told him he would take Hanouf and me with him to sell the whey.

'But remember,' he had warned me, the night before, 'no matter what frivolous trinkets you see in the bazaar, any afghanis you take for the whey are mine. You must bring it all back to me. I know how much the curd will bring, so don't try and cheat me.'

'Of course not, Shaliq,' I answered.

Nothing could spoil my mood. I had a quiet sense of optimism at the thought of visiting the *zyârat*. But overwhelming that was pure excitement. I was going to Jalalabad. I had only ever seen a city in my mind – now I would see a real one.

The small party rode away from the gathering of black tents just as the sun peeked over the lowest mountain. On my first day with the Ghilzai I had thought that the tents had the appearance of butterflies. Now, as I viewed them over my shoulder from a distance, they slumped like giant sleeping toads.

Kaled and two other men, Abdul and Sameer, as well as Hanouf and I, rode in single file along the outer edge of the lush green land near the river. The land was treeless but filled with harvest stalks of corn as well as sugar cane. We followed a path made by hundreds of years of nomads and their animals, the horses' hooves occasionally ringing out as they hit a large, jutting stone. We followed the thread of a trail for some time, then Kaled suddenly swung his horse down through a gully and across a dry stream bed that I imagined would be filled with rushing water by spring rains. As we came up the other side and on to a pebbly plateau, Kaled stopped, and we gathered around him.

Jalalabad lay before us, spread out in a wide, flat plain.

I could never have imagined so many buildings existing in one place. I grew dizzy trying to focus on everything at once, and then, with a start, realised the others were urging their horses downward, towards that place of wonder. I nudged my small, well-muscled filly to catch up.

As we drew ever nearer, I could see the clear outlines of the cupolas of mosques standing out against the pale winter sky. Palm trees grew in abundance. Soon we were close enough to the outskirts, where the huge bazaar was held on this day, to smell the wafting odours of cooking food. And then I heard the shouts of the sellers hawking their wares and saw, on the very edge of the bazaar, kebab stands. I breathed in the rich greasiness of grilled lamb on skewers, and eggs sizzling in mutton fat. Kaled held up a hand, and we drew beside him.

'I have an errand on the other side of the city. I will take Daryâ,' he said. 'Hanouf, stay with Abdul and Sameer.'

The two men nodded, and Hanouf pulled down the dark veil she had attached to her head covering. I did the same.

'Sell Daryâ's curds with your own, Hanouf, and you will divide the money evenly,' Kaled told her, dismounting. 'We will meet you at the horse market before the call to prayer at noon.'

Abdul jumped from his horse and unstrapped the large, sealed jugs I had tied over my saddle, attaching them to his own. Kaled heaped the load of felt he carried behind his saddle to Sameer's pile, and before he had climbed back on his horse, the two men and Hanouf had ridden off to the left.

Kaled and I started on the rough road leading straight into the city. 'It is faster to go through than around,' he said. 'Follow me closely so you don't get lost.'

I saw that on this outer fringe of the bazaar grimy blankets were spread on the dust, with a showing of perhaps six eggs or a poorly brocaded vest. Ragged children sat by the blankets, looking up hopefully as we passed. Next came a row of small stalls selling raw sugar, salt, rice, and low quality cloth, and it took every ounce of my will to keep my eyes on Kaled's back as we slowly rode into the main street of the bazaar.

Luckily it was early, and the streets were not yet overly crowded, so I had little difficulty directing my horse through the wide road of stalls and shops. I spotted young men on some of the roofs, splashing down glittering arcs of water to dampen the fine dust of the street that threatened to coat their polished fruits and vegetables. I kept my head positioned, but under my veil my eyes were darting from left to right, trying to take in all the sights. There were sounds and smells I couldn't identify.

And then I saw a strange man. He was dressed in a short, tight, red jacket. The jacket was decorated with many silver buttons. His skin was pale, his hair the colour of the sun. I had never seen such golden hair.

'Father,' I said, and he turned.

'What kind of man is that? In the red coat.'

Kaled's expression was wary. 'It is a soldier. From Hendustân. The country to the south.' He slowed so that I was beside him.

'He is like the soldiers who fought our men in the war? Many years ago, when I was a child.'

Kaled nodded. 'The First War of the white-skinned *khârejis* and the Afghans.'

'These soldiers killed my father's brother,' I told him.

'And many of my brothers,' he said. 'I fought in that war.'

'But why are they here?'

Now Kaled's face grew even tighter. 'Things change. We are no longer at war with them; they are free to come to our country.'

Suddenly an obstinate donkey, pulling a cart loaded with peppers and green fodder, jibbed in front of Kaled, momentarily barring his path. As we waited for the road to clear, a bird screeched so loudly that I turned to look for it. In an open-air *chây-khâna* I saw a colourful myna perched in a wicker cage, and as he let out a rhythmic, scratchy whistle, I realised he was saying, in Dari, 'Praise Allah! Praise Allah!' It truly was an amazing thing.

Then I saw the huge glass containers of tea leaves – the black tea which I knew came from Hendustân, and the green tea, imported by the Turkomen who lived in the far, north-east corner of Afghanistan. A big brass urn sat on a low table, and behind it, a whole sagging shelf of chipped teapots, all of the thinnest white opaqueness, painted with delicate pink roses. I gazed with awe at the beauty of the old porcelain pots, and had a desire to run my hands over their fragile smoothness.

The donkey was silent now, head down as its owner tugged on the reins. Kaled waited patiently. I quickly looked to my left.

The stall across from the *chây-khâna* sold footwear such as I had never seen – from curly toed, bright red embroidered slippers to the tallest, stiffest riding boots, complete with cruel, pointed spurs.

Hearing a high tinkling laugh, I followed the sound to the stall next to the one with the footwear. Three shrouded women, their heads dainty and round under their ankle-length *châdari*, bartered with a man selling aubergines and pomegranates. The *châdaris* were finely pleated and of thin, soft material, with only a section of gauze over the eyes. As the women moved, the garments swung about them gracefully, and they gave the impression of a trio of small, charming bells.

With an angry belch, the donkey decided to move on, and once again I followed Kaled. We eventually left the bazaar and rode through quieter streets, and I now saw the mosques whose slim minarets I had spotted from the distance. Through the open doorways their cool beauty – floors and walls covered with rich blue- and green-glazed tiles – was visible. Studying the simple yet graceful shapes of the buildings, I thought, with a sudden intake of breath, how grand the barren, mud-walled mosque of Susmâr Khord had seemed to me. Now I realised it was small and poor.

It was as if my eyes were seeing as they had never seen before, as if they were sending words to my brain, filling it with both delight and yet, at the same time, a nudging of discontent. That there was all of this – all of these things to see, to touch, to hear and smell – and yet I was to have none of it. Now the fierce longing to hold the delicate china teapots filled me in a darker, deeper way. I had not expected to feel this way – this swooping, anxious dissatisfaction. This was only a small sample of the life my grandmother had known, and tried to explain to me. This is what she wanted me to know. To live.

On wide, shallow steps which led into a building adjoining the side of another mosque, I saw a group of seven well-dressed boys, no more than eight years old, listening with rapt attention to a dignified, elderly mullah who was instructing them in the teachings of Islam. The balcony of the building, fronted with wooden panels which were carved with circles and hexagons, was supported by pillars of wood also carved with an intricate swirling pattern.

It is a *madrasa*, I thought, a school for boys that my father had once told me about after returning from Kabul. I looked at the earnest young faces and heard the chant of their high, unbroken voices as they followed the mullah's teaching. They were only a few years older than Yusuf, but what were his chances of ever having learning as these boys did? True, the mullah of Susmâr Khord would instruct him, but now I even doubted the depth of that man's knowledge.

I didn't like the heavy, bitter taste – the bile of envy and regret – that grew in the back of my throat, and was glad when we left the area of mosques. Now we emerged on to streets of handsome, high houses with their walled courtyards. I looked at one beautiful house three levels high, its windows covered with carved, latticed shutters to keep out the sun and the prying eyes of the city. A barred gate opened, and as a man walked out, I caught a glimpse of the inner courtyard. There were terraces, planted with flowers and blooming bushes and, in the marbled centre, a huge pruned tree which created a shady haven. Under the tree was a wooden bench padded with cushions of dizzying colours, and on the bench sat a woman, unveiled. A small dog lay at her feet. The woman's face was beautiful, placid, with much kohl and cheek and lip colour. Her hair was heavily oiled and hung in twisted plaits over her breasts. Her dress, a green soft as spring, was sewn around the yoke with sparkling pieces of glass that sent out flashes of light and reflection. The woman touched her reddened lips with her fingertips and fluttered them at the man. As he closed the gate and faced the street, I saw a pleased look on his face.

I looked down at my own dusty pantaloons and *kamis*. My *chapli*, the open-backed sandals of the Ghilzai women, were frayed and worn. I saw my dark, calloused hands clutching the reins, and tried to imagine ever waving to a man with such open, light-hearted affection.

You have not come to see the marvels of a city and to feel sorry for yourself because you grew up a cloistered village girl, learning about life only through the tales of your grandmother. Now you are a nomad's wife. And you came here, through the good grace of your father-in-law, to pray to the Omnipotent Allah to give you power over the curse. You must be grateful, and not measure your life against that of others.

I set my lips into a stern line. Then I raised my chin and straightened my shoulders as we continued to ride down the quiet, orderly street. But I could not shake off the disillusionment that filled me.

Finally Kaled turned on to a narrow side road outside the last of the poorer homes on the far edge of the city. After a short ride, he pointed to a jumbled pile of stones in a small grove of lemon trees. An ancient man, supporting himself with a gnarled branch, hobbled among the trees.

As I dismounted, Kaled held out his open hand. I saw the glint of several afghanis in the wan sunlight.

'Take these,' he said. 'You must buy a small token – an amulet – from the keeper of the shrine. It is thought to help the wish of the devout to be more readily answered. And it's the livelihood of the old one.' He motioned with his chin at the hunched man, whose toothless mouth worked busily as he lurked behind a leafy tree, squinting at what was probably his first company of the day. 'He will make your visit more pleasant if you cross his palm.'

'Thank you,' I said, taking the cool coins and studying them. It was the first time I had held money.

'I will wait for you, just there,' Kaled said, gesturing to a pleasant grassy area under a tall hawthorn tree across the road. He caught up the reins of my filly and led it away.

I hesitantly approached the old man. He came, trembling, from the trees to meet me. He was shorter than I, or perhaps just bent with age. His turban was filthy, his clothes no more than rags. He smelled of layers of dirt and grime.

'Ah, young wife,' he said, in Dari, his tongue poking out between thin, colourless lips. 'I see the eyes of a Tajik, but the clothing of a Pushtun.'

I said nothing.

'And there is more, more to you than that. This I see. You are a stranger among us.'

This last sentence confused me; he stared too intently at me. His eyes were small, the whites yellowed, and yet his look was one of intelligence. I pulled my headscarf lower, so that my face was almost hidden.

'My apologies, young wife. What my eyes see comes directly from my mouth. You have come to ask our saint, Murtaza, to speak directly to Allah for you?'

I nodded.

'And the favour, fine wife? The favour is for . . . ?'

I realised he expected an answer. That I must voice my prayer aloud.

'Fertility,' I said.

'Eh?' he called, cocking his head and moving closer. I leaned away from his foul odour.

'Fertility,' I said, loudly, glancing around to assure that no one else was present to hear me admit my failing.

'Ah-ha, yes. For that I have the amulet of the most special *ta'wiz*. Guaranteed to cure you. Yes, yes, come. You must have the amulet.'

I followed him to the hard-packed ground in front of the shrine, where a large, crudely stitched bag of soiled cotton lay. Muttering to himself, the old man pawed through it until he pulled out a small square of leather. 'This is it. Yes, this is the one,' he said then gave a tiny, high scream of laughter. 'Yes. I knew I had it.' He held it towards me, but as I reached for it he snatched it back and cradled it tenderly against his chest with one dirty hand. I saw a sly glint come to his eyes now.

I immediately opened my own clenched fist, showing the three afghanis on my palm.

'Ahhhh.' A long sigh of pleasure came from the old man. 'Only two, only two afghanis for the amulet, but for all three, why, my fine wife, you can be sure of oh, so much more of the saint's services.' Now, like a small swallow, his hand swooped down with amazing agility, and I stood with an empty palm.

'Keep the *ta'wiz* upon you at all times,' he said. 'It contains sacred words of the Koran.' He dropped the tiny leather packet into my still-outstretched hand. 'And now, come.'

He led me closer to the mound of stones. I saw an assortment of objects stuck between the round rocks – stubs of candles, remnants of cloth, tiny primitive clay figures. His smell was making me ill.

'Before you pray, because of the added afghani, you are allowed a most exalted honour,' he prattled on, reaching behind a particularly large rock and pulling out a dirt-encrusted cloth. He unfolded it and withdrew several small objects, gazing at them with great tenderness. Then he lifted his eyes to mine, and I saw tears shining through the slits of his eyelids.

Suddenly I wondered how I had seen intelligence in his eyes. Now he watched me as a hungry animal watches a smaller one.

He extended the treasure to me, and I automatically reached forward. Then, realising what I was seeing, I snatched back my hand as if I had been burned.

'Take them, take them carefully. Fondle them. Do not be afraid. They are the consecrated finger bones of our martyr Murtaza,' the old man said, nodding at me.

I backed away from the quivering hand holding the grey, mealy bones, shaking my head.

'Now, now, come, fine wife,' he said, his voice reedy and cracked. 'Your ancestors are around you. I see them. They urge you to pray. You have not yet prayed, nor eaten a pinch of the earth of the tomb.' His voice rose as I kept backing away. 'It is Mother Earth herself who can impregnate you. Your body is ripe. I can see this.' His eyes rested on my abdomen. He smiled, but this smile was even more frightening than his words.

I turned and ran from the site, dropping the small square of leather, stumbling in my haste to reach Kaled, who was leaning against the hawthorn tree, arms crossed over his chest as he gazed at a flock of birds winging high overhead. My veil blew back over the top of my head. Hearing my footsteps, Kaled looked in my direction.

'What is it, Daryâ? Did he try to harm you?' he asked at my obvious distress.

I shook my head. 'No. But I was not comfortable in such a place. I did not feel it to be a sanctuary of hope, but one of death and despair.

Please, let's go from here.' I swung myself on to my horse and urged it down the path, towards the city. Within a moment I realised, with shame, that I had taken the dominant position, in front of Kaled. I stopped my horse and lowered my head as he rode beside me. The reins fell from my hands and I sat, slouched, upon the saddle.

He stopped beside me.

'Forgive me, Father,' I said. 'Not only for this rashness, but for wasting your time and afghanis.' I looked at him. 'I fear it was foolishness. I do not mean to blaspheme. I try so hard to believe in the goodness of Allah, but for me, prayer at such a place could do no good. I expected a feeling of enlightenment. Instead, I felt hopelessness. Was it wrong of me not to pray? Is it wrong of me to not always . . . believe?'

Kaled reached over and took up my reins. He started his own horse, continuing to hold my reins so that our horses walked together. Even though upset I wondered at this – that he would allow me to move along beside him, instead of behind, as was my expected place.

'The tombs, the martyrs, prayers, faith in a Higher Being . . . all can be a great source of comfort. But some of us,' he paused, 'perhaps also believe in our own ability, as well as in Allah's will. In determination and perseverance. Some do not need to lean on the crutches as heavily as others.'

I was stunned by Kaled's pronouncement. There came to me then the sense of hope I had wanted to find at the tomb. Kaled spoke to me as if I were his son, not his daughter-in-law. I could tell he now waited for me to speak in response. There was so much I wanted to say, but I knew the ways of men primarily from my father and my husband. It was difficult to speak openly to Kaled.

'I see these things in you, Daryâ,' he said, encouraging me. 'As well as the determination and perseverance I just spoke of, there is strength within you. That is clear. I saw it from the first day, and I knew this would make your life with Shaliq difficult.'

I couldn't look at him. At his unexpected compliments something rose within me, something that had been trapped, waiting to fly into the air. I chose my words very carefully. We still rode side-by-side, both of us looking straight ahead. 'Yes,' I said. 'I also believe this to be so – that lives can be changed through determination and belief in one's own ability – but only if you are a man. Only if you are a man, Father. A man can shape his future; he calls this Allah's will. He can work with it like a good pilau, the rice ready to be held and rolled and moulded, depending on the strength and size of his hands, and the vision of his eye.' I realised my voice had grown stronger, but Kaled did not stop me with a glance or a click of his tongue, and so I continued, bolder. 'But a woman's future is merely a single grain of rice; alone, she is useless, helpless, unworthy of attention. She must multiply, become more than one, and then, with many other grains, can be shaped only as far as the man who holds her wishes, for she has no control, no voice. No freedom.'

My face was hot, and I knew my cheeks were flushed. I had never spoken of such things to anyone, let alone a man – and my own father-in-law, at that. He didn't answer, and I feared I had gone too far. But when turned to me, his face was sorrowful rather than angry.

'I hear your words. I understand your frustration. But even for those of us who are not wholly obedient, who question beliefs, and Allah's wisdom . . .' I stopped breathing, amazed that he would speak of such things. He said *those of us*, not *you*.

We rode in silence, and I thought he had finished, but suddenly he continued. 'As I said, you have a strong spirit, Daryâ. Too strong for my son. You and I both know this, and although he knows it, too, he can't understand or accept it. He sees little beyond the distance of his hand in front of his face. You frighten him, Daryâ, with your quiet strength, your grace. Had I known of these traits, I would not have subjected you to a marriage with him.'

I grew even warmer at his words, at his admittance that he knew the marriage was not a happy one in any way.

'But because of these traits, in order to have a life not filled with misery with Shaliq, you will have to learn to smother some of your fire, Daryâ. Smother it, so that you do not burn so brightly.'

I wanted to cry out: *Why must I? Why must it be that I have to struggle to be less than I am?* But I said nothing, wanting him to speak further.

When he did, his voice was low, full of regret. 'A woman like you, Daryâ . . . you are wasted with a man like Shaliq. But this is the fate that has been given to you, and you can't change it. And so you will have to live this life, daughter. Just live, and try not to imagine what might have been.'

He looked at me with deep sadness, and then urged his horse forward.

As I followed in his dust, it was clear that he knew me much more than my own husband ever would. The words that had been most painful haunted me: *You are wasted with a man like Shaliq.* Wasted. Is this how I would have to think of my life? I knew he was telling me he couldn't offer me any hope for my future with Shaliq. But to say I couldn't change my fate was another.

Yes, Kaled knew me, perhaps more than any of the Ghilzai, and yet he didn't know one thing. For him to tell me to try not to imagine what might have been – what still might be – was like telling me not to sleep, not to eat. Not to breathe.

Had my grandmother truly believed that her fate was written on her forehead? I reached up and touched my own as we rode into Jalalabad.

My fingers touched only skin. My future was not yet written.

PART TWO

Under the Blade of the Indian Sun, Two Years Later

CHAPTER TWENTY

I LIT A LAMP and took off my torn *kamis*. I bathed my wounds with water, then sprinkled a few herbs into a small gourd, added water, drop by drop, and mixed it to a paste with my fingers. Flinching, I patted the balm over the lacerations on my breasts and thighs.

When the solution had dried, I carefully eased a clean loose *kamis* over my head. I poured more cool water on to a wadded cloth and dabbed at my lips, removing the dry blood. Finally, I soaked the cloth and held it to my throbbing eye. It would swell and darken within a few hours.

I knew Shaliq would stay away from me for the next five days of my pollution. Exploring my face very carefully with my fingertips, I also knew I would stay hidden as much as possible, and wear my veil when I left the tent – at least until the worst of the swelling and discoloration had diminished. I hated the shamefulness that came over me now when I walked through the camp after one of my beatings. It seemed that everyone's eyes turned towards me, and there were whispers as I walked by.

While I stayed in my tent Faiza would bring me anything I needed; we visited each other daily, and if I didn't appear for a day she would come to see if I was all right. And if I wasn't, she would care for me.

She was my only real friend here now that Hafeez's family no longer lived with us.

They had left us six months ago. Unexpectedly, in the heat of the last summer, Kaled's brother, chief of a large tribe, had been knocked from his horse and trampled in a wild herd. He died of his injuries, and although he had many daughters, he had no sons to step in and claim their right as chief. Kaled had suggested that Hafeez take over that tribe. Of course, we all wondered at this decision, for was it not expected that Hafeez would one day be our chief? But Kaled insisted on Hafeez taking over his dead brother's tribe. He announced that with Allah's protection he would rule our camp for a number of years to come. And everyone knew, although nobody voiced it, that in those years he could work on helping Shaliq grow into the kind of man who could take over from him in due time.

But since Hafeez and his wives – my sisters – had gone, the camp grew less caring, more full of gossip and disharmony. Kaled was away even more frequently, as if he, too, found the camp less welcoming. Shaliq was of little help in keeping the emotions and morale of the tribe on an even keel.

Without Myassa's maternal affections, Hanouf's cool advice, and Bibi's friendship, to say nothing of the noise and excitement created by their children who called me *tendâr* – auntie – with genuine love, I felt lonely and overwhelmed.

Now, I felt as if I lived my life in an abyss. I woke, worked, ate, and slept. I no longer prayed; I had stopped all my prayers well over a year ago. Nobody knew this, of course, and it hadn't been a conscious decision. It had happened slowly; after many of my beatings, when I lay, dazed and only half conscious, I lost track of the time of day, and often a number of days went by before I realised I had not offered up my prayers. When it was my unclean time I was forbidden to pray, but then there were the days following, when I told myself I would pray as soon as I had finished with the work, as soon as I had prepared the meal, or taken food to Utmarkhail. I told myself surely I would pray the next day.

After a while I did not pray at all, and did not feel wicked for this secret, blasphemous rebellion. I did not think of things merciful. I just lived, as Kaled had told me to do: it became one continual, monotonous circle, with nothing to look forward to, and I felt less and less accepted by the other women because I had not added to the numbers of their tribe. I realised, after my sisters had left, how crucial they had been in making sure the other women accepted me. Worse still was that now Shaliq expected me to care for his mother. Apart from the food I prepared, Myassa had always seen to anything she needed. But with her gone, the duty fell to me.

I was wary of the strange, obese woman; she watched me, as I brought her food and carried away her soiled clothing and bedding, with small, pig-like eyes. Once, as I reached for her empty water jug, she grabbed my wrist and brought it to her nose, sniffing my flesh. Then she dropped it, muttering under her breath.

I tried to find sympathy for her; I knew she was possessed by *jinn* and that her actions were not within her control. But it was difficult, especially after I found out that she made up lies about me to whisper to her son. More than once Shaliq had slapped me or pushed me to the ground because his mother told him I had not brought her food, or had been disrespectful to her when he was not in camp.

'It's not true,' I said, loudly, the first time he accused me of these doings. 'I care for her with respect. I feed her every day, and she is as clean as I can keep her. Why does she say these things? And why do you believe her? You know she is –' I stopped as Shaliq raised his hand again.

'Don't say things against my mother,' he said. 'It is you who try to deceive me, with your lies. I watch you, Daryâ. I know how you talk with the other women against me, how you ignore my mother's needs when I'm not here. You and your talk, your open stares. You have too many words.'

I didn't want to be beaten any more than I could help it. When Shaliq was near I kept my head turned away so he could not accuse me of anything. And I grew more and more silent.

Only Faiza continued to befriend me, but it was difficult for us to spend much time together. She was busy with her two little ones, and was thin and tired. Dark circles surrounded her eyes, and she had a wet cough that had started last spring and continued to grow worse over the summer, instead of clearing up as most coughs did in warmer weather. The trek down from our summer pasture had been difficult for her; I had to help her set up her winter tent a few weeks ago, when we settled in our camp far south. It was apparent she grew steadily weaker.

Her husband Qul had plans to take a second wife from a tribe of Durrani Pushtuns at the end of the winter. Faiza met this news with pleasure; she told me she couldn't wait until spring to have an extra pair of hands to help her, as she was sometimes overcome with a curious weakness that left her sweating and dizzy, unable to care properly for her children or do her work. I worried for my friend, although at the same time I knew that it was also my own selfishness that added to my anxious concern. A tiny, selfish voice told me that Faiza was the only person who kept me from being an outcast.

Now, alone in the dark tent with my injuries, I prepared to sleep. I knew with certainty that my pain would not weaken me. I had grown used to it, my body ever tougher. I used the stories – the stories I kept for the worst of times, not pulling them out to tell myself unless I really needed them, such as now, after a severe beating – to keep the pain from enclosing me in its iron grip. They had become my form of prayer, something to believe in: these stories my grandmother had put into my head. The stories of the *zenana*, the poetry and songs, and also the story of her white-skinned man from England – the beloved with whom she was now in paradise – took on a life and rhythm. I envied my grandmother now in a way I hadn't while she was alive, when I was still too young and foolish, when I dreamed that, like her, I would also have a man who held my heart, tenderly, in his hand.

Now I also made up my own stories, tales that I spun and wove as I imagined the women in the *zenana* had done – to help pass the long night hours.

I was always the heroine of my stories. I was the woman with the painted face I had seen in the beautiful courtyard in Jalalabad; I was a woman who rode a horse, free and wild, over the plains. I was an unveiled woman men gazed upon, captured by my beauty; I was a woman who held a child in my arms, and felt the beat of its heart against mine. I was the British woman with the helmet – the female warrior who ruled even the waves.

All stories which could never be true. Stories I could never tell anyone, for they were only fanciful and childish and bore no weight. They were not stories of bravery or charity or piousness. They were silly and shallow, and I was fully aware that I should create stories of more substance. And yet they helped, and at times I felt they became more true than my own life.

I slept deeply and awoke slowly, groggy and unrefreshed. I saw, by the meagre light around the flap of the tent, that the sun had already risen, and it was too late for me still to be under the quilt. But a listless apathy held me down. There seemed little reason to rise this day: in my unclean state Shaliq would eat his morning meal at another's tent.

Nobody would even notice, for these morning hours, that I was not outside my tent. I would have to prepare food and take it to Utmarkhail soon, though, or there would be an additional beating when she complained to Shaliq.

I moved slightly, awakening the pain. I was thirsty, and yet could not bear the thought of pulling my stiffened body from the warmth of the quilts. I closed my eyes and must have slept again, for I awoke to hear Faiza softly calling me from outside the tent.

'Come,' I said, and when she lifted the flap and the light streamed in, she put her hand to her mouth.

'It grows worse,' she said, hurrying to the jug and pouring me a gourd of water. The water was warm and stale, but I gulped it down, propping myself painfully on one elbow.

I nodded. 'Yes. This time was bad.' I slowly positioned myself and sat up, taking deep, slow breaths.

Faiza touched the side of my face, and I winced. 'I fear for you, Daryâ. Can you not implore Kaled to –'

'He has often spoken to Shaliq, but I am not Kaled's wife. He cannot direct Shaliq's behaviour towards me – especially when he is not here.'

I saw the waxiness of Faiza's complexion as she suddenly coughed so violently that she lowered herself to the ground; it was as if she didn't have the strength to remain standing. She took a cloth from within her sleeve and held it over her mouth, and when she pulled it away I saw a smear of blood before she could tuck it in her sleeve again.

'It is I who worry about you,' I told her.

Faiza held up one hand, putting the other against her chest while she caught her breath. 'It will pass.' She took a shallow breath. 'I wanted to tell you that Shaliq has left camp – he and Qul and some of the other men have ridden into Sala for a few days. They will do some trading.'

I thought of the freedom of Shaliq and Qul and the other men. They could come and go to the villages near camp as they chose.

'Do you ever wish to go to Sala, or any other villages or towns?' I asked Faiza. 'Do you want to choose your own cloth, finger the vegetables yourself? Sit and drink tea with other women, women not of our camp?'

'What are you talking about, Daryâ? Why would I want to go where

I knew no one? I have my family and my friends here. And Qul knows best what we need. Are you fevered?' She put her hand on my cheek.

I shook my head. 'No. I only wish . . .'

'Wish what? I don't understand. Do you want something specific, something Shaliq doesn't bring to you when he goes to trade?'

Again I shook my head. I shouldn't expect Faiza to understand. She had known only this Ghilzai camp all her life. But still – did she have no dreams, no desires? Her face was so kind, so concerned. Like Gawhar, back in Susmâr Khord, Faiza also was a good, faithful friend who didn't understand my longings. How could I blame her for what she didn't feel? 'I'm glad Shaliq is away. It's easier for me when I know I won't have to see his face for a few days,' I said, changing the subject.

'Will you come to my tent and eat, later?'

'I have to prepare something and take it to Utmarkhail.'

'I'll see to it. You rest today, and when you feel well enough, come and join me and the children.'

I nodded, smiling at her pale face. 'I will, Faiza. Thank you.'

The next day I dressed in my new burgundy *kamis* and headscarf. I had made them with a bolt of cloth given to me by Myassa before she left. I had planned to keep them for a special ceremony, but such was my low spirit when I awoke that I put them on. It gave me pleasure to feel the stiff newness of the rich, bright cloth, to see my own fine stitching. My only sadness was that I wore it only for myself, and for no one else.

That afternoon, as I washed clothes at the stream, I looked up, often, at our winter camp, and thought of the long months to come. Although we were situated in a sheltered area, it didn't have the beauty of our summer pastures. We had passed within sight and smell of the smoke from the chimneys of Susmâr Khord on our way south, and although I had, as usual, asked, with exaggerated caution, if I might ride to the village for even a few hours to visit my mother, before I'd even finished the sentence Shaliq walked away, shaking his head. As I'd lain in bed that night, I wondered if the beating he would give me would be worth sneaking out and riding there. But I was afraid that as soon as he discovered I was not under the quilts he would also ride to Susmâr Khord, and then – what was the possibility that he might somehow discover the curse?

So I had stayed where I was, listening to his snores, in the dark.

* * *

I had almost finished my washing when I heard my name being called. It came out in a long wailing cry. I dropped the scarf I was scrubbing on to the rock and straightened, looking around in alarm. Faiza ran towards me.

'Daryâ! Daryâ,' she called, 'oh, Daryâ.' I came to meet her, seeing how truly ill she looked. She pressed both hands to her chest, gasping out my name.

'What? What, Faiza? What's happened? Is it one of the children?'

She couldn't catch her breath, and I tried to make her sit, but she shook her head, grabbing my arms. 'Qul. Qul is – home. He – he came to – he . . .'

'You're frightening me, Faiza. What's wrong with Qul?'

She shook her head again, taking one more gasp. 'It's not Qul, Daryâ,' she said, finally finding her breath. 'He rode home – he left before the others and galloped all the way – ahead of Shaliq. They were in one of the teahouses in Sala, and Shaliq heard – Qul said some Tajiks were talking, and . . .' She stared at me, tears in her eyes – were they from the pain in her chest or something more? 'Is it true, Daryâ? Is it true, what Qul heard? What Shaliq heard? About you?'

I licked my lips, swallowing. 'What is it they heard?'

'A curse, Daryâ. A heathen curse. That your father traded you, knowing you were barren.'

Her eyes held mine. They were brown, the colour of pale tea. I knew Faiza wanted me to deny it, to tell her another story. 'It is true,' I said. I turned my head towards the stream. 'Yes. I was cursed by a Kafir.'

'But, Daryâ, if you knew, if you knew you could not bear a child – all the remedies we tried, all this time of –'

I looked back at her. 'I wanted to believe the curse would be lifted. By my prayers, by my belief in Allah, Faiza. Surely you can understand that.'

Now Faiza glanced over her shoulder, then looked back, holding my eyes with hers. 'Qul says – Qul says . . . I cannot say the words, Daryâ.'

I stared at her.

'Shaliq returns any time. And Daryâ, Qul says he announced to all that he will . . . he will beat you . . . to the death. Because you have been wicked, and lied while speaking the name of Allah, and you were not worthy to come to him as a wife. And so you must be punished.

He is your husband, and nobody can stop him. Nobody but Kaled. As chief, Kaled would protect you. He would not allow –' She looked behind her again. 'But who knows when Kaled will return? Do you hear horses, Daryâ? Could Shaliq be here already? Maybe he only boasts; he would not do as he says, would he?'

'He will,' I said. 'He will.'

'Oh, Daryâ, what will we do? How can I help you?'

I stared at the wide circle of tents, at the smoke from the fires. I heard the laughter and cries of children, women's voices calling to one another, the baaing and bleating of the sheep and goats, the loud nasal complaint of a camel. I looked back at Faiza; she twisted her hands in distress, tears on her cheeks.

I thought of the corrals, wondered if there was time to run there, to take a horse – but the shout of a man jarred me. Was he back? There was no time. I knew what I must do. I grabbed Faiza and held her tightly against me in a fierce hug.

'Daryâ,' she said against my hair, 'what will you do?'

'Goodbye, Faiza, goodbye,' I said, pulling back, staring into her tear-filled eyes.

'But . . . where are you going?'

'I don't know,' I said. 'But I can't stay.'

'Daryâ, you must – it is Allah's will that Shaliq has found out. And so it is Allah who will protect you now.'

I knew she was trying to comfort me, but I could say nothing in reply. Instead, I hugged her again. 'Thank you for all you have done.' I kissed her cheeks. 'Stay well. I will think of you,' I said, and then turned and ran, splashing through the shallow stream towards the forest on the other side. A flock of rooks rose in alarm from the tall grass at the edge of the river, circling above me, cawing with harsh, scolding voices.

I ran from my only home and the only family I had had for almost four years, with nothing but the clothes I wore. My *chapli* were soaked through, my headscarf wound around my neck so that it wouldn't impede my vision. I needed to see the ground and avoid any jutting rocks; I needed to search out the thickest copses of trees, the ones which would prove impossible for a horse to push through, which might best hide the path I broke.

I didn't look back. If it was Allah's will that Shaliq had discovered the curse, it was my will to stay alive.

* * *

I ran eastward, through the forest. I ran until my lungs burned as if the fire there would consume me, and I had to stop, gasping for breath, bent over with my hands on my knees. And then I ran again, my hand pressing the ever-constant pain in my side. At one time, while stopping to catch new breath to run again, I heard, muffled by trees and bushes and distance, the whinny of horses, an angry shout. I hid in the midst of some brambles, my skin and clothing torn by the sharp thorns. Crouching there, my eyes closed, I willed the men to go in another direction, making a picture in my head of them turning and riding away from where I hid. And, as if I had made it come true with my own thoughts, the sounds became fainter and then died away. I waited until I could no longer stay still, and then carefully made my way out, making sure no bits of cloth were caught, fluttering on the brambles, markers of the way I had come.

The patch of sky above the tops of the trees had lost its brightness, and I knew I was safe for this one night, at least. Shaliq would not attempt to find me in the dark.

I sat with my back against the thick bark of a wide tree. Here, far to the south, summer had not completely passed, and the days were still warm, but the the night was cold, and my shivering kept me alert. Around me I heard the sounds of the forest: the cry of the swooping, hungry night bird, the rustling in the fallen leaves by the small animals who only move about in darkness, the wet snuffling of something large, some creature who walked with confidence through the black night, who had surely caught my scent but must have recently filled his belly with other prey. A light rain fell as I sat, alone and afraid. The rain was not heavy enough for water to gather in my cupped palms, just enough to dampen everything. Around me arose the smell of decaying leaves and spongy earth, of moss and mould: an ancient, rotted and yet sweet smell. The patter of drops on the leaves that still clung to these trees was comforting, a rhythm that lulled me, made my heart stop its frenzied beat. I thought of my village, of sitting on the roof of my home in a soft autumn rain, knowing where I belonged.

I thought of how I had not prayed to Allah for protection as I sat in the brambles. And then I thought of the curse, and of Shaliq's wrath. In the dark, so alone, a very tiny idea lit in my mind, an idea I told myself was foolish, caused by fear, by cold and hunger. But . . . could it be that

Shaliq was also cursed – that Allah did not see fit to give him children because of his cruel nature? I was his third wife. It was strange indeed that not one of three women bore a child while married to Shaliq. Could it be that my curse had actually lifted, but it was Shaliq's who stopped me from conceiving?

You think too much, Daryâ. Wasn't it my own father – and then my husband – who had accused me of this? I cast the thought away, and closed my eyes.

With the first lightening of the sky I rose, stiff, shaking away the small snails that had gathered among the folds of my *kamis*. My hands and my face – alongside the still-tender swellings caused by Shaliq – were scratched by the brambles and slapping branches of the bushes I pushed through. In their thin *chapli* the bottoms of my feet were bruised and cut from the sharp rocks and gnarled roots. I kept looking up through the tops of the trees, going in the opposite direction of the travels of the sun. I headed ever-eastward, away from the position of the camp. Occasionally I found rainwater gathered in the curled leaves of a plant, and carefully put my lips to it and sucked it up. By the middle of that second day I had come out of the shadows of the forest into the brightness of a valley. I made my way into the hillside, trying to stay hidden by the bushes and rocks, stopping and dropping to the ground when I heard a sound that I didn't recognise, holding my breath to make certain it wasn't the beat of hooves, the familiar curses Shaliq favoured.

I climbed to a high rock and surveyed what was around me. Far in the distance I saw the sparkling ribbon of a river, and knew that our camp lay near one of the streams that ran from it. I was horrified to see that I had not come far – with all my running and walking, I knew I had not travelled far enough to put a safe distance between Shaliq and myself.

I knew I must drink and eat if I was to continue walking. During the night I had let the idea of trying to make my way back to Susmâr Khord fill my head, but now, in the morning light, I saw my father's face, heard his words to me. I couldn't go home. Shaliq would go there to search for me, and perhaps take back the Kabulis, or intimidate my family in some way. And I knew in this way I would still bring trouble on their heads, and my father would never allow me back into our home.

Now, as I stood on the rock and turned in a slow circle, I realised I was confused with my direction; I thought that I should have headed in another way.

Can someone be lost if they go towards nothing?

I took a deep breath and sat, exhausted and suddenly overwhelmed with hopelessness. Without warning Sulima came into my mind; I had always assumed she had returned to her home when she left that terrible day. But what if, like me, she was no longer welcome in her parents' home, in her village? Where had she gone? Had she wandered as I did now, knowing she couldn't return to the place where she'd been a married woman or to the place where she'd been an unmarried girl? What had really happened to her?

I lay down, pressing my back against a rock warm from the sun, and put my head on my outstretched arm. Suddenly I hoped Sulima had, indeed, been welcomed back in Wamed. That she had married the boy she truly loved, the boy who had also loved her, coming so far to lie with her in the planted fields, and for one brief time taking a chance which changed all our lives. I hoped she now happily raised their dirty, rude children. I wept for myself, and for Sulima. Suddenly I was also weeping for my grandmother, imagining her watching her beloved disappearing with their babies, unable to keep up and losing them for ever. Mâdar Kalân, I cried. I was overcome with deep, painful grief for all of us, for our women's lives filled with, it seemed at that moment, never-ending loss, a need to be loved and yet having it slide away. Or, as in my case, never come at all.

I fell asleep weeping, and when I woke the sun had moved a good distance. I got up and walked again. I didn't know where I went, only that I must not be caught. And I wondered at my earlier moment of weakness, when I'd cried over something as insubstantial as love. I would need all the power I could find within myself to stay alive.

I found a clump of wild licorice and gnawed its roots. They were old and leathery, but it was good to chew, and swallow. Finding a long, stout stick, I used it to help me climb uphill. I walked until the last glimmering rays of the sun were disappearing, and then sat before a cluster of thorny gooseberry bushes. I longed for a flint: something to start a fire. Not only was I cold, but I'd seen the droppings of wolves and jackals as I walked. I didn't know if I would be as lucky as I had the night before.

Clutching my knees, I slowly rocked back and forth, filled with a strange, dead calm. Perhaps it was hunger and thirst causing this; I knew I was light-headed, and yet, at the same time, clear. Surely the following day I would come near to some habitation; I had also seen donkey droppings along a narrow thread of path, and knew it meant that someone had come this way.

I wrapped my arms around myself, but as I tried to settle more comfortably, there came a stealthy rustle behind the spiny gooseberry. I sat perfectly still, and in time whatever lurked there left. I don't know if I slept or only fell into short periods of exhausted unconsciousness through those long dark hours. Soon, as the sky lightened enough for me to see, I rose. As I walked I kept the sun behind me, then let it move over my head and start descending at an angle slightly to the southwest. I found bushes of wizened, chalky berries, limp clumps of acidy sorrel, and a small, unexpected patch of woody wild rhubarb. I ate as many of the berries as I could, and chewed mouthfuls of the sour, tasteless herb and rhubarb stalks. Before darkness fell I spotted what appeared to be the opening to a small cave, high above me on a ridge. I slowly climbed the gradual slope, but at one point my feet slid in the thin gravel, and I half fell, turning my ankle. A sharp pain tore through it, and I clenched my teeth in anger at my clumsiness. I knew my ankle was twisted, and would slow my progress. I limped cautiously to the mouth of the cave and peered in, sniffing. But I could smell nothing, and saw no spoor in the soft earth leading into the cave, although there were many thin, wavery, trailing marks. Breaking a complex entanglement of thick spider webs from the top of the cave opening, I stepped inside. Immediately there were scurrying sounds, and something ran over my sandals. Hundreds of rats scurried about in distressed circles, and I let out an involuntary cry of disgust.

I moved away from the cave. I had felt a small touch of hope on seeing it, imagining a dry, safe place to spend this night, but now disappointment sat heavily in me. I knew I could not stay awake another night. Already I was stumbling with exhaustion and hunger. I walked further, barely able to see in the dusk, my ankle throbbing. Finally I stopped before a cluster of looming rocks. The ground was littered with pebbles; I pulled out a knot of milk vetch and used the thorny plant to sweep a small area clear. Then I gathered a number of rocks, all of a size that fitted my grip. I lay down, my head on one arm, the rocks in a pile in front of me and the other hand resting on them. I told myself that in this rocky area, far from forest and water, few animals would roam. But should one come upon me in the night, I could only hope to defend myself with the rocks. I breathed deeply, trying to push away the panic that had not left me since I heard Faiza's words, and saw the fear for me in her face. But that panic now washed over me with the endless pulse and whisper of water over stones. I stared into the blackness that had fallen around me.

I could do no more.

CHAPTER TWENTY-ONE

SOMETHING WAKENED ME. I sensed I had slept a few restless hours on the hard, rocky ground; I was cold, my limbs stiff. The sun had not risen above the mountains, although the sky had lightened. There was too much noise. I sat up, and the plain below me, although still shadowed in the dull light, was alive, full of movement. I couldn't believe that I hadn't heard the approach of so many horses and men; such was my exhaustion that I slept as if dead.

It took me only a moment to understand what I was seeing. It was the preparation for the most wonderful of sports, an imitation of ancient battles, and known about by even the youngest child throughout the country. The *buzkashi*. The game was meant only for men's eyes; women were not permitted to watch, and so what I knew of it – as was the case for all women – was only through talk. It was a bloody sport involving the finest horses, the most well-trained men, and a dead goat. It was spoken of in reverent tones; it was a game, yes, but also a representation of Afghan life itself, in which brute strength, courage, boldness, horsemanship, and a fierce, competitive spirit must all come together. I had often heard my father speak of the *buzkashi* – he had witnessed it many times during his winters in Kabul – and he said it dated back to the days of the great Genghis Khan, when the men of the north were famous for swooping down on unsuspecting villages to steal sheep or goats – or even enemies or women – bodily whisking them away while at full gallop.

There was no way out of the valley without being seen. My burgundy *kamis* and headscarf – even though covered with dust and streaked with dirt – would stand out like a bright curve of melon or the open wound of pomegranate on a grey plate should I make a move along this rock-strewn rise. I cursed my own pride, my vanity: if I had been less concerned with trying to find pleasure in bright new clothing, had more humility and had put on my usual dull brown *kamis* the morning that Faiza told me Shaliq knew my secret, I might blend into these rocks and slip away. So I would have to stay hidden, and would see what no other Afghan woman was allowed to witness. But there could be no stolen pleasure in this for me.

All I could be thankful about was that I had not chosen to sleep at the base of this rocky hill, where I would have been discovered by the first men to arrive. My life depended upon remaining unseen. If I was detected, I might be thought to be a wilful woman who had defied the rules to watch the *buzkashi*, slavishly following one of the players. In that case I would be beaten soundly, possibly to unconsciousness, and then left under the sun. I imagined myself in this barren plain, vultures swooping overhead, waiting for me to die. Or perhaps not waiting; more than once I had heard of the huge beasts flapping upon a breathing animal, pulling it apart while it still lived but was too weak to fight.

The other possibility was that someone in the crowd of men had heard talk of a runaway wife, perhaps met with Shaliq and any of his men who accompanied him on his search for me, and would know me to be that woman. Not only would blows be rained on me by these strangers, but I would also be returned to Shaliq. It was every man's duty and honour to help another, after all. And then there would be one more beating, delivered with satisfaction – and, to Shaliq – with justification. And that beating would be the final one, ending with my death.

I could not be caught.

In a short time the sun broke free of the mountains, and a soft, golden light covered the slopes. The men knelt as one and pressed their foreheads to the ground. Their murmurs rose, echoing against the rocks around me. When their prayers were over they stood, and something in the very air had changed.

Now I could see the colours and textures. I looked down on the ever-growing crowd restlessly moving in anticipation, and recognised the men of many tribes and villages by their headwear: from the long *longi* to the rounded *kolah* and bell-shaped *qaraqol*. I saw the familiar Pushtun, the Hazaras, Turkomen and Uzbeks, and my own people, the Tajiks. The rich owners of the horses stood out in their silk *chapans* with broad white stripes, their feet shod in supple, costly boots. Swarming around them were the ordinary men in their meagre, worn *chapans*, the long coats grown thin by years of wear, faded colourless by the sun. There were men of every description, all come to watch this game, the *buzkashi*. Some strutted among the anxious, whinnying horses, which were tended to by the syces, the little grooms who dreamed of one day attaining the glory of their masters. Instead of the usual dirty clothing and tattered, greasy turban of a common syce, these boys wore short, richly embroidered leather vests over their long shirts, which gleamed whitely in the sun. Their hats were of loosely curled sheep wool. I had never seen such finely dressed boys.

I watched one who looked up at the man casting a shadow over him. The child's mouth was open, his face intent with concentration and reverence. The man wore a dark green quilted jacket over his striped *chapan*, which floated about his legs in the soft morning breeze. His full black trousers were tucked into knee-high, intricately tooled leather boots with hard soles and curved, high heels designed to hook into stirrups. The man's hair was covered by his *talpak*, a round cap with a crown of astrakhan fleece and a large brim of wolf fur. The hat was the highest honour for a player of the game, awarded only after proof of his courage and ability.

The man's face was dark under the fur-lined hat pulled low on his forehead; he would be, in all probability, a high-cheekboned, narrow-eyed Turkoman or Uzbek from the north.

Now he spoke to the boy; the child nodded. The man tightened his belt around his quilted jacket as he walked away, his gait made slightly awkward by the high heels of his boots. He joined a small knot of men dressed in a similar fashion; some wore the same green jacket, others wore brown. The teams.

And then there was a roar from the crowd, and these men separated and came forward, walking calmly as if to an anticipated meeting with an old friend. From the distance I could not see the marks of honour which would decorate their faces: the scars created by the flesh torn open, over and over, game after game, but I could see their hands. Tucked into their belts were short-handled whips – *quirts* – with cruel leaded tips, but I knew that their hands were the true instruments of the game. Their hands were necessary to grip the goat, to tear its body away from the other players. The rules had never been clear to me – a race of a certain distance, the possession of the goat, its placement at the end of the game. But I did know of the players – the *chapandaz*. Although my father spoke of them with the highest admiration, they were often whispered about by the Ghilzai women in a different tone. The women's eyes glittered with longing when they spoke of these men. These heroes.

I had seen more than one woman's face soften with longing during the whispers; surely some of their bodies, under their dresses and *kamis*, softened as well, weakened with desire for what they could not have. These women were older than I, married many more years, having borne many children. I had never seen a *chapandaz* until that day, but surely the women who dreamed of them must have known that beneath the splendid clothing the *chapandaz* were still men. That their chests, although broader and more powerful than most, were not dusted with gold; that their hair, hidden beneath their *talpaks*, was no less coarse. Surely they knew that the feet of these *chapandaz*, when the glorious high-heeled boots were removed, smelled like the feet of all men. That hidden within their trousers was what was within the trousers of all men, and they should not be confused with their stallions.

Silence fell. The body of a he-goat – the *boz* – was dragged in. It had been beheaded, and its legs cut off at the knees. It was wet, and appeared very heavy, as it had been filled with either mud or sand and then soaked in water. Two men dragged it to the shallow pit and pushed it in.

I didn't know if the game would last one hour, or many. My heart thudded in my ears so loudly I imagined all the heads below turning and looking upward to find the source of the dull hammering. I was afraid for my own safety, and yet I was somehow inexplicably aroused by the horses, the men, and what they were about to do.

It's said that the game could not be a true *buzkashi* without the corpse of a proud *chapandaz* to show at the end. At the very least bones would be snapped and crushed, noses smashed, skin split. The crowd grew wilder as the players waited for their horses to be brought to them. The syces held tightly to the reins of the magnificent gleaming creatures, whose forelegs were wrapped with wool. The stallions pranced and shivered with mounting excitement. I knew they had been trained since birth for the game. They were stunning creatures, their long combed manes soft as a woman's hair, their bay and chestnut and grey and black coats gleaming, the muscles under their silken flesh moving like oiled stones. Their power was evident in their wide chests, their rippling haunches and proudly arched necks. According to the stories I had heard, they were bred so carefully that they were caught before they dropped from their mothers' bodies at birth, so that they would not be defiled by touching the dirt of the ground. They were fed with barley and oats at night, butter and raw eggs in the day. Their lives were those of beloved pampered children. Until it was time for the game.

And now it was time. The sky had deepened to a bold blue, and light, ruffled clouds raced towards the mountains in the distance. The *chapandaz* mounted their horses.

There was a hoarse shout, and the game began. The *chapandaz* surged towards the pit, slashing each other with their *quirts* as they competed for the goat. They lunged and grabbed, their massive hands and wrists swinging the heavy body back and forth with what appeared to be ease. The pack was thick as they fought with their bodies and their *quirts* and their horses, tearing the goat away from each other. Each *chapandaz* who held the goat tried to ride away from the others. Some were successful for short distances, but over and over the goat was grabbed anew; I watched, forgetting where I was, forgetting my own danger, as the *chapandaz* performed unbelievable feats of balance while pulling, pushing, snatching and carrying the heavy goat. Some were able to hang by one hooked foot as they lunged for the goat; others lay almost parallel to the ground against the horse's side to be in a better position to reach for the coveted *boz*. For much of the time – because of the crush of the riders and their horses, and the billowing clouds of dust thrown up by the hooves – it was difficult to see who had the goat. And then, accompanied by a long-drawn-out murmur from the crowd, one rider surged ahead, *quirt* between his teeth, standing high in his stirrups as he gripped the reins with one hand, a leg of the goat with the other, and pounded down the plain. The already torn body of the goat bounced against his thigh. The others raced after him, bent low over their horses' necks, swarming like hornets, arms outstretched as they came ever closer to the *chapandaz* in the lead.

The smell of sweat and blood rose. Caught on a sudden updraft of wind, it climbed so high that it reached me as I pressed into the wall of stone. I breathed it in; I realised I was trembling. I knew this smell;

I had felt the force of strength and power from the hands of my husband many, many times. I had so often been told I had too many words, and yet at that moment the right one – the one that would describe what I was watching – would not come to me. Although what unfolded below me was severe, harsh, still, it moved something in me; I felt similar to when I watched the men of my camp dance. I felt that there was a strange beauty in this brutal game.

How much time passed as the *chapandaz* fought and the goat was yanked from one to another? A horse stumbled and fell; it tried to rise, its neck bulging with the effort of pulling itself upright. I stood without thinking, willing the glorious creature to get to its feet, to avoid the hooves of the other horses. The animal screamed: a long, eerie cry that echoed above the clamour. Its front leg twisted cruelly backwards, broken. The rider, trapped underneath, worked his way free, waving his arms and shouting in frustration as he watched the thundering pack race away from him. A man in a fine silk *chapan* – surely the owner – rode on to the field, pulled out a knife and drew one quick, deep slash across the injured horse's neck. The frantic, futile pawing of the hind legs ceased. The magnificent head crashed to the bloodied ground, mouth gaping and tongue protruding. Three men ran out and dragged it to one side. It lay, alone in the dust, all glory now gone, the sun reflecting off its open eye.

The *chapandaz* and their stallions grew smaller as they rode away. The crowd shuffled, shouting their bets on various players, exchanging coins, buying tea from the sellers, and I dropped to a crouch. Eventually a strange quiet descended, and, as more time passed, the crowd fixed in position, staring down the empty steppe. I shifted in my tight stone niche, but before I could relax into a more comfortable position a small syce scrambled up the rocks, coming ever nearer to where I hid. I stopped breathing. He was intent on the climb, watching his hands and bare feet. And then he clambered to the top of one of the largest boulders, only a few steps from where I hid. He stared tensely into the distance, his back to me. He yelled something I could not understand – neither Dari nor Pashto – and I knew the crowd would be looking up at him. I remained motionless, but dropped my gaze to the ground, like a small child who covers her eyes, believing if she cannot see, then she cannot be seen. My hand rested on one of the rocks I had collected the night before, and I raised my eyes again, now staring at the syce. I closed my fingers around the rock. Should the boy turn in my direction, would I hurl the rock at his head? It was my only option.

Time passed. The sun beat upon me. The shadows on the hills had moved, but the crowd was still, waiting. Sweat ran down my back; it was difficult to keep my breathing shallow and quiet. I suddenly felt that I would choke on my own saliva, cough, give myself away. My thighs quivered with supporting my weight for so long, and it could only be a short time before my legs gave way. Suddenly the young syce jumped up and down, pointing, shouting. I followed the direction of his finger. I saw only a solitary eagle with a white breast circling low over the empty valley, but then I realised the boy was pointing at a thick cloud of yellow dust billowing in the distance. So. The riders returned. The boy clambered back down to join the crowd, never glancing behind him. I fell forward on to my knees, wiping the sweat from my face with my sleeve.

A horse – seemingly riderless – galloped in front of the thundering pack. As it swerved, I saw the *chapandaz*, the high heel of his boot caught in the stirrup. His body hung limp and lifeless by that one boot as his head bounced against the ground. Others caught up, racing past, and the hoof of another horse pounded over his face. Someone in a high, unravelling white turban appeared and galloped alongside on a small mare, catching the stallion's reins, pulling him away from the others. Dismounting, he gently removed the *chapandaz*'s trapped foot, then knelt over him. He removed his own *chapan* and placed it over the dead man's face.

One horse, one man.

Did they feel pain as they played, or did the pain only rise to its full and terrible power after the game had stopped? Or were they so used to pain that they embraced it as an old ally, and bore it with no signs of suffering? I knew so well the pattern of my own body during and after my regular beatings.

And I knew that I no longer felt pain as most women do, and for that gift I broke my year-long silence, and thanked Allah.

CHAPTER TWENTY-TWO

I HAD WATCHED THE death of a horse and the death of a man. I thought about my own death, in the various forms it might take this very day, or within the next few.

Below me the horses and their riders milled and pushed, back near the starting point, where the game must soon end. After many hours of hard galloping and following their riders' directions, struggling in the biting, pawing tumult, the horses were covered with white flecks of sweat and foam. Their nostrils flared, their mouths open as they struggled to breathe around the bit. The flanks of many bled, but in spite of their injuries, each appeared tireless in helping its *chapandaz* gain possession of the goat. And not only had the *chapandaz* lost one brother, but I also saw that others rode oddly, as if an arm or leg were injured. Like the horses, many were bloodied.

A flurry of movement made me turn my eyes from the game. On one edge of the crowd a syce ran, his shirt-tail floating behind him. I watched him come to a place not far below me where boxes and saddlebags were piled; he climbed atop a box for a better view. Unwrapping something, he put it to his mouth and chewed, his jaws working busily. Was it nan? Saliva flooded my mouth at the thought of my teeth closing on a soft thick chunk. Now the boy squatted and reached into a gaily striped saddlebag leaning against the box, bringing out a small skin flask which he tilted over his face, his head thrown back. I saw the flash of water arc into his waiting mouth, the movement of his throat as he swallowed. My own mouth opened, and the scene below me blurred. I swallowed painfully, putting my tongue to my lips. They were dry, cracked and swollen. My last mouthful of water had been yesterday afternoon, a chanced-upon cache of rainwater collected in the hollow of a rock shaded from the sun. I had put my face to the hollow and sucked greedily, as if I were an animal. Apart from the tasteless roots and shrivelled berries I had chanced upon I had eaten nothing for two – no, now it was three – days.

Should I risk discovery, wait for a moment when all eyes looked to the playing field, and then slide cautiously down in the shadows of the rocks to beg water and a piece of nan from the little syce? Would he look less harshly on a woman because of his youth, because it had not been so many years since he left his mother's warmth? But if he had been trained too well, and put up an immediate cry, what could I expect?

Dare I risk it?

I waited and watched, no longer interested in the game. It seemed it would never end. But the spectators must have sensed that the final triumph was inevitable, for they pushed and screamed with new enthusiasm. I saw that the entire crowd was completely caught up, moving further and further from the hills and surging forward to the playing field. The syce shoved the remaining food and flask back into the saddlebag and jumped off the box, disappearing into the crowd.

And I saw then that this might be my only chance – if I were to slither down the hill and take food and water that would allow me to continue my journey, it must be now. Of course I could have used these moments to flee, to try and limp further in the opposite direction while all heads were turned away from the hill. But I knew that if I simply hid myself, when the game was over and the men and horses gone, I would not be able to travel further without water and food.

Better to be caught and returned to Shaliq, I argued inwardly. I would rather die a quick death under his hands, fighting him with the last of my energy, than die a slow and agonising death from hunger and thirst and wild creatures.

I took a deep breath and wrapped my headscarf around my face so that only my eyes were uncovered. Then I furtively made my way down the rocky hill, trying to ignore the pain in my ankle. I arrived at the bottom and crawled through the piled boxes, kneeling beside the large saddlebag. I dug inside and felt the flask of water. I pulled it out and put its string between my teeth. My fingertips explored further; yes, here was nan, and something hard, wrapped – surely cheese. A quick glance behind me ensured that the crowd had worked itself into a frenzy, completely unmindful of all but the fighting *chapandaz*, so near them now. Still crouching, I struggled to get the nan and cheese tucked into the waist of my pantaloons, knowing I would need both hands to climb back up to my hiding place. The sound of the crowd grew even louder. For that one instant, the flask swinging from the string between my teeth, the food held under my waistband, I felt giddy triumph; I knew with certainty that no one would look this way, and all I needed was another few moments, only a few, and I would be safe, hidden securely, with food and water. And then, out of nowhere, brought, perhaps, by *jinn* – for what other reason could there be? – a boot of fine leather stepped into my line of vision.

My teeth remained clamped on the string. I tensed, preparing myself for the tug on my *kamis*, the kick into my spine. Through the narrow opening of my headscarf I saw the edge of the *chapan* which rested on the top of the boot. The *chapan* had wide stripes of black and grey interspersed with a thinner red line, common among the well-dressed men. But then the boot moved, just a shifting of weight, and the *chapan* opened to display the billowing trousers underneath. Again I tensed, but nothing happened.

The noise from the crowd was deafening, although the blood thudded so loudly in my ears that the cries around me grew muffled. Now they were shouting: '*Halâl! Halâl!*' over and over. It was done. The *boz* had been flung into the marked circle, the circle of justice, and the moment of triumph for one *chapandaz* had occurred. The game was over, and a winner declared. Ululating filled the air, the trembling, jubilant song of many dark wild birds.

I inhaled deeply through my nose, trying to clear my senses to deal with what would happen next. I smelled the sweat of the crowd, and the blood spilled from the slit throat of the horse. I smelled my own fear. And then I dropped my shoulders and stood. I would no longer cringe at this man's feet while I waited for my punishment.

I had been caught. I would face this man, as I had faced my father, my husband. I looked at the man, then reached under my headscarf and pulled the string of the flask from my teeth, and threw it to the ground.

The man looked down at it, then back to me. He spoke; his language was Pashto, but so poorly spoken that it didn't make sense. When I stared at him he shook his head and said something else, and this time I understood: '*Lâr sha. Tashtedèl.*'

'*Lâr sha!*' he repeated, louder this time, when I stared at him. Go – go away! '*Tashtedèl!*' he told me. Run!

I blinked, and then turned and scrambled back up the rocks, not looking back. I hid myself completely behind the first boulders I came to. I was aware of everything – the pounding of my heart, the trembling of my muscles from the climb, the dryness of my mouth, the nudge of the nan and cheese into my waist, the pain of my ankle. I heard the continued celebratory noises of the end of the game as I crouched in a small knot behind the high rocks, waiting for my shaking to cease, for my breath to come more slowly.

I pushed my headscarf to my shoulders and pulled out the nan and cheese, but for some moments could not eat it; my mouth was too dry. In the next instant the saliva came in a rush, and I devoured the food, choking in my haste to swallow it. And then I waited. I heard the high, clear tones of the syces, the deeper rumblings of men speaking in many dialects, the coarse shouting of the vendors still hoping to sell the last of their food and *chây* before packing up. There was an occasional exhausted whinny of a stallion, the distant, disgruntled roar of a camel.

The men were leaving.

I had been caught but allowed to escape. It was not my day to die.

I waited until I heard nothing more. The heat was intense. Finally, I peered from around the boulder. In the near distance I could see the wavering trail of horses and camels and men. At the very end, so close that I could still make out the stripes of his *chapan*, was the man who had allowed me my freedom. He walked, holding the reins of a horse, and he spoke to a shorter man who walked beside him, also holding his horse's bridle. The taller man waved his arms as if excited. The gap between them and the men ahead widened.

An idea came to me swiftly as I watched these last two men leave. The food had given me not only strength, but courage. The man clearly would not bring harm to me; he would not have let me go if he wished me ill. I had nothing to lose. The worst he could do was repeat what he had initially told me – 'Go away.'

I covered my face again and climbed down the rocks and hobbled after the two men. They did not hear me, so intent were they on their conversation. When I was very close I called out to the tall man. 'Please. Sâhib. Kind gentleman.'

They both turned and stared, then the taller man called something to me, but I didn't understand him. He spoke rapidly with the other man, but I could not hear their voices clearly. Then the shorter one came forward.

'Who are you? Why do you call us?' he asked, his Pashto strangely accented.

'I – I am a woman alone. I need your help. Please,' I said. I didn't like the expression on his face. His skin was very dark, he wore a turban and *chapan*, and was of a race similar to mine, but his tribe was not of my country.

The tall man came then. I knew I had looked into his face when he found me stealing food, but my eyes hadn't allowed me to actually see him as a man – only as the enemy. I had only thought of my fate. Now I blinked, trying to understand. Was he an Afghan, or not? Like the other man he wore the clothing and *longi* of my country. But his face . . . it was foreign, and yet it could have contained some faint trace of Pushtun. Perhaps it was the eyes, long and dark. But if he were a Pushtun, why could he not speak the language? And so both men were foreigners – *khârejis* – and yet their faces told different stories.

The two voices now spoke in an unknown tongue. And then the shorter man addressed me in his broken Pashto again. 'Sâhib asks why you here? Alone. Far from some place.'

I licked my lips. I could not tell the truth: that I had run from my husband. They would know that they had to return me. I opened my mouth, my eyes looking from the speaker to the taller man. He held the reins of his horse loosely in his hands; the palms were covered with dark rope burns, and calloused, although not so thickly that they would need to be shaved with a knife. The fingers were long and well-shaped, none twisted from being crushed or broken, and the nails, from what I could see, although ragged and rimmed with grit, were intact. These hands were too hardened and dirty to belong to a rich owner of horses, and yet not damaged enough to belong to an ordinary working man. I stared at his hands as if I would find there the answer to who he was.

The shorter man made an impatient noise, and I blinked. But my eyes wouldn't clear; I felt as though I looked through a layer of dust. 'I became lost from my tribe,' I said, my voice raspy with thirst, and speaking slowly, so that the lie had time to form. A ridiculous lie –

could I not come up with something more believable? 'And . . . and' – a trickle of sweat ran from my forehead, under the thin headscarf, and dropped on to my eyelashes. I blinked, and the salt burned one of my eyes, further clouding my sight. I rubbed at my stinging eye with the back of my hand. 'And I wandered for some days and found myself in this place. I need water.'

The man quickly told the taller man what I had said. He nodded, then reached for a gourd attached to his saddle, speaking to the other man, who translated.

'Sâhib says we give water. Your tribe. You go there and –'

'No,' I said, too loudly, and then, seeing the look of puzzlement on his face, realised I had done the wrong thing.

'No? You don't go tribe?' he asked now. 'Go where?'

Where were they going? Surely Kabul.

'I'm going to Kabul,' I said, my gaze again on the tall man's hands, now holding the gourd. I didn't like the look on the shorter man's face; I knew he would not be as lenient as the taller one. The sun was so hot. 'Yes, to Kabul. I will find my brother there. He will help me.'

'Kabul? Far. No walk to Kabul.' He turned back to the other man and spoke.

There was buzzing in my ears – perhaps flies, or perhaps because of the punishing sun, and my need to drink. As the men talked to each other, their voices blending into an indecipherable hum, I put my hand under my headscarf and wiped the sweat from my face. The sand tilted under my feet. I knew that at any time I might faint, fall to the ground at the feet of these men. And then what? What would happen to me? I couldn't show my weakness, my powerlessness. I willed myself to concentrate, to stay upright.

'Please,' I said, my voice barely a croak. 'Please help me. I beg of you.' Could they even hear me? I was enveloped in a white, shimmering haze, and dropped to my knees, swaying, and the taller man stepped forward.

'You speak Dari?' he asked, and I realised I must have unconsciously spoken in my native tongue. 'Yes, yes, I can understand Dari,' he added, and in the same instant I realised that he was speaking to me in the language of my grandmother, in the language she'd sung, had recited poetry to me. Persian. Almost Dari, but even more beautiful. His voice was beautiful to my ears. 'Can you walk? Are you sick, or only weak?'

The Persian flowed from his mouth with ease, and it was music, music that carried memories so precious they were painful. It was as if I had been deaf, and now could hear the melodies I thought were lost to me for ever. Tears came to my eyes, my throat now aching with more than dryness.

'How can I help you?' the man asked.

'Water. Please,' I whispered in Dari, sitting on my heels. 'Oh, please, Sâhib,' and he crouched in front of me, holding out the gourd. The sun was behind his head, and I couldn't see his features, only the outline of his wrapped *longi*. And then the sun grew hotter, and his outline darker, and spots of black jumped before my eyes. I reached for the gourd, trying to close my fingers around it, but then, slowly, as if in a dream, the gourd fell, spiralling gracefully downward, a thin trickle coming from the spout. The man caught it before it hit the ground, and held it to me again, this time closing his own hand over mine to grip it. It was all too confusing; his Persian, the fact that he would touch me . . . and then my hand, guided by his, went under my headscarf and to my lips.

The water was miraculously cool, and I drank and drank with loud gulping sounds, uncaring that the front of my *kamis* grew wet with the water that ran from my mouth and over my chin and neck in my haste to swallow as much as I could. At some point the man withdrew his hand from mine, and when I had drained the gourd, I handed it back.

I drew a deep breath; I knew I must appear strong, even with my clothing filthy and torn, my hands scratched by bushes and climbing among the rocks. 'I am well,' I said. 'It is only because I have travelled far with little to eat or drink that I was overcome,' I said, making my voice as forceful as possible. 'The water has revived me. I thank you.'

'We will give you more water, and food,' he told me. 'Then you will go to your tribe?'

'No,' I said. 'I must go to Kabul.'

'It lies that way,' he said, pointing in the direction I'd come from.

'You don't go there?' I asked, already knowing the answer.

'No. Jalalabad.'

Jalalabad. 'I will go to Jalalabad,' I said. 'I have a brother there.'

'A brother in Kabul and a brother in Jalalabad?' he repeated. 'Now you want to go to Jalalabad?'

I nodded. 'I must go there.'

The man looked at the shorter one, who was frowning, his eyes narrowed. They spoke in their language. The shorter one shook his head violently, his words clipped. It was clear he didn't want me to come with them, but at one loud last sentence from the taller man he stopped, his face now sulky. And I knew then with certainty that the taller man was higher in position, and gave orders to the other. Where had he come from, that he had eyes like a Pushtun but could barely make himself understood in Pashto, and spoke the language from which Dari had sprung?

'All right. You will come to Jalalabad. It is a few hours' ride,' he told me, then spoke to the shorter man again.

The shorter man's mouth tightened, and he stared at me and tossed his head in the direction of his horse.

I went to it and mounted. He swung up behind me; I smelled his sweat and could feel his breath, hot and angry, on the back of my neck, even through my headscarf.

And then we rode on, the taller man in front, and the two of us behind.

CHAPTER TWENTY-THREE

We rode a wearying length of time, through both fertile plains of hues of green and through harsh, rock-strewn hills. I saw the city rise up to meet us as the land became calm and flat again. And then we were at Jalalabad. For this long ride I thought of nothing but the fact that I lived. I did not know why this man let me hide myself from the others, or why he allowed me to come with him to Jalalabad. I could not think beyond this, although I knew that when we reached Jalalabad my future would again be uncertain.

As we started through the city the tall man looked back at me. 'Where is the home of your brother? We will take you there now.'

I didn't answer.

'You wanted to come to Jalalabad. We are here,' he said.

Still I was silent.

'Why do you not speak?'

'I am unsure of how to find my brother's home. I have not been here for some time.'

He made a sound of annoyance and then spoke to the man behind me; the short man sucked his teeth as if to say: You see? I told you she would be trouble.

'It grows late,' the tall man said now. 'We must give the horses food and water. You will come with us for now.'

We were forced to go slowly through the crowded, noisy bazaar, which was in the process of closing for the evening.

The sun flickered through side alleys and the straw matting that acted as walls on the sides of the open stalls. Each time a brilliant ray of evening sun caught my eye in the gloom of the bazaar, it dazed me for a moment, and I had to quickly look down at one of my ragged sandals to clear my vision. We were jostled by hissing camels, plodding donkeys, and hundreds of bodies. The tall man stopped his horse; there was a thick smell of blood. We were in front of a stall where whole sheep and goats, their skinned bodies black with the day's hornets and flies, hung from great clawed hooks. At a word from the taller man, the shorter one climbed down and haggled with the seller – a grizzled Hazara with a brooding expression, his shaved skull gleaming under his small embroidered cap. The Hazara appeared disinterested in making a sale, signalling to a passing *chây* seller carrying a large brass tray of small steaming cups of tea over his head. By the way the tea-seller knotted his *longi* I knew he was a Tajik from the area of my birth. I started to lower my head, but then realised that with my dusty *kamis* and covered face I was just one of many lustreless ghosts who floated through the streets in veils and *châdaris*. Sipping his tea, the Hazara eventually accepted an offered price and wrapped chunks of meat in paper and gave them to the shorter man, who tucked the package under his arm and swung back on to the horse behind me.

We entered an arcade now, passing stalls of costly jewels, silks, furs and carpets, and suddenly were into another arcade, which held an abundance of saddles and *tulwars* – long curved swords. And I saw many *tofangs*, the long-nosed weapons with the noise that sounded like hundreds of crashing pots. Although the men of my camp did not possess these weapons, I had witnessed visiting Ghilzai carrying them strapped to their horses, had seen them draw them out and aim at the sky and with the jump of the open end, the noise exploded. The *tofangs* here were sold by lean, hawk-faced men with ragged locks and unkempt beards. Their chests were crossed with heavy leather belts containing compartments, and in each compartment was a tube-like container that I knew went inside the weapon. Some also wore narrow swords, encased in scabbards, across their chests. These men, unlike any Afghans I had seen before, looked hostile, and I wondered why it was they bore this look.

And it was at this moment that I saw a number of men in identical clothing: short red jackets crossed with straps and decorated with many silver buttons, tight-fitting black pants and high black boots. They wore hard, rounded black hats. It was the clothing of the *khâreji* I had seen when I had accompanied Kaled to this city two winters ago. All of these men in red jackets looked alike, although only a few had the golden hair of that first one. But they were well-fed and sturdy, with a certain cockiness in their walk. They spoke loudly and laughed constantly, stopping to finger pomegranates polished to a gleaming ruby or lift one of the long-nosed weapons or examine an intricately decorated saddle. I saw one season a lamb kebab with the juice of a lemon and, as he ate, boldly watch the passers-by with unguarded, curious eyes.

They have the faces of children, I thought. They enjoy themselves, full of confidence, like dressed-up dolls, eager to play. Again, as had happened when I had come here with Kaled, a hard knot of anger gripped my chest. These were the kind of men who had killed my uncle and so many others, and who now came back to our country and walked through our cities, brushing against our people, touching what we had made, eating what we had produced, as if they had every right.

I was glad when I could no longer see them; we finally passed through the crowded, bustling arcades to a narrow, winding street of flat-roofed houses built of mud bricks, wood and plaster. We stopped in front of one of them, and the tall man dismounted and beckoned for me to do the same. He took the package of meat from the shorter one and handed him the reins of his horse. The other man slowly rode off, surely to nearby stables.

'Wait,' the tall man said, going into the house. Through the open door I heard him speaking, his tone low but with an air of authority. He was answered by a woman's strident voice. Her Dari was coarse. And then his voice murmured, too low for me to make out his words.

'But she could be a thief, or even worse. What will the neighbours think? *Aiiii!!*' The already loud voice rose to a wail, but quieted abruptly as the man's voice rumbled again. There was silence, and then the man appeared in the doorway, his face unperturbed. He waved his hand to me, and I came into the house.

It was a small, dim room. The man pointed to the floor. I stood, uncertainly, but he said, 'Sit,' and I lowered myself to the nearest cushion. The room was very clean; unfurnished but for cushions and carpets, their fabric bright, their patterns still new. The walls were freshly whitewashed. He went through a door on the far wall which I knew would lead to a courtyard, said something I couldn't hear, and turned to me.

I stood. '*Mota'asefam*,' I apologised. 'I am sorry that my presence has brought your wife such unhappiness.'

But the man now looked amused. 'She is not my wife. She is the wife of the man who has allowed me to use this house. Fareed,' he called then.

A plump, middle-aged woman in a sweat-stained shapeless grey dress, her head and the lower half of her face covered with a darker grey scarf, bustled in from the courtyard. She looked at me, raising her chin.

'Greetings, Mistress of the House,' I said.

The woman's thick eyebrows twitched. 'Why, she is nothing more than a dirty beggar, Sâhib.'

I stared at her, my cheeks hot at her words.

The man clicked his tongue. 'Cook the goat I brought for our dinner, but first bring *chây*.'

Fareed disappeared through the doorway, and the man left through the front door. I sat on the cushion again. Fareed reappeared shortly, carrying a pitcher and a bowl, a white cloth draped over one arm. At least she had the courtesy to allow me to wash. She set the empty bowl on to the carpeted floor in front of me with a dull thud, and I held my hands over it. She poured water from the pitcher and I washed my hands, the water in the bowl turning murky. My cuts burned in the warm water.

'I am of the Ghilzai,' I told her. 'Not a beggar or thief.'

She threw the cloth from her arm on to my lap, and when I had dried my hands she snatched it back, a look of disgust on her face as she left with the washing things. She finally returned with a brass tray. On it was a glass of tea, a plate of grapes, and a small round of nan. She set it on the floor in front of me carefully enough not to spill the tea, but heavily enough for me to know she was very displeased to have to serve me.

'My thanks to you,' I said, but she appeared not to hear.

Under my veil I drank the tea and ate the nan and grapes. As I sat in the cool room the aching in my head grew less severe, and my stomach no longer clenched painfully.

The man returned; I stood, flinching as I put weight on my ankle.

'You are refreshed?' he asked.

'Yes. I thank you,' I said. *For saving my life*, I wanted to add, but felt the words carried too much weight at that moment.

He put his fingers to his stubbled chin as if thinking. 'It is almost dark, and will be too difficult to see. You will stay here this night.'

I nodded, relief flooding through me, although I didn't want him to know this.

'Tomorrow morning I will send Fareed with you to find your brother.'

I nodded again. Fareed was making a great racket in the courtyard, banging pots. I heard the sizzle of a fire, smelled cooking meat.

Fareed came in again, carrying an oil lamp, and I realised the room had grown almost dark. 'Your meal is ready in the courtyard,' she said to the man, her tone modest and respectful. 'I have grilled the goat and prepared some aubergines. The *woman*,' she said, then, and her voice suddenly held contempt, 'has already had her food and tea.'

The smell of the meat was tantalising. She had given me nothing but a few grapes and yesterday's nan.

'Show her where she will sleep,' the man said. 'And give her clean clothing.'

Fareed's mouth opened as if to protest.

'You know your husband will be repaid.' And then he walked past her and into the courtyard.

Fareed narrowed her eyes at his back, her expression changing as soon as he didn't look at her. 'Come on, then,' she said, raising her chin at me.

I followed the stout woman into a small room behind a doorway hung with ribbons of billowing material. 'There are quilts here. A container for your private business there,' she said, pointing around the room. 'Now. Remove your headscarf so I can at least see what the *khâreji* is forcing me to deal with.'

I unwound my scarf and pulled it off, shaking my hair free and stretching and rotating my neck. Then I looked at Fareed. She brought the light closer to my face, and pulled down her own veil. Her thick upper lip was darkly bristled, her jaw pouched.

'Well. I thought as much, from your eyes. And what's a pretty young thing like you doing going about without a man? Eh?' This was said in a tone that made it clear she did not compliment me.

I was too weary to explain anything to this bold, rude woman.

'You're married, obviously, with your face markings. So? Where's your husband, then?'

'I don't know,' I said, closing my eyes. The truth.

There was silence, and when I finally opened my eyes Fareed was watching me with a suspicious expression. 'Well, don't expect me to serve you after tonight,' she said. 'I'll do what he', she jerked her head towards the doorway, 'asks, because my husband says I must do so, and he makes it worthwhile to my husband. But he told me you'd be gone tomorrow, and I expect you will be. I'm a good woman. It's sinful for you to be sleeping under the same roof with a man you aren't related to by blood or marriage. Do you have no morals?'

'I have morals,' I told her, my voice hard. 'But for this night I have no choice.'

'Him, out there, obviously doesn't respect you as a decent woman or he wouldn't let you stay here.'

I didn't reply.

'Then again, *khârejis*.' She blew out a puff of sour air. 'What can we expect of foreigners? I should probably sleep here myself, to watch you, but my husband wouldn't permit it.'

I continued to stand silently while she ranted. She had called the men foreigners. But where were they from? I was so weary, and the throbbing in my head had begun again. I would not argue with her and encourage her to stay.

'I'll see if anything is missing when I return tomorrow. So don't even think of making off with any of my pots or quilts in the night.'

'I wouldn't,' I said, my voice as angry as hers, and she set down the oil lamp.

'Because I'd send my husband after you if you take anything. And believe me, he won't be as easy with you as I am.'

Now I said nothing.

'I'll bring you something clean to wear, as I was instructed, and I suppose he'll want me to wash your clothing.' She looked at my *kamis* and pantaloons and shook her head. 'Don't go near the quilts in those filthy things. I don't want vermin in the bedding.'

I wanted to say sharply that I did not carry vermin, but kept my tongue still. She left, muttering under her breath. When she was gone I looked through the window, seeing the men eating in the courtyard. Ignoring the woman's command I sat on a quilt, fighting to stay awake. Finally Fareed returned, scolding me for disobeying and handing me a simple green dress and a pair of black pantaloons. The clothing was obviously well worn, and smelled faintly of sesame oil.

'Give me yours now,' she said.

I waited for her to leave or at least turn away while I undressed, as was only polite, but she didn't. I turned my own back and removed my *kamis* and slipped the dress over my head, then took off my pantaloons and put on the ones she'd given me. I held out my dirty clothing; she took it, along with my headscarf and the lamp, leaving me in the dark.

I lay down, pulling a quilt over me. I don't remember any more than that – the moment the quilt touched my shoulders I slept.

I awoke to low voices in the courtyard and rose, wrapping the quilt around me, as the early morning – the dark had not yet lifted – had a chill. I peeked at the edge of the open window so I wouldn't be seen. Two men were standing beside the small cooking fire, drinking cups of tea. Of course I assumed it was the same men who had brought me here, but as the first streaks of light slowly brightened the courtyard, and the call for morning prayer came from many minarets, I saw I was mistaken. Although it definitely was the shorter, darker man – a Muslim, for he went to the ground for his prayer – the other was a stranger. He wore no *longi*, and his head was uncovered. In the new light his hair was the colour of pale butter, curling over the collar of his long white shirt, which fell to mid-thigh. It was belted at the waist with a twisted rope of fabric in the custom of our men. But I saw that he wore strange pants – not cotton, but wool, wool so fine I could not imagine even the most nimble fingers creating it, and they fit more tightly than the loose trousers I knew men to wear. His body was lean and muscled; I could see the strength in his thighs, the hardness of his shoulders.

I studied what I could see of him, and it was clear that his forehead, where the *longi* protected it from the sun, was shades paler than the rest of his burnished face. A scar – fairly fresh, for it still shone pink – ran from the bridge of his nose down his cheek, under his eye. I hadn't seen this scar yesterday, but I recognised the long eyes. It was indeed the same man: the tall man who had saved me.

He didn't pray, but squatted comfortably on his heels. I studied him further, and in spite of his eyes and sun-darkened skin, by his pale hair I knew then that he must be a white-skinned *khâreji*, an enemy, like the red-coated soldiers who had fought against the men of my *watan*. A man from the country of my grandmother's beloved. England.

CHAPTER TWENTY-FOUR

AT THE SAME moment that this realisation struck me, the shorter man finished his prayers and rose, looking towards the house, and I moved away from the window. I put on my torn sandals and turned to pick up my headscarf – but it wasn't there. Fareed had taken it with my *kamis* and pantaloons last night. And she had not brought me another. I could not venture through the curtain without covering my face from the men. As I stood in the middle of the room, hoping Fareed would return soon, there were footsteps across the carpet, and the ribbons swayed.

'Fareed?' I called quietly. 'Have you returned with my headscarf?'

There was silence, and the ribbons again hung limply. 'No.' It was the voice of the *khâreji*. I snatched up the quilt and held it over my nose and mouth. 'She will arrive shortly,' he said. 'There is food in the courtyard.'

'Thank you,' I said, from behind the quilt, and the footsteps moved away.

Did Fareed not realise I was a prisoner in this room until she returned? The footsteps came again, and once more I held the quilt over the bottom of my face.

'Will you come out?' the voice said from behind the curtain. 'It is time to find your brother.'

'Has Fareed returned? I must speak with her,' I said.

I heard the stealthy whisper of the ribbons twisting against each other, and quickly turned my head. I knew that the man had not come into the room, but had parted the ribbons. 'Fareed sent one of her sons to say she cannot come until much later in the day.'

I stood perfectly still, the quilt over the bottom of my face, not turning towards the man. And then I knew Fareed had done this – had not returned to bring back my headscarf – on purpose and with vengeance, to show her annoyance with me.

'Come,' he said again, his voice irritated. 'We will do what we can to find your brother. I spoke to Fareed of it last night, telling her to go with you. But since she isn't coming I will take you to the bazaar. Someone there may know.'

Did he not see my predicament? Was he blind? 'I cannot come out; Fareed has taken my veil,' I said to the wall.

There was silence, then a murmur of annoyance. 'Wait,' he finally said, and I did.

Time passed; the sun moved, spilling light into the room, warming it. I grew restless, walking about the room or sitting on the quilt, and finally lay down. I didn't think I was tired, but almost immediately I spiralled into sleep again. I was awakened by the hushed twirl of the ribbons, as if they were caught in a sudden breeze. I opened my eyes and sat up, seeing the back of the *khâreji*. At the end of the quilt lay a pale green *châdar*. I picked it up; the fabric was silky and new. As I caressed it I realised the man must have seen my face as I slept, and a flush of shame – that he had seen me in such an intimate moment – ran through me.

I wrapped the veil around my head, holding it over my nose and mouth, and went out into the courtyard. It was empty. I washed my hands and face and drank the cold, unsweetened tea I found, standing as I ate what was left of rice, sticky and studded with pistachio nuts, in the bottom of the pot. I explored the small courtyard. There was an olive tree; its spiky branches reached above the wall of the courtyard. I could see the tops of other trees in other courtyards, as well as a nearby minaret. I stared at the tall spire.

Footsteps came from within the house, and I again covered my face, standing by the tree and fingering a thin leaf. The *khâreji* came into the courtyard; he once more wore his *longi*, and was transformed. He didn't bear any resemblance to the soldiers after all.

'Come,' he said. 'I will take you to the bazaar now, and we will find someone who knows of your brother.'

I didn't know what to do but to go with him. I followed him through the empty house and down the narrow street, filled with veiled women and playing children and chickens scattering in front of us. He knew his way; he walked quickly and purposefully. I hurried to stay behind him, my ankle still making me wince, but it was definitely better than it had been yesterday, and I knew the pain would be gone in a few more days.

As we entered the market place he stopped. 'Go and ask the vendors.'

'But I cannot walk in the market by myself,' I told him. 'I must be accompanied.' In some ways he appeared so sure, with his Persian and knowledge of the city. In other ways – touching me, looking upon my face, thinking I could walk alone – he was ignorant.

Saying nothing, he walked by my side. At the first stall I spoke in Pashto, but the man shook his head, so I switched to Dari, 'Do you know of a Tajik – Yusuf? He is a carpenter.' I told myself that in spite of the lie I used my brother's name and my father's profession. And, as I expected, the man in the stall shook his head. But as we walked away the *khâreji* said, 'Tajik? Aren't you a Pushtun? Layak said . . . from your clothes, and your . . .' he touched his own forehead.

I swallowed. I hadn't considered he'd question me. 'I'm both,' I said.

'Both? But . . .'

'It's possible,' I answered, quickly, and turned to the next man. We moved from stall to stall, every owner we asked shaking his head or saying no, but then, unexpectedly, one man hesitated after I asked my question, and my heart lurched.

'I know of a Tajik carpenter who lives off the lane near the *morgh bâzâr*.'

'The chicken market? How do we reach it?' the *khâreji* asked, giving me time, without realising it, to create a new lie.

'Does this man have only one eye?' I interrupted. 'The other is missing from the socket.'

The stall-owner frowned. 'No.'

'Then it's not my brother,' I said, glancing at the *khâreji*. His lips tightened.

I was weak; the streets were crowded and airless. It seemed that the men stared at my eyes. I saw a boy disfigured by fresh pox scars; I heard the squawk and ensuing thunk of an axe beheading a chicken, the wild fluttering of wings as an old man methodically wrung the necks of pigeons he grabbed, one by one, from a cramped wooden cage. My stomach churned from the smells – animal blood and excrement, rancid cooking oil, unwashed bodies, rotting vegetables. It was a pointless excursion, and yet I had no option but to pretend. The *khâreji*'s thoughts must have been only of being rid of me.

As we walked through a small tree-filled square to cross from one bazaar to another, a high, panicked scream rang out, and all heads turned to the sound. The *khâreji* stopped; I stood by his elbow. A woman in a pale brown *châdari* was dragged through the square by a heavily bearded, scowling man. He bore an uncanny resemblance to Shaliq; the same stocky body, the same expression of rage. The man stopped every few feet and raised a short, stout club and then brought it down with full force on to the woman's head and shoulders. I flinched with each blow, knowing precisely the shocking pain it brought. Under my *châdar* I covered my mouth with my hand so I would not cry out as the woman did. With each chilling thud, as wood hit flesh and bone, she screamed, crying for someone to help her, praying to Allah, and her covered body gracefully floated towards the ground as her unseen legs buckled with the force of the blows. And each time she fell the man brutally jerked her forward, his clutch on her never loosening. At first she managed to get to her feet and stumble along, but finally, as they passed in front of us, she could no longer rise, and he dragged her behind him by her one arm as one might drag a dead dog. She was now silent. A brilliant patch of red spread like a vicious flower near the embroidered eye-patch.

Nobody stepped forward; obviously this was the woman's brother or husband, and she had committed an unworthy act for which she was being punished. Shaliq loomed larger in my head than he had for the past number of days, as did the memory of my own beatings. What if the *khâreji* left me in the bazaar unprotected? What if I was found, alone, and thought to be immoral? I would be beaten like this, or even taken outside the city and stoned to death. As the woman was dragged past us in a state of unconsciousness, her feet lay sideways, one ankle delicately resting on the other. She wore only one finely worked decorated slipper; the other foot was bare. Her toenails were painted with betel, and fine etchings of henna were worked around her ankle. Her skin was smooth; she was very young. And somehow the sight of her beautiful bare foot filled me with a horror and incredible sadness that was even more powerful than the sight of the blood.

I closed my eyes and covered them with my palms, rounding my shoulders as if I waited for a blow. And then I cried, choking with the effort of not making a sound, and my own knees buckled, as the woman's, and I went to the ground.

I grew aware of resumed movement around me, but stayed on my knees, crying as a child, shuddering and gasping, and was deeply shamed before the *khâreji*; shamed that he would see me for a weak woman. I thought he might leave me at this moment, as I had feared.

But when I finally dropped my hands, my eyes still streaming, he hadn't moved. He didn't look at me, but continued to stare ahead into the throng, in the direction the man had dragged the woman. And then he made a sound in his throat, not a word, but a sad sound. He walked a few slow steps, then stopped and looked back at me, and I rose and trailed behind. He led me to another stall; tears still ran down my face as I asked my question of the keeper. I hated my tears, and yet was unable to will them to stop. The keeper simply shook his head as if annoyed, and the *khâreji* turned abruptly, and walked back in the direction we'd come from. Once again I hurried after him, and soon I saw that we had returned to the house. Although I no longer cried, my breathing was raspy and interrupted by stutters, which embarrassed me as much as the crying.

Inside the house, the *khâreji* said, 'Come,' and I followed him to the courtyard where Fareed sat with a board on her lap, chopping peppers and adding them to a pot of lentils.

'She's still here?' she asked, setting down the board and coming towards us.

'Yes,' he said to her, as if distracted. 'She . . .' – he gestured in my direction – 'it is difficult to find her brother. It may take more time. And you know that tomorrow Layak and I leave Jalalabad.'

There was uncomfortable silence, and then Fareed spoke. 'Sâhib? What do you ask?'

I knew what the *khâreji* would say before he opened his mouth.

'Could she stay with you – just until she finds her brother? I will pay you handsomely. You could help her in her search.'

Fareed looked at me while she spoke to him. 'She is a married woman. There is no place for her to go but back to her husband. I will not take her.' She turned and threw the last of the peppers into the pot, stirring with more vigour than was necessary.

'Her husband?' He turned to me.

I lowered my eyes. The tension was so heavy I felt my head would burst open. I didn't answer, but went into the house, back to the room where I'd slept, and sat on the quilts. In only a moment Fareed stormed in, carrying a copper kettle.

I jumped up, my distress replaced by anger. She couldn't even let me sit for a moment, trying to swallow my fears. She had to follow me. I didn't let her start first.

'Where are my *kamis* and pantaloons – my headscarf?' I demanded. 'You had no thoughts of returning them, did you?'

She shrugged. 'When I attempted to wash them they fell apart. They were nothing but rags,' she said.

'That's not true. They were of much better quality than what you've given me,' I said, pulling at the poorly made, worn green dress. I didn't care about my clothes, but couldn't stand to have this woman think she could constantly berate me.

She shrugged, eyeing the pale green veil that now lay on my shoulders. 'Where did you get that?'

'The *khâreji*,' I said, and her eyes flashed.

'Why did he give this to you? What did you do last night to earn it?'

I breathed heavily. 'I did nothing. I could not show myself, as you well know. And so he gave it to me.'

She stepped forwards, her fingers grasping greedily at the fabric. I moved back, out of her reach.

'I can see that it's new,' she said, 'and of considerable worth. Well.' How I hated her voice, her insinuating tone. 'It appears you know how to get what you want.'

As we stood in the middle of the room, glaring at each other, the *khâreji* entered. I quickly pulled the *châdar* to cover my face again.

Fareed lowered her eyes, but her voice carried an impolite edge of boldness. 'I can no longer allow a woman of such low character within the walls of a house owned by my family. Surely she is an adulterous wife, Sâhib,' she continued, 'or she would be with her husband. He has probably turned her away for her wanton behaviour.'

'I am virtuous,' I said, my voice like grinding rocks.

'Oh, no,' she said, loudly, triumphantly, suddenly raising her eyes to stare at the *khâreji*. 'This I knew when I looked upon her face. It is written there.' She nodded. 'She is indeed an adulterous wife.'

'This is not your business, Fareed,' the man said, his voice sharp, and Fareed dropped her eyes but shook her head, her veil swinging from side to side. I wished to take the kettle from her hand and strike her in the face with it.

'But Sâhib, surely you can see that she lies,' Fareed continued, staring at the ground and appearing only slightly cowed by the man's obvious anger. 'It is sure to be adultery,' she repeated. It was as if she couldn't say the word enough, that it gave her pleasure to use it.

'Hold your tongue,' I said, not caring how I appeared. 'Your voice is like the cry of the donkey. And you know nothing, but, like the donkey, bray mindlessly.'

I saw the intake of her veil against her mouth. 'She cannot speak to me like this,' she whined. 'She is a guest of this house and you cannot allow me to be treated so, Sâhib.'

'Fareed,' the *khâreji* said, calmly now, 'leave the food and go back to your own home. I do not need you any more today.'

'This house belongs to my husband; the woman should be punished,' Fareed now hissed, throwing the kettle to the floor. Water flew from its spout as it rolled on its side. 'A woman like her – alone – can be up to no good. Can you not see it?' She slunk past us, and the rankness of her heavy flesh and oily hair followed like an unpleasant cloud. And then there was silence as the *khâreji* and I stood in the empty room. I was shaking with anger, my breath harsh.

'She is a coarse woman,' I said, finally. 'Do not believe her lies.'

'But it is true you're married? And you do not wish to return to your husband? Your tribe?'

'I cannot,' I said, and the *khâreji* waited, but I said no more, turning my back to him, my arms crossed over my chest. Finally he left.

I stayed there, thinking. I knew that the two men planned to leave the next day, and I knew I must take my fate into my hands again, as I had the day of the *buzkashi*.

It was not a difficult decision, for I had nothing to lose. If the two men rode away, leaving me here, Fareed would drive me out of the house and I would be a victim of whoever found me alone on the streets, without a man or family. I couldn't make my way back to the winter camp of the Ghilzai, where Shaliq's wrath awaited. And I couldn't return to Susmâr Khord; my father had made that clear.

Today I had no future. I saw myself lonely, spiritless, wandering from village to village, thrown scraps if the women were kind-hearted, ignored and perhaps spat upon if they were not. I saw myself starving, fighting the smaller of the town dogs for their meals of bone and gristle. I had seen a woman like this when I was a child. She had come to our village in rags, her toenails missing and her feet hard as horns from her years of wandering. She had begged food, had offered to work, but was treated with venom and run out.

There were no choices left.

The men sat in the shade of the olive tree drinking *chây*. Long evening shadows through the leaves cast scattered marks on their faces. When I appeared their talk stopped abruptly; even though they knew I couldn't understand their language, I sensed it was because they spoke about me.

I stood in front of them; I knew I should not stand while they sat, but put back my shoulders and drew a deep breath.

'I wish to speak to you,' I said to the *khâreji*, my eyes lowered, and he set down his cup and also stood, so that we faced each other, although I showed respect and didn't look at his face. He was much taller than me. I realised I was pleating and unpleating the ends of the green *châdar*. I stopped, letting my hands fall to my sides. 'You have helped me without payment,' I said, still not looking at him, 'and for this I am most grateful. But now I ask another favour.' I wanted to say it all at once.

'I plan to take you back to the bazaar this evening,' he interrupted, 'and we will stay until we find someone who has heard of your bro—'

'There is no brother,' I said to the beaten earth at my feet, my voice made loud by fear and my attempt to sound confident. I no longer felt as bold as I had when I planned my words, alone in the room.

'What?'

I kept my head lowered. 'It's a lie. I have no brother here. I only . . . I knew, at the *buzkashi*, that you might not take me with you unless . . .' my words trailed off. 'I lied. I am sorry for this.'

Layak asked, in Pashto, 'What are you saying?'

'I admitted to the sâhib I do not have a brother,' I told him, glancing sideways at him.

Layak looked at the *khâreji*, who studied the evening sky over the rooftops. His cheeks had a dark flush, and I knew he was angry.

Nobody spoke. When I could stand the silence no longer I said to the *khâreji*, still looking at the ground, 'I have nobody here, and you know that Fareed will have nothing to do with me. I cannot be a woman alone. This afternoon – what we saw in the square . . .' The image of the beaten and bloodied woman dragged through the street flooded into my head, and I flinched. 'There is no place for me here,' I said, 'and I have nowhere to go. And so I ask to accompany you when you leave tomorrow.'

'Accompany us? But we leave Afghanistan,' the man said, quickly, as if annoyed. 'We travel into Hendustân. No. It's impossible. You cannot come with us. What are you thinking? Why do you ask this of me?'

I didn't care where they went. I couldn't be left here. Again I saw the flowering blood, rich and dark, on the woman's *châdari*; I could taste its iron flavour on my own lips. In the distance was the steady gong of a bell, the shrieks of laughing children. I went to my knees in front of him, throwing aside any manners and finally looking up, into his face.

'Sâhib. I will die if you leave me here. You owe me nothing, and have already spent much time and energy on me. Your kindness and mercy are great. But without protection, without help, my fate will be like that of the woman we saw today.'

'No.' The word came out with force. 'Get up. I cannot believe this. You would not be treated as –'

I stayed on my knees, now lowering my head. 'Sâhib. Forgive me when I correct you. Fareed spoke of this earlier. Although she was terribly wrong in her judgement of me, in one small way she spoke the truth. A woman alone arouses only suspicion, and is dealt with harshly. A good woman would not be alone; I am a good woman, Sâhib, but . . .'

'Then why are you alone? Why do you not return to your husband?'

'Sâhib,' I said, quietly, 'I cannot speak of my past. I can only tell you that I am worthless. And that I know the fate of the woman in the square, for it was mine as well. And it was that from which I escaped. Why you found me alone, and in such a condition.' I looked up again.

The *khâreji*'s eyebrows and mouth moved, and this small movement softened his face, took away some of the impatience. For an instant I was reminded of the way Kaled had sometimes looked upon me, and this gave me courage to continue.

'I am worthless,' I repeated. 'I ran from my husband with nothing but what I wore. I have nothing to offer but my *halhal*.' I got to my feet and pulled up the leg of my pantaloon, not caring that I exposed my ankle and calf. Bending over, I slipped off my *chapli* and worked the gold circle over my foot. Straightening up again, I held it between us, looking into the man's dark eyes. 'It is little, I know, but I offer it to you in exchange for your help. Please. Take me with you.'

He blinked rapidly, moving his head back slightly as if the *halhal* might come alive and strike him. Layak said something, something hard and low, shaking his head, and the *khâreji* answered sharply. Layak fell silent, but glared at me.

'Put it back on,' the *khâreji* said, and although his voice was not unkind, my heart sank. Did his refusal to accept it mean he wouldn't consider helping me further?

I didn't do as he said, but continued to hold up the gold anklet. He turned to Layak and spoke rapidly; there were questions in his tone. Layak pursed his lips and looked at me. I kept my back straight.

'Leave us. Please,' the *khâreji* said to me.

I went to my room and sat on the quilts. The two men talked for some time in their foreign language, their voices bouncing back and forth, and then the *khâreji* called '*Zan!*' – woman – and I went back out to the courtyard.

'Do you understand that we leave your country? That we go to India?'

I didn't know the last word. 'India?' I repeated, the word coming out clumsily.

'Hendustân,' he said.

'Oh. Yes. You said this earlier.'

He nodded. 'I wanted to make sure you knew . . .' he stopped. 'It is agreed then,' he said. 'You will come with us to Layak's home in India. You will work for Layak's wife. In return you will have a roof and food.'

I looked at Layak, but he studied his thumb. I couldn't tell if he took me as a servant because he believed it was a good idea or because his master had told him he must.

Again I dropped to my knees, this time lowering my head to the ground to press my forehead to the *khâreji*'s feet. Then I lifted my head and took both of his hands in mine. I had never before acted so boldly with a man, and yet I had to show him my gratitude. I pressed his hands to my forehead. He stood perfectly still as I did these things, then said something in a different language, not the language he spoke with Layak, and I let go of his hands and looked at him. But he said nothing more, and stepped away from me as if to leave.

'What is your name?' he asked.

'Daryâ,' I said.

'Daryâ.' His pronunciation of it was perfect. He repeated it once more and left the courtyard. He was so tall that he had to lower his head to avoid hitting it on the low door frame.

'I thank you, Layak,' I said in Pashto. 'Your wife will truly welcome me?'

He rose, his eyes alive but the rest of his face strangely blank. He was shorter than I. 'She be very happy for much money from Burra-Sâhib,' he said, patting inside his shirt, above his belt, and I heard the dull clank of coins. I didn't know the word *burra*, but it was as I had guessed; Layak did not take me to his home willingly, and a small seed of concern over this pushed through the thoughts whirling in my head.

But I couldn't worry about it now; I had asked to be taken away from Jalalabad, and the sâhib had made it so. I could look only at each day, couldn't I?

When Layak left I ate some of the food Fareed had prepared. I chewed and swallowed without pleasure, and only to keep my strength, for I had no hunger after the difficulties of the day. Then I went to my room to sleep, even though it was not yet dark. My head ached from my earlier weeping. I lay on my bed, but sleep did not come, and I wondered if what I had asked for would end in a fate worse than the one I had run from.

CHAPTER TWENTY-FIVE

I AWOKE BEFORE DAYBREAK after only a few restless hours of sleep, and went to the courtyard to heat some water. I washed my hair and tightly braided it, then took another full container of heated water back to my room and bathed. As I did so I kept thinking about what awaited me – a life of servitude, of cleaning another woman's home and caring for any children. Although fed and sheltered, this would not really be a life of my own. I would have less than I once had as a nomad wife, with my pots and quilts and husband and place in the tribe.

Again, I told myself I must be grateful. Why did I find it so difficult to simply accept this offer with relief, be glad and thankful that my earlier visions of myself – wandering and homeless and always in danger – would not come to be? That although it was uncertain, at least I now had a future.

I cooked the meat and vegetables Fareed had left in the courtyard – for at least the first day of the journey – and then prepared a simple breakfast of fruit and nan. By this time the men had risen; I was relieved Fareed didn't appear, and I served them.

As I bent over the *khâreji* with his tea, I fought back the desire to question him. How far would we travel? Where, exactly, did we go? Where would I live now? And did he trust Layak? Would I be safe when I was left with him? But I remained quiet, my eyes lowered, for I was afraid that if I showed my true nature – the talkative, inquisitive manner that had so often created my own difficulties – the *khâreji* would decide I was not worth the trouble, and change his mind.

He and Layak were silent also, although in a different manner. The *khâreji* appeared distracted, immersed in his own thoughts – perhaps that he had made the wrong decision? – while Layak was simply sullen, snatching what I offered him with deliberate rudeness.

Shortly afterwards a boy came to the house with two sturdy donkeys, and the men loaded the small animals with sleeping quilts, a number of bulging sacks they brought from the other rooms of the house, and the food I carried from the courtyard. The *khâreji* had a *tofang* which he strapped behind his saddle.

A stocky bearded man appeared; the *khâreji* put afghanis into his palm, and knew him to be the husband of Fareed. He stared at me, and by the dark, disapproving look on his face I could only imagine what Fareed had told him. And then the same boy appeared with two stallions and a dun-coloured mare, and we mounted. With grunted instructions from Layak I took the leads of the donkeys. And so we left Jalalabad, the *khâreji* leading with Layak and I following, the donkeys strung behind me.

We followed a wide, dusty road away from the city. Although my future was unknown, I felt an odd and unexpected lift in my heart. When I had left the permanence of my childhood home I could not imagine any other life but living in one house in one village. But from the Ghilzai I had grown to like the sensation of movement, the change of sights with the change of seasons. But I knew that today it was more than this – much more. This time I was with two strange men, one miserable, obviously wishing I had never appeared, and the other who . . . my thoughts stopped in mid-sentence. Who what? I knew nothing of the *khâreji*, only that he was not an Afghan, and because of this my fate had changed. He obviously wasn't capable of understanding fully how worthless I was – and so had given me this chance.

I studied his back; he sat erect and yet easily in the saddle, broad-shouldered and slim-hipped. I had seen that his hands were firm and yet gentle as he touched his horse, and in turn the stallion was responsive to his slightest movement. I thought of his hands on mine as he helped me to drink when I had knelt before him, swaying with thirst and exhaustion. His hands had been sure, with no obvious concern or repulsion at touching a strange and possibly unclean woman. Now those hands held my fate as loosely as they held the reins.

I looked over my shoulder at Jalalabad as we left, wondering if I would ever see this place again.

My mare was a warm comfort beneath me; she reminded me of Mehry, so long ago.

We rode through the day towards a mountain range. I was glad that each time the *khâreji* put up his hand for us to halt there were rocks or bushes so that I might have privacy from the men; I had worried about this after the first few hours of riding and my discomfort grew. At one such stop, after the animals had drunk at a stream and Layak had performed his noon prayers, his forehead to the ground, I turned to the *khâreji*.

'You don't pray?' I asked, although it was obvious he didn't. 'You're an unbeliever?' I questioned, and with those words, I suddenly wondered – am I an unbeliever? I no longer prayed. No, I told myself. I was not an infidel, worshipping idols, such as Sulima.

'I'm not Muslim,' he said, tightening his horse's bridle.

'So you don't believe,' I stated. 'You are a believer, or you are an infidel.'

He slapped the dust from his clothes and mounted his horse. 'There are more colours than black and white,' he said, urging his horse away from the stream, and I was ashamed, not only of my obvious ignorance, but that I had appeared foolish in his eyes.

We ate nan and drank from our flasks as the horses plodded forward, the mountains growing closer and closer. We finally stopped for the night near a narrow river, and as the *khâreji* unloaded the animals I prepared food while Layak went to gather brush for the fire.

The three of us shared no common language; I could talk to Layak in one language, the *khâreji* in another, and they shared a third. I knew it wasn't English; while foreign, it wasn't foreign enough. I couldn't describe it in any other way.

'Is it the language of Hendustân – India,' I corrected myself, 'you speak with Layak?' I unpacked a hard square of cheese and put it on a flat stone, wiping the blade of a knife on my pantaloons. The *khâreji* rubbed down his horse with a rag.

'Yes. Hindi,' he said, rubbing vigorously.

'How is it you speak languages that are not your own with such ease?'

He stopped and glanced at me, and I quickly turned my face away. He went on with his grooming. 'I was a child in India.'

'But Persian . . . ?' I looked down as I sliced through the cheese, and Layak arrived with an armload of twigs, calling something to the *khâreji*, and he didn't answer my question.

I was weary from so many hours riding in the thick dust and hot sun, and my eyelids were heavy as we ate cheese and nan and the meat and vegetables I had warmed over the fire. Layak and the *sâhib* didn't speak, and I sensed some underlying discord between them, and also stayed silent.

My eyes burned as I scoured the cooking pot with gritty sand at the edge of the river. By the time I had splashed my face with water and cleaned my teeth with a twig, Layak already slept near the fire, snoring loudly, and the *khâreji*, his *tofang* beside him, sat cross-legged, leaning towards the flames to read a small leather book. Its cover was very creased and worn. I knew it would not be the Koran. He was the first man I had seen read from a book, apart from the mullah with the Koran in his hands. What words did this man's book contain, then? He didn't look at me; I knew he would be the first to keep the fire blazing to ensure our safety from wild animals. I lay down and rolled myself in a quilt, turned from one side to the other, then sat up again.

'Sâhib? What do you read?' I asked. 'Is it a holy book?'

He looked at me, the fire lighting up his straight nose, his strong jaw. 'No. It's a . . . I can't remember the Persian word. A novel,' he said.

'Novel?' I repeated the English word, tasting it on my tongue.

He smiled then, and I realised I hadn't seen him smile before. He looked younger when he smiled. The thought that he was younger than Shaliq went through my mind. 'The name for an invented story.'

'I know stories,' I said. 'Both true and invented.' I immediately regretted my words. I sounded boastful, as if trying to impress him. But I needn't have worried; he was obviously uninterested in what I had to say. He gave a small nod and looked back to the book, and I knew he wouldn't speak again, and so I turned away and closed my eyes, listening to the pulse of the flames and the slide of the turning pages of the *khâreji*'s book.

I was surprised that I had slept so deeply when Layak roughly shook me for my turn to watch the fire. I fed the low flames from time to time but mainly watched as the stars, at first white as pearls, fade with the first streaks of pink light. Wading into the river, I washed my feet and hands and face. Then I boiled water for tea, and both men rose, and so began the next day.

Although it was the turning of the season, past Ramazân, as we went south the sun still shone with the gleam of polished brass, punishing us with its glare. Occasionally clouds slowly rolled in and cast shadows I welcomed with relief, but then they would move on, and the sun would again beat on our heads and backs. In a short time we came to a gorge which wound between cliffs of shale and limestone and led through to the mountains.

The *khâreji* took his *tofang* from its leather strap and placed it in front of him, one hand on its wooden handle. I wanted to call out to him, to ask if there was danger expected, but said nothing. The day before I had tried to convince myself that I must show my gratitude towards him in more ways than my work when we camped, that because he wasn't a man of my country he might not find it offensive if I spoke first. But the two times I had questioned him – first on his faith, and then about his reading – I was left embarrassed and sorry that I'd spoken.

It took us the whole day to wind through this strange pass. In places it was wide and flat, bounded on either side by low, stony hills; we would climb ever upward, the horses' and donkeys' hooves scattering the loose pebbles and throwing up clouds of dust. And then we would descend into small valleys where nomad children tended flocks of sheep and goats. At times I spotted camels grazing on the sparse vegetation. I sensed the *khâreji* didn't want to stop until we were through these mountains. There were many narrow passages, some running with water, but the sound wasn't joyful as is often the way of water. Here it was sombre and foreboding, more of a warning. Occasionally, I felt a sense of being watched, although I didn't see anyone.

As the day drew to late afternoon the animals picked their way carefully along the bed of a ravine. I hoped we would soon be through this mountain range; the walls around us closed in tighter and tighter. At one point the rocky path grew so narrow that two loaded camels wouldn't be able to walk side by side. I looked up at the walls of stone that reached into heaven, forced to tip my head all the way back to see the sky. No sunlight could journey so deep into this opening, and the air was damp and cool. I felt like an insect crawling along the bottom of this long, very narrow pass. The horses' hooves rang eerily.

I grew chilled, and an ominous feeling engulfed me. I must speak. 'What is this place?' I called out in Dari, my voice bouncing against the stone in an unearthly echo.

Both Layak and the *khâreji* turned and looked over their shoulders. 'All day we have ridden through the Khyber Pass,' the *khâreji* replied, his own voice also taking on the same echoing tone as mine. 'It is the only way into Afghanistan from the North-West Frontier, and so a place of much history. Not many years have passed since a massacre occurred where we walk at this moment.'

'The war of your people against mine? When your people came to take our country?'

He didn't answer, but faced ahead again, as did Layak.

'Did you ever wear a red coat, like the others?' I called, my voice suddenly loud. I wanted to know. Had he been a soldier? I thought of the soldiers I had seen in the markets. His face was somehow different, wasn't it? Or was it that he wore the clothing of my people, and so I felt that he wasn't as much of a foreigner?

But again, he didn't answer, and I knew I had once more asked the wrong questions. Could I say nothing to this man except that which made me appear empty-headed, or rude?

I continually glanced up at the crevices and niches in the rocks, imagining how those who rode through could be trapped and killed as easily as newly hatched chickens in this dark, frightening place. The *khâreji* hadn't said who was massacred here, but I could only imagine it was his people. Mine would never be foolish enough to be placed in such a position.

Finally we came to the mouth of the pass, into the thinning evening sunlight, and I breathed deeply, relieved. A huge, coarsely constructed building with a jumble of towers reared up ahead. I didn't know what such a building was erected here for – it was empty, its mud walls in a state of disrepair – and then I realised it would have been a place of protection during the time of fighting. We were on a rise, and I could see for many miles. Spread directly below us was a good-sized town, but far ahead lay a city. Although from this great distance it was only a ragged shape on the horizon, it appeared very large. We stopped our horses and stared at the scene.

'Peshawar,' Layak said, swinging his arm towards the far-off city. 'I am child there. Learn Pashto.'

'Do we go to Peshawar? Is this your home?'

'No longer home,' Layak told me. 'Much further I live.'

We were in Hendustân, then, if Layak had lived in this city. 'Sâhib? We have left Afghanistan?' I asked, urging my horse beside his.

He nodded. 'We're in the North-West Frontier – the furthest northern province of India. The town of Jamrud lies below us,' he said. 'We'll camp on its outskirts tonight.'

A slight tremor ran through me. That I hadn't realised when I had crossed the invisible border between my country and this one somehow shocked me. Although there was no way for me to know, somehow I thought I would feel the difference. But the air here smelled the same, the ground beneath the horses' hooves appeared no different.

The two men started down through the rocky foothills, but I stayed where I was. As I had done when we rode out of Jalalabad, I turned and looked over my shoulder. But then I had left behind only a city. Now it was a country I left – my country. Tears came to my eyes. I loved my land. I was leaving behind the towering purple mountains, the fast-running streams and still lakes, the summer pastures and winter camps, and all the valleys and hills and plains in between. I was leaving behind the village of my childhood and those who had loved me – my mother and sister and brother, even my father, who, I could finally admit, cared about me in the only way he possibly could. I was leaving behind anyone who had ever known me and treated me with kindness there – Yalda, Gawhar, Hasti. I was leaving behind my grandmother's grave.

And there were those of the Ghilzai I also left, the Ghilzai who had cared about me and worried for me, from my sister-wives Myassa, Hanouf and Bibi, to Dulfiya and Faiza. And Kaled, of course, Kaled.

Mâdar Kalân, I thought, *even though it is the beginning of your prophecy, I feel no joy*. And then I heard her answer in my head, her voice, clear, speaking a line from one of her poets, Rumi: *Live where you fear the most*.

And this brought me a strange comfort, and I silently thanked her.

That night as I lay, sleepily staring into the flames, I thought back to the narrow pass, imagining the horrors that had occurred there, and hoped I would not dream of it.

I am in Hendustân. 'India,' I whispered, and the sound of the word on my tongue was foreign, and as yet carried no memories.

CHAPTER TWENTY-SIX

THE NEXT MORNING the *khâreji* sent Layak into Jamrud for rice and meat. As I was packing up the camp, the *khâreji* attending to the donkeys – one had a pebble lodged in its hoof – he stopped suddenly, turning his head as if listening. Then he put up his hand to me, and as I stopped he put his fingers to his lips. He let go of the donkey's leg and silently took his *tofang*, pointing it directly into bushes ahead of him. There came the crashing noise I hated, and I covered my ears in response. The *khâreji* ran into the bush and quickly reappeared, grinning as he held up a large bird, its neck hanging limply.

I had never seen him smile in this manner, showing all his teeth as if unaware of himself. He was obviously pleased as he turned the dead bird over in his hands, and he appeared to be a different man at that moment. Even younger, like one of the boys of our camp who has won his first round of wrestling.

'What do you call this?' he asked me, still grinning.

'A black partridge,' I said. 'They are very beautiful birds – look at the patches of gold. And under here, red – and white.' I lifted the gleaming feathers. 'So bright against the black.' I stroked the softness. 'Beautiful,' I repeated. 'Allah made this creature for us to behold with joy.' Suddenly aware of the silence, I looked up.

The sâhib watched me in a way that made me feel I had done something either very wrong or very right, and took my hands off the bird he still held, trying to think of something to say to cover my confusion.

'You are a good hunter, Sâhib.' Surely a compliment was safe territory, and could not be taken the wrong way.

Now he smiled at me, not the open smile he'd had when he came from the bush, but a smaller, more conscious one. 'Thank you.' He handed me the bird. 'Will you clean it for our supper, please?' he said, and I thought of how Shaliq had never asked me to do anything in this courteous manner; he had only told me what I was to do.

'You are a hunter at home? In your country, England?' I pronounced it carefully, focusing my eyes on the bird I held.

'Yes,' he said, and turned from me.

As I stuffed the bird into a sack I called to him. 'Sâhib? Why did you leave your home and come to my country?' When he didn't answer I glanced up. He was looking at the river, his *tofang* held loosely in both hands now. 'Sâhib?' I said again, but he turned and busied himself with cleaning his weapon, and no more was said as we set out again.

We now followed a twisting, turning river – the Indus, the *khâreji* told me as we camped beside it the first night. We were in a grove of banyan trees; the long roots hung from the branches and grew back into the earth. I heard the repetitive cry of a koel, and when there was a rustling in the underbrush near the river the three of us watched a porcupine stroll lazily by, glancing at us with small, unconcerned eyes.

Layak spoke to the sâhib, and he laughed, nodding. Then he said, in Persian, 'Layak says this animal must be treated in the same way as a mother-in-law.'

I smiled, remembering my conversation with Myassa, in my first days with the Ghilzai, and how she had compared the mother-in-law to a scorpion under the matting. 'It seems in every country the mother-in-law is to be feared and respected.'

He nodded, but I saw that Layak's face had turned sour, as if annoyed that I was included in this conversation. The sâhib unwound his *longi* and combed through his hair with his fingers, as if with relief. Then he took another book from his bag, this one also covered in leather, but not as worn as the first. He also took out a small wooden stick, and made movements over the page with it. I realised he was writing.

'Layak,' I said in Pashto, feeling I mustn't create an even deeper chasm between us, if I were to live with him, work for him, 'where does this river go?'

'Go my home,' he said, surprising me. I hadn't expected him to answer.

'Where is your home?' I asked. I had asked him where his home was twice, but he hadn't answered me, making it clear that he heard, but it was his choice not to speak to me. His home would be my home, I kept thinking, and each time an unpleasant sensation overtook me.

He had been surly and unresponsive whenever I tried to make even simple conversation about the food or setting up camp with him. Now he appeared more relaxed as he sat comfortably with his back against a rock, crossing his ankles and sharpening a stick with his knife.

'Indus go through Punjab, pass many place, then my home. Multan.'

Multan. 'But Multan is not the city of your birth,' I said. 'You said you were born in Peshawar.'

He nodded. 'I leave, young, go Multan for work. Multan is better city for me than Peshawar.'

'It's a good city?'

He shrugged, nodding. 'Some say – city of . . .' he hesitated, searching for the word. 'Holy. Holy men.'

'Saints?'

He nodded. 'City of Saints. But also of dust. Of great heat. Many Muslims.'

The City of Saints. 'Is it the biggest city in Hendustân?' I asked, imagining it would be like Kabul.

He clicked his tongue and shook his head; it was clear he considered me ignorant.

'Many, many cities in Hendustân, woman. Multan only one, not so big.' He scowled. 'Now *khâreji* everywhere, even in Multan. When I come, only few *khârejis*. Sikhs – men of Hendustân – all power. Now five, six years, Sikhs no more so power. Now *khâreji*' – he dipped his head to one side – 'big sâhibs in Multan. In all places in Hendustân.'

I glanced at the sâhib, hoping he was still lost in what he was doing, and didn't understand, with his small knowledge of Pashto, how Layak was speaking of him and his people.

'Will he stay there, as well? Or go home, to England?'

Layak shook his head. 'Go home some time. But first must go through . . .' he made a smooth motion, as if drawing a straight horizontal line, in the air in front of him. 'On flat ground.'

'A desert? Plains?'

Layak nodded. 'Plains. Of Sind. He tell me he go Karachi.'

'Karachi is also part of Hendustân?' I asked.

'Oh yes.' He put down his knife and stuck out his chest, obviously proud to demonstrate his knowledge of his homeland to me. 'Karachi big, big city, by water. Fine. I go there one time. Get wife there.'

The sâhib rose and walked along the river bank. I watched as he sat on a log and again opened his book.

'We disturb him with our talk?' I asked Layak.

Layak shrugged. 'These *khârejis* – who know their thinking? This one, here, he want see Jalalabad, Kabul, go Bamiyan see big stones. Go all the way to Herat. Then back east; he want to see *buzkashi*. We must wait long time for game. Everywhere he always look, look, look. 'Why you look, Sâhib?' I ask him. He no answer, just look. I think he is not like other sâhibs with white skin.'

'What do you mean?'

Layak made a sound of disgust with his lips. 'Except for on horse – he good on horse – he is like woman.' He slapped his chest, hard. 'I am more man. But I must be servant.' He spat into the fire.

I looked at the sâhib. He'd pushed up the sleeves of his long shirt, and his forearms were strong, the golden hair on them glinting in the evening sunlight. Again I saw his broad shoulders, his straight back. 'What do you mean?'

'He . . .' he searched for the word. 'Soft.' Layak again thumped his left breast. 'I see face when he see something, something not . . . not sad. Normal. Dog dying. Bad boy, beat by father. Woman punished. He say nothing, but his face. Too soft. And you,' here he made the same critical sound he had a moment earlier. 'He believe you . . . lies.'

I jumped to my feet. 'I don't lie, Layak.'

Layak's eyes narrowed as he stood to face me. He had to raise his eyes, just the slightest, to look at mine, and I knew this angered him further. He smiled slyly. 'You make him believe. See? He not true man to believe nomad woman like you. I tell him – woman no good, leave in Jalalabad. Will be only trouble, lie, steal. But he look at you, oh, so sad, poor woman. We help.' Layak spat again, but this time not into the fire. The bubbling globule glistened near my foot.

'And I don't steal. You are not a good servant to your master, Layak, to speak of him in such a way.'

Layak's chest went out again. 'Only master short while. Good money. Soon I home, and he no more master to me.'

'Still. You have no respect. I see him – he treats you well. It's you who is at fault.'

Layak smiled, that same nasty smile. 'You know how slave treat master, woman? Soon you see.'

I turned and walked away from Layak, in the opposite direction of the sâhib, thinking of Layak's words, and worse, his smile. I knew then that even if his wife was kind to me, she would not have any say in how I was treated by her husband.

We continued to travel along the Indus, and although it was indeed a mighty river, the further south we went the slower it ran, until it finally widened to a broad, brown, creeping waterway. The stony tracks we followed regularly turned into wider, more beaten paths, and then I would see a tiny village standing in a distant grove of pistachio or date trees. Sometimes I caught glimpses of women, bending in rows as they cut sheaves of corn which reflected golden in the sunlight, or men shaking fruit from trees with long sticks.

The first time we ventured into these towns to buy what we needed, I saw Muslim women in veils, but for the first time I also saw the uncovered faces and exposed neck and arms of a different kind of Indian woman.

'What are those women, Sâhib?' I asked, after we had left the last town. 'The ones with no shame.'

He turned in his saddle to look back at me. 'They're Hindu. And it's nothing to do with shame.' He looked ahead again.

After a minute I called to him again. 'Sâhib? Women in England are open in their faces?'

Again he turned, and this time nodded.

'They're Hindus?'

'No. They're Christian, many of them. Christian women don't cover their faces.'

'There are no Muslims there?'

'I have never seen any,' he said, and turned from me again, but then looked back. 'Have you seen many white men in your country?'

'Only soldiers, Sâhib,' I said. 'None like you.'

He turned then, and urged his horse forward, and we said no more.

Now we plodded through dusty, baked plains, the sun like a blade above us. I was more and more concerned about Layak; I saw the way he watched me, not even bothering to try and hide the fact that he did this when I looked back at him. Once, when I rolled up my pantaloons to wash my feet he stood, arms crossed over his chest, staring at my legs, and I was repulsed by the look on his face. He grew bolder and bolder, and once even followed me as I started towards a clump of bushes for privacy.

'What are you doing?' I asked, whirling at the sound of his footsteps. 'Go away.'

The sâhib heard my cry, and suddenly he was behind Layak. He looked at me, and must have understood the situation, for he grabbed Layak by the shoulder and pushed him, hard, so that Layak stumbled. The *khâreji* then spoke to him in angry, short bursts of language, and Layak, his face dark, turned and stomped away. I was embarrassed to look at the *khâreji* after that, and my misgivings about Layak only grew.

That night I couldn't eat as the three of us sat around the fire. I knew Multan was not many days' ride away. I watched the sâhib as he ate. He looked up suddenly, and I quickly glanced down.

'You don't eat tonight?' he asked, looking at my empty hands.

I wanted to speak to him of my concerns, but how could I?

'You should eat. Are you ill?' His voice carried a thread of something . . . concern?

I shook my head. 'No. I –' I glanced at Layak, and in turn the sâhib also looked at him. Layak stopped chewing and stared from me to the sâhib. He spoke to the sâhib in a polite, questioning tone, but the sâhib said nothing, shaking his head slightly. When Layak rose and went into the darkness, I said, quietly, 'Sâhib? I am troubled.'

He wiped his hands on a cloth. 'What worries you . . . Daryâ?' It was the first time he had said my name since he had repeated it in the courtyard in Jalalabad. He did not say it easily, adding it almost as an afterthought, and for some unknown reason I felt a jolt when it passed from his lips. Embarrassment, perhaps, that it seemed to indicate a closeness between us, a familiarity?

'You know Layak well?'

He raised his eyebrows. As usual, he'd taken off his *longi* when we camped for the night, and his hair, although flattened by the sweat of the day, still gleamed dully in the firelight. It was harder for me to speak to him when he didn't wear his *longi*, for he appeared more foreign. 'I've spent the last number of months with him. I know him in that way, as a bearer, and syce. I needed someone who could speak Pashto to go with me past the North-West Frontier.'

I didn't understand. He wasn't directly answering my question, as a man should to a woman. It seemed he wanted to talk.

'Why did you come to my country, Sâhib?' I asked him, as I had days earlier.

He looked at me, then away, then back to me. He lifted one shoulder. 'I needed to see it. My father was of your country.'

I blinked, my mouth opening. 'Your father? But . . . you are not an *Inglis*, then? Your hair, and, and . . . everything.'

'My mother is English,' he said, haltingly, as if not really wishing to say these words.

I nodded. 'Your father was Pushtun. I know this by your eyes.'

'I only know that he was from beyond the North-West Frontier.'

'So – which is your country? England? Or Afghanistan?'

'England. It's where I spent most of my life.' With his boot he scuffed out a glowing twig which had fallen outside the fire.

I waited, for it seemed he would speak further.

'And I believed myself to be English for most of that time.'

I couldn't think of a reply. After a long time I realised he wouldn't say anything further. 'My grandmother . . . she went to many places,' I finally said. She told me . . . about these places.' *She was in love with an Englishman*, I also wanted to say, suddenly bold, but didn't.

'Your grandmother?' he said, as if distracted by his own thoughts, then continued, 'A friend in Multan, an English friend, asked his own servants if they knew of someone who could go with me, and one of them – Layak's brother – told him about Layak.' He narrowed his eyes as if thinking. 'It wasn't difficult to persuade him to come with me.'

I thought of the greedy glitter in Layak's eyes when he had talked about the money the sâhib had paid him. And would pay him to take me in.

'So you know nothing of his wife? Or how he lives?'

The sâhib's face suddenly changed. 'Oh. I did see his home when I first met him. And his wife – although of course her face was covered.'

'And? You think . . . this would be a good home? For me?' I couldn't believe I would speak so openly, but he made it possible. He watched my eyes as I spoke, nodding very slightly.

'Hmm,' he said, as if unsure. 'I didn't . . . I only thought of taking you from Jalalabad, as you implored me. What other solution is there?

Layak has proven himself to be a hard worker, and . . . what is it? Why do you shake your head?'

But I could say no more. I couldn't do it – voice my concerns as if I were a gossipy shrew. 'It is nothing, Sâhib,' I said, rising and building up the fire. 'Forgive my unnecessary talk.'

He asked me no more, but when Layak returned I saw him watching the short man, a line between his eyebrows.

I'll get to Multan, I thought to myself. Once I'm there I'll figure out how to deal with Layak. I felt strong again. I had come this far, and I could go further.

The sickness came over me gradually. It had started when we were forced to spend a number of hours wading through a muddy sludge, at times thigh-high, to emerge on to the drier earth of a plateau, and then plunge back into the turgid, evil-smelling flow. It was evening when we crossed the last ravine, and my clothing didn't dry. Insects swarmed around us as we unrolled our quilts on the low, sour ground, and I shivered, dirty and damp, through the night. The next morning I awoke with a pounding ache behind my eyes. For the rest of that day and the next I was weary, my body stiff, and the third day when I dismounted my legs wouldn't support me, and I had to hold on to my mare's mane until the weakness passed. The sâhib noticed, and enquired if I were all right.

'Of course,' I told him, for we were only one day's ride from Multan. I would not admit weakness now. It was night, and we sat around the fire.

'You mentioned your grandmother a few days ago,' he said, 'and that she'd been in other places. In Afghanistan?' Why did he choose this evening to speak to me in such a strange, personal fashion? I felt too sick to respond properly, and it was difficult to hide my exhaustion.

'Not only there,' I said. 'Other . . . places. Other countries. The Bosporus . . . Ankara . . . she said in Ankara . . .'

'She was in the Ottoman Empire?'

I closed my eyes, then opened them. 'Yes, Sâhib.' My mouth was dry, and I tried to lick my lips. 'She spoke Persian. Like you,' I murmured, shutting my eyes again.

'You wish to sleep?' he said, and I opened my eyes. He was looking at me across the fire; Layak already snored deeply.

'I'm sorry, Sâhib, I . . .'

'Yes. It's been a long day.' He poked at the fire with a stick. 'Tomorrow we will reach Multan.'

I nodded. It was as if the sâhib wished to say something to me, but didn't. Then I wondered if he was waiting for me to thank him again. 'I am very grateful, as you know, Sâhib. You have given me a new life.' I tried to say it with meaning, but Layak's snores only made me think, yet again, of what awaited me tomorrow. Combining my worry with the deep ache behind my eyes made my voice weak and forced.

'You will be fine, with Layak and his wife?' the sâhib asked. What did he want me to say? No, I wouldn't be fine. Layak would abuse me in any way he wished. I would be a slave. But at least I would be alive. And I would find a way to escape from him. I would have to find a way.

'I will be fine, yes,' I said, and then lay down, pulling off my veil as I turned my back to the *khâreji*, knowing my turn to tend the fire would come all too soon.

'Goodnight,' the sâhib said.

Goodnight, I said in my head, too weary to even murmur the reply.

At some time in the night my body burned, and I threw off my quilt. But next I was shivering, my teeth clattering. As Layak woke me to watch the fire – my turn was always last, before dawn – I fixed my veil in place and struggled to sit upright. All of my joints and muscles ached so deeply that even the touch of my pantaloons against my hips caused pain. I watched the flames dancing before me. But instead of giving comfort, they now took on monstrous and frightening shapes. I squeezed my eyes shut, but still the shapes stayed on the insides of my eyelids, and I knew they were *jinn*, following me to this country. After a time I heard small whimpers, like those of a puppy taken from its mother, and they were so close inside my head that I realised they must be made by my own throat. And as I tried to stop the sounds, to open my eyes so that I could keep the fire burning, a large dark shape came upon me. I fought it, cursing its strength, but it held my arms tightly in its grip, speaking to me in a garbled tongue. I tried to kick it with my legs, but they would not obey, and it was easier, finally, to lie still, and let it cover me with its hot fire.

* * *

I heard the sâhib call my name many times, but it was too difficult to move. I wanted to answer him, say yes, yes, I hear you . . . what was his name? Had he told me his name? I opened my mouth, but nothing came out. It was as if all of my blood had been taken from me, and I was useless flesh stretched over bones which smouldered with painful heat. My throat gulped as I breathed in the dry air, and all I could make were small noises. Except for my own tiny sounds and a slight fluttering – the same rippling sound as a kite when it catches the wind beneath its body – all was silence. Finally I opened my eyes; I couldn't understand the shape above me, although I knew it was not the dark evil that had come upon me before. As I lay blinking, I realised it was simply a quilt, its edges flapping in a slight breeze. Draped over sticks driven into the ground on either side of me, it shaded me from the sun.

I turned my head and saw the *khâreji* sitting on a rock. He held his book and writing stick. He stared at the river and then back to his book, moving the stick across the page. He quietly sang in what I thought must be English – it wasn't Hindi or Persian.

'Sâhib,' I said, but my voice was a whisper, and he didn't hear me. I tried again, and this time he looked in my direction, and put down his book and stick and came to crouch beside me, studying my face.

'What's wrong with me?' I asked, even the effort of holding my eyes open and focussing on him difficult.

'I don't know. Have you been sick like this before?'

'No. I'm always strong.'

'Do you want water?'

'Yes,' I whispered, and he brought me a flask. I shakily raised myself on one elbow and through habit put the flask in position to move it under my veil, and then, in a confused moment, realised that my veil was not in place. I knew I should feel shame, or anxiety that the *khâreji* looked upon my uncovered face, but I didn't. I took the flask and drank, then lay down again, as slowly and carefully as if my body were made of fragile porcelain.

There was a touch on my forehead, and I opened my eyes again. The sâhib still crouched beside me, and I knew he had placed his hand on my face. He poured water from the flask on to a soft cloth, wrung it and placed it across my forehead. Still looking at him, I reached up with shaking fingers to touch the soothing coolness.

'You have a fever,' he said. 'Try to sleep.'

Now I caught his hand in mine and held it. 'Don't leave me here, Sâhib,' I whispered. If he were to go now, when I was too weak to move, the beasts who roamed and howled at night would immediately prey on me. To my horror tears rolled from my eyes. 'Don't leave me,' I repeated.

'Sleep,' he said, as he sat in the dust beside me. 'Don't worry. Just sleep.'

Still holding his hand, I closed my eyes.

I slept and woke, slept and woke. Sometimes I saw the *khâreji* tending the fire or eating, and sometimes he simply looked down on me. Once I reached my hand to him as I had before. This time he took it and gently put it back by my side. My sleep was filled with dreams that were unlike the dreams of regular sleep. I saw my mother with one of Bibi's children in her arms. I wept at the sight of her, calling her name, begging her to help me, but she didn't come. She only stared at me as if she no longer knew me, and this made me weep even more. Another time I saw my grandmother. She sat cross-legged on the ground beside me; I thought that she must have indeed grown younger, as she had said she would in paradise, for she had never been able to sit in this position when I knew her. I cried out to her. 'Mâdar Kalân! Where have you been?'

So far, Daryâ jan, *so far. All the way back to the* zenana. *Do you remember what I told you about the* zenana?

Yes, I remember your stories. All the beautiful women. Dancing, and singing, and the poetry. 'The poetry,' I said. 'Recite to me, Mâdar Kalân. One poem.'

'Daryâ. Drink water.' There was something at my mouth.

'No. I want a poem,' I said, or think I said, turning my head from what pushed at my lips. But Mâdar Kalân was no longer there; it was only the *khâreji*, holding a flask. I was angry with him; he had chased away my grandmother.

'Leave me alone,' I tried to say. 'Leave me alone.'

And then I heard a poem, but it was not in my grandmother's voice. I didn't care, for the gentle rhythm soothed me, and I listened, my face cooled with the damp soft cloth as it moved over my face and neck.

Many wonders are manifest in sleep;
in sleep the heart becomes a window.
One that is awake and dreams beautiful dreams,
he is the knower of God.
Receive the dust of his eyes.

I heard nothing after that, and fell into darkness, where my bones continued to be broken by the claws of the *jinn*.

CHAPTER TWENTY-SEVEN

It was light. I tried to sit up, but the effort was too great. I heard splashing, and the ground vibrated beneath me, and the sâhib was once more bending over me, studying my face.

He picked up my hand and gently pushed back my sleeve and looked at my arm. Then he put his fingers into the top of my *kamis* and pulled it down so that he saw the bare skin of my chest. I tried to put up my hand to stop him, tried to wet my lips enough to cry out, to protest at his immoral treatment of me. Would he take advantage of me, in my weakness? He was not such a man; I was sure of this. What, then, was he doing?

'Sâhib,' I whispered, finally finding the strength. 'Please. What do you want?'

He stared at my chest, and then pulled up my *kamis* to cover me again. He put his hand under my head and lifted it, holding a dripping flask to my lips. I drank; this water tasted like honey. When I had finished he wiped the water from my chin with his fingers, as if I were a small child, and I tried to smile, but couldn't.

'I must take you to Multan,' he said. 'You can't lie in this heat any longer. I know now what it is. You have dengue. Daryâ? Can you understand me?'

I put my tongue to my dry lips. 'Den-gay?' My voice was the croak of a dying bird. 'What is this?'

'Your skin . . .' he struggled for the right word. 'Your body has . . .' He made a circular motion on his own chest. 'The red roughness that comes with this illness. The . . . rash,' he said, nodding. 'And it is appearing on your face now. I thought it was a simple fever, that it would pass . . .

He looked behind him, and I followed his gaze to the grazing stallion and mare, and the donkeys. His face showed worry; suddenly I saw how tired he looked. 'Dengue can last for many days – weeks.

Already you have lain here for three days. Layak has gone ahead. There was no reason for him to remain.'

Layak. I realised I hadn't even thought of him. The sâhib must not have slept, caring for me all this time. I was flooded with an exhausted shame. What had he seen, done for me? I didn't want to think of such embarrassing intimate things, and closed my eyes tightly.

'Does the pain grow worse? I know it affects the muscles and joints.'

I opened my eyes, but didn't look at his face. Instead I stared at his fingers, still holding the flask. 'The same.'

'You're very weak, but you must try to ride,' he told me. 'There's no food left, and you can't remain like this . . .' He stopped. 'I'll pack up the donkeys. It's only half a day's ride.'

'I will die?' I whispered, but he had already moved too far from me to hear. I repeated the question to myself, but even as I heard my own whispered words I knew the answer was no, no, of course not. After all of this, all that had happened, I wouldn't come this far to die here, in the open, like an animal.

'Come,' he said, when he had packed up the camp, and had helped me to stand, his arms around me. I leaned against him, clutching his shirt. I no longer cared that he touched me, or I him.

He lifted me on to my mare. I bent forward, clutching her mane, unable to sit upright. Sâhib came to me with an unwound *longi* and wrapped it around my waist. I watched his hands dully as they tied the cloth securely at my side, too weak to even wonder at this odd action. Then he mounted his horse and took the reins of my mare. He held the end of the *longi* in one hand.

We rode side by side, slowly, the donkeys tied to his horse. In this way we made our way toward Multan. It took an endless time. For much of that strange journey I kept my eyes closed, as the sun in them made my head ache even more. The slow, plodding footsteps of my mare jarred my bones against each other as if a hammer struck them, and I used all my strength to not cry out. Every so often I drifted towards the strange coloured sleep of my illness, leaning further forward or to one side, and at this the sâhib gave a sharp tug on the cloth, and the yank at my waist pulled me back to consciousness. And then I heard the calling of many voices and the cries of animals and birds, and as I opened my eyes there was a new sensation, a rocking motion unlike any I had ever felt before.

'What is this?' I murmured. All around us there were crowds of people and horses and goats and cages of squawking chickens and moaning pigeons on a large wooden structure. And we were on water.

'We're crossing a small river into Multan.'

I nodded, feebly plucking at my *châdari* to pull it up and hide my face. I did not even care to look at the city which would be my home. I only wanted to lie down and sleep.

The sâhib led my mare through a gate in a tall wall. Not far from the wall he stopped at a small mud house with a thatched roof and called out Layak's name as he dismounted.

Layak came to the doorway; a veiled woman stared from behind his shoulder. I saw that she carried a child within, and cupped her hands over her extended belly as if protecting it. In the next instant two small dark children with large round eyes peered around her skirt.

Sâhib and Layak spoke, Layak gesturing at his wife. She answered in a high, chattering voice, looking at me the whole time. Then Layak spoke one more time, still in the doorway, and Sâhib nodded, his face grim. Layak's wife bowed her head at us, then spoke a word to the children, who scampered inside. Layak and his wife followed them, closing the door.

Sâhib stayed where he was, his face fixed as if thinking. Even though my head was so heavy, there could be no mistaking what had just happened. I knew Layak's wife worried for her children and unborn child because of my illness and would not allow me in their house until I was well again. I knew I should worry about what would happen now, but I was too ill.

Sâhib swung back on to his horse and again picked up the lead to my horse and the donkeys and turned us in another direction.

I dully looked around the streets we passed through, but it seemed that my eyes would not tell me what I saw. Finally we stopped again, and the sâhib dismounted, handing the reins to a man with a high white turban, and went towards a house. But this was like no other house I had seen. This one stood alone, surrounded by trees and flowers, big as a mosque and built of square stones.

I waited, swaying on my horse, until the sâhib came out and put up his arms to help me dismount. When he set me on my feet I gripped the mare's mane with both hands, a high ringing in my ears, a brilliant whiteness blinding me. My fingers were useless; they opened and I dropped to my knees, but in the next instant the sâhib picked me up. As he carried me, my head too heavy to lift from his chest, the noise and blindness passed. He took me to a simple hut behind the big house; in the doorway stood a woman dressed in white. There was a small smear of red paste on her forehead.

'You will stay here,' the sâhib said. 'Prita will care for you.' Then he carried me inside and laid me on a pallet behind a screened partition.

The coolness of the hut was wonderful; I couldn't stop the moan of relief as I lay on the softness of the covered pallet. The woman brought me water and I drank.

My last thought was that I would not see the sâhib again, and a great sadness came over me, for I had not thanked him enough for all he had done for me.

I tossed and whimpered on the pallet; the woman came to me often. She wiped my face with cool wet cloths, taking off my sweat and dirt-stained clothing and cleansing my body with water that burned my nose and skin. She dressed me in something soft and put both water and strange-tasting, bitter tea to my lips many times. She helped me in my private business.

At first I thought she had the voice of an instrument, for always I heard high, tinkling music as she came to me. I didn't question any of this; it was as if I were a small child who had no strength or voice, as if the woman I had been had disappeared into the heat and misery of my illness. I wanted nothing but sleep, to try and escape the aching in my body, and yet even that sleep was disturbed by distressing images and voices. Once I thought I saw the sâhib staring down at me, and I put up my fingers to feel if he was real or one of my strange dreams. But my hand touched nothing, and I closed my eyes. When I opened them again the room was empty, and I knew I had been dreaming, for the sâhib would have left Multan.

And then I awoke early one morning – the room was only beginning to show light – and I heard the soft call of a dove from outside the window. I lay there, listening to its sweet voice, and knew with certainty that I had slept deeply, without the fevered nightmares. I felt a different and yet familiar mild ache, and knew it was only hunger, and that this must mean I could no longer be so ill.

I sat up, but moved too quickly in my hope, and was immediately dizzy. There was the rustle of cloth and the sound of the music, and then the woman with the red mark on her forehead knelt by me and laid her cool hand against my cheek. She spoke, using my name. I could not remember if I had been told hers; I pointed at her and raised my eyebrows.

'Prita,' she said, and I had a vague memory of the sâhib's voice saying this name. Her face was gentle and she spoke in a soothing manner, but I could not understand; she spoke the language of the sâhib and Layak – Hindi. She wore many bracelets on her wrists and ankles; they jingled and clinked as she moved, and I knew then it was these that I heard while I lay on the pallet. She brought me water and bathed my face, then went outside and shortly returned with the same bitter tea. Now I could sit up, leaning my back against the wooden wall. I drank the tea, and as I finished, another woman came around the partition.

I knew immediately she was an English woman. She had skin so pale that it appeared she wore a coating of light ash on her face and hands. Her hair was dark, yet threaded with white. Her eyes were very pale blue, and fanned with lines on either side. Deep lines also ran on either side of her mouth. By the white in her hair and the lines on her face I knew her to be no longer young, but she did not look old in the way of the women I had known. Her dress was a soft fabric covered with a pattern of many small colourful flowers; I could not think how these perfect shapes were put on to the cloth. The dress had a high neck and long sleeves, and at her waist drew in very tightly. But then it flared out to a great width. Again, I couldn't understand what held the dress out like this. From the bottom of the wide skirt peeked the toes of dark green silky slippers as she came towards me, but it appeared that the bones from her neck to the end of her back were joined in one solid line, and she must walk carefully, so as not to break them apart. I wondered if she had had some long-ago illness that didn't allow her to move with ease.

She spoke to Prita but looked at me. And then they both left. I stayed where I was, looking about the simple room. There was a shelf on the wall across from me, and on it were idols which appeared to be half human and half animal. There was also a picture painted with many bright colours. It was a man with a blue body, clothed only with a small orange cloth suspended from a string around his waist. Heavy garlands of white and pink flowers were wound around his neck, and on his head a crown of brilliant blue and green feathers with round, white eyes.

I looked away from the evilness of these idols to a picture that hung on another wall. The picture was framed by gold-painted wood. White and blue and red ribbons were looped over it. It was not a young woman, and she had the same white face as the woman in the flowered dress; I wondered if it was her sister. This one's dress was dark and severe. Her expression was also very harsh, unlike that of the woman in the flowered dress. She stared straight ahead in a piercing and somehow demanding way.

As I studied her dress again, I looked down at myself. I realised for the first time that I was wearing a white dress with long sleeves. It was loose, although fitted closely about the neck. I wore no pantaloons, and felt naked without them.

Prita came in with a bowl of rice with mashed lentils; it tasted good to my tongue but my stomach would only take a very small amount. Then I lay down again, exhausted by that simple task, and when I awoke the sâhib was there, and this time my head was clear, and I knew he was not a dream.

I almost cried out with pleasure, surprised at my joy at seeing him. I had believed I wouldn't see him again, and now he was here.

His uncovered yellow hair – shorter now – was soft and gleaming as if just washed, and his face was freshly shaved. He wore unfamiliar clothes – tight-fitting pants and a coat of the same pale brown fabric, and underneath the coat another smaller coat, and under that a white shirt with a stiffness about the neck. A scarf of silk the colour of the early evening sky knotted under the collar of the shirt. So many layers of clothing, like the white woman. He looked like an Englishman now. Even his eyes did not seem to carry what I thought I'd seen: if he hadn't told me of his father I would believe him to be only English.

Again he held the leather book and the stick, as I had seen him do on our journey. He sat on a small wooden stool on the other side of the room, the stick moving rapidly across the page. He glanced up at me, and when he saw my eyes open, put down the stick.

'You are better,' he stated.

'Yes. How long have I lain here?'

'Six days.'

'So long,' I said, sitting up. He stood well back from the pallet and so I did not have to raise my eyes to him. He looked uncomfortable in a way I didn't understand, although perhaps it was just the strangeness of seeing him in English clothing.

'I thought you would have left Multan.'

He turned away, looking out the window. 'I . . . I wanted to make sure you recovered.'

'Will Layak come for me soon?' I asked.

Again, he didn't answer. I wondered if he was still angry with me for causing so much difficulty. 'Where is this place?' I asked.

He turned to face me again. 'A godown – servant's hut. The Hindu woman, Prita, who looks after you is the *ayah* – the *nōkar* – to the lady of the bungalow. The big house.'

'The lady with white skin and the stiff body – is she the wife of a *hâkem*?'

A look of slight amusement crossed his face. 'No. Her husband is not a ruler, although an important man. They are my friends – from home.'

I realised that my face was open; I didn't even know where my veil was. And then I saw that my knees and calves were not covered by the white dress. I knew that in caring for me during my illness this man must have seen me in a way no man should, and my face grew hot, although no longer from fever. I quickly drew up my knees and pulled the thin fabric over them, and the sâhib also seemed embarrassed, again turning away while I tucked the hem of the dress under my feet. As I did so I felt the brush of my gold wedding anklet, and this gave me a sudden sense of peace. I fingered it through the thin cloth of the dress that now covered my ankles.

'Do all the people of England speak Persian?' I asked him.

'No. I studied it when I found out . . .'

There was awkward silence. 'Who is that white woman,' I asked, pointing to the painting on the wall, 'to have such a place of honour?'

'Queen Victoria. The Queen of England.'

'The wife of the king?'

'No. There is no king. She's married, but her husband is a prince. Queen Victoria rules my country.'

My mouth opened. 'But how can this be? A woman is ruler of the whole of your country? She's married and a queen but her husband is a prince, not a king? And he's beneath her in power?'

'Yes.'

I sat very still, staring at the picture of the unsmiling woman. This fact was one that even my grandmother had not known. Although she had told me that the moon might be a woman and preside over the stars, she had never told me that a woman might be a queen, and rule men.

'I know so little of England,' I said, and he sat on the stool again. 'Only a few facts. From my grandmother.'

'And how did she know these things?' he asked, his face relaxing a little.

'She . . . knew an Englishman. He told her that the English will never be slaves. That you must rule everything, even the oceans.'

His smile dropped away, and at his expression I asked, 'So it is true?'

When he didn't answer immediately, I continued. 'England must be very, very big. Bigger even than India.'

Now his face darkened. 'No. It is a tiny country. But very powerful. The most powerful nation on the earth.'

Although the words should have been spoken with pride, instead the sâhib said them with a tone that was almost bitter.

'But this is a good thing for you, isn't it? That your country is so great.'

He drew in a deep breath. 'Greatness comes in many forms. I'm not sure . . .'

I waited. 'Not sure of what?'

'To rule people can be a good thing. Or it can take away their freedom.'

I thought about freedom. 'Your country doesn't rule mine now.'

He shook his head. 'No.'

'So . . . I'm free? You think I'm free?'

He cleared his throat. 'Well, I know nothing of your individual freedom. I meant freedom in the sense –'

'I have no freedom. Nor did my mother, nor will my sister. My grandmother, she was taken to a *zenana* when a child – did she have freedom? When she lived with her Englishman and he took away her children, did she have freedom?'

The sâhib stood, the stool tipping and rolling backwards. I realised, by the strange look on his face now, that I was speaking too loudly, too personally. Had the illness made me forget my manners, my sensibilities?

Suddenly I found that I was standing as well, and was ashamed, and lowered my eyes.

'Even in England,' the sâhib said, 'it's very, very difficult for many of the people. I shouldn't have used that particular word – freedom. All I was doing was . . . I was trying to explain that I'm not sure of my feelings for the country where I've spent much of my life, the country I always thought of as mine, until a few years ago. When I'm away from it I see it more clearly, see what it's done in the past, and what it continues to do. And I'm not sure . . . I'm returning to it, but . . .'

My legs trembled, and I sat again. 'I apologise for my rudeness. It's just that . . . I love my country, Sâhib. I didn't want to leave it, but I had to. And I know I can't return. You left your country willingly, didn't you?'

At his nod I continued. 'And you can return whenever you want, just as you can return to my country – the land of your father – when you want to?'

Again he nodded.

'And yet you show little desire. So. You have two countries, both of which you can go to, and leave, at will.'

He watched me.

'And I . . .' *I have no country now. No home, no family, no country.* 'What will happen to me? What, Sâhib?'

He remained standing. 'Layak. Perhaps it won't be as . . .' his voice trailed away. By the fading of his voice, and his expression, it was clear he knew then that my working for Layak would not be a positive thing. An image of his hut and the mud that surrounded it came into my head. Layak's suggestive stares, the high, demanding voice of his wife, the bony dog slinking under the hut, the flies swarming on his children's faces.

The sâhib shook his head, then, and I saw anger by the movement of his jaw. 'I don't know what will happen to you. How can I know? Hopefully all will go well with Layak and his family. It's all I can do; you've put me in a terrible position, and I –' he stopped abruptly as Prita came in, stooping gracefully to take my bowl of half-eaten food from the floor beside my pallet.

Without looking at me again, he left with her.

CHAPTER TWENTY-EIGHT

I SAT ON THE pallet for a long while. I was shocked by how I had spoken to the sâhib. He had done so much for me – everything he could, everything I'd asked – and I had repaid him by arguing with him, demanding answers when he had none. Was I already forgetting how I had been treated by Shaliq? Could I not simply be grateful to this man, bow my head and thank him? I wouldn't blame him if he didn't come to the hut again.

As the afternoon shadows grew long I felt well enough to walk, slowly, to the doorway of the hut. I looked out at the great expanse of trees and gardens of flowering plants, none of which were familiar to me. A number of Indian men in white clothing bent over the flowers, cutting and trimming and picking up the fallen blossoms and carefully wiping dust from large leathery leaves. Another swept the leaves from beneath the trees and the pathways that led to the big house. The back of it was visible through the trees; a long raised platform with wooden pillars running along its outside wall. On the floor of this platform were many flowering plants in containers, and chairs and tables.

I saw then that the hut – the godown – I stayed in was only one of others; there were a number of similar huts among the trees, and outside them sat men dressed in white. Some looked at me, and I stepped back inside and took a thin white headscarf that must have belonged to Prita, and wrapped it over my head and covered the bottom of my face.

When I again went to the doorway one of the men sitting nearby called to me, but I didn't understand him. And then he spoke in Pashto. 'You are the Afghan woman?' he asked.

I nodded, and he rose and came nearer.

'You come with the sâhib and my brother from the North-West Frontier,' he stated.

'Your brother is Layak?'

He nodded, patting his chest. 'It was I who told the sâhib about Layak. He looked for a man who could speak Pashto to accompany him beyond the North-West Frontier. He asked me to go,' he said, straightening his shoulders, 'for I speak Pashto with much greater ease and understanding than Layak, but I could not leave my job. I am a *chuprassi*,' he said, his expression and voice proud. 'You know this job?'

I shook my head.

'I attend the front door, admitting guests for Sâhib and Memsâhib's visiting. A very coveted position.'

I closed my eyes for a moment, putting my hand on the doorframe. Standing for even these few moments had made the humming in my ears return.

'We all heard of your illness, the one that feels like breaking of the bones. Very bad,' he said. 'There is no such illness to be found in the mountains and high pastures; it hides in the ravines and swamps.'

'I am well now.'

He shook his head as if he didn't believe me. 'So. What will you do?'

'Do?'

'Here, in Multan.'

'I . . . I will work for your brother and his wife.'

He raised his bushy eyebrows. 'I think not. You don't know? Even here they know.' He glanced back at a group of men playing a game with stones on the ground. 'There is so much talk. Talk, talk, talk, always, with these Hindus. Too much talk.' I looked at the men. The evening sun reflected off their white clothing; it made me dizzy. I turned from the man and went back inside.

When the room had grown dark and Prita lit small oil lamps smelling of coconut before leaving again, the sâhib returned. I sat cross-legged on the pallet. I had kept Prita's scarf with me, and now covered my face when he stepped behind the screened partition and sat on the stool. I thought he would tell me about Layak's decision, and waited.

'In Jalalabad,' he started, without even greeting me, 'you said you did not wish to, no, could not – return to your tribe. I should have asked you more then. If I'd realised . . . Now you say you can never return to your country.' But his voice wasn't angry; it was quiet. 'You must tell me what you ran from, and why you can't return to the place you love.'

Surprised, I stared at him. I didn't want to talk about the curse, and my father and Shaliq. He wouldn't understand. For one horrible moment I thought he might try and return me to Shaliq if I mentioned his name. Then I realised this was absurd.

'Why did you run from your husband?' he asked again.

I looked at the wall behind him, at the picture that hung there. The lamplight flickered in the air from the window, and long, wavering shadows were cast over the white woman's stern face. 'Not for the reason Fareed said. But it's impossible for me to return.'

He made a sound, just a murmur in his throat, and I looked back at him. 'So you keep saying,' he said. 'You have no children that you leave behind with the nomads?'

'No, Sâhib.' I didn't like his question; would he think this of me, that I would abandon a child? 'And I am not a nomad by birth. I am Tajik. Born a Tajik but married into the Ghilzai,' I said, although I don't know why I thought it important he knew this. 'And if I had a child I would not have needed to leave. If I had a child I would have stayed.'

He shook his head. 'It seems you speak in riddles. What of your Tajik family, then?'

'What of them?' I stared at his shoes.

'Is there nobody who looks for you? I know the story about your brother was a lie,' I flinched at the word, 'but is there no one who will worry about you if you simply . . . disappear? Wonder where you are, or await your return? Do you have a mother, or fa—'

'As a married woman who has left her husband,' I interrupted, growing more annoyed and yet still keeping my gaze lowered, 'no one will pity me; my father especially would reject me. No one will want to help me, for it would cause bad blood between the Ghilzai and my people.' My voice had begun to rise, just slightly, and I stopped, shutting my lips tightly. I had, only hours earlier, told myself I shouldn't have treated the sâhib so disrespectfully. And yet I was beginning to do it again. But he kept asking questions, kept forcing me to talk, when all my life I had been told I should remain quiet.

'From what you tell me – or do not tell me – I don't understand what could have made you leave your husband. It's clear to me you are determined, and strong of character, and yet surely you were aware you couldn't survive by yourself. Didn't you have a plan, someone to help you? If you knew you couldn't go home, where did you think you would go?'

I was breathing heavily; he was insinuating that either I lied or I was a complete fool. I couldn't help myself; I looked into his eyes. 'Do you listen to yourself? Why do you think I asked – no, begged – to come with you, to leave my country and agree to work for a low man like Layak? Do you think that if I had somewhere to go – anyone who would shelter me – I would journey to a strange place, knowing no one, my future completely uncertain? Yes. I am alone, and no one waits for me. No one cares if I disappear.' My voice was now unpleasantly loud, and, I was sorry to hear, had an edge of self-pity.

'Not even the grandmother you've mentioned? Wouldn't she –'

'She's been dead many years.' There was no self-pity in my voice now, and my stare was unblinking. 'So please don't speak of her again.' He made me feel more worthless than I already did, with his constant questions about no one caring about me, stressing how alone I was.

'I'm sure if you apologised for whatever it was you did, your husband—'

I stood, ripping the white scarf away from my face. My skin was as hot as if the fever coursed through me again. 'You are a fool,' I said. 'You understand nothing. My husband beat me, brutally, over and over. He was a loathsome, cruel man, and my father sold me to him to be rid of me. Do you know why he sold me to this unknown and despicable man? Because no Tajik would have me. Because I'm worthless, Sâhib.' I realised I was shouting, but didn't stop. 'And when my worthlessness was proven to my husband, because I did not give him a son – a child – he meant to kill me, and so I ran. I ran to save my life, Sâhib. To live. So don't tell me to go back, to apologise.' I had twisted the scarf into a tight knot, and now threw it to the ground between us. 'To face my husband again would mean certain death, a long, slow and painful death. Do you understand *now*?'

He stared at the veil, his face stiff, all colour drained and his scar standing crimson. And somehow his disturbed expression pleased me. When he looked back up, his eyes were darker because of the paleness of his face, and I saw it then, saw what Layak had spoken of when he said the sâhib was soft, like a woman. But it wasn't softness. It was simply sorrow, compassion on his face. Layak was too insensitive to know the difference.

He opened his mouth as if to speak, but said nothing. He started to leave, stopped and looked back to where I stood, unmoving, my hands in fists. Then he went through the door.

I walked around the small hut, angry not only at this man, but at everyone and everything. Finally, my head aching again, I extinguished the lamps and tried to slow my breathing.

Now I had truly thrown away any chance I had had that the sâhib would help me further. If what Layak's brother had insinuated was true, that Layak had changed his mind and wouldn't take me, I could expect no further help from the sâhib. In spite of the fact that I knew him to be a compassionate man, I couldn't expect my terrible and disrespectful behaviour to be tolerated. I couldn't blame him if he turned me out into the streets of Multan the next day.

I tossed on the pallet hour after hour, and eventually the pale rays of dawn came through the window. I walked to the doorway and then back to my pallet, back and forth a number of times, feeling my steadiness returning, needing to build up my strength again for what I must face this day. Finally I stood in the doorway. The air was misty and the night dew filmed the grass with silver. Birds called in quiet twitters from the trees, and the servants moved in the garden and on the raised platform at the back of the house. A shuttered door opened and the sâhib stepped out, holding a cup. This time he didn't wear the two jackets, but only the pale pants and white shirt, although without the stiff part around the neck or the tied silk strip of fabric. As he looked across the expanse of grass, the cup halfway to his mouth, he saw me, and his hand stopped. My face was uncovered, and I didn't reach up to pull the white headscarf over it, and after a long moment I stepped back inside the hut.

Even though worried and distracted, not hungry at all, I ate all of the rice and fruit Prita brought a short while later. I didn't know if I would be staying here, or if I would have to worry about finding food soon. Prita smiled as if pleased when she took the empty plates, and returned with warm water for bathing. I was glad to see that the rash that had covered me had now faded completely. As I combed my hair with a wooden comb Prita had given me, the sâhib suddenly came through the door. I was ashamed of my outburst the evening before, weary of worrying when he would tell me to leave. I was glad I wouldn't have to wait any longer. I took a deep breath, clutching the comb. The sâhib's eyes took in my unplaited hair, falling to my waist over the white dress.

'You can see that I am well now,' I said, although I knew how weak I still was.

The sâhib crossed to the window, his mouth in a straight line. He stared at the back of the bungalow.

'Sâhib?' I said, after some time, and he started, looking back as if he had forgotten about me. 'Layak won't take me,' I stated. 'I know.'

He shook his head. 'I misjudged his character,' he said. 'And maybe I misjudged yours.'

I didn't know if this was a criticism or a compliment. 'Do you wish me to leave this place?' I asked.

'Where would you go? You wouldn't be any better off than you were in Jalalabad, would you? At least that was your own country. Here . . .' He walked back and forth in front of me. 'You can't even speak any of the languages.' I felt he spoke – argued – more with himself than me. 'I have always been . . . I don't think things through. I am . . . what?' He said a short word, loudly, in English, and by his vehemence I suspected it to be a profanity. 'I do things without thinking them through,' he finished. 'Impulsive. I have always been this way.'

'As I speak,' I said, hoping he understood this to be an apology.

He stopped walking. 'I can't leave you here. I know only the people in this house in Multan, and they have no work for you. I've asked that they enquire of others, but . . .'

I nodded. 'I understand.'

'I must go to Bombay. I have an arranged passage, home to England, and if I don't arrive in time for the ship's departure I'll be forced to wait two months for another. Already I've been away from home so much longer than I planned – well over a full year. I'm expected home on that ship.'

'Bombay? It is also India?'

'Yes. It's still a long journey from here. Many weeks' travel. And I am so –'

He stopped, and I knew he meant to say that he was so late, so behind in his plans, and that he'd wasted so much time. Because of me.

'And so this is all I can work out. For you,' he said. 'If I offered to find someone to journey back with you, to Jalalabad, would you go?'

I stayed perfectly still.

'I knew you wouldn't. Couldn't. Now I've brought you here, and yet there's nothing for you. You'd be worse off in Multan than you would have been in Jalalabad – at least Afghanistan was your country, with your own people.'

Again it seemed he spoke more to himself than to me.

'So. If you cannot go back, and it is no good for you to stay here . . . I have given this much thought.' He kept touching the tied silk around his neck, today a deep green, stroking it as if it comforted him. 'I have many friends in Bombay,' he said. 'Many. I know I will be able to find you a place – a job – in an English house there.'

I waited, trying to cover my surprise with a blank expression. But it was difficult; my chest rose and fell under the white dress as I breathed rapidly.

'Will you come?' His voice was careful, with no emotion. 'If your answer is yes, we must leave tomorrow. I know you haven't fully recovered, but –'

Silence fell in the hut. Outside the window a man sang in a low voice, the tune punctuated by the sound of a blade cutting through branches. A child's voice called in Hindi, and far in the distance, an ox bellowed. Would I go to Bombay? We stood a few feet apart in the small hut. As well as shocked, I was embarrassed by his kindness. I couldn't understand his concern over my future after my lies in Jalalabad and my most recent display of ill temper and forwardness.

And yet he also seemed . . . not embarrassed, but uncomfortable, as if he, too, couldn't understand why he would confuse his own life by continuing to help me.

I had come this far with this man, and no harm had befallen me. There seemed no other option. 'I will be ready tomorrow,' I told him, my voice matching his in its toneless quality. I couldn't yet sort out my thoughts at the idea of this next plan. 'I thank you, Sâhib. Again.'

He inclined his head, and then left me in the hut.

We left Multan early the next morning. As the sâhib and I rocked back and forth in a bullock cart, I was shocked to realise that on our arrival in this city I had been so ill that I had ridden through the streets as if blind and deaf.

Colour was everywhere; it was the first time I had seen women in *châdaris* which were not the shades of the earth – here were women in flowing, voluminous, pleated coverings of vibrant shades of scarlet and orange and saffron. Some of the *châdaris* had a small peak at the top, which gave them an added joyful look. There were also unveiled Hindu women in beautifully coloured skirts and separate bodices, some with gold or silver threads running through the fabric, but these bodices were shamefully small, exposing all of their arms and the brown skin of their midriffs. Their heads were often uncovered as well, and their hair, fastened tightly against their heads, gleamed richly. I saw that the sâhib gazed freely upon these women, and I looked down at my own clothing.

Prita had given me many things for the journey. She had packed everything inside a bag woven with multicoloured threads. There were three long-sleeved shirts – *kurta* – she kept saying, which reached to my thighs. One was dark green, another the grey-blue of the morning sky, and the third soft gold; they all had beads and small pieces of coloured glass sewn around the neck and sleeves, and simple embroidery decorated the bottom edge. 'Muslim,' she said, nodding, also giving me pantaloons which matched the *kurtas*. There were new sandals of thin leather and two square headscarves which Prita insisted were *hijbas* – one a deep orange with knotted fringes and the other sheer pale gold. I chose to wear the gold outfit; its colour and softness against my skin brought me a simple pleasure.

Prita had also given me the wooden comb, soap and cloths for washing and drying, and an oil which she called *neem*. She demonstrated that I was to rub it on to my skin to keep insects from biting, as well as another oil, which she made clear I should use on my hair to control its weight, and so that it would shine like hers. And just before I left the hut she slipped a number of bracelets from one of her wrists and put them on to mine. I was grateful for her many kindnesses, and hugged her before we parted. Now I kept the bag firmly between my feet on the floor of the cart. In it was all I owned – all I had to travel with me to such a far place.

The city was alive with birds and animals: from shrieking, whistling bold parrots and gloriously coloured parakeets in brass and wooden cages to elephants with bells tied around their ankles. The monstrous wrinkled creatures patiently shuffled with their bells chiming through the crowds behind their keepers. There were small creatures with black faces and tiny clever hands and long curled tails. Crouching on the shoulders of men, their tails wrapped around the men's necks, these little animals were obviously cherished pets. They stared about with bright, bead-like inquisitive eyes, and occasionally screeched in a demanding manner, grimacing and baring their small sharp teeth.

As we rumbled through the main streets I understood why Layak had called Multan the City of Saints – everywhere were beautiful mosques and temples and tombs of Sufi saints. The buildings we passed were such as I had never seen; many were of designs created with a delicate placement of bricks, while others were covered with mosaics and coloured glass. Grand homes had protruding windows, sometimes decorated with friezes of blue-glazed tile and painted with what looked like gold, and these opened on to ornately carved balconies. At times there was a whiff of sweet incense as we passed these balconies, and I breathed it in.

I realised I was clasping my hands to my chest when I saw the sâhib looking at me. 'Such a wondrous city,' I said, and he nodded.

'Yes, the architecture here is truly . . . wondrous, as you say,' he agreed, and held his open hand towards a domed mosque, its windows covered with grills of marble and ornamented with a dizzying design. 'It is an ancient city,' he said, and as we rumbled through an entry with a high, pointed arch, he added, 'Haram Gate. There are six such gates leading in and out of Multan.'

I thought for a moment how wonderful it would be to live in a city of this beauty, and then I remembered what I could of Layak's simple structure, with its crumbling walls and unshuttered windows and dusty thatched roof. I realised that what I saw today was for those who possessed wealth and power; as a servant I would not have been welcomed here.

We arrived at the banks of the Indus River; the sâhib had told me that for the first part of the journey to Bombay we would travel many miles down the river to the city of Sukkur. I looped the strap of my bag over my chest as we stepped off a muddy bank and into a flat-bottomed boat. The sâhib had a number of leather and camel-skin bags; so many for one man. He didn't wear his English clothes, but again dressed in loose cotton trousers and a *kurta* much like mine, but his was made for a man, in heavy striped cotton. He had also wound a white *longi* round his head, and once more I was struck by how he did not immediately appear to be a *khâreji* when his hair was covered.

We sat on low wooden boxes attached to the floor; at our feet were sacks of mangoes, pomegranates, oranges and dates, peppers and aubergines and onions, as well as a crate of grumbling chickens. Coconuts rolled back and forth in the bottom of another box, and tin cookware rattled in the corners. We were pushed away from the shore by boys who walked along the wide edges of the boat, deftly manoeuvring long poles. They sang, their voices blending into a low, simple melody.

Again I turned, as was now my custom, to watch the place I left, not knowing if I would ever see it again. As the city grew smaller, and the boys' voices louder, I still couldn't put a name to my emotion. I was going ever further from my home.

But I no longer have a home, I suddenly thought, and without warning, it was as if the toe of Shaliq's boot kicked my stomach, so that it was difficult to breathe with ease.

Was this how my grandmother had felt as she moved from place to place, always searching for contentment, for freedom?

CHAPTER TWENTY-NINE

WE WERE SIX women – four Hindu and another very young Muslim woman – and nine men, one the Muslim woman's husband. The sâhib was the only white man, but he was comfortable with the others as if he were of their country. It was clear they accepted him openly, although I saw that he carried an inner, unspoken power which commanded a quiet respect. I watched him sitting on the crate of chickens, in his *longi* and Indian clothing, talking and laughing with the men. His teeth were white and strong in his dark face, and I thought at that moment that he appeared more real to me like this than he had in the hut behind the big house in Multan. There, in his tight layers of clothing, he had grown rigid, like the white-faced woman, even his words pinched. Although perhaps, I argued with myself, that was only my interpretation, as our conversations had all been uncomfortable.

I longed to be able to understand the other women. Some of them smiled at me in a friendly manner and greeted me, but I could only hold out my hands in apology. The Muslim woman – her eyes wide and bright above her veil – continued to question me; I answered in both Pashto and Dari, but she only shook her head.

We floated, that first day, through broad, flat plains on the lazy, meandering river. The sâhib came to sit beside me, and told me that the cooler, dry weather was the best time of year to make this journey, as the river was low and wide and slow. In the beginning of the warm weather, he said, it would swell and expand with flood waters of melting snow from the north.

The sky was a brilliant blue and cloudless, the weather pleasantly warm as we floated – we were only poled by the boys when we drifted into shallows.

In the evening we stopped and the boat was tied to stakes driven into the shoreline, and the boat boys killed some of the chickens and cooked them with vegetables over small braziers. The food was plain but tasted better than any I had eaten in a long while. When it was time to sleep I went with the other women into one of the rough huts built at the back of the long boat, and the sâhib went with the men into the second. As I lay on matting in the quiet hut, the boat rocking gently, I heard the howling night-song of the jackals, the jingle of camel bells from a distant village, and smelled the cool river air, carrying the hint of dung fires. I was reminded of my life with the Ghilzai but, for the first time in a long while, was not overcome with fear or sadness. I wondered if in spite of what I had endured over the last few years, perhaps this was the way fate had intended my life to go.

The next day we travelled through a desert area called the Cholistan, and beyond the banks of the river the sand stretched endlessly. Occasionally we passed men and boys fishing, and women gathering tough reeds which I knew they would weave into baskets. In areas where channels had been dug to lead streams off the river I saw small fields of cotton growing near the villages. Birds flitted everywhere; I didn't recognise any of them and knew they were birds of the water, for there were no trees for them to roost in. And then I saw the strangest sight, and stood in my excitement, pointing.

'Sâhib,' I cried. 'Look! What is it?' Everyone turned in the direction I pointed, and some nodded and murmured.

The sâhib smiled. 'The river dolphin.'

I watched the large playful fish as it swam and dived so near the boat. I had never seen such a large fish; it was the size of a full-grown ram. It was grey-brown, and when it turned on one side, its hard fin up as if waving, I saw that its belly was pink. It had a long, slender nose that was more like a beak than anything I had seen on a fish.

'Such a huge fish in this shallow water,' I said to the sâhib, and suddenly other fish of the same kind appeared, and a group of them swam and dived beside us. I laughed and clapped my hands in delight, as did the other women, and when I turned to look at the sâhib again, I saw that he wasn't looking at the fish, as everyone else was, but at me. Suddenly conscious of my open laughter, I closed my mouth, even though it was hidden beneath the *hijba*. But I still smiled. 'You've seen this fish before?' I asked.

He nodded. 'This dolphin favours these silt-laden, slow waters of the Indus. But look, look at their eyes. Because the water is so muddy, they've become almost blind. They're all born that way.'

I unconsciously gripped his arm as I leaned over the edge of the boat to be closer to the dolphins, studying them, and saw that indeed, their eyes were fine slits with little more than a hole the size a needle might make. I watched them until they disappeared and then sat back, closing my own eyes tightly, making a picture in my head that I would always remember.

When I opened my eyes I realised I still held the sâhib's sleeve, and I took away my hand without looking at him.

We travelled down the Indus for a number of days, and every morning I awoke with a small sense of excitement at what I might see. It was a time of unexpected calm for me, sitting in comfortable silence with the other women. I was reminded of my life with the Ghilzai women, their quiet companionship, and the sense of being a part of something larger. I realised how alone I had felt since I ran from Faiza at the stream. I thought back to my fear and hunger and thirst as I hid those first days, and the uncertainty I had felt when imploring the sâhib to help me. And even when he had taken me from Jalalabad, I could think of little but what would await me with Layak, in Multan.

I still should be uncertain – now what awaited me in Bombay? And yet for those first few days I let all of that concern wash away, for there was no going back, only ahead. And it seemed that like me, the sâhib was also at peace; he smiled easily and his face was calm as he wrote in his leather book or read from the others he carried in his bags. And because of this ease it was now natural to speak with him; although I always kept my lower face covered, I no longer felt it necessary to lower my eyes when we talked.

'Sâhib?' I asked him, one afternoon. 'Bombay. I will . . . fit, there?'

He lowered his book. 'Fit? What do you mean?

'Are there many Muslims, as in Multan?'

'There are many kinds of people in Bombay; I like it because it is not as' – he searched for the word – 'rigid as either Calcutta or Madras, the big cities to the east of India.' He ran his fingers over the cover of his book. 'In Bombay are many Hindus and Parsi, Gujaratis and Europeans, such as the Portuguese from Goa. And the British, of course.'

I could not take in this surprising information, and all the names he spoke flew from my head like bright parrots, swiftly leaving the trees. 'I don't know of any of these people except for Hindus.'

He smiled. 'Parsi are originally from Persia, many years ago. Now they're highly regarded in Bombay because they are business people, and more receptive to European influence – more willing to embrace the morals and work ethic – than the Hindus. And the English favour dealing with Muslims, because we worship one God, the Christian God,' he raised his eyebrows, 'as you worship one God.'

His words inwardly shamed me. I did worship, but did I ever call on Allah any more? It seemed that my prayers were now to something I couldn't name. I believed in the good of Allah, and the comfort he brought to so many. Just not to me. I had changed in more ways than I realised.

'The many gods of the Hindus upset our overly sensitive beliefs,' the sâhib said then, with a laugh, but it was a scornful sound. I wanted to ask him about his Christian God, but he continued.

'European refers to anyone not native. And so there they all are, these people of Bombay, with their different religions, different languages, but they live together fairly peacefully.' He stopped, looking at my eyes. 'As I said, it is less restricted than other cities, and for you I think this will be a good place, Daryâ. Maybe you will find . . .'

'Find what?' I prompted.

He shrugged. 'What is it you wish to find? What would make you happy?'

Nobody had ever asked me this question. I thought of how my grandmother had said those who are not content must spend much time searching for happiness. 'I think I would like to feel that I belong.'

He smiled, a strange smile. 'I think we would all like that.'

'But – surely – if you say England is your country, you must belong when you are there.'

'Do I? I don't know. I don't seem to be able to settle anywhere. But you – do you want to belong as you did once? In your village, or with . . .' he hesitated, 'with your husband?'

I shook my head. 'I didn't fit in my village. I didn't behave as I should have. I was always bringing trouble upon myself.'

His smile was now playful. 'I can see that. How you would have been as a child.'

His word and smile made me see that my childish disobedience and misbehaviour wasn't that serious. And then I thought of Sulima, and how the deeper changes within me had begun because of her presence. I didn't realise my face reflected that sad time, but it must have, for the sâhib's smile faded.

'And with the Ghilzai – my husband's tribe – I was never one of them. I tried to belong, and some were accepting of me, but . . . again, I was a disappointment. Especially to my husband.'

'A disappointment?' he repeated. 'You disappointed him?'

I nodded, and then turned away, not wanting to think any more about Sulima, or about Shaliq.

As we approached Sukkur the river narrowed. Groves of date palms and eucalyptus grew along the river here, and many boats were tied along the banks. Bullock carts and drivers were waiting when we finally stopped, and all the Hindus hurried from the boat and into one of them, talking excitedly, the women waving to me. The sâhib said they were on a pilgrimage to the caves and temples located outside the city; many made this pilgrimage, he added.

I waited with the Muslim woman while her husband and the sâhib went into Sukkur in another bullock cart. Within a few hours they returned on horses, leading two others. The Muslim woman and I mounted, and the four of us went at a brisk pace along a road outside Sukkur until we reached a small caravan.

'I heard this group started for Karachi today,' the sâhib told me. 'It's best not to travel this road alone.' He left me with the Muslims then, and rode towards the others. There were three white women and five white men, as well as three Indian men. The Indians who packed the small but strong, shaggy-maned Pegu ponies with supplies were syces who would also set up camp and cook our meals.

We began the journey to Karachi, and right from the start the sâhib no longer treated me with the same ease as he had on the barge. It was now as if he wasn't sure how to be with me. Although still dressed as a native, with Afghan blood running through his veins, he proved to me that he was definitely an Englishman. All that first day the sâhib rode alongside the other white men and women, although he often glanced behind, where I followed with the Muslim couple and the syces.

That first evening, after preparing our meals, the syces set up a small shelter of mats woven from date leaves for the Muslim couple and me, then rolled themselves in the thin shawl-like garments they wore over their shoulders, and, without speaking, immediately fell asleep in the dust close to the horses.

The sâhib ate his meal with the other white people, then came to where I sat. I stood up.

'You are well?' he asked, shifting from foot to foot.

'Yes, Sâhib,' I answered, and for an unknown reason there was a discomfort between us that made me feel I should lower my eyes. But I didn't.

He eyed the rough shelter of mats.

'You are also well?' I asked, and he nodded. It was as if we were strangers in spite of all the time we had been together. All the ways he had seen me.

'Yes. Yes,' he repeated, then said, 'Goodnight,' and left to sleep in one of the daks – the small, simple structures along the side of the road, built, obviously, for the white people who travelled this route.

This same routine took place every day: we didn't speak or come near each other in the day, although every evening after the food was eaten he would approach and ask if I was well. I always said, yes, Sâhib, and then he left again and returned to his people.

I tried not to dwell upon this; I felt a strange annoyance with his behaviour towards me, and I didn't enjoy this part of the journey as I had earlier, although there was much to see and wonder at.

I noticed, as I had when we had ridden from Jalalabad until I became ill, what command the sâhib had upon a horse. It appeared he and his animal moved as one, as if there was an inner language they shared. I sensed this was due to his Afghan father, for none of the other Englishmen appeared quite the same upon their horses.

The white women sat strangely upon theirs. The saddles were attached to the sides of the animals, and so the women were forced to sit with both legs to one side, knees raised. I was surprised that they managed to ride at a steady pace sitting in this peculiar fashion, but they were at ease in their many skirts and very odd headdresses. The English women and men – except for Sâhib, with his *longi* – wore hats of a hard white substance which had been shaped into what looked like an inverted bowl, pulled low on their foreheads. One of the women had decorated hers with a snake skin and small feathers. I found it amusing; the first time we gazed upon her the other Muslim woman's eyes also laughed.

We often stopped in groves of hard-barked sheesham trees growing in sandy soil by streams. The large, leathery leaves of the trees afforded good protection from the sun. Oblong, flat pods hung from the branches, and groups of white-backed birds of prey nested in the tops of the trees. There were many travellers on this deeply rutted, well-used road. As well as people walking and riding horses and camels and being pulled in wheeled wagons, there were other odd means of travel for white women: flat beds piled with cushions. High poles and crossbars covered with material created a curtain they could pull closed to keep out the dust, but it also meant they travelled in blindness. A handle protruded from each corner of the bottom, and four bearers ran with each cart. Sometimes they stopped at the same shaded area as our group, and as I watched the women climb out of their tiny prisons, I knew, by the way they hobbled and limped about, that they were very stiff and bruised. I wondered at this choice; it was much more comfortable to ride than to be bounced and rattled along on hard wood all day, jarred with the footsteps of the bearers as their legs pumped endlessly on the narrow trails through groves of trees and marshy land.

Occasionally rugged-looking native men rode past us, glaring suspiciously at the white men, and then I understood the sâhib's comment about travelling in a group.

I loved looking into the rich green leaves of tall trees, spotting the blue, yellow and red of parrots and other small birds. Along streams there were humped cattle up to the middle of their legs in mud, and sometimes small white birds sat upon their backs. Near them women squatted, pounding clothing against the stones at the edge of the water, and as I watched the remembered rhythm, knowing the heaviness of wet cloth against rock, I thought of how long it had been since I had been a woman like that. Although in reality not a great stretch of time had passed, because of all that had happened it felt that I had been away from that life for many seasons.

I was still thinking of this as we settled for the night, the area I slept in divided from the Muslim couple by a draped mat. When the camp was still except for the chirring of crickets and I assumed everyone but me slept, I heard the rustle of clothing from the other side of the mat. Although they were discreet, almost silent, I knew what was happening, and lay perfectly still, holding my breath. I was strangely aroused by what I heard and envisioned, although it wasn't as much the act that moved me, but their quiet murmurs afterwards. The obvious companionship the Muslim man and wife shared, and the warmth of their whispered voices, a stifled laugh, made me put one hand over my already closed eyes.

What kind of woman was I now? I had nothing of my own, nothing to distinguish me but my *halhal* and the *harquus* which marked me as a married woman. And yet I was no longer a wife. I would probably never again know the sensation of a man joining with me, and although Shaliq's actions filled with me with disgust, I knew with certainty there could be more, so much more. It was not as my mother had told me: that there was no enjoyment, no fulfilment, for a good woman. Her life was so narrow, and she had never attached any importance to her own wishes. My mother had believed so strongly in this life, in performing in all ways what she thought were the right and proper ways to please Allah, and to please her husband. And yet had it brought her any pleasure?

I listened to the unknown words the Muslim woman breathed to her husband as they fell asleep, and longed to know what it was she knew and felt.

There could be no sleep for me after that, both my mind and body stirring with an unnamed frustration. I sat up in the doorway of the enclosure until the stars faded and the moon grew pale and distant. Finally the misty morning came, covering everything with dew that danced like fireflies in the first light, and I hoped that with the start of this new day I would no longer feel the darkness I had through that lonely night, listening to the sounds of love I would never know.

As we made our way south to Karachi the air was dry, the heat heavy and the blinding sun oppressive. We often travelled many miles in silence but for the constant buzzing and grinding of insects and the swooping of the wide wings of vultures overhead. At times I saw white clouds crouching on the flat horizon, but then they would slowly move and disappear. Again we passed distant villages, the spire of a mosque or the dome of a temple standing against the sky like a small dark mark. If we passed close enough for the village dogs to smell our presence they would bark and howl as if we were unseen spirits, and the sound was unpleasant as it echoed across the fields.

And then, one afternoon as we rode through rolling plains, I detected a change in the air. I breathed deeply, and a moist, fresh smell chased away the dustiness that had lodged in my throat and nose for many days. We made our way up a hill, and when we came to the top we stopped, as one, and looked at what unfolded below us.

It was the city of Karachi, sprawled on a gentle rise facing the sea. On one side was a tangled mangrove forest that would have taken days to ride through; on the other a wide river formed a natural barrier. The city itself was surrounded by mud and timber walls; from our position the walls looked to be the height of at least three men. There was a gate leading into the city from this side, and none other. The only other entrance would have to be from the water, and I knew this was a city that could not easily be attacked.

Beyond it all lay the sea. To see an ocean for the first time was mesmerising: that expanse of reflected silver in the sun's glare, and its size and beauty were so overpowering that tears came to my eyes. I was glad I was behind the Muslim couple; I didn't want them to see my tears and interpret them as weakness.

But I couldn't take my eyes from that gleaming surface as we wound our way down and then back up to the city. We passed through the gates, and I was immediately aware of soldiers and more white people than I had ever seen at one time. The Muslim couple left us, the woman and I exchanging fond goodbyes, for even though we hadn't been able to speak to each other I had liked her company. I followed the sâhib and the others to a high stone building. There we stopped and the syces were paid and took the horses, and the white men and women spoke with the sâhib and then went into the building.

'From here we'll take another boat to Bombay – this one much bigger – on the sea,' he said. 'It leaves tomorrow, so we'll stay the night in Karachi. I'll take you to a place near the docks and find you a room with other native women.'

He didn't look at me as he said this last sentence. It would be now as it had been on the caravan from Sukkur: our differences – not just man and woman, but colour and position – completely clear.

We went through the city on a creaking wagon pulled by slow-moving bullocks. This was a place of much stone, but it in no way resembled the buildings in Multan. These structures were newer, square and unadorned, as if they had been built for purpose, not beauty. I didn't understand why there were so many soldiers here, although I saw, facing the sea, weapons like the largest imaginable *tofangs*. Beside them rested piles of heavy dark balls the size of ripe melons.

When we came to what the sâhib called the docks – high platforms that ran out over the edge of the sea – we stopped at a tall building, but this one was not stone. It was wood, and the wood had been bleached to near-white by the salty air.

Outside the building the sâhib bought me food: chupattis with chickpeas and peppers, and sticky sweetmeats on a large green leaf. He handed it to me, then went with me – up many steps – to a room filled with native women and children. He stopped at the door. 'I'll come for you tomorrow,' he said, and I nodded.

It was very hot, and as I looked around the room I saw that the one window had curved bars across it, and wondered, uneasily, about this. I turned to ask the sâhib why the window was barred, and how early he would come back for me, but he had already left. I hurried out, but the stairs were crowded with men and women walking up and down, and I dared not leave the room in case I could not find my way back. It was growing dark, but there was no lamp, nothing in the room but rows of bare pallets and three pails of water with a tin cup floating on the surface of each, and behind a curtain a covered pail. The noise was terrible; the women spoke loudly and called to each other, babies screamed, and footsteps pounded on the steps outside the doorway. I sat on a pallet and ate, hardly tasting the food. The woman beside me had covered her face with her headscarf and wept. The room began to smell as the covered pail was used, and it sweltered with the day's accumulated heat. I felt the pressure of this odour and heat as though it were a thick blanket over my face, and found it difficult to breathe. Finally the footsteps stopped and children and other women slept – except for the one beside me, who continued to cry quietly – and I lay down. In the hot, low-ceilinged room a frenzy of buzzing came from the flies behind the curtain, and outside on the docks there was endless clanging and the hoarse shouts of many men. Their voices rose over the grinding and thudding and screeching; the noise broke into pieces and scattered like glass, and then began again.

In the stinking darkness I grew more and more distressed, as if my own life was about to break apart as well, and I realised, with a sickening thud, that I was afraid. The last time I had felt this particular, deep fear was as I travelled through the forests and hills, running from Shaliq, alone and lost. Now I was in a strange place, again isolated, for here I could not speak to anybody or understand even the simplest sentence. I had not even one coin to buy myself food. What if the sâhib did not return? What if he was attacked and killed, and was now lying dead in one of the filthy alleys we had passed? Or what if he simply decided he did not wish to take me to Bombay after all, and got on the big ship without me?

I tried to picture the concern on his face as he spoke to me in the hut in Multan, his easy smile on the barge. But now he was with so many of his own people. What if he decided that he had made a mistake? If he were going to abandon me, it would be here.

I tossed in a miserable state throughout that long and dreadful night. In the first light of morning I rose, unrested and sticky with the heat, and looked out of the barred window. I had never been so high above the ground, and looking down at the people and animals and carts moving on the docks below made my stomach lurch. Any sight of the sea was obstructed by buildings. A line of crows had gathered on the straight edge of the roof across from me. They lifted their wings and shook themselves, their greasy feathers standing out from their large bodies like spikes. They cried loudly, as if blaming Allah for their fate.

In groups of twos and threes the women gathered their children and bags and left, and I was overcome with panic, not knowing if I should just wait patiently for the sâhib, or whether I would be better off following the women. Maybe they, too, went to the ship. Finally the room was empty but for me. I waited and waited, sitting very still, trying to breathe quietly, preparing myself for what I would do if he did not come. Loud, heavy footsteps rang on the steps and I ran to the doorway. It was a *khâreji*, but not mine. This man did not even glance at me as he hurried by, a large package in his arms, which knocked my elbow and hip against the wall.

I went back inside the room; I was thirsty and drank the last of the warm, stale water. I told myself when the crows stopped their rough crying he would come. They eventually flew off in a beating of hard wings, but still he didn't come. A woman in a ragged sari entered and moved a broom slowly between the pallets, humming to herself. It seemed she didn't see me, as the man in the hallway hadn't. Had I become invisible? I walked between the pallets, counting the times I walked up and down, and told myself when I had walked ten times he would come; then ten more times and ten more. Still he didn't appear.

The woman finished her sweeping and took the pail from behind the curtain and, carrying it carefully, left. I sat on the pallet, pulling up my knees and resting my head on my arms. I knew he was not coming.

In the distance there was the noon call to prayer. I heard still more footsteps on the stairs; I fought from running to the doorway as I had done another four times since the first time. I stared at the doorway, willing it to be the sâhib. And my wish was answered: it was him. As he came into the room I jumped up.

'Come now,' he said, smiling. 'All is well, but we must hurry.'

I was so relieved that at first I felt joy in seeing his face, but, the next minute, deep anger flooded through me. 'All is well, you tell me?' My voice came out harsh as the calls of the crows. My hands clenched my bag. 'It is already past noon, and I have waited here, alone, not knowing –'

He frowned. 'Were you bothered? Harmed in some way?' He looked at me as if suddenly confused, obviously so unaware of the worry he had caused me. He was once more dressed in his English clothing, and now he put his fingers inside the stiff collar, pulling it from his neck as if it were too tight.

'No.' I lowered my voice. 'But . . . I didn't know where you were. I can look after myself when I know what I must do, Sâhib. What is expected. But here . . . I thought . . . I didn't know if you were coming –' Suddenly embarrassed at how childish I sounded, I pulled up my scarf to cover my nose and mouth, but he reached out and stopped me, one hand on the end of it.

'There was difficulty in purchasing the passage tickets; the boat was already full, and I had to wait hours, and then persuade . . .' His voice had become deeper, tinged with annoyance. 'It was impossible for me to be here any earlier. I didn't think you would worry.' He looked around the empty room. 'I told you I would come back for you,' he said. His voice still held a thread of anger, and I was suddenly ashamed.

'I should know the language of the country I am to live in. It is humiliating to be speechless,' I said, turning and going down the stairs, his steps a few behind mine. Now my anger was with myself.

CHAPTER THIRTY

WE JOINED A group of others, native but for a few soldiers, in a line on the dock. We didn't speak, and I was sorry I had made the sâhib angry. His shoulders were stiff, and he didn't look at me as we went to stand at the back. As one, the natives moved aside so that he could go to the front of the line, but he shook his head. With that I realised the power of English blood in India, and thought of the English song again. I also saw the natives' curious glances at me, so close at the sâhib's side.

We eventually walked up a long wooden bridge that led into this big boat that waited in the crowded harbour. The boat had tall poles that rose into the sky, and the poles were covered with limp, white cloth.

There were wooden benches lining the sides of the boat, and stairs leading both up to another level, and down, beneath the floor. As we stood, gently rocking, there was a sudden strange vibration beneath my feet, and then, as if moved by unseen rowers, we slowly began to move away from the docks, and the white cloth above us billowed and flapped with the sound of many wings. I couldn't understand the ease with which the boat moved forward, although I knew that it was partly due to the wind in the white cloth.

That first day I learned many English words about the boat – steam, sails, smokestacks, engines, decks, cabins, dining room, sailors – from the sâhib. 'It's just a small steamer that goes regularly between Karachi and Bombay on this sea – the Sea of Arabia – carrying . . . I don't know the Persian word. Letters which people write to each other.'

We sat beside each other on a bench, me pointing to the parts of the boat and repeating the words he said, as if I were a child. But he didn't make me feel childish. He seemed pleased that I was interested, smiling and nodding as I pronounced the words, and I was relieved he was no longer angry with me. It surprised me that I cared this much that he not be unhappy with me.

'Hindi will come to you quickly, once you're settled in Bombay,' he said, as if answering what I'd complained about hours earlier.

'I like English, I think,' I told him. 'Sails. Sailors. Deck,' I said again, slowly and clearly, and this time he laughed aloud, not mocking, but friendly. I saw he treated me once again as he had on the barge from Multan to Sukkur, and knew it was because there were no other English – apart from the few disinterested soldiers, who were caught up in playing games with hard pieces of coloured squares – to judge him. Or perhaps, I suddenly thought, it had been to prevent the other Englishmen and women from looking upon me with the wrong thoughts.

'You'll learn English when you begin to work. The memsahibs expect their servants to understand and speak a little, at least.'

Again, apprehension came to me, as I tried to imagine what would happen when he left me in a strange place, with unknown people. 'How many days will we be on this boat?'

'Ten, if it goes as planned.'

I had ten more days before we reached Bombay. Ten days.

Food was set out on tables in a large room upstairs during the day, and at night, the sâhib and the soldiers slept in rooms on this top floor, and I slept with the natives below, in one big room strung with rope beds and separated into areas for men and women by a long curtain. The boat continued to go forward even through the night; the humming from beneath the floor a rhythm that was like comforting music.

Such was my excitement that I found it difficult to sleep that first night, and came up the stairs to watch the reflection of the moon break into long, wavering fragments on the rippling water, the stars brilliant overhead.

I spent all the next day outside, either on a bench or standing with my arms on the railing, looking at the changing shoreline, silently repeating the English words I had learned. To be at sea! Moving through the water, the wind cool and fresh, the boat stayed close to the shoreline of vegetation or rocky projections. My body relaxed into the gentle rocking, and I found it calming to rest my eyes on the water: always moving, but always the same.

The sâhib joined me and we gazed at the shoreline together. 'Do you like the sea?' he asked.

I nodded. 'I especially liked sleeping with the movement of it last night.'

'I was told there are no storms predicted; it should be a good, smooth voyage.'

We stood in easy silence, and then he spoke again, still looking at the waves. 'To move about the world is my passion.' He smiled. 'It's only when I'm moving that I feel at peace.'

'Like a nomad.'

He smiled more broadly, his head to one side as he now looked into my face. 'Like a nomad,' he agreed, and I knew he thought what I was thinking: was I more the nomad, or he?

'So your passion brings you peace,' I said.

'I suppose so.'

I looked out at the waves, searching for the words, the old words my grandmother had taught me, so long ago. Then I recited:

Passion makes the old medicine new:
passion cuts off the bough of weariness.
Passion is the elixir that renews:
how can there be weariness when passion is present?'

There was more, but only those four lines came to me in their entirety.

He was silent for a long time before he spoke. 'Rumi. You know the poetry of Rumi?'

'Yes. And others.' The wind had risen, and I pushed aside a long piece of hair that had come unwound, and blew in front of my eyes. 'I know Rudaki. Sadi, and Hafiz.'

Then he said, still looking at the waves, 'I know nothing of you but your name, and that you can quote Rumi. Not how old you are, or anything of the life you've lived. I don't know anything about you,' he repeated, 'except that you must have, within you, a certain power, to survive as you have.'

Power. I kept my face fixed, blank, to give away nothing, but a tremor of joy ran through me. So he saw it, then. This *khâreji* saw what nobody else had seen – or at least spoken of – since I was eleven years old, and had watched my grandmother die.

After a moment I said, 'You know more of me than I of you, then, Sâhib, for I don't even know your name.'

He turned to me then, and I saw surprise on his face. 'I'm David Ingram,' he said. 'I didn't tell you?'

'Sâhib David Ingram,' I said, then repeated it, meeting his eyes.

'Yes. Sâhib Ingram.'

The wind blew stronger, the waves higher, lined with foam. We watched their shifting movement as though they might hold a secret. I thought of Rumi again. *O furious wind, I am only a straw before you; how could I know where I will be blown next?*

'I have almost twenty years,' I said then. 'It was my grandmother who taught me poetry. She was not born an Afghan, but came from the country near the Black Sea.'

He looked startled. 'The Black Sea? Russia?'

I shrugged. 'She was a Circassian, she said.'

He nodded. 'You're not of pure Afghan blood, then.'

'Nobody spoke of such a thing in my family, or village. She was made a Muslim while a child, and became a Tajik upon marrying one. So she was a Tajik, and a Muslim. As I am.'

He looked at me again, and then away, at the waves. 'I am twenty-three,' he said. 'And although believed to be English by all who know me, carry Afghan heritage, and also have India in my blood.'

'In your blood?'

He made a strange sound, close to a laugh, but not quite. 'It's an expression. Some English who were born in India never stop hearing the sounds of India, never stop missing the colours, the smells. Even though my home is England, when I'm there I have a longing, almost a sickness, at times, to return to my first home. To India.'

And I have no home. 'You are lucky, then, Sâhib Ingram, for as I have already said, you have the luxury of two countries – no, three – to call home, and also the opportunity to choose where you wish to be.' I tried to cover the edge of bitterness in my words.

'Yes,' he said. 'You're right. I should consider myself lucky.'

That evening after the meal, when I went on deck, Sâhib Ingram sat on the bench, in the same spot we had been in earlier. He was writing in his leather book, frowning with concentration, and I didn't want to disturb him, so went to the other side of the deck.

After some time I went back, and saw he'd left the book on the bench. I glanced around to see if he was nearby, but by now it was growing dark, and the deck was deserted. I picked up the book, feeling a tiny stab of guilt, but I wanted to see what made this book so important to him.

I opened the first page and saw rows of small, neat dark markings, not at all like the writing in the Koran. I turned the page to more English writing, but here there was also a picture he'd drawn. It was of a bazaar, filled with men of my country, the women in their *châdaris*, floating about like apparitions. I kept turning the pages, seeing scenes I recognised, and then I knew this to be a book to record what the sâhib experienced. There were many pictures of the *buzkashi*; I could not believe the sâhib – Sâhib Ingram, I corrected myself, glad that I now could call him by his name – could recreate the scenes with such accuracy. The efforts of the horses and the expressions on the faces of the *chapandaz* – their strain and exhaustion and pain – were clear. There were other pictures – of Layak sitting under the olive tree in the courtyard at the house in Jalalabad, of Fareed's broad back as she bent over the fire there, and then pictures of the countryside as we rode towards Multan. There was a small picture of the black pheasant he'd killed, and an eerie one of the tall cliffs of the Khyber Pass.

When I turned the next page, I saw a sleeping woman. She lay beside a fire, one hand curled under her cheek. Looking closer in the fading light, I saw the markings on the woman's forehead, and, startled, realised it was me. I looked around quickly, suddenly even more uncomfortable with my stealthy touching of the sâhib's book, but then stared at the picture again. I was grateful that at least I wore my veil, and only my closed eyes were visible. I turned the page, not wanting to think of being watched while I slept. With relief I looked at the picture of the Haram Gate of Multan. And then – when I turned the next page, I drew in my breath sharply. In this picture I lay on my side on the pallet in the godown. I wore the dress Prita had put me in, and my legs – I saw the *halhal* on my ankle – were bare to the knees. My hair was loosely braided over one shoulder, and my face was completely uncovered, my eyes open. It was as if I stared out of the page and at myself.

I was shocked and almost frightened at seeing myself in this way, and dropped the book back on to the seat as if it burned my hand. In the next instant I rearranged it, closing it and placing it as Sâhib Ingram had left it. I went back downstairs to my bed, not wanting to be present when he returned for his book. I felt, somehow, that by capturing my face and body with his hand on the page, that he knew me in a way that was strangely unsettling.

On the last night on the boat I was overcome with sadness as I stood alone on the deck. As long as we had travelled over land I felt I was still connected to my country. But now . . . after nine days and nights on this sea, I couldn't imagine ever finding my way home again.

I had truly left everything that I knew.

I stayed outside that whole night, eventually lying on a bench and staring up at the sky, trying to find joy in the sweet-smelling breeze, the rippling of the sails in the star-filled sky, trying to find peace within myself. I was still there when dawn coloured the sky, and in small groups the others came to the deck, chatting quietly, and we all stood and watched as we approached Bombay. Sâhib Ingram was at my side.

Even before I saw the city I smelled it. The early morning wind carried the scents over the water, and there were smells sweet, as flowers and incense, and rotting, as vegetables and human waste.

The bay curved gently, sloping hills rising behind it, and houses became visible – tall and constructed of white stone, which, I knew from our stop in Karachi, the foreigners favoured. Domed temples – some gold – gleamed in the morning sun, and it was a comfort to see the spires of many mosques. As we drew nearer, into a broad bay that would take us to the city, I could see that Bombay was huge – so much more so than even Karachi.

'You are not too late for your next ship, Sâhib?'

He shook his head. 'No. We made the journey more quickly than I had expected.' He stared at the city in front of us. 'This was only a trading port on a quiet backwater . . . but it is now what you see – a teeming, expanding city,' he said. Usually I enjoyed hearing him speak, but this morning I was distracted, and found it hard to concentrate on his words. 'But its growth has been slow and peaceful, and it still has – to me, at least – much more appeal than most Indian cities,' he went on. 'Although I was a child in Calcutta, I've spent more time visiting here than there. Bombay,' he said, with pleasure in his voice. But just as I didn't listen closely, he spoke as if more to himself than to me, for he didn't look to me for any reply, and it seemed that although we stood beside each other, we were far apart in our thoughts.

It took a long time to approach the dock and depart from the boat.

Finally we descended a long wooden platform on to the grimy, crowded dock. It was unpleasant; the sun blazed down, bringing out the dirty odours, and everywhere were stern-looking soldiers, not only English, but also Indian.

'Sepoys,' Sâhib Ingram said when I asked him why natives were wearing the red coat. 'They're in the Indian army, under the English,' he said, and I found this odd, that natives and – what had he said? Europeans – would be in the same army. Had they also fought against my people, then?

There were fly-covered oxen, squawking crows, bony, cowering dogs, and so many people crowded shoulder to shoulder. Standing out was a group of giggling, olive-skinned women in short, shining skirts of brilliant hues; they wore flowers in their hair and a great quantity of gaudy jewellery. I saw them approach the white soldiers shamelessly, and turned my face from their immoral gestures.

There were many disfigured beggars with only stumps of arms and legs; some had no noses or ears. They pulled ceaselessly at the clothing of the white men and women who ignored them or kicked them away, speaking sharply. I hated the sight of the children: smaller naked ones toddled about on the horrid filth underfoot, and older ones in rags carried sick-looking babies on their back and hips. They all cried piteously, their small hands held out, adding to the terrible noise. The stench of so many people and animals and the leavings of their bodies was everywhere. I pulled my veil closer and only looked straight ahead, while the sâhib piled his bags and boxes into an open cart. Then we climbed in and the driver shouted to the team of oxen, slapping their backs with the slack ropes.

'Where do we go now?' I asked him, looking around.

'To the home of some good friends, good people from England. I'll make arrangements for you there – even if they can't take you, they'll know someone who can. I'll stay the night and then I'll go on to the Bombay Club for the remainder of my time before the ship leaves. A lot of unmarried men stay there and I'm hoping there will be some of my acquaintance.' As he spoke I suddenly realised I hadn't even wondered if he were married. If he had children.

'You have no wife?' I asked, my tone matter-of-fact.

He turned to me. 'No,' he said.

'Why not, Sâhib? At what age do the men of your country marry?'

'It depends,' was all he said, and we sat on the wooden bench that ran across the cart without speaking for a while. I watched the houses, the people, and then I had to ask. 'And so now you'll leave me? And your friends . . . they're kind?' Not like Layak, I thought to myself.

'Yes.'

Suddenly the enormity of it came over me. I stared around the crowded, narrow streets, rocking from side to side as the cart slowly rumbled over the hard-packed mud road. Although there had been impressive European buildings along the waterfront, now we travelled through narrow streets of tall, colour-washed poorly constructed houses with leafy trees jammed between them. We passed mosques and temples with rounded tops and others, pyramid-shaped and half hidden behind high, latticed wooden walls. I heard bells and gongs. And then the cart rumbled through a crowded area where there were only native faces, and where the houses were in disrepair, although painted in gaudy pinks and yellows.

Finally we came to a row of fine, large houses with beaten earth areas separating them from each other. As we stopped in front of one and the sâhib gave the driver a number of coins, I climbed from the cart, trying to take in the house. But I had little more than a fleeting impression of handsomely carved pillars and a high roof of red tiles as the sâhib went up the pebbled path leading to it, and I followed. There were stairs, and then a wide, deep area shaded from the sun by an extension of the roof. It was similar to the outside room on the back of the big house in Multan, with chairs and tables and plants. And there were servants, two men dressed in white, standing outside the door. At one end two small boys, naked but for squares of cloths suspended on strings around their middles, crouched, shoulders touching, watching us with big eyes.

'What is this called, Sâhib?' I whispered, not sure why I felt I should lower my voice. 'This room with a roof but no walls?'

'Verandah. Wait here, please.' He spoke to one of the Indian men, who bowed his turbaned head and opened the door for Sâhib Ingram. Both men followed him inside and I stood, uncertainly, on the verandah, waiting. The boys continued to stare at me. I heard voices through the open window – Sâhib Ingram's, and a woman's – speaking English. I was overcome with the memory of the young and untouched girl sitting behind the curtain in her father's home while he spoke with the

Ghilzai. Now, as then, I would be forced to wait while decisions were made by others about my future.

Only this time I was not that girl who knew nothing of the world and the ways of men, and with the knowledge I had acquired I had lost all traces of naive dreams.

Finally, Sâhib Ingram returned with a white woman. She was older than both of us, but had a pleasant face and a warm smile.

'Memsâhib Andrews, Daryâ,' Sâhib Ingram said, and I bowed my head, then lifted it and looked into the woman's face.

She said something to me in English, and the sâhib said, 'You may sit there, Daryâ,' pointing to a chair a little apart. One of the servants who had been standing at the door when we arrived came out, carrying a tray with three glasses filled with pale yellow liquid.

The woman and Sâhib Ingram sat on woven chairs, and I on mine, and the turbaned man bent before them, offering them a glass. They each took one, setting it on the table, and then Sâhib Ingram spoke in Hindi. The man with the turban looked at me, frowning, his eyebrows meeting over his nose.

He came to me and stood in front of me with the tray. I had never been served by a man, and was uncomfortable. But I was very thirsty, and obviously my sâhib had told this man to serve me, and so I reached for the glass. The servant pulled the tray back, just the slightest, his eyes narrowing, and I knew he felt it was beneath him to serve me. But I firmly took the glass, ignoring his expression.

The woman and Sâhib Ingram spoke rapidly in English. She continually glanced at me. I was very thirsty, but didn't want to drink until either she or the sâhib drank first.

I knew by her tone that the woman asked questions as she looked between me and Sâhib Ingram. I sat very straight, holding my glass in both hands, my ankles touching, and tried to look as I thought I should; subservient and yet slightly eager. I had dressed carefully, saving my last clean *kurta* and *hijba* for this moment.

Usually Sâhib Ingram answered her in one or two words, although a few times he looked at me, as if unsure of the answer, before he spoke again. Finally the woman paused to take a sip of her drink, and I did the same. The drink was sweet, and tasted of lemon.

I looked at Sâhib Ingram, who didn't drink, but stared into his glass.

What did he say about me? What questions did the woman have? She kept nodding as she drank, blinking rapidly, as if nervous, or perhaps because of a problem with her sight. Although her hair was light brown, her eyebrows and eyelashes were almost colourless, giving her a strange appearance. Her lips, too, were very pale, and looked rough, as if she bit them. Although she was very thin, her dress, made of cloth striped blue and white, looked too tight, and flared out from her waist. She set down her glass, her forehead wrinkling, and spoke more quickly.

They continued to talk in low voices, but were interrupted by a native woman dressed in white – a Hindu, with the red mark on her forehead, as Prita had worn – coming through the door with a small child of under a year. The child's skin was so white it seemed to glow, except for two bright pink spots standing in odd relief on its cheeks. Fine purple veins ran in its temple. It had eyes of such a pale blue that they, too, were almost white. I had never seen eyes like this. I didn't know if it was a boy or a girl; it wore layers of white lacy clothing, and its straight, thin pale hair clung damply to its scalp. It looked like a child possessed by *jinn*, its hair and skin so colourless, its eyes too big, bright with fever. It was whining, holding its arms out to the woman, and she rose and took it from the Hindu woman, patting the little back in a distracted way. Then she stood with the child and simply looked at me, her face a mixture of mild dismay and exhaustion. She spoke once more, then left, the Hindu woman following.

'What did she say?' I asked Sâhib Ingram. 'What was she asking you?'

'Questions you'd expect. What you could do. Your character.'

'And? You told her . . . ?'

'I said . . . that I didn't know exactly what you could do, but that you learn quickly. That you're honest and hard-working.'

Although I should have been pleased at these positive remarks, I knew he wasn't telling me all they had discussed. They had spoken too long for such easy questions and answers. And although I was glad that Sâhib Ingram found me honest and hard-working and quick to learn, it made me sound so uninteresting. Was this how he saw me? As a simple woman who could wash clothes in a stream and cook over a fire? Was this, in reality, all I was? No. I was so much more. I just needed the chance to show it.

CHAPTER THIRTY-ONE

'Does she have work for me?' I asked, pushing that thought from my head.

'Her youngest – the little girl – is quite ill. There are two other young children as well, and it's difficult for her, even with her ayahs. Her husband is away much of the time, and she now has many visitors, here to enjoy the cool season. She said there will surely be something you can do to help the ayahs with the children. She'll come back out and discuss it further when she's settled the child.'

I nodded. Children were children, whether European or native. It wouldn't be difficult; I was good with children. This was much more than I had expected, and I smiled with relief.

'It would please you?' Sâhib Ingram asked.

I nodded. 'I like children.' *Although I will never have one.* The door opened again, but it wasn't the woman. It was another man, and he walked right past me, straight to Sâhib Ingram, who rose and took the outstretched hand of the other man. Although this man smiled broadly, Sâhib Ingram looked first surprised, and then slightly disturbed. But he almost instantly rearranged his face, although his smile wasn't the natural one I had come to know.

As they spoke to each other in English I studied this second man, assuming him to be the woman's husband.

His features were not as even and fine as Sâhib Ingram's, although this could have been because he was older by a number of years – he was almost as old as my father. His body was thick, solid, and his face appeared slightly bloated. His skin – like the child's – was too pale, his cheeks marked in a faint pattern left by the old scars of a pox. This skin, with its slight sheen, reminded me of a plant left in the dark.

But in spite of his poor colour, for a *khâreji*, this man was not entirely unattractive. His straight hair – a colour such as I had never seen, dark, rich red, with a few threads of pinkish-grey running through – was combed back from his forehead and touched his collar. He had a long, square-cut growth of hair the same burnished colour down each cheek, as well as a moustache. Without warning he turned from Sâhib Ingram and looked at me. I immediately stood and dropped my eyes.

'Daryâ,' Sâhib Ingram said, in Persian, 'this is Sâhib – Mr Bull. Visiting from England, and a guest here.'

Not the woman's husband, after all, but one of the too many guests. It was very hot on the verandah, and my mouth was dry, even though I had finished the glass of lemon drink.

'Miss Daryâ,' the other man said. I assumed *miss* was a polite English formality, as was the English word *mister*. 'I am so very pleased to meet you. What an unexpected surprise – that Mr Ingram has acquired you along the way.' His Persian was as flawless as if he had been born with the language on his tongue. Although his tone was fluid, his low voice soothing, I didn't like the word *acquired*, as if I were an object, and lifted my gaze at it.

Sâhib Ingram knew me well enough to understand what was in my eyes, for he quickly spoke to the other man in English again. Mr Bull raised his eyebrows, asked a question, and, on Sâhib Ingram's reply, slowly smiled.

'So you've had some trouble, I understand,' he said then, 'and are hoping your luck will be more fortuitous in a different country.'

I assumed *fortuitous* meant better. I nodded, and Mr Bull gave a sharp command to the boys in the corner, and almost immediately there was a steady thunk, thunk, thunk from overhead. I looked up to see a square of white fabric on a wooden frame moving back and forth to stir the air. There was a rope attached to one side, causing this movement, and as I followed it, I saw that it led to the small hand of one of the boys.

'It must have been quite an interesting journey,' he said, sitting down and putting one leg over the other, so the foot swung in the air. I had never seen a man sit in this way. He looked at Sâhib Ingram and then back to me. I understood that he was expecting something of me, and so I nodded again.

'Your knowledge of Persian was well worth the study, obviously,' Mr Bull said to Sâhib Ingram. 'Your ability in it is quite exemplary.'

'It was most useful in Afghanistan.'

'Will you continue your study of languages, then?'

'I haven't completely decided what I'll do on my return to England,' Sâhib Ingram said, 'although I may go on with further studies.'

I realised, with a start, that they spoke to each other in Persian in order to include me in the conversation, and I felt a surprising swell of pleasure at this consideration.

'He's a clever fellow. Don't you agree, Miss Daryâ?' Mr Bull said, and Sâhib Ingram looked down, obviously uncomfortable. 'Although wild as a hawk. Not given to predictability, or much discipline.'

I grew warmer, flustered by this completely strange Englishman speaking so directly to me, as though I were another man, saying such personal things about Sâhib Ingram.

The talk between Sâhib Ingram and myself had been different, I suddenly realised. I looked at him now for some indication as to how I should respond, but he didn't look up.

Mr Bull cleared his throat. 'You may speak, if you wish, Miss Daryâ,' he said, smiling kindly.

I tried to compose my voice, to sound assured in a way I didn't feel, sitting with two men unrelated to me in any way, and being served by a third. What could I say? I had never been invited to take part in a male conversation. I thought of his talk of Sâhib Ingram's study of Persian. 'You are a teacher of languages?' I asked this pale man.

'Charming tone,' he said, and in the next instant continued. 'No. Although I have been known to instruct others – those with interests similar to mine – in travel, and a love of the exotic. The study of older civilisations, other cultures.' He turned to Sâhib Ingram again. 'We have had the odd interesting discussion on our various travels to the East, the cultures and so on, haven't we, David?'

Finally Sâhib Ingram glanced at me. His face was strained, as if fighting to remain fixed in a pleasant, blank expression, and I instinctively knew, in that instant, that he didn't like this Mr Bull. 'Yes,' he answered, the word clipped.

'Have you known many Europeans, Miss Daryâ?' Mr Bull asked.

I shook my head. 'Only Sâhib – Mr Ingram.' The word *mister* was strange in my mouth, but Mr Bull appeared to enjoy my attempt to pronounce it. He smiled openly at me.

'So you know little of our fine Empire – of Britain?'

At the word Britain I hesitantly smiled under my *hijba*. 'I know a song of Britannia.' *Rule Britannia, Daryâ* jan. *Sing it to me.*

'A song?' Mr Bull looked at Mr Ingram, rubbing his hands together and smiling. Again, he said something to Mr Ingram that made him shake his head, as if displeased. 'Would you sing it for us, then?' he asked, in Persian, ignoring Mr Ingram's response.

I quickly shook my head as Sâhib Ingram had. Why had I told this man I knew a song?

'Perhaps another time, then,' Mr Bull said. 'Mr Ingram? Are you staying long?'

Mr Ingram again spoke in English. And then the memsâhib returned with the same Indian woman who now looked at me, unsmiling, from my headscarf to my sandals. Mr Ingram and Mr Bull both stood up. Memsâhib Andrews spoke to Mr Ingram, and he nodded at me.

'Memsâhib Andrews says you can help the ayahs with the children. This one – Unma – will instruct you.'

Unma said a Hindi word and made a motion with her head, and I looked back at Mr Ingram.

'Yes. Go with her. She'll take you to a godown where you'll stay.' The verandah seemed impossibly crowded at that moment, with the memsâhib and Mr Bull and Mr Ingram, the two servants by the door, the staring little boys, and the ayah. I was overwhelmed, suddenly, and wanted nothing more than to be back on the steamer with Mr Ingram, chugging along the peaceful shoreline. It was happening too quickly, even though I knew this was why Mr Ingram had brought me here.

'I will see you tomorrow, Daryâ,' he said now, his voice expressionless, his face unreadable.

'She doesn't appear to be ayah material, David,' Mr Bull said in Persian, and I looked from him to Mr Ingram. Mr Ingram stood very stiffly. 'Are you sure you know what you're letting yourself in for, Miss Daryâ?' Mr Bull asked me now, that same slow smiling coming to his lips.

I didn't know how to answer. The ayah started down the steps, and there was nothing for me to do but to follow her.

The godown was behind the big house, and much like the one in Multan. But Unma was not gentle and accepting as Prita had been. She scowled as she rattled to me in Hindi, even though it was obvious I couldn't understand anything she said. In the privacy of the godown I pulled my *hijba* aside, and she shook her head as if disgruntled at the sight of all my *harquus*. She kept talking, waving both hands at me, obviously very angry.

She finally left, and I sat on a pallet, wondering what I was to do, when a younger ayah, also marked as a Hindu, entered, carrying a plate of chicken and mashed lentils and chupatti. I breathed a sigh of relief when she hesitantly addressed me in Persian. 'Unma send me to you, to speak,' she said, handing me the plate. 'I work for Parsee family, learn Persian. I am ayah here too.'

'I am Daryâ,' I said, and she smiled, although hesitantly.

'And I Kavindra,' she said, obviously not wanting to meet my eyes. 'Evie-*baba* always sick, take much care. Unma be with her, you help me with little sahibs George and Teddy. You have baba?' she asked, finally looking at me.

I shook my head. 'Baby? No. I have no baby. But I've always looked after the children of . . . others. I know children. And you?'

'I have two,' she said. 'But only girls,' she added, with a helpless shrug.

'Where are they?'

'With mother-in-law. I see them sometimes.' She gestured at my plate. 'Eat. I think much better you stay here now, not see Unma.' She hesitated, but only said, 'Tomorrow you work.' And then she left.

I wondered briefly why I caused Unma's anger, and why Kavindra treated me slightly fearfully. Then, suddenly hungry, I didn't think of them any further, and ate everything on the plate. When I had finished I went outside. It was late afternoon, and I sat with my back against the wall of the hut, watching the big house. The verandah from the front ran all around the back of the house, and white people came and went, sitting there, being served drinks, and talking. I watched for Mr Ingram, but didn't see him. Mr Bull was there, though, and his voice, louder than the others, carried to where I sat.

Eventually I went inside and tried to sleep; Unma and Kavindra didn't return to the godown, and I assumed they slept near the children in the big house.

In the morning Kavindra came with white clothing such as she and Unma wore, and I dressed in it, covering my face with the ends of the white headscarf. I followed her to the back verandah, where Unma already sat, holding Evie-*baba*, while two small boys played at her feet. The little girl looked even more ill today, lying quiet and wan against Unma's breast. The boys, unlike their sister, were both dark-haired and lively, and wore the same white hats – like inverted bowls – as all of the other Europeans I had seen in India.

The little sahibs, who looked to be about three and five, spoke both English and Hindi. I heard Kavindra say my name, and the boys stared at me. I pulled aside my face covering and smiled, kneeling beside the younger one, Teddy. He touched my *harquus*, asking something in a high voice. Kavindra answered him, and he nodded. I held out my arms to him and he came to me easily, obviously trusting, and settled on my lap, holding a book. I looked at the pictures on the pages as he turned them, and I wanted him to go more slowly, for the pictures were of children and animals, and were interesting.

Absorbed in the pictures, I didn't hear Mr Ingram come out on to the verandah, and only looked up when I heard him speak in Hindi. How long had he been here? Had he watched me? I covered my nose and mouth and stood, holding Sahib Teddy in my arms, and Mr Ingram said one sentence in Hindi. Unma looked even more annoyed than usual, her lips set in a thin line, and rose with Evie-*baba*, now sleeping, and went inside the house. Kavindra took Sahib Teddy from me, and holding Sahib George's hand, led them down the steps and settled with them beneath the shade of a spreading tree behind the house.

'I wish to say goodbye,' Mr Ingram said, and at that moment his face was suddenly so dear to me that the thought of not seeing it, ever again, filled me with a sadness I had never expected.

'You are leaving? Now?' I didn't like the thread of panic in my voice.

'Yes. Mrs Andrews is overwhelmed with guests, and I don't want to add to her burden. As I said yesterday, I'll stay at the Bombay Club until the ship leaves.'

I nodded, and he looked at the godown, and then back to me. 'It will be well for you here? With the children?' he asked.

I hesitated. 'Yes.' There was no reason for me to suspect it wouldn't be fine, and yet . . . 'I am reminded of my own young sister and brother,' I said, although of course Sâhib George and Teddy were nothing like Nasreen and Yusuf. But I wanted – needed – to reassure Mr Ingram, to let him know that I understood that this was a good thing he did for me, that I should be very pleased, and grateful, even though at this moment my heart was so heavy. 'At least as they were when I last saw them, some years ago.'

'You never spoke of them,' he said.

'We never spoke of many things.' Did he have brothers and sisters? What of his life? I wanted to know. We had had so much time alone together, and yet it hadn't seemed proper for me to ask him personal questions. And although so many times I sensed he wished to speak to me, perhaps to also ask me about my life, we had both carefully stayed within our boundaries of English sâhib and Afghan woman. Yet now, now that he was leaving, I wanted to know about him, about this strange, kind Englishman with Afghan blood who – once my eyes had grown accustomed to him – was so fine to look upon, with his hair like the sun, his eyes dark and expressive, his finely curved lips.

Something, some presence, hovered in the air between us, but it was not evil, like *jinn*. It was something good, and comfortable, and yet at the same time the weight of it sat upon my chest, making it difficult to breathe normally. Neither of us said anything; I had too much to say, and couldn't sort out one thing. Was it the same for Mr Ingram?

Mr Bull's voice came from within the house, echoing through the open doorway, and we both looked towards the sound. 'This Mr Bull – he is a man like yourself?' I asked, not caring about Mr Bull, but needing to break through this thick atmosphere, say something that was trivial, and therefore safe.

'Like me?' Mr Ingram started, looking back at me. 'Do you mean . . . his bloodline?'

I shook my head. 'No, no. Only . . . is he a true sâhib? A fine gentleman?'

Mr Ingram frowned slightly. 'We are not alike in any way.' He reached up to brush his hair from his forehead, and I remembered how I'd first seen his hands in the dusty plains, the long, slender, undamaged fingers. 'As well as India, and other eastern countries, he lived in Persia for some time. He did encourage me to study the language.'

'But . . . is he also your friend?' I hadn't forgotten the expression Mr Ingram tried to cover when Mr Bull appeared on the verandah yesterday. Why was I wasting our last moments together discussing this man?

'Friend?' He shook his head. 'No. He was a friend of my – the Englishman I knew as my father – in Calcutta. Now he lives in London, the city where I live with my mother. He took it upon himself, a few years ago when I was considering my education, to give me some advice. My mother . . .' he hesitated. 'She and Mr Bull sometimes see each other at social events, although my mother has made it clear she'd rather not associate with him.' He hesitated, then said, 'She has an uncanny sense when it comes to assessing people.'

He cared deeply for his mother; I saw it in his face, heard it in his voice when he spoke of her, even so briefly. He lived in a city called London. It seemed there were many pieces to this man, many secrets. And these small pieces were all I would ever know of him. When I said nothing more, he asked, 'Will this position, this new life with Memsâhib Andrews . . . do you feel more certain about your future?'

He had done all he could; there was nothing more possible. 'Is anyone's future certain, Sâhib? Is yours?' *O furious wind.*

He looked at me sharply, and opened his mouth to say something, something I knew would be important, and Mr Bull stepped through the open doorway.

Anger flooded through me. Why did this man have to be here, at this very moment? Couldn't he give Mr Ingram and I a chance to say goodbye to each other? I could tell Mr Ingram felt the same way at the other man's sudden appearance, for he stepped back – I hadn't noticed he'd been standing so close to me – and spoke in English, politely but with an edge of impatience, to Mr Bull.

Mr Bull held a short glass filled with amber liquid. He answered Mr Ingram in English, took a long drink and lowered himself into a wooden chair with a sloped back, sighing with pleasure. He sipped from his drink, watching us. He obviously intended to stay, in spite of what Mr Ingram might have said to him.

'I must go now,' Mr Ingram said quietly, turning his back on Mr Bull, looking into my eyes as if searching for something. 'Goodbye, then, Daryâ. I wish you . . . I hope . . .'

Like him, I could think of no words, and my heart beat with a slow thudding that hurt my chest. I had known all along that we would part. But now that he was actually going . . . I put one hand on his arm as I pulled aside my headscarf with the other, suddenly wanting him to see my whole face one more time. 'Mr Ingram,' I said.

He looked at me, then down at my hand. I left it on his sleeve, the wool soft and warm under my fingers, and beneath the fabric his forearm felt hard and muscled. I remembered the golden hairs there, and knew they would be as soft as the hair on his head.

'I wish to thank you,' I said. 'I haven't thanked you for all you've done for me. You . . . if you had not . . .' I stopped, removing my hand and crossing both hands on my chest. 'My heart is full of gratefulness.'

He nodded, his face unreadable.

'I won't disappoint you; I will act as a proper servant here,' I said, aware that Mr Bull could understand and that he was listening. Mr Ingram and I weren't alone in our circle of language, as we had been from the time we left Jalalabad, and because of Mr Bull's presence my words came out woodenly.

I wished I had more time to speak to Mr Ingram, to be near him. Just one more day.

'I know you will,' Mr Ingram said. 'I have trust in you.' His voice was as strained and awkward as mine.

I took his hand with both of mine and pressed it to my forehead, lowering my eyes. I breathed in the clean scent of his skin. 'Go in peace, David Ingram,' I said. Confusion and regret swirled in my head. Why hadn't I . . . hadn't I what? What was it I regretted not doing? *I will never see you again.*

'And peace be upon you,' he replied, in the way of my people, and put his hand over mine, and pressed it with such intensity that I knew the imprint of his fingers would be left on my skin. I was so overwhelmed with an unexpected – and unknown – feeling that I couldn't look up at him, afraid that if I did he would see something written on my face, something that shouldn't be there.

And then he let go of my hand.

There was a whisper of stirred air as he went through the open doorway, back into the house, but I stood where I was, my eyes on the floor, my hand warm from his.

Mr Ingram had been near me for the past – I couldn't count the time, surely it had been nearly three months? – and although we had attempted to stay without our own worlds, I had always been in the comfort of his familiar presence. I had known what to expect of him, and had felt secure. And now I realised how little I knew of him, or his life. He had, at first, been only a sâhib – my sâhib, as I had started to think of him, even though I had always known that he had never been mine – to use that possessive word. I thought of all he had done. When I had begged him to take me with him from the *buzkashi*, he had. When I again had begged to leave Jalalabad with him, he had also allowed this, even securing a place for me with Layak's family. When I grew ill he could have left me by the river to die, for no one would have ever known what had happened to me, but he had brought me to the hut, with Prita to care for me with her gentle generosity. And he could have left me in Multan to fend for myself, saying he'd already done enough. But he hadn't.

I remembered him soothing me during my sickness by the river, with his cool hands and poetry, and carrying me into the hut behind the big house. I remembered our long journey, on horseback, on barge and steamer. Of the pictures he'd made of me, and how he must have watched me, his eyes and fingers knowing me well enough to recreate, with astonishing likeness, my eyes, my hair, my mouth . . .

And now that part of my life was finished. He had brought me here, to Bombay, and now he was gone, and with his abrupt departure the last thin thread of my former life tore, and I floated, completely alone, in this strange place.

CHAPTER THIRTY-TWO

I LOOKED AT THE empty doorway, unaware of myself and where I was for those few moments after Mr Ingram left. And then I heard my name, and turned.

I had forgotten my face was open, forgotten Mr Bull sat on the verandah. 'Miss Daryâ,' he said again, his eyes lingering on my *harquus* before I could fix my scarf in place. In that instant a curious expression came over him, his eyelids lowering just slightly, as if heavy, and something in his stare made me shiver, although the air was so warm. In the next instant he blinked and smiled, showing straight strong teeth discoloured only slightly from tobacco, and in one swift movement he stood, stepped closer, and picked up my hand. The hand Mr Ingram had held, only moments earlier.

I was dully surprised at his unexpected touch. Although it was inappropriate, he did it with such confidence, his grip so sure, that I momentarily assumed he was unaware of his error, that he simply acted in what might be the usual behaviour of an Englishman to a woman. But no – he had lived in the East; surely he knew of the proper way to treat a Muslim woman. I pulled back, and he immediately released his fingers.

'Don't be upset, Miss Daryâ,' he said. 'I can see you're shaken by Mr Ingram's departure. I only meant to comfort you.' He gestured at the chair beside his. 'Sit and talk with me.'

I shook my head, confused. 'I have to work now,' I told him, glancing out at the grass, seeing Kavindra with the small sâhibs. She shaded her eyes and looked at me.

'If you must,' he said, and sat again. He put his feet on a stool and said a word to a boy sitting cross-legged on the far end of the verandah. The boy jumped up and ran to him, carrying a fan made of long, colourful feathers, and stepped behind Mr Bull's chair. Then he slowly waved the fan over the man's head. Just before I turned to join Kavindra, Mr Bull raised his hand to drink from his glass again, and I saw a glint of gold on his smallest finger – a ring set with a black stone.

The rest of the day was long and confusing. I was surrounded by languages I didn't understand, tried to follow the routines for the children, tried to stay out of Unma's way. I wondered, briefly, if her anger was because I was Muslim. There was another ayah; this one tended to Memsâhib Andrews' needs, and she was a Hindu as well. All the other servants were male. I couldn't lose the sadness that lingered whenever I thought of Mr Ingram – that he was elsewhere, and would soon leave this country. While I would remain. I was surprised that I felt his loss so strongly.

I saw nothing of the inside of the big house except for the separate room for the children. Kavindra took me to it through doors which, like all the doors off the verandah, were made of wooden slats, open to catch the breeze. The room had two high beds and a third, even higher, with bars around it. Evie-*baba* lay here, and as I watched her, turning feebly, whimpering, on the thin bedding, I understood the bars would prevent her from falling to the ground. The legs of all the beds sat in small dishes of water, and when I saw the many insects creeping or scuttling on the floor, I knew then that the water would deter them from climbing up the legs of the beds to bite the sleeping children. Draped over each bed, enclosing them completely, was white, sheer material, making the little boys and baby girl appear unearthly, as if pale ghosts in their filmy prisons. It seemed sad that they would sleep alone; no small child of Afghanistan – or any native children I had seen in India – slept without the comfort of a woman.

As darkness fell and the children had been fed and bathed and settled in their beds, Unma and Kavindra lay on pallets along one wall of the children's room. There was a third pallet, but as I went to it Unma shook her head and waved her hand dismissively at me, muttering crossly.

'Unma say you sleep godown, Daryâ,' Kavindra told me, and so I went through the wooden doors and across the space of trees and flowering bushes and beaten earth, the path to the godowns lit by flaming torches. I lay on my pallet in the hut, hearing the sounds from the big house – the clatter of dishes and tinkling of glass, and English voices and laughter – especially that of Mr Bull, clearly recognisable to me, far into the night, it seemed.

Although the mournfulness at leaving my country and the loss of family and friends would perhaps stay with me always, my escape and my long and uncertain journey to safety were over. I had not become the victim of Shaliq's rage, nor was I that ragged outcast of my nightmares. I had food and a place to sleep. The memsâhib appeared kind; the children made me smile. Kavindra, although timid, wasn't unfriendly, and as for Unma – I could deal with her.

I was safe here, and all was well.

So why couldn't I pull my thoughts away from my journey with Mr Ingram? Although for my time with him I had never been sure of my destiny, now I wished I had understood the freedom I had. That time grew large, Mr Ingram's face so clear in those night thoughts. I concentrated on the expression on his face as he'd said goodbye to me. Was it regret? Sadness? Or was I imagining it all? Was it simply relief, freedom that he was finally rid of me? I argued back and forth, thinking of the pictures he'd drawn of me, the way I'd sometimes seen him looking at me – when I'd laughed at the dolphins, or recited Rumi, or watched the waves. The way he held my hand, with more pressure than I'd expected, just before he left.

But he was gone for ever, and, I told myself I should think no more about him. I should think no more about my old life in my own *watan*. This was my new life, and my new country. I would learn its languages, and I would become the best ayah I could be. That was all I should hope for.

Is such a small life all you really dream of, Daryâ jan*?*

I opened my eyes in the darkness. *Have I not tried hard enough,* Mâdar Kalân? *How can you expect so much of me?*

Daryâ jan, *are you certain you do not ask: Why should I expect so little of myself? If you are willing to accept this life, you must be very sure it is all you are capable of.*

I turned on to my side, trying to still my grandmother's voice in my head, and closed my eyes tightly.

The second day of work followed the pattern of the first, although Unma was even more brusque, slapping my hand when I couldn't master using the silver English tools to help Sahib Teddy eat, muttering nastily under her breath and casting burning stares at me. I refused to be dismayed by her treatment of me, or the confusion I had over the way the children were cared for. They were denied nothing, and had only to point at something and one of us would hurry to supply it. I didn't know if this was because they were boys or because they were English, or both; Evie-*baba* was too placid to demand anything, but I knew this was due to the illness which seemed to have drained her of all her colour and strength.

It was obvious Unma gave me the less desirable jobs, such as changing Evie-*baba*'s sodden, soiled clothing, or killing the insects in the children's room. She also had me take the painted china bowl the little boys used for their private business out to an elderly Hindu in a tattered loincloth who appeared to wait for it, hunched in the dust at the side of the house with a trembling, scrawny hand extended.

This is what I must do, I whispered to myself through that second long day. *It is my job. I am an ayah now.* We were of no importance to the white men and women who came and went from the house, or sat on the verandah with glasses in their hands, the men smoking tobacco in dark leaves that had been rolled into long thin tubes. The servants bowed and served these English as if they were still the ages of Sâhib George or Teddy, with every need met before it was even spoken. There was no task too small – from wiping the dust from a shoe to refilling a glass before it was empty, or to keeping the insects away with the constant fanning of a small whisk – and all were done with no obvious gratitude from the guests.

I thought of how the natives at the docks in Karachi had moved aside for Mr Ingram. It appeared that English blood was in some way superior.

Like the other servants, I moved silently, and it was as if I were invisible.

Except to Mr Bull. Twice I looked up to see him studying me from a window opening on to the verandah where I played with the children; both times I turned away from his smile.

Later in the day Memsâhib Andrews came to where the three of us sat with the children, looking at me while speaking to Unma. Unma answered too quickly, too loudly. Memsâhib appeared to soothe her with quiet words, glancing at me and then back to Unma, putting her head to one side as she spoke, as if reasoning with her.

'Is big upset,' Kavindra whispered to me, when the memsâhib had left. 'Unma's daughter third ayah, but now you here, Unma's daughter must go home.' I looked at Unma, who combed through Evie-*baba*'s wispy hair with her fingertips. Although her hands were gentle, she muttered under her breath, paying no attention to us. 'Unma cannot be angry at Memsâhib. So must be angry at you.' Kavindra leaned closer, her mouth uncertain. 'Daryâ, Unma is so long time Memsâhib's favourite. Memsâhib say to Unma don't worry, say she must take you for now, because tall sâhib who bring you here want this, but when he leave soon on big boat . . .' She shook her head. 'Is maybe not good for you, Daryâ, I hear. Our memsâhib very nice lady, but when boat is gone she put you another place to be ayah, so Unma be happy again.' She shook her head. 'All ayahs know that sâhib where you will go. Not good.'

I tossed in the godown again that night. Was what Kavindra told me true? Her face had been sincere. Was nothing ever to be sure in my life again?

The next morning Kavindra and I sat on the verandah with the small sâhibs. Teddy had cried when Kavindra gently insisted he keep on his hard white hat – his *topi* – even when in the shade, and to cheer him up she made simple music, banging sticks and ringing small bells. Teddy forgot his distress, and both boys joined her with enthusiasm.

I did what Unma had instructed me to do before she went inside with Evie-*baba*. On my knees, I spread black paste on the small leather shoes of the sâhibs, rubbing it in with a soft rag until the leather shone.

'That is the job of the Sudras – our lowest caste – like the one who takes the flowered pots,' Kavindra told me when Unma left. 'But Unma says now you do. You . . . allow touch leather; you are not like good Hindu.'

Good Hindu. At the words I thought of my lack of prayer, my uncharitable thoughts towards Allah. My more human thoughts about Mr Ingram. I was no longer a good Muslim woman, I knew that now.

I rubbed vigorously at the little toe of the shoe, as if trying to scrub away the thoughts of my faithlessness. As I did so, gleaming toes of a different pair of shoes stopped in front of me. Sitting back on my heels, I looked up. It was Mr Bull.

He murmured as if dismayed. 'This is a most distressing sight,' he said. 'A woman like you shouldn't be reduced to such drudgery. Please, stop.'

I shook my head. 'I can't, Mr Bull. If Unma sees me, she will report to the memsâhib that I am not –'

He waved his hand dismissively. 'I am a burra sâhib. A most important gentleman. If I request you to stop, it's me you must obey, not Unma. Now, join me, Miss Daryâ.' He sat on a woven chair padded with cushions, and patted the chair beside it.

Glancing at Kavindra, I set the paste and rags back in their wooden box, wiping my hands on a clean cloth as I got to my feet. I hesitated, but again Mr Bull patted the seat of the chair. I perched on its edge, clasping my hands in my lap.

'Now. I just must see . . .' he reached over and gently pulled the scarf from the bottom of my face. I jerked away, staring down so he wouldn't see the anger on my face at his appalling familiarity with me. I was glad Kavindra was still busy with the boys, and wasn't watching.

'I'm sorry,' he said, and my head darted up, knowing my expression didn't hide my displeasure at his behaviour and his obvious lie – it was clear he wasn't sorry at all. 'I'm so fascinated by your facial markings. Since I saw them the other day I haven't been able to stop thinking about them. About you.' His smile was open and friendly, and I knew then that Mr Bull's behaviour was not the result of a lack of knowledge or manners. He was simply so full of confidence in himself that he didn't consider – or care – how his actions might be viewed, or what effects they might have. He was like a bold child, one who is used to being forgiven, and assumes that he always will be.

'I understand your culture, Miss Daryâ,' he said, as if capable of seeing the thoughts in my head, 'and do know you're uncomfortable with me viewing you in this manner,' he went on. 'But I sense that you're . . . different from many other Muslim women. Am I not right?'

Of course I was different. All that had happened to me, all that I had caused to happen, made me different. But he wasn't expecting me to answer his question. 'You must tell me about them, these marks. Although I've travelled through – and lived in – a number of Eastern countries, I haven't seen this particular pattern. What are they, exactly? Mr Ingram said you were of the Tajiks.' He stood then, and took my chin in his hand, turning my face to one side. 'I am absolutely intrigued,' he said. 'Can you explain how they were done? Different peoples use different techniques.' He stood so near that the edge of his jacket brushed my shoulder. He smelled of tobacco and something powdery, flowery, although it didn't disguise the faint odour of sweat trapped in the wool of his clothing.

I struggled to remain calm. Could I continue to blame his outrageous behaviour on his own personality, or, I suddenly thought, was it simply because he was English? No. Mr Ingram had never behaved so. He had always treated me with respect, even when I was at my lowest moments. But then . . . he was not a true Englishman.

'Don't be shy. Please. Tell me,' Mr Bull said, taking his fingers from my chin and again sitting down.

I swallowed my anger. There seemed little recourse but to respond. I told him about the simple procedure as briefly as possible.

'Did it hurt?' he asked. He licked his lips. Beneath the thick, dark red moustache his lips were full, perhaps too full to be truly manly, I thought.

I looked away, staring at what lay beyond the verandah – the trees, the flowering bushes, the walkway leading to the godowns.

'A little,' I said. 'I don't remember now. It was a number of years ago.'

'It's a Tajik ritual, then? Of womanhood, perhaps?'

'They're not Tajik. Tajik women are not decorated with *harquus*.'

'*Harquus*.' He rolled the word on his tongue as if it pleased him. 'But if you're Tajik . . .'

'They're for good health, for fertility, among the Ghilzai. They're also to add beauty.'

'Why were you marked by the Ghilzai?'

Finally I turned and looked at him. 'For my husband, a Ghilzai Pushtun. He wished it.'

'Your husband? You were married?'

I didn't know whether this pleased or displeased him, but he stared at me harder now. 'Yes,' I said, turning from him again.

'It grows more intriguing,' he said, 'for David Ingram told me you were a young woman alone in the world.'

'He told the truth in this. I no longer consider myself married.' This was true; although I was still bound to Shaliq by Islam, I carried out no wifely duties. It seemed that Islam was becoming lost to me in many ways. I picked at the black paste caught under my fingernails.

Then I looked at Mr Bull again, and he now wore that sleepy look, the one that had flashed over his features when he saw my uncovered face the first time.

'I must work,' I said, rising.

'Just another moment. Please?' he asked. He cocked his head. 'You have such a lovely voice. Would you do something for me?'

I waited.

'You said you knew a song about Britain. Did Mr Ingram teach it to you?'

'No.'

'Who, then? Who taught you an English song? Have you known many other English gentlemen? Are you keeping something from me, Miss Daryâ?'

'No,' I said, not liking the suggestive way he spoke. 'It was my grandmother who taught me.'

'Your grandmother?'

'She knew about many things in the world.'

He took my hand again, and I stood very still. 'Miss Daryâ,' he said. 'I won't let you go until you sing for me.'

I studied his face; he was smiling, looking at me with the unblinking stare of a snake. I knew that although his tone was teasing, he meant what he said.

'I know only a few words,' I said.

'That will be fine.'

I took a deep breath. 'Rule, Britannia,' I sang, my voice very low, hoping Kavindra would keep on making the banging, ringing music with the boys, not hear me singing to this man as he held my hand. I didn't even know if I remembered the right rhythm, but sang quickly, almost breathlessly, only wanting it to be over. I was ashamed, and angry at Mr Bull for putting me in this position.

'Britannia, rule the waves: Britons never will be slaves,' I sang, then stopped. 'That's all I know,' I said.

Mr Bull let go of my hand to clap his own, still smiling. 'How wonderful! Simply adorable, Miss Daryâ, to hear English roll so prettily off that native tongue. Aren't you a clever girl?'

'Now I will work,' I said, and he sighed, heavily, as if overly sad, and put his hand on his heart.

'What a disappointment that brings,' he said, and I went back to the leather shoes, and when he left the verandah a moment later I sighed with relief. Unlike his, my sigh was real.

That night as I sat in the godown, looking through one of the children's books by the light of a candle, there was the shuffle of shoes on the finely ground shell path outside. My hand, turning a page, froze. I hadn't asked permission to take the book, simply picking it up from a table as I left the children's room, thinking it would help to pass the time before I could fall asleep. What if Unma had watched me, and told Memsâhib Andrews that I had stolen it? Surely Unma would love to create this trouble, to be rid of me even sooner for a reason nobody would argue with. I jumped up, still holding the book. To try and hide it would make it appear that I really did act as a thief.

But it wasn't the memsâhib. It was Mr Bull, with a small oil lamp in one hand, a glass of the amber liquid in the other. 'Don't be alarmed, Miss Daryâ. And don't bother fumbling for your scarf.' But I had already covered the bottom of my face, and he sighed again, as he had earlier. 'The evening has turned very tedious, the company so dull and predictable. I decided to stroll through the garden, and saw the light from the candle. Why are you still awake? All the other servants, except those needed, are sleeping.'

I shrugged.

Mr Bull sighed again; how annoying for a man to show such petulance. 'I'm terribly bored. Thankfully I'll be leaving in a few days.' He suddenly put his hand on his stomach and breathed deeply, wincing, as if he were in slight pain.

'Where do you go?' I was relieved to hear he wouldn't be here much longer, although I hoped my voice didn't show too much eagerness at this thought.

'Home. To England. This will be my last trip to India. Although I've lived with this climate for so much of my life, suddenly I can no longer tolerate it. I've been ill, off and on, since I arrived months ago.' Again he pressed his palm against his stomach. 'I thought the cool season would help my symptoms, but I'm afraid I must face the truth. I shall sail home, and have to be content with my little India in England.'

'Little India in England? What is this?'

'I've tried to recreate the Indian life at home.' He rolled the liquid in the glass, bringing it closer to his mouth and staring down into it. 'I do love it so – the richness of colour, of taste and smell. And the servants – so much more loyal and concerned than ours at home. Of course my attempts in London are very small, but I do what I can.' He took a drink.

I nodded, rubbing the cover of the book with my fingers.

'What's that you're looking at?' He came closer, setting the lamp on the low table beside the candle, and as he straightened up, so near me, I instinctively stepped back.

He smiled, cocking his head as if about to scold me. 'Come now, Miss Daryâ.'

I held the book between us. 'I will return it tomorrow. It belongs to the little sâhibs. I only wished to look at it for one night. I will return it in the morning,' I repeated.

'In the bungalow there are books much more interesting than those simple childish sketches. I'll bring you a few, shall I? Tomorrow.'

'As you wish.'

I didn't know where to look; he had his eyes fixed on me in that same unblinking stare.

'Do you find me attractive, Miss Daryâ?' he asked, and the forwardness of his question so startled me that I dropped my head immediately, fixing my eyes on my feet.

'Can you not look up and answer? I hope you do. I find you very appealing.'

'Mr Bull.' It was the first time I had uttered his name. 'I do not wish you to be here. Please. Go back to the house.' I kept my head bowed.

'Don't be frightened.'

'I'm not,' I said, although I was, indeed, very uncomfortable with his presence, alone, in the godown filled with shadows cast by the candle and his lamp.

'I believe you. You're truly a brave young woman. So far from your home, with an obvious spirit of adventure. Able to adapt to new surroundings, and circumstances.'

Although I still didn't like him being here, his words sent a sliver of pride through me. His were the words I had wanted to hear from Mr Ingram's lips as we sat on the verandah a few days ago with the memsâhib. Not that I was a hard worker.

But I didn't want Mr Bull to know his words pleased me. 'I am no one, Mr Bull. Just a woman – a homeless, childless woman who does what she must to survive.' Finally I lifted my eyes.

He raised his eyebrows. 'I don't see you like that, my dear. You're very exotic.'

'Exotic? And exactly what makes me so?' I didn't want to keep talking to this man, and yet his compliments were like the smell of cooking food when one is hungry. 'I am ordinary.' It was only pride, pride that was false, that made me want to hear what he had to tell me about myself.

'You would not be seen as ordinary in England. There is a fascination there with the lives of other places – especially, right now, the lives of the East. There are many paintings of women such as yourself – young and beautiful, seductive with the allure of the unknown – being exhibited in London.'

Did he mock me? I was not beautiful, or alluring. I was too tall, and although I had the tattoos the Ghilzai found favourable, nobody had ever spoken of my appearance in these terms.

'Would you ever entertain, Miss Daryâ, the idea of life in London?'

'What do you mean? What do you speak of, Mr Bull?'

'David Ingram must have aroused your imagination with images of England. Didn't he?'

I shook my head.

'He didn't speak of the glories of our fair land? Well, not completely surprising, considering he is more at home here than in England. No, not surprising at all, knowing what I do of the fine young Mr Ingram, with his flights of fancy and lack of proper decorum. Although I've seen for myself how that dark, brooding expression drives the young English ladies to distraction.' His voice had taken on a mocking tone. 'Now, you wouldn't see it, Miss Daryâ, if you had other – true, proper – Englishmen, such as myself, for comparison.'

I didn't like what he said, or how he said it. It was if he was trying to make me see Mr Ingram in a negative light, without him able to defend himself.

'You mustn't base all Englishmen on David Ingram. Not fair at all. Anyway,' he said, with an annoyed shake of his head, 'to go back to what I've been thinking . . . Miss Daryâ, would you ever care to see the sights of our wonderful Empire?'

I kept looking at him. He took another drink. 'It's quite simple, really. I can get you a passage on the ship. You'd have to stay below, with the other natives, and it's a devilishly long voyage, but once we've reached England's shores, why . . .'

Now I shook my head. 'Why would I come to England? What would be there for me?'

'What would be there? Why, pleasure. Simply pleasure. Don't you feel you deserve pleasure?' He drained his glass. 'Or would you rather remain an ayah, working for a few rupees a year?' Without waiting for an answer, he continued, 'As I told you, I've recreated my own Indian world in my home in London, living a similar lifestyle to the one I've always so enjoyed here. And I like to open that world – my home – to others. There are many who enjoy my hospitality, and my exotic offerings. I like to think of myself as a bit of a nabob, my dear.'

I didn't know what a nabob was, and didn't care. 'I think your idea has no sense. It's like a cup with no bottom, a dry river bed. A woman with no child,' I ended, with a hint of bitterness in my voice. 'Why would you wish me there?'

'Wouldn't you enjoy seeing the very British Empire your dear old grandmother spoke to you about? It's quite an offer I'm making you, Miss Daryâ. Quite an offer indeed.'

An offer. 'And what,' I asked, speaking slowly and clearly, 'would be expected of me in return?' My face was hot.

A slight breeze blew in through the open doorway, and Mr Bull's face became darker, just slightly, although perhaps it was the wavering of the candle flame just before it sputtered and died. 'Really,' he said, his voice low. 'All that distance, from Jalalabad to Bombay, with David Ingram? Just the two of you? You must have grown to know him – and he you – very, very well. I'm sure you – shall we say – repaid him for all he did for you. And I would ask no more than he.'

Now my whole body heated. 'Mr Ingram is a good man,' I answered, trying to cover my shock at his suggestion, fighting for dignity, distressed and insulted not only at Mr Bull's view of my character, but of his view of Mr Ingram's. 'He treated me, always, with respect. And I – I, Mr Bull, am a virtuous woman.' I was breathing rapidly.

He didn't answer for a moment, and then he smiled a sly smile. 'And you expect me to believe that?' he said, leaning against the wall. 'You really expect me to believe that?' he repeated. 'You were a married woman; it's not as if you're a frightened girl with your virginity at stake,' he said, and I drew in my breath again, in shock, at his speech. 'I'm a good man too, in my own way, Daryâ,' he said, 'for I could extinguish this lamp and take you right now, if I weren't such a gentleman. Don't you think this will be your eventual fate with another of the burra sâhibs? Word travels quickly through these tight little British enclaves. Who will you tell, when – not if, but when – it happens? And further, who would care?'

My heart beat harder, my thoughts spinning. 'I am a good Muslim woman,' I repeated, 'and I—'

'Stop your tiresome protests, Daryâ. No good Muslim woman travels hundreds and hundreds of miles – lives for months – alone with a young man. Do you think Mrs Andrews doesn't know you have no morals, in spite of whatever Ingram tried to tell her? And don't you see why the other servants treat you without respect? You're what is known among the English as a fallen woman. Who knows what the Indians call you? But this I do know: you're not worth very much here, Daryâ.'

I stared at him. Worthless, he was saying. Again, I was called worthless.

'So you will be used at will by men who so desire you. And of course in time there'll be a child – a half-caste, no less – and then you'll be out of a job. And the only job you'll find will be in the clamorous brothels of Bombay.' He cocked his head. 'Oh, no, I've forgotten. You're virtuous. In that case you'll join the beggars down on the docks.'

I put my hand over my mouth at the pictures he was drawing of my future.

'Have I upset you? Well, think about these images, and then think how it could be for you in England. I would treat you as a princess. My own exotic princess. Think about it, Daryâ *jan*,' he said, and at that term of endearment, which nobody but my grandmother had ever used, all the heat fled from my body, and it was as if the icy waters of the Panjshir ran through me.

'We'll talk about it further tomorrow,' he said, his voice suddenly strangely kind. 'I know it's difficult to hear certain things. To know what others truly think of you. But I'm offering you a way out – a way to have a life you've never dreamed about, a life of luxury and freedom – a life only a lucky few ever know. Think about what I've said.' He took up the lamp, and as the darkness closed around me, his own face came more clearly into focus.

Then he turned, but before he left he looked back over his shoulder. 'Not many people have a chance to choose their fate,' he said. 'So think carefully, very carefully, about what life you want.'

CHAPTER THIRTY-THREE

I WALKED UP AND down the length of the hut, my eyes burning with fatigue but my heart still racing with shock that Mr Bull would offer such a completely inappropriate proposition. I couldn't imagine that any man of my culture would suggest such a thing to an ordinary, decent woman. I finally lay down in the darkness of the godown, staring at the ceiling until the sun rose. I continued to tell myself that what this bold *khâreji* said was appalling and insulting as I washed, and ate my simple breakfast and went to the children's room.

But I understood with more depth what Unma's face showed when I walked in. I now knew her treatment of me was not wholly because I had temporarily taken her daughter's job. She looked on me as a woman of low breeding, of immoral behaviour, much as Fareed had in Jalalabad. And what I had presumed to be timidity on Kavindra's part was really shocked fascination – that the memsâhib would allow one such as I into their midst.

It was even more difficult to work this day; I was distracted, the children's demanding voices shrill, Evie-*baba*'s whimpers endless. I felt that Unma – and even Kavindra – judged my every movement, and I wanted to shout at them that I was not the kind of woman they believed me to be. Is this how it would be wherever I worked in Bombay? This judging, the whispers, or open hostility following me wherever I went? Or worse, as Mr Bull had remarked – men feeling they could use me at will?

And he, Mr Bull, seemed to be everywhere, watching me from the open windows or doors, sitting on the verandah, one leg crossed over the other, foot swinging as he followed my movements. I didn't look at him, and he didn't speak, but I knew his thoughts, and this made me anxious, tripping over my own feet and dropping what I carried.

I found myself glancing at the others on the verandah. Was the sâhib with the long, drooping moustache staring at me? Why was the memsâhib frowning as she watched how I held Sâhib Teddy? As I passed one of the servants who stood in attendance on the verandah, did he make a low sound of disgust in his throat, or was he simply clearing it?

It seemed the day would never end. I was confused by my own fears, distracted by my thoughts, and Unma never stopped glaring at me, hissing commands which Kavindra translated, making it clear I was not following directions, that I was not giving the children the proper attention. When the little ones were finally in bed I stumbled to the godown in exhaustion, my lips trembling as I fought back tears.

You are only tired from not sleeping last night, and weak because you were too anxious to eat, I told myself as I entered the godown and pulled aside my headscarf with shaking fingers. Tomorrow will be better.

But would it?

On my pallet lay a large book with a hard cover of pale yellow silk, and I knew Mr Bull had left it for me. I lit a candle and sat, slowly turning the pages all the way to the end, and then went back to the beginning to study the pictures again. Each time I looked at the same picture I saw something new, something puzzling or fascinating. The pictures weren't in colour like the paintings on the walls in the children's room, or the ones in Prita's hut in Multan. These were in shades of grey and white and black, and as I ran my fingers over them, I could almost feel the hard shapes of the tall buildings, the texture of the leaves of the trees that lined wide stone roads, the coarse manes of the horses that stood harnessed in front of boxes that looked like small houses.

The pale-faced women wore hats resembling heavy birds, and very tight dresses with huge skirts like Memsâhib Andrews and her friends. There was a picture of a bear on his hind legs. A wide strap around his neck had worn away his fur. His mouth opened in a roar, but his teeth were short and square, and I wondered how he killed his food.

'Do you like the photographs of London?' Mr Bull asked, making me jump. I hadn't heard him approach; again he held a glass. He drained it and set it on the windowsill. 'Photographs,' he repeated, and then told me of a box which captured these people and buildings and animals inside itself and made them reappear again, on paper. I didn't believe him; surely he made up this story to impress me. Although a powerful *khâreji*, he was still a man.

'There are bears that walk the streets of England?' I asked, turning to the page of the animal.

He sat beside me on the pallet. I moved my knees further away and pulled my arm against my side so his body didn't touch mine. 'No,' he said. 'That one is in the . . . hmmm, is there a Persian word? In English, a circus. And others live in a zoo. People come to look at them.'

'The bears don't hurt them?'

'They're kept in cages at the zoo, along with many other animals and birds.'

'All in cages?' When he nodded, I asked, 'What do they wait for?'

Mr Bull leaned closer and ran his fingers over the bear's image. 'Wait for?' He looked at me, his face too near. The pupils of his eyes were pinpoints. 'They wait for nothing.' The odour of the amber liquid was on his breath, sharp and unpleasant, reminding me of the soaked cloths Prita had bathed me with during my illness. 'They're for the amusement of the people who come to see them.'

I watched his hand on the page. His fingers were blunt, the nails a little too long and very smooth, as if polished to an even glow. The black stone of his ring winked in the lamplight. 'In England a bear is exotic, then?' He removed his hand from the page, and I closed the book with a slam, holding it against my chest as I stood. 'And so I will be like this bear? For your own amusement?' My voice was low but strong as I looked down at Mr Bull. 'Tell me the truth, Mr Bull. If I came to England, as you suggested, would you put me behind bars as well?'

'Of course not,' he said, and there was anger in his voice as he rose and faced me. His brow was damp with sweat, and his face contorted in a spasm periodically, and I knew that the illness that plagued him was causing him great discomfort. 'I'm not forcing you to come to England. If you don't wish it, say now, and you can stay here, and be a servant for the rest of your life.' He pulled the book from my hands. 'I'm doing you a favour, Daryâ.'

I noticed he no longer put the formal *Miss* in front of my name.

We stood in silence; I found him easier to talk to with this annoyed expression, instead of the idle, slightly amused one he usually wore when he looked at me.

'If, Mr Bull, if for even one moment I did think about coming with you . . .' his expression altered, just the slightest, and I was shocked at the words coming out of my mouth 'could I return if I didn't like it there?' I asked him. What had I just said? Had I actually thought about going with him, to England?

One corner of Mr Bull's mouth pulled up. 'You're not a prisoner, Daryâ. You can return to your own country right now, if you wish. Nobody is stopping you. Isn't this so?'

I watched his mouth. No, I wasn't a prisoner. But there was no way for me to get back to Afghanistan, nothing to return to there. And if I went to England there would be nothing to return to in India. It seemed I grew further and further away from anything familiar. The further I went, looking for . . . for my life, I realised, the further away it seemed. Always out of reach. And yet I couldn't give up, stop trying to reach out and touch it, could I?

'What's that look I see on your face? I just said you wouldn't be a prisoner. Nor would you be mistreated in any way. In fact, you would have more luxuries than you know exist. You would never have to polish shoes or deal with spoiled, pasty-faced children again. Never have to do anything but enjoy your life. As I told you yesterday, what I'm offering you, my dear, is freedom.'

He picked up his empty glass and put the book under his arm, then walked slowly up the path, stopping, twice, to bend forward slightly, his arm across his middle. I watched him, but he didn't look back.

I blew out the candle and went to the open window. The moon rose, huge and white over the top of the big house and its surrounding trees, bathing everything in a mystical, silvery light. I thought of my grandmother's face, and of the homeland I had left. I thought of Mr Ingram saying goodbye, and of Mr Bull's offer.

Again, I thought of the future he had described here: that the memsâhib would put me in another house soon, and how word of my character would spread. I would not have a home or family to go to on days of celebration, for other ayahs would see me as Unma and Kavindra did, and would never invite me to join them. At best, I would belong to one memsâhib or another for the rest of my life in Bombay. Perhaps it would really be true, that I would be used by men of bad character, for I had no one to protect me. This *khâreji* offered me something completely unknown.

I thought of my grandmother's talk of finding a way to feel alive, of freedom. But in spite of what Mr Bull tempted me with, my life with him would still not be free, for I would belong to him and he would use me as he pleased. And yet, I had always belonged to somebody. First my father, then my husband, and now Memsâhib Andrews. And later I would belong to another memsâhib.

I had always worked hard, and received little thanks and few pleasures. If I chose to stay here wouldn't it be the same now – a life of servitude and loneliness?

In England, according to Mr Bull, I would have no work and no duties, save for the nightly one. I thought of Shaliq, and the nothingness I had eventually felt – after the first few horrid months – when he came upon me at night. There was no pain, physically or in my spirit, but simply a distasteful, rhythmic irritation that was over quickly. Would it be so different with this man? At least I would be in the great British Empire, in the city of London. I would see the world, as my grandmother had predicted. She could not have foreseen the shape her prediction would take, but she must have known that there is little in this life that is given without a layer of thorns.

If I went to England as Mr Bull's possession I would knowingly disobey the laws of Islam by committing the act of joining with a man outside of marriage. To make this choice would mean I would not be welcomed into paradise at the end of my days.

I put my arms on the windowsill and leaned my forehead on them. Why couldn't my decision be an easy one? Why couldn't I be a good, fearful Muslim woman, who would never, ever consider such an openly wicked proposition, or an evil non-believer, an immoral woman who would say yes as easily as the snuffing of a candle? Was there nothing in between?

There are more colours than black or white, Daryâ, Mr Ingram had once said to me. And yet in my case it appeared I had only these two to choose from.

Mr Ingram. There hadn't been room in my head to think of him since Mr Bull had come to me with his offer last night. And now suddenly he stood there, clearly. Would he know? Had he already left, or . . . I tried to think of what Kavindra had said. *But when the English leave soon on big boat* . . . did that mean there was only one, that Mr Ingram would be on the same boat as Mr Bull – and possibly me? If I did go with Mr Bull, would I be able to look at Mr Ingram without falling to my knees in shame, in apology? Would I be able to explain my choice to him?

Should I let my thoughts of Mr Ingram – and my need for him to not think poorly of me – direct my choice?

I raised my head. No. He had left me here, said goodbye, and walked away. I was of no importance to him, and I must not think of his expression, of the touch of his hand and how it had made something leap inside me.

I stared at the moon, suddenly remembering Mr Ingram telling me that England was ruled not by a man, but by a queen. 'I see you shining upon me, Mâdar Kalân,' I whispered to the glowing orb. *Do you see me from paradise? Is it wrong that I feel I must exchange one life – one of predictable unhappiness – for an unknown one, one in which I give a small part of myself in the hope of some measure of happiness – in order to know the world? Is this what you did? Or should I try and be what is expected of a good woman, hidden and silent, invisible, with no power of her own?* 'Please show me what to do,' I whispered.

I knew nobody could tell me which path to choose. But as I watched the sky, knowing that I had only myself to trust, a dark, ruffled cloud sailed across the face of the moon, veiling it, hiding its glory, and the night lost its magic.

The next morning Mr Bull came to me as I sat beside Sâhib George, who knocked down his small metal soldiers with a wooden sword, making ferocious sounds. 'Well, Daryâ? Have you thought further about my offer?'

When I didn't immediately answer, he continued. 'Please don't disappoint me,' he said, his face sincere, his voice low and pleading, and somehow this was comforting. 'The boat sails tomorrow, Daryâ. There's no more time.'

I stood and faced him, taking three deep breaths before answering. 'I will do it,' I told him, my mouth tight, as if not wanting to let the words out. 'I will go with you, Mr Bull.'

He smiled, showing all of his teeth as he lifted his chin. 'You've made the right choice, Daryâ,' he said. 'It wasn't so difficult, really, was it? To give up this' – he waved his hand towards Unma, trying to soothe Evie-*baba*'s high, squalling cries, and Kavindra, again wrestling to secure a *topi* on Sâhib Teddy – 'for a life of luxury.'

I let a moment of silence pass. 'It was my grandmother. I asked her, and she advised me to go.'

'Your grandmother? But I don't understand –'

'There is much you do not understand, Mr Bull,' I said, and he frowned at my tone, but I didn't care, turning to help Sâhib George find his sword, which had slipped from his hand into the oleander bushes which grew in profusion at the edge of the verandah.

I didn't speak to Unma or Kavindra the rest of the day; I was glad they ignored me, for I had no wish for them to know of my departure – and its meaning – while I had to work with them. I assumed Mr Bull would tell the memsâhib, and I would simply leave without saying anything to the other ayahs. I knew they would be relieved to see me go.

That night Mr Bull – as had been his routine for the past two nights – again held his glass as he came to the godown, although this time he didn't carry a lamp.

I sat outside in the moonlight, leaning against the wall.

'I wanted to again tell you how pleased I am at your decision, Daryâ *jan*,' he said, and again, the coldness went through me at his casual use of that intimate term.

I stood to face him. He was tall, although not as tall as Mr Ingram. 'When do we go to the boat?' I asked. 'In the morning?' I had made up my mind, and now I wanted to be away from here as soon as possible. Especially knowing that with my decision I would truly be as Unma and Kavindra already thought of me.

'Mid-morning,' he answered, and I was glad. 'I've already purchased your ticket, and have told Mrs Andrews that you're joining me.'

I closed my eyes at the thought of that conversation.

'It's very far to England?'

'Yes,' he said.

'As far as from Karachi to Bombay?'

'Much, much further.' He ran his finger over the rim of his glass, smiling as if very pleased with himself. 'All the way across the Indian Ocean, and then the Atlantic Ocean. We'll go on a great ship that carries goods to England – cotton and silk, tea and spices, as well as people. It's a long, long journey to the ports of London.'

I nodded, and he looked at the white ayah's dress I wore.

'Do you have any belongings?'

'Only one bag.'

'I'll send someone to the market first thing in the morning, to get you what you'll need for the journey,' he said, rubbing his hands together as if even more pleased, and I wondered exactly what it was he would decide I needed.

CHAPTER THIRTY-FOUR

At the dock I again saw the women in their revealing clothing and painted faces. But this time I didn't have the same reaction to them as I had had less than a week before.

I looked down at the new shimmering yellow and orange sari with its draping shawl to cover my bodice and arms Mr Bull had brought to the godown as I waited there before we departed. When he left, I'd put it on, smoothing down the silky folds. I covered my face with the delicate gold *hijba* he'd also given me, and tightly folded the other three saris he'd provided into my woven bag.

How had these women, I thought, watching them now, made the decision that they would not live like the gaunt, reeking beggars with their outstretched palms? Were these women really as terrible as I had first imagined, or, like me, did they simply do what they must in order to survive with some tiny sense of command over how their lives would be lived?

A huge ship with sails that reached high into the sky lay far out in the water. Now Mr Bull directed me, his hand possessively on the small of my back – into a small, crowded boat with about twenty others, both European men and women and children as well as three Hindu women in plain white saris. I knew them to be the memsâhibs' ayahs, as they all held English children upon their laps.

We were rowed across the stretch of murky water by two very dark-skinned men wearing only a scrap of cloth which hardly covered their lower bodies. These near-naked men kneeled as they rowed, their thin arms surprisingly powerful as we cut through the water. One had very protruding yellow teeth and smiled at me in too friendly a manner, and I glared at him and then looked away with my chin in the air, holding my *hijba* tightly across my face. I wished now that I wore a plain white sari, as the ayahs; it was clear, by his smirk, that he knew that I was little better than the loose women on the dock. I had seen him look at the firm grip Mr Bull had on my arm as I stepped into the boat, and run his eyes up and down the silky and costly sari.

I made sure not to look at him again from my seat at the side of the boat, Mr Bull beside me. As we were rowed further into the dark water I clutched the splintered sides until my knuckles grew pale. Although I had been on the flat boat on the Indus, and the mail steamer from Karachi, this small, low boat was very close to the water, made rough by all the other boats surging around us. I feared we would tip and be plunged into the sea. I glanced at Mr Bull and saw that he was watching my hands. I put them in my lap, not wanting him to see my anxiety.

As we approached the big boat its many levels rose high above us; it was as high as a building in the city. At its side the white men helped the memsâhibs and older children on to a stout ladder lowered at our arrival, and they climbed to the top. Shading my eyes and looking up, I saw a *khâreji* in a *topi* and white English clothing decorated with brass buttons who reached out his hand to assist the women and children on to the deck. And then he helped the *khâreji* men who climbed next, carrying the smaller children, and he took these children and put them into the arms of the waiting white women. Mr Bull climbed up; I saw that he was unsteady and climbed with difficulty, and the man with the brass buttons called another man, and each took hold of one of Mr Bull's hands as he neared the top. Finally the ayahs climbed the ladder, bunching their saris in one hand, but the man in the white trousers and jacket and *topi* didn't reach out to help them. I was last, twitching away from the yellow-toothed man who tried to put his hands on my waist in the pretence of assisting me – as he hadn't with the ayahs – as I put my foot on the ladder. When I reached the deck Mr Bull sat on a low wooden chair, his head back and eyes closed, breathing quick, shallow breaths, his hands clasped over his abdomen. I stood near him until the man with the brass buttons said something sharply to me. Mr Bull opened his eyes and answered the man.

'He'll show you where to go, Daryâ,' Mr Bull said, and again closed his eyes. Now his skin had a sallow cast, his lips dry and colourless beneath the moustache.

I followed the other *khâreji*; with a motion of his head and hand he indicated that I was to go down hard, clanging stairs. I did, clutching my bag, and followed a narrow hallway to the sound of women's voices chattering in Hindi. I stopped at the doorway of a small room with two rows of beds made of rope. They were attached to the walls with huge hooks, and blankets were folded on them. There was no window, and already the room, lit only by lamps attached to the wall, was dim and hot. This was the room for the ayahs – I recognised the three from the small boat, as well as three more, and another native woman who didn't wear the sari of an ayah, but a beautiful coloured one. They all sat on the beds, but stopped talking as I came in. I went to the one empty bed and put my bag on it.

The woman who did not appear to be an ayah called to me, but I couldn't understand her, and shrugged. She tried another language, and finally said, 'Persian?' and I was relieved that there was somebody I could speak to.

'Yes,' I said, smiling.

She didn't smile back. 'You are not an ayah,' she stated, looking more intently at what she could see of my face. 'And your eyes are not Indian. Are you a Portuguese?' she asked, her voice growing louder.

'No, I'm from beyond the North-West Frontier,' I told her, and removed my *hijba*, wiping the sweat from my face with my arm.

'Hmmmph,' she said, shaking her head as she looked at my *harquus*. 'Now I must also share a room with a tribal woman. Who takes you to the land of the dirty sky?' she asked.

My heart sank, but I spoke boldly, as if not ashamed. 'I travel with a very powerful sâhib. He takes me to be a guest in England.'

She raised one eyebrow, and a sly smile came to her lips. 'Hmmm,' she murmured now. 'I would not think this to look at you. Your sâhib likes your face like this? Does he not insist you cover those marks with white powder?'

'What of you, then?' I asked, ignoring her expression and questions.

'I am European,' she announced. 'English father, Parsee mother.'

Her skin was paler than the ayahs', although I quickly realised her face and neck were covered in a fine creamy mixture, difficult to detect unless one was close. Her eyes were very black, her eyebrows finely arched. She didn't look like the Hindu women, but she also didn't look like the memsâhibs. And she was very beautiful and delicate, her hands and feet dainty. 'And you are not an ayah, either,' I said, looking at her sari of blue and green silk, spun through with gold thread so that she resembled a small and lovely parakeet. Her large eyes were ringed with kohl, her profusion of long black hair was oiled like the ayahs', but she wore a flower of shiny white fabric over one ear, and strings of small paste pearls were woven through her hair.

'No. And I should not be here, in this pitiful room of natives,' she said, 'but it is difficult for us, isn't it? I also travel with a great sâhib,' she said, but I didn't like her tone, sly, like her smile. 'My Englishman. He takes me home.'

'England is your home?'

'Yes. Although I haven't been there before,' she said, tossing her head as if this were an unimportant fact. 'But he will make me a true English lady, as I was born to be.'

'He's your husband?'

She made a clicking sound with her tongue, shaking her head and grinning in a way that didn't suit her face. 'We are blessed, are we not, to have fortune bring our sâhibs to us?'

I didn't answer. The other women looked at us with disapproving stares. Although I doubted they could understand Persian, clearly they didn't wish to be near us.

'I am Blossom,' the woman said, 'named by my mother. She always told me, from when I was a very small child, that some day I would go home. My mother is very happy now.'

'And I am Daryâ,' I told her, and the ayahs went as one out the door.

'Where are they going?' I asked.

Blossom lay back on her bed lazily, inspecting her fingernails, which were stained scarlet. 'We will depart now,' she said, closing her eyes. 'I, for one, although happy to see the last of Bombay, wish only to look upon my true home.'

Unlike Blossom, I did want to watch as we left the city, and so I followed the ayahs. I went to the deck that ran around the whole ship, and stood beside them, but they pointedly moved away so that I stood alone. The deck above, which sat further back than the lowest one that I stood on, was crowded with white people, all looking at the mainland, talking and laughing, waving their arms to those tiny figures standing on the dock we had left across the span of water. It seemed that the *khârejis* on deck were happy to be leaving this country and going back to England.

Mr Ingram, I thought, looking away from the *khârejis*, pulling my *hijba* tighter, suddenly not wanting to see him, not wanting him to see me, even though I knew he wouldn't recognise me in this clothing, my face almost completely covered. I hadn't seen Mr Bull as I glanced up at the Europeans, and thought of how poorly he had looked after the climb to the deck. I presumed that now he rested in his room.

Down from me, the ayahs showed little expression, although I saw one put her arm around another's shaking shoulders, and I knew she wept to leave her home.

All of the business of loading the mountains of bags at the docks and the rowing of all the passengers across the water and settling them on the ship had taken hours; it was now early evening and a breeze had risen. There were lamps being lit along the dock and shining from the windows of the buildings close to the water. I thought of the people in those homes, moving about, eating, preparing to sleep, talking to each other, knowing what lay ahead on this night and for the next days of their lives. I envied them at this moment, and didn't know how I felt; I had already left my homeland, and knew little about this place we sailed from now. And I knew nothing of what waited for me in the land I went to, except for its queen and the pictures Mr Bull had shown me. The ship rocked very, very gently under my feet; the railing I held was damp and slippery. The ayahs were completely silent; two wiped their eyes with the ends of their headscarves.

'This is a Chinese clipper.' I jumped as Mr Bull spoke behind me. His voice was loud, so as to be heard above the noise of the other voices and calls. 'The finest vessels to sail the seas.' His face was still yellowish, and I smelled, from his breath, that he had been sick, and tried not to breathe as he spoke.

The ayahs moved even further away, two talking behind their hands as they glanced at us.

'They have so much material in their sails' – he pointed above us at the billowing expanse of white – 'which harnesses the wind. In a strong wind it's almost as if we fly over the ocean.'

I ignored the ayahs' stares and looked up at the sails which, from the dock, had actually reminded me of kites. I liked this image, and thought how wonderful it would feel, how smooth and free, to fly like a kite – or large bird – over the water.

'These clippers are known as the Kings of the Seas. With their marvellous sails we'll make the journey in record time – under a hundred days.'

'A hundred days? One hundred?' I repeated, shocked. Even though Mr Bull had told me the journey was further than the one from Karachi to Bombay, and had spoken of the different seas we would cross, I hadn't asked how long it would take. *One hundred days?* This was the time for a crop to flourish from the planted seed, for the plum tree to blossom, grow fruit, and the fruit dried and made into sweet jam, for the moon to present its glowing fullness three times.

At that moment there was a grinding, as terrible as if devils gnashed their teeth, and I clutched the rail, my shoulders rising.

'The anchors are being lifted so we can set sail,' Mr Bull shouted into my ear, smiling as if amused, but the smile immediately dropped away, and he put his hand to his abdomen again, wincing.

And then we were moving, and the wind whipped my *hijba* about my face, and I clutched it under my chin. But a mighty gust pulled it from my hand with a sharp tug and it flew up into the air. I put back my head to watch it. The square of pale fabric floated like a golden bird high over the billowing sails, and then disappeared into the heavens.

That first day I learned that the room I was to spend the next hundred days in was not only too crowded and always hot, but was also terribly noisy, and was situated beside rooms where the sailors stayed and where supplies and live animals were kept. There was a constant unpleasant odour, and the sailors passed by our room at all hours, and, because we were forced to leave the door open for air, we had no privacy. We had to go down the long, dark hallway, often passing and brushing against these men in the narrow space, to use a bucket in a tiny curtained corner. In another corner were pails of fresh water to wash, but the area was not kept clean. We ate our meals in a large room one floor above on splintery wooden tables and low benches. Beside this room was a much bigger, brighter cabin with round glass windows and a separate compartment for each bed. There were hooks on the walls from which hung simple dresses of white women, and there was a large spotless area for washing.

'What's this room?' I asked Blossom as we passed it that first day at sea.

'The room for the white servants,' she told me. 'We are given the worst, at the bottom of the ship, for the lowest fare. My sâhib of course wanted me upstairs, in a lovely spacious cabin, but it was not allowed, for the captain of the boat refused to recognise my heritage.' She scowled. 'It's not right. I'm not one of you.' She touched the silk flower she always wore in her hair. 'The natives are not even allowed beyond this second floor, except for the ayahs. They're given the right when their ladies call for them to attend to them or care for the children when they eat and enjoy entertainment. But they must remain out of sight, inside their memsâhibs' cabins.'

Although I wondered at Blossom's story of being half English, she was the only person I had to speak with, and I was glad for her presence.

'So we don't see our sâhibs?' I asked her.

She smiled, that same, sly smile I already knew. 'Unless they call for us and make arrangements that we go to them. As long as our presence isn't detected by the other guests upstairs, my sâhib has assured me that the sailors will act as if they don't see us.'

I hoped Mr Bull wouldn't call for me. Not here, on this boat. I thought of his yellow complexion, the smell of his breath.

But did this also mean I wouldn't see Mr Ingram? I didn't know what answer I wanted to hear when I questioned Blossom. 'So the Europeans never see us, then?'

She shrugged. 'I believe they are free to go anywhere on the boat – as I should be,' Blossom said, again shaking her head, 'with this fine English blood running through me. But they won't be bothered to come to the lower deck; why would they? My sâhib says those upstairs will spend their time eating fine food and playing games, listening to the music provided by a group of musicians, sometimes dancing – men and women together, as is the English way, of course – and even acting out small performances.'

'And how do we spend our time, here below?' I asked.

She made a face. 'We simply sit, and wait,' she said. 'No one worries about our entertainment. Not yet. But when we reach England it will be different. Then our sâhibs will make sure we are part of all the festivities. In that land the sky is not like the Indian sky, Daryâ,' she said. 'There, my mother heard from my father, before he went home when I was but a small child, the sun is pale and distant, and rarely shines, and without its glow, the sky is dull, the colour of a smudged silver plate. But I don't care – what do I care for the sun when I will have so many riches, so much to do, as my sâhib promises?'

I wondered at her words about the sun. Would the moon also be less bright, then?

The next night – our second at sea – after the ayahs and Blossom lay quietly on their beds, I was too hot, and the smells from the animals and food the sailors cooked made it difficult to breathe. I went up to the lower deck and stood in the dark, taking deep breaths of sea air, looking at the star-strewn sky. Muted melodies played by unfamiliar instruments floated in the still air.

It would be as Blossom had told me, then? Did the English dance? Would I dance with Mr Bull when I was in England? Assuring myself that there were no sailors in sight, I went up the steps. This upper deck was deserted, and I stood well back from the large windows that ran all around it. From my shadowy spot I watched the sâhibs and memsâhibs laugh and talk, some sitting at tables that ringed the room, eating and drinking. And indeed, some did shamelessly dance together in the centre of that long room, their bodies touching for all to see. I didn't see Mr Bull among them as I glanced at each table. But in the corner furthest from where I stood, sitting alone, was Mr Ingram. He watched the dancers, unsmiling, and a book lay open on the table in front of him.

Mr Ingram. Although it had been less than a week since I'd last seen him, it felt as though a year had passed. He looked to me – as usual – not right, somehow, in his English clothes. But more than that, as I watched him watch the others, it occurred to me that he was lonely, and also uncomfortable in some way that had nothing to do with the tight English clothing. I thought of the ease with which he'd sat on his heels among the Indians on the barge, in his loose cotton trousers and *kurta*, his head thrown back with genuine laughter, his face and voice alive. But now, among his own people, he didn't appear certain of his place.

Was he so different to me, then, looking for a place to be at peace? But at that moment hands clutched my shoulders. I cried out at the shock of it, twisting around to look into the face of one of the sailors, a big man in a spotless white jacket with the rows of brass buttons that

I knew indicated his importance. He spoke roughly, shaking me, and I grabbed my headscarf and pulled it across the bottom of my face.

'I do no harm,' I said, my voice rising. 'I'm only looking.'

Of course he couldn't understand me, nor I him, but he continued talking, shaking me as he pushed me towards the stairs. There were other voices, and then silence – the music had stopped – and I saw that while some watched through the big windows, a small group of men and women clustered in the open doorway of the long room.

I breathed heavily, holding my scarf so that it covered most of my face, feeling the stare of eyes upon me as I now silently struggled against the sailor's hands. Suddenly the deck tilted with a swell of the waves, and the sailor lost his grip on me, and I let go of my scarf to grab a post for support. The scarf slid back from my forehead and on to my shoulders. One of the women in the doorway made a loud, annoyed sound.

'Savage,' she called, and then spoke quickly and loudly, repeating the word as she stared at me. *Savage.* Although I didn't know its meaning, the hiss with which she uttered it and the look on her face made it clear she found me loathsome. And then Mr Ingram pushed through.

'Daryâ?' he said, coming closer. 'Daryâ,' he repeated, disbelief in his voice, looking at my sari.

I lowered my eyes, not wanting him to see me like this, humiliated.

'What are you doing here?' As the ship rolled again he reached out one hand to me, as if to stop me should I fall, but stopped when it was halfway between us.

The sailor again took hold of my upper arm, but Mr Ingram spoke to him, and he let go. Then Mr Ingram simply said, 'Go downstairs, please, Daryâ.' The crowd murmured, watching as he followed me down the deck towards the steps.

When we were finally in the dark shadows of the lower deck, I turned to face him. 'I'm sorry, Mr Ingram,' I said. 'I only meant to watch. I didn't think . . .'

He shook his head, his voice hesitant. 'But . . . why are you here?'

My breath came quickly; I'd known from the moment I gave my answer to Mr Bull that this might happen: that I might have to face Mr Ingram. But there was no way to explain, no right words to admit to him why I was on the ship.

'Daryâ?' he said again, waiting, and the shamefulness of what I had chosen came over me with such fierceness that I had to turn my head, and as I did I pulled my scarf across my face.

'Why do you hide your face from me? How have you come to be here . . . your sari . . . Daryâ, tell me.'

I looked back at him. 'I am going to England, Mr Ingram.'

'Obviously. But –'

It was hard to speak calmly; my breath was ragged. 'It was Mr Bull. He invited me,' I said, my voice louder than I intended, and inwardly I cringed at the quivering, yet bold sound of it. But if I gave in to what I was truly feeling my words would come out in an apologetic whisper, and I wanted desperately to cover my disgrace.

'Osric Bull? You've come . . . with him? With Osric Bull?' he repeated, as if I'd just told him I'd swum through the water, following the boat all the way from Bombay.

There was a steady pulse of the wind rippling the sails against the night sky; I shivered, although the wind was not cold. 'I am to be his guest,' I said, but this time my voice was weak, as if I didn't believe my own words.

'His guest.' It wasn't a question, and now it was Mr Ingram's voice which had grown stronger, louder. 'You are coming to England as the guest of Osric Bull,' he said again, as if needing to ensure he was correct.

I nodded, still watching his face, wanting . . . wanting what? His approval? His understanding? Or did I wish his lack of understanding, his belief that what I did was innocent, and simple.

But Mr Ingram's face – the shocked disbelief turning to something dark, something hard and distant – spoke too clearly. He took a step back. 'The position as ayah was not to your liking?' he asked, his voice so unfamiliar, so cold that I wanted to weep.

'It wasn't . . . Mr Ingram.' *Please put out your hand. Touch mine like you did on the verandah in Bombay. Understand who I am, and why I have done this.* 'When you left, Mr Ingram . . .' But what could I say? How would I complain, tell him what I feared would have become of me? How could I make him understand that what I was about to become was not who I really was?

Another moment of silence passed.

'Can you not try to understand, Mr Ingram? I could not stay . . . Mr Bull offered me something – a way out of a life of servitude, of humiliation, he offered . . . can you understand? Should I beg for your forgiveness? I know you thought the life in Bombay would be –'

But Mr Ingram backed further away. 'No, Daryâ, no. You needn't beg my forgiveness.' His jaw tightened. 'It's you who must now forgive me. For how stupid I've been . . . I understand completely. You have agreed to be Osric Bull's whore. Of course I understand,' he said then, in a horrible, final way, each word like a firm slap across my face.

He turned and walked away from me, his back straight as he climbed the stairs, his footsteps ringing in my ears, through my head, each like a shot from a *tofang*.

CHAPTER THIRTY-FIVE

FOR THE FIRST few days after that night I felt ill, my head pounding and my stomach rejecting food. It had nothing to do with the motion of the ship; it was brought on by thinking about Mr Ingram, his face and voice, first the surprise at seeing me – the way his eyes had lit up – followed by shock. And then, as he listened to my clumsy words, the growing expression of cold disgust, as if he smelled something rotten. I couldn't stop thinking about what he must be thinking of me – if he still thought of me at all. He had said he understood, but he didn't. He didn't understand my need to not accept what it appeared would be my fate.

I didn't see him for the next twelve days, although I sometimes felt he might be looking down on me from the upper deck. Each time I felt this I turned, quickly, looking up, but he was never there. I wanted so badly to see him, and yet I couldn't bear it if he looked at me as he had in the shadowed lower deck. I watched the waves, my future as lonely and dark and endless as they appeared to me now, and I wondered how I would get through the rest of what would surely be an endless journey. Now when I recalled what happened between us on the verandah in Bombay, it was dirtied, spoiled. I knew Mr Ingram thought of me with hatred, and this pain was deeper than I could have ever imagined. *Mr Ingram, I'm sorry.*

'I'm sorry,' I whispered to myself, over and over. If only I could say it to his face.

One early evening a sailor came to me and said my name. I nodded, but he spoke to me in English, so I went down the deck to fetch Blossom. She listened to the sailor and then told me that he brought a message from my sâhib. I thought he meant Mr Ingram, and put my hand to my throat, my heart leaping, but when Blossom said, 'He says you are to go with him, and he will take you to his room, because your sâhib wishes to see you now', I realised it was Mr Bull who was now my sâhib, not Mr Ingram. I had thought, regularly and with distaste, of Mr Bull, and was glad he seemed content to remain above while I lived below. Now I swallowed and stared at Blossom. She winked, smiling, and I thought *no*. I could not bear to go to Mr Bull, not here, on the ship, but knew I had no choice.

I followed the sailor up the stairs and along inside passages. He stopped in front of a door and rapped upon it, and there was a low reply from inside. The sailor opened the door and I stepped in, and it shut behind me.

Immediately the smell – sweat and the undeniable stink of sickness – made me hold my hand over the *hijba* already covering my nose and mouth. Mr Bull was propped up on pillows on a wooden bed attached to the wall. His skin was very yellow, and his face thinner than it had been when I last saw him.

'Ah. Daryâ,' he said, showing his teeth in more of a grimace than a smile. 'Come in.'

I went further into the dim room. It could have been pleasant, with its pictures attached to the walls, its gleaming wooden furniture also attached to the walls and floor with polished pieces of brass, and a small window. But the window was closed firmly, and only a bit of grey evening light made its way through. Mr Bull was covered with layers of blankets, although his face shone with the sweat that filled the enclosed space.

'I apologise for my state,' he said. His hair lay lank and greasy against his scalp. 'Terrible business, pancreatitis. Although the symptoms include an inability to digest properly, the motion of the ship hasn't helped. I'm unable to keep anything down at all.'

I tried not to choke on the acrid odour; a wooden bucket covered with a cloth sat on the floor at the side of his bed, and I knew the smell came from it. I wanted to turn and run back, out into the clean sea air.

'Will you sit here, on the bed by me, and keep me company?' he asked, stretching his hand to me. So close to him, I could see that the ends of his moustache were wet, and I pulled my head back the slightest. 'I've missed seeing your lovely face.' He dropped his hand limply on to the bed. 'Uncover it for me,' he said now, with complete authority, and I let my scarf fall.

Instantly a stealthy grin came over his sallow features, and he beckoned with his hand for me to come closer, sitting up from the pillows. But as he struggled to move into a comfortable position, a peculiar look came over his face, and he breathed heavily, reaching down, fumbling to pull the cloth off the bucket.

I turned and hurried through the door, closing it behind me. I wouldn't stay and be a witness to his illness, and he was in no state to demand that I remain.

I went back to the lower deck, and although I told myself it was uncharitable of me to be glad that Mr Bull was ill, I couldn't help but feel relieved that he was obviously too sick to expect anything from me.

Blossom was still standing where I'd left her. 'Why have you returned so quickly?' she asked, frowning. 'I didn't expect to see you again this evening.'

'He is sick,' I said. 'Very ill.'

'This isn't good,' Blossom said, studying my face. 'Hope he does not die, Daryâ,' she added, and I opened my mouth in surprise.

'Why should he die?' The idea hadn't occurred to me.

'They do, the pure English,' she said, 'if they get sickness in India. I worry for my gentleman; he is no longer young, and it is difficult for him to walk on the ship. If they die, then what becomes of us?'

'Don't talk of this, Blossom,' I told her, and she shrugged, and in the next instant was chattering about something else.

She tried to teach me the English she had learned from her mother, and laughed with good nature at my mistakes. She told me I should no longer eat with my hands, for this was the sign of a native, and in England was not allowed. So I struggled with the tools – the knife, so dull – and the fork and spoon that I'd first held when attempting to feed little Sâhib Teddy. The food we were served on the long wooden table every day – the meat and fish and vegetables – was all dry and tasteless, with no spices. We were most often given meats from the pig, which I didn't touch, and Blossom told me the Hindus couldn't eat beef so it wasn't served. I longed for something familiar, something that awoke my mouth, but the closest thing was an occasional meal of rice and a thin curried mixture of an unidentifiable meat. I was often hungry, and ate it in spite of the possibility of it being pig, telling myself if I didn't know for sure I couldn't blame myself.

Blossom moaned over the state of the plain black tea, making a face of disgust as she drank from a tin mug. 'I am used to true English tea, drunk with milk from a china cup, and it seems we are not good enough to be allowed this treatment.' She commented bitterly that the ladies upstairs would be drinking very milky tea, surely, and 'with proper tea service, I can imagine'.

In spite of her complaints, I liked her. It was difficult to resist her smiles and whispered, funny comments about the memsâhibs. And more than anything, we were company for each other. I realised just how much I had missed the company of another woman, one I could talk to. We exchanged stories from our pasts, and Blossom occasionally made me laugh, although nothing could make me forget the way Mr Ingram had looked at me in the shadows of the lower deck.

At times Blossom grew pensive and sullen, and I saw that her mood depended on a piece of white silk with a black symbol on it brought to our cabin by an older sailor who looked upon Blossom with open disdain. When the white silk was not brought for a few days she appeared worried, restless, but with its arrival she was immediately cheerful again, singing as she chose one of her saris – she had many – and fussing with her hair and applying more of the pale cream to her face and bathing her arms and throat with rosewater. Those nights, when the ayahs breathed quietly in sleep, she would creep out of our room, although she was always in her rope bed in the morning. But if I awoke when she returned, I no longer smelled the sweetness of the rosewater, for she bore the distinct scent of a man upon a woman, and I knew she had gone to her sâhib.

And at these times I was even more glad that Mr Bull lay sick in his cabin.

One windy afternoon Blossom and I stood on the deck together. Suddenly she smiled over my shoulder in a particularly dazzling way, lightly pinching my arm. I turned; it was Mr Ingram, walking towards us.

My heartbeat suddenly pounded in my ears. I had wished so much to see him again, and now that I did, I was frightened of what he might say, that he might look at me with disgust as he had earlier, and I didn't think I could bear this again.

He stopped beside me, and before he had a chance to speak Blossom lifted her chin and extended her hand in front of me, forcing me to lean back. 'Good day, sir,' she said in English, dipping one knee. He looked at her hand and then took it, holding it for an instant.

'Good afternoon,' he replied.

I knew these simple phrases of greeting now.

'Lovely day,' she said, and I was pleased that I also understood this.

'Yes.' He let go of her hand.

'I will introduce you,' Blossom hissed to me in Persian. 'Act in a charming manner.' Before I could speak she put her hand on my arm and spoke in English to Mr Ingram, too quickly for me to understand anything except my own name.

'Yes. Miss Daryâ and I know each other,' he said in Persian, and Blossom's mouth opened, then closed, then opened again.

'This is Mr Ingram, Blossom,' I said, when I realised she was looking at me, waiting for me to say something. 'He speaks Persian,' I added, unnecessarily. 'Mr Ingram, this is Blossom.'

'Well,' she said, looking from Mr Ingram to me. 'So. You are Daryâ's gentleman friend,' she said, reverting to Persian as well. 'I do hope you are feeling better,' she added with a small laugh.

Mr Ingram didn't answer, looking at me with an expression I couldn't read.

Blossom looked from me to him, the tension growing, then she dipped her knee again, her eyelids lowered coyly. 'I shall leave you to your conversation, then, sir,' she said, 'for you and Daryâ obviously have much to discuss.' She again put out her hand, and again Mr Ingram took it. When he let it go, Blossom moved slowly down the deck, her hips swaying under the thin sari, and his eyes followed her.

'She's teaching me English,' I said, flustered, wanting to delay what Mr Ingram might say or do. As if to demonstrate that I spoke the truth, I repeated what Blossom had taught me only the night before. 'You biggee man, Sâhib. So-very-please-meet-you.'

He shook his head, frowning. 'Don't do that,' he said, his tone, again, cold and unfamiliar. 'It's only *che-che*.'

'*Che-che*?'

'Just a silly, sing-song version of English. Used by uneducated servants. It's demeaning – it doesn't suit you.' When I said nothing, he continued, his voice rising. 'Or perhaps it does. I always thought you to be a proud woman, but . . . go on, Daryâ. Learn your *che-che*.' He looked down the deck again, to where Blossom now stood, leaning over the railing. 'So,' he said. 'There are others like you aboard, then.' He was angry. He clenched the rail in front of him; his knuckles stood white.

My cheeks flamed; again, it was as if he had struck me. Yes, I knew that Blossom and I were the same kind of woman.

He blinked rapidly, muttering short, angry English words, but then his expression changed, and he ran his fingers through his hair. 'I'm sorry,' he said, as if suddenly tired, and I saw new lines on either side of his mouth. 'I didn't come here to speak to you like this. It's been very . . . difficult for me to think of you in this way. This new way.'

I waited. At least he still thought of me.

'But I have – I have thought, much about it. And I know I have no right to judge you. It's not my place. I've made enough of my own –' he stopped. 'I had come down here to apologise for my earlier reaction – when I first saw you here, on the ship.' He cleared his throat. 'But I'm not doing it well. I'm sorry,' he repeated.

I looked down. 'I, too, am sorry. I am sorry, Mr Ingram.' I had said it so many times, in my head and aloud. Now it sounded weak.

We both looked at the waves, and then I turned to watch his profile, and said, quietly, in English, 'Thank you, sir.'

He finally looked at me.

'This is proper, or *che-che*?' I asked in Persian. 'If not, can you tell me the right words?'

He didn't answer my question, saying, 'So. I will go back upstairs.' But he didn't; he stood where he was, as if waiting for something, and my hopes rose again. Then suddenly he turned, swiftly, and walked away, and something like desperation shot through me.

'Mr Ingram?' I called, my voice too high, breathless, and he stopped and looked back. 'Will you . . . talk to me? Would you stay and talk to me?' I realised how much I wanted this. I wanted to have him back as my sâhib, the sâhib I had spent so much time with between Jalalabad and Bombay. Even though I had disappointed him, angered him, was I so repulsive now that he wouldn't even speak to me? That he couldn't bear to be on the same deck as me?

He didn't answer, but cracked his knuckles, something I'd never seen him do before. 'I don't think so. I only came to apologise. I believe it's best if I . . . if we . . . don't see each other for the rest of the journey, Daryâ.'

Something small and cold closed around my heart. 'But why?' I asked, knowing the answer, knowing that in his eyes I was no longer a proud woman, but had fallen to the level of one like Blossom. And so I was too far beneath him.

He stared at the waves, then looked back at me, his face fixed in an expression that was at once hard, and yet carried the same odd, lonely look I had seen when I watched him through the window upstairs. 'I just believe it's better this way,' he repeated, and left, his strides long and sure on the wooden deck.

When he disappeared Blossom hurried to me; she had obviously been watching. 'Daryâ,' she breathed. 'You have such a fine sâhib. So young and handsome.' She lowered her eyelids again. 'Did he come to arrange a meeting? I am surprised he has been able to last so long without you going to him. Or have you been sneaking out when I was not aware—'

'He's not my sâhib,' I interrupted, my words clipped. 'And I don't go to him.'

'What do you mean?'

'Mr Ingram is not the sâhib who takes me to England. He is . . . someone else. Someone I knew . . . before. The sâhib I came with is nothing like Mr Ingram.'

'But . . . I see how he looks at you. And you at him. You have already been with him – to his bed. And he wants you to come again, and you also wish to go. I can see this clearly. So why don't you go to him now? If the one who takes you to England is ill, he'll never know.'

I needed to be alone, to think about what had just happened. 'It's not that way between us,' I said.

Blossom said nothing more, but I knew by her expression that she didn't believe me. I told her my head ached, and I was going to the cabin to rest.

I went to my rope bed and lay there, thinking of Mr Ingram, thinking about what Blossom had said about going to his bed. Thinking about his hands, and what their touch on my body would be like.

I was unable to cry, as if frozen with grief. As if I had experienced a death.

Strangely, it was death that brought Mr Ingram back to me.

After a few weeks of quiet seas, during which I simply sat on the deck, waiting for each day to pass, trying so hard not to look upward, at the deck above where I knew Mr Ingram stayed, a harsh wind blew up one night. It created a storm that tossed our ship as if it were a small vessel of flimsy twigs, and all of us in the room at the bottom of the ship grew very ill. It was a terrible time – because of the motion of the ship, which felt as if it were being shaken by the huge hands of the *jinn*, we could not even walk to the bucket down the hall. The floor of our cabin was a foul mess, and the Hindu women screeched and cried out the names of their idols in the dark. I clung to the ropes of my bed and prayed silently to Allah, suddenly remembering my old prayers, but this prayer was only for the storm to pass. For an unknown reason I knew with certainty that my destiny was not to die in water, and so did not fear death here as the ayahs did.

And their fears were realised; one of the ayahs refused to tie herself to her bed with scarves and saris as the rest of us had. She was afraid, Blossom told me later, that if the water rushed into the cabin she would be trapped, and would drown. And so at some unknown hour in the black horror of that night storm she was thrown from her bed and struck her head on a protruding beam. We didn't know this until the next morning, when the sailors brought lamps and pails of salty water to dash upon the floor. The terrible discovery was made by all of us at the same time. We roused ourselves, covering our noses from the stench we had created, and in the flickering light of the sailors' lamps saw the poor woman's body gently rolling back and forth under us in the layer of slime. The ayahs screamed with shock and sorrow as the sailors lifted their lifeless friend and wrapped her in a sheet and took her up the stairs. Later, after the sobbing women had cleaned her and dressed her in her best sari I watched – with the other natives and a few of the memsâhibs – as her body was wrapped and tied in a white sheet and then gently deposited into the sea by two sailors. The memsâhibs had brought offerings of cakes and small gifts; they gave these to the ayahs, who threw them, weeping softly and praying, into the water after the small white form had disappeared beneath the now calmly rippling waves.

I watched the deep, dark spot in the ocean where the ayah had been left, so alone and far from her home and all who loved her. I wondered if a soul could make its way to the Hindu paradise from such a place.

As I turned to leave, saddened for this unknown ayah, wondering when and how the family she had left behind in India would learn of her death, Mr Ingram rushed down the deck towards me. He was breathing heavily from running, and yet his sun-burnished face was uncharacteristically bleached of colour.

'Mr Ingram?' I said, not only surprised at his presence, after what he had told me days earlier, but also at seeing him looking so strange.

As he caught his breath a more natural shade returned to his face. 'I just heard,' he said, panting out the words, 'there was talk of one of the native women . . . dying . . . last night, and I . . .' He stopped, wiping his lips with the back of his hand.

'It was a Hindu ayah,' I said, seeing the tremble of his fingers. 'She has already been put into the sea.'

He looked at the water, foaming along the side of the ship, not looking at me now. After a long moment he asked, 'Was she a friend?' but his voice was not his own.

I shook my head, even though he still watched the water. 'No. I didn't even know her name. The ayahs won't speak to me, because of who they see me to be, even though . . .' I paused. 'Even though they refuse to see who I truly am.' *In this way they are similar to you, Mr Ingram.*

Finally he turned to me, and his colour and voice were as always. 'Osric Bull is quite ill,' he said. 'He is unable to rise at all. Fortunately there is a man trained in medicine on board, who cares for him.'

'I know he is ill.' The sea was so calm now. It was hard to imagine its fury and strength, its ability to kill. I watched the rolling waves, thinking of Blossom's warning. 'Do you believe he will die?'

Mr Ingram shook his head, smiling, but it wasn't an amused smile. 'I've been told he has an illness called pancreatitis.'

I nodded, remembering the strange English word uttered by Mr Bull.

'It affects his . . .' he put his hand on his abdomen. 'I don't know the Persian words to describe it. His drinking of alcohol has made it worse. He's very uncomfortable, but he'll survive. Men like Osric Bull seem able to withstand almost anything.'

'What do you mean – men like him?'

Now his face, so pale only moments earlier, flushed. 'You know nothing of him, Daryâ, nothing, and yet you would agree to accompany him, to – to live with him, in England. How could you do this?' I heard the returning undercurrent of confusion and anger.

'I knew nothing of you, Mr Ingram, and yet I begged you to take me with you. Twice. From the *buzkashi* and from Jalalabad.' I waited a moment. 'Desperation has a forceful hand.'

'And you were desperate in Bombay?'

I stared into his eyes now. 'Yes.'

'And so you asked Bull to—'

'No,' I interrupted. 'It was he who asked. I was shocked – insulted – by it, and wouldn't consider it at first. But then . . .' I shook my head. 'I didn't make the decision lightly, Mr Ingram. It was very difficult. And I still don't know if what I've done is right.' I stopped. 'No. I know it is not right. What I mean is . . . I don't know if . . .' I stopped again. I didn't know how to explain, to tell him that I wanted to find a place where I could live not only in safety, but also with hope, and even some joy, without sounding full of my own desires and importance. Would I find this in England? I didn't know. I only knew it would not be mine as a scorned woman in Bombay.

Now he looked uncertain. 'But I thought . . . I assumed you would be – well, content as an ayah. Mr and Mrs Andrews are fine people.'

'I'm sure they are.' I would not tell him what had happened after he left, what I had learned his fine friends would do with me.

'What did Bull promise you, to make you decide to go with him?'

I didn't want to answer. Finally I said, 'You said it would be better if we didn't speak further. And yet now you stand and talk with me. Why have you changed your mind?'

He looked into the water at the side of the ship again, and in my head I saw the small figure, the white shroud secured with a *hijba* from each of the other ayahs, heard the tiny splash – so sadly insignificant in the huge ocean – as the body slid over the side and into the water.

'You imagined it was me who died,' I stated, knowing this to be true from the moment I saw his stricken face.

He looked at me, neither nodding nor shaking his head. 'I realised ignoring you would do no good, that to treat you so . . . I knew it would accomplish nothing.' He inclined his head at me and left, but this time as I watched him go, I knew he would come back. If he hated me as I had made myself believe, the thought that I may have been the native woman who died wouldn't have brought him running down the deck, shock and fear standing strongly on his face. Wouldn't have made his hands tremble, his voice falter.

I felt a surge of power, knowing that no matter what he had called me, and no matter how he struggled with his feelings, Mr Ingram did still care about me. And with this understanding came the first moment of calm I had known since he left me on the verandah in Bombay. At that moment I didn't care what would happen when we arrived in London; I didn't care what would happen the next day. I held on to this thought – that Mr Ingram couldn't stop his thoughts from turning towards me – and turned my face to the sun.

CHAPTER THIRTY-SIX

THE NEXT MORNING a white woman came to our cabin – I had seen her at the ayah's funeral on deck the day before. She had stood with the other memsâhibs, but had looked very different to them. She'd held a book with a very worn black leather cover, and had read from it in a murmur as the ayah was lowered into the sea.

Unlike the highly decorated clothing of the memsâhibs, this one wore a simple dark blue dress with a yellowed lace collar. The dress hung limply on her, and was stained under the arms, and as she had stood on the deck that day, her plain face so sorrowful, tears filled her eyes.

Now she wore the same dress, with the same discoloration under her arms. A large cloth bag was slung across her flat chest. She was tall and too thin; the bones on her face stood out in an unpleasant manner. Both her hair and eyes were the faded brown of weak tea. She once more carried the leather book in her hands, and I saw that for all her thinness, her hands looked as strong as a man's, the nails short and ridged. She smiled fondly at us, as though we were her own dear children whom she had not seen in some time.

She spoke to us in Hindi, but the Hindu women wouldn't look at her, defiantly turning their backs. Blossom laughed out loud at something the woman said; the woman didn't flinch at the laughter, but only smiled benignly.

'Who is she? What does she want?' I asked Blossom.

'She's a woman who carries the word of the white God,' Blossom told me. 'In English, a missionary lady. There are always missionary ladies wherever there are memsâhibs.'

'Mish-in-ary lad-ee,' I repeated, and the woman's washed-out eyes brightened and she came to me. She took my hand and put it on the book. The leather was creased and soft from much use, and warm from the woman's hands.

'Be careful,' Blossom warned, laughing again. 'She wants to put her Christian God inside you. You must leave room for your sâhib.' She laughed even louder, in her high tinkling laugh, at her own crude joke, and I ignored her.

Now the missionary lady's large, square fingers covered mine. She spoke Hindi, in an urgent, earnest tone, into my face, until Blossom rudely tossed off a brief sentence. The woman's face grew perplexed as she questioned Blossom further.

She put the book on my bed then, and laced her fingers together in front of her chest, speaking loudly into my face as if the increased volume would make me understand. Blossom continued to laugh; the ayahs paid no attention. Finally she unclasped her fingers, and I saw that her face was wet with effort. I didn't know what she wanted from me; all I knew was that she was the only white woman who had ever looked into my face and spoken to me, and she didn't have the demeanour of the other memsâhibs.

She turned and went through the narrow doorway; her dress was wet down the back. I followed her, and when we came up on the deck I put my hand on her arm. She looked down at it, and then at me.

'English,' I said, patting my chest.

She shook her head slowly, gently touching my *harquus*. 'No English,' she said.

I shook my own head in annoyance; did she think I was another Blossom with ideas of my own self-importance? I put my fingers to her mouth, then to mine. 'English,' I repeated. 'You say. Me. English.'

Her fact lit. 'Ahhh,' she said, nodding vigorously. She motioned for me to sit on the bench beside her, and opened the book. 'God,' she said, touching the page and then pointing to the sky.

'God,' I repeated. *Allah.*

She pointed to her left breast.

'Loves.'

I repeated this word, and then she patted her chest. 'Me.' She said the three words together, and I echoed them, feeling like a small child.

Her eyes shone and she nodded even more vigorously, her head bobbing on its thin neck. 'Yes, yes,' she said. 'Oh yes. God loves me,' she told me, 'and He loves you.' Her teeth were soft and browning at the gums.

I understood what I had said. It wasn't that different then – her God and mine – although I wondered if hers would be more forgiving, wouldn't see me in the way I knew mine must.

I wanted to learn what English I could from this memsâhib, so that I could show Mr Ingram that although he might see me as a woman like Blossom, at least I wouldn't speak only *che-che*.

Sometimes the ship stopped at strange harbours, and people left and others came on, and always huge boxes and crates were carried on to the ship by snaking lines of sweating men. I had no way to keep track of one hundred days; I stopped counting after twenty, the day that Mr Ingram came back to me.

And from that day on I was happy, and didn't care if the journey was two hundred days, or more; I didn't care if we stayed on this ship for ever, floating between two worlds – his and mine.

It was three days after the ayah's funeral, a warm afternoon, and as I watched the sea from the railing, Mr Ingram suddenly appeared beside me, not speaking, and looking at the water as I did. I didn't turn to him at first, didn't want him to know that I had been waiting, that I knew with certainty he would come to me. From the corner of my eye I finally saw him look at me, and I faced him. I didn't wear a *hijba* any more. The constant wind whipping the fabric around my face had grown unbearably annoying, but more than that, it seemed unnecessary. I was only with women; to the sailors I didn't exist. The rules I had once known weren't the same here, with water instead of ground beneath me, wearing foreign clothes, learning a new language, with no reminders of my former life. I told myself that when the land was once again firm under my feet I would put on my veil again.

'Good day, Mr Ingram,' I said in English, carefully, having practised greetings with the missionary lady a number of times. And this time he smiled, his genuine smile, and it was so familiar that an unexplained melody sang, high, in my head for an instant.

'Good day, Miss Daryâ,' he said, and I returned his smile at his use of *Miss*. 'Is your cabin comfortable?' he asked, reverting to Persian. *Is your cabin comfortable* – it was as if the last weeks no longer existed, as if the grief I'd experienced hadn't occurred. It was as if we were old friends, separated briefly, but now were meeting again.

I took a deep breath. 'It's fine,' I lied.

'Your friend Blossom is well?'

'Yes. She's sleeping. She sleeps a great deal.' Especially when she's been with her sâhib half the night, I thought, but wouldn't say.

'She's still teaching you English?'

I shook my head. 'The missionary lady teaches me. I want to learn the proper English.'

He cleared his throat.

'She speaks a great deal about your God,' I said, and frowned. 'You once said we shared a similarity in that we believe in one God. But she talks of three,' I said.

'Three?'

'She talks of *pâdar*, and *pesar* – son – but . . . something else. Another God she cannot make me understand, a God called' – I sounded out what she'd told me – 'Holyghost.'

'Father, Son, and Holy Ghost,' he said, in English, shaking his head. 'They're not three Gods, but what Christianity sees as the parts to make up the one God.'

'It's confusing.'

'Yes,' he said, and we both turned back to watch the waves.

Father, Son, and Holy Ghost. 'What of your fathers, Sâhib? You spoke of an English one, and the other.' I looked at his profile.

Even though his expression didn't change, I sensed a difference in him. 'The Englishman I thought was my father died. Of malaria.'

I assumed this was an illness. 'You were very close to him?'

He shook his head and didn't answer. Finally he turned to me. 'I don't remember him but for a few shadowy images. I was only a small child in India when he died. And then my mother brought me to England.'

'But what of your . . . the other father? The one whose blood you carry? He lives?'

Again he was silent. Finally he said, 'I've never spoken of him, Daryâ, to anyone.'

'I'm sorry,' I said. 'I'll ask nothing further.'

He nodded, and I asked him something inconsequential, something about the sea, but he didn't answer. And then he said, as if continuing his last sentence, 'Although I know I can speak of it – of what I know – to you, because . . .' he shrugged and looked at me. 'It's a different situation, with you, isn't it?' He seemed to be waiting for an answer.

I didn't know what to say, not sure how our situation was different, but I was quietly pleased by his admission. That he would admit that what he had with me was different – in some way – to what he had with others. It created a fleeting sense of something close to intimacy. I wondered if this showed on my face.

'Because you're not English,' he said then, as if he had seen into my mind, and knew I wanted more of an explanation. 'And because you won't judge me for what I played no role in – my own heritage,' he said.

'I have no right to judge you in any way,' I said, as he had said to me days earlier. 'No right,' I repeated, and then he looked away from me, back to the water, and fell silent again.

His face was still as if he was lost within his own thoughts, or perhaps he was weighing carefully what he would say next. He crossed the deck to a bench and sat there, and I knew I could follow him, could sit beside him, and did so.

I folded my hands on my lap and waited, aware of the closeness of our arms, our thighs, on the narrow bench. Not touching, but so close I thought I could feel the heat of his body.

'I really have no idea if the man who fathered me is alive or not,' he said, putting both hands, palms up, on his thighs, looking down at them as if they held an answer. 'I only learned I was not who I assumed I was two years ago. It was then my mother came to me to confess the truth. She told me she had promised herself she would do this when I turned twenty-one.' He looked up from his hands, out to the ocean once more. The water had the same lulling sense as looking into a pulsing fire; it made speaking easier. 'That's why I came to your country. I wanted . . . needed, to know something of it.'

'You searched for your father?' I asked quietly, watching his profile.

He shook his head. 'I don't even know his name. My mother wouldn't speak it, and said I could never find him, for she herself didn't know what became of him. She knew him only a brief time, she said, and that was all she would ever know him.' His voice grew slightly louder, as if remembering an argument.

'But . . . did you find what you hoped for in Afghanistan?' What had he been looking for when he travelled through my – his, I corrected myself – country, when he watched the *buzkashi*, when he saw, in the markets of Jalalabad, the English soldiers, the beaten woman? Was he looking for a sense of who he was, of a sense of the man who had fathered him? Had he waited to feel something pull deep inside him, something that brought comfort, or relief?

Finally he turned to me. 'I don't know what I was looking for,' he said, in an unsettled voice that carried the thread of anguish. The wind blew my hair over my eyes, and when I pulled it away Mr Ingram pointed upwards.

'The English word is *sky*. Do you wish me to help you learn English?' he asked, and I nodded, my eyes wide that he would offer.

'Sky,' I repeated then, and knew he would speak no more of his fathers.

Mr Ingram came to the lower deck every day after that – sometimes in the morning, sometimes in the afternoon, sometimes in the early evening. He spoke English with me, carefully and patiently. I tried with all seriousness to copy the correct sounds, but at times it was difficult to be serious, for I made many mistakes, laughing at myself and causing Mr Ingram to laugh as well. Sometimes he brought me books to look at, books with paintings and sketches both of people and of the English countryside.

He asked many questions about my homeland, talking about what he'd seen and asking me about my childhood. I stared at the sea and spoke of the seasons, of the spring light dancing through the new leaves of the mulberry trees in the courtyard of my home, of the fields of golden wheat that surrounded it, the smell of the wind as it came down from the mountains in winter. He watched me as I spoke, and when I stopped he was quiet, but still watched me, and at this I had to turn my head, for I was suddenly ashamed by the emotion I knew my voice carried.

'You speak with such a deep love for your country,' he said, and I looked back at him, realising, by his words and expression, that I needn't regret my honesty. 'I envy you this, this certainty of feelings. I wish I could . . . my own feelings – for England – are confused.'

'I'm sorry,' I said.

'And so I can imagine how sad is must have been for you to leave this beloved home of your childhood.'

I nodded. 'And especially to leave my family – my mother, and my sister Nasreen and brother Yusuf.' When I said the children's names I heard an unexpected tremble in my voice. They would be growing up now, no longer the babies they had been when I left. Did Nasreen even remember me? Would my mother keep her own rules about not speaking of things from the past that were painful? Eventually Nasreen might not have even the slightest shadowy memory of her big sister, the sister who had watched her birth, had carried her on her back, had comforted her while she cried and held her while she slept. No one in the village would speak of me except perhaps old Yalda, who might already have gone to paradise. And I wondered if by now I was also dead – to my parents, to Nasreen and Yusuf, to the whole village.

To my horror my eyes filled with tears, and I turned my head quickly, wiping my eyes with my palms.

I felt Mr Ingram's hand on my back.

'I'm afraid I'll never see them again. That I'm dead to them,' I said, my voice distorted with the attempt to not weep openly.

'I understand,' he said. 'You are going so far. But surely they'll always remember you, as you remember them.' The pressure of his hand increased, and I closed my eyes, suddenly wanting to be held, to have someone comfort me. But Mr Ingram removed his hand then, and I took a deep breath and cleared my throat.

I asked him to tell me, again, the days of the week in English.

If the sun shone and the wind blew sweetly we stood at the railing; when it wasn't as warm, or when it rained, we sat, slightly protected, on a bench that was sheltered by a doorway and the curve of the deck. As well as books he occasionally brought me a sweet treat; it appeared he ate well, and I would not tell him that now the food given to us in the lower deck had been reduced to dry biscuits, a mush made of oats, and heavily salted meat which I knew with certainty was pig. I ate it anyway, inwardly asking for forgiveness, but telling myself that what I was already doing to survive was much worse than eating a forbidden food.

Blossom stayed away when she saw me with him, sometimes winking or raising her eyebrows; the ayahs, on their frequent walks around the deck, hugged the railing when they passed us, as if we might contaminate them.

'Mr Ingram?' I asked him one sunny afternoon. 'What if in England people look on me as the woman on the upper deck – the one who hissed a name at me, who looked at me as if I were poison?'

He was silent for so long I thought he wouldn't answer. And then he said, 'I understand your fears. As I left England this last time – to come to Afghanistan – I kept hearing, in my head, an inner voice, a worrying presence making me wonder how things would turn out at every stage of the journey. At times I asked myself why I did this, why I put myself into situations that were unfamiliar and uncomfortable, at times even verging on danger.'

I thought of my own situations. The fear and danger. 'And did you find an answer to these questions?'

'I believe now that voice is simply part of the spell of a journey. Maybe that's what you're hearing. And I found that somewhere along the route another voice chimed in, struggled to be heard. It was quieter than the first, less demanding, and I had to listen closely to hear it.'

I waited.

'The second voice was telling me to trust. To put my faith in my own strength and knowledge, and not to try to understand why the world around me was different, but to surrender to that difference. Surrender to the fact that as long as I conducted myself in the best possible way, my fate would turn out as it should.'

I smiled. 'These are the teachings I know, Mr Ingram, although for a long time I have not . . .' I stopped smiling, and looked at the rolling waves. 'I was taught to put my faith in Allah, and my fate would then unfold as it should. What is written, is written.'

'It is a good belief for those who need it.'

I thought of his earlier words. 'As long as we don't surrender completely – to a new life, or to believing that we cannot change it.'

He put his hand into his pocket and when he withdrew it, held something on his open palm.

'What is it?' I asked, leaning closer. 'Oh. A *ta'wiz*.' It was a small amulet like those so many men of my country wore, the words on the paper inside blessed by a mullah.

He stroked the rolled leather with his thumb. 'It was given to me when I first arrived in your country, as a welcome from a kind villager. And I've carried it with me since then; the man who gave it to me told me it would bring me safety.' He shrugged and smiled. 'I know it is only a superstition, but –'

'It is a superstition to you. To the man who gave it to you it was a talisman of faith, and he believed in it. If you took it you should have also believed in its power.'

He looked down at it. 'I think I did. Otherwise . . . why would I still carry it?'

I took it and closed my hand around it. It was warm from his own hand. Then I gave it back, and looked into his dark eyes. 'Perhaps because you carry Islam in your heart,' I said. 'Passed from the father.'

He looked uncertain, shrugging. 'Perhaps,' he said.

The weather grew cooler, and Mr Ingram said we were far into the Atlantic Ocean, and on the last stretch of the journey. I had just eaten the piece of dense coconut cake he had brought me, and he took a small, hard case out of his pocket, opening it, and I saw the likeness of a woman. It was a similar picture to those in the book of England Mr Bull had shown me, although this one had a browner tone.

'I know this,' I said, not wanting to say Mr Bull's name and cast an unpleasant mood on our time together. 'Pictures from inside a box?' I asked, tilting my head and smiling, waiting for Mr Ingram to tell me the real way they were made.

But he didn't. 'Yes. It's a daguerreotype – a type of photograph.'

I nodded, somehow annoyed that Mr Bull had been telling the truth.

'This is my mother.'

I took the case and studied the photograph. I saw little of Mr Ingram in the image, except for the light hair and firm chin. 'I think you must be like your father,' I said, and again he grew still.

'What did you think of her – when she told you about this other father?' I asked.

'What do you mean?'

'Did you think . . . less of her? For her betrayal to her husband? Her adultery?'

Mr Ingram opened his mouth as if surprised at my question, shaking his head vigorously. 'No. No, I never thought poorly of her. She must have had her reasons.'

'Others know this? That you are . . .' I thought of the word Mr Bull had used, when he told me what might happen to me if I stayed. I thought of Blossom. 'That you are a half-caste?'

He shook his head. 'No one, no one except . . .' he stopped.

I waited.

'My mother told me that Osric Bull always suspected the truth. Something that had happened between them in Calcutta.'

I thought of the way Mr Bull spoke with open disregard of Mr Ingram, and nodded.

'It is bad, to be a half-caste in England?'

He made a wry face. 'Oh, yes.'

We both stiffened, and I wished the conversation had not turned to Osric Bull.

'It is the same in India?' I asked. 'That half-castes are not respected?'

He nodded grimly. 'Among the English in India, many of the memsâhibs, especially, hold deep scorn for the Indian offspring who were fathered by their own countrymen. Ironic, isn't it?'

'Blossom is a half-caste,' I told him. 'She says her father was an Englishman.'

'That's usually the case. In my case . . . my mother being the European . . . it's unusual, and much, much worse for a white woman to be involved with a native man. And twenty-three years ago, it would have been certain tragedy for my mother should I have been born with too strong a resemblance to a native child.' He took the case from me and ran his finger over the image. 'She managed to conceal the truth. My mother is an extraordinary woman. Very strong.'

'When your English father died – did another man marry her? Your uncle, perhaps? In my country it is the brother of the dead husband who has the responsibility.'

'No. She didn't marry again. And I have no uncles, or aunts.'

I frowned. 'You have brothers and their wives to look after her? Or sisters who are not yet married?'

'No. I have no brothers or sisters. There's no other family at all.'

'But – when you are not there, in England, to care for her, who looks after her?'

'She . . .' he shrugged, smiling in a slightly apologetic way. 'She looks after herself.'

'How can this be?'

'It's possible in England, Daryâ.'

I thought about this strange fact. 'She is very sad, so alone?' I looked down at the image again and pictured my own mother with my father, and Nasreen and Yusuf. A sharp pain tore through me as I thought, again, that I was going further and further from them. It was now even more difficult to bring the images of their faces to my mind, to think of their lives, and their fate. Even though I hadn't been able to see them when I was still in my country, I realised that I had always felt, in some way, connected to them. I had lived with the hope that one day Shaliq would allow me to see them, or someone would bring me news of them. But now . . . in the place I was going, so far, across so many oceans, the connection would be completely broken. I wouldn't know if they lived, or succumbed to an illness or injury. If one distant day Yusuf would bring a wife to look after my mother in her old age. If Nasreen would grow to maturity and marry and leave Susmâr Khord. I put my hand to my chest and drew a deep breath.

'My mother is definitely not sad,' Mr Ingram said, not appearing to notice my own sudden melancholy. 'And she's not alone. She has many friends, and a particular man she is very close to, and who brings her much happiness. But she chooses not to marry again. She's not like most other Englishwomen.'

'Why?' I said, trying to take my mind away from my own family.

'She's difficult to explain. She's always been very loving towards me, but in spite of the fact that I'm her only child she's never had trouble letting me go off on my own, to do what I need to do. In fact it seemed, at times, as if she even encouraged me to be different from the other boys at school when I was growing up, although now I . . .' he stopped. 'Now I understand – that she knew I *was* different, and perhaps secretly pleased.'

'And your English father?' I said. 'She kept his memory alive for you?'

He shook his head. 'She didn't speak about him, and didn't appear to keep in contact with any of his friends. I remember one year – I suppose I was eleven or twelve – when I wouldn't stop asking questions about him, wanting to know. She tried to answer, but it almost seemed as if she didn't have many memories of him to tell me. She could go on endlessly about she and I in India, what my favourite foods were, the games she and I played, the songs she sang to me, the loving ayah I had, the servants' children I ran about with, descriptions of our house and garden, but nothing specific about my father. No special name he had for me, no stories about his life, nothing, and my questions seemed to agitate her. I finally decided it was sorrow, grief, that had erased her memories and that it was unkind of me to force her to think of him. But now . . . knowing what I know, and remembering her strong reaction, I don't think it was sorrow. It was something else.'

We sat in silence, rocking on the waves. 'I've come to think her time with him was very unhappy,' he finally continued. 'And maybe she turned to someone else for happiness. That's how I imagine it.'

I nodded.

Suddenly he shook his head. 'I don't talk about my mother, usually. In fact I never talk about her – not the sort of thing an Englishman does,' he said, with a slightly embarrassed smile.

I smiled back, my hand caressing the smooth leather cover of the case. 'A Muslim man believes that heaven lies beneath his mother's feet,' I said. 'She is the most important woman in his life. He can have a number of wives, but there is always only one mother.'

Mr Ingram looked at my mouth as I spoke. I held out the case to him when I'd finished. He didn't seem to notice, and I reached up and touched my lips, wondering if a piece of coconut from the cake had caught there, but didn't feel anything.

I put the case into his hand, and he looked down at it, then back at me, his eyes again going to my mouth, and unexplained heat rose from my neck, flooding my face, and I stood quickly, going to the railing, and let the cold rain that fell cool my cheeks.

CHAPTER THIRTY-SEVEN

AND THEN ONE afternoon as I lay on my bed, looking at the paintings in one of Mr Ingram's books, Blossom came to the doorway, her eyes wide.

'It's a gentleman, Daryâ. He asks for you.'

I threw down the book and jumped up, smoothing back my hair, smiling.

'It is not your Mr Ingram, Daryâ. It's another one – the sick one, I think.'

My stomach dropped. I pushed past Blossom and slowly went down the hallway and up on to the deck. Mr Bull stood, supported by two sailors, one holding each arm.

'Mr Bull,' I said, shocked at his appearance, but keeping my face still. He had lost a great deal of weight, and his skin hung on his neck and face. He had no colour at all in his face, and even his hair seemed to have faded, the red was flatter, duller. 'I'm glad to see you are finally able to walk about.'

'I've been terribly ill,' he said, petulantly. 'I should have returned to England earlier, before the symptoms had grown so severe, and where I could be cared for properly. But I believe the worst is over, and now it's simply a matter of recovering my strength.' He seemed to be waiting for sympathy, but I said nothing. 'Well,' he said. 'Unlike me, you look as if the life at sea agrees with you.'

'I go very well,' I said, slowly, in English. 'Thank you.'

He frowned. 'What's all this? Who's been teaching you English?'

'The missionary lady,' I said, knowing instinctively it wouldn't be wise to mention Mr Ingram.

'Hmmph,' he grumbled. 'I don't like the sound of it coming from you. You should stick to what you know,' he said. 'I prefer you speaking Persian.' He frowned. 'Remember that. Only Persian.'

I nodded.

'We'll be arriving in London within the week.'

Again I nodded.

'All right, then. Wait at the doorway – there – once we dock, and I'll send someone to bring you to me.'

'Yes, Mr Bull,' I said, and went back to my cabin and lay on my bed, now disinterested in the book, not wanting to talk to Blossom. The voyage was nearly over, and this filled me with a deep and terrible foreboding. And an even deeper sadness.

It had grown colder and more blustery over the last weeks, and the next day the wind was raw and the sea grey, gleaming dully, like tin, whenever a shrouded, pale sun broke through the cloud-laden sky. For the last week, looking at this often cloudy, dark sky, I had thought of Blossom's words about the land of the dirty sky, and understood what she had tried to describe.

It was already evening when Mr Ingram finally came to the windy, deserted lower deck. I sat in the sheltered area, my arms hugging my knees with my feet on the bench, my sari tucked under my sandals. I had wrapped the thin, coarse blanket from my bed around my shoulders.

'I planned to come earlier,' Mr Ingram said, his back against the rail, facing me. 'But Osric Bull was in the dining room for dinner. He's feeling better, and kept me cornered for hours, boring me with his tales of past adventures.' He looked away. 'We'll be in London in a few days,' he said. 'A few days,' he repeated. His dark eyes did not look as I expected for one who is arriving home after a long journey.

'Is there nothing that awaits you there that pleases you?'

He didn't answer for a moment. 'It will be good to see my mother again. And some friends. I expect my mother will be at the docks; I had sent word to her from Karachi that I was taking this ship.'

In the cold, wet air my sari hung damp and limp against my chilled skin, and I shivered, but not from the cold. It was knowing that once we arrived in London I would go with Mr Bull, and Mr Ingram would go to his life, and we could never again be together. I put down my legs and pulled the blanket more closely around me.

Mr Ingram suddenly peered down at my sandals, then back up to the blanket. 'Didn't Bull provide anything but those flimsy saris and shawls for you?' he asked. 'No boots, or a warm cloak?'

'The blanket is warm,' I said, but he made an impatient sound of annoyance, which I knew was directed at Mr Bull, then shook his head, muttering in English as he took off his own thick wool jacket.

'Come here, Daryâ,' he said, and I stood, the blanket slipping off me. He held the jacket out and I turned my back to him and slipped my arms inside, the silk lining smooth and still warm from his body.

I wrapped my arms around myself and faced him. 'Is there anything in England that will be familiar to me?' I asked.

'There is beautiful countryside,' he said. 'Outside of London. Meadows, and rolling hills. Forests. Birds, and flowers – mostly different birds and flowers to those you've known, but birdsong is birdsong,' he said, and then smiled. 'And a rose is a rose.'

'I know a story about a rose,' I said. 'A rose and a nightingale. Told to me by my grandmother. It's very old, and was told, over and over, in the *zenana*, where the women talked at night to keep away the sadness of missing their homes and families.'

I began, aware of Mr Ingram watching me closely. 'In many lands, nightingales were the most precious of all the birds.' I looked at the horizon, imagining that instead of the cold grey waves it was the warm and glorious Sweet Waters my grandmother had known that rippled beyond the rail. 'Once a nightingale gazed at the beauty of a sleeping rose, and sang to her in darkness blessed by the glow of the moon. The rose, aroused by his velvet voice, awoke . . .'

I thought of the moon, of my grandmother. 'It was a white rose, like all the roses at that time – white, innocent and pure. Virginal,' I said. 'As the untouched rose listened to the song, her heart stirred, and she trembled on her stem. The bird came to her, blinded by the reflection of her white beauty in the moonlight, and sang, in a whisper, of his love.' I paused, licking my lips. ' "I love you, rose. How I love you, for you are unlike anything I have ever known." ' My voice had dropped as I spoke, looking straight ahead at the waves. And then I looked at Mr Ingram again.

'At those words, the delicate heart of the rose blushed, and in that instant, pink roses were born. The nightingale came closer and closer, and though Allah, when he created the world, forbade the rose to know earthly love,' I closed my eyes, seeing the pictures my words made, 'the rose opened her petals and the nightingale came upon her, and stole her purity. In the morning, the rose, shamed by what she had allowed, knowing she had displeased Allah, coloured to a deep red, giving birth to red roses. Since then the nightingale, having known such beauty of sensation, comes nightly to ask for that divine love once again.' My voice was little more than a whisper now. 'But forever more you will see that while the rose trembles at the voice of the nightingale, its petals, sadly, remain closed throughout the night. For it was a love that could never be.'

I took a deep breath, and as I let it out, heard it quiver. For those few moments I had forgotten where I was. I was lost in my own story, hearing the lonely voice of the nightingale, smelling the delicate scent of that sad rose. When I opened my eyes I was horrified to have to blink away tears, overcome with my own emotion, and quickly turned so that Mr Ingram wouldn't see them, wiping my fingers under my eyes.

But he put his hands on my shoulders and turned me, and what I saw on his face filled me with a light, bright air unlike that which swirled around us. It was as if something had shifted, delicately, as if something off balance had been righted, and the feeling was so smooth, polished as if it were a perfect gem, that my whole body trembled, very slightly.

Saying nothing, he pulled the jacket around me as if to button it then, but it was too big. He lapped one side over the other, and just the touch of his hands stilled my trembling. We stood so close that I could smell his skin, the soap he used, and see the glint of golden whiskers along his jaw. His scar had grown fainter, and it was as if my hand had a will of its own, and I couldn't stop myself from reaching up and running one finger along it. As I did so, a slight shiver ran through him, and he closed his eyes for just a second longer than a blink.

'You're cold now,' I said, in almost a whisper, for our faces were so close that it seemed impossible to speak in a normal voice. 'You need your coat.'

'No,' he said. 'I'm not cold.' His hands still on the front of his jacket, he pushed me, very slightly, so that I had to step backwards. When my back was against the wall of the ship, he took my hand in his as if to warm it. 'Your hands have grown soft on the voyage,' he said.

I tried to slow my breathing. 'I do no work, and the sea air is . . .' I stopped as he ran his thumb over the pads of my fingers.

'Touch me again,' he said, in English, and so softly that at first I didn't think I understood. 'Touch me, Daryâ,' he repeated, and opened his hand. I took my hand from his and reached up to his scar again, this time with all four fingers, and ran them over the faint jagged ridge, from the bridge of his nose, under his eye, and then to his cheekbone. He looked into my eyes the whole time. I let my fingers stay on his cheek, finally moving them down his jaw, feeling the faint bristles there.

He put his arms inside his jacket then, around me, and it was as natural as the sun sinking into the sea for me to lean my head against his chest, to breathe in the clean scent of his white shirt, to feel the skipping of his heart against my cheek. We stood like this for a long, long time, and the heat from the length of his body against mine gave me a warmth I had never known before.

'Daryâ,' he finally whispered, and I knew I had to look up into his face, and when I did, he lowered his mouth, and for the first time I felt a man's lips upon mine. I returned the pressure, and felt his lips part slightly, softening, and then he moved his mouth on mine. I did the same, and it seemed that I had always known how to do this, and that David Ingram and I had been doing this all our lives, and I never wanted it to stop.

But it did; eventually he pulled his lips from mine and I again rested my cheek on his chest. His heart now drummed with a frantic rhythm, but in spite of it I heard him utter the name of his God.

'Jesus Christ,' he said, very softly, and I looked up at him again.

'You pray?' I asked, and he smiled, a sad, beautiful smile, and shook his head.

'No. I haven't prayed for a long time.'

'Nor have I,' I said, 'David.' I wanted to keep saying this name, wanted him to kiss me again, and stood on my toes, so that I was closer to his mouth, and as he bent his head a sailor's voice called out, close by, and was answered by another, and Mr Ingram – David – stepped back.

Two sailors came around the end of the deck, and as they walked past us they nodded at David, one speaking to him in English as his eyes swung over me, and I looked down and fingered a button on the jacket. When they had gone I expected David to come back to me, and smiled, my own heart hammering as I'd heard his do. But he didn't. Instead, he looked strange, uncertain, his face telling a story I hadn't seen before as he took another step away from me.

'David?' I said. 'Please. What is it?'

'I shouldn't have done that.'

'I liked it,' I told him, shy and yet wanting him to know.

'It's being on this ship,' he said. 'You're not in your country, and I'm not in mine. We're both somewhere in between, and it feels as if the rules of life – of my life, and surely of yours – no longer exist. Once we arrive in England I shall have to be the person everyone expects me to be, and you will be . . . you will be . . .' He stopped. 'I'll see that you get some warmer clothes,' he said, and I reached out to him, but he only looked at my hand, and then left.

I thought, from what he'd said, that he would soon return with warmer clothing, and retrieve his jacket, and so I waited where he'd left me. After a while I walked up and down the damp deck, my arms wrapped around myself in David's jacket, trying to stay warm, but eventually, as the sky grew dark and there was no more sound from the upper deck, I knew he would not come this night.

When I went to my cabin and lay the jacket over the end of my bed, smoothing it, I felt a lump in the pocket, and reached in. It was the amulet. I took his jacket under my blanket, holding it to me as I fell asleep.

The next day I went out early, watching for him, knowing it would be all right when we saw each other again, only sorry that it was a bright day, and too many people were about for him to put his arms around me and kiss me again. I waited, missing the noon meal, but still he didn't come. Finally it was the missionary lady who arrived, carrying a thick wool cloak and high black boots with rows of small black buttons like the eyes of a fox, and my heart dropped within my chest.

She demonstrated how to put on the English stockings, and how I was to hook the buttons of the boots together, and I dully followed her instructions. The boots pinched like a trap across the top of my feet and squeezed my toes. My ankles felt rubbed raw by the leather. Although I tried to walk as I had seen the memsâhibs walk, one foot gliding smoothly in front of the other, my legs were heavy and awkward, my footsteps clomping like a horse's hooves.

And then I was glad David hadn't brought them, for I wouldn't want him to see me stomping clumsily up and down the deck. And yet I couldn't understand why he hadn't come to me. Was he not thinking of how it had felt to kiss me? It was all I could think about.

When I prepared for sleep I saw that my feet and ankles were crossed with angry red lines where the leather had bitten into my skin, and knew I would never get used to wearing English boots.

The next morning a subtle change in the movement of the ship woke me. The hall outside our cabin was still in complete darkness, but I knew the change in the rhythm of the ship signalled the boat slowing. I threw my cloak over my shoulders and went out on deck, and by this time the hard blackness of night was leaving. But it appeared that we were caught in the clouds. Was the sea near England like the mountains at home – so high as to meet the clouds? A damp, cold layer of mist covered everything; the door I had come from was little more than a ghostly outline.

I gripped the wet rail in front of me, and as the cloud lifted, I saw we were sailing between flat marshes. The river was broad and slow-moving, and filled with boats of all sizes. I wondered how we didn't collide with any of them, but the vessels passed alongside one another with apparent ease. We moved steadily and slowly, eventually travelling on a great loop of river towards a distant forest of looming masts fluttering with strips of cloth decorated in various colours and symbols. Behind ships which already sat alongside the rows of docks, black smoke billowed from chimneys stretching high into the air. The smoke belched out into the grey air in bursts, and was blown sideways by the damp wind. There were no buildings gleaming whitely in a high sun, no lush greenery, no golden domes or elaborate mosque spires such as I'd seen as we approached Bombay. Here were only row upon row of blackened stone buildings, a foul odour of human waste, carried on the wind, and the dirty sky.

'London,' I whispered.

As we drew nearer I made out tiny figures moving along the shoreline of the city. Eventually I was able to see that they waded into the cold water, and I recognised that some were only small children. They were digging and sifting through the slimy shore in search, it seemed, of whatever might be washed in by the lapping grey water.

The noise grew more and more intense as we drew alongside the docks: the shouting of voices, the grind and screech of the swinging chains that carried boxes from ships and deposited them on to the docks, the general noise of the crush and swarm of bodies.

Any peace I had felt on the water blew away like the smoke from the chimneys. I still believed David would come; his jacket lay on my bed. He had to – he couldn't have kissed me in such a way, held me the way he did, and then not come to me again.

When the ship had finally stopped, and its anchors had been lowered with shouts and great splashes, and still he hadn't appeared, I slowly returned to my cabin. I carefully folded the jacket, putting it into my bag, unable to believe I might not see him again.

Blossom and I said goodbye on the lower deck. She had dragged out her large leather case with all her clothing, while I stood, waiting, as Mr Bull had told me, with my bag across my chest.

She loudly repeated, 'Cheerio, cheerio', to the obvious amusement of two memsâhibs standing nearby. She was dressed as one of them now, in a beautiful dress of pale blue wool with a collar of snowy lace, a burgundy cloak trimmed with soft black fur and a hat with gleaming bird feathers. She didn't wear her kohl, although she had painted her face with an unusually thick layer of the white cream.

'Goodbye,' I told her. 'I'll think of you.'

'And I you,' she said, smiling, but I saw a new uncertainty in this bright smile, and for all her boldness it was clear that she was as anxious as I. I put my arms around her, and she hugged me tightly, and I knew how lonely I might be without her friendship – or any friendship – in this new country. Then she pulled away from me, straightening her shoulders and touching her hat with fingers that shook slightly. 'Remember, Daryâ, you will never get what you don't ask for. Surely you see that the Englishmen are different to the men we have previously known, and you must use this knowledge to your advantage. This my mother taught me.' Her smiled trembled then, and she drew in a deep, shaky breath.

We embraced again, and as she held me against her for a long moment I smelled her rosewater and the chalkiness of her face paint one last time. I watched as she went to an old, very heavy man with a face red and mottled. She was forced, by her clothing, to move in the same stiff and unnatural way of the memsâhibs. She linked her arm through the man's, laughing up into his face as they walked down the long wooden bridge that led from the boat to the dock. Because of his age and weight the man walked very slowly, using a thick, carved gold-headed stick to aid him.

She turned and waved her gloved hand at me, and I waved back, hoping that she would become the true English lady she believed herself to be.

Men swarmed over the decks, heaving bags on to wheeled carts and going down the broad bridge to pile them on the dock where our ship was anchored. I waited where I had been told, the smell of waste and rot even stronger now, the air floating with tiny black flecks which I knew fell from the smoke from the chimneys. Young boys worked alongside men on the docks, hauling baskets of dirty black stones, their hands and faces as black as the stones, the whites of their eyes standing out in a frightening stare. In other places little girls held out small bunches of wilted flowers, or small boxes, hoping to sell them. I was saddened to see these children. Although they didn't beg as they had at the docks in India, to see them work like this – some alone, in such a dirty and cold place and barely older than Nasreen or Yusuf – was distressing. As I watched them, thinking of my own sister and brother and what they would be doing in the safety of Susmâr Khord, a tall, thin man in a dark coat and hat came towards me. His grey hair was long, with greasy ends sticking out from under the hat. He spoke to me with a questioning tone; I heard my name and Mr Bull's, and nodded. He waved his hand at me and I followed. But he walked very quickly, and as I went down the bridge and on to the dock, it was suddenly as if my legs no longer remembered how to walk upon the earth. I could barely keep up with him, and was afraid of being separated in the crowd. I stumbled and lurched behind him, at times tilting into someone who walked beside me.

He stopped at an area heaped with bags. 'Stay here,' he said, and I nodded again, understanding. I stood uncertainly, holding my *hijba* over my nose and mouth as people pushed around me, some staring at me openly, some glancing at me and then away. I searched the crowd, hoping I would see David before Mr Bull came for me, my legs still so shaky that at times I reached out to steady myself on one of the stacks of piled bags and boxes. Languages I had never heard before were all around me, and one group of sailors with hair the colour of corn sang a boisterous song, slapping each other's shoulders and grinning as they passed.

I realised some of the stench came from huge open bins of the skins and horns of animals that sat beside the bags and boxes. But I also caught the faint scent of unknown spices and the familiar tarry odour of ship ropes. Shouts, steady hammering, the rattle of chains and the occasional whinnies of horses filled the air. I stepped back as an empty barrel rolled along the stones towards me, its hollow rhythmic thumping a lonely tune in spite of the noisy masses.

And then, as I looked up, I saw him – David – walking towards the bags, towards me, and I wanted to run to him. But as I tried to go to him my legs felt as though they had been stretched so thin they wouldn't carry me, and when he was close enough I stumbled against him. Did I stumble, or did I actually throw myself at him? I don't know, only that I felt the hard width of his chest against my breasts, the pressure of our thighs as our legs met. At the same time he instinctively grabbed my upper arms. Our faces were so close, and I wanted nothing more than to put my mouth against his. But of course I wouldn't, couldn't, what was I thinking? A woman stepped up beside him, and I backed away, and he took his hands from my arms.

'Are you all right?' he asked, and I nodded, embarrassed by what my body had done, by the way the woman beside him studied me.

'My legs. I can't walk – from the boat,' I stammered.

'Yes, yes, it's always that way,' he said. 'It will take a few days for you to feel right on land again,' he continued in Persian, then switched to English. 'This is my mother, Mrs Ingram,' he said, drawing the woman forward. 'Mother, this is Miss Daryâ.' He spoke to her again in English, quickly, and she nodded.

'Miss Daryâ,' the woman said, smiling. 'I am pleased to meet you.'

'I am pleased to meet you,' I repeated, looking at the pale oval of her face, her brown eyes flecked with gold, the faded yellow hair pulled back simply under a plain velvet plum-coloured hat. Her smile was warm and genuine; she hadn't been smiling in the photograph, and I hadn't known that she and David shared this same beautiful smile. I took David's jacket from my bag and handed it to him. He accepted it without speaking, and his mother stared at it passing from my hands to his.

'You are from Bombay, Miss Daryâ?' she asked now, speaking slowly enough for me to understand the question.

I looked at David, then back to her, shaking my head. 'Afghanistan,' I said. 'I am home Afghanistan.'

She started, and looked at David. His face was drawn; he frowned and looked down at his jacket as if it were something foreign that he'd never seen before.

Mrs Ingram spoke to me again, but this time too quickly, and I couldn't understand. 'I am sorry,' I said, shaking my head. 'I . . .' I looked at David, wishing he'd tell me what she'd said. But he spoke to her instead, and I heard Mr Bull's name, and Mrs Ingram drew in her breath sharply, and her words all ran together as she spoke to her son in a questioning tone, her voice rising.

'Miss Daryâ,' Mrs Ingram said, taking both my hands and looking intently at me as if trying to make me understand something, although she didn't speak. I felt the strength in her hands, and remembered the things David had said about her. As I looked into her face, I knew the compassion I had seen within David was from this woman. I also knew she would never harm anyone, in words or action, and yet she was in no way frail or meek.

And then the greasy-haired man in black came to me and said, 'Come now. Mr Bull is waiting in his carriage', and I looked back at David, wanting him to say *Don't go to Mr Bull, Daryâ, stay with me.*

As the man pulled on my arm David dropped the jacket on to the muddy ground and reached into his pockets, as if looking for something, and then spoke quickly, almost urgently, to his mother. She nodded, digging into the small silky bag she carried, pulling out a small, hard creamy piece of paper and handing it to him.

'Just a moment, please,' David said to the man, who stopped, but didn't let go of my arm. 'Take this,' David said, in Persian, putting the square of paper into my hand.

I looked down at it sitting on my palm. The unknown words written on it pulsed, seeming to grow larger and smaller as I stared at it.

'If you . . . you must give this to a carriage driver on any street. He will bring you to me.'

'Carriage driver?' I asked, confused by the paper, and by his words. I looked back at Mrs Ingram. The expression on her face, combined with David's strange request, caused a slow, heavy premonition of dread to grow within me.

'David?' I asked, twitching my arm away from the man and stepping closer to him again. 'Will you come to Mr Bull's? Will you come to see me?'

He nodded. 'Yes,' he said, flatly, 'yes. Don't lose this.' He gestured at the paper I now held between my thumb and forefinger. 'This is how you can find me. If you . . . if you need me,' he finished, and I wanted to reach for him, to say *I need you now*. I wanted him to put his arms around me, and say it was a mistake, you shouldn't go with him, you should be with me.

But he didn't. Of course he didn't. What was I thinking? Although born with Afghan blood, he really was a fine English gentleman, one of proper manners and obviously of better morals and higher ideals than Mr Bull. He could never be with a wild tribal woman, one marked with the ownership of a husband, and with no knowledge of his world.

And yet – the open, joyful way he laughed when with me, the obvious pleasure he showed as he listened to my stories, the conversations we shared about our lives . . . I may have imagined some things, but not the look in his eyes and the tremor that ran through him when my fingers traced his scar. Not the insistence of his body, the strength of his arms around me. Not the pressure of his mouth on mine.

'Goodbye, Daryâ,' Mrs Ingram said, and I nodded, whispering goodbye to her while still looking at David. Then I pulled my eyes from him and turned to follow the greasy-haired man, listing slightly on legs that no longer felt as if they belonged to me.

PART THREE

LAND OF THE DIRTY SKY

CHAPTER THIRTY-EIGHT

MR BULL'S BAGS were tied with thick rope to the back of a very fancy box – carriage – with large wheels. A man in a tall black hat sat on a high seat on the roof of the carriage, holding the reins of two horses harnessed to the front. The greasy-haired man opened the door for me, and I ducked my head and climbed the single step. I sat across from Mr Bull on a bench covered with fabric, and the man slammed the door. There was a shout, and then a mighty and unexpected jolt which threw me forward, so that I had to put my hands on Mr Bull's thighs to stop myself from falling. I took my hands away as if burned, pushing myself back on to my seat and turning my head to stare out the window, trying to see David in the crowd. But there were too many people, too many carriages and too much confusion. The carriage rocked and jerked as the wheels rolled over the hard stones of the ground.

'Terrible place, Wapping Docks,' Mr Bull said, and I looked at him. 'Filth and squalor. As with all docks, it seems. And yet it's good to be home.' As he turned to watch through the open window he showed his teeth in what I assumed was a smile. 'The British Empire never stops expanding. She owns the West Indies and Canada now, and great swathes of Africa, of Australia, New Zealand, and, of course, India.'

Did he think I knew these places, except for India? Did he try to impress me, when I could think of nothing but David, standing at the docks as I was pulled away from him?

'Yes,' he continued, now looking back at me as if waiting for me to nod in wonder and awe, 'and of course we do hold influence over so many of the seas. This great empire,' he said, and leaned back as if pleased with himself, as if he had played some role in his country's greatness.

I looked away from him, out the window, and as the carriage moved slowly along the crowded passages I saw still more children working, some loading carts, some trying to sell small objects. Many of the structures were storehouses, filled with crates and boxes and bins, and as we drove from the docks the area was lined with low buildings, their front windows displaying objects I knew from the ship – sailors' clothing, rope, tins displaying pictures of meat and the hard biscuits I had been served every day, jars of brass buttons, and other instruments I couldn't name. And then we passed tiny dwellings, dismal homes with their windows covered with brown paper, and everywhere were children, dirty children in ragged clothing, some carrying babies when hardly more than babies themselves, some crying, some sitting. Just sitting, blankly watching the fine carriages passing.

I looked away then, suddenly dizzy with so many sights rushing past the window, and let my head fall back against the padded wall behind me. I closed my eyes, and still the outlines of the images – people, buildings, horses pulling open carts and closed carriages like the one we sat in, and the small empty faces of the children – moved on the insides of my eyelids in a jittering motion as if dancing, taunting me. I had seen nothing I recognised, nothing that was familiar except for those things related to the ship, and I tried to breathe deeply in order to push down the panic.

'Are you ill from the motion of the carriage, Daryâ?' Mr Bull asked.

'No,' I said, opening my eyes. 'But I cannot watch.' I thought about my words. I always wanted to see new things, and now I could, and was choosing not to.

'Oh, but you must. There is so much to see.' He again leaned forward to look out the window, and once more opened his mouth in that wolfish grin. The grooved lines on his face were deeper with his lost weight. 'Ah, London. In all its glory and its chaos. In all its power. Possessing men of greatness and wisdom.' He stared at me. 'Do you realise that I am one of these men, Daryâ? Great, and powerful?' he asked, licking his lips, and I thought of Mrs Ingram's face – her obvious distress when she learned I was with Mr Bull – and turned away.

'Well?' he insisted, demanding an answer. 'Do you not see me as this?'

'Yes,' I said, not looking at him, because it was the answer he waited for, and I could not defy him within these first moments of being in London with him.

* * *

We travelled for a long time, stopping and starting, over and over, and the shouts and cries and rumbling and clattering from outside were often so loud that I wanted to cover my ears. But after a while it grew less noisy, and I felt myself drifting towards the edges of sleep, my head rolling against the padded wall, thinking of the feel of David's cheek against mine, the hardness of his chest against my breasts. And then the carriage stopped, and I opened my eyes.

Mr Bull had opened the door and was being helped outside by the greasy-haired man; I realised he must have ridden on the outside of the carriage. The carriage rocked slightly, and there were thuds, and I knew Mr Bull's bags were being untied. The door closest to me was opened, and I stepped down.

I followed Mr Bull up some steps to a gleaming black door while the other man struggled behind us with Mr Bull's bags and boxes. Through the fabric of my own bag I fingered the hard corner of the paper David had given me.

The door was swung open as if someone waited. I again followed Mr Bull, and we stood inside a wide room. Facing us was an elderly man; although dressed in English clothing he was an Indian. I was surprised and yet reassured at the sight of his brown face. His skin was lined and eyes sunken, his white hair thin, but he bore himself with great dignity, and his expression was gentle. His eyes flickered to me, and then he bowed low to Mr Bull, his hands pressed together under his chin.

I expected that Mr Bull would speak in Hindi to him, but I heard English instead. 'Good afternoon, Govind,' he said. 'I – we – are home, at last.'

The greasy-haired man came through the open door, piling Mr Bull's belongings in one corner. When he'd finished, Govind put a coin in his hand; the man touched his hat and left.

Govind bowed again and took Mr Bull's hat and coat, and held out his hand to me without looking into my face. I gave him my cloak, and he draped it over his arm together with Mr Bull's, then gestured again, and I knew he meant I was to give him my bag.

'No,' I said in English. 'I keep. Please.'

As Mr Bull fussed with removing soft grey gloves, Govind disappeared with our coats, and then reappeared almost immediately. Limping badly as if one leg slept, he started up many wide stairs, and Mr Bull followed him, and I trailed after him, clutching the strap of my bag slung across my chest. We went into a large room, and I drew in my breath.

We were in England, and yet I felt I was in a place somehow familiar, and at least this was a relief. The tall windows I stood near were covered with thick red velvet, putting much of the room into shadows. In the dimness I inhaled deeply, shutting my eyes, and suddenly I was once more beside my grandmother on our roof in the twilight; I ran barefoot past the village mosque with its waft of sweet incense; I lay on my pallet amid the comforting dusty heaviness of rich carpets and embroidered pillows. I was so overcome with the odours I had not smelled for such a long time, and which came so strongly and unexpectedly that a gasp – almost a sob – escaped before I could stop it, and my eyes flew open at the sound I made.

Mr Bull didn't notice; he was being helped by Govind to a deep red chair. He sighed as he sank into it. 'Well. It's amazing what being in one's own home – and on terra firma – can do. I feel better already. And so we have finally arrived, my Daryâ *jan*,' he said, and I hated that he used the endearment immediately. He waved his arm in front of him. 'What do you think of my home?'

I swallowed around the painful stone lodged in my throat, blinking away the tears that had come to my eyes. 'It is . . . like India, as you said,' I told him. My hands hurt; I looked down and saw how tightly they still held the strap of my bag.

His eyebrows lifted. 'Of course as a townhouse it can't compare to some residences,' he said. 'Mrs Ingram's, for one. But it is quite suitable for my lifestyle.'

I pulled aside the curtain, uncovering a tall sheet of glass and letting in thin early evening light. But I could see nothing but a row of tall stone buildings with many windows across from me. It was as if I was enclosed within brick walls; there was no sense of direction, of where the sun would rise or set, of anything that might lie beyond these houses, this room I stood in. I wanted – needed – to rest my eyes on land, on sea, or sky. Suddenly it was hard to breathe, as if there was no air in the room, and I put my hands on the glass, looking for a way to open it. I pushed on it, but it was solid, and my panic grew.

There was a sudden ringing and chiming and bonging that

surrounded me, that came from beneath and above me, and I whirled to face Mr Bull.

'You'll soon get used to the hourly reminders,' Mr Bull said. 'I'm a collector of clocks.'

When the noise finally stopped, a low, cackling voice came from across the room. I blinked into the far, dark corner, and saw a parrot perched on a wooden rail in a huge brass cage. The cage sat on the floor and was higher than my head.

It called 'Hello, hello', in English, murmured something in an unknown language, and then shouted the Persian greeting.

'*Salâm! Salâm!*' it croaked. I walked across the room, cautiously approaching the cage as I echoed '*Salâm*' in reply, and then leaned closer. I felt foolish, and yet asked, '*Che hâl dâred?*', not expecting a reply. But the bird, with its brilliant red and green feathers, its clever black eyes, responded with a screeching whistle and then, '*Khub astom, tashakor!* Fine, thank you!'

How long had this bird lived in his huge cage in this closed room? Now it shuffled down its perch and cocked its head, admiring itself in a small brass mirror that hung on the side of the cage, and the house settled into a creaking silence.

From behind me I heard the heavy, slow breathing of Mr Bull and the more rapid, noisier sound of Govind, who breathed through his open mouth. I turned, suddenly nervous, and brought the edge of my *hijba* towards my face.

'There is no reason to veil yourself in this house,' Mr Bull told me. 'Consider it your own protected place – although you are now in a new life, Daryâ. It will go better if you allow yourself to feel at ease with me. And to be the woman I expect.'

I let the veil drop.

'You'll be very weary from your long journey,' he continued. 'And surely overwhelmed. I know it will take some time for you to feel familiar in a strange country. I myself well know the feelings of being a stranger in a strange land, and will do all I can to help you settle into my home.' His words were sincere, but his face, so thin now, was almost frightening with its hollows and shadows. 'And I also understand that it may have been difficult for you to once again say goodbye to David Ingram.'

I froze. Had he been watching me with David and his mother? Did he know something of my time spent with David on the boat?

'He . . . he is . . .' I couldn't think of anything I wanted to say about David. Not to Mr Bull.

'As I told you in Bombay, he's a strange young man. I was a friend of his father's, in Calcutta, and knew his mother as well. After his father died and his mother returned to England, I lost touch with her, but I came into contact with her here in London a few years ago. Of course, although she attempts to cover it, I can tell she considers herself above me. Which is laughable, really,' he said, and his eyes narrowed.

'Laughable?'

'She doesn't deserve the lifestyle she's able to afford. Somers Ingram – her husband – left her enough money to never have to worry about anything again. It should be me in that position, not a woman like her.'

I was upset at his sneering tone when he spoke of Mrs Ingram.

'He didn't divulge anything of his life to you, then? Young Mr Ingram?' He rubbed his hands together as if they were cold, although I found the house overly warm, a fire burning brightly in the bricked opening near Mr Bull's chair.

I shook my head, not wanting to talk about, or hear anything more of, David and his mother.

'Nothing at all? No lovely, deep and dark secrets?'

Again I shook my head.

Mr Bull put his hand to his forehead. 'I must lie down.' He studied me, rubbing his temple in a slow, circular movement. 'Are you not pleased to be here?' he asked. 'I would hope you are grateful for all I have done.' From the corner came the lonely, moaning calls of the parrot.

I did what I knew I must then, in my role in this house. I knelt at Mr Bull's feet, lowering my head, and when I rose I witnessed on his face a deep pleasure that was laced with some other very small, but troubling aspect.

'Govind will show you to your room – there is a lovely room I'm sure you'll enjoy. Some fruit and cheese will be brought for you.' He spoke in his perfect Persian, and again rubbed his hands together, and now I wondered if it was impatience. 'We shall better acquaint ourselves tomorrow, when we're both rested,' he added, slowly rising and going to the parrot's cage. 'I think it best if I rest quietly tonight, and regain my . . . vigour,' he said, and I understood his meaning, and looked away, trying not to show my relief that I would not have to tolerate his attentions immediately. The bird flapped its wings and whistled with excitement, but Mr Bull lifted a large dark cloth and draped it over the cage. Immediately the parrot was silent.

He turned back to me and took my hand, bowing low over it. Through the thinning dark red hair on the top of his head I saw his scalp, pink, and then felt his lips – slightly moist and too soft – upon the back of my hand. I fought the impulse to pull away.

'My affliction has been resolving itself steadily for the past few weeks, and by tomorrow . . .' he smiled again, letting the sentence trail off. 'I know you won't mind waiting one more night.'

I swallowed, sour saliva suddenly rising in my throat.

'Please. Go with Govind now, and sleep well,' he said, releasing my hand.

Govind put out his hand for my bag again, and this time I gave it to him, and he put it over his shoulder. We had to go up yet another flight of stairs; I saw how slowly the old man climbed, dragging one leg. His breathing grew to an alarmingly ragged wheezing. I knew by the way he walked, one hand heavy on the railing, that he was in pain, and I thought of my grandmother in her last days.

In a wide hall Govind grasped a handle on one of the doors, swinging it open and handing me my bag. I thanked him in Persian, and then in English; he didn't move or blink.

In the room a fire burned, and lamps were lit. The room had high windows with thin slatted shutters painted white. They were folded back, and while Govind closed them I looked around me. There was a very high bed with a cover and a curtain that draped down over it – the material was painted Indian cotton in bright hues of green and blue and yellow, and I thought of Blossom the first time I had seen her. The floor was covered with a thick carpet of dark green, splashed with dull blue shapes, and on the wooden top of the brick opening for the fire was a collection of Indian idols.

Bowing to me, as he had done to Mr Bull, with his hands together, his fingers under his chin, Govind backed out of the room, closing the door.

I wandered about the room, touching the smooth, gleaming wood of the furniture, seeing the water in the jug, a thin cloth draped over the plate of food. I discovered a bowl under the bed; although it was of fine china and decorated with painted flowers, I understood its use was the same as the one for the children in the bungalow in Bombay. I thought it far too beautiful for such a lowly function.

I extinguished the lamps and took off my hated boots. I opened my bag and took out a sleeping dress, and the *ta'wiz* fell from its folds. I had kept the amulet, and now I held it to my nose, hoping for a tiny reminder of David's scent. The dragging step of Govind thumped past the door, and a little while later his shuffle was overhead, and I thought of my grandmother again. Still holding the amulet, I went to the window and pushed between the shutters, again trying to force this glass open. But I couldn't, and so I twisted my neck to try and see the moon, its size and shape. But my view was restricted by the roofs and chimneys, and not only could I not find the moon, but I could also only see a slice of the sky. I felt the same growing panic I had experienced in the room with the parrot. I wanted to smell the air, to feel it on my skin. How did the people of London live like this? Was it the same at David's home? No, it couldn't be. I knew that like me, he would also need the air and the sky.

I stared at the strip of night sky visible to me. It wasn't black, but an odd and unnatural glow, and there were no stars.

No moon, and no stars.

I tossed on the high bed, disliking lying so far above the floor, one hand or foot always reminding me of its edges. Unable to sleep in this new place, although at least not having the worry of Mr Bull coming to me this first night, I listened to the clocks chiming the hours of the night. There were sounds outside – the rumbling of carriage wheels, horses' hooves clattering on the stones, muted voices and hurrying footsteps. I wondered how one learned to sleep amidst such noise, on such a high, soft bed. My head ached dully.

I thought of all the places I had slept in since I left Susmâr Khord – the tents and yurts of the Ghilzai camp, and then, when I ran from it, the forest and the hard stony ground. In Fareed's bedding in Jalalabad, rolled in quilts beside fires and rivers as I left Afghanistan and travelled through northern India. In the godown in Multan where I tossed, so sick, and then the comforting rhythm of the rocking barge on the Indus. In date-mat huts along the road through the Punjab, in a stifling, crowded and yet lonely room high over the city of Karachi. On the steamer across the Arabian Sea, with the hum of its engines, then the isolation of the godown behind the big house in Bombay. The rope bed on the Chinese clipper, listening to the the billow of the sails that blew me ever farther from home.

And now here, on this overstuffed English bed high as a table.

I was used to new places, new foods, new situations. Just as I had quickly adapted to my home with the Ghilzai, and to the travel with David, I could do this, too. I could adapt.

And yet as I thought of all of the places I had been since I left my village, I knew that none of them had truly felt like home, and I cried, softly, at that sorry realisation, holding David's amulet tightly.

Had Sulima ever felt at home in our mud and straw house in Susmâr Khord? Had my grandmother felt at home in the *zenana*, or the room she shared with the Englishman in Ankara? Did she even feel at home after she was brought to Susmâr Khord to become the wife of a Tajik?

We were women, brought to places by men. We went with them looking for freedom from danger, for freedom from slavery. But did we find it?

I thought of Sulima, of my grandmother. Of myself, lying in this high, dark English house in a strange land. Had any of us found the freedom we had hoped for? I sat up then, pressing the amulet to my chest, the Indian cotton cover to my face, wiping my tears and trying to take deep breaths. The paler darkness falling through the half-open shutters cast long horizontal strips across the room, giving the shadows an ominous feeling of bars. The room smelled of old candle wax and seemed filled with the memories of others.

What had I done by agreeing to come here? What had I done?

Finally, exhausted by weeping, I did sleep, and dreamed of my grandmother. She climbed the ladder to the roof of our house, but with an ease I had never before seen, her steps light and easy. She looked down at me, extending her hand. I reached for it, but to my horror saw, as I stretched my hand in front of me, an old woman's hand, wrinkled and spotted and gnarled. I looked up again, and saw my own face looking down at me. And then I was falling from the roof, and after that, I dreamed no more.

CHAPTER THIRTY-NINE

I AWOKE ON THE carpet beside the bed, curled on my side, my shoulder sore and my legs cramped from one position, the Indian cover twisted about them. As I stretched the cries of the parrot came, muffled, up the stairway and through the closed door. He screamed and squawked as if very disgruntled; I imagined his cage had been uncovered and this was his morning ritual. My eyes burned, and I had no sense of time in the darkened room. As I lay there, the clocks began, and I counted the chimes: nine. I quickly changed from my sleeping dress to a sari, not putting on the boots, or my veil – as Mr Bull had requested – then opened the shutters all the way. The sky was the colour of metal, and, looking down, I discovered that I no longer found height distressing as I had so long ago, in the miserable room in Karachi.

The scene outside my window was strange but not overly interesting. There was a very narrow walkway between high brick fences, and directly across from me were the windows of other houses, with most of the curtains closed. Govind knocked and then entered, setting down one tray and picking up the one I hadn't uncovered the night before.

'Do you speak Persian?' I asked, hopefully, in that language, but his face remained fixed. 'You talk me English?' I tried again, but he turned and left as if I hadn't spoken.

I picked at a boiled egg and ate a piece of the pale English bread. Again thinking of Blossom, I poured milk into my tea, but didn't like the taste. What was she doing now? At least she . . . I thought of what Mr Bull expected from me. Blossom didn't have this to worry about – giving herself to her gentleman was already a part of her life with him.

What was David doing now? I tried to picture him in a house like this one, but I couldn't. I could only think of him as I'd known him on our journey through Afghanistan and across the North-West Frontier and then down through India – his skin darkened by the sun, the dust caught in the sweat of his cheek, his arm coming up to wipe it away. His hair long and uncombed as he sat on the ground around smoky fires. His nails rimmed with dirt as he tore at the meat he had cooked. His ready smile natural.

Govind returned and motioned for me to follow him. We passed a small plain room beside mine, containing only a narrow bed, and then a bigger room at the front of the house. I noticed the large bed, the profusion of Indian chests and rugs and carvings, the elephant tusks on the wall, and one of Mr Bull's cases on the floor, and knew this was his own bedroom. Govind led me down the stairs and back to the room with the parrot. The curtains were partly open now, and although still shadowed, the room was made brighter by many lights on the walls and tables; there was a faint hissing which I thought came from these wall lamps. Mr Bull stood by the bird's cage. My heart gave one low thump. His colour was better, and he looked rested.

'You slept well, Daryâ?'

'Yes, Mr Bull. Thank you.'

'I instructed Govind to allow you to sleep as late as you wished this first day,' he said, glancing at a clock on the wall. At that moment the clock whirred and clicked, and Mr Bull nodded approvingly, taking out a small, rounded, gold case from his pocket. He pressed on it and the top sprang open, and he looked down at it expectantly. And then there was the chiming and musical ringing again. Another hour. Mr Bull closed the lid of the gold case and returned it to his pocket. 'Good,' he said. 'All in order. I was just about to have some tea.' He gestured to a delicate blue and white pot on a low table, surrounded by matching cups and small plates that fitted under them.

I knew what was expected, and so I went to the table and put my hand on the handle of the teapot. 'Would you care for sugar?' I asked.

His smile grew, and he came to the table, putting his hand over mine on the handle. It was hot and dry, and I eased mine away. 'Allow me,' he said, and poured two cups of tea. 'Please, sit down.'

I sat by the fire, crossing my ankles and keeping my back straight, the little plate that held the cup in my hands. The fire crackled cheerily. Mr Bull sat opposite me and crossed one leg over the other at the knee, as he had in Bombay. I couldn't imagine him ever crouching on his heels, or on the ground with both legs crossed, as the men of my country did. As David had done with ease. He drank his tea, and I mine, and I realised that I had been too overpowered by all that was happening yesterday to take in all that was in the room.

The lamps illuminated shelves of books lining two of the walls. The floors were covered in luxurious fringed carpets, smaller ones on top of larger ones, and I recognised the tree and bird designs of the Kashmiri and Turkish rugs in the mosque in Susmâr Khord. On the walls without bookshelves were paintings; I couldn't make out the images without going closer. A round table, draped with a shawl with trailing silk fringes, sat in the middle of the room. On it was a beautifully decorated *chelem* with a snaking tube wound about it. The mouthpiece had been well-used, and I knew that Mr Bull must like his smoke. There were low stools with brocade tops and many other chairs and small tables. Along one wall was an odd, high chair that was long enough for three people to sit on. It had half a back and an armrest on one end; it was, like the curtains, of red velvet. The long shelf over the fireplace was crammed with objects – as well as more Indian idols made of both brass and painted wood, there were figures of women in fancy dresses, round glass balls of red and blue glass, a display of pipes of different sizes, tall candles in silver holders, and a number of small and useless-appearing objects that I had no name for. They were all reflected in the long mirror behind them. There was a tangled profusion of plants in brass and painted china containers throughout the room; I wondered how they flourished in this dull light.

The parrot watched me from his corner, lifting one foot and bringing it to his beak. He nibbled on his curved talon, then slowly lowered it to the perch and lifted the other with the same precise movement, his eyes never leaving me.

Mr Bull finished his tea and set the cup on a table beside him, then uncrossed his legs and leaned forward. The fire created a rosy glow on one side of his face; his eyes were pale blue ringed with a deeper blue. There was something so intimate in the way he looked at me that my heart fluttered wildly. I jumped up, setting my empty cup down so quickly that it clattered on its little plate, and I went to the window. That look filled me with dread for what I knew would occur this night.

I stared out the window, although all I saw, in the glass wet with rain, was Mr Bull's reflection, blurry and pale. I looked down.

The street here was much busier and wider than the one I could see from my window, which I now knew to be at the back of the house. When I leaned far to one side I could see the leafy tops of trees. 'All of London is like this, Mr Bull?' I asked, trying to make my voice interested, hoping he didn't realise what I was doing, stalling, not wanting to have to be so near him. Across the street was a tall white building which stretched far on either side. There were many doors, some dark wood, some painted colours, and, I counted – four rows of windows on top of each other. What had he called his house yesterday? A townhouse. 'London is all townhouses?' I looked back at him.

'No, no, the city is huge,' he said. 'There are different types of homes in different areas. This area is Kensington.'

'I see trees.'

'Kensington Square,' he said. 'A nice place to take a walk.'

I turned to him. 'Could we go there?' *Now? Could we go outside so I don't have to sit alone with you, in this room, and have you look at me in a way that makes me shiver as if a cold wind is blowing about my ankles?*

'Some time, surely.'

'And does Da— does Mr Ingram and his mother . . . do they live close to you?'

He snorted, as if my question annoyed him. 'No,' he answered, his voice short. 'They live in Richmond. Too dull for me out there, with all those gardens, and the solitude. I like to be closer to the city – the life of the streets, the shops, my circle of interesting friends. Much more suited to my lifestyle.' He licked his lips and his mouth pursed under his moustache.

I nodded, turning back to look out the window.

'Come away from the window. Sit down.'

As I did as he asked, he shook his head. 'I quite envy Mr Ingram his journey: all the way to Kabul and far beyond, witnessing the wonders of your country, and, to make it all so much more glorious, rescuing a beautiful young woman. It's all a bit like a fairy tale, isn't it, one of the glorious tales of the Arabian nights?'

I knew David would never have used that phrase – rescuing me – for he hadn't, had he? I had saved myself, at least at the *buzkashi* and then in Jalalabad. I had refused to give in, had convinced him take me with him.

'What is that dismayed face, my dear? Is it that you don't believe in your beauty?' Mr Bull said, and I jumped, for I hadn't been listening to the last few sentences, and didn't realise my face was reflecting my inner feelings. He put his head to one side. 'While it's true that you do not have the fragility and paleness so prized in young women here, there is something very . . . strong about you that I've always found appealing in women. I like my women to be of the earth, not of the air. I always have and, I daresay, always will. I do love women with fight in them, ready for a bit of a struggle. Isn't that what I see in you?'

I looked at my cup, lying on its side. 'My grandmother was very strong. I think I am like her,' I said, trying to push away thoughts of this man coming to me.

Rain ticked against the glass, matching the sound of the clock on a table.

'May I please drink more tea? My throat is dry from talking,' I asked, and he immediately rose.

'Of course.' He went to a long cord hanging near the fireplace and pulled on it. 'I shall have Govind bring us a fresh pot.'

When the tea came Mr Bull poured me a cup, then picked up a small brown bottle that was also on the tray. 'This will put you at ease,' he said. 'Just an English tradition,' he added, opening the lid and pouring a few drops into my cup. He added sugar and stirred it. 'Why don't you take it to the divan' – he lifted his chin at the long chair – 'and get comfortable.' I did as he said, sitting near the armrest and sipping my tea. It had a strange taste, slightly masked by the sugar, but wasn't unpleasant.

As I let the fragrant liquid soothe my throat I thought that England and Afghanistan shared at least one social custom – and in the silence I grew sleepy and relaxed, and leaned against the armrest.

'Do you feel better now?' Mr Bull asked, his voice soothing. 'The laudanum I put in your tea is very helpful.'

I looked at him, feeling completely calm. The reflection of the flames danced across Mr Bull's cheekbones, and his face was no longer menacing. 'Oh, yes,' I said. 'My grandmother lived in a *zenana*,' I went on, dreamily, not sure why she came to me so clearly at this moment. 'In a place far from my homeland.' The fire crackled softly. 'The Sweet Waters,' I murmured.

'The Sweet Waters? On the Bosporus?' Mr Bull asked with a delighted smile. 'Ah yes, one of the greatest harems of the Ottoman

Empire. How intriguing,' he said, smiling even more fondly at me. 'It only becomes richer.'

'Richer?' I echoed, but he didn't answer. 'She predicted I would know many lands. I would move across the earth as the moon moves across the sky.' I closed my eyes. 'And she was right. I am . . .' I wanted to say I am a star, brilliant and alive, but it seemed too much of an effort to speak further. Why had I never before realised this – that yes, I was like one of the stars in the heavens.

'Perhaps she was a bit of a seer,' Mr Bull said, and I opened my eyes to see him watching me, smiling as if very pleased.

I smiled back, slowly, wondering with no real concern how my tongue had loosened to let the words spin from my mouth with surprising ease, and with a rippling, musical quality that I didn't know I possessed.

There was a comfortable silence except for the parrot muttering under his breath, then the ringing of a bell from somewhere within the house.

Mr Bull looked annoyed at the sound. He went to the door and opened it, putting his head out, then called to Govind. 'No visitors,' he said, but then I heard Govind's voice, and Mr Bull went out, closing the door behind him.

When he returned it was hard for me to tell how long he'd been gone – I had lost all perception of time.

'You appear sleepy, Daryâ *jan*,' he said, and I was so relaxed that this time I didn't mind his use of the name. 'Why don't you go to your room and rest? I've instructed Cook to prepare some specialities for your first formal meal. We'll enjoy our food, and then later, tonight . . .'

I stood, my limbs warm and supple from the heat of the fire, and as he leaned over me, I felt no anxiety even though he made it clear he would take me that night. 'Have a pleasant slumber,' he said, and as I left I languidly waved my fingertips at the bird in its cage in a manner that was unlike me in every way.

I fell asleep immediately, and when I awoke, sitting up on the high bed, a girl perhaps a few years younger than I stood nearby, holding a rag and jar. Her hands were red and scabby. She stared at me, but then turned and dipped her rag into the jar and polished the wood furniture, glancing at me over her shoulder all the while. A neat bow was tied in the tails of a limp white skirt wrapped over another dress, this one black. Her hair was dark, with lighter brown streaks. Stray pieces had fallen from under her small white cap, and hung around her collar.

I didn't know if I should speak to her, but she appeared very interested in me. Her mouth was partly open, her bottom teeth small and sharp. Covering her pale skin – her face and neck and hands – were tiny, soft brown marks that seemed a part of the skin itself. But when Govind came to the door she hurried from the room.

I rubbed my eyes and smoothed back my hair; my head was pounding, my mouth dry.

Govind gestured for me to follow him again, and I went down after him, one flight, and then another, back to the door where we'd entered yesterday – was it only yesterday? – into another room. Mr Bull stood beside a very long table which held plates and cutlery and a number of large covered dishes. Even though it was only early afternoon, the light in the room was so dim that a huge stand of silver holding many candles sat in the middle of the long gleaming surface. Mr Bull had changed into a different suit of clothing, and his dark red hair shone in the candlelight. 'You've had a refreshing rest, Daryâ *jan*?' he enquired.

I couldn't speak; it was as if my tongue were too large, and I only nodded.

He pulled out the chair in front of me, and as I stood, puzzled, he gestured for me to sit on it. I did, and he sat across from me. One by one, very formally, Govind stepped forward and took the cover off each dish. As Mr Bull had promised, there were tempting foods that I had not seen since before I boarded the ship in Bombay: saffron rice with nuts and raisins, chunks of spicy grilled lamb, and circles of mashed vegetable, fried crisp and golden. Govind wore white cotton gloves now, and he spooned the food on to the large ivory plate rimmed with gold which was set before me on the table. When Mr Bull picked up his fork I picked up mine. It was so heavy – much heavier than any of the cutlery I had used on the ship – and was decorated with many swirling circles. In the middle of the biggest circle was a symbol.

We ate in silence for the first few minutes. I drank three glasses of water; Govind stepped forward and refilled my glass as soon as it was empty. I was more hungry than I remember feeling for a long time, and the food . . . it was too delicious to try and describe. I had to use all my energy to eat slowly and politely, as Blossom had instructed, even though at this meal my instinct was to chew and swallow quickly. I noticed that Mr Bull ate very little, mainly moving his food around on his plate, occasionally taking a deep breath and putting his hand to his middle. As I swallowed my last piece of lamb, Mr Bull set down his fork and knife and came around the table, standing behind me. He put his hand on the back of my neck, under my braid, caressing it lightly, and at his touch the last bite of lamb came back to my throat, and I had to fight to swallow it again.

Mr Bull then squeezed my shoulders. I couldn't see his face, and was glad. I ran my thumb over the symbol on the handle of the fork, preparing myself for . . . I didn't know what. I smelled tobacco and a hint of musky fragrance.

And then suddenly he stepped away from me and went to the door. As he put one hand on the brass knob, he looked at me again, and I watched him, realising I was trembling, ever so slightly. One of the clocks ticked loudly. Mr Bull's breath was even as he studied me.

'I have a bit of business to take care of,' he said, 'but I shall see you in the drawing room in about an hour.' And then he left, closing the door with a careful, studied movement.

I sat, unmoving. I tried not to imagine what I knew with certainty would happen in a short while. I wasn't the innocent girl I had been when I was taken to Shaliq, untouched and not knowing what would take place under the quilts. I wasn't frightened as I had been then, but now it was a sad and heavy coldness of my spirit that so distressed me, the knowledge of who I had become, a woman paid for her services with the gifts of a luxurious life. I was worse than Sulima, for she had been married to my father. I was possibly even worse than Blossom; she had spoken of her gentleman with genuine fondness, and had at least known him intimately in India.

Very slowly Govind stepped from the shadows and cleared the table. He leaned close to me as he lifted my plate from the table. 'Where Missy come from?' he whispered in English. It was the first time I had heard his voice.

I raised my head. 'You talk me English?' I asked, as I had earlier in the day, also in a whisper, although I wasn't sure why.

'Yes, Missy,' he said.

'I come Afghanistan. North, from India.'

'Far, Missy,' he said, 'you come so far.' He still whispered in that raspy tone, and I realised that he could not raise his voice above this, and wondered what had caused this to happen.

I twisted my head so that I could look into his face.

'You must go careful, Missy. Go careful,' he said then, and something I read in his expression – was it pity, or merely concern? – was enough to make me weep. Suddenly the food in my stomach sat like a lump of clay. It had been too rich, after the small, simple meals I'd been used to on the ship, and I'd eaten too much. A cold sickness came over me as I looked into the old man's kind face, wondering, again, what I had done by coming here, remembering Mr Bull's hands moving with such familiarity, such . . . ownership, on my neck, my shoulders. I knew soon I would feel them on my body. There was a hissing as one of the candles in the tall silver stand in the middle of the table burned itself out.

And then the lamb did slide back up my throat. I retched, covering my mouth with my hands. Govind came with an empty silver bowl, and stood, patiently holding it, while I embarrassed myself.

CHAPTER FORTY

WHEN I HAD wiped my mouth with the damp cloth Govind gave me, and drunk more water, I went back to the drawing room as Mr Bull had told me to do.

Nervous, not knowing how long I would wait, unable to sit quietly, I looked at the shelves and took out various books, caressing their soft covers of smooth animal hide or of silk. Most of them contained only pages of English writing, but then I discovered one with photographs of women, and sat and looked through it. They were dressed in various exotic clothing. Some of the women had very narrow eyes, like the Hazara, but were of another race. They wore tight silky dresses and their hair was made to look like an elaborate headdress. Their faces were round and powdered very white, their mouths painted into the shape of tiny flowers. There were other women, darker skinned and wearing filmy clothing and great quantities of jewels. They were almost like Pushtun women, although of finer features.

Studying the photographs, I didn't hear Mr Bull when he appeared in the doorway. Govind was behind him, carrying the tea tray. I jumped, the book falling from my hands to the carpet with a dull thump.

'Sit down, Daryâ,' Mr Bull said, smoothing his moustache with one hand.

I sat on one of the cushioned stools beside the low table as Govind set down the tray and left. Mr Bull sat on the divan and lit the *chelem*. The dark sticky wedge which he had pushed into the bowl with a practised dip of his middle finger gave off a smell that was not tobacco, but another that I recognised. The sweeter and heavier aroma was the ground seeds of the poppy; Dulfiya had given it to those suffering from injuries. Sometimes she gave it before setting broken bones, or when she had to stitch torn flesh together, and I knew it took the edge off pain, and made the injured person quiet and sleepy.

Mr Bull looked up after his first long pull on the mouthpiece, smiling slightly. He held out the mouthpiece to me, but I shook my head. 'This helps my headache,' he said, and inhaled again as the heated water bubbled merrily. 'I suffer from terrible headaches.' He held in the smoke, finally letting it out with a long sigh. After a few moments I saw that this smoke must have truly helped, for his features grew more relaxed, the lines on his forehead visibly smoothing. He shifted, reclining on the long red divan, his ankles crossed. As I watched him, his eyelids grew heavy, although they did not completely close.

I stood, but Mr Bull's eyelids flickered. 'Where are you going, my dear?' he asked, his voice slow and deep.

'I thought you would sleep now,' I said.

'No, no. Stay with me.' He put his hand to his temple. 'Come. Please, come closer.'

I went to him. He took my hand and put it on his temple, sighing deeply. 'Your lovely hand is so cool, so soothing,' he said, his eyes closed. 'Rub my head; it will help.'

I took a deep breath and kneeled at the armrest where his head lay, moving my fingertips in small circles upon his temples. His skin was hot and dry, and he made a sound of pleasure in his throat, and I clenched my back teeth. I looked down at his face; it was in repose, and content.

'Do you miss your home?' he asked, quietly, continuing before I answered. 'I already miss that other life – the life of the East. So warm. Comforting. I spent time in so many places, places where I was . . .' He tried to lick his lips; they appeared as dry as his skin felt under my fingers. 'Damn body, betraying me.' His voice faded, then came back. 'Please. My head, Daryâ. Don't stop.'

I gently rubbed his temples again.

'Have I told you', Mr Bull's eyes opened, startling me, my fingers losing their rhythm, 'that I knew David Ingram's mother?' I sat back on my heels as he slowly sat up and put the slender ivory mouthpiece between his lips, lighting the *chelem* again. After he had inhaled, he continued. 'In Calcutta. Long ago.' Of course he had told me this, but I didn't want to correct him. 'Strange young woman back then,' he murmured. 'Secretive. Kept to herself. I found her intriguing. I've always liked a woman with a secret.'

His eyes were closed, his voice dreamy and relaxed. 'It is strange, I suppose,' he continued, then fell silent. 'Her secret . . . of course I . . . David . . .'

I lowered my head at the sound of David's name. Mr Bull put down the mouthpiece and slowly poured a cup of tea, opening the small dark bottle he pulled from his jacket pocket.

'Let me give you some of this again.'

'No, Mr Bull,' I told him. 'My tea will be fine as it is.'

He shook his head as if sorrowful. 'Osric. You must call me Osric. Now do as I say, Daryâ *jan*. It's only the laudanum again. Everybody uses it. It won't do you any harm.'

Would it do for me to create discord over such a small thing? He poured a few drops of the clear liquid into my tea, then another spoonful of sugar. He stirred it for me as if I were a child.

I drank it in silence while Mr Bull smoked. 'I see you were looking at a book of photographs,' he finally said. 'I don't suppose you know what those are. Photographs.'

Before I could answer he continued, 'The word photography comes from Greek – its meaning is "drawing with light".'

'I know of photographs,' I said. 'You showed me a book of England. In Bombay.'

'Ah yes,' he said slowly, as if distracted, or talking to himself. 'Based on principles of light. Of combining chemistry with what the eye beholds. Optics – mirrors and lenses. Fascinating. Fascinating,' he repeated. 'I take photographs as well.'

I didn't understand what he spoke of, except for his last sentence. 'You take photographs of England?'

'Of England? Oh no. That would be tedious. I take photographs of people.'

'People? What people?'

He smiled, a slow, pleasant smile. 'Only beautiful people, my dear. They must be beautiful.' He roused himself to pour a cup of his own tea, then another for me, again adding to it from the dark bottle.

As I put the cup to my lips he lifted his chin. 'Would you like me to take your photograph, Daryâ *jan*?'

I raised my eyes over the brim of my cup. 'I . . . I don't know.' I thought of his words, long ago, about being captured in a box.

'Finish up your tea,' he said, and I drained my cup and set it down. 'Now come and I'll show you my darkroom.'

He held out his hand and I put mine into it, knowing the laudanum was making me agreeable, unquestioning. He led me to a room beside the drawing room. I was immediately struck by the smell, a strange odour I couldn't identify. The room was dim, bathed in the early evening's murky glow due to a thick double layer of yellow fabric stretched across the long window at the back of the room. Mr Bull lit a lamp that sat on a square table with drawers, and the objects in the room came into focus, although still blurred, made unreal by the eerie light and perhaps by my own altered state. On the walls were maps and heads of dead animals. Under my feet was a rug of black and white stripes that had the shape of a deer, or a small horse. A big chair with arms sat in front of the square table. Quills in a decorated jar were on the tabletop. I ran my fingers over their feathered ends, then lifted the stopper from a bottle of black liquid beside them and held it to my nose. It had a rubbery smell, but this was not what I smelled in the room.

'Leave the ink and come here,' Mr Bull said, standing near the window, and I put the stopper back into the bottle.

As I came to him his face was unearthly in the yellow light. He stood before a long narrow table. On it was an assortment of objects – deep metal trays, wooden squares clamped together, big brown bottles and narrow clear ones filled with transparent liquid. Squares of glass were neatly stacked one upon another in a tall pile. To one side of the table was a big box on a three-legged stand.

'Sit there, just there,' he said, gesturing to a wooden stool in front of the table. 'I want to show you something.' He pulled a box from a shelf under the table. All his movements seemed slow and fluid in the odd light.

I studied a clear bottle in front of me. Like the ink, its stopper came out easily, and as I touched the wet mouth of the bottle with the tip of my finger, a silvery brown ring seemed to grow out of my skin where it had rested on the glass. Replacing the top, I picked up the bottle beside it. This one was larger, one of the brown ones, and as I held it up to the yellow light to try and see inside it, shaking it slightly, Mr Bull spoke sharply.

'Stop, Daryâ. Put that down. Carefully,' he demanded, and I lowered the bottle to the table. He came and took it, setting it on a high shelf. 'Collodion is highly explosive if handled roughly or exposed to flame,' he said. 'More than one photographer has found that out, unfortunately.' He picked up a small soft brush and flicked it over the top piece of glass. 'After I take the photographs I turn them into pictures here, and all these things – including the yellow light – are necessary for their development. Now, look at this.' He put a piece of paper into my hand.

I studied it; it was a photograph of shiny, purplish-brown. A woman stood with her back turned, looking over her shoulder. Her head was bare, and she was dressed in a sari, the middle of her back exposed by the short bodice, the sheer skirt wrapped around her hips. The shape of her legs was visible through it. Although her clothes were those of an Indian woman – although more suggestive than I had seen in India – and her skin dark, her features were not like the women of that country. He handed me another. This was two women. The first reclined against a stack of pillows, one arm under her head, and she was swathed in delicate clothing that clearly suggested the outlines of her body. She wore a circle of jewels in her hair, and much jewellery on her arms and around her neck. Her expression was one of boredom. At her feet knelt the second woman; this one was sharply in contrast, wearing only a short plain dress and a head covering that partly obscured her face. She held a pitcher over the first woman's feet, as if she were about to bathe them. Again, the women were dark-skinned, but there was something fake about their clothing and demeanour.

I knew by the furniture that all the photographs were taken in Mr Bull's drawing room.

'It takes skill and patience to produce these photographs,' Mr Bull said, handing me another of an equally odd woman in foreign clothing, sitting in a languid and crude pose, her knees apart.

'These women are your friends?' I asked. The women appeared coarse.

'Friends? Of course not. I paid them to sit for my photographs.'

'This is their job?'

He smiled, looking into my face. 'They do another sort of work entirely, Daryâ *jan*, but are only too happy to earn extra shillings in this manner. They're easily found.'

'Found? But where are they from?' I picked up the first photograph again. 'She's not an Indian,' I said. Then I reached towards the box, to look at another, but he slid the cover on to it, and something in his movement was too fast, as if he didn't want me to look further.

'It's of no consequence where they're from. I enjoy the process. And the result.' He smiled at me. 'But you, Daryâ. You are entirely different.'

I looked back at the last photograph, and then at him. His hand caressed the lid of the box.

'You are different because you are a proud Tajik,' he said. 'And because you possess a true beauty, not a mere transient and fleeting false attempt at the exotic. Do you know how lovely you are? Come,' he said, again extending his hand, and leading me to a mirror that hung on a wall near the door. Standing behind me, he put his hands on my upper arms, his fingers warm. 'Look at yourself, Daryâ,' he whispered into my ear, his breath hot, dark and smoky, stirring my hair.

I looked, blinking, for what I saw was a wavery blur, as if seen through yellow water. And then I saw myself, but my eyes did not look like my eyes. I couldn't see any green; they were black. I leaned closer, looking into them, and saw, reflected over my shoulder, the leering face of Shaliq. I cried out, turning my face away, wrenching my upper body to one side, and the grip tightened.

'What's wrong?' It was Shaliq's hard voice. But Persian, not Pashto.

'I . . . I don't want to look any more,' I said.

'You must,' Shaliq said, forcing me with his strong hands to face the mirror once more, shaking me, lightly. I looked, and this time saw myself as I always was, and there was Mr Bull, peering over my shoulder as his hands held my upper arms.

'There, there,' he said. 'Are you all right now?'

I nodded.

'Good,' he said. 'Good.' He ran his hands up and down my arms, and my flesh puckered at his touch. 'You're cold,' he whispered again, this time his mouth against my neck. 'We mustn't let you be cold. Come,' he said, 'come, my princess.' And, putting his arm through mine, he led me upstairs, to his room with the wide bed.

It was not as I had expected . . . what had I expected? All I knew of the act I knew from Shaliq; he had simply mounted me in the same way every time, his movements as dull and unfeeling as the routine scrubbing of a dirty shirt upon a rock. Mr Bull – Osric – was neither quick nor rough, and yet, afterwards, I was as filled with as much – possibly more – shame and disgust than when Shaliq had first taken me.

After I had crept back to my room, silently, along the dark hall, I closed my door and removed the sari I had put back on only moments ago to leave the front bedroom. I washed my body, scrubbing with a cloth until my skin felt raw. But I wanted to feel this stinging discomfort, knowing that I would have preferred to be treated in the way I knew, with nothing but a hurried, meaningless rhythm. Osric Bull's studied movements and whispered demands, his sighs and murmurs and final low cries of pleasure now made me clench my jaw as I worked with the soap and wet cloth, trying to clean away all traces of him.

Mr Bull had extinguished the gas lamps, and only the fire glowed. He went to the fireplace and picked up one of the idols – they sat on the fireplace ledges in every room.

'This is Kali,' he said, 'wife of Shiva the Destroyer. Come and see her.' I did, immediately glad I didn't have this one in my room, for it was ugly and fierce, with a protruding tongue, a frightful stare, and a necklace of human skulls around her neck. As I looked at the idol's ugly face the laudanum still made me slow in both my thoughts and movements.

'I have other idols,' he said, and went to a cupboard with drawers. He opened one and took out another statue. 'Look at this one,' he said, and held it out to me.

I took it, studying it in the firelight, trying to understand the two-headed creature with many twining arms and legs. And then, with a dull shock, I saw that it wasn't a two-headed creature at all, but a man and a woman, their bodies twisted into an unnatural position as they performed an indecent act.

I shoved it back at Mr Bull as though it burned my hand. He stared down at it, running his hands over it, and then looked back at me, slowly.

'Are you still relaxed from your dose, my dear?' he asked. When I didn't answer he went on. 'I'm feeling rather serene myself.' He set the revolting statue on the fireplace ledge. 'Here, let me,' he said, and went behind me and untied the thread at the end of my braid. Then he slowly pulled my hair free, gently raking through it with his fingers. When he was done he lifted his hands, holding my hair to his face and breathing in, finally exhaling with a deep sigh that verged on a moan. He sat in a chair near the fire, his legs stretched out in front of him, his hands on the arms of the chair, staring at me. 'Take off your sari.'

I instinctively crossed my arms over my chest. 'Mr Bull, I don't –'

'Tut. Osric. You may only call me Osric. Say it.'

'Osric,' I whispered.

'That's better. Now. Off with it. But slowly. Slowly, my dear.'

I had never in my life stood naked before anyone. I couldn't look up as I unwound the folds of the sari and pulled the bodice over my head, dropping it all in a pile at my feet. I was trembling, my quavering breath sounding like that of a pony who has run for too long.

'Ah, yes. I thought you would be like this. I have imagined you so often, my dusky princess. You are even more beautiful than I could have ever hoped.' He rose, and I flinched and drew back.

'Are you afraid of me? Because you have no reason to be. I've given no indication that you will come to any harm, have I? That I would hurt you in any way? And really – I have been told by many, many women that I have pleased them greatly. Wouldn't you like me to please you in that same way? Aren't you lonely, my Daryâ *jan*, lonely for a man? You are surely a hot-blooded woman – that's what so attracted me to you in the first place – you have vitality and fire. And it's common knowledge that dark blood runs with more heat.' His voice murmured on, his eyes, under the heavy lids, glowing as they continued to take in my body.

'Swooning, pale and pinched English women have never been of interest to me – I like a woman who is rather . . . lusty. So this wide-eyed demeanour is a little disappointing. Or is it something David Ingram liked . . . an attempt at prudery?' Suddenly his voice grew louder, his eyes more focused. 'Did he encourage you to be this way, so you were more like a wilting English flower?'

At the sound of David's name I closed my eyes. Why did he say it now, when I stood like this, so vulnerable and shamed, filled with distaste and dread?

'I'm sorry, Daryâ, but I expect more than this from you,' he said, his voice changing again, verging on impatience now. 'I do expect you to perform in a certain way, with anticipation and, perhaps, even slight . . . aggression. If you don't – if you prove to me that you're not what I was led to believe, by your bold eyes and rather direct manner of speaking, and your full understanding of what I want from you – well, things may not go as smoothly as we'd both hoped.'

You must go careful, Missy. Go careful. Govind's earlier words rang in my head, and a shiver ran through me. I had misjudged Osric Bull. His pretence of being a gentleman, his manners . . . I thought of the photographs of the young women, the strange, listless expression on many of their faces, as if they either didn't want to be doing what they did, or . . . I pictured Mr Bull's drowsy, unperturbed expression as he ran his fingers over the statue, as he looked at me . . . as if they also had smoked the poppy.

I took a deep breath and opened my eyes. 'I am not afraid, Osric,' I said, forcing confidence into my voice. 'But at this moment it is as though I'm a camel on the selling block in the market place.'

He laughed at that, a loud, long laugh, and then came closer, removing his jacket and unbuttoning the cuffs of his shirt, and I turned from him and went to the wide bed, and did what I had agreed to do in order to escape the life in Bombay.

CHAPTER FORTY-ONE

MY SLEEP HAD been dark and deep.

A thin line of light came through the shutters. I rose and opened them to pale sunshine, and put my fist to my mouth, repulsed at the thoughts of what I had been forced to do the night before.

Osric Bull was my master now. He could call me to him whenever he wanted, and I would have to do whatever he asked. Or be subjected to whatever he desired.

I went to my bag, digging through the saris still folded there, and my fingers touched the hard edge of the card David had given me. I pulled it out and studied the English words. He had said I could come to him if I needed help. But . . . I couldn't. I didn't need help, did I? All that was so horribly wrong was that I didn't want to be here. I wanted to be with David, not with Osric Bull.

There was a bold knock on the door. 'Come, my dear,' Osric said as he opened it. 'I have a surprise for you.' His face was calm as he held out his hand, but I didn't take it, and a frown, little more than a twitch, passed over his features.

We went to the drawing room. Today all the curtains had been pulled open, and the room was flooded with light. The parrot's cage was not as brilliant as it had appeared glinting in the light from the fire and the lamps: the brass was tarnished, turning green in places. The deep richness of the velvet divan and curtains now appeared washed out; the brocade chairs and stools had a number of worn patches, as well as stains impossible to see in dim light. There were missing fringes on the shawl over the table. I saw streaks of dark ash on the tiles around the fireplace, and smears and fingerprints on the glass of the lamps. There was a heavy woman sitting in a chair by the table.

'Mrs Allen will make you new clothes, Daryâ *jan*,' he said, smiling, and his use of my grandmother's term annoyed me again. 'You are badly in need of them.'

'I will wear English clothes now?' I asked, knowing that as it was with the boots, I would never be comfortable in such tight garments. The woman took a long ribbon from the small drawstring bag she carried.

'Oh, no,' he continued smoothly. 'You shouldn't dress as an English-woman. What would be the excitement in that? No, the seamstress will create garments that reflect and complement your body and features.'

'Will they be Tajik?' I asked, carefully. 'You know that this' – I gestured at my now faded Indian sari – 'is not of my homeland.'

'The clothing will be of my vision,' he said impatiently.

He spoke rapidly to the older woman, and she kept nodding as she studied me. Then she put the long thick ribbon around all the parts of my body – my breasts and waist and hips, the distance across my back and down it, and the length of my legs. I didn't like her familiar touch of me; she was perspiring heavily and muttering to herself, stopping occasionally to write on a piece of paper. She had me put my bare feet on a piece of brown paper and drew around them. When she was done she and Mr Bull left the room together.

I sat at the round table, but stood when he returned a few moments later. 'You don't have to stand in my presence,' he said, and as I sat again he continued, 'I know you will be very, very pleased with your new clothing, Daryâ.' He licked his lips quickly, as if excited. 'It will all be quite elegant. Draped and flowing, and many details. Beads, tiny crystals, the finest silks and sheer fabrics of jewel hues. Delicate slippers.'

'And to go outside? I have the cloak from the missionary lady, and the boots, but will the woman also make me something –'

'Don't worry yourself about that, my dear,' Mr Bull interrupted. 'I do not intend that you go outside overmuch, so there's no need for anything other than what I've arranged. Mrs Allen is in possession of a stunning collection of exotic clothing. With all her seamstresses at work, altering the specific pieces I've requested will take only a matter of a few days. She assures me they'll fit you to perfection. Does that not please you? I wish you'd smile. You're quite lovely when you smile,' he said, and I forced my lips upward.

'In fact, when newly attired, you might resemble your grandmother as a concubine in the *zenana*. Strange, how history repeats itself.'

I didn't like him speaking of concubines, or my grandmother. 'Mr Bull,

I know that on the boat you requested I speak Persian,' I said, changing the subject. 'But I wish so much to learn more English, and I—'

Mr Bull interrupted me, shaking his head. 'Yes, I did tell you I didn't want you learning English, and that's how it will be. You and I can communicate so wonderfully in Persian; I love speaking this glorious language. Why would you spoil what we have by attempting to speak in English?'

I ran my fingers over the raised design of the shawl on the table. 'But then I can speak with no one else. Will I not have the opportunity to meet other people – English people?'

'You mustn't even think about that, my Daryâ *jan*,' he said, his voice low and soft. 'It's so special to live within our own little world, isn't it?'

He came to me and picked up my hand from where it lay on the table. 'Just the two of us,' he repeated. He pressed my hand between his own; his hands were large and square, the palms damp, and I could feel their force. 'It will be a secret language for us to share.'

'And Mr Ingram,' I said. 'Mr Ingram speaks Persian.'

He let go of my hand.

'He said he would come soon, to visit,' I told him, my voice sounding as though I were trying to convince him. And myself?

Mr Bull's eyes narrowed. 'He's a very busy young man, with his studies and many friends of his own. In spite of what he may have promised, don't expect him to come. He's no longer responsible for you. You realise that, don't you?' he asked, raising his eyebrows.

When I didn't answer, he smiled, but without warmth. 'He's back to his own life now, and there's no more reason for him to think about you. His responsibility of bringing you to Bombay ended there, as did any hold he had over you.' He went towards the door. 'I must rest now. My strength is coming back, but slowly, and I don't want to overdo it. I've already been out this morning.' He studied my face from across the room. 'You shouldn't think of David Ingram any further. It's best if you forget him. I'm sure he'll forget you very quickly, too,' he said, then paused. 'If he hasn't already. His intended will be taking all of his attention.'

'Intended?' I asked. 'What's that?'

He smiled, this time a slow, lazy smile. 'Why, his betrothed, my dear. He's pledged to marry the lovely Gwendolyn Liston; surely she'll be anxious to set a date for the wedding now that he's back in the country.' He went on further, but I heard nothing more.

David was betrothed? But . . . I swallowed, although it was difficult, my mouth suddenly dry. I reached up and ran my fingers over my lips; he had kissed me. He . . .

The bell I'd heard yesterday jangled again, and there was a quiet knock on the door. Osric opened it to Govind; they spoke, Osric shaking his head, then Govind left and Osric closed the door and looked back at me.

'Are you not feeling well, my dear? You've grown quite pale. I'm going to lie down now. And you should have a rest as well,' he said, and left.

I lay on the divan in the quiet, warm room, a brocade cushion under my head, my arm over my eyes. After a long while I sat up and looked at the parrot. Holding a nut in his claw, he delicately worked the meat from the shell, his thick black tongue flexible. It was as if I was regaining consciousness after one of Shaliq's beatings: I hurt everywhere, and felt a similar sickness to the one last night, at the table. But this churning, nauseous sensation had nothing to do with too much rich food.

I folded my arms across my abdomen and bent over them. That David had kissed me . . . the reaction of his body – was he only thinking of the woman he loved, the woman he'd been away from for so long when he'd held me? Were those moments in the failing light – the pressure of our bodies, our arms around each other and our mouths moving together until it was as though I had been lifted out of the dark lower deck and held into a clear, bright sky – only him dreaming of her, this woman . . . what had Mr Bull called her? Was it nothing more than simple lust David had experienced, wanting to remember a woman's body, kissing me while he thought of her?

Govind came in, refilling the parrot's water dish and cleaning its cage. The bird flapped its wings as if distressed, and I heard Govind whisper to it – 'Suleyman, Suleyman the Magnificent, yes' – over and over, and the parrot calmed down.

I stood and paced, unable to stay still any longer. Govind put the dirty paper from the cage into the fire and turned to me. 'You are good to Mr Osric, Missy?' he whispered.

Heat flooded my face, and I looked away.

'Missy?'

I had to look back at him, but as before, I couldn't understand what I saw on his face. 'It will go much better if you are always good to him.' And with that he left, his hoarse whisper repeating in my head.

'*Salâm*,' Suleyman called, then turned his back as if annoyed, and sat, hunched and petulant, in his huge and gleaming cage.

The sound of the unknown bell came again. I stopped pacing and listened, heard the low murmur of voices through the closed door. And then it opened again, and Osric came in, rubbing his hands together, squeezing his fingers as if they gave him pain.

'I couldn't rest comfortably; unfortunately I'm suffering one of my headaches again,' he said as he crossed the room and closed the curtains. He settled into the red chair near the fireplace; there was a dish of nuts on the small table beside him. Through the window and curtains came the muffled sounds of wheels on the stones, an occasional called greeting. I needed to breathe air not made stale by the closed windows, needed to move my legs – not only up and down the stairs, but in long strides. My muscles felt too tight, stiffened through so little exercise.

I went to the window and parted the curtains, standing between them. People passed by below; I watched a man and woman, her arm linked through his. Her skirt blew around her ankles, and she put her hand on her hat, tilting her face to the man, smiling. What was David doing on this – no. I wouldn't think of him. 'Can we go outside?' I asked. 'It's sunny.'

'I don't think it's the right time,' Osric said, his voice very firm.

'When will the time be right?' I asked, purposely keeping my own tone light. I knew I should stop, stop questioning him, but for some reason couldn't.

'When I tell you,' he said, and put a nut into his mouth. It made a bulge in his cheek as he chewed.

'I would wear my warm cloak,' I insisted. 'I would like very much to go outside, to the square where I see the trees. Please' – I hesitated – 'Osric.' The name was hard, its edges sharp in my mouth. 'Just for a shor—'

He cut off my sentence by sighing, carefully setting down the dish of nuts and putting his fingers to his forehead. 'Daryâ, don't upset me.' He leaned forward, his elbows on his knees, and closed his eyes, rubbing his forehead with great agitation.

'Come,' he said, without looking up. 'Help me. Soothe this terrible headache. You know what to do.'

I went to him and stood behind his chair, putting my fingers on his temples. Immediately his shoulders – which had been high and tight – relaxed, and he leaned back against the chair.

'Ahh. Yes, yes,' he murmured, his head dropping further back. I pressed with more force.

'Umm. Good. That's the way,' he said, and I went on in this manner for some time, my fingers moving in soothing circles. After a while I grew unaware of my fingers as I looked around the room, watching Suleyman admire himself in his mirror, his head tilting to first one side, and then the other. And then, without warning, Mr Bull reached up and caught my wrist in a tight grip so quickly that I started, letting out a small cry.

'It's all right,' he said, in a husky, unfamiliar voice. 'It's all right,' he repeated, and then drew my hand down his cheek – I felt the rasp of his whiskers – until it rested on his neck, just above his stiff white collar, where his skin hung loosely. The drum of his blood beat beneath my fingertips; the skin was thin and stubbled.

'You do know what I need, don't you, Daryâ *jan*?' he said, in that same voice.

I stood very still.

He let go of my hand, standing to face me, and his cheeks were flushed, his eyes heavy-lidded and his lips loose. The look was unmistakable. There was a sliver of nut caught between his bottom front teeth.

It was after noon; the clocks had chimed twelve times while I stood behind his chair.

'Let us retire to my room,' he said, his voice low, but then the bell again rang, insistently, over and over, and Osric's face lost its drowsy yet expectant look. Now he was angry.

'Damn,' he said, and went to the window, yanking back the curtain and looking down. Since I had last stood at the window the sky had darkened, clouds hiding the sun. Then, with the same brisk, annoyed movements, he pulled open the drawing-room door. Govind already stood there, his hand raised to knock. They spoke in quiet tones, Mr Bull shaking his head, and then he left with Govind, shutting the door behind him.

I lowered myself into the red chair. It was still warm from Osric. Would he not even wait until nightfall, until it was at least dark? He would take me in the daytime, with Govind and the girl with the spotted skin moving about? What if they heard, and knew what we did?

I shook my head at my ridiculous thoughts. But of course they already knew why I was here. The glances the girl cast at me when she thought I didn't see, and Govind . . . especially Govind. They knew my purpose in this house. Although they had to serve me, and treat me with civility, they did not have to respect me. I would never be a memsâhib, a lady of the house. To them I was no more than a common whore.

You have agreed to be Osric Bull's whore. David's words came back to me now.

I went to the window and looked down to see the closing door of a carriage parked outside. The driver slapped the reins and the carriage left, and within a moment Osric came back to the drawing room.

I stared fixedly at the coloured glass pieces on the mantel, hoping his mood had been shattered. He came to me and pulled me by my hands to face him, then he fussed with my hair, pushing it back from my forehead, running his fingertips over my *harquus*, but my wish had obviously been answered. He was agitated now, his movements forced, and I knew his desire had been banished by the ringing bell and whatever it had meant.

He stepped away from me finally, shaking his head with annoyance. 'I'm going out for a few hours,' he said. 'But I'll be back early this evening. Wait for me, Daryâ, and we shall have a lovely time.' His voice was low, heavy with meaning, and I knew our time together had merely been postponed.

I went to my room and stood at the window, watching the soft rain come down with a steady, insistent rhythm. Two people – a man and a woman – hurried along the narrow passage between the houses, their heads down against the rain. I couldn't escape the picture of David and his woman. I was warm and dry, and yet it felt as though the rain had seeped deep inside me.

As I raised my eyes I saw a child in the window across from me; she waved, and after a moment's hesitation I raised my hand. She had long dark hair in curls, and a bright bow on the top of her head. And then a woman appeared behind the girl, glanced out of the window, and drew the child away.

Nasreen would be near the age of this other girl. I again remembered how my mother had once told me that it was best not to speak or even think of things from the past, and that her own mother had taught her the only way to drive away the pain of remembering was to bury the memories. I had tried to do that while I was with the Ghilzai, when Shaliq wouldn't allow me to visit Susmâr Khord. I had tried hard to push the memories deep, let them lie still and dead at the back of my thoughts.

But I couldn't. I closed my eyes and saw the courtyard with the apricots drying on the roof under the brilliant sun, heard the soft whinny of Mehry. I felt Nasreen's small arms around my neck, smelled the warmth of Yusuf's thick, soft hair.

And I felt the loss of it all – of home and the people and everything that had been my life – more keenly than I had in a long, long time. I had experienced such an unexpected, quiet and yet joyful power when David had kissed me – and had wanted me, I was certain – that I believed I could never feel this loneliness again. But now, knowing what I knew, it was as if something was dying, and I was powerless to stop it.

I want to go home. Even though I knew what I had run from, I let myself imagine it as a welcoming place. And waiting for me there were my family and the people who cared about me. As darkness fell outside the window I felt like the child I had once been, wanting someone to lay a soothing hand on my forehead, someone to rock me and to murmur to me that it would be all right.

Was I losing my senses? Nobody had done these things for so many years – since my grandmother and mother had in Susmâr Khord. I was a woman now, and should think like a woman, not a child.

I looked up; at home after a rain, the stars shone more brightly. But it was not to be here. As I stared into the strip of night sky that I could see between the roofs, it seemed that the cloudy, unpure air that hung over this city would never allow the stars to shine with their full power.

Finally I lay on my bed, turning my face to the wall and weeping. Govind brought in a tray, but I stayed where I was, and knew I couldn't eat.

I lay on the bed, waiting, until Osric Bull returned home and came for me.

CHAPTER FORTY-TWO

HEARING SULEYMAN'S SQUAWKS from below, I sat up in my rumpled bed the next morning, my eyes sore. I rose and looked at myself in the mirror attached to a small table. My eyes were red-rimmed and swollen from crying after I'd returned from Osric's room in the middle of the night. I stared into the mirror, telling myself sternly that I must not – *must not* – turn into a woman who lay weeping into her pillow, made hollow by what she couldn't have. I smiled bitterly, for I felt far from hollow. Instead, it was as if my limbs were filled with sand, and I thought of the headless goat in the *buzkashi*. But of course that brought back the image of David, holding the gourd for me to drink that day I ran after him, begging him to help me.

I straightened my shoulders and lifted my chin. In the mirror I saw that my mouth now looked straight and firm, although there was a small line between my eyebrows that I hadn't noticed before.

There was a light tap on my door and Govind entered with a tray, setting it down and leaving silently. Within minutes came another knock; this time it was the girl who had cleaned my room. She dipped her knee at me – as I remember Blossom doing to David when she first met him. I stepped aside and she came in; I spoke slowly to her, asking her name, and she hesitantly told me.

'Lucy, Miss,' she said, again dipping her knee. She opened the shutters and I watched the way she turned the handles and pushed up the window. Warm air blew in, lifting the edges of the curtains around the bed so that they danced and swirled like dervishes, and I breathed deeply. It was the first outside air I had known since I had arrived at Osric's house, and although it smelled less than fresh, I was glad to feel it on my face.

'It's a beautiful day,' Lucy said, as sunshine washed across the floor, and I saw that the blue shapes on the rug were flowers. And then she got down on to her knees in front of the ashes of the fire and scooped them out, putting them into a bucket.

I watched her work, seeing the worn-through bottoms of her shoes as she knelt there, and felt deep shame as I sat on the edge of my bed as this girl cleaned my room. She was probably no more than thirteen or fourteen.

'Mr Bull says he wishes you to come to the drawing room. Please, Miss, you're to dress and eat,' she said as she stood, gesturing to the tray on the table.

I looked at her, and at the thought of what had been done to me the night before, I turned away.

'He's been up for quite a while now, Miss. Mr Bull don't like to be kept waiting.'

She spoke quickly, and, as I'd noticed before, her words didn't sound like Osric's or Mr Ingram's, and it was a little harder for me to understand her. As she worked I put on my sari and then sat at the table, but had no desire to eat the food there. When she'd smoothed the blankets on my bed Lucy picked up my comb and hesitantly approached me.

'Shall I help you with your hair, Miss? I'm only a parlourmaid, but Mr Bull asked that I do what I can to help you. Of course we don't have a lady's maid yet; I'm sure he'll hire one soon.'

Was she saying she would comb my hair? I looked at her as I translated her words, and she must have taken this as yes, and began working through my hair. Nobody had combed my hair for me since my grandmother, the last time when I was perhaps six years old. It was calming; I sat, quietly, trying to enjoy the sensations as she gently combed my hair from my scalp to the ends, and then braided it as I always wore it, tying the end with thread.

'Your hair is so lovely and thick, Miss,' she said. And then she stood in front of me, her own head down, her hands clasped in front of her.

I stood, not knowing what she waited for. Finally she lifted her head and said, very quietly, 'You're to put on your boots, Miss, and go downstairs to the drawing room. Mr Bull is waiting.'

'Thank you,' I said in English, and she dipped her knee. I didn't understand the meaning of this movement, but did the same, to be polite, and she smiled. It was the first time I had seen her smile. It was a good smile, and I returned it.

★ ★ ★

When I went to the drawing room, my feet encased in the hated boots, Osric threw the paper he was reading on to the table and stood.

'Good morning, my princess,' he said, and saliva flooded my mouth. He had murmured that phrase to me a number of times the night before, and I found it hard to meet his eyes now, not wanting him to see the disgust in my expression.

He came closer; I held my breath. 'Have you nothing to say, this morning, Daryâ *jan*?' He stood in front of me and picked up my hand. 'Nothing at all?'

I looked into his face. He was smiling in a light-hearted way, his chest out. I knew he was pleased with himself, pleased with his performance the night before. Did he expect me to thank him, to fall to my knees in gratitude?

'I slept well,' I said, when I knew he would wait until I spoke.

He raised his eyebrows. 'I feel quite hearty today, and as it's a glorious Sunday, the perfect day for a carriage ride, I've summoned my brougham, and it's already waiting at the front door,' he said. 'I thought you would enjoy an outing. A small treat. After last night,' he added, looking down at me suggestively.

I lowered my own eyes so as not to have to see his expression. 'Shall I take my cloak?'

'It's far too warm. And you won't need it in the brougham,' he replied, then took my hand and put it on the inside of his elbow, in the same manner as I had seen the men and women outside when they walked together on the street. He led me down the stairs and out the front door as I fixed my veil in place.

We rode along the street of townhouses, and as we turned on to another street, and then another, we came to buildings that didn't look like homes, for there were large windows lining their fronts. I took in their brightness and colour, leaning close to the open carriage window to look at the objects displayed there – painted china plates and men's pipes of different shapes and sizes, ladies' hats with ribbons and feathers, and wonderful wooden animals made for children's hands. The wide street was teeming with horses and small carriages and the longer carriages packed with many people. Omnibus, Osric said when I pointed to one.

People were everywhere: men, women and children walking near the buildings or dodging their way through the dangerous street, avoiding the moving carriages and stepping around great piles of horse droppings which swarmed with hovering flies. Women stood against the buildings, holding out flowers or fruits, calling to the passing people. One of them reminded me of a woman in Osric's photographs – the same rough, dark appearance.

'Do we go to the square . . . Kensington?' I said the remembered name carefully.

'No. There are only walking paths there. We'll go through Hyde Park, where you – we – can stay in the brougham.'

The tall buildings rose from the hard ground into the sky. I thought of my own land, of the curves, the soft lines, the village houses growing softly from the earth itself. Of the fabric and skin tents and yurts, malleable, temporary. Here I felt chilled – not by the air which blew in the open windows of the carriage, warm and stinking of the droppings on the dusty streets, but by the squareness and permanence of these solid buildings. Even in the carriage I felt the pressing closeness of the stones, blackened by time and the dirty air. It was difficult to breathe; I put my head to the window and looked up at their tops but couldn't see enough of the sky.

All this time I had longed to go outside, and yet now that I actually was, the feeling I had of being closed in was even more powerful than when I was within the walls of Osric's house. It wasn't only that there was no beauty. I was suddenly overcome with a sense of panic and captivity, of having nowhere to run, no horizon to set my eyes upon.

I stopped looking at the buildings and instead watched the people, especially the women. I saw how they were dressed, many in even more elaborate clothing than the memsâhibs I'd seen on the ship. As we stopped and other carriages rumbled by, I studied one woman who walked beside the carriage; her hair was piled and woven in an elaborate style, a high hat perched upon it. Her dress was silk, the colour of the silvery leaves of the wormwood that grew wild at home. There appeared to be many layers of white lacy skirts under her dress, and when the warm gritty wind blew, all the skirts swirled with a whooshing sound, and as the skirts lifted her dainty boots gleamed.

I looked down at my sari again; I could not walk the streets dressed like this – people would stare at me. I suddenly thought of the woman on the boat, the woman who had hissed at me, judging me only by what I wore, by my *harquus*. Was this why Osric wouldn't allow me out of the carriage – because of my inappropriate clothing? Or because he didn't want to be seen with me by other English people?

'Here we are, Daryâ,' he suddenly said, as the carriage turned again, and I saw green open spaces, and the glint of light playing on water, and tall trees and full bushes. A rush of tears came to my eyes. It had been so long since I'd seen anything alive, apart from the plants in Osric's house.

The carriage went slowly along a road of crushed yellow stone. There were bright flowers growing in mounds of earth; it was obvious they were tended carefully. Men and women walked slowly along winding paths, sometimes with a dog on a rope, and children ran by; I smiled to see them. There were wooden benches where people sat and talked. As we slowly continued, the branch of a tree brushed against the carriage, and I reached out and caught a leaf, pulling it off its stem. I gazed at it as I held it: the broad, deep green with its network of tiny lines fanning from its centre to the delicate, trembling edges. Then I brought it to my nose and breathed in its faint odour, closing my eyes.

As the carriage stopped to allow another to pass across the road in front of it, two men walking by greeted Osric. As he leaned out of his window, speaking to them rapidly in English, his voice low, one of them looked around Osric at me, his eyebrows raised and a sly smile on his mouth. I was ashamed, for the look on the man's face made it clear that Osric had explained my presence.

I looked away from the men and out of my window, idly watching people walking or standing near a body of water where large white birds floated. And then I saw him. David was standing and talking with a small cluster of other men and women on one of the narrow pathways. I stared at him, my heart pounding with the joy at simply seeing him. Already it seemed that his face had lost some of the sun's colour while under the thin skies of London; his skin was still darker than many of the men walking around him, but to me he appeared too pale. His hair was neatly cut and held in place with some potion, although it would not be completely tamed, springing up in a few curls at the back of his collar.

And then, as I watched, leaning out of the carriage window, a young woman moved to stand beside David. She balanced on her toes, speaking into his ear, her hand laid casually upon his arm, and he nodded. Even though her skin was so pale as to be almost translucent, her lips were a deep pink which matched her dress. Surely to touch her with anything but a whisper of fingertips would bruise that skin: even from here I could tell that it was so fine that tiny blue threads would be visible at her temple, like Evie-*baba*'s. She had silky hair a shade paler than David's, and I knew that when the curls were loosened they would fall like a sheet of gold over her shoulders. Her wrists were small and fine, and I was sure that her delicate hands had never done work. I imagined that when she walked the heels of her small boots would tap like an impatient pony's. She was so slender and her dress cinched so tightly about her narrow waist that David's hands would fit around it easily. Her breasts, too, were small and high.

All this I saw in that first moment as I watched David and the woman I knew must be – by her familiar behaviour, her touch – his betrothed. By comparison to this woman I was too tall, my body too angular, my skin too dark, flawed by its markings.

The sounds around me suddenly grew louder: people talking and laughing and calling in one monotonous rhythm, horses and carriages rumbling by, the sawing of greedy insects, wind rustling the leaves of the trees. One of the men who spoke to Osric had a loud, hard voice, but now the rustling and buzzing grew to such intensity that it blocked out everything else. I was too hot, and the quick flashes of the sun on the carriage windows were dizzying. I breathed in quick, shallow gasps as I watched David and the young woman in pink.

And then David looked in the direction of our carriage, and I threw myself back, away from the window, but he was still within my vision. He walked towards the carriage, the girl holding his arm and moving beside him as if floating on the cloud of her dress, and it was as if I could hear that pink cloud whispering, laughing at me as if it was alive. I gripped Osric's arm.

'Osric,' I said, 'please. Please let us go now. I am sick, Osric, please,' I said, realising that I truly did feel sick, overcome with the shock of seeing David with his betrothed, of the thought of having to speak to him while the woman he loved clung to him, stared at me, at my *harquus*. 'Osric!' I said, the faces of the men outside his window receding in and out as he nodded and then reached up and rapped on the window behind his head with his knuckles.

I was breathing heavily, not daring to look out the window again, so afraid David would see me. We rumbled away, and I opened my clenched hands and saw the leaf, now crumpled. As I watched, the fragile form slowly unfolded itself and lay, creased and still on my palm. Unexpectedly I thought of Yalda the night Nasreen was born, remembered asking her what she saw in my hand. And I also remembered that she hadn't answered, but had gazed at my palm with a strange and troubled expression.

When we had driven far enough so that I knew David could no longer see me, I looked at the clouded window beside me, but all I saw was my own face, bloodless as a dead fish.

When I awoke my room was dark. I had gone directly there when we came in, telling Osric I needed to lie down.

I had ripped the laces from the boots and pulled them off, throwing them across the room so that they hit the tiles on the front of the fireplace. Then I sat on the edge of my bed, my face in my hands, and finally I lay down, pulling the Indian cotton cover over me. Even though the room was warm I shivered as I fell asleep.

Now I stood by the windows, watching the glowing orb of the light at the top of the tall post closest to the house, seeing the insects that fluttered close to its light and heat. The clocks chimed ten times, and I knew I'd slept many hours. I went to the cupboard and took out my embroidered bag, feeling to the bottom. I touched the paper David had given me, and then the rolled leather. I pulled it out and considered throwing it into the fireplace, but couldn't do it. I squeezed the amulet, hard, and then returned it to my bag. The door opened and I turned to see Osric, aware that he had not even knocked.

'I'm disappointed that you didn't join me for dinner, Daryâ,' he said from the doorway. 'I looked in on you, but you were sleeping soundly. Would you like to have something to eat now?'

I shook my head.

'Why are you standing there in the dark?' He crossed to the table and lit a lamp, and as the room grew brighter he held out a small black velvet bag.

'For you,' he said. 'A present. Come and see what it is.'

I went to him and silently took the bag from his hand.

'Go on, Daryâ. See what I've brought you.'

I jammed my hand inside and pulled out three thin gold bracelets. They were of different widths, and the thickest carried marks that had been beaten into the gold. I ran my thumb over the design.

'Put them on,' Osric told me, and even though I wanted to say no, I knew there was no use. As I slipped them over my wrist they jingled with a small, pleasing sound. 'There's something else in there,' he said, and I again felt inside the bag and drew out earrings. They were also thin gold, long hoops strung with small, delicate pale blue pieces that I sensed were not glass, but true gems.

'Blue tourmalines,' he said, lifting the lamp and bringing it closer, so the stones shone in its light. 'Blue is an important colour for you, isn't it?'

I looked at the earrings in my palm. 'Yes. The *jinn* don't like it.' The word *jinn* sounded odd when uttered in this English house. I hadn't thought about them for a long time. Did I still fear them as I had at home? Here, in this land of heavy, grey sky they didn't seem to carry their normal threat and strength. I touched my ear lobe. 'I haven't worn earrings since . . . a long time,' I said, suddenly remembering that I had not put on any earrings on the day I had run from Shaliq, because one of my ears was bruised and swollen from his beating. So long ago.

I reached up and jabbed the thin gold wire into the hole in my lobe; it still went through easily. I put in the other and shook my head slightly, and the earrings gently swayed against my cheeks.

'I also bought this,' he said, reaching into his pocket and pulling out a small jar. 'For your eyes.'

I took it, opening the top, and saw a substance that I knew was similar to kohl.

'Let me,' he said, and when I took a step back, he said, his voice husky, 'Don't you trust me, Daryâ *jan*?'

Trust him?

He dipped the end of his smallest finger into the dark creamy powder. He put his other hand under my chin and tilted my face towards the lamp. Then he ran his finger under my bottom eyelashes with a touch as light as the small white moths I had watched fluttering about the gaslight.

'Lower your eyes,' he said, his voice deep, almost a whisper, and he repeated his movements on my eyelids. 'Now look at me.'

I did, and he took a deep breath and stepped back.

'You are my beautiful odalisque,' he said, in that same husky whisper, turning me so I could see my reflection in the mirror. 'Your eyes are like jewels,' he whispered, and I looked at him and saw that his own eyes were strangely black. His breath smelled of smoke and alcohol as he leaned closer. 'Like jewels,' he repeated.

A mysterious woman whose green eyes, within their black outlines, were huge and bold and elongated stared back at me from the mirror. In the lamplight my eyes did glow like jewels, or like stars. I was suddenly aware of the deep rug under my bare feet, the coolness of my wedding anklet on my skin, the whisper of my hair against the back of my neck.

Osric's voice was as soft as his finger had been when it traced the outline of my eyes, and yet still it startled me, because for that one instant I had forgotten about him, even though he stood so close. 'Do you like what you see?'

I didn't answer. I no longer looked or felt like the woman I had been in Afghanistan, or in India, or on the boat sailing over the seas to England. I couldn't recognise myself, and for a moment felt as if I were looking at something I shouldn't be looking at. I found it difficult to lower my eyes, to look away, not only because I looked – was I beautiful, as Osric told me? – but also because . . .

I thought of David and the woman who had spoken into his ear, and I knew then that what Osric had told me was true, that David could never be interested in a woman like me. The woman he loved was like a kitten, with soft fur and tiny paws. Helpless and winning so that one must protect her, hold her softness close. A woman who would make a man feel powerful, not one who spoke of her own power.

As Osric lowered his face to mine, and I felt the touch of his tongue on my *harquus*, and then the dampness of his lips upon my eyelids, I knew that David Ingram was lost to me, and would never think of me again.

CHAPTER FORTY-THREE

When I went downstairs the next morning, I became aware for the first time of other people who moved within the house like ghosts. There was a thick-waisted older woman in a dark dress and white collar, her hair pulled back severely, a jumble of keys on the belt around her waist. She passed me on the stairs, turning her head from me, her lips knotted into such a tight pouch that I knew she was very displeased at me being in the house. A gaunt young boy, bony wrists protruding from too-short sleeves, slipped along a hall with two pairs of Osric's shoes in his hands, his shaved head lowered. Another girl, like Lucy except even younger, knelt on the tiles in front of the main door, washing them with soapy, steaming water, her hands bright red from the heat of the water. I heard the rattle and clank of pots, and the busy chopping of a knife against wood as I stood near the stairs that led to the lowest level, under the house, and knew this must be the cooking area for those who prepared the food and put it on the trays Govind brought to my room or to the dining room.

All these people to run Osric's house, people like the servants in the house in Bombay, the kind of person I had been, for those few short days. Invisible, silent, doing what must be done without being noticed. And now – now I was not one of them. I was one they served.

'Good morning, Daryâ *jan*,' Osric said as I entered the dining room. 'Help yourself to breakfast.'

I nodded, and as I went to the table I passed him, and he put his hand on my back, his fingers caressing me for a moment. Wasn't this a little like the life my grandmother had described – where she was free from work and responsibility, and had food prepared and brought to her, and could sit and think and dream whenever she pleased?

And yet it felt so wrong.

* * *

After breakfast Osric went to the drawing room and read a book. I walked up and down the many stairs of the house, trying to stretch my legs. I idly gazed through the open doorways: on the ground floor was the grand dining room and behind it another room with a smaller table and chairs and sitting area among many plants, and the stairs going down to the kitchen; on the next floor up was the drawing room and Osric's darkroom; the three sleeping rooms were on the third floor. There was still another stairway leading up, to the top of the house, the stairs narrow and uncarpeted, and I remembered Govind's dragging step above me and knew it was where he – and maybe some of the other servants – slept.

I knew the walls of the house joined the walls of the homes on either side; sometimes I heard faint voices on the other side of my wall as I lay in bed. I was trapped within a many-chambered place, only able to go up and down. It was like living in a hive, with the quiet buzz of others who circled but didn't come near me.

As I went down to the first floor again Lucy wiped a mirror in the long hallway beside the front door.

'You talk to me?' I asked.

'Oh no, Miss. I couldn't,' she said, startled.

'Yes. Please. My house now.'

She looked over her shoulder, then up the stairs, as if someone were watching, then said, 'Only for a minute, while Mr Bull's busy, and Govind is in the kitchen, with Cook. But Mrs Wimby – if she sees me talking while I should be working . . .'

I couldn't understand all she said, although it was clear I made her uncomfortable. 'Mrs Wimby?'

'The housekeeper. She tells us all what to do – Cook and me and Ella and Pete and the others – what work downstairs. Even Govind, sometimes. She gives us all our orders.' She lifted, then dropped her shoulders. 'Well, not you, of course, Miss.'

There was the same tinkling bell I'd heard so often, very loud now, and Lucy quickly stepped away from me. Govind appeared and opened the front door and I realised, finally, that this bell meant that someone had come to the door and wished to come in.

It was a young man carrying brown packages; Osric had come down from the drawing room and took them as Govind gave the man a coin.

'Daryâ,' Osric said, 'look. Your new clothing. Come back to the drawing room and we'll look at them,' he said, and I followed him.

My main hope was that these new clothes would surely be more acceptable should I wish to go outside, and walk on the streets. Osric took a small folded pearl-handled knife from a drawer in the table that held his bottles of alcohol and, one by one, he cut the string wrapped around the brown paper. The fabrics were beautiful: very fine blue silk the colour of the summer sky over Susmâr Khord; green, deep as the oceans I had sailed over; the gold-brown of the richest tea; red, brilliant and gleaming as Suleyman's tail feathers. There were three pairs of satin slippers decorated with intricate embroidery. As he shook out the pieces of clothing, I saw pantaloons with full, shimmering legs, long tops with sheer sleeves and embroidered bodices covered with patterns made of tiny glittering beads. Some had lace so fine as to resemble the web of a spider. There were intricately worked belts of shiny pieces of some metal, or perhaps shell, glowing warmly in the light. And there were translucent veils of varying shades, which surprised me, as Osric had made it so clear that I wasn't to wear a veil in his presence.

And in spite of the beauty of the fabrics and colours, my heart sank, for I knew that this clothing was far more revealing than my saris, and unless I was covered from neck to ankle with a cloak I could never venture outdoors.

Osric nodded approvingly, not seeing the concern I knew was on my face. 'Take these,' he said, draping a pair of red pantaloons and a bodice of red and gold over my outstretched arms, and putting a pair of slippers into my hand, 'and put them on.'

I went to my room, and when I was dressed and stood in front of the long mirror, I was horrified. I felt almost naked; my arms and throat were bare, the tops of my breasts visible, and the outline of my legs easily seen through the billowing pantaloons.

Anger grew inside me like the opening of a flower, and I stared at myself again, scowling. How dare Osric plan this clothing for me? How dare he think I would ever agree to walk about – even within his house – in such an immodest manner? In spite of the richness of the materials, I still looked like a woman of the lowest standing, like the women in his photographs. I sat on the bed, breathing heavily, waiting for him to come so I could voice my rage.

Finally he opened the door. That he never knocked added to my anger. 'Daryâ? Let me see,' he said, coming in.

I raised my chin. 'Osric,' I said, loudly. 'I cannot wear this clothing.'

He frowned. 'What do you mean? Why not? Stand, stand right now, and show me.' His voice grew harder.

I shook my head, looking down at my feet in the beautiful gold slippers with their red and purple embroidered flowers. 'It's little more than the covering of a shadow,' I said, quickly and angrily. 'It's improper. And shameful.' When he didn't answer I looked at him.

His eyes were narrowed, his brows meeting. 'I cannot believe your insolence. And your ingratitude.' There was a globule of saliva on his lower lip.

I said nothing, still staring at him. There was a darkness in his face that wasn't caused entirely by anger; I realised I was playing a game he enjoyed, one that allowed him to dominate me.

'Are you forgetting yourself, Daryâ, forgetting your role here? Besides, what have you to hide? I've known you, haven't I, in the most intimate manner. So playing coy is rather belated.' He was breathing heavily now, his eyes moving up and down my body, the tip of his tongue touching his front teeth.

'It is different to that,' I protested. 'For Govind, and Lucy, and Mrs Wimby and the others . . . to see me like this . . . I am shamed.'

'Shamed?' He laughed slyly. 'Were you shamed these last few nights? I detected no signs of it. Come now, Daryâ.' He came even closer, and smiled down at me, running the back of his hand under my chin, down my throat and brushing his knuckles over the tops of my breasts. 'I won't have you arguing with me. I thought I made that perfectly clear. I really don't care how you feel in the clothing.' He was almost whispering, his face so close I could see the veins in his eyes. 'It's all expensive, and beautiful, and you'll wear it because you have no choice. And because it pleases me. That's why you're here, my dear. To please me.' He continued to brush my skin with his knuckles, watching his own hand now.

I looked away.

His voice returned to normal, and he took a step back. 'So you'll wear this clothing every day.' He glanced at my sari on the bed, and walked to it, gathering it up and crumpling it into a ball, then tossing it to the floor. 'What I've had made for you is what you'll wear, and nothing else. Do you understand?'

I nodded, keeping my face expressionless, and he left. I sat before the table with the mirror, and then opened the drawer and took out the leaf I had brought home yesterday. But it had already become brown and brittle and curled in upon itself, and now it crumbled at my touch.

And then Lucy came to my room, carrying the rest of the new clothing and putting it away in the long cupboard in one corner. She hesitantly took my saris, glancing at me, and I knew she was following Osric's orders.

Neither of us spoke.

I finally went downstairs when I could stay in my room no longer. Seething indignation danced within me, and I had felt like a caged animal as I strode back and forth in the narrow confines of my room. Before I left I studied myself in the mirror once more, shaking my head in disgust, and then I wrapped one of the long veils around my shoulders so that I wouldn't feel so naked.

The house was quiet, the drawing room empty, and I was filled with angry relief that Osric was out. I didn't want to think what I might say or do if I came face to face with him so soon after he had made my position very clear, and my lack of a say, even in what I would wear. That he had not only forced me to dress in such shameful clothing, but had also had my comfortable, discreet saris taken away was a final blow. I tried to push away the repulsive picture of how his eyes had travelled down my body, his tongue touching his teeth, and the memory of his hands on me with such ownership, and I shuddered, once, as if an unexpected cold draught had blown over me.

But in the drawing room I couldn't calm myself; the ticking of the clocks beat within my head, and Suleyman's mumbling and sudden screeches annoyed me. I went back out to the hall, walking briskly up and down, trying to drive out my indignation and rage with more movement. Every time I passed the darkroom I stared at the closed door, thinking of the way Osric had quickly covered the box of photographs.

Everything in this house was his – including me. His air of superiority, his sense that I must do – must be – exactly as he demanded . . . I had known this in one way with my father, and in another with my husband. But Osric Bull's sense of ownership and complete authority was more than that I had known in my village or with the Ghilzai. In spite of my restlessness in those former homes I had still had freedom of movement, still dressed as I wished, and had others around me who might be a comfort or companion. Here . . . it was only Osric Bull, and his wishes.

Knowing it would only bring trouble should he discover me, I turned the knob of the darkroom, stepping in and closing the door noiselessly behind me. I waited until my eyes adjusted in the dull yellow light. Then I went to the long wooden table with the trays and solutions and took the box from the shelf under it and opened the lid. I quickly glanced through the photographs he'd shown me, and then took up another pile of them, these tied with a piece of string.

As I looked at the top photograph I knew this was what he had hidden. And I knew why. I put one hand to my chest, my heart beating so hard it caused a thumping pain.

I undid the string so I could look at all of the photographs. I didn't want to see them, and yet couldn't pull my eyes from them.

These photographs were not just women in suggestive clothing, as Osric had shown me. These were of two women, or sometimes three. They were unclothed, their bodies entwined in positions of intimacy with each other. Some reminded me of the vile statue of contorted bodies he had shown me. Some held and used instruments – whips, and sharp objects – to inflict pain. In these photographs the women who were the victims might be bound, or their eyes and mouths covered. I had never seen or imagined such depravity, and couldn't understand why these women would partake in these horrible activities. Nor why Osric Bull would wish to witness this – to photograph this. I imagined him watching the women, giving them instructions – as he instructed me – in that low, forceful voice. Had he owned these women as well?

I dropped the photographs to the floor as if the images there carried a disease. As they fluttered to the ground like broken wings there was a creak behind me. I whirled, stumbling against the table so that the glass bottles tinkled.

'Missy,' Govind whispered. 'You cannot be here. It will be big trouble for you.' His eyes went to the photographs on the floor. 'Mr Osric is home now, in his room resting. Put them back, quickly, before he looks for you. If he finds you here, with his photographs, he will be . . .' he stopped.

I studied his face in the queer yellow light, then knelt and gathered the photographs. I stared at one I hadn't yet seen, picking it up with a shaking hand.

This naked woman lay in a chair with her legs disgracefully spread. There was something odd about the tilt of her head, the way her hand hung limply over the arm of the chair. I looked closer; her eyes were fixed and staring, and what I had thought was her hair around her neck was a cord or thin rope. I closed my eyes, then opened them at the understanding of what I was seeing.

She was dead.

I slowly stood. Govind was watching me.

'Govind?' I asked, holding the photograph out to him. 'You know woman?' The paper trembled violently in my hand; I knew he was too far away to see the image, but still, he immediately shook his head.

'I do not know these women,' he said.

'But . . . this, this photograph', I said, sounding it out carefully, my voice slowed by the shocked reaction of my body, 'is here. In drawing room. You must see women, you open door for them, or . . .'

Govind now wrung his hands as if distressed. 'Please, Missy Daryâ. This is not a good business for you to talk about,' he said, his whisper louder than I'd ever heard it. 'Come away.'

'No,' I said. 'You tell me. About women.'

Suddenly his hands grew still and his kindly old face lost its benign expression. As I faced him his features appeared stronger, and I suddenly saw Govind as he might have been when he was younger, straighter, his voice undamaged and clear. 'They are only for play for Mr Osric,' he said. He stared at me. 'You understand play?'

I nodded, looking at the photograph and then back at Govind. He came to me then, glancing down at what I held.

'But only for a short while. And then Mr Osric is tired of them.'

'Tired?' The coldness was now deep inside, in my blood, in my chest as I breathed, and I heard its icy rattle.

'He is easily bored. When he doesn't want them any more, he pushes them aside. Dismisses them. Or . . .'

We both looked at the photograph. Govind took it from my shaking grip and put it with the others. He retied the string around the pile and put it into the box and returned it to the shelf under the table.

'Come now, Missy,' he said, touching my arm, and I followed him as if under water, my legs heavy, my mouth open to pull in each slow breath. Once we were in the hall, Govind shut the door silently but firmly behind us.

I sat in the drawing room, still in shock.

The women had been women from the street, hadn't they? They hadn't lived as I, in this house, as Osric's mistress. He would never . . . he didn't look upon me as he did those women, did he? No. He gave me jewellery, fine clothing. He took me in his carriage. Had he done this for any of the other women?

The bell tinkled, and I jerked as if roughly awakened. Through the open door I heard Govind's slow shuffle, then a voice. A man's voice. I jumped up, my heart swinging heavily like the hanging brass disc on the standing clock in the hallway. I rushed to the top of the stairs and looked down. There, in the open doorway, with the light from the street behind him, was David, holding his hat in one hand, his other firmly holding the door open. Govind had both his hands on the knob, as if trying to close the door against David.

I made a sound in my throat, and both of them looked up at me. David's scar was losing its colour, turning silver. And his face looked different in some small way, as if something within was not as bright.

I couldn't speak; my heart and its heavy beat seemed to have pushed up into my throat. I gripped the railing at the top of the stairs, frozen to the spot and unable to rush down, to run to him, as I wanted.

The terrible photographs, and now David here – here, finally – looking up at me, his face so familiar, so concerned. I think I whispered his name.

'Daryâ?' he said, and stepped forward, into the hall. Govind stood there, frowning, and finally closed the door and started up the stairs.

'I will fetch Mr Osric,' Govind said. 'He rests.'

'No,' David said to him, and spoke rapidly, in Hindi. Govind looked back at him, shaking his head, answering in Hindi and appearing slightly confused. He continued up the stairs, brushing past me, and I went down.

'Daryâ, are you all right?' David asked, immediately stepping closer as soon as I reached the bottom of the stairs. I was suddenly aware of my clothing; I must have left the veil in the drawing room. I looked down, seeing the tops of my breasts, my legs visible through the sheer pantaloons. Did David notice? He peered intently into my face. 'You're not ill?'

I swallowed. 'I am very well,' I said, finally finding my voice, although it came out breathless, lower than usual.

'Are you really?' He was still studying my face.

'Why do you look surprised?' I asked him, in that same low voice, wanting to touch his scar again, knowing how it would feel under my fingertips.

'Because . . . I've come every day, Daryâ. Every day, sometimes twice, starting the day after we arrived in London,' he said, his eyes dropping, for only a moment, to my chest, and then quickly coming back to my eyes. I fought the impulse to put up my hands to cover myself. 'And every time I've rung the bell either Govind or Bull himself has told me you were ill, or sleeping, and would not receive company,' he said, his voice edged with anger. 'I was turned away every time, Daryâ. Every time,' he repeated, stepping even closer and shaking his head. 'But this time I refused. I pushed in before Govind could close the door. I had to see you. To make sure . . .' his voice trailed off, and again his eyes momentarily dropped to my clothing, and I felt a flush rise from my neck.

I thought of the number of times I'd heard the bell ring. 'But I've not been ill at all, nor sleeping.' I wanted to say his name, but wouldn't let myself. 'I've been here, every day but . . . but yesterday, when we went for a ride in the carriage . . .' *When I saw you with your woman.* At the remembrance of the beautiful woman in pink, the woman who held his arm, I stepped back, and my voice returned to normal. She was his woman. 'Osric didn't tell me you'd come.'

As I said Osric's name I sensed a subtle change in David's expression. 'I did see you, yesterday, Daryâ. That's why I refused to be turned away today. Because I knew you were well enough to go out. I saw only a glimpse – your veil, and your eyes above it in the carriage window. I tried to get to you before you drove off; I wanted to –'

Again he came closer, and my body reacted almost as though I had no control, softening, moving towards him as if pulled by invisible silk. My arms lifted, and then I thought of the cord around the woman's neck in the photo, and caught my breath.

'What is it? Daryâ, look at me. Tell me what—'

'This is an unexpected visit,' Osric said, his voice booming as he came down the steps. He was buttoning his jacket, and his hair was uncharacteristically uncombed, his shirt collar crooked. His skin had the colour of uncooked dough, his lips colourless. He rubbed his hands together in a dry, raspy rhythm as he stood beside me at the bottom of the stairs.

'Is it, Mr Bull? It's no different to my calls over the last few days. Except this time it's obvious Daryâ is able to receive a visitor.' David's face was stiff, darker now. His voice was cold, his words polite and yet the tone disrespectful.

Osric straightened his collar. 'What is the nature of your call?' he asked, in a bored tone.

David lowered his chin. 'I wanted to see Daryâ. To make sure that all was well.'

'Why wouldn't it be?' Osric asked. Now his voice matched David's: thinly disguised anger.

I looked from one to the other, and then David said, more quietly, 'Daryâ? You do appear as if you're able to go out now. So I'd like to invite you to join my mother and me for dinner, at our home. Perhaps Wednesday, or Thursday?'

Before I could reply Osric put his arm around my waist. I stiffened, feeling his hand, hot, through the almost-transparent fabric.

David looked at it.

'That's very kind, but Daryâ has other plans for the week. Plans with me. Don't we, Daryâ *jan*?' Osric said.

I couldn't answer, shamed at Osric's display in front of David, and then felt his fingers exert more pressure against my waist. 'Don't we, my dear?' he repeated, slowly, and I again thought of the woman in the photograph. I nodded, looking at the floor, not wanting to see David's face.

'And I'm sure, Mr Ingram, that you're very busy with your own life,' Osric went on. 'I have explained to Daryâ that there must be so many people, so many social events for you to attend, after being away for so long.'

'Daryâ?' David said to me. 'Are you sure you wouldn't care to come for dinner? When you're not . . . as occupied. I could send a carriage for you . . .' He waited.

I raised my eyes to look at him, and thought of the girl in pink again, her hand on David's arm. And it all came back to me: how he'd made me feel that I was something special to him, that what he felt for me was . . . I raised my chin. I was not proud of what I had become with

Osric, but I could still show some dignity in front of David, pretend to be the proud Tajik woman he had once known. I would not run to him, cling to him and say *I am beginning to be afraid here, David, I think Osric is not what he tries to appear.* I would not beg David to help me as I had too many times before. And I would not sit at a table and try to eat, the food dry as ashes in my mouth, while I watched David with his beautiful woman.

I was worthless now, although in a different way to how I had been in Afghanistan. I would not show this shame to David. He had his betrothed, the woman he loved. He would soon forget me, and the sooner he did, the less I would feel this pain.

'No, thank you,' I said firmly, lifting my chin. 'As Osric has said, we are very busy.'

He blinked rapidly. 'You don't wish to see m—'

'As I said, once before . . .' I interrupted, although my voice faltered. I took a deep breath, 'I'm very grateful for all the ways you have helped me. I owe my life to you. But now I am in England, and no longer your responsibility,' I said, echoing Osric's former words. 'There is no reason for you to see me again. Please don't come any more. I am . . . I am happy here.'

Osric's fingers now caressed my waist.

'With Osric,' I added, my voice barely above a whisper, and yet it appeared that I had shouted, so strange was David's expression, and the way he drew back his head as if he'd been struck.

He didn't reply for a moment, then said, simply, 'Daryâ,' in a voice that was strangely intimate, even though I stood with Osric's arm around me, his hand tight on my waist, his breath in my ear. David speaking my name in that particular tone made me feel as if we were on the lower deck of the ship, in the dark, with the glorious stars above us, the mysterious ocean beneath us.

I felt as though I might sway as I had when walking on land after months at sea.

I looked into his eyes, wanting him to know why I said what I did, why I asked him – told him – to never come again.

But it was clear he didn't understand. His face grew very still when I didn't say anything more, and then became paler, his scar more apparent again.

'Govind,' Osric said, and there was a movement behind us. 'Show

Mr Ingram out.' He spoke slowly, the words heavy and filled with satisfaction.

As Govind went to the door and opened it, David turned as if to leave, but then looked back and spoke one final time, staring at me with a look I couldn't identify. 'Well then. Good.' His voice was too loud, as unnatural as his expression. 'I'm pleased for you, Daryâ. That this has actually turned out to be what you hoped for. That you're happy.' He put on his hat. 'And free. That's what you wanted, wasn't it? To be free.' His eyes ran over my clothing, the earrings I still wore from the evening before. Had I washed my face this morning, or were my eyes smudged with the kohl Osric had applied?

I opened my mouth, wanting to say something, wanting to make him understand, but he left then, slamming the door with such force that the knob was pulled from Govind's hand.

The noise echoed in my head, slam, slam, slam, loud and final, and I sagged heavily against Osric. He held my arm, firmly, as he led me back up to the drawing room. He ordered tea, and as we waited he walked back and forth in front of the fireplace, smoothing his hair with one hand over and over. I watched him, my heart so heavy I couldn't speak.

'Well. That was a less than pleasant experience,' Osric finally said, his voice sharp and loud. 'Such arrogance, arriving here unannounced with no other purpose but to bother us,' he said, stopping and looking into my face. 'Really, you look quite pathetic, Daryâ. I can't imagine what David Ingram said to upset you so.' He smiled down at me almost fondly; I had curled into a big chair with my knees drawn up. I laid my cheek on them, not wanting to see Osric, not wanting to hear his voice. 'And I'm proud of you for putting him in his place. He won't be bothering you any more. Well done.'

Govind brought in the tea, and I asked, for the first time, for laudanum. I wanted its powers to help me through the next long hours, when I would have to face the fact that I had lost David Ingram for ever.

I drank my tea and what it contained, keeping my head down so Osric wouldn't see my wet eyes, or guess what might be written on my forehead.

CHAPTER FORTY-FOUR

FIVE DAYS HAD passed since David had come, five days since I had told him I did not wish to see him ever again. Now I had been in London almost two weeks, and the house was always warm, the fireplaces no longer lit. The foul smell of the streets came in through the open windows, and my fingers came away dark and gritty when I put my hands on the sill to lean out. My unclean time had come, and, unlike the monthly dread this had caused me when I was with Shaliq, knowing it would bring on his rage, now I was pleased, for it meant Osric would not come to me for at least this brief time. I looked at the darkroom door every time I passed it, thinking of the photograph of the woman with the cord around her neck.

In the warmth of a late afternoon I sat in a chair by the drawing-room window and Osric lay on the divan. When Govind came in to remove the tea tray I glanced at Osric. His eyes were shut, his mouth open, and tiny, huffing sounds came from between his lips. He had smoked his *chelem* for a long time. I said Govind's name and he shuffled to me.

'Yes, Missy? You wish something?' he whispered.

'Sometimes . . . you want home, Govind?' I asked.

He bent near me. 'Home, Missy?' He shook his head. 'India is too far for me now. I am too old.'

'But you think of India? You think of home?'

'Oh yes, Missy. Always.'

'You are sad then?'

'Sad? No, no longer. It is too hard to be sad.' He straightened. 'But' – he looked over my head, out the window – 'I dream I will die in my true home. My body floating on Ganga Ma – Mother Ganges – not lying under cold English soil.' He shook his head. 'I am only a foolish old man,' he said, still gazing out the window. 'It cannot be.'

'I think I go home soon,' I said, looking up at him.

He glanced over his shoulder, at Osric, and then back to me. 'Maybe,' he said, his whisper even softer, and put his hand, lightly, on my shoulder.

When he left I stood and pulled the curtains open wider.

'Close them, Daryâ,' Osric grumbled, stirring and putting his hand over his eyes. 'Too bright.'

I went to him. 'Can I go outside, Osric?' I asked.

He sat up, smoothing his moustache with his fingers. 'No. Of course not. Maybe in a few days I'll take you for another ride in the brougham,' he said. 'Other than that, you stay inside.'

I remembered his words in the godown in Bombay, when I'd asked him if he would put me in a cage, like the bear in the photograph. Then I turned away, angry at him for his lies, angry at myself for believing him.

I stared over the rooftops at what I could see of the sky. 'At home at this time of day the sky is freshly washed, a clean blue that smells of . . . of hope. It trembles above us, this sky, trembles lightly, as if leaving room for our thoughts to fly up, fly away, into that fragrant air. But here,' I went on, 'here the sky is like a basin of dirty water in which the city sinks. Into which we sink. Our bodies. Our minds.'

He stood, stretching.

'What's brought on this discontent?' he asked, obviously unconcerned as he lifted his half-full cup of cold tea to his mouth and drank.

My jaw was tight, aching with the effort of holding my temper as I tried to explain. 'I need something to do, Osric. I have nothing to do. With my hands or,' I touched my temple, the way he did when one of his headaches was starting, 'or here.' He didn't answer, and I walked up and down in front of the window, turning sharply at the end of the room and walking back again. 'I must move, Osric. Move and think. Don't you see that?'

'Don't be so dramatic, Daryâ. It's tiresome.'

'Tiresome? But . . . I must have something to *do*; I must keep my body busy so that my thoughts can flow. Without my body moving it's as if my head, too, is idle.' This wasn't true; I had too many thoughts, thoughts that swirled around in confusion – of my family, of my country, of David – of all the things that were now lost to me. All sad thoughts.

'Very well, my dear,' he said, patting the seat beside him. 'You have been a good and patient girl. And you have pleased me in many ways.' He raised his eyebrows, and saliva came to my mouth at his suggestive leer. I swallowed, but went and sat beside him.

'So you should be rewarded, have something you enjoy doing,' he said, pushing my hair back over my shoulder. 'Let me think.' He looked towards the window, then nodded. 'Yes. You could wind the clocks for me,' he said.

'The clocks?' I asked. 'Wind the clocks?' My voice rose in disbelief at his suggestion.

'Yes. It requires some time, going to every room and winding each of them. Govind is getting slower and slower, and I'm afraid he's not keeping up with all his duties. Mrs Wimby has made it clear the job is beneath her, and I don't trust Lucy or little Ella to handle them. But you could do it, with those quick hands, those clever fingers.' His tone was as if placating a bad-tempered child with the offer of something sweet to quiet an outburst. He picked up my hand and pressed his mouth to my fingertips, and at the feel of his damp lips I grew more and more angry.

Wind the clocks. I, who had carried weight on my back like a sturdy pony as we moved camp, who had stood in icy streams up to my knees and pounded heavy clothing against rocks, who could put up a goat-hair tent in less time than it took a full pot of water to boil over the fire. Who had travelled through foreign lands, who had endured illness and loneliness and fear. And now I was to be given the task of turning little keys to ensure that the minutes and the hours of the day could pass with the ticking reminder of lost time. I couldn't think of an appropriate reply for a few moments. There was a persistent pounding behind my eyes.

And then I snatched my hand from his grip, and held up both my hands; they were shaking. 'Do you really think these fingers would be made happy turning keys?'

Osric stared at me, his face so close that I saw the dull gleam of dried spittle on the edge of his moustache. 'Don't talk to me like that, Daryâ. We were having a perfectly pleasant time. You asked for something to do, and I've assigned something to you. But again you react ungratefully. You've completely annoyed me,' he said then, his voice taking on a warning tone. 'Again.' He stood and pulled down his cuffs. 'I won't stand for this. I've told you more than once.' Now his jaw clenched. 'Do you not yet understand? Who do you think you're speaking to?'

Better you be good, Missy. Govind's words rang in my head. *When he doesn't want them any more, he pushes them aside . . . Or . . .*

I turned away.

'I'll get Govind to show you the routine with the clocks,' he said. 'I'm glad I thought of it. You can start tomorrow, and I'll expect you to do it every day,' he said, his voice harsh. 'Well?'

I looked up at him.

'Do you not have something to say?'

'Thank you, Osric,' I said, tonelessly, and he nodded, and left.

The weather grew hotter as the weeks passed, and occasionally a stinking yellow fog floated over the street outside. As Lucy cleaned my room one morning she told me to keep my bedroom window closed at night, as the warm air now carried disease.

'It is summer?' I asked her, and the way she looked at me before she answered, 'Yes, Miss,' gave me an uneasy feeling. Her look and voice had suggested a kind of surprised pity, and I was ashamed at my ignorance. I had no knowledge of what went on outside the windows.

Osric never again took me outside, although he frequently left the house, and every morning I stared out of my window, seeing only what I had seen every day since my arrival at his townhouse in Kensington: the back windows of the house across the lane. I didn't see the little girl with the dark hair any more, and after some time wondered if I had only imagined her, thinking of Nasreen. When I thought like this I wondered if I might be losing my mind, might be becoming like Utmarkhail, shuffling aimlessly, mindlessly about, although, unlike her, I had no desire for food, and ate only enough to keep from feeling ill.

Since I had said the final goodbye to David, and my life had narrowed down and become trapped within the walls of this house, I often felt as though I wore a heavy *châdari* which not only shrouded my sight and made it difficult to move with ease, but also seemed to darken my thinking with its heaviness. I asked for the laudanum in my tea every afternoon now; it was the only thing I looked forward to, for it provided a few hours of escape, and I would lie on the red divan and doze until dinner was served.

I had also instructed Govind to bring me another cup of tea with laudanum in the evening, before I went to Osric's room. Govind brought it to me faithfully, his face expressionless, and once I said, without fully knowing why, 'I am sorry, Govind,' as I drank it, standing in front of him.

He took the cup from my hand and just shook his head, saying, 'Missy', before leaving.

But the laudanum made the time on the wide bed less sad and distasteful for me. With it my body became more pliant, slipping languorously into the positions Osric requested, and while he enjoyed himself I could float in a half-dream, the words he wanted to hear me say emerging from my mouth as if spoken by someone else.

One afternoon when Osric was out I lay in the hot, airless drawing room, the teacup loose in my fingers. I had tried to look through a book of paintings I'd taken from a bookcase, but I couldn't concentrate, and had let the book slip to the carpet. Govind came and touched my hand, and I opened my eyes and looked at him.

'You have visitor, Missy Daryâ,' he whispered, his face slightly disturbed.

David? I ran my hands across my eyes, touched my hair. And then I stopped. It wouldn't be David.

'I bring her,' he said then, and I frowned, not sure if I'd understood the feminine *her*. I heard Govind's footsteps followed by lighter ones, and stood up. A small woman came in, and my mouth opened.

'Oh,' I said, my eyes widening in surprise. 'Mrs Ingram.'

'Hello, Daryâ,' she said, her voice quiet and yet carrying undeniable force. She seemed slightly distracted as she looked at me, tilting her head to one side, her smile so familiar – so like her son's – that I felt my own mouth tremble as I attempted to smile back.

When I'd seen her at the dock I'd been disoriented, distressed over saying goodbye to David, about going with Osric, and I hadn't taken in much more than her pale hair and dark eyes and warm smile. Now she smiled again, and I realised she was pleasant to look at, and would have been attractive in the quiet English way when a younger woman. The gold flecks in the brown of her eyes were more apparent now, and her blonde hair, threaded with greying, darker blonde, was twisted into a smooth knot, although wisps framed her face, and a few tendrils tried to escape at her collar. I knew her hair, when unpinned, would be like

David's. She wore a pale lilac dress that accentuated her small frame, and a matching bonnet and white gloves. She carried a small silk bag of a deeper purple hue.

Govind hovered behind her, and Mrs Ingram turned to him. 'When do you expect him back, then?'

'He did not say, Memsâhib. He has been gone a few hours.'

She nodded. Govind was obviously distressed by having her here without Osric present, and I felt he hadn't wanted her to come in, but she'd insisted. Like David had. Now he gestured to a chair.

'You will wait for him, Memsâhib?' he asked.

But instead of sitting she just nodded in a slightly occupied manner and then came to me. 'I'm happy to see you again, Daryâ. You're adjusting to our English weather, and feeling well?' she asked, speaking very slowly, smiling, but as she studied my face and her eyes took in my clothing, the smile faltered slightly.

'Yes. I am well,' I said, and she looked at me with that same intent stare.

'David has told me that he had difficulty seeing you,' she said.

I didn't know what to say.

She glanced back at Govind. 'You may leave us,' she stated, with authority.

He nodded and bowed his head, his hands under his chin, and backed out.

'But you are truly well?' she asked again, even though I'd already answered her. 'You . . .' she still studied my face, my eyes in particular, and then she took my hand. 'Come. I want . . . I need to speak with you.'

We went to the divan and sat beside each other. 'I took a risk coming here. Not knowing whether Mr Bull would welcome me into his home,' she said. 'We do not care for each other.' She stopped, then said, 'And even if he allowed me in, I didn't know if I'd have the chance to speak to you – alone like this. Can you understand me?'

'If you speak . . . slow. Yes. I do not know to say all words, but understand many.' I had to concentrate deeply as she spoke, and it was difficult. I wished I hadn't had the laudanum earlier; I wished my mind was clear, sharp as it had once been. Why had she come? I was confused.

'I've worried about you.'

This was even more confusing. 'About me? But . . . why?'

She glanced at the *chelem*. 'David doesn't know I've come. He has seemed very disturbed since he's been back. Not himself.' I tried to picture his face as the young woman in the pink dress spoke to him. Had his face been disturbed? I couldn't remember now. 'I know the voyage was a difficult one for him,' Mrs Ingram went on. 'He told me . . . that he spoke to you about why he'd gone to Afghanistan.' She glanced away, pulling off her white gloves, setting them in her lap, then looked back at me. 'David has told me a little about you. You were married to a Pushtun?' she asked. 'Of what tribe?'

David had told the truth about his mother – she was indeed different, in some way that I couldn't name. She was not like the other memsâhibs I had seen, both in Bombay and on the ship, but seemed genuinely interested in me, and to find my appearance – my *harquus* – neither offensive nor overly curious.

'The Ghilzai,' I said, realising, as I did, why she had asked. Who David's father must have been. I looked at her hands, tightly clasped. They were delicate, the nails neat and short.

As if reading my face, she nodded. 'David has told me he confided in you; you know that his father was not my husband, not an Englishman.' She sat straighter, squaring her shoulders, and spoke firmly. 'I was not myself when I went to spend time far in the north of India one hot season. It was there at Simla, near the North-West Frontier, not far from the border of your country . . .' She stopped as a horse and carriage rumbled by outside the window, with cries of '*Hoy! Hoy!*' 'I surely did not plan such a thing, but unforeseen circumstances were such that I . . . grew close to a man there. A man such as your husband.'

I grimaced, shaking my head rapidly. 'No. Not like my husband.'

'I only meant he was a Pushtun,' she said, quickly. 'A kind and thoughtful man.' She looked to the window now, and I thought of Kaled. David's father could have been a man like Kaled.

'But no one knew,' she continued, shaking her head slightly and looking back at me. And then, when I discovered that I carried the child that was David . . .' She glanced towards the closed door. 'There may not be time to say all of this – I didn't know if I'd even have the chance,' she repeated. 'But . . .'

I looked into her eyes, again seeing the flash of gold.

'When David told me that you would come here, to live with Osric Bull, even before I understood that you meant a great deal to my son, I was terribly worried.'

I waited, watching her mouth, struggling to understand as much as I could. Had she said I meant something to David? Is that what she'd said?

'I knew Osric Bull in Calcutta. He was a friend of my husband's.' She picked up her gloves from her lap, twisting them, and I realised that she was very nervous, in spite of her calm face. I sensed she was capable of keeping her emotions disguised, and knew how and why she had learned to do this, keeping David's secret for so many years. 'Osric appeared the perfect gentleman in public. Like my husband,' she went on, and a sudden brief loss of control flitted over her face as she uttered this last phrase. Was it the same look that had been on my face only moments before, when I had thought of Shaliq?

'I was visiting an Indian midwife – one who would help with David's birth. Do you understand?'

I nodded.

'I went to her in secret.' She dropped her gloves and unconsciously put a hand on her abdomen, and I imagined her terror at what she faced. How alone she must have felt. 'White women were not to associate with these women, but I went because . . .' she hesitated, then said, 'I was afraid, before David was born, that if he looked . . . I had no one to turn to, and she offered comfort, and help.' She licked her lips and suddenly her face gave way, and I saw her as a young woman, perhaps the age I was now, and felt compassion, understanding what strength it must have taken to go through such an ordeal. 'While I was there one day, Osric arrived. With an Indian girl. The midwife tried to help her, but it was too late. The girl died within a few moments.' She shook her head, still saddened at that old memory.

'Because of baby?'

'No. She did carry a child, but there were other things . . . she was no more than twelve or thirteen, Daryâ. And she'd been . . . misused . . . can you understand?'

'No. Not this word.'

'She'd been hurt. Her body . . .'

I nodded, swallowing hard. Osric had been hurting girls – women – all these years, then?

'When Osric saw me he said he had found her, that she was one of his servant's daughters, but I understood. He wouldn't have brought her to this place if what he said was true; her family would have cared for her. And I also knew by the way she was dressed what he'd used her for.'

I sorted it all out in my head, translating her words. Osric had brought a young girl to the midwife. She carried a baby, but he'd hurt her. She died. Mrs Ingram didn't go to an English doctor when she carried David. I looked down at my pantaloons. The sheer blue fabric appeared to swim and ripple, and I knew my legs were trembling. Had he dressed the young girl he'd hurt – he'd killed – in a similar fashion to how I was dressed now?

'I knew what he'd done, but he also saw me in a place I shouldn't be. The way he looked at me . . .' she paused again. 'As I understood what had brought him to the midwife, he had an idea why I was there.' Her face was now as white as her collar.

'I would not have been forgiven, Daryâ. I would have been cast out not only by my husband, but by the rest of the English in Calcutta – and the disgrace would have even followed me back to England, if it was known that I carried another man's child. Not just another man's, but a man of . . . another race. I didn't care what happened to me, but I had to think of my child. David. I had to, didn't I? That's what a mother does.' The strain showed around her eyes and mouth now. She suddenly leaned heavily against the back of the divan.

'Mrs Ingram? No one see what I see when I look David? His eyes – when I first look him, I see Pushtun.'

She spoke again, so quickly that I shook my head, and she stopped, then spoke again, much more slowly. 'I worried about the shape and darkness of David's eyes . . . of course *I* saw David's true father when I looked at him, but in the polite English society of Calcutta no one seemed to suspect – or if they did, they wouldn't speak of such a thing, because my husband clearly believed David to be his. And my husband was a man no one dared anger. He was like Osric Bull in that way.

'But he – Osric Bull – being the kind of man he is, guessed the truth when he saw me, in my obvious condition, at the Indian midwife's. He didn't speak to me, Daryâ. He just looked into my face and smiled.'

I knew the smile she spoke of, the one of superiority, of smug certainty that he would have what he wanted.

'Of course I couldn't tell anyone where I'd seen him, or what he'd done to that poor child, because it would be questioned why I was there. But whenever Osric Bull saw me after that, once David was born, he'd always look at him, and then at me and smile, that particular smile, and nod. He knew that David's father was a native. No words were ever spoken, but I saw it in his face, the knowledge of the truth about David. He knew.'

Mrs Ingram's whole body was now trembling from reliving that emotional time. 'And I know the truth about him,' she said, and the door opened, and Govind stood there.

'Mr Osric's carriage arrives,' he announced, and Mrs Ingram closed her eyes, breathing deeply. When she opened them she fixed a smile on her face, raising her chin. Her face was completely composed again, as if we'd been discussing nothing more serious than the weather.

She moved from beside me to sit on a chair.

Footsteps sounded on the stairs, and suddenly Mrs Ingram turned to me as she put on her gloves, whispering urgently. 'Do you still have the card – the one David gave you at the dock?'

Before I could answer Osric came into the drawing room, rubbing his hands. 'Well. Mrs Ingram,' he said, his voice brisk. 'I was very surprised when Govind told me you had come. Rather unusual, you stepping down in this way.' He raised one eyebrow. 'Just out for a drive, were you, and decided to stop in? How uncharacteristic, Mrs Ingram, for one of your class.'

I didn't understand what he meant, but obviously Mrs Ingram did, for her lips tightened, and a crease appeared between her eyebrows.

'And it's apparent your son has the same lack of decorum; are you aware he also made a habit of calling without being invited?' He shook his head as if sad, but immediately a half-smile that was oddly menacing came to his lips. 'So it is a pity you've had to wait for me, but of course you should have sent a calling card to avoid this embarrassment. Shame on you,' he said. 'Tut tut, Mrs Ingram.'

Now I knew he was somehow mocking her; it was unpleasant and I was ashamed for him. But Mrs Ingram's frown smoothed, and she smiled in an almost girlish way.

'I apologise, Mr Bull,' she said, her voice high and light. 'As you guessed, I was simply out for a drive, and well, it was a whim, terribly rude, I know.' She spoke with such surety that even I didn't doubt her, although I knew she didn't speak the truth, that she had come specifically to see me. It was clear she and Osric played a game of words with each other.

'David introduced me to Miss Daryâ at the docks, and as I came through Kensington this afternoon I suddenly thought of her and wondered about her adjustment to English life.' She smiled brightly and patted her forehead with a small lacy square she took from her bag, glancing at me. 'We haven't managed to have much conversation, but she appears well. My, it's warm.'

'Yes,' Osric said, still standing. 'Were you offered refreshments?' He said this unconvincingly, as if simply pretending to be polite.

Mrs Ingram stood now. 'Oh please, don't trouble yourself. But thank you. And now I really must go.' Her politeness appeared natural, unlike Osric's attempts. She started across the room, then stopped and looked back at me. 'Daryâ? I shall tell David I saw you, shall I? And that you are fine.'

I nodded, trying not to think of him with his betrothed, holding her as he'd held me. Kissing her lips.

'Did you wish to send him a message? Something you'd like me to tell him?'

I glanced at Osric; his face was dark. He crossed his arms over his chest, one foot tapping impatiently.

'You will say to him . . .' What could I tell him? 'I hope he is happy. In his marriage.'

Osric cleared his throat as Mrs Ingram frowned. 'His marriage?'

'To Miss Gwendolyn Liston,' Osric said, loudly. 'Did I not hear word of their engagement even before David left on this last trip?'

Mrs Ingram shook her head. 'You must be mistaken, Mr Bull,' she said, her voice surprised. 'David and Miss Liston have known each other since childhood, in Calcutta. They see each other at social events, as they have many friends in common, but . . . where would you have heard that?'

They were speaking too quickly; Osric was mistaken, Mrs Ingram said. Mistaken about . . . I heard the woman's name, the name of David's betrothed. I stepped up to Mrs Ingram.

'David does not marry woman in pink dress?'

She shook her head. 'I don't know who you mean. But no, he's not marrying Gwendolyn Liston or anyone.' She looked at Osric again, but he merely raised one shoulder.

'Govind will show you out,' he said then, and Govind stepped forward.

'Goodbye, Daryâ,' she said, and I echoed, 'Goodbye', and watched her leave, her back straight and her shoulders firm.

When the front door closed Osric shouted for Govind as he sank into his red chair. 'Pour me a drink,' he said, when the old man appeared. Govind went to the collection of tall bottles on a brass-topped table, and poured half a glass of amber liquid, bringing it to Osric on a small silver tray.

Osric took it roughly, some of the liquid slopping over. 'You had no right to allow that woman – or anyone – in when I'm not here.' He glared up at Govind. 'I've given you strict orders, and yet you seem to open the door to anyone. You're becoming more and more useless. I should have been rid of you years ago, should have someone who knows how to take orders.'

Govind stood silently.

'Remember what I've told you, Govind. If you're no longer able to carry out your duties properly, I can't keep you in my employ.' He drank, his expression brooding. 'And you know what that will mean for you,' he said, staring at Govind over the rim of his glass. 'It *is* clear, isn't it?'

Govind hadn't moved, holding the empty tray, and I was still in the spot I had been in when I'd looked into Mrs Ingram's face and asked her about David, where I'd stood when she told me that he was not betrothed, would not marry.

I watched Osric drain his glass and then demand another, and I thought about what Mrs Ingram had told me about him and the Indian girl, and about the photograph of the dead woman.

Of the lie he'd told me about David.

Osric gulped down his second drink and then pulled me by my arm up the stairs to his room, slamming the door. But he was angry, the smell of the alcohol strong on his breath, and although I was in that room with Osric, my mind was somewhere else, somewhere far from him, my body limp and unresponsive. It didn't go well; he wasn't pleased with his performance and blamed me, telling me to get out, to go back to my room.

After a long while, when the light began to fade, I went and stood at my window. In the early evening light the little dark-haired girl came again to the window across from me. This time her hair was tied with a white ribbon.

She was real, then, and not a figment of my imagination. I waved at her, and she held up a small pretty doll with yellow curls, pressing it against the glass to show it to me, and I smiled, nodding at her.

David, I mouthed against the glass, fogging it with my breath.

He was not betrothed. All this time, he had not been in love with another woman, had not dreamed of, or held, or kissed another woman.

I smiled again, although the little girl was no longer at her window.

CHAPTER FORTY-FIVE

DAVID WAS NOT betrothed. It was all I could think about all through that night, and then the next morning. Now I had to find a way to take back the words I had said to him, to let him know that I was not happy with Osric, that I had lied. That yes, yes, I would come to his home. For dinner, as he had once asked. For anything. I would come to him. Yes.

The house was oddly busy that whole day; Mrs Wimby hurrying about, following Lucy and Ella, giving them directions in a low, sharp voice, and speaking to Osric more than I had witnessed before. Govind carried in a number of large vases of flowers, placing them in the drawing room and dining room and hallways. The thin boy, Pete, and Lucy moved furniture into different positions in the drawing room, directed by Osric, and I wondered at it all.

I stayed quiet, sensing Osric was still not pleased with me over the recent failure in his bedroom, and I didn't want to anger him further. I knew that if I were to find a way to see David again, I must do exactly what Osric wanted, what he asked.

Towards the end of the afternoon Osric came to find me. 'Daryâ,' he said, and I was relieved that both his face and voice were normal, as if there had been nothing unsatisfactory between us. In fact, he appeared excited. 'I shall have company tonight,' he said, smiling. 'An evening of guests.'

'Guests?' Would he have me come out, or keep me hidden in my room?

'Yes. And you will feel very comfortable, I can assure you. There's no need to worry about anything.'

I was surprised at this, and even more so when he continued.

'I'm sure you'll enjoy yourself with these particular friends. Unbraid your hair, and wear it loose. Apply your kohl, and put on the red and gold – my favourite.' He tilted his head, looking jaunty. 'It's the summer solstice, and we're celebrating with a Midsummer Eve party.'

He pulled me to my feet with both hands, and then said,

'And the glow-worm came,
with its silvery flame,
and sparkled and shone
through the night of St John.
And soon has the young maid her love-knot tied.'

I stood, watching his mouth, realising he was reciting English poetry, although it didn't make sense.

'Off you go now,' he said, calling after me as I went up the stairs. 'Tonight it would be most appropriate to wear a veil. Wait in your room until I fetch you.'

As I waited for Osric, I hoped for a brief moment that David would be among the guests, but immediately let the thought go, for I had seen how Osric had looked at David, how he'd treated him the day he'd come to the door.

The noise from below grew louder and louder – the arrival of many carriages outside, voices laughing and calling, the shake of the house as feet went up and down the stairs.

When Osric finally opened my door I gasped, drawing back. He wore an eye mask that sparkled with minuscule pieces of blue glass. It had a moulded pointed beak that fit over his nose.

'Don't be alarmed, my dear,' he said, shouting to be heard over the music and rumbling of men's voices and the shrieks of women's laughter coming from below. He stepped into my room and closed the door, muting the sounds. 'It's part of the celebration. All the guests are in fancy dress. I considered having a costume devised for you, but with your luminous eyes above your veil, and your *harquus* standing out in such a wonderful pattern on your forehead, you are quite enough of a vision. I can't wait to exhibit you to those below.' He held out his arm, and I took it.

As we descended the stairs, there was too much for me to take in. I saw only a crush of bodies moving as if they were a wave of water. The air was hot and smoky, and a wall of smells – tobacco and powdery fragrances, underlaid with a whisper of sweat – rushed up to meet me. Music floated from the drawing room. And then I was able to see individuals more clearly. I watched a man lift his mask – of a horse with a horn growing from its forehead – to drink from his full glass. Another man, in a one-piece costume with a long, forked tail attached, shamelessly put his mouth to the naked neck of a young woman who wore a mask of glorious, spiked red feathers. He took small, playful bites at her white throat.

Osric took me into the drawing room; here the air was even thicker with smoke, for both men and women not only smoked long, thin dark cheroots, but also took turns at the *chelem*. Everyone drank from long-stemmed glasses served by men in fine black suits and white gloves. Some also carried trays of small foods; I didn't see Govind, and knew he would never manage in this mass, trying to make his way up and down the stairs with a heavy silver tray. Three men dressed similarly to the men who served the food and drink made music with stringed instruments, but nobody gave them the respect of watching or listening.

Osric threaded his way through the crowd, holding me close at his side, stopping constantly. 'This is my newest guest, Miss Daryâ,' he would say. 'Isn't she magnificent? I found her in Bombay,' he might add, or, 'Mind you, she did not shine as she does now, with my influence.' He held my arm tightly, and his smile never wavered. I wanted to stop, to listen and try to understand what I could of conversations, to try and speak, but Osric wouldn't allow it. It seemed he must present me to every person, and accept their compliments as they agreed with him on my exotic beauty, on my fortune in travelling to England to be a guest of Osric's. And then suddenly he looked over my head, frowning. 'Excuse me,' he said, 'I'll return in a moment,' and he left me in front of a small group of people.

I smiled in a friendly manner under my veil, knowing they could see this in my eyes, but they paid me no attention, talking rapidly amongst themselves. The women who didn't wear masks wore too much false colour on their faces, their cheeks and lips unnaturally red. The men laughed too loudly, blowing smoke into the air, and some already walked unsteadily from the effects of alcohol. The behaviour of both the men and women was less than dignified; I instinctively knew they were not honourable people. This didn't come as a surprise, knowing what I did of Osric.

I wandered towards the hall, wanting to be away from the smoke. As I started down the steps a woman in a mask of white china that covered only her eyes stopped me with her hand on my arm. She leaned close and touched the *harquus* on my forehead. 'What have you painted those on with?' she shouted into my face.

I shook my head. 'Not paint. *Harquus*.'

'What's that?' she asked, louder still.

I tried to remember the English word. 'Tattoo,' I said.

A man stopped with a tray; she took a tiny triangle of bread spread with dark paste, and I took a glass of ruby liquid. But as I lifted it to my lips and smelled alcohol I lowered it, holding the stem between my fingers.

'Why are you tattooed, then?'

Before I had time to answer she turned to the man beside her. He didn't wear a mask, but had a band with horns over the top of his head. 'Look at the strange lightness of her eyes, Bith,' he said.

'Open wide, darling,' the woman said, as if she hadn't heard him, and as the man opened his mouth she put the piece of food into it, and he closed his lips around her fingers, sucking on them. She tapped his chest with the fan she carried, her laughter a high trill. The man chewed, staring at me. Others pushed past us, and I looked down the stairs into the milling entrance hall. Even if there were the slightest chance David were actually here, how would I recognise him in this sea of masks? But he would recognise me, and come to me, wouldn't he, even though I'd told him the lie of my happiness? And then I could tell him the truth. That I wasn't happy here, that I wanted to leave, as soon as possible. That I didn't want to have to look upon Osric Bull's face one more night, and that it was his face – David's – that I thought of.

'Quite different, isn't she?' the man with the horns asked the woman, and she said, 'I suppose so.'

'If you'll excuse me,' the man said, and in the next instant reached up and pulled away my veil, taking it into his hands. I was so shocked at his forwardness that I didn't react except to squeeze the fragile stem of the glass. 'I'm a painter. What do you think, Bithia? Doesn't she have something – the longing and, perhaps, the sensuous loneliness of the young woman in the seraglio?' He stepped back, cocking his head as he stared at me. 'Yes. Perfect. The lonely *houri*.' Other masked people closed in, surrounding me like a pack of crows around a newly dead animal. I wanted my veil back, and put my hand out towards it.

'Oh, Osric,' the man said, looking behind me and unintentionally moving the veil out of my reach. 'I must talk to you about this enchanting woman.'

I turned. Osric was on the step above me; he took the glass from my hand.

'Wherever did you find this treasure?' the man asked.

Osric frowned slightly.

'I would love to paint her, Os. Will you lend her to me?' He smiled at me, an open, friendly smile. I didn't smile back, shamed by these strangers who stared at my open face, by this unknown man who now reached out and, like the woman, touched my *harquus*. I pulled away.

'Bith knows all too well the time I've spent attempting to capture the nuance of the voyage to the East. Lovely paintings of the oeuvre – this muse of a new kind – in South Kensington Museum at this moment. You understand more than most what I mean, Os. The journey that's become a rite of passage, one by which a double truth is reached: that of knowledge,' he paused, 'and that of desire.' He ran my veil through his hands. Then he looked around at the growing crowd stopping on the stairs, and at those at the bottom, looking up at us. His voice rose; he obviously enjoyed the attention. I didn't understand what he was talking about, but it was clear that it displeased Osric. Why didn't he speak? I looked both up and down, wanting to get away.

The man took another long drink. His eyes had trouble focussing on me. 'And so, the new muse of which I speak is not that of love, but is the *almée* – the muse of desire.' He shook his head. 'What a wonderful discovery on this night of love and lovers, isn't that right, Bith?' He put his arm around the woman's back, and ran his fingers lightly up and down her bare arm. She stared at me through her china mask.

'Since Ingres's *La Grande Odalisque* in the Louvre,' he continued, 'the odalisque has become the symbol of exotic and erotic splendour.' He looked at Osric. 'So what do you say, Os? I could do a marvellous painting, given the right props. Is she available for a sitting?'

'I'm afraid not,' Osric said, smiling now, but in an unfamiliar way. 'She doesn't care to leave my side. Do you, Daryâ? Certainly not for something as time-consuming as sitting for a portrait.' He reached out and pulled my veil from the man's hand, and as he attempted to arrange it over my nose and mouth I snatched it from him and did it myself.

'Now we must move on. There are many others I haven't greeted yet,' he said, and led me back to the drawing room.

'What was he talking about?' I asked Osric, pulling on his arm to make him stop in front of an open window. 'I didn't understand.'

'He's just a young fool,' Osric said impatiently. 'Pumped up with his own shallow talent, spouting nonsense he doesn't know the meaning of. Tiresome.' He took a long drink. 'And you – you didn't stay where I left you,' he said, his voice now chiding. 'I don't like it when you go off on your own.' There was a warning tone in his words.

'How could I be on my own with all these people? Do you expect me to stand, fixed, in one place, Osric?' *Like the women in your photographs.* 'I only went—'

'There are details I have to attend to,' he interrupted, his eyes moving about the room, not even listening to what I said. 'Now. Stand right here,' he said, still not looking at me, 'and this time wait for me. There are others who haven't yet seen you.'

'Osric,' I called as he stepped away, but he didn't hear me. I knew he would be very angry, but I couldn't stay in this noise and confusion any longer. I wanted to go back to my room, open my window and lean out. The heat from the glowing lamps and many dripping candles was terrible, and as I picked up the edge of my veil to wipe my forehead, a short man wearing the mask of a bird, similar to that of Osric's but with a longer and sharper beak, came to me and bowed. When he raised his head I stared through the eyeholes, but they were too shadowed for me to see clearly. And then he pulled the mask up from his chin, over his face, and let it rest on the top of his balding head. The beak pointed to the ceiling like a finger, showing the way.

'Good evening, Miss Daryâ,' he said, bowing again. 'Allow me to introduce myself. I saw you in the carriage with Mr Bull not too long ago. In Hyde Park. I'm Mr Sutcliffe.'

'Good evening,' I said, trying to remember the face of the man who had peered at me with such interest through the open carriage window.

He stepped closer. Long dark hairs sprouted from his nostrils. 'May I fetch you a drink? I see you have nothing.' He stared as if trying to see through my veil.

'No, thank you. I do not take drink.'

'Oh, come now. It's very warm. You must want something.' He

patted his upper lip with a folded burgundy handkerchief he pulled from his jacket pocket. He wore gloves so white they gleamed in the light, and a small button winked at the wrist. 'These masks only make it worse. You've chosen not to wear one tonight?' he asked, stepping so close that I felt the touch of his knee against mine, and moved back. The edge of the window pressed into the small of my back. He put his hand on my arm. I looked down at it.

'No.'

'Then again, you don't need to. Your own face is mysterious and provocative enough.'

Because of both the noise in the room and the unknown words it was hard for me to understand him. I wanted to be away from him, and yet again, like on the stairs, there was no escape; the window was behind me, and he blocked my path. Over his shoulder I saw an approaching woman in an eye mask of golden beads strung with brilliant blue feathers.

'Silas,' she said, touching his shoulder, and he turned. 'Your lady in yellow looks for you.' She pulled off her mask. She wasn't an Englishwoman.

'Oh,' Mr Sutcliffe said, his face lighting up. 'Oh yes. Thank you, Urbi.' He turned back to me. 'So lovely to see you again, Miss Daryâ. I know this won't be the last time.' He fixed his mask over his face again, then threaded his way through the crowd.

I smiled at the woman, grateful she had sent Mr Sutcliffe away. She was shorter than I, and her body very full and curved. She was not Indian, but something else. Her skin was bronze and completely unmarked everywhere – face, neck, exposed chest and arms; it had the texture of satin. Her hair, wound in strange loops about her head, gleamed black under the gaslights, and her eyes were so dark as to also appear black. She had very heavy eyebrows and full lips.

'I am Urbi,' she said, returning my smile. 'You Daryâ, yes?'

I nodded, strangely pleased. 'How you know me?'

Her smile grew very wide. Her teeth were straight and white, except for one front tooth, covered in gold. 'I am very good friend of Osric. Like everyone here. All good friends for special party.'

She moved her hands as she spoke, and rings were on many of her fingers. She was missing the last joint of the end finger of her right hand, but still, she wore a ring there. And on her thumb was a wide gold ring with a glittering black stone – it matched her eyes. The ring was familiar; I recognised it as the one I had seen on Osric's finger in Bombay.

'Where you come?' I asked her. 'What is your home?'

'My home? I am English!' she said, laughing, a sweet, smoky scent on her breath, and of course I thought of Blossom. 'Long time I'm English. I live in English house, eat English food, wear English clothing when I go out. Me, and other women.'

'Other women?'

'Yes. Women come, some women go, other women come. We are a family, sometimes big, sometimes small. We have the Englishmen, like Osric, to look after us.'

I unexpectedly thought of my grandmother's *zenana*, with its kept women.

'Soon you are English too.' She stopped laughing, brushing her cheek with the feathers of her mask. 'But I am born in Egypt. You know Egypt? Cairo?'

I shook my head.

'It is far,' she said, and then smiled brightly again. 'England is much more good place than Egypt. I never go back. You too, never go back?'

I stood in the hot, noisy room, her simple question knocking into me with an unexpected and swift force. Was this my life now – this useless, empty life? For the last five years my life had been about movement, about trudging through mountains and valleys with people who knew hard work, who might witness birth and death on the same day, who believed in themselves and those around them. Of the whole sky wrapping me in its wide embrace. Of travelling through heat and dust and illness. It had been about staying alive.

And now it was filled with inactivity, and waiting for each day to fade into the next with the ticking of clocks. Of decorating myself with fancy clothing and jewellery, of headaches caused by the hissing gas that lit the rooms. Of one dull view from a window, and people like these crowded around me who amused themselves with drink and idle gossip and shameful displays of intimacy and immoral use of their bodies.

'I go back. Soon,' I said, surprising myself to speak the words aloud, knowing with certainty that I wouldn't – couldn't – stay here. I would find a way somehow. I could do it. As I had found the strength and determination to run from Shaliq, then to leave the uncertainty of a life in Jalalabad and the sad certainty of what waited for me in Bombay, I would find a way to leave this life with Osric Bull. But Govind's words wouldn't be silent in my head. *When he doesn't want them any more* . . . Suddenly my heart hammered. I would have to go, soon. I couldn't wait until Osric had tired of me, as he had tired of the woman in the photograph.

'Don't be a sad girl, Daryâ,' Urbi said then. 'Come. We will dance and be happy.' She shoved her mask into the top of her bodice, between her full breasts. She clapped her hands over her head, swinging her hips, and I watched her, my body wooden. When she lifted her arms the tight bodice pulled up so that her waist was exposed, the flesh there too soft, hanging slightly over the band of her skirt. The feathers of her mask bounced against her breasts. She winked at a tall, very thin man in a simple black eye mask who stopped, drink in hand, smiling lazily at her around the wreaths of smoke that arose from the cheroot between his lips.

He took Urbi's hand and led her away. She looked over her shoulder at me, grinning, and her gold tooth glinted.

I edged my way through the crowds and up the stairs; I wouldn't stay any longer, no matter what Osric had told me. As I put my hand on the doorknob to go into my room, a low moan came from the stairway that led to the top floor. I walked silently down the hall and looked around the corner, then immediately drew back. It was Mr Sutcliffe; I recognised the ridiculous long beak on the top of his head. One of his hands was under the the skirt of a small woman in a costume of yellow feathers. He pressed her against him, and his face was buried in her breasts, rising like small white hills from the low feathered bodice. Her head was thrown back, her eyes covered by a yellow mask that matched her costume.

Osric's friends were all like him, of low character. That's why he didn't mind letting me out of my room in front of them; he knew they would accept me for what I was, would commend him on his dirty secret. Would see me as one of them.

That's why David hadn't been here; he was not Osric's friend, not like these people.

In my room I looked into the mirror over the washstand as I drank a glass of water and then splashed some on my cheeks. I was grey-faced with fatigue, and there was a smear of crimson face paint on my sleeve. My toes were sore; many people had stepped on my satin slippers.

Bursts of laughter rose like swirling veils from below, and I went to the window and opened it wide, leaning out and drawing deep breaths to rid my head of the smoke and noise. Then I slid down so that I sat on the floor, the wall at my back and the window over my head letting in a whisper of a cool breeze on this night of the English midsummer.

Finally I lay on my side, thinking of David. And I knew then that I had been fooling myself, that I might have only the memory of his kiss to last through the rest of my life.

I awoke to the sound of laughter and sat up, blinking in the first early rays of daylight. I was surprised I had fallen asleep on the floor, and as I rose to go to my bed, I heard the laughter again – a woman's. Did the party still go on?

I went to my door and opened it, and heard another laugh, quieter now, and voices murmuring, and knew that it came from Osric's bedroom. I quietly closed my door and leaned against it.

Osric had taken another woman to his bed. Did this mean he had grown tired of me already?

CHAPTER FORTY-SIX

I SLOWLY WALKED AROUND the drawing room, picking up the pretty objects sitting on tables and shelves and putting them down. There was a light rain falling outside, its murmur soft through the half-open window, but instead of cooling the air, it only made everything damp. My skin felt as if it were covered with a thin sheen as I went to the window and watched the rain fall on to the long, straight street.

The drawing room – and the rest of the house – had been as orderly as always when I came downstairs, with no sign of the party the night before, and I knew that Govind and Lucy and Ella would have worked many hours to right everything.

Now it was early afternoon, and when the drawing-room door opened, I discovered, as she came in on Osric's arm, that it had been Urbi who had shared his bed last night.

Was this really the beginning of him wearying of me, or was it only that he was still angry that I'd been unable to make him happy the night before the party? I didn't look at him, afraid, suddenly, of what I might see on his face.

Urbi looked tired, her face puffy, her smile not quite as bright as it had been last night. She came to me and took my hands, and I felt the little finger with a missing part against my palm.

'You are well today, Daryâ?' she asked.

'Yes,' I said. 'And you?'

'I am always well,' she said. 'I would like to drink something, Osric.' She went to the divan and sat on it, her legs stretched out in front of her. She wore satin slippers like mine, and of course the same revealing outfit as she'd had on at the party. I sat beside her.

'Sweet sherry?' Osric asked, going to the table that held the tall bottles.

'Brandy.'

Osric brought her a large glass with a rounded bowl; she took it almost too eagerly, immediately putting it to her mouth. Her tongue came out over the lip of the glass to touch the rich amber liquid before she drank. It was small and pink, but looked slightly rough, like a cat's.

After she had swallowed she turned to me. 'What do you do, Daryâ? You go to many parties with Osric?'

I glanced at Osric, but he was busy pouring his own drink. 'No.'

'So then, what do you do?' She drank with small, steady sips, her black eyes staring into mine.

'I . . . I stay here.'

'Osric!' she called. 'Why Daryâ stays here? You don't take her out for fun?'

Osric came back with his drink. 'You two are just lovely,' he said, ignoring her questions, speaking English. 'A very lovely pair. May I take a photograph of you together?'

It was suddenly hard to breathe. I put my hand to my chest and coughed with a sputtering sound.

'What's the matter, Daryâ?' Osric asked, tilting his head. 'You don't wish to be captured in a photograph?'

I shook my head. 'No,' I said loudly. 'No, Osric. No photograph.'

'Don't be silly,' he said, dismissing me, and I knew that in this, as in all things, he would have his way. 'Urbi, you're happy to sit for me, aren't you?' he added, with full certainty.

I looked at the girl, and she nodded, wide-eyed, smiling first at me, and then at Osric.

'Fine. I'll get what's needed.'

When he had gone out, shutting the door, I grabbed Urbi's arm. 'Say no photograph, Urbi. Please. Photograph is . . . bad. Bad,' I repeated, shaking her arm slightly.

Urbi looked down at my hand on her arm, then pulled away, standing and finishing her drink. She went to the table and poured herself another, then shrugged as she brought the glass to her lips. 'Osric likes to photograph.'

'You . . . photograph before?'

She came back to the divan, nodding and pointing at one of my earrings. 'From Osric?'

'Yes. But –'

'I have this,' she interrupted, and touched a ring – a round green stone surrounded by smaller ones, set in gold – on her middle finger. 'Emeralds. This,' she held up her thumb with the black ring, 'and this,' here she wiggled the half-finger with an oval ring with a milky stone. 'Opal. And soon he gives me more rings,' she said. 'Urbi means princess, in Egyptian. Osric says I am a princess now, in England. Urbi is not my name from my home, but Osric likes.'

My grandmother had had another name, in another life. She'd forgotten her true name. Did Urbi remember hers?

'You like Osric?' Urbi asked, but before I could answer she touched my *harquus*. 'Why you have these?'

'At home. I have husband.' I tried to remember Shaliq's face. 'But no more.'

She made a puffing sound. 'Husband is no good for me. One man is no good. You like it here, with Osric?'

I raised one shoulder. 'He . . . make me this house.' I wouldn't call it home.

'And other men? He bring you other men?' She looked at me slyly.

I understood, thinking of Mr Sutcliffe, of the man who talked about painting. 'No. No other men.'

'You know only Osric? No other man in London?' She sounded surprised.

David, I thought, but unlike Shaliq's fading image, David's face stood clearly in the front of my head, as if it were a photograph with a light shining on it. I stood. I wouldn't let Osric photograph me. If he didn't photograph me, he wouldn't hurt me.

'Only Osric?' she repeated, winking as she had at the tall man the night before. 'But he like something else, uh? Something special.'

Suleyman gave a sudden squawk, and Urbi whistled, loudly, as the Ghilzai boys whistled for their goats, and the bird cocked his bright head and whistled back.

I looked at the parrot, shuffling up and down his perch. Now he bobbed his head as we watched him. I thought of an old proverb: *Even in a golden cage, the nightingale yearns for its native land.* I tried to see Suleyman in the land he had come from. What memories could a bird keep alive? Did he still retain a whisper of his land, where he had lived in the wild lush greeness of sweet air and brilliant, pure light – not in a cage in an overheated drawing room kept in semi-darkness.

At that moment Osric returned with the box on the three-legged stand. Behind him, Govind carefully carried a wooden frame with a sheet of glass clamped into it. I stared at Govind, but he didn't look back, gingerly handing the glass, which glistened wetly, to Osric. As Osric slid it into a slot in the box I kept looking at Govind. Govind wouldn't let anything happen to me, would he?

Now Osric placed the *chelem* on the floor beside the divan, moved it away and then put it back again. Then he had Urbi and I sit together on the divan, our shoulders touching. He pushed us this way and that, his hands firm and damp, as always, and I shied from that familiar touch, thinking of what those hands had done to me, what he had done with Urbi only hours earlier. When he was satisfied he stood behind the box, putting his face to the back of it and reaching in front, placing his fingers on a round cap that projected there.

'Urbi is used to this, aren't you, Urbi?' he asked, looking up over the top of the box. He smiled, a lazy, indulgent smile, and slowly put his tongue out to lick his already wet lips. I glanced at Urbi. She was smiling back at Osric with that shining gold tooth.

'Darya! Don't move,' Osric demanded. 'I had you just as I wanted. Tilt your head. No, to the right. Lower your chin.'

I did as he said, and he nodded, his eyes flat and dark. 'Now. Look at the circle of glass on the front of the camera, Daryâ. Just here, where my fingers are,' he told me, in Persian. 'All right. That's it. Stay very still and look at the circle.' He gave that same pleased smile once more, and I swallowed, my mouth suddenly filled with saliva. He lifted away the cap, and I stared at the round glass eye; after a very short time he put the cap back on it. He pulled the framed glass out of the box and handed it to Govind, who slowly left, and I panicked again, watching him go.

'Good. Now take up the mouthpiece of the *chelem*, Daryâ. Put it in your mouth.'

'You know I don—'

'You're not going to smoke it,' he said impatiently, shaking his head. 'Just put your lips on it.' His voice lowered. 'Urbi, you lay your head on Daryâ's shoulder.'

The mouthpiece was cool and smooth, smelling of the dark sweetness so often on Osric's breath. Govind came back with another square of wet glass, and again Osric slid it into the box and tapped his finger on the cap, murmuring, 'Here, Daryâ,' and when he removed it I stared at the glass eye until he covered it again.

Then he told me to stand. 'I'll do an individual one of you. There, by the plant. Let the fronds fall in front of your face.'

'Osric. I am tired. Please. I don't want to do any more.'

'Don't argue.' Now he pursed his lips. 'Why can't you behave as Urbi? She's a perfect subject. Very obliging.' He looked at her and winked. 'In every way.'

She giggled, saying '*Naughty Osric*,' and I had to look away from their exchange.

'Now, Daryâ. Stand there, as I said.'

I did as he told me, and after the exchange of glass with Govind he looked through the box. He straightened and shook his head and came to me, fussing with the plant, tugging my bodice lower and pulling a piece of my hair forward. His damp fingers lingered just a second too long on my breast as he arranged my hair, and again he licked his lips. I recognised the look – the lowered lids, the full, wet lips, the slightest flush to his pallid skin, so that the pox scars were more visible, and knew his pleasure and excitement. He was enjoying himself immensely to have Urbi and I at his command.

He looked through the box again and spoke as if to himself. 'Your mouth is too wide – not the rosebud favoured now. Your cheekbones too prominent. But your eyes! The green of the ocean. Sea-green . . . if only I could capture you in colour.'

Again, he removed the cap and I looked at the circle. 'One last one for now,' Osric said, arranging us in another pose, pressing against me as he did so, and I knew with certainty then how this aroused him. Urbi stood behind me with her hand on my shoulder while I sat on the divan. He placed Suleyman on my other shoulder. But the bird would not stay still: first he nibbled on my earring with his hard, curved beak, then he pulled at my hair with one talon. Finally he edged down my arm and I lifted my elbow to support him, and he settled there.

'That's good. I can see his face more clearly. Let him stay there; it's a better position,' Osric murmured. 'Stay very still so he doesn't move.' My arm began to tremble from Suleyman's weight, but finally Osric was pleased, and uncovered and then recovered the glass eye, nodding. He pulled out the glass frame and handed it to Govind.

Osric took Suleyman from my arm, stroking the bird's sleek head with his knuckles before putting him back in the cage. The bird made a chuckling sound. 'Come. That's enough work for now,' Osric said. 'And a good sitting. I'm sure the results will be very satisfactory. Very satisfactory,' he repeated, rubbing his palms on his thighs, and then he began preparing the *chelem*.

It was over, and I breathed a heavy sigh of relief.

'I will go to my room now, Osric,' I said, but he shook his head.

'Oh, but we're not done. Stay,' he demanded, in the voice I knew I couldn't argue with, and I closed my eyes for a brief second. *We're not done*. 'Govind is bringing tea,' he added.

I stood by the fireplace, watching as Osric sat on the divan and Urbi on the cushions on the floor. They smoked the *chelem*. Govind brought the tea tray, and when he put it down Osric rose and went to it. He turned his back so that I couldn't see what he was doing, but in a moment brought a full cup of tea and gestured for me to sit on the divan, handing the cup to me.

'Drink it,' he said, and I took a sip. There was a metallic taste stronger this time than ever before, and I knew he had added a great deal of laudanum to my tea. Too much. I put the cup down. He immediately picked it up and held it to my lips. I shook my head, but he said in a low but strong voice, 'You *will* drink this, Daryâ,' his hand on the back of my neck. I was very afraid of him at that moment – of the strange, unfocussed look in his eyes, his voice, the force of his hand on my neck, and I tried to twist away, but his grip was too strong.

I looked at Urbi as I silently struggled with Osric, but she said nothing, simply sitting and watching us as she smoked the *chelem*. And in the end I had no choice but to drink.

After finishing the cup Osric held firmly to my lips I felt momentarily nauseous, the metallic taste sickening me, and I lay on the divan, my arm under my head. I tried to watch Urbi and Osric as they passed the mouthpiece back and forth many times. My own eyelids felt as heavy as Urbi's looked; I was lulled by the bubbling of the *chelem* and the rhythmic sound of their breathing. Then their individual breaths moved into one, long, sighing sound, and the room was warm and quiet, dark, the smell of the smoke sweet, and I was in deep peace. In a small, still lucid thought I realised that the laudanum must also be like the poppy. I tried to rise. I wanted to go away from this room with the box on three legs and its evil eye, and I attempted to push myself up, but my arms had no strength.

Although I struggled to keep my eyelids open, they wouldn't obey. The last thing I saw was Urbi whispering to Osric, leaning her head on his shoulder; with the other hand she reached up and played with his ear, then traced her fingers down his jaw and over his lips, sliding back and forth over their wetness. Osric opened his mouth, and Urbi's fingers dipped inside, then out. They moved up into his hair. And then my eyes closed, and this time I knew they wouldn't open again, but it was all right, it was all right, for I saw David then. I wanted to cry and laugh at the same time; it was as if I had lost some treasure from long ago, and suddenly came upon it, thinking I would never see it again. David. *Da-veed.*

He no longer wore English clothes, but Indian cotton trousers and a soft shirt. His fingers, long and narrow, stretched towards me, and I put my face to them as the grass reaches to the wind. I heard him laugh, softly, and then his laughter broke apart into many pieces, scattering inside my skull like small blossoms that blow from the trees in the spring wind. But then they came together again, easily and smoothly, all the edges fitting into each other as if they were fluid, and it was beautiful.

There was a rush of cool air – were we outside? – and I needed to feel this freshness on my skin. My clothing was too tight, its touch bothersome, and I struggled to be rid of it. Then David's hands stroked my hair, my face, my bare skin as he lay beside me. The sound of the sea came through my head, and I knew we were once more sailing on the waves. There was the salty scent of the wide, wide ocean on my lips and tongue, and at the same time the warmth of David's body, his skin so unbearably soft against mine. His breathing was quiet and even, and I matched my own to it, and together the sound echoed the rolling in and pulling back of the waves as my body rose in the same rhythms that were so old and yet somehow new. I wanted to stay like this for ever, rising and falling with the waves, with David, and I tried to open my eyes and look at his face, to speak, to tell him of the unbearably wonderful sensations and emotions he brought to me, but the words wouldn't form, and my eyelids were weighted as if with small stones.

A deep contentment washed through me as the seas calmed. I let myself fall into darkness, David's arms around me, keeping me safe.

I shivered, the bedding damp and heavy. My head ached, and my mouth was dry and tasted as if I had eaten spoiled food. Sudden flashes came to me, the dreams of David and I, the sensations that were so real, Urbi . . . I shakily put my hand over my closed eyes.

The photographs. I opened my eyes; I was in my bed. I was safe, then. Nothing had happened. Was it day or night? My room was dark, but perhaps only because the shutters were closed. Everything was a confusing swirl of images and voices that I couldn't sort out. I turned fitfully and slept again, and when I next opened my eyes Govind was in the room. There was the slight tinkle of glass and china.

'You wish to eat, Missy?' he whispered, coming to the side of the bed.

'Water, please, Govind,' I said.

He poured me a glass and as I sat up to take it I realised I wore nothing, and yanked the covers to my neck with one hand. Not looking at him I drank, water running down my chin and on to my neck. He opened the shutters; the feeble daylight was oddly sharp.

'Thank you, Govind,' I said, and as I handed him the glass he would not look at me, and I sensed something in his face – disapproval, or was it sorrow? – as he slowly left.

I dragged myself out of bed, stepping over my pile of clothing, pulling on my nightdress and splashing water on my face. The door opened again; it was Osric.

'Well,' he said, coming to me, his face smooth, unperturbed. 'You've slept the day away.'

My head thudded as if someone beat a drum there; the clocks struck four times as I looked into his face.

'I'm going out, but I expect you to be dressed and waiting for me upon my return.' He continued to stand in front of me, studying my face, and his eyes narrowed. 'Did you enjoy our little party with Urbi yesterday?' he asked, in a toneless voice.

I put my fingers to my temple. 'I . . . I don't remember . . . the laudanum, Osric. You gave me too much. I . . . I slept. And dreamed.'

'I see,' he said. 'And what were your dreams of?' His skin shone damply, unnaturally white, as if no blood flowed under his skin. As if he were a corpse, laid out for burial.

I lowered my eyes. 'Just . . . confusing images. I don't know,' I said, knowing I would never tell him what went on inside my head. My thoughts and dreams were all that I owned now.

'Hmmm,' he said, and lifted his hand to smooth his moustache with his fingers. 'And are you confused today?'

I had to look up at him again. 'What do you mean?'

'Are you still confused about our party?'

I shook my head, shrugging my shoulders, and as he continued to stroke his moustache, I saw silvery brown marks on his fingers, and knew I should know what caused them, but my headache made it difficult to think clearly.

After I heard the slam of the front door and the clopping of hooves as Osric's carriage left, I sat on the edge of the bed with a growing unease, something tugging at me as I thought of Urbi. I couldn't remember saying goodbye to her, or coming back to my room, or removing my clothing and getting into bed. I only remembered my dream, the softness of David's mouth and hands on my body. I wanted to bring it back, dream the same beautiful dream.

I got up and went to the cupboard, taking the amulet from my bag again. I looked at it and then tilted my hand so that it rolled from my palm, over my fingers, falling to the bottom of the tall cupboard among my slippers. It didn't matter. It meant nothing, really.

As I stood there, my hand still palm up, I suddenly remembered the brown ring on my own finger after touching the solution in his darkroom, and knew this is what I had seen on Osric's fingers.

Still in my sleeping dress I went to the darkroom. The photographs were in plain view on the top of the long table. The first ones were those I remembered Osric taking, the ones of Urbi and me on the divan, of me by the plant, with Suleyman on my arm. But then . . . I put one hand over my mouth to prevent any sound from escaping. Urbi sat on the divan, her dress pulled up to show her naked calves and knees, her bare feet resting on a low stool in front of the divan, her ankles crossed casually. And I lay on my side, my head in her lap, one arm up so that it touched her neck, as if stroking her skin, or waiting to take the *chelem* from her. She held the mouthpiece between her lips with one hand, and her other rested on my breast, which spilled from the top of my bodice. My naked breast was visible, Urbi's hand resting lightly and yet with deliberation on its fullness. And I was smiling. Smiling, my eyes half closed as I looked out of the photograph. And then I looked in even more horror at the next photograph, of me on my side on the divan, my head on my outstretched arm. I was shameless in my nakedness, for although my unbraided hair hung over me, it did not completely cover my breasts. My top leg crossed over the bottom one, but still, I had not hidden myself. My eyes were half open, my mouth in that same empty, pleased expression. The next was of Urbi and I. She was also unclothed, and she kissed my cheek as we lay together on the divan, our arms and legs tangled.

I bent over, closing my eyes, and then opened them and looked at the next two pictures. These were only Urbi, lying naked on the divan. And she . . . I looked closer. Her hands were tied together, over her head, the same cord that tied them running down, attached around her throat. I could see the cord digging into the flesh of her neck. Her mouth was parted slightly, and the gold of her tooth was only a dark square; her eyes were open, but the look there was not the sleepy, languid gaze as earlier, as the one I wore. Her eyes were wide, staring upwards . . . they did not look as if they saw, but . . .

I pushed the photographs away with both hands as if the paper crawled with vermin, breathing as if I had run a great distance in the blazing heat. I would destroy these photographs, tear them into many pieces. I grabbed them, unable to stop looking at the rings on Urbi's fingers, the cord around her wrists and neck, her mouth, laughing only yesterday. . . I started to tear one, as if by destroying the image I would change the truth about what I knew had happened to Urbi.

Suleyman screeched from the next room, and it was as if this scream swooped into my head, clearing it of the clouded terror and confusion, and my fingers let go of the photograph. If I tore them up, Osric would know I had seen them, would know I knew. And then my time – for I knew completely that it would come, that he would enjoy me for a little longer and then find even further pleasure in one final, terrible moment – would be finished. Who would know what had happened to me? No one except the servants even knew of my existence in this house. Would any of the people at Osric's party remember me, or if they did, would they care? David, after what I'd told him, wouldn't come to this townhouse in Kensington, and Mrs Ingram had assured herself I was fine. If she came to the house again Osric could easily explain me away, and who other than she might question him, or accuse him of anything? Govind? Govind could barely walk or speak; he was an old Indian in a land not his own, living at the mercy of Osric Bull.

I carefully arranged the photographs, trying to put them exactly as I had found them. And then I crept from the darkroom, and as I closed the door with a quiet click, and turned, there was Osric, leaning against the wall with his arms crossed over his chest, waiting for me.

CHAPTER FORTY-SEVEN

'WHAT WERE YOU doing, Daryâ?' he asked, his voice flat.

'I . . . nothing. I . . .'

He came to me slowly, and I drew away. 'I think it might be best if you went to your room,' he said, his voice frightening in its intensity. 'And stayed there.' He shook his head. 'I trusted you, Daryâ. And yet here you are, sneaking about.'

What had he done with Urbi? And where had I been in those last terrible moments? I looked at his hands, imagining them winding the cord around Urbi's wrists, her neck. Had I lain there, maybe only feet away, drugged with the laudanum, while he . . . I had to look away from his hands, but as I did, I noticed that he again wore his black-stoned ring.

'Go to your room, Daryâ *jan*,' he said, very softly now, as a father might to a beloved but naughty child. I went past him, turning sideways so that I didn't touch him, and climbed the stairs on heavy feet. I closed my door and stood in the centre of my room, listening for Osric's steps. I went to the cupboard and reached to the bottom of my bag, feeling the square of hard paper David had given me at the docks. Then I went to my knees and scrabbled on the floor among my slippers, my fingers searching for the small roll of leather.

I would do as David had told me. I would go to him, this very night, when Osric slept. I wouldn't stay here, waiting for something terrible to happen. I would take my fate into my own hands, and leave this place.

But fate is only fate because we cannot predict it. Later, when the house grew quiet and the streets dark, I dressed, putting my bag over my chest and wrapping myself in the cloak the missionary lady had given me.

Then I went to my door and put my hand on the brass handle. I turned it, but it didn't move. As quietly as I could I tried again, gripping it firmly as I turned, but the handle stayed in one position. And then panic came over me, and I didn't care how much noise I made; I rattled and shook the handle, yanking on it, but it stayed fast, and I knew, then, that it was locked, and I had truly become Osric's prisoner.

I went to my bed and sat on it. A long time passed, but I would not lie down, wouldn't close my eyes. I had to stay awake, to make sure Osric didn't come to me, didn't . . . and as I thought of what might happen to me there was a stealthy grinding from the keyhole, and then the doorknob turned, and I jumped up.

The door slowly opened; it was Govind, and instead of his spotless uniform he wore a long blue and white striped shirt, past his knees. His feet were bare, and his usually neat, sparse hair stood up on one side. He looked at me standing beside the bed, his face relieved, and I knew he had been afraid of what he might find when he unlocked the door. He put his finger to his lips as he silently shut the door behind him.

'Govind,' I whispered, going to him and taking his hands. 'Help me. I must go to David Ingram. I must go now.'

He shook his head, his pouched eyes glittering in the dark of the room. 'You cannot go out, Missy Daryâ. Mr Osric sits downstairs. I think he will not go to his room this night.' He squeezed my hands.

'I am afraid, Govind. Last night . . . you know Urbi? What happened to her? You see her go home? She is good?' I wanted so badly for him to tell me he'd opened the front door for Urbi, seen her get into a carriage and drive away.

He closed his eyes for a moment, then opened them. 'Mr Osric told me to go to bed. You sleep on the divan, he and Miss Urbi smoked the hookah. I go when he tells me. This is how it always is. I do as Mr Osric says. I must.'

'But . . . tomorrow, then? You help me tomorrow? I go in carriage. I have,' I fumbled in my bag, holding up the card. 'I have place. I go in carriage. You help me . . .'

He shook his head. 'I am old, Missy Daryâ. I cannot stand up to Mr Osric. He has told me that he will put me in the workhouse if I can – or will – no longer carry out my duties. Do you know of the workhouse?'

I shook my head.

'A very, very bad place. For the old, the sick, for those who have nothing and no one. It is bad to live there, and worse to die there. I do not wish my life to end so, Missy. I wish to help you, but I am old. I cannot fight Mr Osric, but . . . I do not wish for you . . .' he held his hands, palms up, to me. 'You understand?' he whispered. 'What can I do?'

I licked my lips. 'I understand, Govind. But what I ask – it will not be this trouble for you.' I reached into my bag again and took out the amulet. 'You take – paper and *ta'wiz*. Send to David Ingram. Only go to street, or ask Ella, give to carriage man. Osric will never know you do this, so no trouble for you. Yes? You do this for me, Govind? Please?' I thrust the paper and amulet at him.

He looked down at the objects in my fingers, his face so weary, so lined with age and worry that I felt my chin tremble. I saw his scalp through the last fine threads of hair. He was such an old man. How could I ask him to help me, and expect that he had any strength or power to really do anything? And then he looked up at me, and what I saw in his eyes shocked me. It was pity. As I had pitied him, so he pitied me. I knew that he understood everything. Everything.

He took the objects from me, his warm, dry old fingers brushing mine. I wanted to believe he nodded, although it could have only been a tremor.

And then the door closed, and I heard the stealthy grind of a key in the lock, and I went back to sit on my bed and wait for the night to end.

But it didn't. It was still dark when the door opened again, this time with no furtiveness. A key was clattered into the lock and turned sharply.

'Why are you sitting in your cloak, my dear?' Osric spoke with little emotion, his voice hard. 'Were you thinking of going somewhere?'

I jumped up, speaking loudly and clearly. 'Yes. I will leave here, Osric. I don't wish to stay any more.' Osric liked a bold woman; he had made it clear he despised those who were weak and clinging.

He laughed, a short, mirthless bark. 'You don't wish to stay. How amusing. But I don't appreciate your behaviour.' His voice had grown even harder, and he came towards me as I stepped back.

'He who wants the rose must respect the thorn, Osric.' I was fighting to keep up this brave front. 'Why did you lock my door?'

He stopped and crossed his arms over his chest. 'Why did I lock you in? Because I can. I can do anything I choose, Daryâ.' He was almost growling now. 'You've become a less than grateful guest.' His voice rose. 'All I've given you, and yet the moment my back is turned I find you going through my personal belongings, touching my photographs.' A glob of spittle flew from his lips on the last word, and landed on my cheekbone.

I wiped it away with a brisk swipe of the back of my hand. I couldn't let myself waver, show any fear. I sensed the only thing that was keeping him from . . . from what? From hurting me in some way at this very moment, was my attempt at standing up to him.

'Fine,' I said. 'You do not wish me to stay, and I wish to leave. So I will go.'

He shook his head, smiling now as if amused. 'You think you'll go? You think you can walk out the door, after the expense and trouble I've gone to, arranging for your passage, feeding and clothing you, to say nothing of the pleasure I've brought you? Why are you looking at me like that? Don't deny you didn't savour my attention in bed, even though I've concluded you could never be as imaginative as I'd hoped. A disappointment, really.' He shook his head. 'Nor could you have ever imagined the life I've provided for you, and yet you couldn't be grateful, wouldn't cooperate, would you?' He laughed again, that horrible, harsh sound. 'Don't you realise you belong to me, Daryâ? You are my chattel and I can do with you as I wish. You are worthless without me.'

I finally turned from him, looking at the window. 'Osric,' I said then, suddenly exhausted, my voice no longer brave, but quiet, pleading. I stared at the strip of sky over the rooftops. A shadowed half moon hung over them. 'I do not wish to be harmed. Like Urbi. Like the others,' I breathed. 'I only wish to go from here. I ask for nothing, and will leave behind all the clothing, the jewels, anything you've given me. Please,' I said, looking back at him and knowing, as I did so, that what he had said about my worthlessness was true.

He was still smiling, his arms still crossed over his chest. One lock of his hair now hung over his forehead. 'Harmed, my princess? I think you're letting your imagination run away with you,' he said, his smile fading. 'Whatever are you talking about? Is it the dreams that haunt you that you're confusing with reality?' He suddenly came even closer, and I cried out, running to the window and struggling to push it open.

'Whatever is the matter?' he asked, from behind me. 'What are you planning to do?'

I looked over my shoulder at him, then down at the stones, so far below.

'Now. You must calm down.' Something in this quiet voice made me more fearful than his anger. As I watched, he took the glass from beside the flowered jug and pulled the familiar brown bottle from his jacket pocket. He poured the clear liquid into the glass, filling it halfway. 'Drink,' he said harshly, holding the glass towards me.

'I won't, I cried, shaking my head. 'I don't want it.'

He stared at me, shaking his head. 'When will you realise it doesn't matter what you want?' He came to me, and I had nowhere to turn, the open window behind me. I flung up my arm, knocking the glass from his hand. It flew towards the fireplace, hitting the tiles and shattering into shards which sparkled dangerously in the faint moonlight. Osric looked at them, then grabbed both my wrists with one hand; I was shocked at his strength and the brutality of his grip. I stared into his face, and it had changed even more drastically. Now it had the appearance of one of the leering masks at the Midsummer Eve's party.

'Govind!' I screamed, panicked, 'Govind, help me,' knowing, as I called the old man's name, that it was useless. I struggled to free myself from Osric's grip, bending my knees and pulling back. But he held me to him easily with one hand; I realised how weak I had become in this time in the dark house. He pushed the bottle against my lips with his other hand, and although I fought him, twisting my head away and trying to keep my lips closed, I eventually heard the clink of the glass hitting my teeth as he forced my mouth open. And then he poured the laudanum down my throat.

Someone called, '*Mâdar! Mâdar! Please help me*,' and I listened, opening my eyes and realising the voice was mine, although so faint. I recognised the ceiling above me, and knew I was in the drawing room. I tried to move, but it seemed I was bound. Suddenly I saw myself from above, lying on the divan, and then saw myself with my wrists tied with rough rope, swinging from the tree in the village square of Susmâr Khord.

But unlike the girl who had so long ago turned and twisted there, now I saw a woman who hung limply, head forward, defeated.

Another woman came, an unveiled woman with a dark and sinister glow around her, and I watched in horror, knowing it was Sulima. She was screeching, pointing and shouting her curses at the hanging woman, at me, but I was powerless to stop her, to respond. I simply dangled there, shoulders slumped, and I wanted to cry out to that other Daryâ, cry out, 'Lift your head. Open your eyes. Help yourself', but there was no sound but Sulima's screeching. And then the screeching lowered, suddenly it was not a woman's voice at all, but a man's, and I moved my head and my soul returned to the body on the divan.

The man's voice was Shaliq's, also shouting, although not in Pashto but in English. How did he learn this language? Had he come to take out his final terrible vengeance on me for my lie? Doors slammed and footsteps pounded, and then I realised the voice was not Shaliq's, but Osric's, and I whimpered, for his leering face appeared inside my head, that smile, the wet lips and damp hands, and such was my horror that I swooped out of my body again, hovering somewhere near the ceiling.

I looked down at myself again, and saw, studying my utterly still face and body, my bound hands, that I was dead. That's why I couldn't move, couldn't make a sound.

I no longer had to fear Sulima's curses, or Shaliq's wrath.

Osric had killed me, and now I lay alone and dead on his divan, in a tall dark house in a strange land. And then the thought came to me that my mother would never know what had become of me. She would not know that her daughter had taken her fate into her own hands, had found the courage to travel so far, to sail across oceans to this distant, foreign land, and had learned so much. She would not know the strength and power her daughter had once possessed.

And then I was again looking upward, but no longer saw the shadowed white ceiling, streaked with black from the lamps. Instead I saw my village, as if in a book of photographs, except in true colour. Over me the sky sat like a blue plate, and I saw the low buildings of my village. I prayed to Allah then, the old words coming back to me as easily as if I'd said them only yesterday. I prayed that all those I had loved at home – my mother and father, Nasreen and Yusuf – were still there, safe and well, even though we would never see each other again.

And then I saw, in the pictures on the ceiling, veiled women, winding their way along the path to the graveyard on the edge of the village. Did they go to visit my grave? No. I was not there, buried in the quiet, tree-shaded area. Suddenly I found that I was behind the others, a shadowy, undetected figure of no substance, and, ahead, the line of women flowed like dark grass at the edge of a river. There, in the graveyard, I went to the stone that marked my grandmother's grave.

Although the others wept, I didn't, for I knew that my grandmother was happy in paradise. And, sitting near the stone, I did feel my old strength flow through me again.

I know you are with your Beloved, and you are happy, Mâdar Kalân. But throughout this long and strange journey of my life you were always with me, always in the face of the moon.

As if in answer, moonlight washed over me, in a light so bright that even with my eyes closed I was blinded by the glare. And then I heard the voice of my Beloved calling my name.

'Daryâ. Daryâ, please. Please,' David said, again and again, and I felt his hands stroking my face, my neck, my shoulders. I wanted to tell him I heard him, that I was ready to come with him, all the way to paradise, but I couldn't answer, because I was dead.

But I didn't mind, for David was dead too, wasn't he? He must be, to be calling for me from paradise, and I felt beautiful, truly beautiful, for the first time in my life, as my grandmother had predicted happened in paradise. And still David spoke my name, and then my body was lifted up, up, so high that I became one of the stars in the heavens. But it was a long, long voyage, and I was jolted and rocked from side to side, and voices spoke in garbled tongues all around me, and I wondered if one journeyed to paradise by horse, by camel, by boat or by carriage.

How did one reach paradise? I thought, and then all was dark and still.

I came to consciousness, trying to remember . . . I licked my lips, then bit on my lower lip with my teeth. I felt the pressure. I was not dead then. But the light, and David's voice, calling me . . .

And then I remembered Osric and drew in my breath in a sharp rasp, my eyes opening wide into brightness. At the sound there was a rustle and a thump, and I turned my head to see Mrs Ingram standing in front of a chair, a book at her feet.

'Osric?' I asked, in a breathless whisper. 'He is –'

'You are safe, Daryâ,' Mrs Ingram said, her voice kind. 'And free of him.'

'Free?' I whispered, and she nodded, pouring a glass of water and coming towards me. She helped me to sit up, her arm around my back, and held the glass to my lips. 'You're at my home. Mine and David's,' she said. 'You needn't fear Osric Bull any longer.'

'He won't look for me?' I tried to clear my throat, but my voice was still hoarse.

Mrs Ingram smiled wryly. 'No. David has assured me of that.'

I sipped the water; it helped the dryness in my mouth and throat. I wore a sleeping dress of a fine white material, the sleeves trimmed with lace. 'How did I come here?' I asked, looking around the sun-dappled room, delicate sheer curtains lifting and billowing with the air from the opened windows. Beside me on a small table were roses, delicate pink roses in a glass vase. Mrs Ingram's small, cool hand pushed the hair from my forehead as she settled me against crisp white pillows.

'It was old Govind who came in a carriage, all the way here in the dead of night, with only a jacket over his nightshirt, his feet bare, pounding on our door. Poor old fellow,' Mrs Ingram said, shaking her head slightly. 'As soon as David saw him, trembling violently – even before Govind pressed a small charm into his hand – he ran and saddled a horse and rode to Osric's. Some time later he returned in a carriage, carrying you in. You've been here since yesterday, and in that time David's done little but pace about, asking about your well-being every half-hour.'

David. It really had been his voice, then, when I thought he called me from paradise. It had been his hand stroking my face. He had come to me, and taken me from Osric Bull.

I pushed myself into a sitting position, wiping my eyes with my fingers, the tears flowing from weakness and relief, from the thought of David and what he had done for me. Mrs Ingram brought a soft cloth and a brush, and as I held the cloth to my eyes she sat beside me, silently brushing through my hair. I wanted to lean against her; the long, slow strokes of the brush were soothing, and when she had finished I knew my tears were done as well.

Then she stood, and said, in a low voice, 'David has reported Osric Bull to the authorities, and I have arranged to speak to them as well.

Govind has also promised to tell them of what he has seen and heard in Osric Bull's house.'

'Govind?' I asked, and she nodded.

'He's here. He was obviously terrified of returning, and David convinced him to stay with us.' She put down the brush and stood. 'Can you stand?'

I licked my lips. They were still dry, and there was a painful buzzing in my head. Mrs Ingram studied me.

'Osric used something to keep you still and quiet – was it laudanum?'

I nodded, thinking of the brown bottle.

'Did you drink it often?'

Again I nodded, now shamed by what I saw in her eyes.

'It will take some time for you to not desire it, for the need to leave you entirely.' Her face darkened, and again I wondered at what her past held. 'I understand its grip. I'll help you until you are completely well. Now. Take my arm, and come to the window.'

Slowly we went to the long windows, and she pushed them open further. I breathed in, smelling not horse droppings and rotting food and the press of bodies and dirty air, but the sweet scent of those things which grow in the earth. As I stared over the green open spaces and tall trees there was a sudden flutter, and a flock of small brown birds rose as one and wheeled over the treetops.

'Larks,' Mrs Ingram said, standing at my side, her arm around my back. 'How lovely they are.'

'What is this place?' I asked, staring at the birds until they were out of sight.

'I've told you, dear. It's our home.'

'But this is not like London,' I said, letting my eyes rest on the wide, blue sky.

'No. It's outside of London. Richmond. You're overlooking Richmond Park.'

I thought of how long it had been since I'd smelled this kind of air, seen a sky that was clear and high. Heard birdsong. How long it had been since I had been able to look as far as the eye could see.

And then there was the crunch of a foot against stone and I looked towards the sound. David strode up and down a short path edged with flowering bushes. A black dog – big and sturdy but old, I knew, by its grey muzzle and swayed back – walked at his side. The dog's long tail slowly swung back and forth in quiet pleasure, and every so often David absently ran his hand over the dog's head, and at this the tail swished furiously.

I watched David, saw the worry on his face, the agitation in his movements. I thought of how well I knew his many expressions, the way he moved.

David.

As if hearing the name I'd spoken only in my head, he stopped his restless pacing and looked up.

I lifted my hand in a half-wave, and his mouth moved, and I knew he'd said my name. He started back along the stone path towards the house, striding briskly at first, but then breaking into a run.

The dog loped at his heels, ears back and tongue lolling in delight, his pace surprisingly quick for such an old animal. And I knew, watching them come ever nearer, come to me, that the dog had run at David's side all of its life.

EPILOGUE

EIGHT MONTHS LATER

There is a Persian saying: Where your heart goes, your feet will go.

It is night on the sea now; we sailed from the London docks this morning. One journey has ended and another begins.

I go out on the deck, carrying a white bowl with its fruit, remembering the voyage here, my future so uncertain. Now the comforting rise and fall of the waves is an undulating motion which unexpectedly reminds me of the rhythmic gait of a camel.

'I've been waiting for you,' David tells me as I stand beside him at the railing. His hair is blown about, his face flushed from the fresh wind.

I extend the bowl. 'Will you try one?'

He puts a pomegranate seed into his mouth. 'Sweet,' he says, and I smile, again thanking him for bringing this special fruit aboard for me. The pomegranate is the symbol of fertility in the land of my birth; he brought it for me because of what I whispered to him only days ago.

Our child will be a girl, for I saw a cloud in the shape of a crowned bird on the day I knew I carried her. We will name her Pari – the Persian word for fairy – because will she not be like a creature of magic, strong enough to drive away a curse, and yet light enough to live on this earth?

Already she stirs, tumbling like a tiny leaf within me. The ship sails smoothly on this first night of its journey to India, carrying me as I carry within me the child who will be born and begin her life there.

David's mother accompanies us; she says it is time for her to go back for a brief time. She will see the face of her grandchild as she enters the world, and forget the unhappiness she once suffered in that land of glorious colour. She says she will remember the joy.

The ship also carries Govind. He is very frail, but his determination to set foot on his native land will see him there safely. David and his mother and I will tend to him on this journey, and make sure that he is comfortable and with friends for his final years in the land he has not seen for so many years.

David and I both have much to face, some of it known, some undiscovered. But it is no longer difficult to face the unknown when the present is so undeniable. Now my fate shines like the full, bright face of this moon we watch on the cloudless night. I lean against David's chest, and his arms come around me and wrap protectively over our unborn child.

This is my dream: that when she is old enough for a journey we will venture further north, retracing our steps. I see myself holding up my child to my father, and putting her in my mother's arms. I want them to look upon me and see that I have survived, and that I have found what I needed to find in my life. I want to see for myself that their lives are unfolding as they should – that my father sits on the roof in the twilight with his son, that my mother finds pleasure with her husband and children and home and friends, that Nasreen – who was never like me, wicked and disobedient – is content, knowing her place and accepting it with grace.

Will this ever come to be? There are many obstacles, but for now I will not think of them. I will think, instead, of the fact that Allah has forgiven me; the child under my heart is His blessing. I will start with that.

And now it is time to ask you: was I wicked to let my beliefs fade, to believe instead in myself? Was I deluded to think that I possessed power – and that I used this as an excuse for immoral behaviour, lying with an evil and destructive man in exchange for what I thought would be freedom?

Whatever you think of me for all of this, I do believe that life is pre-written, woven by fate and circumstance, and yet I also know now that those circumstances can be altered, that we can work with our own power to change the pattern of the tapestry. Please remember this in your judgement of me, and be kind.

The moon sends its long, wavering light across the waves. I watch the shadowed, round face, and think of my grandmother as I turn to David.

Breathe into me, my head sings.

Breathe into me.

ACKNOWLEDGEMENTS

Huge thanks must go to my agent, Sarah Heller, for her suggestions and her endless encouragement. This book would not be what it is without my wonderful editor, Harriet Evans, as well as Catherine Cobain at Headline Publishing. I appreciate their faith in me, their instinct, and their ability to gently keep me on the right path throughout the long course of this novel. I am deeply indebted to these three women.

I also must thank those who support me in different ways – Peter Newsom, Kim McArthur and all at McArthur and Company – thank you for all you do. And Anita Jewell, Andrea Downey-Franchuk, Joanne Renaud, Shannon Kernaghan, Donna Freeman, Holly Kennedy, Irene Williams, Kathy Lowinger, Carolyn Langill, Randall Freeman, Carole Bernicchia-Freeman, Tim Freeman, Zalie and Brenna, and the rest of you – you know who you are. True friends and beloved family, they wait patiently through my long silences and frequent absences, supply me with food for the soul when I hit the wall, and are always there for me at the finish line. Special thanks to my son Kitt for his particular understanding of living with a writing mother – I appreciated his new-found culinary skills, his generosity in understanding the freedom necessary to lose myself in the writing, and his ability to remind me of what is important in life.

All the books and resources I used in researching this novel are far too numerous to list. But those of particular influence and importance to my understanding of the fascinating country and peoples of Afghanistan include: *Afghanistan* by Louis Dupree; *A Short Walk in the Hindu Kush* by Eric Newby; *Among the Afghans* by Arthur Bonner; *Under a Sickle Moon: A Journey Through Afghanistan* by Peregrine Hodson; *Afghanistan: An Atlas of Indigenous Domestic Architecture* by Albert Szabo and Thomas J. Barfield; *Caravans to Tartary*, by Roland and Sabrina Michaud; *Afghanistan: A Short History of its People and Politics* by Martin Evans, and *Beyond the Khyber Pass* by John Waller.

GLOSSARY

Author's Note: I have tried to the best of my ability to confirm proper spelling and word usage in both Dari, the language of the Tajiks, and Pashto, the language of the Pushtuns. Any inconsistencies within these translations are due to the difficulty in the blending of dialects and the variety of spellings found in different sources.

Dari

boz – goat
châdar – headscarf or veil
châdari – veil for body; burqa
chapli – sandals
chây – tea
chây-khâna – teahouse
chelem – hookah
hâkem – ruler
halhal – ankle bracelet
jan – dear; loved one
jinn – evil spirits
khâreji – foreigner
kolah – rounded cap
longi – turban
mâdar – mother
mâdar kalân – grandmother
madrasa – religious school
nōkar – servant
pâdar – father
qaraqol – bell-shaped Astrakhan hat
sâhib – gentleman; sir
salâm – peace – as a greeting and reply

sandali – brazier
ta'wiz – amulet; charm
watan – homeland
zan – woman
zenana – harem

Pashto
atan – time-honoured dance
bas – enough!
buzkashi – 'goat grabbing' – Afghanistan's national sport
chapandaz – buzkashi player
chuptiya – silence; be quiet!
dai – midwife
degcha – pot
halâl – permitted; granted or religiously sanctioned
harquus – female facial decoration
kamis – long shirt worn over pantaloons
landay – couplets sung at celebrations
naswar – type of chewing tobacco
quirt – riding whip
shâbas – well-done; bravo
talpak – sheepskin cap with brim of wolf fur
tofang – rifle
tendâr – aunt
turbruganay – play on words; hidden insults
zyârat – tomb of saint